*Ararat*

by STELLA WILCHEK

*Harper & Brothers · Publishers · New York*

# ARARAT

FIRST EDITION

K-L

*For my husband,*
*who made this possible*

*Though based on historical facts, this book is a work of fiction. Hitler existed. There was a Jewish emigration to South America and there are today Jewish colonies in every South American country. But there is no place called El Paramo, and the characters in the novel bear resemblance to characters living or dead only inasmuch as any fictional character, to be believable, must have human traits common to all of us.*

*I hope the book will throw light on a little-known phase of the Jewish emigration. It was a labor of love and desperation. My special thanks go to Miss Elizabeth Lawrence of Harper & Brothers, without whose invaluable editorial help the original manuscript would never have attained its final form.*

S.W.

# Part One ❦ *Male and Female*

*And of every living thing
of all flesh, two of every sort
shalt thou bring into the
ark, to keep them alive with
thee; they shall be male
and female.*

GENESIS 6:19

*Tuesday, January 13, 1939.*    They say I made money on the visas!

After I risked my life traveling to Hamburg with their black market dollars in my pocket to bribe the consul of El Paramo, they say I made money on the visas! If not for me and my friendship with Josef Blumenthal, where would they be today? Still in Nazi-dominated Vienna and not on their way to South America!

Like a fool, I had expected gratitude. But yesterday, when I came down to the cabin to get my sunglasses, I overheard Goldmann saying to Jakob Kramer:

"Of course he made money on the visas. Leave it to Professor Bernstein to put two and two together. He isn't a professor of mathematics for nothing! How much did he ask from you?"

"Two hundred dollars. In dollars, mind you! The consul would not take the bribe for our visas in any other currency, he said!"

"You got off cheap. It cost me three hundred dollars at the black market price."

"But your family is larger than mine, Goldmann. With Eva we're only three, and he threw her visa into the bargain though she isn't yet a part of the family."

"I'm sure he went fifty-fifty with the consul. That would leave him enough to pay for his passage."

"So what can we do, Goldmann? He *did* get us the visas! Did you know of a better deal?"

"No."

I wanted to rush inside then and say—but what do you say in such a case? Should I remind them that I had not forced the visas on them but that *they* had come to me for help? As soon as they had learned that El Paramo still admitted Jews and that I had a friend there who could procure visas, they had all appealed to me for help. First Walter Kramer, after his abortive attempt at an illegal border crossing. Then shortly after he left for El Paramo, his parents had come to me. Next Eva, Walter's fiancée. And last Goldmann, the father of Eva's friend, Trude. Goldmann had just been released from the concentration camp and given one month to get himself and his family out of Austria. How he had pleaded with me then!

"For God's sake, Professor Bernstein, you have to get me the visas! I have a wife and a daughter and an old, widowed sister who isn't quite right in the head to think of!"

And now that he was safe all he could think of was that I had made money on the visas!

Should I have told Goldmann and Kramer when I caught them talking how I had groveled before the vice-consul of El Paramo on their behalf? ("Yes, your Excellency, of course, your Excellency, we will always appreciate your kindness, your Excellency," as if I did not know that you don't address a vice-consul as your Excellency! But what harm could it do to soften up a man who was known to be a Nazi sympathizer and an anti-Semite?)

The way he talked down to me!

"You know of course, Professor—uuhh—Bernstein that El Paramo requires a landing money of five hundred dollars per family and an additional one hundred dollars per capita. Also, you will have to sign a pledge to dedicate yourself either to industry or to agriculture. El Paramo only wants immigrants who will contribute to her economic expansion. Also, there will be considerable gastos consulares (this he said in Spanish), which will have to be paid in dollars."

The lies I made up to convince him that Kramer and Goldmann were wealthy manufacturers of ladies' lingerie! What else could I have told him? That they were both farmers? Or the truth, God forbid? ("Your Excellency, for all I know there are no Jewish farmers in Austria or anywhere else in Europe.") I don't even know what made me hit upon ladies' lingerie. Unless I was thinking of the famous poster for Aronoff lingerie: the blue rose on the pink cushion, and the caption beneath: Blue Rose Lingerie for the Discriminating Woman.

What difference does it make now? Still, I should have spoken up when I caught Goldmann and Kramer talking about me. There is nothing worse than swallowing one's resentment.

All night long I kept tossing on my cot, making up stinging and witty retorts to the accusation. It was stiflingly hot in the cramped cabin, and I was furious at the two other men for being able to sleep. At about four o'clock in the morning I knew that if I could not talk to somebody I would go out of my mind.

But who was there to talk to? Kramer and Goldmann were the accusers and had ruled themselves out as confidants. Frau Kramer would be loyal to her husband and Frau Goldmann would not take my side either. Trude Goldmann? An intelligent girl—but she might back her father even if she does not seem to think too highly of him. Or Goldmann's sister Paula, who is beyond loyalties, a mumbling, feeble-minded old woman?

Of course there is still Eva. Ah, Eva! I have to keep reminding myself that I am past sixty while Eva is only seventeen and engaged to be married to Walter Kramer as soon as we arrive in El Paramo. Besides, I am a man who has only recently lost his wife under the most tragic circumstances and who is still supposed to be in deep mourning.

Supposed to be in mourning! How could I explain to anybody about Alma if I dare not explain about her even to myself?

The sky was beginning to turn pink outside the porthole when the idea of a diary came to me. I had never really thought of keeping one, not even when I was still young enough to consider every one of my thoughts a combination of brilliant wit and profound wisdom. But this time the purpose was not so much to record my immortal thoughts for posterity as to get out of my system the poison which has accumulated inside of me.

I remembered that in one of my suitcases I had a notebook in which I used to jot down remarks for my university lectures. I climbed out of bed and pulled my suitcase out from under my cot.

Goldmann, who sleeps in the cot above me, woke up and stuck his head over the rim of the bed. His shaved skull gleamed in the dull light of dawn which seeped through the porthole. His mouth hung open as he watched me riffle through my suitcase, the four missing teeth which had been knocked out in the concentration camp forming a dark gap between his lips.

His eyes strayed to the porthole and then back again to me.

"What time is it?"

"About five o'clock."

"What the hell, are you out of your mind, Professor Bernstein, waking people at five o'clock in the morning?"

He rolled heavily over on his side and resumed his snoring.

When I had finally found the notebook I got dressed without turning on the light and sneaked out of the cabin. I went upstairs to the room which doubles as a day room and a dining room. There the light was brighter, and although the air was hot and moist, it did not smell of three men sleeping and digesting in a small cubicle.

And here I am sitting now, writing like a maniac, while the ship rolls softly from side to side and the boards whine with the constant movement.

I feel like a thief, waging a one-sided quarrel on paper with my fellow passengers. I suspect nothing I have written makes much sense, but at least it has given me some relief.


*Wednesday, January 18, 1939.*     Reading back over my first entry, I was struck by the fact that Alma's name should have cropped up in it. What has Alma got to do with my quarrel with Kramer and Goldmann?

Of course she has a great deal to do with it. If not for Alma's suicide, I would hardly have taken it upon me to save my present companions. By now it is clear to me that I only helped them to buy myself free from my guilt.

I still feel that I killed Alma.

When Werner Heggern brought us the news of the death of our son I shouted at her: "It is *your* fault that he had to die! *You* would not let him go with Walter Kramer!" (This before I knew that Walter had never got across the border.)

Can I truthfully say that I only cried out in my grief, or was I trying to transfer my own guilt feelings to Alma? Could I not have foreseen the tragic results of such an accusation? Worse yet, did I secretly wish for these results?

How little man knows about himself. It had been up to me, not Alma, to save Arthur. If I had taken Josef Blumenthal's letter seriously, Arthur might have been out of the country by the time the Gestapo came for him.

I felt doubly guilty because I had to use Werner Heggern to find out what had happened to Arthur. If Alma had had her wits about her when he broke the news to us, how would I have explained to her my acquaintance with a Sturmtruppenführer? Should I have told her that I knew

Werner Heggern because his sister had been my mistress for almost ten years?

Christine. Christine Heggern; the Baroness von Heggern; but that I found out only in the third year of our friendship, when Christine asked me up to her home while her parents were away on a trip, and I saw the coronets embroidered on the linen.

I am not a promiscuous man. I did not turn to a student in my class—almost twenty-five years my junior and a Gentile—out of fickleness. There were too many things missing in my marriage with Alma: some which had never been there; some which went out of our life after Arthur's birth, when she became mother and feeder instead of mistress and wife.

Perhaps what made me hate Alma was the urge to confess to her at long last; and hating her I accused her of having killed our son when all the time I knew that I had really killed him.

It would have been different if I had never received Josef's warning letter. How was I to know what he meant when he wrote about the Anschluss three months before Hitler marched into Austria? I might have been better able to understand his letter if over the years our correspondence had not deteriorated into an occasional postcard for birthdays or holidays.

You know a man as a boy. You grow up with him in a small Polish village; go to school with him; follow him to Vienna; attend university together. Then you get married and something happens to your friendship. And when your old friend leaves for South America, to build roads and bridges there, you are almost glad that he is gone, for he has turned out to have been right about your wife, and you wrong. ("Don't marry Alma, Norman. She'll never understand you. She's a cow.") You are ashamed because he has been right, and you even feel a grim satisfaction when five years later he writes you that he, too, has got married, to a South American woman, a Gentile, and your wife says triumphantly: "I knew your friend Josef Blumenthal would come to a bad end." (As if he had been decapitated and his head shrunk by Amazon head-hunters!)

But you still keep on writing to him, infrequently now. And then, years later, out of the blue, you suddenly receive a letter from him. You turn the letter over in your hand before opening it, vaguely wondering what ill news it will contain. A death notice? A plea for money?

At last you reluctantly tear it open and read, without quite comprehending: . . . this would be the time for you to quit your job, sell your belongings, and move your family to South America as soon as possible because of the imminent Anschluss of Austria. Above all, you want your son out of the country . . .

You read the letter over and over again, refusing to believe its implications because they are uncomfortable to believe. You do not want to give up your chair at the university; you do not want to leave your home and your friends; you still think that you can make up with Christine.

So you write back to Josef that there is no cause for alarm, that all is well in Austria. And six months later your son jumps out the window at Gestapo headquarters.

How do you feel then? Can you face yourself, or do you blame your wife for your son's death, killing *her* too?

Alma did not really have enough influence on Arthur to keep him from going with Walter Kramer. In spite of all her efforts, the only tie she had ever been able to forge between them was by catering to his unsatiable appetite. Arthur was fat and sluggish, and when Alma implored him not to go with Walter he made a gesture of pleasing his mother, when he was actually pleasing himself.

He was so much like me in this respect, and for that very reason I should have insisted on his leaving!

How many nights have I lain awake, arguing with the dead and trying to reshape the past? But the dead always win the arguments because they are silent.

And now when I thought that I was finally through with these nightly ordeals, I am again lying awake, arguing with Kramer and Goldmann instead of being grateful that they *let* me save them. After all, it was I who needed redemption. And who am I to quarrel if my redeemers are not perfect?

*Thursday, January 19, 1939.*   The first pages of my notebook were scribbled with remarks and equations. I tore them out only today. Now they lie before me on the table, half crumpled and strangely dead without a classroom full of students to whom to expound the rules and theories.

Occasionally, when Alma wanted to make me feel a failure, she would ask: "What good is mathematics?" I would try to argue with her on her own level, saying that without mathematics it would be impossible to build houses and bridges and roads. Of course I knew that men had built houses and bridges and roads long before they had a grasp of mathematics. The great miracle is that man's mind is inventive; the reasoning is largely an afterthought. The lever and the wheel were invented before man knew why they lightened his work.

It has always been my great disappointment that I do not have a creative mind. I am a good teacher but I am neither an inventor nor an innovator. Perhaps what is missing in me is the spirit of adventure.

I remember when Josef first left for South America, twenty-five years ago, I used to dream of running away and joining him. I had some wild ideas of black-eyed, olive-skinned girls whirling in fiery dances, and of myself riding into a hacienda on a white steed. It was always a white steed. No doubt, some sort of symbol, though I have no idea what. I also remember that Alma and Arthur never figured in the dream, and that I felt secretly guilty about their omission.

Once I made the mistake of mentioning something to Alma about going to South America. Her reaction was horror mixed with ridicule.

"So what are you going to do there? Teach the monkeys mathematics and leave me to live among heathens and Indians and wild beasts?"

This was Alma's idea of South America. Well, perhaps it was no more distorted than my own.

But now that my dream has come true, even to the point of omitting my wife and my son, it has lost its flavor. Old dreams, like old beer, tend to grow stale. Especially dreams whose realization has been forced upon one by outside circumstances.

*Friday, January 20, 1939.* The long voyage is beginning to get me down. Sixteen days aboard this miserable, small Dutch freighter, and we have not even sighted our first port of landing, Curaçao. I am beginning to hate the ship. Why couldn't I be rich enough to book passage on a large steamer where one can avoid one's fellow travelers when their company becomes unbearable?

We are an oddly assorted crowd: outside of my own little group of refugees, the *Mariejke* carries only another nine passengers: three Dutchmen destined for Curaçao; one Dutch girl, going as a bride to Aruba; and five Germans, one of them a woman, returning to Chile from a Nazi convention at Nuremberg.

Whenever the Dutch are late for a meal, an icy silence reigns in the dining room until they appear to make a convenient barrier between our table and the Germans. Only then does the conversation return to its normal pitch.

Outside of an exchange of greetings there was little fraternization among the passengers until today, when a swimming pool was set up on deck. The pool looks like a huge canvas bathtub, some fifteen feet long and eight to ten feet high, tarred outside and supported by sturdy metal framework. The upper rim can be reached only via a slippery stepladder, an approach which has made it off limits for us older people. Frau Kramer said she had never aspired to becoming a monkey; besides, she had not even brought a bathing suit along, an omission for which all of us ought to be duly thankful.

Eva, of course, has brought a bathing suit.

Right after breakfast Eva and Trude went down to the cabin to change, while we older people repaired to the deck and sat down in our deck chairs. The Germans and the Dutch had already put on their bathing suits, and as if the shedding of their clothes had erased a barrier between them, they were beginning to throw snatches of conversation back and forth. Two of the German men were cavorting in the pool. We could not see them, but they kept splashing water over the rim as they swam around, and we could hear them frolicking in their raucous Prussian.

After a while Trude and Eva came on deck, both wearing bathrobes. Trude modestly sat down in her deck chair before she untied the belt of her robe, throwing it open to display the heavy, bluish-white thighs of her short legs. She took off her glasses, stuck them in the pocket of her robe, and shut her eyes before she slipped her arms out of the sleeves, as if by closing her eyes she could make herself invisible. She is deeply conscious of being a pitifully ugly girl. I have seen her look into a mirror with an expression of outraged surprise, as if she could not believe that what she saw was really her face.

Eva did not use such modesty for disrobing. On the contrary, she made quite a display of it. As if the deck alone were not a fitting stage for her, she climbed the ladder to the swimming pool and, balancing on the narrow metal platform at the top, cast off her robe and threw it casually over the railing running alongside the pool. Then she remained posing for our benefit with her head thrown back, her shoulders squared, and her legs slightly parted.

Something like a hush fell over the deck. The Dutch stopped chattering and laughing. The two Germans in the pool stopped shouting. Herr Kramer leaned forward. Herr Goldmann leered. Frau Kramer gasped and looked stunned.

Eva had on a white, two-piece bathing suit, revealing a lot of skin which, though not yet tanned, had a clear, golden hue as if it had retained the color of many previous tans. From where I sat her slender legs looked incredibly long, supporting her lithe, young body, thin-waisted, with small girlish mounds of breasts curving beneath her halter. Her long, blond hair was blowing in the breeze and her eyes reflected the deep blue of the sky and the sea around us.

I could see the Germans gaping admiringly at their ideal of a slimmed-down Walkyrie. Only this Walkyrie was Jewish.

Eva gave us another minute to look at her and then she dived into the pool.

A little later, when she stood beside me toweling herself, I told her of the effect she had had on the Germans. She seemed contemptuous and even angry.

"Should I really feel flattered by the admiration of a bunch of Nazis? Last summer, in Vienna, I was stopped in the street by an SA man carrying a camera, who wanted me to pose for the picture of the 'Perfect Aryan Girl.' I managed to get away from him before he took the picture, but I was too terrified to tell him that I was Jewish. Afterward it bothered me for days that I had not told him I was Jewish. I would lie awake in bed, making up things that I should have said to him. But I guess I never would have dared say them. I'm just a coward at heart."

(So Eva too is having her nightly conversations!)

I told her that she had done the one sensible thing, but she still looked doubtful. Probably she feels that she passed up her one big chance of becoming a heroine. She does not yet know that the best place for futile acts of heroism is in one's imagination.

*Saturday, January 21, 1939.*    This morning Eva had her redemption. One of the Germans came up to her as she lay in her deck chair and said:

"What is a pretty Aryan girl like you doing with a bunch of Jews?"

For a second Eva remained petrified, then she sat bolt upright and shouted:

"Why don't you leave me alone! I'm Jewish!"

I hope she can sleep in peace now.

*Sunday, January 22, 1939.*    Why do people tend to pour out confidences aboard a ship? Is it because the confinement makes them more talkative or because it is impossible for the listener to get away?

Take Frau Kramer, for instance: today, without the slightest provocation, she gave me an account of her past. She also made a few remarks which revealed how she felt about her future daughter-in-law.

The tropical sun had become too hot for me and I had sat down beside Frau Kramer in the shade. Possibly she thought that I was seeking her company rather than the shade, for she gave me a coquettish smile and said:

"Yes, we old people had better stay out of the sun."

I must say I resented her remark. Although I am nearly sixty-one, I do not think of myself as an old man. Of course I have gained some weight since my younger days, but I am tall enough to carry it. My hair may be white now, but at least I have lost none and I feel that it adds distinction to my appearance, especially since I wear it a little longer than is customary. (A few days ago Eva teased me about the length of my hair. "Who do you think you are? Professor Einstein?" she asked. She has no idea that I really know Professor Einstein.) My face has been called handsome so often that by now I believe it myself. Even my curved nose cannot distract from that. (Besides, Christine always said my nose was not curved like a Jewish nose but like the nose of a Roman senator.) Altogether I think I am still a good-looking man and I was annoyed when Frau Kramer implied by association that I was old.

Actually, I have little right to resent the implication. Frau Kramer is only fifty-two, and I certainly think of her as an old woman!

If I had not seen her passport I would have taken her for older. I doubt that she was pretty even in her youth. In fact I doubt that she ever was young. She is a big woman with iron-gray hair, a bulbous nose, and protruding lips. Like so many fat women she has a weakness for large-flowered print dresses with ruffles and bows, which only add to her bulk. The seams of her stockings are always crooked (stirring in me a resentful remembrance of Alma), and she wears sensible oxford-type shoes, laced up tightly right to her thick ankles.

I cannot help wondering if she can still kindle desire in her husband. Of course this is not what I discussed with her. It was she who brought up the matter of her marriage—or rather marriage in general. After inquiring about a few people whom she felt I ought to know from Vienna (I did not) she shifted the conversation to Alma.

"Your late wife, may she rest in peace, I understand she was from Przemyśl?"

"Yes, she was from Przemyśl."

"I lived there myself for a while. May I ask her maiden name?"

"Finkelstein. Alma Finkelstein."

"Her father, he was dealing in feathers?"

"No. He was a furrier."

"Ah. She must have had a nice dowry. So who arranged the match for you?"

"I met my wife at her aunt's house in Vienna." (I said that rather stiffly.)

"You mean there was no schatchen?"

"No schatchen."

Frau Kramer paused briefly to digest this stupefying discovery.

"May I ask when you were married?"

"In 1906. Thirty-three years ago."

"And there was no schatchen? Most unusual. Most unusual."

(My father-in-law had thought so too. In fact he had thought it a scandal when his daughter returned from a visit to Vienna with a suitor. The selection of the proper suitor was the privilege of the father. If I had not already had my doctor's degree then, he would have flatly rejected me. Even so he made me understand that a girl with his daughter's dowry could expect to marry, at the very least, a doctor of medicine, not a schnorrer of a mathematics teacher. If he eventually gave his consent it was, as Frau Kramer had remarked, most unusual.)

"My marriage, of course, was arranged by a broker. It was the proper way to do things," Frau Kramer said in a tone of slight criticism. "Besides, I was not a very pretty girl. I was more of an intellectual."

I suspect I just sat gaping at her. Heaven knows, she had never struck me as an intellectual!

"You are surprised? I used to read Schiller and Goethe, and I went to concerts. I also wrote some poetry. Naturally, I had high hopes for my future husband, but how many cultured men do you find in a small Polish village? The first suitor Papa brought to the house I insulted at the dinner table. I told him not to stick his knife in his mouth. He walked out right after dinner and never came back."

Frau Kramer chuckled happily at the recollection, while I thought that she had not done so well in the end either. Herr Kramer's table manners are anything but appealing.

"Before Papa brought home the next husen, he strictly forbade me to open my mouth at the table. That's how I met Jakob. All evening long I sat there like a dumb golem, and Jakob did not say a word either. But my father and his father kept talking about how much money I would be getting, and how many sheets, and pillow cases and tablecloths; and how much china and silver. Well, at least he did not take me without a shirt on my back. Not like Walter is taking *her!*"

She pointed with her chin at Eva, who, eyes and nose covered with cotton pads, lay in a deck chair, absorbed in the daily ritual of the sun bath.

(I know that Eva carries with her an enormous wardrobe trunk full of clothes, and two large wooden crates in the hold of the ship, containing household effects for her future home. She also has her landing money. One could not say that Walter is taking her without a shirt on her back, but then perhaps he would not mind at that.)

"My Walter, he could have made a better match any time! If not for Hitler and the emigration, he would never have thought of marrying Eva! Who ever heard of a grown man, twenty-five years old, an architect with a degree, going to a party, falling in love with a seventeen-year-old girl with not a penny to her name, and asking her to marry him? Why, rich girls were actually throwing themselves at my Walter! But he always had this idea of a romantic marriage. Ever since he was a kid he wanted to get married to any girl he kissed once. I just laughed and told the girls not to take him seriously! That's what I told Eva right away when he brought her home: 'Don't take him seriously, he won't marry you.' I warned her! At least she'll never be able to say that I didn't warn her."

With an expression of mingled outrage and hope on her face, Frau Kramer glared at Eva, as if deep inside she still expected Walter to tell her that it had all been a monstrous mistake.

"Romantic love," Frau Kramer said bitterly. "So tell me, what's wrong with being in love with a rich girl? A nice girl, a girl that has a little respect for his parents, a girl that at least looks Jewish! You think I like having people ask me in a confidential whisper: 'Your son's fiancée, is she . . . ?' So, say yourself, Herr Professor, if your son—" she hesitated and caught her breath "may he rest in peace, would want to marry a girl like Eva, would you approve?"

Looking at Eva stretched out in the deck chair, I said, perhaps with too much enthusiasm:

"Yes, indeed, I certainly would!"

"Ah." (A quick, nasty look of suspicion.) "And your wife, may she rest in peace, how would she feel about it?"

I remembered Alma's jealousy tantrums when she could no longer deceive herself about the promiscuity of her son.

"My wife? I doubt that my wife would ever have approved of any bride for my son."

"You see! A mother knows. Your wife must have been a very smart woman. What a pity this . . . accident . . . had to happen. We would have understood each other very well."

I was tempted to say: I'm afraid so. But there are such things as taste and good manners.

*Monday, January 23, 1939.* Sometimes I think Eva works like a catalyst on the people around her. She brings out all sorts of hidden emotions simply by her presence. This morning, without speaking a single word, she managed to throw Herr Kramer into a rage. Considering that he is a choleric little man to begin with, this does not take too much doing.

I remember when Herr Kramer first came to me because of the visas. He brought with him an important-looking briefcase and carried a walking cane. All through our conversation he held on to his cane, tapping it on the floor to underline every single one of his statements, however unimportant. With my weakness for forming hasty judgments I thought: Here is an uneducated man, trying to hide his ignorance behind authority.

During the time we have spent together aboard ship I have also learned that Herr Kramer is something of a family tyrant. He will interrupt his wife in the middle of a sentence to switch the conversation to a topic of more interest to him. Once or twice he has done the same to Eva, with the result that she now hardly opens her mouth in his presence. This he interprets as haughtiness. Add to it that Herr Kramer thinks of all women as creatures of inferior intellect, and you have quite a situation.

The clash this morning was bound to come sooner or later. For the past few days Herr Kramer has taken it upon himself to protect Eva's virtue, or whatever he thinks he is doing.

Ever since Eva started to take her revealing sun baths, a young sailor has been watching her from the upper deck. He cannot be older than Eva, seventeen or eighteen perhaps. Recently he has been working stripped to the waist, baring a tanned, muscular torso with an anchor tattooed on his chest.

Of course Eva knows what he is up to, though she makes a show of keeping her eyes tightly closed. But now and then she betrays her knowledge of being watched by protectively folding her arms over her breasts—a recognition of virility she has never extended me.

Herr Kramer was quite outspoken about his annoyance with the sailor.

"Outrageous," he said to me. "And she's shameless enough to provoke him! I forbade her strictly to put on this bathing suit again! But does she listen to me? Believe me, I'll be glad when I'll have the responsibility for her off my hands!"

I doubt that anybody entrusted Herr Kramer with the responsibility for Eva. He strikes me much like a self-appointed guardian.

This morning Herr Kramer discovered that the young sailor had added a new stroke of insolence to his activity. Leaning far over as he scrubbed the railing he softly sang and whistled down at Eva. She acknowledged this tribute by smiling amusedly with her eyes closed.

The Kramers, the Goldmanns, Trude, and I were sitting in the shade, watching this scene. Herr Kramer kept drumming with his cane on the boards, while his face turned darker all the time. Finally he rose and said with venom:

"Enough is enough. I'm going to put a stop to that."

Kramer strutted across the deck and came to a stop by Eva's deck chair. Glancing around him, he discovered her bathrobe draped over the back of the chair; he snatched up the robe and spread it over the girl. Without speaking or opening her eyes, Eva moved her arm, casually, almost languidly, and the robe slid off and fell on the floor.

Herr Kramer looked close to apoplexy. He knew that everybody was watching him, but there was nothing he could do without making an even bigger fool of himself. The sailor above, who had interrupted his whistling when the object of his admiration was being draped, gaily resumed his former occupation. Herr Kramer glared up and raised his cane as though to shake it at him, but thought better of it, executed a sharp turn and walked away, smacking his stick at empty deck chairs. Avoiding us, he began a prolonged march around the deck.

"You see," Frau Kramer said with satisfaction masking as indignation, "you see how she acts. No respect whatsoever for her elders! God only knows how *this* marriage is going to work."

I wonder whether Frau Kramer has the slightest inkling that many of her sinister predictions are wishful thinking.

*Tuesday, January 24, 1939.*    Since yesterday Herr Kramer has not spoken to Eva, a circumstance which hardly affects their relationship. Even before, their conversation was limited to mere essentials.

What surprised me was to hear Frau Kramer urging her husband not to show his resentment. "Why give the Goldmanns more food for gossip? I bet they've been pitying us all along."

If the Goldmanns have been gossiping, they certainly have not taken sides. Especially Frau Goldmann has been reluctant to condemn Eva.

"Poor child," Frau Goldmann said to me in an unguarded moment. "Traveling around the world all alone, without her parents! The things this criminal did to us! Just imagine our Trudi going on a trip like that without us!"

The gruesome image of her daughter making this voyage unescorted made tears well up in Frau Goldmann's eyes. By now I know that she is an emotional woman with an exaggerated sense of the dramatic. Her appearance would certainly do credit to a great dramatic actress: a woman in her middle forties, with a statuesque figure, splendid legs, a beautifully molded face with smoldering eyes, and a white streak running through the ebony-black hair. Unfortunately, her emoting is restricted to little domestic scenes, which she overdoes to the extent of rendering them ridiculous. ("Oh, Trudiiii! Did you have to *put* on this *terrible* dress? What are *people* going to *think* of you?")

Sometimes I wonder what sly trick of nature presented such a beautiful, foolish woman with an ugly, intelligent daughter like Trude. Trude is not even fortunate enough to resemble her tall, haggard father, who always makes me think of a scarecrow. She is short and fat like her deranged aunt.

I remember when I first saw Frau Paula Gruen. Goldmann could read the shock on my face as I gaped at the mumbling, wild-eyed woman.

"So what am I going to do with her? Leave her behind? She's twenty years older than I am, and she brought me up after my mother died. She never had children of her own; I was her baby! Can I leave her now?"

I knew he was arguing with himself rather than with me. He stood running his fingers over his bald head, in a gesture of hair remembered.

Of course he had to bring her along. In her own weird way she rounds out our odd assortment of people.

I don't know why I feel so critical of my fellow passengers this morning. I did not sleep well last night and rose in a mean mood. The steward tells me it is the closeness of land. We are to reach Curaçao tomorrow.

*Wednesday, January 25, 1939.*     First day in Curaçao.

It is a strange sensation not to feel the ship moving underfoot. The heat is unbelievable, heavy and sticky. I feel as if I could reach out with my hands and knead the air into balls. Everybody is complaining except Eva and Trude, who seem to like it.

The Dutchmen and the bride have disembarked, and we are left alone with the Germans in the dining room. The meals pass in arctic silence, which is the only cold and quiet thing about Curaçao.

The city of Willemstad is certainly bubbling with noise and movement. From the ship we can see the long, wooden bridge spanning the harbor, the dismal shacks close by the docks, and on the opposite side of the harbor large oil tanks between the palm trees. It is all very strange and exotic.

We have been walking the streets most of the day. What struck me most was the absence of white faces. The majority of the population seems to consist of Negroes, interspersed by mulattoes. Some of the dark-skinned girls are breath-takingly beautiful.

The center of the city is neat, with store crowding onto store in the narrow streets. The girls were agog staring at the exotic merchandise in the shop windows: carved ivory objects; intricately wrought jewelry; richly embroidered kimonos. The storekeepers stand in the open doors, trying to snare their victims from the street. We were startled to be repeatedly addressed in Yiddish.

"Nu, perhaps a nice bracelet you need? A kimono for the pretty girls? So where are you from? Vienna! I was there once before the war. You are going to El Paramo? Woe is me!"

This last remark greatly upset Frau Goldmann. "If these cutthroats don't like El Paramo, it must really be bad," she kept arguing.

"Well, what do you want us to do, Else? Turn around?"

The girls love it all: the heat, the noise, the stores, the Negroes, the smell of oil over the bay, the bustling city, the ringing of the bell before the bridge swings open, the gabled Dutch houses painted in bright colors. They enjoy themselves as if they were on an outing, not part of an exodus.

Eva says she is going to buy herself a kimono.

"That's all she has on her mind," Frau Kramer said. "Primping herself, while we worry about the future."

Do we really worry? I believe we are still too numbed by the anesthesia of novelty to worry seriously.


*Friday, January 27, 1939.*   Our last day in Curaçao.

Yesterday Eva made a conquest. A handsome young man in a white convertible followed her all over town, trying to persuade her to go for a ride with him. But she would not hear of it.

"I wouldn't mind going for a ride with a good-looking oil millionaire," Frau Goldmann said.

"How do you know he is an oil millionaire, Mama?" Trude asked. "Perhaps he is a white slave trader."

I think it was Trude's remark which suddenly made Frau Kramer encourage her future daughter-in-law to go for a ride with a strange man. This was her last chance to see Eva sold into white slavery.

But a few hours later Frau Goldmann made everybody forget about lost chances.

We had sat down in the dining room, everybody except Frau Goldmann, who had gone to the cabin to freshen up. The unloading of the ship had stopped and it was strangely quiet. Suddenly the air was rent by a piercing shriek. Herr Goldmann jumped up, white in the face.

"That's my wife! One of those beastly stevedores has attacked her! I knew it would happen, I warned her not to take one step by herself!"

He rushed outside and we all ran after him.

Frau Goldmann stood in the ship's corridor, shaking with terror as she clung to the hand railing along the wall. Her black eyes were screwed up with fear and her mouth still stood open from the scream.

"What is it, Else? For God's sake, what happened?" Goldmann asked, gripping her shoulders and shaking her violently. "Where did he go, the villain, tell me so I can kill him!"

"There! There!" Frau Goldmann shrieked, raising herself up on her toes as if she were trying to take off from the ground. Following her pointing finger, I turned fast enough to catch a glimpse of a mouse scurrying down the corridor.

Herr Goldmann moaned and wrung his hands.

"You can give a man heart failure with your foolishness, Else!" And then, turning to the spectators who had gathered around Frau Goldmann: "And this is the woman who is supposed to stand beside me in times of tribulation!"

But in spite of Goldmann's efforts to shame her into acting sensibly, Frau Goldmann would not consent to walk to the dining room under her own power until we had checked the entire corridor and had made sure that the mouse had moved to more hospitable surroundings.

One would think that living under Hitler for almost a year would make a person immune to little idiosyncrasies. But observing the people around me—myself included—I have discovered that as soon as an imminent threat is removed, people will return as speedily as possible to the original pattern of their lives. Perhaps this is one reason why we can't learn from history.


*Saturday, January 28, 1939.*    We have again lost sight of land. Although Panama is only two days away, we might as well be in the middle of the Atlantic. Our small world is again bordered all around by water, and the shared confidences go on as before. This morning it was Trude who poured out her heart to me.

"Wasn't it terrible the way Mama carried on yesterday evening?"

"There are plenty of women who are afraid of mice, Fräulein Trude."

"I don't know, sometimes I feel Mama does it on purpose, this . . . this being afraid of the wrong things. Do you remember when the SA came around to get Jewish girls to wash the windows of their barracks? Some of the girls were pushed out of the windows and fell to their death! Yet when they came for me, all Mama was afraid of was that I would ruin my hands from the water. And just now she isn't worried about how we're going to make a living in El Paramo, but whether we'll be able to live as well as the Kramers. She is convinced that during his three months' headstart Walter has already prepared a sumptuous home for his family. And Papa only keeps encouraging her in all this nonsense: 'You've never starved with me, Else. I promise you, you won't starve now!' How can he promise her *anything?*"

"Don't you have confidence in your father, Fräulein Trude?"

(It is easy for me to talk, knowing that I have a position waiting for me! What if the Labor Department of El Paramo had not been planning a social security program and Josef Blumenthal had not suggested me as the proper man to organize it?)

Trude looked sadly down at her hands and shrugged.

"I don't know. When I was younger" (she is twenty now!) "I used to have blind faith in him. It's always a shock to find out that your parents are human and fallible. And now, especially since he developed this delusion of grandeur—if you know what I mean . . ."

I know indeed. After all, it was I who converted Goldmann into a fictitious manufacturer of ladies' lingerie. But now he has reached the point where he is telling me (me!) all about his factory in Vienna. The number of his employees and the size of his plant keep increasing proportionally to the distance which we put between Europe and us. Listening to him, I sometimes wonder whether I have not created a monster.

"Mama *and* Papa, they're both impossible," Trude said with sudden, vicious disgust. "Do you know what Mama did when she heard that Eva was shopping for a trousseau? She ran out and bought a trousseau for me! God knows she could have found a better use for the money. And the worst part is that now she's harassing me with the argument that if Eva can get married at seventeen, I certainly ought to get married at twenty!"

"Don't you want to get married, Fräulein Trude?"

"Don't I want to . . . ! And *who* is going to marry *me?*"

"Why shouldn't a nice young man want to marry you?"

I am very clumsy at this sort of thing. It was written all over my face that I knew as well as Trude why it would be hard to find a nice young man for her. Again I had to question nature's capricious ways.

Why couldn't Trude have inherited at least a semblance of her mother's beauty?

Trude also seemed to think of her mother, for she said bitterly:

"You would expect the daughter of Else Goldmann to be a pretty girl! But no, I have to take after my aunt Paula. I just hope I won't turn out like her in the end—crazy!"

"Isn't that a cruel word to use?"

"Well, maybe there are better words. I always tried so hard to find the right word. Of course now it doesn't matter any longer."

I realized that somewhere along the way I had lost her. Her mind had jumped and I could not follow.

"What on earth are you talking about, Fräulein Trude?"

She cast a furtive glance about her, the precaution of a person about to impart a conspiratorial secret.

"You know what I was going to be, Herr Professor? I was going to be a writer! What else could I be with my face? I happen to have a very beautiful soul" (she giggled deprecatingly) "and my face wouldn't show in a manuscript. This was the only way for me to be beautiful."

I was startled by what she presented as her incentive for writing.

"Do you think this is really a good enough reason for wanting to be a writer?"

She looked at me and laughed.

"Of course not. Don't ask me what makes people want to write. I suppose the best answer is because they can't help it. Something like breathing. Well, what difference does it make now? I won't be a writer now, ever!"

Only a minute ago she had been laughing, but now she had clapped her hands to her face and was crying, blubbering between sobs:

"I sold my first story when I was sixteen. By the time I was eighteen I had two more accepted. When Hitler came I was working on my first novel. The night when they were shouting in the streets 'Kill the Jews!' I tore it up. I tore it up in little pieces and trampled on it. I'll never again write a word in German! I'll never be a writer now! I'll be ugly all my life!"

She was sobbing heartbreakingly.

I was just about to argue her out of this unfortunate obsession when we were interrupted by the Goldmanns, taking their daily stroll around the deck. Trude quickly turned away and hid her tear-stained face.

"Aha, intellect drawing to intellect," Herr Goldmann said when he saw us together.

Frau Goldmann surveyed her daughter with a critical mien.

"Trudi, why are you wearing this shabby old bathing suit? You have as many nice suits as Eva. What are people going to think when they see you every day in the same old suit?"

"For God's sake, Mama, who cares?"

"Who cares! You hear that, Markus, who cares! And then you ask me why she never looks neat. I care! Your father cares! The Herr Professor here, he cares, don't you? Now go immediately and change!"

She took Trude's arm and forcibly marched her off the deck. Goldmann looked after them glumly, mumbling:

"Why can't she look like her mother? Or Eva?"

As he looked at Eva stretched out on a mat in the sun, his eyes brightened and he gave me a cordial nudge in the ribs, accompanied by a lewd wink.

"Not bad, eh, Herr Professor?"

At forty-nine Goldmann wants it clearly understood that his virility is still at its peak. He tries to prove this by heavily lacing his speech with obscene remarks and injecting an ambiguous meaning into the most innocent phrase. Several times during our voyage he has asked me not to come to the cabin in the afternoon.

"What the hell, I don't know about you and Kramer, but I'm not a eunuch! And with the women in a separate cabin, how am I going to get mine? I can't very well ask the ladies to wait outside for three minutes! Why, they might get jealous and start a riot!"

He grinned lewdly, considering himself irresistible with the gap in his teeth and his bald pate. Looking at him, I asked him why he did not have his teeth fixed before he left Vienna.

"Never! Not as long as this cur, may he drop dead, is still alive!"

Goldmann never refers to Hitler by name and inevitably adds a curse after whatever he calls him. This turn of the conversation had brought him to his favorite subject next to sex, namely, politics. He was about to expound some of his absurd views when his sister came weaving her way about the deck like an erratic spider.

"Excuse me, Herr Professor, but I have to walk with her for a while. She is always calmer when I am with her."

As he walked away from me he no longer looked either lewd or animated. The thought suddenly struck me that he was really the most tragic of us all: a lonely, frightened man, saddled with three women, facing an insecure future. For the first time in all those weeks aboard the ship I noticed how closely his naked head resembled a skull, and that his ears stuck out from his bald head. Leading his sister past me, he waved apologetically. His smile was sad, and the sun filtering through his ears made them look like large, pink shells.

*Sunday, January 29, 1939.*   We are getting closer to Panama, and I am again sensing the proximity of land. The steward claims that the smell of the shore wakens the animal within us.

Lately the animal within me has been giving me quite a bit of trouble. Since Alma's death—it is six months now—I have been living without a woman. I keep telling myself that at sixty the so-called desires of the flesh should no longer bother me. But they do.

What contributes greatly to my restlessness is Eva's presence. Whenever she flaunts her perfect body before me I have to keep reminding myself that she does not try to tempt me on purpose. I believe she could not consider me less susceptible to her charms if I were dead.

But time and again, under cover of fatherly benevolence, I find myself seeking her company. She suffers me as a young girl will suffer an old man, answering my questions with the condescension of the very young toward the old. Trying to draw her into a conversation is at best a difficult task. Whenever she is not in the mood to talk (and quite often she is not) she withdraws behind some inner bulwark which it is nearly impossible to penetrate.

This morning, though, she seemed in a more talkative mood. She had been the first one to go up on deck, and I found her there sitting in her deck chair, her knees pulled up to her chest as she stared dreamily into the distance.

"Dreaming about your fiancé, Fräulein Eva?"

She glanced at me with a quick, guilty smile.

"Oh, just dreaming," she said, a faint blush deepening the gold of her skin.

I could not help wondering what a girl like Eva would be dreaming about. On the spur of the moment I asked her:

"Tell me, my dear, what would you have done in normal times?"

She darted a suspicious look at me. I had touched on the forbidden, implying that she had not really planned to get married at seventeen and emigrate to El Paramo. I swiftly amended:

"Of course a pretty girl like you would have got married sooner or later!"

"Not before I was twenty-six."

"And why set such an arbitrary date?"

"Because it takes that long to study medicine."

"Is that what you wanted to be, a doctor?"

"You don't have to look at me like that. A girl isn't necessarily stupid just because she has a pleasant face and straight legs. I know I would have made a good doctor."

"Hmmm. So you were dreaming about becoming a great, famous doctor!"

I realized immediately that I had used the wrong tone of voice; as if I were teasing a five-year-old about her ambition to become a nurse.

Eva's eyes narrowed angrily, and she replied with mockery:

"No, I wasn't dreaming about becoming 'a great famous doctor.' That was just something to please my parents, so they could say 'our daughter, the doctor,' the way Frau Kramer says 'my son, the architect.' Isn't that what every middle-class Jewish family wants: to breed at least one doctor? I had the ability and I would have been a good doctor, but I wasn't dreaming about it just now! Do you really want to know what I was dreaming about?" She was very angry now, almost shouting at me. "I had the most stupid, silly dream! All I really wanted to do, I mean *really,* was to go to the Opera Ball when I was eighteen! Well, so much for that stupid dream!"

She turned away quickly, obviously ashamed of her outburst and appalled that she should have said so much to me. I did not dare speak to her for fear she might think I was laughing about her. But I was not laughing. For there, in a nutshell, was the dream of every young girl: all she had said—and the few things she had not said but which, nevertheless, must have been in her heart—was that she wanted to go to the ball in a beautiful gown and glass slippers; that she wanted to meet Prince Charming, have him take her by the hand and walk with him into never-never land to live happily ever after.

And here was Eva, all of seventeen, wavering between the dream and the stark reality into which she had been thrust so young. I wanted to reach out to her, comfort her, and tell her that I understood. But she had walked away from me and stood leaning against the railing, with her back to me. I was not sure that she was not crying.

I am very clumsy with young girls. Yesterday I had Trude in tears; today Eva. Perhaps I would do better to stick, as Frau Kramer calls them, to people my own age. The young may be putting up a brash front, but deep inside they are not yet resigned to the loss of the dream.

*Wednesday, February 1, 1939.* After two hectic days in Cristobal we are again afloat. But now we can dimly see at all times the coastline of South America to our left. Somehow I felt happier when we were surrounded by water. Now the proximity of land has brought back all my Jewish fears.

The fears and qualms began right after our arrival in Cristobal. Shortly after we had dropped anchor a letter from Walter Kramer was delivered to his parents aboard ship. In it Walter instructed us—our entire party—to go to a merchant in Cristobal who would sell us certain articles much in demand in El Paramo at good prices. The idea is to bring these items in custom free—in other words, to smuggle them in and make some profit on them. Altogether we have filled three suitcases, bought especially for that purpose, with men's shirts, socks, pajamas, and ladies' underwear.

I can't say that I am much taken with that enterprise, but I was outvoted by Kramer and Goldmann. Staring coldly at me, Kramer said:

"Perhaps other people also want to recover their traveling expenses."

I wanted to ask him what he meant by "also" but thought better of it. Why start an argument over the profit which I am supposed to have made on the visas?

One consolation at least: Walter wrote in his letter that he has good connections with the customs officials.

*Friday, February 3, 1939.*    Tomorrow is our last day aboard ship. The day after we will reach our port of debarkation, Rioverde. We are all restless and edgy. Now that our arrival is imminent, certain fears for the future become more concrete in my mind. So far I have been able to delude myself as to the severity of the language barrier. (Goldmann: "So who wants to talk to the Indians, anyway?") But now, shortly, the little Spanish that I have taught myself will be put to the test.

It is a great relief to know that Walter will be there to pick us up from the boat and chaperon us on our way to Esperanza.

*Saturday, February 4, 1939.*    Last day.

We spent most of it on deck, mentally saying good-by to the ship which, in six weeks, has become home to us. Shortly after breakfast we men became embroiled in an argument over how much to tip the stewards. None of us can afford to squander money, and Goldmann was of the opinion that we ought to tip as little as possible.

I argued that there would be other Jewish refugees taking the trip after us; by tipping properly, we would ensure their good treatment in the future. Goldmann grumbled, but finally consented to tip twenty dollars for his family of four. Kramer settled for fifteen, and I volunteered ten.

"Believe me, we're crazy," Goldmann said. "I bet the Germans don't tip a cent. They just go around shaking everybody's hand and saying a hearty Dankeschön!"

Probably Goldmann is right; but the Germans don't mind being disliked. We do. For two thousand years we have pathetically tried to be liked by our hosts. I wonder whether we will succeed in El Paramo.

I am so tense that my thoughts come only in fits and starts. For some reason I keep remembering Frau Kramer ironing one of her flowered, ruffled dresses and shining a pair of fancy shoes which she has not worn on the ship. She flutters as if she and not Eva were the future bride.

In the afternoon Eva brought a geography book up on deck, explaining that she had taken some of her schoolbooks along in her luggage. This again brought her youth startlingly back to me. A schoolgirl with books in her trunk traveling to South America to be married!

For a while we sat around studying what facts we could find about El Paramo. Strange that we should have put off facing reality for so long —as if we wanted to enjoy our artificial vacation aboard this ship to the last moment. When I went down to the cabin I borrowed the book from Eva to copy some of the information. This might prove interesting in comparison with our future experiences. I am trying to condense here what seems most pertinent to me:

. . . El Paramo borders on the Pacific Ocean . . . includes steaming jungles as well as perpetual snow fields . . . more than twenty active volcanoes cause frequent earthquakes . . . (Frau Goldmann should have read that!) . . . some minerals occur: silver, gold, copper, petroleum near Aguas Calientes . . . capital city Esperanza situated in the Andes at an elevation of about 10,000 feet at the foot of the volcano Grampico (inactive, we hope) . . . most of the population of El Paramo lives in this healthful region: Indians, mestizos, whites—with a few Jews now being added . . . main port of El Paramo is Rioverde, located about a mile inland at the mouth of the Rio Verde . . . it has frequently suffered from earthquakes. . . .

Why all this insistence on earthquakes? Josef never mentioned anything about earthquakes in his letters. Neither did Walter. Well, what do we have to lose? Our lives? I am still glad though that Frau Goldmann did not get hold of the book.


*Rioverde, Sunday, February 5, 1939.*    A day of catastrophe!

It is past midnight and I am deadly tired, but I cannot sleep. Now that I have finally become used to the narrow cot in the cabin and the rocking of the ship at night, I have been thrust into this nightmare of a hotel room. Walter says this is the second best hotel in Rioverde (we cannot afford the best), ironically named Hotel Royal.

The house is a crude, wooden structure, cleverly designed to trap the humid, tropical heat and to allow for free passage of sound from one room to the other. The dividing walls between the rooms do not reach all the way up to the ceiling but end in a sort of open grillwork, obviously meant to allow for a better circulation of air. Instead of admitting a refreshing breeze, the open slats in the wood let in the desperate whining of Frau Kramer from one side ("Oh, God, oh, God, how are we going to survive in this climate!") and the ceaseless, wild babbling of Frau Paula Gruen from the other.

Even without the noises of my neighbors it would be impossible to sleep. Outside a torrential downpour is flooding the streets. The hard prattle of the rain surges through the open window into my room, a sound as if water were spurting full force from a thousand faucets.

As if the heat and the rain were not enough, the air is buzzing with myriads of disgusting cucarachas. They cling in vile clusters to the lampposts, crawl on the walls of the buildings, and drop out of the air onto the heads and shoulders of pedestrians. Frau Goldmann has been reduced to a state of shrieking hysteria and refuses to leave the hotel, even to attend Eva's wedding.

Eva and Walter are to be married day after tomorrow. Frau Kramer was stunned when Walter broke the news to her. ("What's the hurry? Why not wait until we get to Esperanza, until we're all settled? We could furnish a home first, invite a few people—besides, your sister wrote in her last letter that she and Alfred might still decide to come to Esperanza. So the whole family would be there, and what difference would another three, four weeks make now?")

Walter patiently explained to his mother that he had already rented a house for them, and that the arrangement of rooms was such that he and Eva had better get married before they moved in. Failing to persuade him to change his plans, Frau Kramer has been sulking ever since. In fact, she has been sulking since Walter came aboard to pick us up.

This morning I was the first one up on deck, long before the others came out of their cabins. I watched as the tugboat steered us into the

Rio Verde, winding its way among the perilous, small islands which clutter the mouth of the river. In the distance the city lay asleep in the haze, but around us were messengers of human life: orange peels and bits of refuse floating on the slimy, green water of the river.

It was not until after we had dropped anchor and were surrounded by a fleet of small rowboats from which dark-skinned boys shouted up offers that the others came on deck. I looked around for Eva. Apparently unaffected by the murderous heat, she stood by the railing, watching the scene below. She was dressed entirely in white and wore a white ribbon in her hair. The skin of her bare legs and arms gleamed golden in the sun. From the bridge above the young sailor was watching her wistfully.

Frau Kramer, lips pursed in disapproval, also was observing Eva.

"She will get herself all dirty. I told her to wear something more sensible, but does she listen to me?"

Glancing down at her own flowered-silk dress, Frau Kramer heavily bent over to flick a speck of soot from her freshly shined shoes. I had never seen her so meticulously dressed and combed. Even the seams of her stockings were straight.

Herr Kramer kept himself at some distance from us, walking up and down and swinging his cane. On the whole he deported himself like a king expecting his crown prince.

The Goldmanns emerged on deck as a solid group, Herr Goldmann herding his women before him, as if he were afraid to lose one of them at the last moment. Catching sight of Eva in her white dress, Frau Goldmann viciously turned on her daughter:

"I told you to wear your pink silk! Look at Eva! Why do you always have to go around looking like a schlemasel?"

Trude shrugged impatiently and went over to Eva. Frau Goldmann mournfully looked after her.

"She just doesn't *want* to look pretty. And I bought her such beautiful dresses! Why are children so ungrateful? The sacrifices I made to buy her clothes . . ."

It was at this point that Frau Goldmann noticed that we had dropped anchor in the middle of the river. Her eyes anxiously began to measure the distance between ship and shore, while her face grew more and more alarmed.

"Tell me, Herr Professor, how is our luggage supposed to get across?"

I passed on the information the steward had given me earlier: that we and the luggage would be picked up by barges and ferried across the river.

"You mean to say they're going to load our trunks on one of *those* boats? On one of those rickety things down there? And what if it sinks, God forbid!"

"Else, don't be foolish, why should it sink?"

"With our luck it just might!"

"All right, if it sinks we'll all buy fig leaves and walk around naked. You'll look very pretty in a fig leaf, Else!"

Goldmann grinned lasciviously, nudged me in the ribs and giggled like a goon. Frau Goldmann flushed angrily and stamped her foot, but before the Goldmanns had a chance to erupt into an argument Frau Kramer began to bob up and down with excitement.

"Here he comes! Here comes my Walter! Everybody come look at my Walter! Isn't he handsome?"

(It takes the imagination of a mother to call Walter Kramer a handsome man. He is of medium height and stocky, with sharp, Jewish features, light-gray eyes, and the fleshy mouth of his mother. I remember Arthur's telling me that Walter had great charm and was something of a Don Juan. Even if I can't see it, there must still be some reason why Eva was drawn to him.)

Spurred on by Frau Kramer's shouting, everybody hurried over to the railing to get a better look at the approaching motorboat. Four men were sitting on its crude benches. There was no mistaking Walter among them: he was wearing gray pants and a short-sleeved sports shirt, and he was the only one without a hat. The other three men, obviously the immigration officials, wore black suits and black hats which, in the glaring sun of forenoon, gave them the eerie appearance of undertakers.

As the boat drew nearer Frau Kramer's shouting and bobbing became more agitated. Waving a big, white handkerchief, she almost fell overboard in her effort to attract Walter's attention. Even Frau Goldmann was so overcome by excitement that she burst into tears.

I glanced quickly at Eva. If she was excited she certainly showed admirable self-control. She had moved away from Trude and stood by herself, aloof and composed, her hand fluttering gently in the saluting gesture of visiting royalty. The murderous heat had wilted nothing of her morning freshness, and she still looked cool and virginal in her white dress. Though she barely smiled, there was a breath-taking radiance about her.

The motorboat had pulled up by the side of the ship and a rope ladder was lowered into it. Walter was the first one to climb it, his face turned up with a grin wavering between embarrassment and joy. When he jumped on deck, Eva was the first person in his path. He grabbed her by the shoulders, held her away from him and rapturously gazed at her for a moment.

"God, you're beautiful!"

Then he took her in his arms and kissed her.

Halfway across the deck to hurl herself into her son's embrace, Frau Kramer stopped dead in her tracks. She stood panting as she watched Eva and Walter kiss for what—even to me—seemed a very long time. Then Walter let go of Eva and turned toward his mother. He made a move as if to embrace her, but Frau Kramer turned sideways and stood caught in his arms like a sulking child. Her face was a grimace of outrage and hurt as she said to him:

"You kissed her first!"

"But, Mama, she's my bride!"

Frau Kramer was by no means mollified by his answer, but as Walter moved on to greet his father and the rest of the party, her ill humor was momentarily lost in the hubbub of shouting and handshaking.

Presently we were all marched into the dining saloon, where the immigration officials had set up their office. With Walter as interpreter, the passport control proceeded swiftly and painlessly.

By the time we came out on deck again the unloading of our luggage had begun. We all watched tremulously as the big steamer trunks and crates were piled into crude nets and lowered onto the barges. Even I could see that the men handling the nets were not skilled in their labor. The transfer of the heavy crates from the ship's hold onto the barges was a haphazard operation, accomplished with much waving of arms, running to and fro, and repeated shouting of words which were not, as I later learned from Walter, orders, but untranslatable obscenities. Just as the last load was about to be piled into the net, Frau Goldmann suddenly lurched forward and threw herself over one of the trunks.

"Not that one!" she cried desperately. "You can't put that one in with the rest! The net will tear and everything will fall in the water and my Trudi's trousseau will be lost!"

Walter tried to persuade Frau Goldmann to release the trunk, but she sat on it and would not budge. Finally it was agreed that Trude's trousseau should be lowered by itself. But apparently there was a misunderstanding on the barge: as soon as the last large load had been accommodated, the towlines which fastened the barge to the ship were pulled in, and when the net with Trude's trunk came swinging down, the barge had already moved a few feet out into the water.

While the net swayed precariously over the ever-widening gap between ship and barge, Frau Goldmann hung over the railing, shrieking and gesticulating with despair. In the barge below the men raised their arms, shouting:

"Bájelo! Bájelo!"

"No, no, súbelo!" Walter screamed.

After a few minutes of utter confusion, the men on deck began raising the net. But as they raised it, a rip which had been widened by the previous heavy loads, split along the entire width of the net. Before the disbelieving eyes of Frau Goldmann, the trunk popped out the way a ripe chestnut pops out of its green husk, plunged down into the water, submerged, bobbed up once more in a brave try to stay afloat, but finally was swallowed by the burping, slimy waters of the Rio Verde.

Frau Goldmann collapsed with a loud scream. Her voice came out racked between sobs:

"Oh, the trousseau! Oh, my poor Trudi's trousseau!"

Trude knelt down beside her crying mother and tried to calm her.

"Mama, please, control yourself. What does it matter? I'm not getting married, anyway."

"Yes, you are!" Frau Goldmann screeched. "You are so going to get married!"

The rest was sheer bedlam. How Walter ever got us to the hotel, between the crying, sulking women and the men who could not speak Spanish and therefore were of no help, is still a miracle to me. By the time we were halfway settled it was too late to go to the customhouse for our luggage. This would not have mattered but for the fact that the train for Esperanza leaves only every other day, and by missing tomorrow's train we will have to stay two additional days in this rathole.

And this is only the beginning!

*Monday, February 6, 1939.* This morning I was awakened from a leaden sleep by the most unearthly screams, coming from the street. I fumbled for my watch and found that it was only five o'clock, but I was unable to go back to sleep. So I lay in bed, listening until the words shouted in the street began to make sense. "*El Día! El Día!*" (The newspaper, I learned later.) "Las uvas!" (Grapes.) "Naranjas!" (Oranges.) And something which sounded like pecado, but turned out to be pescado, fish. Pecado, Walter said, meant sin and was being sold in another sector of town. Goldmann was all in favor of going there, but Walter was not to be won over to this cause. After all, he is getting married tomorrow.

Later in the day we went to pick up our luggage at the customhouse. Fortunately Walter's friend was around to help pass our "imported" suitcases through the inspection. Walter told us only afterward, on our way back to the hotel, how lucky we had been: prior to our arrival there had been a short revolution in El Paramo and most of the government officials had been changed. If I imagine what might have happened . . . Ah, the recklessness of youth!

In the evening the revolution which Walter had so casually mentioned in the morning was discussed once more. Frau Goldmann immediately launched into a dramatic scene.

"A revolution! You hear that, Markus, a revolution! Oh God, why did we have to come here?"

This last with an accusing look at me.

Walter tried to calm her.

"Don't worry, Frau Goldmann. A revolution here is of no significance. It takes a day at the most, and half the people don't even know about it. Of course the entire government changed, but that won't affect our status here at all."

"And what is our status here?" I asked.

Walter gave me a withering look.

"Here," he said, "we are welcome."

*Tuesday, February 7, 1939.*    For a man who has always slept very soundly, I am beginning to develop a serious case of insomnia.

Outside, the rain is again pounding the pavement. The heat, which is bad enough during the daytime, becomes even worse at night—or rather less bearable, because one expects it to cool off.

Frau Gruen is mercifully quiet tonight. But now, during a lull in the rain, a strange noise seeps in from the room of the Kramers. I know the noise but keep telling myself that it can't be. And yet, there it is: the rhythmical whining of bed springs.

This is unbearable!

No, not the thought of Herr Kramer's enjoying his wife (if he can still enjoy her), but the suspicion of what brought on the act of love next door. Eva and Walter were married this afternoon, and their room adjoins the one of the Kramers. Surely some of the sounds of love-making must come through the open slats in the wall!

Oh, God, I wish they would stop!

Am I really enraged by the thought of Herr Kramer's drawing stimulation from the sounds of young love, or is this only jealousy masquerading as indignation?

I spent ten minutes by the window, watching the lights of solitary cars swim by in the rain. Then I went to bed, but I was still unable to fall asleep under the white mosquito net that perches above the bed like a nightmare.

Next door it is quiet now. I have already begun to tell myself that the sounds which I thought I heard were an illusion, conjured up by my overwrought mind. Perhaps I have been thinking too much about the wedding night of Eva and Walter.

In the afternoon, shortly before they left to get married, Walter decided that nobody but the two necessary witnesses should accompany them. He gave a number of reasons for his sudden decision: the civil marriage was a mere formality; we would not understand a word of the ceremony; it was raining much too hard for any of us to venture out.

Actually, I believe that Walter has detected some of the tension between Eva and his parents and that he would rather be alone with his bride on this occasion.

Eva seemed calm enough, looking considerably less a bride today than on the morning of our arrival. She wore a gray raincoat and sturdy shoes but she would not relinquish the token gesture of wearing a little white hat with a veil.

"You're only going to ruin it," Frau Kramer chided.

"What should I save it for? My next wedding?"

In the early afternoon the two witnesses, who under the law have to be citizens of El Paramo, came to pick up Eva and Walter. They greeted Walter in profuse Spanish, vigorously slapping his back just above the kidneys. If they had not switched to Yiddish after they realized that none of us spoke Spanish, I would never have taken them for Jews.

They were certainly an odd-looking pair: one short, dark and shifty-eyed, introducing himself as Dubrovsky; the other one tall, bony and sporting a beard of at least three days' growth, as Grushka. Staring at them, I thought that this was indeed going to be a very informal wedding, with the two witnesses looking as if Walter had just fished them out of the gutter.

While Grushka went out in the rain to call a cab, I managed to ask Walter just where he had dug up those two suspicious-looking characters. He answered evasively that they were two friends of his from Esperanza who had come on business to Rioverde. I must say Walter is picking some strange friends!

But now, the more I think of Grushka and Dubrovsky the more I am convinced that they must be the recipients of our merchandise. They certainly look as if they were engaged in some sort of illicit business! At least they had sense enough not to return to the hotel with the bridal couple.

We were all assembled in the lobby to await the return of the young people. The air was exceedingly close, and the rain hung over the entrance to the lobby like a solid curtain of crystal strings. One could barely see out into the street, and Eva looked like an apparition when she suddenly dashed in. Her hat had become thoroughly drenched, and the veil, which she had thrown back over her head, hung down limp and bedraggled. There was a faint smile on her face, but with the raindrops on her cheeks she looked as if she were crying.

Walter came in after her. For a second he stood brushing raindrops from his hat while he foolishly grinned at the reception committee.

As upon a signal, we all converged on the young couple, congratulating them, embracing them, kissing them.

After the endearments were over we stood around for a while, looking foolish. It was still too early for dinner—only three o'clock in the afternoon—and the rain outside made it impossible to propose a walk. Besides, it was obvious that Walter was casting about for a tasteful excuse to retire with his bride.

Twisting his hat in his hand and gazing at it with profound interest, Walter said slowly:

"Well, I guess Eva and I will go and change now. We're both soaked to the skin."

An expression of genuine alarm spread over Frau Kramer's face.

"But you can't . . . I mean, you're not really *that* wet! Let Eva go and change, and in the meantime you can tell us all about the wedding, and where did your two friends go, why didn't they come and eat with us, you should have invited them . . ."

As she talked rapidly, holding on to Walter's arm all the while, Eva walked away and began to ascend the stairs to the second floor.

"I'll tell you all about it later, Mama."

Walter tried to disengage himself from his mother.

"Let him go, Rifka!"

Herr Kramer suddenly snapped at his wife in such a gruff manner that she instantly let go of Walter's arm. Walter quickly slipped away, caught up with Eva on the steps, and together they disappeared around a corner. As soon as Frau Kramer realized that her son had escaped her, she turned on her husband:

"What kind of a father are you, not even interested in the wedding of your own son!"

"Wedding, shmedding, he'll tell us all about it at dinnertime."

Frau Kramer sniffed, pulled out her handkerchief, blew her nose, and went to sulk in one of the wicker chairs by the window. There she sat for a long time, glumly staring at the misty glass panes on which the rain ran down in wide, undulating rivulets.

Frau Goldmann and Trude also went upstairs to rest, while we three men remained in the lobby.

"Well, I for one am glad that they got married so fast," Herr Kramer said. "What that girl needs is a husband to keep her in check."

He sat down and clamped his ever-present cane between his legs, freeing his hand to light a cigarette. As the match burst into flame, his features were briefly illuminated, displaying what impressed me as a faun-like grin of contentment. I imagined Herr Kramer thinking of his son as an extension of himself, imposing upon Eva the one act of mastery which in the future would render her an obedient wife. The cane between his legs stuck out like an obscene, phallic symbol. For no good reason I suddenly felt like striking him.

Goldmann stretched and rubbed his eyes with the back of his hands.

"I guess I'll also retire. The honeymooners won't come down before dinner, if they come down at all."

It turned out that Goldmann had guessed correctly: Eva and Walter did not come down for dinner.

Frau Kramer could barely be restrained from carrying some food upstairs to her son. She was so fidgety throughout the meal that she made us all nervous. After dinner we wanted to go for a walk, but the sodden air outside was humming with mosquitoes and we fled back into the lobby. There we sullenly sat around for another hour until Trude sensibly suggested that we ought to go to bed. Our train for Esperanza leaves tomorrow morning at six o'clock. That means getting up at three.

I should have been asleep a long time ago. The slamming of doors in the hotel has ceased and even the dripping of the rain outside has become fainter. It is almost two o'clock. I will have to rise in another hour. Well, I can always sleep on the train.

*Wednesday, February 8, 1939.*    This is only an overnight stop in a place called Nariz del Diablo, Devil's Nose. Tomorrow we continue our trip to Esperanza.

My insomnia has become persistent. It seems that the wearier I am the harder it becomes for me to fall asleep. The moment I close my eyes the impressions of the last twelve hours begin to reel through my mind. Ah, the sights and smells, or rather the stench of the trip!

We left the hotel in Rioverde at four o'clock in the morning. Even among the hubbub of the departure everybody kept staring at Eva. But if each of us, according to his preconceptions, searched her face for a change, we were all disappointed. Though she was officially a woman now, she looked as pure and virginal as the day before.

A cab took us down to the Rio Verde. From there we were ferried across by another rickety barge to the railroad station, which is located on a peninsula. As soon as we debarked we were surrounded by a horde of howling cargadores, offering to carry our luggage to the train. Many were just half-grown boys, extremely dirty, ragged and evil smelling.

With the help of one of them we reached the train, which consisted of a few dilapidated, overcrowded coaches. Some of the overflowing passengers were crouched on top of the coaches, laughing and shouting obscenities at each other. Most of them got off at villages in the vicinity of Rioverde.

As the hours passed I realized how lucky we were to have a first-class compartment to ourselves. Even so the train ride was trying enough. We must have halted in a hundred villages. In each one vendors swarmed out of their huts and surrounded the train to peddle their wares. Some sold fried bacon rind and cooked beans, which they scooped out of the pans with their dirty hands, piled on a piece of newspaper and handed to their customers.

After repeated loud screams of horror, Frau Goldmann refused to take another look out the window. Whenever we pulled into a station she sat with her hands clamped over her eyes, moaning and cursing the day Hitler marched into Austria.

"Why did we have to come here? Oh, God, why did we have to come here? Who ever heard of people in their right minds emigrating to El Paramo?"

"Come now, Else, don't make things worse than they are! Just take a look at the bananas I bought! A whole cluster for one and a half pesos, ten dollar cents! Why, at this rate we can go on eating forever."

Goldmann stood there like a bald King Kong, swinging the cluster of bananas in his hand. In spite of his boisterous demeanor, I knew that he was frightened. He wears his constant optimism like an armor. Later he even naïvely suggested that he was really going to manufacture ladies' underwear, but Walter only laughed at him.

"Where will you get the machinery?"

"Where will I get the machinery? Buy it, of course!"

"And how much money do you have?"

"I don't see that this is any of your business!"

(I happen to know that Goldmann has seven hundred dollars; five hundred landing money for himself and his wife, and a hundred each for Trude and his sister.)

Goldmann retired behind a barrier of hurt dignity, but a couple of hours later he was back, sparring with Walter.

"So what do people do for a living in Esperanza?"

Walter shrugged.

"Well, Walter, what do *you* do for a living?"

"You really want to know? I've been teaching Spanish to new immigrants."

"You mean to say we're not the only maniacs coming to El Paramo?"

"You'd be surprised," Walter said.

Goldmann retired into a corner to brood about his future prospects and soon fell asleep.

The train ground on and on. There were fewer villages now, and the encroaching jungle almost spilled over the narrow railroad tracks. For some reason I suddenly had the foolish vision of Josef Blumenthal singlehandedly hacking his way through the jungle to lay the tracks for the train. Josef Blumenthal, young and virile, in boots, tight breeches and a white helmet, like a shining knight out of a fairy tale.

Imperceptibly but steadily the train began to burrow into the mountains. One after the other, my weary fellow travelers dozed off to sleep.

Walter and I were the only ones whose eyes remained open. I tried to carry on a whispered conversation with him, which consisted more of pantomime than of words. Pointing at Goldmann, I formed the question:

"What *can* he do in Esperanza?"

Walter pulled up his shoulders, raised his hands, palms upward, and lifted his eyes to the ceiling as if to say: God only knows.

I felt a brief stab of guilt because I had a job waiting for me. God bless Josef Blumenthal, I thought.

The train was climbing steadily now, and the air got considerably colder. Eva opened her eyes and shivered. One after the other the rest of our fellow travelers awoke and began to complain about the cold. With the profound gloom of a sybil, Frau Goldmann kept predicting that we would all catch our death on this trip.

The hairpin curves around which the train snaked its way became steeper and steeper. The grade had become so perilous that the train had to zigzag its way up the mountains. Walter explained that this point was called Nariz del Diablo, the Devil's Nose. For the last two hours heavy clouds had hung around the mountains and darkness fell suddenly as it does in low latitudes. Half an hour after we had passed the Nariz del Diablo the train stopped for the night in a village of the same name.

Again we were herded into a hotel, almost the replica of the Hotel Royal in Rioverde. Only this one is cold and damp.

After dinner we all retired, and here I am sitting now, trapped once again in a forbidding hotel room while I long for something resembling home.

But I shall be living in a home soon enough. During dinner the conversation had turned to living conditions in Esperanza. I asked if there were any small apartments available for an old widower like myself.

"Of course you'll be living with us," Walter said matter-of-factly.

I muttered a feeble protest, something to the effect that I did not want to be a burden to anyone.

"Nonsense," Walter said. "After what you did for us, this is the least we can do for you. You'll have a nice, quiet room to yourself. The house I rented is large enough for all of us. We'll live upstairs, the Goldmanns downstairs. I bought beds for everybody, nothing much, but at least we'll have a place to sleep when we get to Esperanza."

Frau Goldmann cried and called Walter a saint.

Considering all the times aboard ship when I could hardly wait to be rid of my companions, I feel oddly relieved to know that I will have a home with them. Alas, man is a social animal!

Now that I have a job and a home, what else is there to worry about? I wonder whether Josef will come to meet me at the train.

# Part Two ❧ Ararat

*And the ark rested in the seventh month, on the seventeenth day of the month, upon the mountains of Ararat.*

GENESIS 8:4

*Friday, February 10, 1939.*     I was too exhausted yesterday to write down anything about my meeting with Josef. If only I had not fashioned in my mind this silly picture of Josef in breeches and a tropical helmet, the encounter with him would have been less of a shock. Perhaps my weariness after the long train ride added to my feeling of disappointment.

We had boarded the train at daybreak. By the time we reached Esperanza, the city was shrouded in the twilight of early evening. All day long rain had fallen, the gray masses of water almost entirely blotting out the landscape outside. Only now and then could I get a glimpse of the mountains rearing up through the swirling mist, or of a jagged peak swimming like a phantom above the low-hanging clouds. The country through which we traveled was depressingly desolate, and the long-drawn, mournful brays of a solitary mule only added to the nightmarish feeling of the trip.

I dozed off repeatedly. Every time I woke up I had to remind myself that I was not dreaming. The others also slept in fits and starts, but as we kept coming closer to Esperanza a restiveness spread among us. We began getting up from our seats, stretching, and jostling each other away from the window to get a better look outside.

The huts by the railroad track had become more numerous. In the lead-colored light of late afternoon we could see figures crouching on the ground outside the doors. While the train slowed down I observed an Indian woman meticulously delousing her child. From time to time she stopped to stick her fingers in her mouth. Walter explained laconically that she was disposing of her offspring's lice by eating them.

Eva turned away and retched. If I had not been on the lookout for Josef I would have done the same. But I was already too keyed up to relinquish my post by the window.

Even before the train came to a complete halt I lowered the window and stuck my head outside. This unwary motion was taken by the cargadores as a signal to advance on our compartment like a band of howling dervishes. Among their flailing hands and bobbing heads I was unable to locate anybody even resembling Josef.

All up and down the platform welcomes and salutations were in full swing, accompanied by much backslapping. Most of the people wore unrelieved black, as if the entire nation were in deep mourning. The women looked nunlike, with their heads and shoulders swathed in black shawls.

I was unable to spot Josef among the milling crowd. (For some reason I still expected him to be wearing a white tropical helmet.) When we finally left the train my disappointment about his failure to meet me was sharp and smarting. While Walter went to get a cab and we stood fighting off the pressing phalanx of cargadores, a portly man suddenly forced his way through the shouting, snatching crowd.

I immediately recognized the man, though I could not say that I recognized him as Josef Blumenthal. Staring at him, I felt transported fifty years back when, on a Saturday afternoon, Josef's father, Reb Mendel Blumenthal, had come to call on my father. Surely Reb Mendel had been younger then than his son was now, but he too had been stout, with sparse, reddish hair and a shiny, high-colored face. And his black caftan had looked not unlike the black suit Josef was wearing.

It took me a few seconds before I was able to adjust the picture of Josef Blumenthal—of a young Josef Blumenthal in breeches and tropical helmet—to the appearance of the man before me. I had never been separated from a close friend for a long period; now, for the first time in my life, I had the shocking sensation that time had passed and I had grown old.

I believe Josef had a similar experience. For quite a while he only stood gaping at me, his expression wavering between shock and deep emotion. Then, almost simultaneously, we both took one step forward. The next moment Josef had embraced me, vigorously pounding my back and greeting me in profuse Spanish. His welcome left me with the uneasy feeling that I had been met by a complete stranger.

The next few minutes were extremely awkward ones. Josef told me that I had not changed at all, and I reciprocated the lie. Then I introduced him to my companions. With every hand he shook he said gravely and courteously: mucho gusto. The introductions over, Josef offered to take as many of us as he could accommodate in his car to our new home. A reverential silence fell over our group: Josef Blumenthal owned a car!

Just then Walter returned to announce that he had found a cab. I knew that Walter and Josef had met before (I had given Walter a letter of introduction to him), but what I did not know was that there seemed to be some sort of bad feeling between them. They greeted each other with cold civility, and then Walter tried to hustle us off to the taxi. Of course there was not room enough to accommodate nine people in one cab, and we were only too glad to take Josef up on his offer.

Most of the ride from the station to our house passed in deep silence. Outside it had become so dark that hardly anything could be seen. Beneath the street lamps, sickly yellowish cones of light hung in the mist. The store windows were covered with wooden shutters, and there were no electric signs anywhere. Aside from a few pedestrians hurrying along the narrow sidewalks, the whole city looked deserted and dead. Even in the darkness I could see the black mass of mountains looming oppressively close.

Our ride took us up and down hilly streets, over uneven pavement that jolted us in our seats. Josef tried intermittently to make polite conversation. All the time we did not look straight at each other, but only snatched secret glances. We were like two strange dogs, sniffing each other.

We had crossed the entire city, and after a while I dimly realized that we had reached the suburbs. The streets had become wider, and on either side were small houses surrounded by gardens. It looked as if we were being taken to a neighborhood much too exclusive for our circumstances, but I was too weary to question anything just then.

When we arrived at the house which Walter has rented for us, it was raining again. The house, still in the last stages of construction, offered an uninviting sight. Behind the unfinished garden wall heaps of rubbish and mangled boards were scattered over what, I suppose, would someday be a garden. The walk to the front door consisted entirely of mud puddles, and the women complained bitterly as they picked their way through the sticky clay. Frau Goldmann lost the heel of one shoe in the mud, an accident which only strengthened her in the belief that she had been singled out by fate for a life of grief.

Inside, in its bareness, the house seemed of palatial dimensions. The entrance hall extended in height through both stories, with a curved stairway sweeping up to the second floor. Frau Goldmann and Frau Kramer immediately began taking stock of the place, restricted only by their weariness from engaging in a heated discussion about the merits of the upstairs apartment versus the downstairs apartment.

Josef gravely said good night to me, inviting me to call on him as soon as I was settled. Then he walked out, stout and somber in his black suit, a stranger who had once been my friend. I could not help feeling that he was glad to get out of the inhospitable-looking house with its unwaxed floors, spattered windows, and the air still smelling of fresh paint and cement.

I think two or three days will be a good time to let the shock of our first meeting wear off. By then I will also be rested enough to talk with Josef about my job. In the interim I am sitting here alone, facing the third strange room in the past week. Save for my suitcases and the large, canvas-covered couch, the room is completely empty. There are no curtains on the windows, and in two spots water is seeping through the cracks around the window frames and running down over the freshly painted walls, leaving narrow, wet tracks. (The rain has not stopped since our arrival.) It is cold and damp, a dampness which seems to penetrate to the very marrow of the bones. As I write with stiff fingers, my notebook propped up on my suitcase, I keep wondering whether this will really be home someday.

*Saturday, February 11, 1939.* Everything looks better on a bright day!

This morning, when I woke up, my room was filled with sunlight. The gushing of the downpour last night had made me think that it would never stop raining. Only the chorus of frogs in the night reminded me that we were on dry land. Well, land at any rate!

I was once awakened about midnight. A rooster whose sense of time had gone haywire kept crowing and crowing, rousing the dogs of the neighborhood to a furious exchange of barks. They yapped insults at each other across the gulf of the night until they tired of it and fell asleep again.

The next thing I felt was the sun on my face. I got up and stepped to the window. The air outside was transparent, as if the rain of the previous night had washed away every last particle of dust. Opposite my window, appearing deceptively close, the mountains reared up against the brilliantly blue sky. From a snow-capped peak at the center of the range the slopes broke away in velvety green folds. (This mountain is the famous Grampico. The name is an abbreviation of pico grande, large peak. Goldmann was delighted to learn that there is a double-entendre to it: pico grande also means large penis.) Here and there the crests of the mountains were dotted with the feathery outlines of trees, and the rectangular shapes of the fields were etched in various shades of green upon the slopes, as if by the meticulous hand of an artist. Above a solitary hut, a white flag of smoke unfurled against the dark-green background.

I was overcome by a vacation mood. For a moment I even forgot what had brought me to El Paramo. I opened the window, took a deep breath of mountain air, and my stomach began to grumble inside of me.

I went to the kitchen, passing the bathroom on the way. Walter was standing outside the bathroom door, waiting his turn. His hair was tousled, his skin dark with beard, and he wore blue-and-white striped pajamas which made him look like an escaped convict. He had bad news for me.

"Don't use the toilet if you don't have to," he said. "The plumbing doesn't work."

"I'll try my best," I promised without conviction. "How about washing?"

"I had one of the workmen bring up a pail of water from next door. If you want to wash, you have to get a pitcher of water from the kitchen."

When I came into the kitchen I found Frau Kramer there, virtually tearing her hair. Instead of a modern gas range, an outdated, wood-burning stove not unlike the one my mother had used fifty years earlier had been installed in the kitchen.

"Barbarians in this country! How am I supposed to cook on this contraption? Oh, God, why did we have to come here?"

This last question, as usual, was directed at me.

"You want some water?" Frau Kramer asked me. "That's all you can have anyway. You'd think my son would get up in the morning and buy something for us to eat! But no, he lies in bed like a prince and doesn't even answer when I knock on the door. For all he cares we can starve to death in this god-forsaken country!"

Frau Kramer was very angry at the world this morning. Her gray hair stood around her head in an unkempt mop. Her robe was sloppily tied, one side pulled up, the other side hanging down at the hem. She already wore her sturdy shoes, but her stockings were rolled down, and her varicose veins showed blue and knotty beneath her grayish white skin. She reminded me so much of how Alma used to look in the morning that I shuddered.

"Walter is still ahead of me. I'll come back later for the water."

I fled from the kitchen and walked out onto the gallery which runs around the large center hall. A gust of wind blew up from the open front door. Workers were passing in and out at a leisurely pace. From below I heard the voices of the Goldmanns, embroiled in a heated discussion about the faulty plumbing. I could imagine Frau Goldmann asking why we had to come here.

Why indeed?

I passed the open door to the bedroom of the Kramers. On the unmade bed, Herr Kramer sat in his long underwear, frowning as he cleaned his nails with his pocket knife. He was so absorbed that he did not even see me pass. In a way I was glad. He and I do not have much to say to each other. I know nothing about the drygoods business; Herr Kramer knows nothing about mathematics; and we often find each other at opposite ends about politics. What else is there for men to talk about? Women, of course. But by a silent conspiracy everybody seems to think that I am already past that age.

And yet heaven knows I'm not! All it takes is the sight of Eva to remind me that I'm not. I could see her through the glass door which leads from the gallery to the large, crescent-shaped terrace in front of the house. She was standing with her back to me, her face lifted up to the mountains, her robe of multicolored India silk fluttering behind her, revealing her long slender legs. Her blond hair shimmered in the sun, and she was pleasant to look at after the Kramers in their morning attire.

When she heard me opening the door she clutched her robe around her and turned to face me. She wore no make-up in the morning and she did not look older than fifteen. Her face was grave and her eyes red-rimmed, as if she had been crying.

Just then Walter's voice burst through the open door in an angry shout: "Eva, where the devil are you? Why aren't you in the kitchen, helping Mama?"

Eva pouted and her eyes filled with tears. Without a word she ran past me into the corridor. Walter, still in his pajamas, came out onto the terrace and stood beside me, scratching his head. He looked puzzled.

"I don't know what's the matter with her," he said. "This morning I woke up, and there she was in bed, crying. Is this what marriage is like?"

He has been married less than a week now and he already asks if this is what marriage is like! I found myself thinking, foolishly, that if Eva were married to me, she would not be crying in the morning. Before I could make some sage remarks about marriage, Eva came back to the terrace.

"There's nothing I can do in the kitchen. I don't see why I should just stand around and listen to your mother curse the stove!"

"All right," Walter said. "I'll get dressed and buy something to eat. By the way, Eva, Mama tells me she's been knocking on our door this morning. Did you hear anything?"

Eva did not answer, but it was written all over her face that she had heard Frau Kramer knock.

"Why the hell didn't you wake me?"

"It was six o'clock in the morning and you were fast asleep! She could see you were asleep! She was standing right there by the door, looking in! You should have made them put a wall between the two bedrooms while they were building the house. A wall without a door! I won't have people look at my bed at six o'clock in the morning!"

She put her hands to her face and quickly turned away.

I felt that under the circumstances I had better leave the young couple alone. But I can understand Eva's outburst.

The bedrooms of the younger and elder Kramers are connected by a large door, the upper half of which consists of glass panes. There are no curtains on the door, and one can see from one room into the other. Having been left the choice of the rooms, Frau Kramer picked the one containing a large double bed which during the day serves as a couch, while Walter and Eva were left with the room furnished with two narrow couches running around the corner. ("I don't see how Papa and I could possibly be comfortable on the narrow couches," Frau Kramer had said. Sometimes I ask myself whether she really has no idea of what she is doing.)

But Walter should have had more sense. Perhaps I ought to speak to him. But I doubt that he has offered me his hospitality in order to give me a better chance to meddle in his private affairs.


*Tuesday, February 14, 1939.*    I have asked Walter to get me a plan of Esperanza in order to familiarize myself with some of the street names. So far we have not yet ventured out alone, but tomorrow morning we are to go for a tour of the city.

Walter has pointed out on the map the few places of interest: the central plaza, called Plaza de la Libertad; the few blocks of shopping center, bordered on one side by the Avenida Bolívar and on the other by the Avenida Rioverde; the Calle Manuel Araujo, named for the national hero of El Paramo, and the two other streets named for the day he was born and the day when, after he had fallen from grace, he was seized by the populace, tied to the tails of two horses and dragged to his death through the streets of El Paramo. (I do not know whether the fact that these three streets run parallel to each other speaks of the Parameños' sense of historical perspective or of their macabre sense of humor.)


*Wednesday, February 15, 1939.*    We got home from our tour of Esperanza about an hour ago, just beating the rain. (Every day the rains start punctually a few minutes after one o'clock. The first clouds, billowing around the Grampico, are suddenly followed by a gray mass which seems to break over the ridge of the mountains like a huge wave. Seconds later heavy drops begin to fall, gaining momentum until the mountains and the valley below are swallowed up by a churning mass of water.)

But when we set out the morning was perfect. Everybody except Frau

Kramer and Frau Goldmann came along. They had decided to stay home and unpack the trunks, which arrived yesterday. Since we still depend upon Walter as an interpreter, we all stuck close to him, even in the rickety, evil-smelling bus, where we were so confined by the crowd that we could not possibly have got lost.

At the Plaza de la Libertad we were glad to get out and leave the stench, the jostling people, and the trespassing fleas behind us. Our eyes were assaulted by the riot of colors splashed all over the plaza: the brilliant hues of flowers in their beds, the green of palm trees, the tarnished bronze of the Bolívar monument, the red and blue ponchos of the Indians mingling with the dark, somber clothes of the gentry. Our own girls in their light summer frocks looked like frivolous butterflies among them. People were staring at us and saying "gringos."

Walter showed us the squat-towered, massive cathedral built of gray stone, one of the oldest in South America, and on the far side of the plaza the long row of white government buildings. (The thought that I might be working there next week, possibly with a view of the colorful plaza below and the green Andes in the background was not at all unpleasant.) Then Walter led us through the shopping arcades beneath the second story of the buildings around the plaza toward the business center of Esperanza. There were open stands between the legitimate stores, heaped with all sorts of merchandise. Most of the transactions were conducted in the street at top voice. All along the way beggars kept swinging out from the shade of the arcades, holding out their hands, clinging to our clothes, whining as they ran along with us. Walter said that begging was a profession here and chided us for giving away all our loose change.

In the Avenida Bolívar we passed the store of the wealthiest Jewish merchant in town, one Isak Levy. Like Grushka and Dubrovsky, he belongs to the old immigration, but his business is strictly legitimate—or almost so—Walter told us.

We reached our next important stop, the post office, via a very steep street. Mail is not being delivered in Esperanza and has to be picked up from a postal box, an apartado. So far Walter has been unable to secure a private apartado for us and we will have to have our mail sent c/o one Señor Peter Fleischer.

On the steps of the post office we met Frau Fleischer, a tall, handsome woman with reddish-blond hair, in her mid-thirties I would say, carrying herself like a woman who knows that men like her. She seemed quite familiar with Walter, and as she talked to him, smoothing his lapels and brushing dust off his coat, I had to wonder again what women can see in Walter Kramer. After she had walked away, swiveling her hips, Goldmann asked Walter with a lewd wink whether he knew her well. Walter put on the innocent air of a man who has something to hide and said:

"Her husband is quite a wolf." (As though this proved something or other.)

Eva frowned and I wondered whether she was jealous. But then she is so much prettier than Frau Fleischer!

By the time we left the post office we'd all had enough new impressions and were glad when Walter took us home. After the heat and noise of the city it was good to come back to my own room. Though it is still cold and bare, I realize that I might have ended up in a much worse place. Once I have a regular working routine I think I could be perfectly happy here.

What more can a man ask than a home and a family who is not his blood relation and whom he can leave any time he pleases?

*Friday, February 17, 1939.* Trying to while away the morning by writing in my diary.

Yesterday evening Josef sent an Indian with a note, asking why I had not called on him yet and inviting me for lunch to his house today. I have brushed my good suit, polished my shoes, and laid out a fresh shirt. Now I am just sitting around with the tense feeling that used to plague me as a young student before every examination. But why should I be so anxious to please Josef? There is really nothing I want of him except the job, and that is already agreed upon. Still, I suppose we all crave approval.

Outside I can hear the clatter of footsteps on the bare floor and the whining of angry female voices. Although workers are still walking in and out, brooms are being wielded, pails keep clanging and doors slamming, while the house is being turned into an inferno of cleanliness.

All in all, the emigration seems to be easier on the women than on the men. Now that the women have their treasured household effects, they can go back to doing what they always did: making a home.

With the men it is different. Goldmann and Kramer keep wandering about the house like lost souls, getting in the way and making the women nervous. I keep to my room, anxious for the day when I shall start on my job. Walter is kept busy doing the marketing and acting as interpreter. Today he gave us a long list of instructions what to do, or rather what not to do: don't eat fresh fruit unless it has been thoroughly washed and soaked in permanganate for half an hour; don't drink water unless it has been boiled for twenty minutes; don't drink unboiled milk; don't eat salads; don't buy ice cream in the street, it is made from unsterilized water. It almost sounds like the ten commandments. Sanitary conditions in Esperanza are simply frightful.

The girls are not much help either. Poor Trude is almost as much of a nuisance as the men. Her mother will not let her do any manual labor. Her argument: "This is not what we brought her up for. Besides, Trudi might ruin her hands."

Perhaps Frau Goldmann has a point there. Trude has beautiful, white hands with long, tapered fingers. A girl with so few attractive features can't risk spoiling what little she has. Trude is of a different opinion.

"I wonder whom Mama thinks she's saving me for? Prince Charming?"

A while ago Trude came up to my room, asking if I would lend her some books. I did not bring too many things with me, but I had sense enough to have my entire library crated. While Trude pulled out a few books at random, I kept watching her. She looked heavier to me than she had when we left Vienna. (I have seen her eat candies, greedily stuffing the sweets in her mouth as if the movement of mastication could actually assuage her mind.)

After what she told me on the boat, I really don't know why I asked her if she had done any writing since we arrived here. (Perhaps it had something to do with my urge for sharing the secret of authorship.) She gave me a withering look, as if I had suggested that she defile a grave.

Her sadness oppressed me, and I felt guiltily relieved when she left.

Once I am settled I might perhaps find some work for her in my office. Of course it would be much more pleasant to have Eva around to look at, but I doubt that Walter would consent to her working— though I don't see how he is going to support a family of four with his Spanish lessons.

During the meals he seems absent-minded and worried. I wonder how much money he spent on advance rent and furniture. Sometimes he looks at me as if he were on the brink of speaking to me. Perhaps he did not mean to offer me free lodging when he invited me to live with him. I really don't know what made me interpret his offer that way. As soon as I get back from Josef, I shall offer to pay my share. For the present at least it looks as if I am going to be the only breadwinner around the house.

*Later at night.*     The world has come to an end. I have no job.

I should collect my thoughts and try to think of something for the future, but my mind is blank—as blank as it was when I learned of Arthur's death. I know that this numbness is nothing but a protective measure, but I cannot help it. Or perhaps I do not want to help it.

It is raining again, and the heavy air keeps pressing down the putrid smell of burning offal. The smell has been with me ever since our arrival here, but tonight it seems worse than ever. Or perhaps I am more sensitive tonight. A bruised man always is.

My feeling of despair is heightened by the melancholic music which wafts in through my window. In the rear of our house is a small hut, surrounded by a cornfield. The Indian who lives in the hut has been playing on his reed pipe for the past hour, the same sad, primitive bars over and over again. For some perverse reason the mournful music makes me think of the gay summer concerts at Huebner's in the Stadtpark. I remember how Christine and I used to listen to the music drifting across the park, while we watched the swans, impeccably white and elegant, gliding over the lake. It was June and the air was heavy with the scent of blooming acacia trees. The memory makes the smell of the smoke here even more irritating.

But what I really think about is that I have no job.

*Monday, February 20, 1939.* The most amazing quality of the human mind is its resilience. True, it took me three days to recover from the blow of losing my job, but now I am collected enough to go back over my visit with Josef step by step.

Walter had accompanied me on the short walk to Josef's house (I am still afraid to venture out alone) and had left me at the garden gate. I pushed the bell and had hardly time to pull back my hand before two huge German shepherd dogs hurled themselves against the gate, howling and snapping at me through the iron bars. Presently an Indian came running to unlock the gate. He took hold of the furious dogs and said something to me in Spanish which I understood to mean that Josef was expecting me. I walked up the garden path to the house, all the time listening to the snarling of the dogs behind me. What a welcome, I thought.

The house—a sprawling building painted a pale pink, with little turrets jutting up here and there, and flowers and vines trailing down from a row of balconies on the second floor—looked like a castle out of a sugary fairy tale. The garden was riotous with flowers, and the loggia which formed the entrance to the house was overgrown with blazing, purple bougainvillaea.

Josef met me in the loggia, a proud patrician waiting for his guest. He wore a black suit again, but he no longer seemed as strange as on our first meeting. (The image with the white tropical helmet has since vanished from my mind.) Nor was I particularly surprised when he threw his arms around me and began slapping my back. I even made a halfhearted attempt to return the salutation, but, awkward as I am, ended up slapping his buttocks instead.

As I made some flattering remarks about the house and the garden, I could feel Josef mellowing toward me. Several Indians, obviously servants, trotted past us while we stood exchanging amenities. A woman, an infant sucking at her bare breast, peeked around a corner. All the time I wondered where Frau Blumenthal was, but I did not ask. (Before I left, Frau Kramer had whispered to me: "I understand that the wife of Herr Blumenthal is not Jewish." She made it sound as if I were setting out on a dangerous mission into enemy territory.)

Finally, after I had run out of compliments, Josef showed me into the house. We walked through a long series of rooms, all furnished with dark, ornately carved chests and tables, stiff brocade upholstery and hangings, and very bright carpets which reminded me of the flowers in the garden. In all the rooms the windows were tightly closed, and the air had the musty odor of a vault. The only bright room was the one in which I met Señora Blumenthal at last. It was much airier than the rest, with two large French doors opening into the garden. The chairs and the small coffee table had gilded legs, and the upholstery was a pale, silvery blue. The sun fell slantingly through the window, tracing the lacy pattern of the curtains on the floor. In the garden outside the birds were twittering.

I was startled to come upon Señora Blumenthal in this cheerful room, not so much by her sudden appearance but because she looked so somber in comparison, dressed entirely in black, as if she had recently lost a close member of her family. (Josef told me later that she had lost a sister two years ago, and that for close relatives it was customary to wear mourning up to four years.) She looked amazingly young, with the finely chiseled, melancholy features of a madonna, bare of make-up, and huge, brown eyes in the pale face. Her hair was black and luxuriant, severely pulled back from the forehead and twisted into a knot at the nape of her neck. Her only piece of jewelry was a small silver crucifix at her throat.

Extending her hand, she came forward to greet me with the elaborate Spanish salutation of which I still do not understand a word. I glanced helplessly at Josef, but he only beamed upon us without any attempt to help me. After I had desperately searched my vocabulary I came up haltingly with:

"Buenos días. Como está?"

The señora clapped her hands in delight, turned to Josef and rapidly chatted to him.

"Consuelo says you speak Spanish very well."

I felt childishly flattered.

We sat down on the delicate chairs. The señora shook a little silver bell, a sound which brought in an Indian with a large tray loaded with canapés. While the Indian walked around noiselessly on his rope-soled shoes, Josef poured drinks for us. I noticed that he did not pour for his wife. Raising my glass to Josef and the señora, I said:

"To the future!"

Josef blinked (or perhaps this occurs to me only now, as an after-thought) and replied:

"Salud!"

Again we sat silent. In my embarrassment I found myself devouring large quantities of canapés, as if I were at the brink of starvation. The señora kept looking from one to the other with the bright, alert movements of a bird listening for a worm in the ground.

"Consuelo does not speak German, but she understands some," Josef said.

We made some plodding conversation about the weather and the new impressions which I had gathered during my short stay here. Feeling the eyes of Señora Consuelo on my lips, I found myself talking more and more to her, though I was sure that she understood only a fraction of what I said. I was relieved when the Indian came to announce that luncheon was served. He respectfully addressed Josef as Don José.

(Little Jossele Blumenthal, who years back had sat beside me on the floor of the cheder, had become Don José. I felt very strange.)

All through the meal Señora Consuelo tried to carry on a conversation with me, slowly enunciating every Spanish word as if she were speaking to a deaf person. I smiled foolishly and kept staring at the crucifix at her throat. It reminded me of the one Christine used to wear, only Christine's had been made of gold. The formality of the meal made me miss our casual lunches at home (I already think of our unfurnished house as home!) and Frau Kramer's ranting about the kitchen stove with which she spices every meal.

We returned to the parlor—the sala—to have our coffee. Afterward Señora Consuelo retired saying smilingly to me—and this time Josef was gracious enough to translate—that she was leaving us to talk about old times.

I watched her as she left the room, a girlish, slender woman in a black dress.

"A very beautiful woman," I said to Josef.

"And a wonderful wife. This year we have been married twenty years."

"But she looks so young!" (I had forgotten how long ago Josef had been married.)

"I should not tell you, but she is going to be thirty-nine."

I was on the brink of asking him whether there had never been any difficulties because of their different religions, but I realized in time that it was too soon to ask. Though we had been friends once, we were little more than polite strangers now.

Instead of talking about old times we sat in awkward silence, smoking and looking out into the garden. Through the frayed leaves of a palm we could see the ridge of the Andes chipping into the blue sky. The first clouds were gathering around the Grampico. The sun was still shining brightly, but soon it would be raining.

Josef was clearing his throat with an embarrassed cough.

"Norman, I am terribly sorry . . ."

So convinced was I that he was going to talk about Arthur and Alma that I made an almost disdainful gesture with my hand, the sort of gesture a man will use to cover up the fact that the topic about to be broached is still too painful for discussion.

But Josef continued:

"I did what I could, but the new Minister of Economics and I just don't see eye to eye. I'm afraid there won't be any job for you."

I just sat there dumfounded. Such a possibility had simply never entered my mind. Mistaking my stunned silence for sulking, Josef added apologetically:

"You know, of course, about the revolution . . ."

"Yes, Walter Kramer mentioned something about it when he picked us up in Rioverde. But he said it was all over and it would have no effect on us!"

"I'm sure your status as immigrants will be in no way affected. But where social reforms are concerned . . . to be more concrete, the social security project on which you were to work . . . well, to put it bluntly, the new government is reactionary and won't consider any plan of the sort!"

"But there was a revolution! How can there be a reactionary government after a revolution?"

Josef gave me a long, grave stare.

"Look, Norman, this is not Europe. Here revolutions are not made by an oppressed populace; they are made by the military. You'll notice that after a revolution the new head of the government is usually a general. Any small, dissatisfied faction in the country can stage a revolution, so long as they can get the backing of the army. Take a group of reactionaries who are closely related to some high-ranking officers—and everybody here is closely related—and you can figure out the consequences yourself. Of course this does not mean that after a few months we cannot have a complete reversal of policies."

I just sat gaping at Josef, bewildered by the sudden lecture on South American politics. The idea that I was without a job was so all-encompassing that I was unable to grasp what he was talking about.

Josef finally realized my consternation. He bent forward and consolingly patted my knee with his hand. His hand was freckled and pudgy, with fine wrinkles crisscrossing the red skin. The hand of an old man. I kept staring at the hand while he spoke to me:

"Don't take it so hard, Norman. The new government probably won't last long."

He shook his head, as if disputing with himself.

"I tried talking to Alfonso Andrade, the new Minister of Economics, but you don't know Alfonso! He comes from an old family who owns huge haciendas here and at the coast. He still keeps peones, Indians who live in semislavery. When he talks about his Indians he refers to them as 'animales.' You just don't know the man!"

At the moment I could not have cared less about Alfonso Andrade and his relationship with the Indians. All I cared about was my lost job.

"But what am I going to do?"

Josef took his hand off my knee and began jingling his watch chain.

"I understand your friends are going into industry or agriculture. Maybe you could go into business with them."

"Josef, you are not serious! These people know as little about industry and agriculture as I!"

He looked startled.

"But those were the conditions . . . They signed the papers!"

"My God, can't you understand that these people were trying to save their necks! If necessary, they would have signed on as lion tamers! There must be *something* we can do here. Some jobs . . ."

"Jobs! Do you speak Spanish? And even if you did—do you realize what salaries are being paid here? A salesman in a store makes about eighty pesos a month: four and a half dollars. An office employee makes little more. No, no, you will have to go into some sort of business for yourself."

"But what?"

Josef shrugged.

"I don't know. I really don't know. If at least you spoke the language, I might try getting you a teaching position. But this way . . . Look, Norman, I suppose you have a little money to tide you over the first months. Give it time. Think it over. If you need anything, I'll gladly . . ."

I pulled myself together. He was right, I had a little money. And there was always time later on to beg and accept charity.

I left soon afterward. When I reached home I did not tell anybody what had happened. Frau Kramer asked so many questions about the visit that I thought Alma had returned from her grave to harass me. I believe I was quite rude to Frau Kramer.

Not until next day did I mention the fact that I had no job. Walter looked extremely upset, and I am sure now that he expected me to pay for my keep. But I did not have the strength of character to offer him a contribution just then.

In the meantime, though, I have gone over my resources. Seven hundred dollars in cash and a crateful of German books. If I only knew how much Walter expects me to pay him, it would be easier for me to make him an offer.

I am a contemptible old miser and coward. If I had any sense I would immediately destroy these notes. Why keep a record of my own weakness?


*Wednesday, February 22, 1939.* This morning was marked by two arguments.

Number one: making an inspection visit upstairs, Frau Goldmann found ours to be the choice apartment. She was quite outspoken in her opinion that since the Goldmanns were sharing the rent alike they should have been given a chance to voice their preference. Better yet, they should have decided by drawing lots who was to live where.

Walter, enraged by what he termed petty female intrigues, offered Frau Goldmann a cut in rent, a move which only partly appeased her.

Number two: Eva again brought up the matter of the dividing door. It seems that Herr Kramer had walked in on her while she was dressing.

"I'm going to put a curtain on the door, and I'm going to lock it permanently!"

"You'll do no such thing!" This from Frau Kramer. "We'll need both rooms for entertaining!"

"Entertaining!" Eva literally spit out the word. "Who are we going to entertain? And where are we going to get the money for entertaining?"

"Don't talk about things you don't understand," Herr Kramer said. "You're only a child."

Eva pouted and ran out of the room.

"Well, you *could* knock on her door before you walk in on her," Walter said to his father.

"Knock on the door! Knock on the door in my own house! Who is she to tell me to stay out of any of my rooms!"

"She's my wife," Walter said. He didn't exactly say it, he shouted it. His face was very red and thick veins stood out on his forehead.

I don't think Walter is too happy about his father's barging in on Eva while she is dressing. Still, he has not backed her up in her request about locking the door.

In comparison to the morning, the afternoon was pastoral. Just before the rains started two hired Indians came to plant a few dry sticks in the ground. This was called preparing a garden. I understand that these sticks are supposed to take root and someday turn into rose bushes, but I cannot help being skeptical. I am reminded of the curse put on Tannhäuser: "Sooner will this barren stave sprout leaves . . ."

If Tannhäuser had not lost hope he would have lived to see salvation. Perhaps it is wrong to emulate him too soon.


*Tuesday, February 28, 1939.*    Looking at the date of my last entry I realize that another week has passed. Where has the time gone?

I cannot have been too busy to write a few words. On the contrary, I had nothing to do. It seems that the lack of purposeful occupation brings on complete inertia.

My mornings were spent outside on the terrace, where Eva is taking her daily sun bath. She has resumed the habit as if she had never left the boat. As soon as she has straightened up her room she comes outside, peels off her silk robe and lies down to bask in the sun.

I hope that Eva is not aware of my real purpose on the terrace. I always make a point of holding up a newspaper before my face, rustling the pages to indicate that I am reading. My knowledge of Latin helps with the Spanish but Eva's presence is distracting.

From time to time Frau Kramer makes brief appearances on the terrace, always carrying a broom in her hand, as if she were about to take off on it. She glowers significantly at Eva lounging in the sun, but Eva keeps her eyes tightly shut and pretends not to see her. I hold up the newspaper before my face to avoid being drawn into a conversation. Finally Frau Kramer retreats, defeated. I know that Eva ought to be helping around the house, but I much prefer to have her with me on the terrace.

Evenings, after dinner, are spent in "conferences." These conferences are a free-for-all and take place either on the upstairs veranda or downstairs in the living room of the Goldmanns.

The living room has been furnished with a crude, unpainted table and a few chairs bought at the market. The emptied crates have been cut down, and the leftover lumber used for adding shelves; these are the book cases, china cabinets, etc. One crate, left its original size, had a crossbar added and serves as a closet. There are no possibilities of locking these doorless closets, and neither Frau Goldmann nor Frau Kramer, who owns similar furniture, will leave the house unless somebody stays at home to guard their treasures.

But to get back to the conferences: the ever-repeating theme is, of course, WHAT ARE WE GOING TO DO?

Goldmann is still decided to go into the manufacturing of ladies' lingerie. He has even worked out a plan: Frau Goldmann will disassemble a slip and a nightgown and copy the pattern. Herr Goldmann will buy some piece goods and a sewing machine, and will set aside one of his rooms as a "factory." There Frau Goldmann will produce slips and gowns, a one-woman industrial force, so to speak.

We all try to make light of this plan, but I think the scoffing is mostly due to jealousy. Goldmann's plan might work at that. And in a slightly oblique manner it is even within the stipulation of his visa.

The Kramers have no concrete plans for the future, neither have I. Walter is still giving Spanish lessons, but an income which was enough for him no longer suffices to support a family of four. I know that the Kramers have been dipping into their resources.

By the way, yesterday I finally offered Walter to pay my share. He seemed immensely relieved and so was I, once I had done it. (This probably is the reason why I feel like writing again today.) We settled on fifty pesos a week for my room and board, a fair price for both parties, I believe. This means roughly $180 a year. With seven hundred dollars in my possession—even if I figure some extra expenses—I should be safe for close to three years.

The two girls, Trude and Eva, were all for going out and seeking work in a beauty parlor. But Walter was dead set against it. He insisted that ladies did not work in El Paramo.

"We're not ladies, we're refugees," Eva said spitefully.

Frau Kramer sided with Walter, although not to save Eva from the hardship of work. Her argument ran along a different line: "What will people say?" Eva commented on Frau Kramer's reservation with a vulgar obscenity. Everybody was shocked, even I.

At times Eva makes me think of a young colt that has to be broken, but I am beginning to doubt that Walter is suited for the job. (I of course am. Hah!) Walter's disadvantage in dealing with Eva is that he, too, is still very young—a disadvantage I would gladly trade with him.

But with all the arguments back and forth nothing has as yet been accomplished. Somehow time seems to stand still here and the air is pregnant with postponed decisions.

I am beginning to understand the meaning of the word "mañana." It does not really mean tomorrow. It may mean the day after tomorrow, or a week, a month, a year hence; possibly never. There is only one undisputable meaning to it: not today.

Our life is now running much along the mañana line: we will, eventually, have to make some important decisions. But not today. Mañana.

*Friday, March 3, 1939.*    Tomorrow is Purim. Frau Kramer proposed a little celebration, but she met with opposition from all sides.

"Much reason *we* have to celebrate while this twentieth century Haman, may he rot in hell, is persecuting the Jews," Herr Goldmann said.

The young people were even more averse to marking the holiday, and so we decided to let Purim go by quietly.

*Sunday, March 5, 1939.*    Today we had our first taste of culture in Esperanza: Walter took us to the movies.

Every Sunday afternoon there is a première in the Cine Paraíso. Though we arrived there well ahead of time we already found a large crowd milling about in the narrow street. All the people were dressed in their best clothes, the men in dark suits, the ladies wearing fox stoles over their silk dresses and large, lavishly trimmed hats. It was raining cats and dogs, and our girls wore sensible raincoats. But I could tell that Eva was sorry that she had not dressed up too.

As soon as the box office was opened a near riot ensued. The men who had stood in a casually scattered line all surged forward at the same time, nearly crushing those nearest to the ticket booth. Soon voices were being raised and fists began to fly as they tried to push each other out of the way, some adventurous ones even attempting to climb over the backs of the others. All the time the ladies kept demurely in the background, watching their men with anxious pride, like Roman matrons witnessing the entrance of their lovers into the arena. Walter lost a button off his raincoat and had his sleeve ripped in the hustle, but he seemed to consider it all good, clean fun.

Finally in possession of our tickets, we followed the crowd inside. While the lights remained on, the ladies kept walking up and down the aisles to show off their dresses, and even after the lights were dimmed none of them removed their tremendous hats.

From what little I could see from behind those hats I gathered that we were shown a wild West picture, but its action was an anticlimax compared to the battle which had taken place outside the theater.

When we got out it was still raining, and in a spendthrift mood we took a taxi home. The driver refused to enter our street because of the mud, and Walter retaliated by paying him less than the agreed-upon fare. Finally the cab pulled away, leaving us standing in the downpour while the driver shouted back at us: "Gringos de mierda!"

And this, I think, really culminated an afternoon of culture.

*Saturday, March 11, 1939.* We are all very excited because of what is happening in Czechoslovakia. I am only beginning to feel how handicapped I am by my poor Spanish in reading the newspaper. Again we depend on Walter for interpreting the news for us.

Tiso, the deposed premier of Slovakia, has gone to visit Hitler in Berlin, and Hitler has given him his promise of support. The general feeling among us is that Hitler will invade Czechoslovakia within the next few days. There is only one exception among us: Goldmann.

"You mark my word, the French and the Russians will never permit it. The British, I spit on the British, but the French and the Russians have always been friends of the Czechs. You'll see!"

*Wednesday, March 15, 1939.* An hour ago Walter came home with the evening paper. What we all feared has happened: German forces have occupied Bohemia and Moravia. The Czechs—let alone the French or the Russians—did not even fire one shot in their defense.

Goldmann is sheepish, but this is poor consolation when we think of all the Jews in Czechoslovakia—those who live there and those who fled there from Germany, Austria, and the Sudeten in the foolish hope of finding a haven in Europe. At the moment we are so glad about being in Esperanza that we even forgo our customary complaints.

*Sunday, March 19, 1939.* The young people have again gone to the movies, but I begged off this time. I don't see why I should spend five pesos for the privilege of being half trampled to death in order to watch the back of a lady's hat for two hours. Goldmann invited me to come downstairs and have coffee with him, but I have no patience for listening to his foolishness. He has completely recovered from the Czech debacle and is now busily airing his new theory: the Russians were not quite prepared to take on the Germans but, mark his word, by June they will attack Germany and before the year is over we will be back in Vienna.

The occupation of Czechoslovakia seems to have thrown a great scare into the Jews of Europe. Yesterday four letters arrived, two for me, one for Eva, one for the Kramers, all pointing in the direction of a large-scale exodus. The two letters addressed to me were from men I have never heard of before. One from a Dr. Erwin Landau, who got my address from my former colleague, Professor Koerner. The other letter from a Leo Horowitz, a distant relative of Alma's old aunt Perla. Both Landau and Horowitz asked if I could get them visas for El Paramo. Their reasons were the usual ones: they were born in Poland and Rumania, respectively and were unable to obtain visas to the United States. They did not even mention the possibility of a temporary refuge in another European country.

The trend toward leaving Europe was borne out by the other two letters. The Kramers' married daughter, Frau Ruth Lipschitz, wrote from Paris that her family's French visa had expired and they had been denied an extension. Consequently, they were now planning to emigrate to El Paramo. Would Walter speak to me, etc. etc.

Eva's mother wrote from Vienna that Hans Braun and his wife were due to arrive in El Paramo by the middle of April. I had had no idea that Eva knew the Brauns, and we both reacted with the unexplainable delight which the discovery of mutual acquaintances seems to produce. Hans Braun's father had been our family physician for years. I assumed that he had also been Eva's doctor, but she said she knew Hans because his wife had been friendly with her mother. Frau Braun had brought her young husband to Eva's house a few times, and from Eva's enthusiastic reminiscences I gathered that she had had a crush on the young couple.

Hans Braun was a geologist for an oil company, and for their honeymoon he and his wife went off to Burma or Pakistan or some such place, Eva said.

"For a while I thought I was in love with both of them. Or perhaps I was in love with what they meant to me: the perfect union of two perfect people. Of course I was only twelve at that time and I had different ideas about perfection. I still believed that people got married and lived happily ever after."

She looked wistful, like a child who has discovered that fairy tales are not true.

I wonder what is wrong with Eva's marriage. This living together is certainly not a healthy thing. If I were asked, I would make a few suggestions—but nobody has asked me. I think I had better stick to requests directed at me: the procuring of visas. I am sure Josef will jump at a chance to do something for me. He seemed to feel so guilty about my lost job. And I won't even have to ask him for a visa for Hans Braun, who comes here under contract to the Pan American Oil Company. This will put him into a category apart from us: a man with a steady income. We sorely need an element of security in our small community.

What else is there to write about? The weather of course. It still rains daily, and the evening concerts of the frogs always begin on schedule.


*Tuesday, March 21, 1939.*    Today I went to see Josef about the visas. As I had expected, he was eager to be of help.

It was early in the morning when I called on him. We sat on wicker chairs in the loggia in front of the house. The sun was upon the mountains and the view was breath-taking, but I could not wholeheartedly enjoy it because of the dogs sniffing around me.

As we sat talking I was again struck by Josef's resemblance to his father. Unexplainably, I found myself growing hungry upon looking at him—this shortly after I had had my breakfast.

After a while it dawned on me what had brought on the pangs of hunger. Josef's father, rich Reb Mendel Blumenthal, the shohat, had been an obese man who had loved food. Whenever he came to our house there were stains of food on his long, black caftan. We, on the other hand, were never well fed on what my father scraped together as a tailor. I recall staring at the food stains on Reb Mendel's caftan, trying to figure out what he had eaten. Looking at Reb Mendel invariably made me hungry, and now I felt the same way when looking at his son.

Still, this was a different kind of hunger. Not for food, but rather for the feeling of security which Josef exuded. He was well-fed in an emotional sense while I was starving.

Enough of this nonsense.


*Friday, March 24, 1939.*    More bad news. Yesterday Hitler annexed Memel. Now he has begun talk about the German right to Danzig and Pomorze.

"And he'll get it too," Walter predicts somberly.

"Not a chance," Goldmann says. "Just let the rabid dog, may he choke on a poisoned bone, touch Danzig, and you'll see the Russians pounce on him."

Herr Kramer drew me aside and asked if, under the circumstances, I could not press Josef to rush through the visas for his daughter. I told Herr Kramer that Josef had promised to act as speedily as possible. I am sure he is as well aware of the danger surrounding the Jews in Europe as we are.


*Saturday, March 25, 1939.*    This morning Josef came to tell me that the visas for Landau, Horowitz, and Ruth Lipschitz and family have been cabled to the consuls in Europe.

It was about eleven o'clock in the morning when Josef called. He came unannounced, throwing Frau Kramer into a wild tizzy. She almost fell over herself showing him up the stairs and out onto the terrace, where I was sitting at the time.

Eva was with me on the terrace, taking her sun bath. Josef appeared so suddenly that she had no time to put on her robe, and she held up her halter with one hand as she scrambled to her feet. To say the least, Josef was startled to come upon Eva in this state of undress.

"Sit down! Please sit down!" he almost shouted at her.

He looked around quickly as if he were afraid that somebody had followed him into the house. After Eva had excused herself and left us, he whispered to me:

"Tell her not to do that . . . not to show herself like this . . ."

"But why not? Aren't women here wearing bathing suits?"

"Not where they can be seen by strangers from the street! It's indecent! It isn't done here!"

While he was at it Josef instructed me about something else which isn't done here. Eva and Trude have taken over the marketing. Once a week they go to one of the large, open markets and bring home their purchases in woven wicker baskets.

"It isn't done here," Josef chided. "Tell them to hire an Indian woman to carry the baskets for them. No white lady ought to be seen carrying anything in the street."

(Eva's democratic feelings were outraged when I told her, but she admitted having been stared at in the street.)

Josef did not stay too long. We had a brief conversation about the recent political developments, which was interrupted when Frau Kramer joined us on the terrace with a tray of cookies. While Josef dutifully sampled her latest baking accomplishment, she gave him a detailed description of her difficulties with the stove.

I was glad that Herr Kramer had gone on a walk and was not around to make a fool of himself. The way I am embarrassed by their acts, one might think that these people were really my relatives.

*Tuesday, March 28, 1939.*     Goldmann has actually bought a sewing machine.

We all went downstairs when the machine was delivered, swarming around as it was carried inside, much in the manner in which, I imagine, the Israelites used to mill around the Ark. After all, this is the first concrete sign of our industrial future in El Paramo.

All day long Goldmann reveled in the wildest fantasies of wealth just around the corner. He strutted about the house, his chest sticking out, the gap in his front teeth revealed by a wide grin. I asked him whether he would replace his lost teeth as soon as he began to reap his great expected earnings.

"Never," he said. "Not while this cur, may he roast in hell, is terrorizing all Europe. These missing teeth are a reminder! We must never forget what happened, ever!"

As if we could forget. Whenever our conversation does not revolve around some wild scheme for the future it dwells on the past. Mostly we talk about what has been, with an occasional variation on what might have been if . . . We rarely talk about the present, a fact on which Eva angrily commented a few days ago.

"We're living now and we ought to make the most of it, not just drift through the present!"

This is exactly what we are doing: drifting through the present. We have been here over a month now, but except for the purchase of the sewing machine we have taken no decisive steps. Perhaps we older men (here I am, including myself among the old people!) have an excuse for not trying: we don't speak the language. But what is Walter Kramer's excuse for not looking for work?

He is almost never at home. I often wonder what keeps him busy all day long, sometimes until late into the night. There are days when we sit down to dinner without Walter. Eva rises time and again to look out into the street, while Frau Kramer speculates in a mournful voice on a number of gruesome mishaps with which her son might have met. Herr Kramer is usually less concerned, and with good reason.

Walter always shows up, sometimes two or three hours late, apparently oblivious of the fact that he had been expected earlier. Devouring his food with an absent-minded air, he neither notices that Eva has retired to her room nor that his mother looks grim while serving him his solitary meal.

I really cannot figure out Walter Kramer!

*Friday, March 31, 1939.* Today I discovered by chance what keeps Walter occupied in the evening. He gambles!

I had gone to Esperanza in the afternoon to pick up my mail. (I have learned to find my way to the post office, a trip I look forward to every day because it gives me a chance to get out of the house and meet some people.) When I came to our apartado, Herr Fleischer was sorting out his mail from among the other letters. There were no letters for me, and to cheer me up, Fleischer asked me if I would like to have a cup of coffee with him in the Jungle Café.

This was to be my first visit to a coffeehouse since our arrival here, and I felt childishly excited over the prospect. I had already fashioned an elaborate mental picture of the Jungle Café—some sort of exotic place with palm trees, revolving fans, and monkeys swinging in cages between the tables. I could not have been further off the mark.

The Jungle Café is not what one would call a coffeehouse, though coffee is being served there. It is not a restaurant either, although one can order food. Nor is it a bar, in spite of the availability of spirits. It can best be described as a dump.

One enters through a narrow door which is half blocked by a huge expreso machine, half by the owner, an equally huge, red-haired Jew named Brody. He belongs to the Grushka-Dubrovsky group of earlier immigrants, and (this I learned later in conversation) is known to have great influence with a number of government officials. It was also mentioned that he is an informer and that he was once active in white slavery. But this last accusation I firmly refuse to believe. Altogether, though, not a very attractive personality.

Herr Fleischer made a point of introducing me to Brody with all my titles, as if I were being presented at court. Brody, cigar stub hanging from the corner of his mouth, made noises to indicate that he was delighted to meet me. We shook hands and then he ushered me into his establishment.

First we walked through a narrow, dark corridor. Then we entered a large, oblong room whose dark-brown, battered tables and chairs were dimly visible through the smoke there. Along the wall were built-in booths from which emanated the rhythmic rattle of dice being shaken in hard leather tumblers.

I discovered Walter sitting in a booth, rolling dice with Grushka and Dubrovsky. I had been under the impression that he spent his days giving Spanish lessons.

To say that I was alarmed would be an understatement. I walked over with Fleischer to watch the game for a while. Walter gave me the icy, absent-minded stare with which people involved in any kind of game greet a new arrival. His hair was disheveled, his eyes had a glassy expression, and he alternately chewed his nails and bit his lips. Needless to say, he was losing.

I stayed around until dinnertime, hoping to persuade Walter to come home with me. By that time he was winning and could not get up. (I learned that it is virtually impossible to pry a gambler loose from the table. He will not get up while losing and he obviously cannot get up while winning.)

Finally, after Walter's winnings had dropped to five pesos, Grushka made use of his privilege as the loser to call it a day. By then the Jungle Café was almost deserted. Fleischer had long gone home, and Walter and I were alone when we walked to the bus. I simply could not refrain from admonishing him.

"Walter, you must be out of your mind! At one point you were losing over two hundred pesos, half a month's rent!"

"What else am I to do in this rotten town for entertainment? No theaters, no concerts, no lectures, no new books . . . nothing! One new movie a week is not enough!"

"You have a young, beautiful wife!"

He gave me a long, gloomy look which ruled out Eva as entertainment. Again I was on the brink of asking what was wrong with his marriage, but reminded myself in time that this was a topic where angels fear to tread.

"Besides, you have an obligation toward your family," I said. "You ought to be trying to earn money rather than gamble it away!"

"Earn money! All right, I could start earning money tomorrow. Grushka and Dubrovsky employ a fleet of peddlers to sell their 'imported' merchandise from house to house. Two thirds of the earnings go to the bosses, one third to the vendor. The income depends upon how good a salesman you are. Today Grushka asked me if I would like to work for him."

"But, Walter, you're an architect!"

"Ah, you see! If *you* take this attitude, can you imagine how my mother would carry on if I told her that I was going to be a peddler?"

I could see his point, but whatever I could have said to defeat it was cut short by the arrival of our bus. So far we have had no chance to come back to our discussion. And yet, this is no time for petty, bourgeois considerations. We will have to get rid of a lot of prejudices if we want to survive!

*Saturday, April 1, 1939.*    Goldmann's idea of a joke was to bang on our doors early this morning and to shout that Hitler had dropped dead. Later Frau Goldmann came upstairs to apologize for her husband.

"I don't know what gets into Markus sometimes. He's really very smart otherwise."

That's loyalty for you.

Politically, there is a ray of hope now. The British and the French have pledged their help to Poland in case her independence should become threatened. But Goldmann, the smart man, keeps insisting that if the Russians will not come to the help of Poland, nobody will.

*Monday, April 2, 1939.*    This morning Josef paid me an unexpected visit, mainly to reproach me: I never call on him unless I need his services. To make up for my negligence I went for a long walk with him. I was anxious to get away from home, since Frau Kramer is already turning the house upside down in preparation for the Passover holidays.

As Josef and I strolled aimlessly through the suburbs, he talked about himself for the first time. He had retired from business five years ago, and except for some interest in real estate and afternoons in the Club Grampico, his life was as idle as mine. (This reminds me: we have begun talk about founding a club for Jewish refugees.) But time and again Josef's thoughts veered back to his more active years, when he was still building roads. He told me that he had once been trapped in an earthquake when he was building the road to Aguas Calientes, the village beyond which the Panamerican Oil Company is presently drilling for oil. None of Josef's laborers had been killed, but the natives of Aguas Calientes had grabbed the nearest image of the Virgin and fled into their church. The church, an adobe structure, had collapsed on them and over three hundred had perished beneath the rubble.

Ever since this conversation with Josef I keep having the same foolish daydream over and over again: everybody in our house is killed by a terrible earthquake—everybody but myself and Eva, whom I manage to save in some miraculous manner (not yet figured out). Finding herself all alone, Eva naturally turns to me for love and security. And they live happily ever after. End of dream.

I have a homicidal mind. Apparently I would be willing to sacrifice all my friends in order to have Eva to myself—provided, of course, an earthquake would relieve me of having to kill them with my own hands. I remember having a similar dream when I first began going with Christine. I kept hoping that Alma would die in her sleep, quietly, painlessly, without much fuss. I wonder how many people would turn into murderers if they were not afraid of the consequences?

These are disturbing thoughts. The lack of purposeful occupation and the continuing rain must be making me morbid.

*Wednesday, April 5, 1939.*    Yesterday was the first Seder.

Walter had ordered several boxes of matzoth from the United States, but they did not arrive on time. In spite of the missing matzoth, Frau Kramer prepared a festive meal: stuffed fish; soup without the traditional matzoth balls; chicken; potato pancakes; and cake and stewed prunes for dessert. (By the way, Frau Kramer has long done away with the pretext of keeping a kosher household. It is simply impossible here.) Whatever one can say against Frau Kramer, she is a marvelous cook, even if she diminishes the pleasure of each meal by a detailed description of her cooking difficulties: the wood is green and will not burn; the chimney is clogged and will not draw; and Eva is of no help whatsoever.

Actually I doubt that Frau Kramer really wants Eva in the kitchen. She stresses Eva's absence only to impress upon Walter that he still depends upon his mother for food. How much she reminds me of Alma!

Eva hardly touched her food at the Seder. Since everybody else was also glum on our first Seder away from home (home!), Eva's explanation that she was not hungry was not questioned. But I believe I know what was really wrong with her appetite.

The previous day Frau Kramer had bought two chickens at the garden gate. An Indian had come to the door, carrying a bunch of live chickens on his back, tied together by their legs like a bunch of radishes. They were hanging head down, peeping faintly and gasping for air. The Indian dropped his entire load on the ground and, selecting two chickens, held them up for Frau Kramer's inspection. As if they knew what awaited them, the chickens screamed piteously.

Eva, who was on the terrace at the time of the purchase, fled into the house. This was nothing for my stomach either, so I followed her. Frau Kramer took quite a while haggling over the price of the chickens in her ridiculous, broken Spanish. She has learned to use two words very effectively: no; and caro, expensive. Finally the price was agreed upon and the chickens were being killed in the customary manner: the Indian was wringing their necks.

Their screams were heart-rending, and Eva sat with her hands clamped over her ears, tears streaming down her cheeks.

"We're nothing but wild beasts," she said. "I never used to think of a chicken as something that was once alive. I only saw them cleaned and dressed in the window of a butcher shop. It's enough to make you turn vegetarian."

Frau Kramer was less affected by the carnage. As the feeder, she cannot permit herself to think of a chicken as a suffering creature. Eva is still too young to accept the idea that survival is often linked with brutality.


*Saturday, April 9, 1939.*　　The Italians have bombed and invaded Albania!

Goldmann is filled with grim satisfaction because, once again, neither the British nor the French have made a move to help the attacked nation. More than ever his hope is pinned on Russia, especially now that Spain has joined the Anti-Comintern Pact.

Who knows, perhaps Goldmann isn't such a fool after all. Perhaps nobody will dare attack the Germans unless the Russians do.


*Sunday, April 16, 1939.*　　Today we talked nothing but politics all day long. Last week the French and the British pledged their help to Rumania and Greece—after they had let Mussolini gobble up Albania.

And as if to top off the irony, President Roosevelt sent a letter to Hitler and Mussolini, asking assurance against attack on thirty-one nations in Europe and the Near East! Assurance from those two criminals! It is amazing that the leader of such a large nation should be so naïve.

*Tuesday, April 21, 1939.*    I have made a habit of visiting the Jungle Café every afternoon. Even the daily downpours cannot stop me from going there. Considering that I do not like the place, this is quite astonishing. I suppose I am driven by the urge to get away from the women. Seeing the same people for breakfast, lunch and dinner can become monotonous. Our conversations are slowly turning stale. How often can one rehash the past?

Eva has become so sullen that she hardly opens her mouth at mealtime. She displays a hostile attitude even toward me, and often her eyes are filled with tears. Yesterday I overheard her saying to Walter:

"I am sick of looking at old people day in day out."

This was something of a shock to me. I had the idea that she did not consider me old. At least I never feel old when I look at her. Of course this is entirely due to self-deception. Since I can see only her face and not mine, I think that I too am seventeen. At times I suspect that I am seriously infatuated with Eva. If only I did not see so much of her, especially at times when I am not supposed to see her at all!

My room is built over the garage, which juts out at a right angle to the house. None of us has curtains, and from my window I get a good view into Eva's bedroom window. I can see part of a wall on which she has hung a mirror, right next to the much-disputed door. (The door is still a topic of daily argument.) In the evening, after I have turned out the light in my room, I can see Eva, in a filmy nightgown, brushing her hair before the mirror. No wonder my imagination tends to run away with me.

Sometimes, after Eva has already retired to bed, the connecting door opens and in walks Herr or Frau Kramer to—to do what? To bring Walter a late snack? To talk with him about some important matter which could not have been discussed earlier?

I sit up waiting for their exit while I think of Eva in her sheer nightgown and of what a fool Walter Kramer is. If he had any sense, he would have picked my room for himself and Eva.

Well, it is none of my business.


*Friday, April 25, 1939.*     Yesterday the Brauns arrived in Esperanza.

Eva and I went to pick them up at the airport. It was a beautiful morning, with the Andes rising green against the azure sky and a clean wind sweeping down from the mountains. The grass around the landing strip trembled in the breeze, and twittering, white-bellied swallows darted back and forth among the bushes.

Eva remarked how different this was from our own arrival in Esperanza.

"Some people are fortunate."

She has already made up her mind that the Brauns are the most fortunate people on earth.

The plane arrived on schedule, but we still had to wait quite a while before the passengers emerged from the door. I recognized Hans, tall and bony, ambling down the stairs. With his plaid sports coat and his camera slung over his shoulder, he looked like a tourist. Behind him came his wife, leading a little girl by the hand. They disappeared into customs, from which we were barred by a fence, and after a considerable while came outside.

Frau Braun immediately rushed toward Eva and stood on tiptoe to kiss her.

"My, you've grown over my head!" she exclaimed.

Hans shook my hand and introduced his wife to me. (She is not nearly as pretty as Eva made her out to be, but with her dark-brown hair and her light-gray eyes she might be called an attractive woman. What makes her gain immensely is her pleasant smile and the easy way she has with strangers.)

Eva has nothing of that ease. Though the Brauns are old friends of hers, she was extremely self-conscious at first, even tittering like a stupid teen-ager when Hans bent down and kissed her cheek. I just hope that little gesture of affection will not revive her old childhood crush on him!

On the ride from the airport to the hotel she glanced at him repeatedly.

Every time their eyes met, she blushed. I could see that Hans was surprised to find a woman instead of the child he had remembered, and he looked at her slyly, a man scrutinizing a pretty girl in the presence of his wife. Frau Irene did not seem to notice anything and chattered gaily all the way to the hotel.

Perhaps I am attaching too much significance to the exchange of glances between Eva and Hans. I really don't know what Eva sees in him. I always thought young girls didn't go for men who wore glasses. Also, there's quite a bit of gray in his hair, and his hairline is receding. I think I am jealous.

We accompanied the Brauns up to their hotel room and watched them unpack. Their room is much better than the one I had in the hotel in Rioverde, but Frau Irene said that they would have to start hunting for a suitable house right away.

"Eva can be our guide," Hans proposed cheerfully.

Aha, I thought.

Frau Irene seemed to consider it a splendid idea that Eva should be their guide. She had better be very sure of her husband.

Watching her move awkwardly between the suitcases and the dresser, Eva said:

"I don't know, Irene, but you seem to have gained weight, and you walk funny."

"Of course I've gained weight. I'm going to have a baby. That's why we're in such a hurry for a house."

Eva was so stunned by the news that she could not even congratulate her. I suppose none of us considered the possibility of Jewish children being born in the emigration. But was there ever a disaster or holocaust to stop nature in her course?

At least this gives us something to look forward to: the birth of a Jewish citizen of El Paramo.


*Wednesday, April 26, 1939.*   By now I have established a daily routine. Twice a week I call on Josef. Weather permitting, we sit outside in the loggia, from where we have a splendid view of the garden and the mountains. This helps, since we often have trouble keeping the conversation going. During the long silences we watch the hummingbirds, hovering luminously green above the brilliant flowers. Most of the time we avoid discussing the present, thus burrowing deeper and deeper into the past. One might think that we had stopped living thirty years ago.

I rarely see Señora Blumenthal. She visits her large family in the morning, calling on a different member every day. At least her absence saves me from groping through a tortuous Spanish conversation. Another comfort: the dogs have come to know me, and on my last visit one of them licked my hand. It was a pleasant feeling; warm, moist and friendly.

After leaving Josef I usually go for a long, solitary walk. I rarely meet anybody but Indians in the street. The men usually ride mules; the women trudge behind them on foot with heavy loads strapped to their backs. Every once in a while I become an unwilling witness to their appalling habit of eating lice or relieving themselves in the middle of the street without the slightest shame. (A few days ago I came upon Goldmann, urinating against our garden wall. When I asked him what the devil he was doing, he said he was just adopting the customs of the country. A pig this Goldmann.)

Except for the two mornings when I visit Josef, I spend an hour or so on the terrace, reading last night's newspaper and watching Eva take her sun bath. Her body is now a deep, golden bronze, like the statue of a golden goddess cast by the ancient Incas.

Occasionally I accompany the girls on their marketing trips. Among the open-air markets in Esperanza my favorite is the Mercado Santa María. There, behind stands spilling over with produce in riotous Van Gogh colors, squat the vendors, sometimes on turned-over boxes and sometimes on the ground. Most of them are flat-nosed Indian women, who often open their shapeless, white cotton blouses and bare their sagging breasts to nurse their infants right in the middle of a business transaction.

No purchase is made without loud and wild haggling. It is safe to offer half and pay two thirds of the exorbitant price asked of gringos. But Eva and Trude have already become steady customers of certain vendors, and the purchases are made with a minimum of dramatics. Even the yapa—an extra piece of fruit or vegetable—is thrown in without much coaxing. The girls are well liked, and the Indian women indiscriminately call both linda and bonita, pretty one. Only the last time one vendor, pointing at Eva, winked at me and whispered admiringly:

"Que alhaja la señorita!"

When we got home I looked up the word in the dictionary. Alhaja—precious, also precious jewel. The word fits Eva. Alhaja, the golden goddess.

*Thursday, April 27, 1939.*    Walter does not seem to think of Eva precisely as a jewel. Today I had a long, unexpected talk with him when I returned to the house from one of my morning walks. Eva was not at home. I had seen her and Trude walking in the distance, but before I could catch up with them, they had turned into a side street and disappeared. I could not help feeling that they had intentionally avoided me. I made some jesting remark about this to Walter. Actually, though, I was hurt.

Walter said that his wife and Trude were having long, serious girl talks.

"I wonder what they are talking about," I said.

Walter shrugged.

"Trude is still a virgin and wants to know what it's like."

Expecting him to look amused, I was surprised to see Walter looking grim.

"Walter, are you a prude? You can't possibly object to their conversations?"

"Object! I wish to God Eva were qualified to tell Trude what it's like! I doubt that she knows herself!"

He had spoken with sudden fury, and once he had gone so far he could not stop himself from blurting out his complaints.

"Look, Herr Professor, I've got to talk to somebody. This thing has been eating at me for weeks. I don't know what's the matter with Eva. I don't seem to be able to reach her! If I were inexperienced, if I hadn't had a good number of love affairs before I got married, I might be blaming myself. But it's not my fault! I just don't understand why she doesn't . . . I mean why I can't . . . the hell with it, she's frigid!"

He stood there shaking, enraged, on the brink of tears. Walter Kramer is not a handsome man, and when he is upset his features become distorted and he is decidedly ugly. I stared at him with mixed emotions, knowing that I ought to commiserate with him. But all I could think of was that he was trying to smash my golden goddess. The next worse thing to calling a woman a whore is to call her frigid. It could not be true, I thought. He was lying. He was a blundering fool.

"I just can't understand it," Walter went on. "Before we were married she seemed quite passionate. She enjoyed having me touch her, she got excited. Now she pulls away, shuts herself up into herself. She is always tense, on edge, as if she were listening for something while I'm making love to her. Honestly, I'm at my wit's end! I was counting on financial troubles, language troubles, job troubles when I started out on the emigration. But I never thought that my own wife would make me feel inadequate as a lover! It's something you can't blame on Hitler and the emigration. And the worst part of it is that I'm in love with her!"

As a wise elder I was clearly expected to know of an easy solution for this problem. I asked Walter if he had tried talking this out with Eva.

"How can I talk to Eva? The moment I utter the slightest criticism of her, she begins to cry. And when I ask her why the hell she's crying, she tells me she doesn't want to share an apartment with Mama. I don't see what our troubles have to do with my mother!"

I still don't know why I didn't tell Walter what I think about his living with his parents. Now I am beginning to question my motives. Can it be possible that I secretly wish for Walter's marriage to fail? Is this something akin to my earthquake fantasies?

I think I know what Eva is listening for when Walter makes love to her: she is listening for his mother tossing in bed next door. I should have told Walter so. But I missed out on my chance to warn him, and we are just not on intimate enough terms for me to broach the topic on my own.


*Sunday, April 30, 1939.*    The young people have gone to the movies. This time Walter didn't even ask me if I wanted to join them. Ever since our conversation he has been avoiding me. I think he is embarrassed and already regrets having made me his confidant. For the past few days he has been coming home very late at night, and I could see Eva standing by the window, staring out into the darkness as she waited for him.

Yesterday evening she did something very strange. After I had turned out the light in my room I glanced once more at her window before I went to bed. Eva was standing in front of her mirror, a diaphanous scarf draped over her shoulders and her breast. She kept smiling at herself in the mirror, delicately passing her fingers over her cheeks, her throat and her breasts, as if she were trying to find out how it felt to touch her. It was exciting to watch and I trembled in the dark.

Perhaps Eva is already transgressing from her marriage in her imagination. I simply refuse to believe that she is frigid.

*Wednesday, May 3, 1939.*    Eva has her own innocent way of giving rise to rumors.

Today we were sitting in the Jungle Café; that is, Goldmann, Kramer and I were sharing a booth. (Variation here consists of meeting the same people in a different surrounding.) We were still talking about the speech Hitler made last week in the Reichstag as a reply to Roosevelt's letter.

"Letters he's sending him," Goldmann said bitterly. "A planeload of bombs the Americans should drop on Berlin, that's the only language this criminal would understand. And this is exactly the medicine the Russians will give them come June, mark my word!"

Shortly after Goldmann had uttered his favorite prophecy, Fleischer came and joined us. We ordered a round of tintos, black coffee with the texture and taste of ink, and talked some more about politics. Suddenly Fleischer said to Herr Kramer:

"Say, who is this man your daughter-in-law is running around with?"

The question was probably not meant the way it sounded, but it still made me gasp. Herr Kramer certainly looked dumfounded.

"I don't know that my daughter-in-law is running around with anybody," he stated stiffly, but he looked as if he believed the worst.

"Oh, I thought he must be a friend of the family"—Fleischer was now trying to blunt his initial remark—"you know, a tall, thin fellow with glasses, about my age . . ."

"Dr. Braun, of course!" I exclaimed. "Eva has been helping the Brauns to shop around for a house."

"Ah. I didn't know that there was a Frau Braun."

Herr Fleischer looked aggrieved, the image of a man who had been deprived of a delicious morsel of gossip. Herr Kramer seemed almost as dour as Fleischer. I doubt that he had known anything about Eva's squiring Hans Braun around town. But he was resolved to make it clear that no member of his family did anything behind his back or without his consent. He stood up, the way he does when he wants to put special emphasis on one of his statements, and declared:

"Of course Eva is assisting Dr. Braun! The Brauns are old friends of Eva and Walter."

Fleischer had to accept this statement at its face value. He was in no position to know that Walter had met the Brauns only recently. In fact, Walter had seemed somewhat miffed by the interest Eva showed in Hans Braun. One morning last week I witnessed a near-argument just as Eva was about to leave the house.

"Are you going to see the Brauns *again?*" Walter asked.

Eva said testily: "I promised to help them find a house."

Walter addressed me in the voice of a parent trying to castigate a child by embarrassing it in front of a stranger:

"You know, Professor Bernstein, I think my wife has a crush on Dr. Braun. A schoolgirl crush on an older man! Nothing else could make her skip her daily sunbath. She wouldn't go without it to help Mama in the kitchen!"

"All right, have it your way," Eva said in a trembling voice. "I just go there to jump into bed with Hans, while his wife and his daughter sit on the other bed and applaud our performance!"

"That was in very bad taste, Eva," Walter said, sobered.

"This whole conversation is in bad taste. All I said to begin with was that I was going into town to help the Brauns find a house. And that's exactly what I'm going to do!"

She stalked away without saying good-by. I noticed that she was wearing the white dress which she had worn when Walter came to fetch us from the boat. Her blond hair shone in the sun like a helmet of gold. The goddess striding off in martial wrath to fight—fight for what? Her right to help her friends find a suitable house?

Walter looked after his wife, puzzled and worried.

"Tell me frankly, Herr Professor, do you think that Eva has a crush on Hans Braun?"

I shrugged and made noncommittal sounds. Should I have told Walter that I had the same suspicion and that I liked the idea as little as he did?

*Saturday, May 6, 1939.*    Thank God, the Brauns have found a house! Eva has gone back to her old sunning schedule, and I see more of her now than I had for the past two weeks. This morning I tried slyly to question her about her feelings for Hans Braun. I am ridiculously jealous of him.

Although I framed my question as a jest, Eva immediately caught on to what I really wanted to know.

"Look, Herr Professor, I don't have a crush on Hans Braun, if that's what's bothering you. I just—well, I just respect him."

Eva tried to make this sound like a clinical statement, but disproved her detachment by blushing violently.

"Oh, so you respect him!" I mocked. At the same time I cursed myself for acting like a jealous eight-year-old.

Eva caught the tone of derision.

"You can laugh, but I do respect him! He's so reliable. All he worries about is to keep Irene from any kind of exertion during her pregnancy. He just worships her! I think they have a perfect marriage."

"Eva, what do you know about the marriages of other people? By what standards do you measure a perfect marriage?"

"By comparison to mine. I don't have one!"

Here she was, condemning her marriage after a trial period of three months. How could I explain to an impatient girl of seventeen that the making of a marriage took years of adjustment from both parties? And even then there were often stirrings of discontent beneath the smooth surface of outward happiness. Or hadn't she noticed the way Hans Braun had looked at her in the cab?

"Eva, you're a child!"

"That's what everybody says to me: Eva, you're a child." She looked terribly angry. "Well, I'm not a child! I'm a married woman! I have a right to voice an opinion! I have a right not to be afraid all the time!"

"Are you afraid, Eva?"

It had never occurred to me that this girl, beautiful, cool and composed, could be afraid of anything.

"Of course I'm afraid! Sometimes I lie awake at night and worry about all those stupid people around me. They all live in a make-believe world of the past and refuse to admit that there is a present. Besides, I know that Walter is gambling. Do you think we can afford it? Do you think we can afford living the way we're living? Walter hasn't made a cent in the three months we're here. He hasn't even looked for work, and what's more, he enjoys being idle!"

"Now, Eva, this is a very strong accusation!"

"Is it? But it's true! He enjoys not working, and so does my father-in-law, and Herr Goldmann, and Herr Fleischer, and . . . well, I know it's hard for you, you're an older man."

By exempting me from the obligation to work she had added insult to injury. I tried to defend myself by defending the other men.

"Really, Eva, I don't know where you get this foolish idea that all those men are pleased with their idleness!"

"Sure I'm foolish. I'm nothing but a foolish child! I'll let you in on a little secret: when Hitler came to Vienna, I stopped going to school in the middle of the term. I guess I had always wanted to play hooky, but as a good student I didn't dare. Now I suddenly had a perfectly legal reason for playing hooky: I wouldn't attend classes as a second-rate citizen. I was very righteous about the whole business, but actually I enjoyed not having to go to school. And that's exactly what the men here are doing. They're playing hooky from their responsibilities, and they enjoy every minute of it!"

"Eva, you don't really believe what you are saying!"

"Of course I do! And that's why I respect Hans Braun. He's not a drifter, he's a doer."

"You're not being fair, Eva. Hans came here with a working contract. He'll be paid in dollars. His situation is entirely different from ours."

"But even if it weren't, he would still be trying. That's what I can't forgive Walter: he isn't trying. If he would only try, or even if he would let me try, perhaps we could still make enough money to be able to move out and live by ourselves."

So it all boiled down again to the need of living alone with Walter. If I were Walter, I thought, I would go and work in a quarry to please Eva. Alas, I am over sixty, and there are no quarries around Esperanza.

But the other things she said—about our loafing—well, I don't know. Perhaps she is right at that. Perhaps we are really looking for a good excuse to spend the rest of our lives in idleness.

*Monday, May 8, 1939.* An abominable day today. It is raining so hard that I have had to skip my daily visit to the Jungle Café. A little while ago I went looking for Eva and Walter, but in spite of the bad weather both were out. Since I did not feel like listening to Herr Kramer giving a lecture on the drygoods business nor to Frau Kramer snoring on her large double bed, I returned to my room.

But I am still restless. I think I shall go and look for Goldmann. On a day like this even his foolish talk is cheering. He is still convinced that the Russians will attack Germany by the end of June.

*Tuesday, May 9, 1939.* Something most unexpected has resulted from my visit to Goldmann: since yesterday evening, he and I are business partners.

I had nothing of the sort in mind when I first came downstairs yesterday. In fact, Goldmann was not at home. Wringing her hands, Frau Goldmann told me that, deluge or no deluge, her husband had insisted on going into town.

"Would a man in his right mind go out into this rain? I'm telling you, Herr Professor, he's going to be worse than his sister, God forbid! The altitude and the emigration have damaged his brains. He will catch his death, he will ruin his clothes, and he will mess up my floors when he comes home." Frau Goldmann enumerated the perils of her husband in this order.

"Mama is exaggerating, as always. It's her one luxury!"

But Trude has little cause for mocking her mother. Frau Goldmann has turned out to be a veritable pillar of strength. While Goldmann spends most of his time in the Jungle Café and Trude lies sprawled on the bed, stuffing herself with candy and devouring books, Frau Goldmann putters about the house, washing floors, cleaning windows, preparing meals, cutting ladies' underwear and keeping the sewing machine whining until late at night. Now and then, when the work becomes too much for her, she breaks into tears and vigorously curses Hitler. These outbursts seem to bring her great emotional relief and renewed strength.

Trude is not quite that uncomplicated. Her only antidote seems to be food. In what ought to be a period of privation, Trude has become appallingly fat. Little sausages of fat ripple above her waist, and her buttocks press through her skirts. She can no longer close any of her zippers, and she looks sleazy and unkempt, given over to complete hopelessness.

Seeing me scrutinize Trude, Frau Goldmann seized on the opportunity to express her dissatisfaction with her daughter. (Again the method of shaming children in public!)

"Just look how she walks around! Does she comb her hair? Does she give herself a manicure? Does she care at all about her appearance? Her father"—Frau Goldmann disclaiming any relationship with her husband —"goes into town when he should be staying home, but Trude stays home and won't go any place! I keep telling her she ought to go with her father once in a while. I'm sure there must be some young men in this Jungle Café."

Trude stamped her foot in embarrassment.

"For heaven's sake, Mama! Haven't we got enough troubles without you trying to marry me off?"

At that point our conversation was interrupted by a wild banging on the window.

"That's one of Papa's brilliant jokes," Trude said when she saw me start. "He does it to frighten Mama."

Frau Goldmann dashed past Trude to beat her to the door.

"So there you are, Markus! I bet you were the only lunatic in the café! Probably you'll be sick tomorrow! That's all I need, to have you sick in bed! Don't go one step further—my floors!"

Conditioned by years of married obedience, Goldmann stopped dead in his tracks. He had gone without an umbrella and was soaked through. Water was dripping from the brim of his hat and a small puddle was collecting on the floor around his shoes.

"Well, what am I supposed to do?" he howled. "Stand here until I turn into a pillar of salt? Trude, my slippers! Your mother would sooner turn me out like a dog than let me walk over her floors!"

"You know how hard I worked to get these floors clean, Markus. If I had carpets, like the Kramers, I wouldn't mind so much."

"Oh, God, why can't I keep my mouth shut?" Goldmann moaned.

He bent over clumsily, untying his shoelaces and placing his wet shoes on a newspaper which Trude had brought him. He was still wearing his hat, and his voice sounded muffled from his bent position.

"I know the Kramers don't have more money than we," Frau Goldmann said. "They ordered curtains and a new dining-room table, and Walter gambles, and Herr Kramer is a very heavy smoker . . ."

"All right, Else, so they don't have more money! They're just show-offs, that's what they are!"

". . . and Frau Kramer said they're going to throw a big party and invite all their acquaintances as soon as her daughter arrives here," Frau Goldmann continued as if she had never been interrupted.

"So what do you want, Else, to give a party too?"

"Why not? Would it be so bad for Trude to meet a few people?"

"Please, Mama, leave me out of this! If you want carpets, it's strictly between you and Papa!"

"In other words, you also want carpets," Goldmann said, as if until now he had had no idea of what was behind his wife's badgering.

"Only one," Frau Goldmann said modestly. "Only one, for the living room. Unless, of course, we can't afford it."

"If the Kramers can afford to buy carpets, so can we. Nobody is going to say that Markus Goldmann's wife has to suffer privations!"

Goldmann pulled out his wallet and began extracting bills with quick, jerky movements, as if he were furiously plucking the petals from a flower. Frau Goldmann greedily snatched up the bills. (It seems that when it comes to taking their husbands' money, women don't care much whether it is given joyfully or in anger, so long as they get it.)

"Anyway, a carpet is an investment," Frau Goldmann said, unwilling even to relinquish the last word. "If we need money, we can always sell it again."

"Sure, sure."

Goldmann took off his hat and shook it, spattering water all over the floor. Frau Goldmann only gasped but did not protest. Then she gave Trude a crisp order to come along and help her set the table, and both women went to the kitchen.

I was alone with Goldmann. He raised both his arms in a helpless gesture, silently calling me as a witness to all this madness.

"So what can I do? Tell her we can't afford it? The woman is working her fingers to the bone, how can I deny her a little pleasure? She wants a carpet, let her have a carpet! The trouble is, it won't end there. You heard what she said: a dining-room table, curtains, a party. . . . I tell you one thing, Herr Professor, we can't last much longer unless I find some way of making money. I wouldn't tell that to anybody else, you know how people talk right away. But you . . . after all, you saved our lives!"

I did not realize immediately that this belated recognition was only a prelude to making me understand that, since I had saved the Goldmanns' lives, I was also responsible for keeping them alive.

Goldmann shuffled up to me, a crafty expression in his pale eyes. Baring the gap in his teeth with what was intended as an ingratiating grin, he whispered confidentially:

"Say, Professorlein, how would you like to go into business with me?"

"I? Go into business with *you*? What do I know about the making of lingerie?"

(Here I was, just as Eva had said, rejecting the first chance of starting some sort of enterprise.)

"Oh, forget about the lingerie business! There's no money in it, anyway. It's just something to keep the immigration authorities happy. What we really ought to do is buy a little merchandise and try to sell it in the provinces."

"You mean work for Grushka and Dubrovsky?" I said with open distaste.

"Who wants to work for those crooks! I mean going into business for ourselves. What they can do, we can do. And Levy would give us the merchandise wholesale, well, almost wholesale, one third down, the rest payable in ninety days, and no cut from the profit."

"And why should Herr Levy want to make you such a generous offer?"

"I suppose he has confidence in me."

(This I didn't believe, and I still wonder what sort of deal Levy really offered Goldmann.)

"Now, tell me just one thing, Herr Goldmann, why would you want me for a partner? Can you imagine me selling merchandise from house to house? Why don't you ask a younger man, like Fleischer or Walter Kramer?"

Goldmann rubbed his nose thoughtfully. He glanced at me and immediately looked away again. "There's just one trouble. I've hardly any money left to invest."

"Oh!"

"Now, what I thought—" Goldmann spoke very rapidly now, his words tumbling over each other—"I thought if you would put up the money, I would offer to put up the work, you know, save you the traveling around and all that, and we would still share the profit fifty-fifty, now you could use an income, couldn't you, and I thought since you did so much for us, I might do something for you in return, of course I would need the money, say two hundred dollars."

"Two hundred dollars!"

"Well, you can spare two hundred dollars," Goldmann said resentfully. "I know you have the money." (Implying, possibly, money which I had made on his visa.) "And how much do you need, a man your age? You're not paying the Kramers so much, and a mistress you haven't got, eh? So what do you want to keep your money hidden away for when you can get some income out of it? It's not going to get more that way, is it?"

I resented Goldmann's insolence, especially the crack about not having a mistress, but I also had to accede to the logic in it. The money was not going to increase, and the longer I was in Esperanza the more certain I had become that I was not likely to find suitable employment. But I was still hedging for time.

"Look, Herr Goldmann, this proposal has come very suddenly. Let me think it over."

But Goldmann could sense his advantage and would not let me go. He insisted that I have dinner with them, and before I could refuse he had sent Trude upstairs to inform Frau Kramer.

At the dinner table Goldmann blithely introduced me as his new partner. Frau Goldmann embraced me and blessed me for my sense of enterprise and the confidence I had in her husband. I was too embarrassed to make it clear that I had not yet consented to give Goldmann the money.

Trude seemed angry when she heard the news. She scowled at her father and sulked all through the meal. Frau Paula Gruen, whom the Goldmanns keep isolated most of the time in the "factory," caught on vaguely that something pleasant was going on, and her mumbling was incessant and more feverish than ever.

We ate in the kitchen at a crude table. Frau Goldmann had prepared a cold supper, but she insisted on warming up some leftover meat for me. I realized that by accepting all this hospitality I was committing myself, but I think I was also grateful for being pushed.

After dinner Goldmann and I retired to the sala for further business talks. Goldmann outlined the merchandise he wanted to buy: cheap ladies' stockings, some underwear, men's shirts and socks. He was going to sell everything on the installment plan, making weekly rounds to collect the money. By the end of the evening he had me so far that I promised to give him the two hundred dollars. But we still have to draw up some sort of contract.

Now that I have promised Goldmann the money I feel much calmer, the way one feels after deciding to go through with an operation. After all, what can happen? If Goldmann cannot sell the merchandise, I suppose Levy would be willing to buy it back. And if bad comes to worse and Goldmann can't collect the money for the sold merchandise, I'll simply start starving to death one year earlier than I had intended.

*Thursday, May 11, 1939.* Frau Kramer is still piqued because I had dinner with the Goldmanns. Why the sudden hospitality? she asked. She insisted on a detailed description of what I was served, trying to coax

me into the admission that her cooking was better than Frau Goldmann's. I believe she suspects Frau Goldmann of trying to snatch her
boarder.

I did not mention having promised Goldmann two hundred dollars. As
if it were any of Frau Kramer's business what I do with my money!
Somehow I cannot help the feeling that she is Alma's representative on
earth, just as the pope is God's.

I would have liked to get Walter's opinion, but he had been out all
day and, as usual, was late for dinner. I sat waiting for him with the
Kramers long after Eva had retired to her room. Her light was on, and
I could see her moving around restlessly. She had used the excuse of
being tired only to get away from us.

"That girl," Herr Kramer said (he usually refers to Eva as That
Girl), "you'd think she would help my wife with the dishes. She acts
as if she were a guest here, or a queen! Too arrogant even to sit with us
and have a civil conversation. I'm going to have a word about her with
Walter."

Herr Kramer has had several such words with Walter. These discussions generally end in an all-around shouting bout, with Walter threatening to move out if his assorted relatives cannot get along with each
other.

Frau Kramer also voiced her complaints about Eva while we sat
waiting for Walter.

"Why does she act that way? What have we done to her? After all,
we are the parents of her husband, and she owes us some respect."

I was sorely tempted to tell Frau Kramer that respect has to be earned
before it can be owed. To wit: what happened only a half hour later.

Walter had finally come home. (Eva must know the sound of his
step on the stairs, for she came to the door and stood looking in through
the glass without coming into the room. That's another thing: Walter
always drops in on his parents first before he goes to his wife.)

Frau Kramer greeted her son with the customary reproaches: she
had been worried; they had waited with dinner; now he would have to
be served separately. Trying to calm her, Walter said that he had already
eaten in town. This only added fuel to Frau Kramer's anger.

"So why do you think I cook, if not for you?"

"Mama, you make it sound as if you were cooking for me alone!"

"Well, who else cares? Papa and I wouldn't mind just eating a piece of bread and butter! And the Herr Professor here, do you think he cares?" (I do, very much so!) "And your wife, she eats with a face as if I were serving her poison, God forbid!"

Having received his cue, Herr Kramer stood up.

"Walter, I have to have a word with you about Eva."

"Not now, Papa. I'm very tired. If you don't mind, I'd like to go to bed."

Ever since he had come in Walter had been holding one of his hands awkwardly, as though he were hiding something behind his back. Now, as he turned toward the door, he was too slow to hide a small, white paper bag from the suspicious eyes of his mother.

"What have you got there, Walter?"

Walter blushed deeply, like a child caught stealing a penny.

"Oh, nothing. Just some candies for Eva," he said.

Frau Kramer made a little gurgling sound of disbelief.

"Candies? For Eva? And what did you bring me?"

"Mama, for heaven's sake! Eva and I have been married three months! Can't I just once bring her some candies?"

"I've been your mother for twenty-five years," Frau Kramer said bitterly. "If you bring her something, you might bring me something too!"

Walter opened and closed his mouth, sighed and edged closer to the door. His nose seemed to have grown longer, and his homely face was tired and puzzled. He forced his mouth into a crooked smile.

"All right, Mama, I'll get you something tomorrow. You tell me what you want and I'll get it for you."

"I don't want anything now! You should have thought of your mother before!"

Walter shrugged and opened the door.

"Well, good night then," he said.

Eva was still peering through the glass panes. Her eyes were wide and horrified, and she looked close to hysteria. When she caught me looking at her she dropped out of sight. I am sure that she heard every word of the conversation.

As I said before: respect has to be earned.

*Saturday, May 13, 1939.*    Today, for the first time since we arrived in Esperanza, we had no rain all day. When the sun went down behind the Grampico, at about six-thirty, the air was full of the long blue shadows of early evening which I had almost forgotten. Then, within half an hour, it was dark.

The frogs are not croaking tonight, and my ears ring with the unaccustomed silence.

I called on Josef this morning for our biweekly chat in the loggia. The colors around us were incredible: the mountains lush green against the blue sky, framed between the pink pillars of the loggia and the purple sprays of bougainvillaea. I noticed that one of the dogs was not around. Josef told me that the bitch had had puppies, and we went to the garage to have a look at them, but the mother would not let us come close.

Her tits sagged with milk, and she snarled as we approached, baring her fangs even at Josef. She had made her lair behind a stack of firewood, and all we could hear was the faint squeaking of the puppies. Josef said that the Indian who fed the dogs had counted three, but that he had been unable to get very close either.

On the spur of the moment I asked Josef if he would let me have one of the puppies as soon as they had been weaned. I don't know yet how I am going to break the news to Frau Kramer, but I think that Eva would love to have a puppy.

*Sunday, May 21, 1939.*    I am beginning to understand why Levy has shown himself so co-operative toward Goldmann.

Today Levy and I were invited for lunch at the Goldmanns', sort of getting to know your new business relations meeting. This time Frau Kramer did not mind so much being rid of me for one meal. She is expecting her daughter day after tomorrow and has thrown herself into an orgy of cooking and baking for the event. When she heard that Levy also had been invited, she pricked up her ears.

"Ah, so Herr Levy is invited too. Well, well. Pretty smart that Goldmann."

For a second I felt my stomach contract, while I wondered how she had found out so fast about the deal between Goldmann and Levy.

"What do you mean?" I asked sheepishly.

"Well, I understand Herr Levy is a bachelor. And quite rich, too. They say he is no longer young, but then Trude isn't pretty and hasn't got a dowry either."

It took me a while to follow the mysterious workings of the female mind but I soon realized that Frau Kramer might be right. I recalled wondering about the easy terms Levy had offered to Goldmann. For all I knew Goldmann had promised, in return, to act as a matchmaker between Levy and Trude.

I began to see Levy in a new light. The few times I had met him in the Jungle Café, I had not paid too much attention to him. In spite of the awed whisperings about his wealth, all I could see in him was an insignificant little red-haired man with unpolished manners. Though he speaks a perfect Spanish, he always makes it a point to speak German to us—a faulty German, heavily tinged with Yiddish. Like so many of us he seemed to have forgotten that Yiddish is one of the richest and wittiest languages, and I often found myself wishing that he would revert to it without any further pretext.

I don't know how much Goldmann had told his daughter about Levy, but Trude seemed tense and nervous when I came downstairs. She wore a black skirt and a white cotton blouse, which was too tight across her bust and gaped where the fabric strained away from the buttons. A little piece of her pink brassière showed through the openings, but on Trude this did not look suggestive, only slovenly.

Goldmann, dressed in a dark suit as if he were going to a funeral, glared at his daughter in open disapproval.

"Is this what you're going to wear, Trude?"

"You didn't expect me to put on an evening gown," Trude replied testily.

"I begged her, Markus! I begged her, just for once . . ." Frau Goldmann said.

"Mama!" Trude said sharply.

The argument was quelled by the arrival of Levy. We heard a car stopping in front of the house, and then we saw Levy walking up the garden path, his head and torso completely hidden behind a huge arrangement of flowers. With his vision thus blocked, Levy missed one front step, stumbled, but finally recovered his equilibrium. Watching him, Trude giggled nervously. Goldmann ran to the door, his mouth split in an inviting, toothless grin.

"Come in, come in, Herr Levy! How are you? Here, let me take the flowers from you!"

Goldmann tugged at the basket, but Levy would not let go. Peering around the flowers, he caught sight of Frau Goldmann and stiffly walked toward her.

"Madame Goldmann," he said, "I have taken the liberty of bringing you a little present."

He dropped the huge basket into Frau Goldmann's arms and took one step back, gazing at her with his head tilted to one side as if he were sizing up a masterpiece. Next he pulled forth a large candy box which he had carried clamped under his arms and looked questioningly at Goldmann.

With the springy step of an affable salesman, Goldmann walked over to Trude and began pushing her toward Levy.

"And this, Herr Levy, is my little girl!"

Trude winced and shot her father a withering glance.

"How do you do," she said stiffly, remaining in the spot where Goldmann had stopped pushing her.

I waited for the first signs of disappointment to show on Levy's face. No doubt, Goldmann must have told him wonderful things about his daughter's charm and beauty. But Levy did not look so much disappointed as bewildered.

"Fräulein Goldmann?" he asked doubtfully, as though he were trying to adjust the picture of Trude in the flesh to the image he had fashioned from her father's reports. The adjustment seemed to come swiftly enough, for the bewildered expression was shortly replaced by a cheerful smile. "Fräulein Goldmann, I have taken the liberty of bringing you a box of sweets. Your father was kind enough to confide in me that you like chocolates."

He thrust the box at Trude. It was, like the basket of flowers, enormous, and I could envision the contents adding another layer of fat to Trude's hips. But perhaps Herr Levy liked girls of generous proportions.

"Thank you, Herr Levy, you should not have bothered," Trude said formally.

"No bother, no bother at all. As a matter of fact, it was a pleasure! How often does a bachelor have the honor of being invited to such a nice home?"

He looked with exaggerated admiration around the sparsely furnished room, which looked hospitable only because Frau Goldmann had moved the festively set kitchen table there for the day. Goldmann eagerly offered to show Levy the rest of the apartment, but this invitation was canceled by his wife.

"I am sure Herr Levy is hungry," Frau Goldmann said quickly. "We will show him the place some other day, when we have all our furniture."

"Ah, yes, we should be getting our furniture any day now," Goldmann said, catching the broad hint from his wife. "You must excuse this crude table, but everything takes so long here!"

"I know, I know, mañana," Levy said knowingly.

Trude looked from her mother to her father and squirmed as if she had reached the first stage of purgatory.

Frau Goldmann ushered us to the table and we sat down. Levy picked up his napkin, wiped his mouth and his forehead, and then neatly tucked the napkin into his collar. Trude watched him with morbid fascination. They sat across from each other, both red-haired and homely, and for a frightening moment I saw them surrounded by a bunch of ugly, red-haired children. But my imagination might have been overactive, for Trude behaved anything but invitingly.

As soon as Frau Goldmann had left for the kitchen, Trude rose with the unlikely excuse that she must help her mother. Herr Goldmann looked pleased with what he considered an act to impress Levy.

"I'm telling you, Herr Levy, my Trude is a regular little housewife, the way she cooks and sews . . ."

"My father is only joking! If I sew on a button it's a disgrace, and I don't know how to boil an egg!"

Levy stared at her in open consternation.

"But, Fräulein Goldmann, your father told me that you went to university! Why should you have to know how to sew and cook? You will have a maid to do these things for you . . . I mean, once you get married," Levy corrected himself, flustered by his clumsiness.

Trude looked cornered and frightened. She made another attempt to leave the table, but before she could escape Frau Goldmann was back with the first course.

"Where are you going, Trudi? I'll worry about the kitchen! You stay here and entertain our guest!"

The conversation during the meal was anything but brilliant. Trude spoke little, but what she said was expressed in choice words and clearly enunciated, as if she wanted to make Levy feel semiliterate.

Trying to watch his table manners, Levy was nervous and awkward. He slurped the soup with little sucking sounds, and Trude looked miserable. Frau Goldmann kept urging him to have seconds of everything, and since he ate very slowly and finished later than the rest of us, we had the pleasure of hearing him eat. For dessert we had stewed prunes, and Levy daintily spit the pits into his plate.

After the coffee we still sat around for a while and made small talk. Frau Goldmann refused to let Trude help with the dishes, and the poor girl had to suffer out the afternoon with us. All through the meal, up to the time of Levy's departure, we did not once mention business.

On leaving, at about three o'clock, Levy thanked the Goldmanns profusely, saying something about a good Jewish meal in a good Jewish home. While the Goldmanns walked their guest to the garden gate, Trude hung back with me. In her embarrassment she began fussing with the flowers Levy had brought.

"I guess I better put them in water," she said.

Pulling out one rose and then another, she found that the flowers had been snipped off just beneath the chalice and that they were tied to long pieces of wire in lieu of stems. Trude held the roses away from her body, stiff-armed and with an expression as if she had touched some loathsome form of vermin.

"My God, how horrible," she said, shuddering. "A basketful of guillotined flowers!"


*Tuesday, May 23, 1939.*    An emotional day for the Kramers: their daughter Ruth with her husband and her two boys arrived from France.

Walter went to the station to pick up his sister while the rest of the family waited at home. Frau Kramer had decorated the entire house with flowers for the welcome, even winding garlands around the banister of the stairs. The hall looked like a place prepared for a bacchanalian orgy.

Everybody was dressed in his best clothes. Eva, in a light-blue dress which picked up the color of her eyes, looked lovely but sullen, as if she did not particularly relish the idea of getting more relatives.

In the morning she had had another argument with Walter, this time concerning the accommodations for his sister. Walter has found a house for the Lipschitzes into which they will move as soon as it is finished. In the meantime they will have to live in a hotel. Eva asked why she and Walter could not move into the house and his sister live with his parents. Walter said something about the children making Frau Kramer nervous, and Eva said she wished somebody would for once worry about what made her nervous.

"I wish I was five hundred years old and had a long, white beard so that people would show me some consideration!"

"Eva, please not today! Just for once don't spoil it!"

"All right. I'll be oozing with charm."

Of course Eva was anything but oozing with charm when the Lipschitzes arrived. She was stiff and frightened, and she kept in the background while Frau Kramer fell upon her daughter and her grandchildren, weeping copiously as she embraced them time and again. Herr Kramer virtually had to force his way into the weeping, kissing crowd.

Eva waited cautiously until she was approached by her new relatives. The first one to meet her was her new brother-in-law who, not being a true-blue blood relation, had not been completely smothered with affection.

"Alfred, meet my wife," Walter said.

"Aahh!"

This was the deep, throaty aahh of appreciation, the sort of sound that comes from a hungry crowd when the doors to the dining room are finally flung open to reveal a splendidly set buffet table.

Clearly, Dr. Lipschitz is a man who appreciates the good things in life. He even looks the part of the Epicurean, with his blandly handsome face and his sensuous, pink mouth embedded in a generously padded chin.

The way he kissed Eva, I thought he was contemplating taking a bite out of her.

Frau Ruth, still engaged in endearments with her parents, seemed to learn through some sixth sense that her husband was carrying brotherly love too far. She struggled out of the parental embraces and quickly came across the room, with the short, ungainly steps of a plump woman too tightly encased in her girdle.

"All right, Alfred! Perhaps you will give *me* a chance to kiss my new sister-in-law?"

For a second the two women stood appraising each other, Eva fair and aloof, Frau Ruth pudgy and full-busted, with her blue-black hair and the delicate, white skin of the typically Jewish beauty, reminding me of Alma when she was a young girl.

I suppose Frau Ruth has been a woman long enough to know that a girl like Eva will tempt a man without half trying. At any rate, as she kissed Eva she carefully interposed herself between her sister-in-law and her husband. Then, releasing Eva, who had stiffly suffered the kiss, she stepped back and emitted an exaggerated sigh.

"Ah, Walter, she's a lovely girl. And you better keep an eye on Alfred. She's just his type," Frau Ruth said jestingly, but she looked worried.

Eva did not seem to relish being the center of attention. She seemed relieved when the two little boys were called over to be introduced to her.

"This is Paul, my baby, and the big boy is Kurt."

Paul, the baby, is three, Kurt seven. The little one was so weary from the trip that he fell asleep almost instantly, but the big one, a regular little monster, made up for him in liveliness.

Kurt walked up to Eva and stared at her unblinkingly.

"Who's she?"

"This is your new aunt Eva I told you about."

"She doesn't look like an aunt," Kurt said sullenly.

"Why not?"

"She's pretty."

"Well," Frau Ruth said, exasperated. "Well. Let's all go and sit down and talk with Mama and Papa."

But we had no chance to do much talking. The meal we were served was hectic, with all three women filing in and out of the room in a procession of serving. In their eagerness to outdo each other, they kept snatching away the plates before one had a chance to finish eating.

"You had enough meat, Herr Professor? You finished eating, Walter? All right, pass the plates on down, Eva. Sit, Ruth, sit!"

All attempts at a reasonable conversation were throttled by one or the other of the women coming back from the kitchen and asking what we were talking about. Kurt did his share to keep the gathering from getting dull by drumming with his feet against the table. Most of the time Eva looked incredulously outraged, as if she were witnessing the ceremonial feast of some primitive African tribe.

Kurt finally managed to knock himself out and fell asleep on the bed beside his brother. In the ensuing silence we had a brief chance to talk about a few mutual acquaintances and what had become of them. Within five minutes at least half a dozen countries, spaced neatly over the globe, were named in connection with people one had once known. The Jews were certainly getting around these days.

It was after ten o'clock when the Lipschitzes gathered up their sleeping children and started out for their hotel. Everybody except Eva accompanied them downstairs.

In the hall below, Dr. Lipschitz pulled Walter into one corner and whispered to him:

"Tell me, Walter, this big house and the way you're living here . . . I mean, what do you do for a living?"

Walter raised his shoulders and turned his palms outward in the traditional gesture of God only knows.

"Everybody lives like this," he said vaguely.

"What are you two whispering about?" Frau Ruth called back over her shoulder. "Oh, I know what you're doing! You're looking at Eva!"

"Well, you caught us! Doesn't she look lovely standing up there?" Dr. Lipschitz said.

Eva gave us a faint smile. She stood on the upstairs gallery, and from below we could see her long legs tantalizingly disappear into the shadow of her flary skirt. (No matter how often one sees a woman in a bathing suit, one still wonders about her legs the moment she puts on a skirt!)

"Good night, Eva!" Dr. Lipschitz blew Eva a flirtatious kiss, which she acknowledged with one of her royal waves. As she leaned over the banister, her long, blond hair fell forward over her shoulders.

"The Lorelei, luring unwary sailors to their doom," Dr. Lipschitz rhapsodized.

"She is beautiful. Isn't she beautiful, Ruth?" Walter asked with possessive pride.

"Yes, she's very pretty. But just between you and me, Walter, this isn't the real color of her hair. She dyes it, doesn't she?"

*Thursday, May 25, 1939.* Another visit with Josef. I told him about the arrival of the Lipschitzes.

"They're lucky," he said. "Just in time. It's only a matter of months, weeks perhaps, before there will be a war in Europe."

"You really think so?"

He looked at me as if he seriously questioned my intelligence. I had to think of the letter in which he had forewarned me of the Anschluss of Austria. Perhaps we are not yet detached enough to evaluate what is happening in Europe.

Later we went to look at the puppies. They have turned into the most irresistible, wiggling bundles of fur. Their mother is beginning to become indifferent to them. She hardly turned her head when I picked one up and petted it. Josef says in another week I may take one of the puppies home.

*Sunday, May 28, 1939.* Today I provoked a stormy debate by mentioning what Josef had said about the probability of a war in Europe. Most of the shouting took place between Dr. Lipschitz and Goldmann, who always drops in after lunch now.

Ever since their arrival, the Lipschitzes have been regular guests for every meal except breakfast. Frau Kramer cannot abide the idea of any of her brood eating in the hotel. Of course Goldmann's curiosity will not permit him to miss the political discussions which develop after the meals, especially since he has found out that Dr. Lipschitz is as much of an armchair strategist as he is.

During the first few days, before the novelty wore off, Dr. Lipschitz held court. He would pull a chair into the middle of the room and straddle it, facing us and lecturing like a teacher to his class. Unfortunately, for a man who likes to hear himself talk, he has a habit of overloading his sentences until he loses the thread and finishes without a verb.

Eva also seemed to notice this weakness, for every time Dr. Lipschitz blundered, I could see a gleam of malicious amusement creep into her eyes.

It would be nearly impossible to reconstruct any of these sentences, but the general style is something like this:

"Now, of course, if the Germans keep massing troops at the border which, as you know, is the Maginot Line, but on the other hand, the English are not willing to fight yet, and naturally, the Americans will perhaps want to remain neutral, and the French have never been good soldiers and cannot alone, then the time will come for all the Jews in France."

This is only a very inept sample of Dr. Lipschitz's political theories. But the gist of it all is that he does not believe there will be a war in Europe, at least not in the near future—a statement which almost made Goldmann jump down his throat.

"No war? Of course there will be a war! Mark my word: by June the Russians will attack the Schweinhunde! By September it will be over, and within a year we will be back in Vienna!"

Eva, who usually does not get involved in these debates, sat up and glared at Goldmann with cold, blue eyes.

"You wouldn't really want to go back there? Not after what they did to you? What do you want to do, go back and say thank you?"

"Eva," Herr Kramer said sharply, "what do you know about these things? You're only a child!"

"I'm old enough to know that we ought to hold on to the little dignity we have left as Jews!"

I had never seen Eva so excited. Among us all, she has always seemed the one who carried her Jewishness with the greatest indifference.

"My, my," Dr. Lipschitz said, making smoldering eyes at Eva, "a regular Jewish Joan of Arc."

"Oh, shut up," Eva said softly. She said it under her breath, and only Walter and I, who were close enough, heard her.

From that moment she kept out of the discussion, and the rest was a shoutfest between Goldmann and Dr. Lipschitz.

*Tuesday, May 30, 1939.*    Dr. Lipschitz is a habitual name dropper. Into every account of his stay in France he manages to weave the names of certain celebrities he claims to have met there.

Today he finally goaded me into mentioning that I knew Professor Einstein. The effect on him was as if I had said that I knew God. Instead of stopping my bragging right there, I found to my horror that I could not keep from reeling off the names of the other famous guests at the dinner which Frau Aronoff had given in Einstein's honor.

At least I had sense enough not to tell Dr. Lipschitz that Professor Einstein and I had given an impromptu rendition of the Kreutzer Sonata. And now that I think back to the event, it seems like something I dreamed up in a moment of wild fantasy.

What year was it—1930?—when Alma went to spend the Christmas holidays on the Semmering? It must have been 1930. I had promised her a stay in the Panhans Hotel—rather expensive for a man with my salary, though not entirely a gesture of generosity. I had to buy myself off for two weeks in order to spend all the time I wanted with Christine.

I remember New Year's Eve. Christine and I went to an obscure little restaurant where nobody would recognize us. When we stepped out into the street, long after midnight, the city had been blanketed by snow. I remember the clean smell of snow in my nostrils; how radiant Christine looked in her winter coat with the fluffy, white fox collar; the feeling of happiness. Ever since the smell of snow and the feeling of happiness have always gone together in my mind. I doubt that I shall ever smell snow again.

Alma came back early in January, full of tales about all the important people she had met in the Panhans. I had the horrible vision of Alma pushing herself on strangers who did not have the slightest desire to meet her. The story that Frau Aronoff—the renowned Frau Aronoff who gave literary teas and soirées and whose husband was one of the few Jewish industrialists in Austria—had promised to invite her to one of her parties, I quietly discarded as a figment of Alma's imagination.

I had practically forgotten about it when we received a note from Frau Aronoff, inviting us for dinner. Alma was triumphant, but I worried for days over why Frau Aronoff should have asked us. I was neither a writer nor an artist, and it dawned on me only later, after I had met Professor Einstein, that we had been invited because of my academic standing.

It turned out that my apprehension about the party had been unfounded. Instead of the large, glittering crowd which I had expected, there were only eight people present. (Later I learned that Professor Einstein loathed large parties.) But who really put me at ease was Frau Aronoff. For some reason I had pictured her as a variation of Alma —a scantily educated woman buying distinction with her husband's money. I was pleasantly surprised to meet a lady of the type Schnitzler used to idolize in his plays: cultivated, slender, unusually tall, with dark, intelligent eyes. Only her mouth kept her from being a perfect beauty; the thin-lipped mouth of a woman constantly on guard against herself.

She made the introductions with charm and ease. My knees went soft when I shook Professor Einstein's hand, and I had to keep reminding myself that he was a few years my junior. But even then there was about him an aura which commanded veneration. After Frau Aronoff had introduced us to all her guests, I noticed that her husband was missing. Since nobody else asked about his absence, I did not either, but on the way home Alma told me that it was common gossip that Generaldirektor Aronoff never attended any of his wife's parties.

All through the meal we discussed music, literature, politics—anything but physics, to my great relief. For once Alma did not make a fool of herself. She hit it off very well with Frau Einstein, a heavy, prematurely old woman.

After dinner we retired to have a demitasse in the salon. The room was dominated by a magnificent Bechstein grand, and as I walked over to the piano my attention was caught by a photograph displayed on it. It showed a handsome boy of about sixteen, I guessed, no doubt Frau Aronoff's son. He had the same deep-set eyes, the same lofty brow, the same narrow nose. But from the nose down it was a different face: the full-lipped, square-chinned face of a spitefully sensuous young faun. Tucked into the frame of the photograph was a snapshot of the same boy with boxing gloves, holding a trophy in his hands. And beside him a man, a little shorter than the boy, with a paunch and a double chin, but with the same full, pleasure-loving mouth: Generaldirektor Aronoff beaming upon his son.

I kept glancing from the picture to Frau Aronoff and back again, wondering what had brought about the union of such contrasting partners. Frau Aronoff mistook my interest in the photograph for interest in the piano.

"Isn't it a beautiful instrument?" she said. "We bought it after my boy refused to go on with his violin lessons. I thought something more vigorous, like a piano, might appeal to him. But his only ambition at the moment is to become a boxer!"

"What a shame!" Alma exclaimed; and then, to gloss over her tactless remark: "My husband plays the piano."

I felt like murdering her.

"Well, my husband plays the violin," Frau Einstein said. "And since Frau Aronoff mentioned having a violin, perhaps you two could play a duet!"

Before I could protest, Professor Einstein said that we would be delighted to entertain the other guests. He was so devoid of self-consciousness that he made me feel foolish. Frau Aronoff produced the music for the Kreutzer Sonata, and we picked our way through the score. I doubt that our performance deserved the applause it received, but it was a rewarding experience in itself. Afterward I sat in a pleasant daze and was only startled back into reality by the hard banging of the door.

When I looked up I saw that the boy had come into the room. He was even handsomer than in his picture, exuding an air of barely bridled animal strength. It was hard to think of Frau Aronoff's son as a fighter, but perhaps that was what nature had intended him for.

"Egon, we have a very famous guest here tonight," Frau Aronoff said to her son. "Professor Einstein."

"Oh," the boy said without enthusiasm.

"My God, is that all you have to say?"

"Well, what else am I supposed to say?"

The boy glared defiantly.

Frau Aronoff began apologizing to Professor Einstein, but he seemed genuinely bewildered by her embarrassment. He insisted that he did not see why a young boy should be interested in him.

"You would not expect me to feign an interest in pugilism, would you?" he said to Frau Aronoff.

Even Frau Aronoff was taken aback by such forthrightness and humility. She fumbled and then sent the boy out of the room, almost brusquely. After he had left, Frau Einstein turned to her hostess.

"A very handsome boy. How old is he? Fifteen?"

"He's tall for his age. He's only thirteen."

A little later Frau Einstein discreetly whispered that she and her husband were not in the habit of staying up late. We all rose and began saying our good-bys.

On the way home Alma kept talking about the furniture and the carpets and the china and the silver and what Frau Aronoff and the other ladies had been wearing, and there was a stain on Professor Einstein's lapel (only Alma would notice such a thing!) and Frau Einstein was such a nice woman, so unassuming, and young Egon Aronoff was a very handsome boy, but terribly rude, and she would be ashamed to be his mother. (What she actually hoped was that Frau Aronoff would feel humiliated because of her son.)

"And why should a mother feel ashamed of a son who looks like a powerful young panther?" I asked, thinking of our own overfed Arthur.

Alma stared at me, aghast.

"So who wants a panther in the house?" she said.

*Thursday, June 1, 1939.*    Our place is utter bedlam. I brought the puppy home today. He was terrified by the new surroundings, leaving a trail of puddles behind him as he scampered through the house. Most of the time he hid under beds and in corners, but once he managed to escape onto the terrace, where he wriggled through the wrought iron grating and sat on the narrow ledge beyond it, balancing precariously above the one-story drop below him. He had sense enough—or perhaps it was instinct—to remain there motionless. Eva was even more frightened than the dog.

"Here, puppy, here, baby," she cooed, trying to coax him back again.

But the puppy was too scared to move, and finally Eva swung one leg over the banister, placing herself in as much peril as the dog, and pulled him in. She held him to her breast, crooning to him, and I thought that what she really wanted was a baby. A helpless creature upon which to release all her pent-up tenderness. Sensing that he was safe again, the puppy wagged his short, stubby tail for the first time since his arrival.

I left it to Eva to name the dog. On the spur of the moment she came up with Don José. (I wonder how Josef would feel about that?) For delicacy's sake we have abbreviated his name to Don.

The biggest surprise was the way Frau Kramer took to the puppy. He has completely captured her heart with his ravenous appetite.

*Sunday, June 4, 1939.* Yesterday it was my turn to go to the railroad station. Leo Horowitz and Dr. Landau arrived together from Rioverde, and I, as the old, experienced immigrant, had to escort them to the hotel.

To say that my Spanish is shaky would be paying myself a compliment, but I would not let on about my difficulties in front of the new arrivals. Thus I made a great display of haggling with the cargadores, eventually overpaying them horrendously just to put an end to the bargaining.

As we walked to the taxi I noticed that Horowitz picked his way through the milling, unwashed crowd, wrinkling his nose and walking with mincing steps like a woman daintily lifting her skirt before she skips across a puddle. I had thought that Landau, the doctor, would be shocked by the filth, but he was saddened rather than horrified. Looking at the dirty infants sucking at the unwashed breasts of their mothers, he said:

"It's a miracle that any of them survive. But then life is full of miracles."

I asked him whether he was a religious man. He looked appalled.

"Religious! How can you expect a man—a Jew—to believe in God after what is happening in Europe!"

Still, something in his voice failed to convince me of his lack of faith. This was neither the time nor the place to engage in a profound, theological conversation with him, but I find the prospect of such future discussions quite cheering. God knows I could do with an intelligent exchange of opinions once in a while!

It was not until we sat in the cab, out of reach of the jostling cargadores and begging urchins, that I really had a good look at my two wards. One feature had caught my attention the moment they stepped from the train: they were both very short, like twin midgets. But there the similarity ended.

Dr. Landau is the much older man, about my age, I would say. His hair is short-cropped, with the odd, greenish tinge which a liberal sprinkling of gray brings to blond hair. On the back of his head is a neat, bald circle, resembling the tonsure of a priest. His face is small and mournful, breaking into a hundred tiny, overlapping folds, like a toy balloon that has lost most of its air.

Horowitz must be about forty, but perhaps he is older, only feigning the youthfulness of the perennial bachelor. His hair, thick and brown, is cut an even length all around and stands about his head like an indomitable brush. For reasons of his own he looks perpetually angry, his small mouth grimly set and his eyes glowering.

"Filth, squalor, poverty," he recited. "Just look at how those poor Indians live! No doubt exploited by their white masters!"

He glared at me as if holding me personally responsible for the living conditions of the Indians. I expected him to ask me any minute why I had brought him here.

Dr. Landau was less concerned with the Indians and more with the cost of living in Esperanza. He questioned me minutely about my monthly expenses, until Horowitz remarked with venom:

"What do you care about the cost of living, Dr. Landau, you're filthy rich anyway!"

"Why must you always exaggerate, Horowitz? I will probably have to live on what I have for the rest of my life. I'm not allowed to practice here, and I'm too old to start all over again. Besides, I promised to engage in industry or agriculture. Who knows, I might end up delivering calves instead of babies."

"And what's wrong with delivering calves? Or is it too proletarian an occupation for you? I might become a farmer myself . . . get up at daybreak . . . till the ground . . ." Horowitz rhapsodized.

"Till the ground! You with your manicured hands!"

I cast a quick glance at Horowitz's hands. They were small and delicate like a girl's, his nails neatly trimmed, filed and buffed to a pale shell pink. Horowitz blushed and thrust his hands into his pockets.

"Horowitz, the manicured farmer," Dr. Landau teased.

"You could stand a manicure yourself! You're much too sloppy for a doctor, anyway!"

I left them at the hotel, where they probably went on bickering and nagging each other like a long-married couple. I thought that only army life, prison life, and emigration could bring two total strangers to such a point of familiarity within one brief month.

Tomorrow morning I will have to look in on them again. Subtly, without saying it in so many words, they too made me feel that since I brought them here I am responsible for their welfare.

*Monday, June 5, 1939.*   Frau Kramer told me to bring Dr. Landau and Horowitz for lunch. Her urge to feed is all-encompassing and extends even to strangers.

The two men were certainly grateful for the invitation. When I got to the hotel in the morning I found them in very low spirits. The water had stopped running while they were shaving, and the coffee they had ordered had been an abominable brew. These things have become so familiar to me that I had forgotten to warn Horowitz and Landau about them.

I never thought I would relish the role of a guide. On the whole, I talked as though I had arrived in Esperanza twenty years ago. The very strangeness of the other two men made me feel more at home.

Both Landau and Horowitz were overawed by our house and the way in which we live, or rather seem to live. At first sight it is impossible for the outsider to discern the frightening hole of insecurity beneath the external gloss.

"Tell me, are those people very rich?" Dr. Landau wanted to know.

"No, not particularly," I said, giving my own version of the truth.

"Then how come they live like this?"

I borrowed an explanation from Walter: "Everybody lives like this."

But Dr. Landau is not a man to be easily satisfied. He wanted to know how much rent the Kramers paid, and how much I paid them. When I told him that I paid two hundred pesos a month, he was outraged.

"Why, you're practically paying half their rent! They're exploiting you!"

We were sitting in my room prior to the meal, and fortunately nobody heard his remark.

"I'm paying for room and board," I said. "And Frau Kramer is an excellent cook."

(Besides, there is Eva in the house. But this I did not tell Dr. Landau.)

Of course my guests could not help noticing Eva's attractions for themselves. Especially Horowitz could not take his eyes off her. I even think she flirted with him. She kept smiling at him until he became flustered and edgy like a man who wears itchy underwear and does not dare scratch in public. She left Horowitz reduced to a state of blubbering admiration.

"Oh, what a girl! Oh, what a beauty! Are there more of that sort in Esperanza?"

"Not that I know of."

"And even if there were, Horowitz," Dr. Landau said, "what would they want with *you?*"

"They might still prefer me to you, in spite of your filthy lucre!"

I don't know why Horowitz keeps referring to Dr. Landau's wealth. God knows he does not act like a rich man! He even let Frau Kramer wrap a piece of cake for him to take back to the hotel. Frankly, I was embarrassed.

After they had left, I could not resist asking Eva how she had liked my new protégés. She smiled wryly.

"They're a fitting addition to our zoo here," she said. "Dr. Landau looks like a morose pinscher. And Horowitz, with his hair standing up all over his head, like an enraged porcupine."

Eva has a sharp tongue, but at least I no longer think she was smiling at Horowitz. She was just laughing about him.


*Thursday, June 8, 1939.*    Yesterday Goldmann went on his first overnight trip to the provinces. When he returned today he looked dirty and beaten, and he had a number of unkind things to say about the bus service, hotel accommodations, Indians, and Hitler. But when I asked him how business had been, he perked up and insisted that it was very good, reeling off a long list of items he had sold.

I don't believe a word of what he told me.


*Saturday, June 10, 1939.*    With the instinct of a huntress Frau Goldmann has smelled out the arrival of two eligible bachelors. This afternoon, when I was about to leave for the city, she waylaid me at the garden gate.

"So your friends have already arrived? They seem like very nice gentlemen."

How she could have formed this judgment by peeking at them from behind her curtains is beyond me.

"Yes, they're very nice."

"Younger men?"

"Well, one might be called a younger man."

"Ah. And what are they going to do here?"

"I have no idea. Landau is a doctor, but he isn't allowed to practice here."

A gleam of deep interest had crept into Frau Goldmann's eyes.

"This Dr. Landau, he would be the younger man?"

(Was there ever a Jewish mother who could resist the idea of having her daughter married to a doctor?)

"No, I'm afraid Dr. Landau is about my age."

Frau Goldmann heaved a deep sigh, sadly parting with the short dream of "my son-in-law, the doctor."

"And the other one, what is his name?"

"Horowitz. Leo Horowitz."

"He would be around thirty, thirty-five?" Frau Goldmann suggested hopefully.

"He's closer to forty, I suppose."

"A mature man has his advantages."

Without once mentioning Trude, Frau Goldmann and I both knew what we were talking about. I thought I had given her all the information she craved for the moment, but as I was about to step into the street, she caught me by my sleeve and whispered:

"Now, Herr Professor, don't mention anything about this to Frau Kramer, but perhaps one of the gentlemen would like to rent a room from me? I could move Trudi's bed into the dining room, and he could have a nice, sunny room with a view of the mountains. You'll talk to him, won't you, Herr Professor?"

I noticed that she had advisedly dropped the plural, and since we had last talked of Horowitz, I had to assume that she had already selected him to be her boarder.

"Well, I don't see how I can tell one without telling the other about the room," I said.

"You tell them both, of course," Frau Goldmann said, flustered because I had caught her. "And about the price . . . I think I would ask the same you're paying upstairs. But we can always talk about the price. Just don't mention anything to Frau Kramer before the deal is settled. And not to Trudi either. You understand, I want to tell her myself."

"I understand perfectly."

Poor Levy, with his guillotined flowers, is going to have an unwitting rival, at least where Frau Goldmann is concerned. It seems that Trude is becoming quite a prize!


*Sunday, June 11, 1939.*     If I had known that the puppy would add to the tension between Eva and Frau Kramer I would never have brought him home. My idea was to give Eva a live toy, but Frau Kramer has made the affections of the dog a matter of fierce competition between them. Of course the poor animal is bewildered. He is torn between

Frau Kramer, who feeds him, and Eva, who is his playmate. If I could think of a plausible excuse I would return the dog to Josef.

But when I broached the subject, both Eva and Frau Kramer for once aligned themselves on the same side: parting with Don was out of the question!

*Monday, June 12, 1939.*  Horowitz mentioned today that he and Dr. Landau were looking for accommodations in an inexpensive pensión. This was a good chance to bring up Frau Goldmann's offer. Before he committed himself, Dr. Landau cautiously inquired about the rent. When I quoted a price, he made a face like a bulldog sniffing the chair where the cat had slept.

"I'm not as charitable as you are, Professor Bernstein. I don't see why I should support the Goldmanns with my rent."

But Horowitz seemed quite interested, especially after I mentioned (very casually) that there was a young girl in the house.

"Tell me, is she as pretty as the one upstairs?" he asked with a confidential wink.

"W-e-l-l, Trude is a very *nice* girl."

Horowitz's face fell. "I prefer them pretty," he said.

Nevertheless, he told me to go ahead and ask Frau Goldmann to keep the room for him. Frau Goldmann was overjoyed, throwing herself into a renewed frenzy of cleaning in preparation for Horowitz's inspection visit tomorrow. No doubt Horowitz will be pleased with what he finds.

*Thursday, June 15, 1939.*  Our Kaffeeklatsch in the Jungle Café is gaining members daily. Every week brings more refugees to Esperanza, and with the arrival of the first Czechs here, the number of Jewish families has increased to about a hundred. We are really beginning to feel the need for a club of our own.

Most of our conversations revolve around the founding of such a club, and though we have not even agreed upon a name yet, certain members of the community are already vying for the post of president. Goldmann insists that Levy can financially afford the position and fiercely backs his nomination. Herr Kramer, for reasons best known to himself, thinks that he ought to be chosen. Behind his father's back Walter has asked me if I would accept if nominated, and when I declined he came up with the surprising proposal that I ought to approach Josef Blumenthal with the idea.

But all this is still neither here nor there. For the most part we just talk. Our discussions can be divided into three categories: top priority is given to the founding of the club; next comes the political situation in Europe; last, what are we going to do to survive here.

Officially we are all either industriales or hacienderos. But only a handful of immigrants have bought or leased haciendas. Farming is not a Jewish business, though I understand that Jews in Palestine have made a success of it. But perhaps it is different working your own land.

Our industriales are all more or less of the caliber of Goldmann: one-man productions, selling their output to one or two stores, or peddling their wares from door to door. Some of the more enterprising have set up their plants in empty garages, turning out floor wax, soap, and clumsily fabricated, leaking tin cans. The output of all these manufacturers is so small that their income does not cover their living expenses, which most of them have to supplement out of their landing money.

A few cunning individuals have managed to wangle permits to open stores. The new immigration chief, Señor Moran, has turned out to be a liberal-minded man, open to persuasion in the form of currency. In the face of a strong enough argument, he will find ways to circumvent the provisions stated in the immigrations visas. Thus several groceries and small restaurants, catering mainly to refugee patrons, have sprung up in Esperanza. This is not as good as it appears at first sight. Since most of the money spent in these establishments comes from Jewish customers, and these same customers have no source from which to replenish their income, we are put much in the same position as the worm which unwittingly feeds upon its own tail.

The real Croesuses among us are all members of the old immigration, like Grushka, Dubrovsky and Levy. It must be said to their credit that they support a number of the new arrivals by employing them as peddlers. Their headquarters are in the Jungle Café, which not only saves them the rent for an office but also gives them a chance to keep an eye on each other.

Levy officiates in a booth at one end of the café, while Grushka and Dubrovsky occupy a booth at the other end. Between them their peddlers keep fluctuating back and forth, presumably to find out by eavesdropping what sort of merchandise is being handled and at what price. The competition, though, is rather amiable.

The only time discussions become really heated is when they turn to politics. Instead of being a consolidated group, we are split into numerous factions. But this is generally the Jewish fate. We have not only the East and West Jews here, but we have also the orthodox, the assimilated, the German, the Austrian, the Czech Jews, the Jews who are Zionists and those who are anti-Zionists, the Jews who want to go back as soon as it is "all over" over there, the Jews who want to go on to the United States, and Horowitz, who says he is a Communist.

I could not say that Horowitz's political color has come as a complete surprise to me—not after he kept referring to Dr. Landau as a filthy and stingy capitalist. What enrages poor Horowitz is that nobody takes him seriously. He is continually being heckled by one faction or the other and has, in the short period since his arrival, managed not to be on speaking terms with a number of people. That is, he refuses to speak to them. But generally these rages on his part last no longer than two or three days.

Personally, I think that Horowitz is about as much of a Communist as I am. He just suffers from our common malady of liking to hear himself talk, and Communism is almost as inexhaustible a topic as philosophy, religion, or sex.


*Saturday, June 17, 1939.*    Goldmann has given me another of his business reports, but he is vague and evasive, and I am beginning to worry. I offered to accompany him on his next trip to the provinces, but he was dead set against it. Still, I think I shall insist.


*Sunday, June 18, 1939.*    Once again Eva and Walter are conversing in monosyllables, if at all. Their hostility might have something to do with our visit to the Brauns, where we were invited for lunch today. (Frau Kramer wanted it understood that she felt slighted because she had not been asked.)

It is amazing how much Frau Irene has accomplished with her house in a few weeks. Of course she had most of her furniture shipped from Europe, and her rooms do not have the makeshift quality that results from uncurtained windows, bare floors, and crude furniture hastily knocked together from dismantled crates. The Brauns' house looks warm, hospitable and secure. This is nothing like the feigned prosperity of the Kramers.

Eva certainly liked the atmosphere. She could hardly tear herself away and kept gazing at Hans with something amounting to idolatry. The godfather-provider. But isn't this what all women want?

Walter felt very bitter about Eva's behavior.

"She enjoys making me feel an all-around failure," he complained. "Her pet peeve now is that she can't understand why we need a club and why I should spend time and effort planning one. 'The ridiculous urge to band together like sheep,' she calls it. She really believes that man can get along by himself. Well, I can't! And she's wrong if she thinks that Hans Braun can. He's just lucky! We can't all be employees of the almighty Panamerican Oil Company."

I believe Walter tries to find excuses for having to make a living by giving Spanish lessons. I just can't understand why he never tried getting work as an architect. Perhaps I ought to speak to Josef about Walter Kramer.

*Wednesday, June 21, 1939.*   Our community—at least the Viennese section of it—has been rocked by a new event: young Aronoff has come to Esperanza!

Why, everybody keeps asking, why Aronoff with all his money—why should Aronoff, who could certainly take his pick among the countries, come to El Paramo?

There are two theories about it: some people claim that Aronoff has smuggled out a fabulous fortune and that he has come to a small, obscure South American country to hide out for the duration. (Why he should be hiding out nobody bothers to explain; but then logic is never a strong point of guesswork.) Others say that his father's capital is entirely tied up in Austria and that Aronoff escaped penniless. Be that as it may, young Aronoff's arrival here has brought us a new distraction, not completely limited to speculations about his finances.

Yesterday morning I saw Aronoff for the first time. We—that is, Goldmann, Fleischer, Jakob Kramer and I—were standing on the steps of the post office. Eva and Frau Fleischer stood a little way off, chattering about one of the parties that now have become weekly fare. Suddenly both women stopped talking and stared. Frau Fleischer raised her hand and began fluffing her long, red hair. Eva's mouth gaped a little and she looked breathless.

Fleischer was the first one to turn around to see what the women were staring at. Whistling softly through his teeth, he said:

"Say, isn't that young Egon Aronoff? I used to see his photo in the *Wiener Illustrierte,* usually stripped to the waist and with some sort of sporting trophy in his hand. Well, if he's in Esperanza, we husbands may as well declare a period of mourning."

By then we had all turned to look at Aronoff. I could not honestly claim that I recognized in him the boy whom I had seen only once, nine years ago. There was still a resemblance to Frau Aronoff, but now the heavy, sensuous features of his father seemed to have gained the upper hand in his face. Not so much the features as the expression of a man deeply appreciative of the material pleasures of life. He was tall and quite dark, his sun tan set off by the light-gray suit which fitted him the way only a good, custom-made suit can fit. He came ambling up the stairs with the easy, graceful gait of an athlete, his head held high, his dark hair gleaming bluish in the sun.

The behavior of the two women seemed to bear out Fleischer's gloomy prophecy. Frau Fleischer virtually simpered when the young man passed her. Eva just stood petrified, gaping at him.

Aronoff scrutinized Frau Fleischer with great interest, but did not give Eva a second glance. It was impossible that he had not seen her. But perhaps a miracle had happened; perhaps he was blind to Eva's charms the way some people are unable to see certain colors. (Instead of pondering this phenomenon, I want to be grateful.)

An hour later I met Aronoff again in the Jungle Café. He sat by a table, half lying on his chair, his long legs stretched out before him. He looked perfectly at home, as if places like the Jungle Café were his natural habitat and he had not been raised in Frau Aronoff's culture-bristling household.

With him was the strangest-looking person I have ever seen: a man well over six feet tall, his enormous chest bulging out of a loud sports coat, which was patched at the elbows with leather hearts. The coat, fitting snugly over his shoulders and his arms, seemed much too small for him, ready to pop from the single button which held it together. One could sense the muscles rippling beneath the tight fabric. On the shoulders of this Gargantua sat the most ridiculously small head, with astonished, guileless blue eyes, a gently curved mouth, and the golden ringlets of a cherub. This creature was being addressed as Rudi.

(I have since learned that his full name is Rudolf Brueck and that he trails young Aronoff everywhere.)

It was unavoidable that a number of rumors should have sprung up around young Aronoff, son of a scion of Viennese Jewry, and Rudi Brueck, of uncertain antecedents and widely suspected of not being a Jew.

Frau Ruth Lipschitz has her own theory about those two: Brueck, she claims, is obviously a Nazi spy, attached to young Aronoff to watch him —and all of us—here.

Aside from the fact that there is hardly anything worthwhile spying out in Esperanza, I doubt that Herr Brueck has the acting ability with which Frau Ruth credits him. His chimpanzee grace and the doglike devotion with which he looks at young Aronoff appear entirely genuine.

Dr. Lipschitz has another explanation for the odd twosome: they are, of course, homosexuals.

But from what I have seen of young Aronoff I am afraid that this is merely wishful thinking on Dr. Lipschitz' part.


*Friday, June 23, 1939.*   One should not meddle. At least I might have asked Walter Kramer's consent before I spoke about him to Josef. That way I would have found out that Walter had talked to Josef about a job months ago.

Josef was angry when I brought the matter up.

"Don't talk to me about Walter Kramer! I tried to get him a job right after he came to me with your letter of introduction. A builder I know was willing to pay him two hundred pesos a month, fifty pesos more than he would pay any of his own countrymen. But Walter said he could make more money giving Spanish lessons or working for those two crooks, Grushka and Dubrovsky. More money! When I came here I was ten years older than Walter Kramer and I didn't make more money in the beginning!"

A sense of loyalty made me back up Walter Kramer. I said that Josef did not have to support a family when he first came here. Josef dismissed my remark with an angry gesture.

"Look, Norman, what difference does it make how much a man is paid in the beginning? El Paramo is still a land of opportunity where the gringo is considered a miracle worker. There's no competition if you have any aptitude at all. True, I started with a small salary. But two years later I was partner in the firm, and five years later the sole owner. I got government contracts to build roads and bridges, and the fact that I was a foreigner worked for me, not against me. Believe me, Walter Kramer could have a splendid future here if he would only try!"

This is exactly what Eva always says: if he would only try.

And that goes for all of us.


*Sunday, June 25, 1939.*    Frau Kramer is getting ready to throw the big party with which she has threatened us ever since our arrival here.

The house is so far in order now that it appears quite presentable. The curtains are up in all the rooms, and the couches have been upholstered in a brocade-like fabric. Frau Kramer's large double bed, done in a rich green, looks like a square of meadow. I cannot help snickering at the thought of Herr and Frau Kramer cavorting on the green. (What am I laughing about? I would not mind having a woman myself. Horowitz tried to induce me to visit a brothel with him, but the idea did not appeal to me. There ought to be another possibility. What, for instance? Eva? And yet sometimes I think that the privations of celibacy weigh heavier on our minds than our bodies. It is not so much what we need as what we think we ought to have that bothers us.)

This evening Frau Kramer made out a tentative list of the people who are to be invited to the party. She arrived at a staggering number. First of all, there are the regular members of the household: the Kramers, Eva, Walter, and I, which makes five. The Goldmanns, Trude and Horowitz, from downstairs; nine. The Lipschitzes; eleven. Walter said he wanted to ask the Fleischers, a suggestion for which he received a suspicious look from Eva. The Fleischers were accepted, making thirteen. Eva retaliated by insisting that since they had been to the Brauns', they ought to ask them back. Frau Kramer reminded her that she had not been asked, but Eva won. The Brauns; fifteen. I proposed Dr. Landau, who is all alone here. Frau Kramer permitted me to invite him, adding with a bashful twitter that I might also ask Josef. With Dr. Landau and Josef, the number of guests for the party was up to seventeen.

Later, when Goldmann came upstairs for his daily after-dinner chat, he firmly requested an invitation for Levy.

"One of our most distinguished citizens and the benefactor of many members of our community," Goldmann said.

Many members? Goldmann must be thinking of himself in the plural. Well, maybe Levy is also my benefactor. I don't know yet. So far I have seen no money from Goldmann. But I shall accompany him on his next business trip this coming Thursday.

*Tuesday, June 27, 1939.* This evening, when Goldmann came upstairs to set a departure time for our trip tomorrow, Eva said to him:

"Herr Goldmann, today is the 27th of June."

Goldmann blinked his eyes.

"Anybody's birthday?" he asked.

"No. But there are only three more days left in June. Wasn't that the month when the Russians were supposed to attack Germany?"

Everybody had to laugh, even Herr Kramer.

*Friday, June 30, 1939.* It is a miracle that I am still alive after my trip with Goldmann. What an irony if I had escaped Hitler only to end up mangled and broken at the bottom of a ravine! Even so, I have not yet recovered from our adventure.

We started out yesterday, at five o'clock in the morning. As we rode the trolley into town we could see the Grampico looming starkly against the brightening sky. The undulating ridge of the cordillera looked like the humps of gigantic animals huddled together for warmth during the night.

When we reached the Plaza San Juan, from where the buses start out for the northern and southern provinces, most of the buses were already crowded to capacity. I expressed doubts that we would find a seat, but Goldmann told me not to worry: the bus driver, his amigo, was keeping seats for us. (Goldmann had gained his valuable friendship by giving him two pairs of cheap silk stockings for his inamorata.)

As it turned out, the grateful bus driver had not only kept seats for us, he had kept the doors of his bus locked until our arrival. We had to fight our way through a crowd of infuriated would-be passengers who had surrounded the locked bus, pounding at its door and showering the driver inside with insults which dealt explicitly with his perverse love life, his lack of virility, and the questionable reputation of his mother.

The moment the driver unlocked the door we were shoved head-long inside. Goldmann immediately threw himself across the seats right behind the driver. I hardly had a chance to sit down before the rest of the passengers surged past me, screaming, cursing, pushing, sweating, dragging and accommodating their bundles, and, now that the driver had ceased to be the object of their ire, trading insults with each other.

I soon began to understand why Goldmann had made such haste to grab the front seats: the stench soon became overpowering, but was alleviated when the bus got into motion and the wind blew the odor away from us.

The trip, which under different circumstances ought to be a delight to the senses, was a grueling nightmare. Our driver—no doubt a frustrated race driver—tore at top speed through the city and out onto the open road.

Open road! The road kept burrowing into the mountains, winding its way around perilous hairpin curves which, completely unprotected by any sort of barrier, broke down on our left into a yawning abyss hundreds of feet deep. On our right the mountains reared up in a straight, rocky wall. There was hardly enough room on the road for two vehicles, approaching from opposite directions, to pass each other. But this did not in the least influence our driver to reduce his speed. He kept leaning on the horn as he raced around the curves, probably trusting that the Virgin, whose flower-wreathed picture was tucked up above his seat, would keep the road clear for him.

It took us five hours to reach the village of Tarqui in the northern province of Grampico. In spite of my exhaustion, Goldmann insisted that we had to start on our round of cobranzas right away if we wanted to make use of the two hours left before the midday siesta.

The streets of a predominantly Indian village may look quaint and picturesque to a visiting tourist, but to a salesman bent on collecting they look more like a bad dream. All the houses resemble each other: adobe chozas, many of them windowless, with only a door to admit some light and air. How Goldmann keeps track of his customers in these identical houses is beyond me. But I have to hand it to him; he is an able salesman.

Carrying his two grips full of merchandise (he had refused to let me carry one; whether out of respect for my academic title or because he considers me too old and decrepit, I don't know) Goldmann led the way. At some of the houses he stopped and opened his grips to display his wares. The "ladies" of the house, filthy, evil-smelling, their unkempt hair hanging into their faces, would appear to inspect the merchandise. Goldmann never let any of them touch the articles, but held them up at a safe distance from the buyer.

Every transaction took a lot of time, especially since Goldmann is anything but fluent in Spanish. He has taught himself the most important words for his business: barato—cheap; precio fijo—fixed price; a plazo— in installments; deposito—down payment; yapa—no, absolutely NO, no yapa!

The collections were even more difficult. Many doors which had stood ajar were quickly slammed at our approach. In spite of Goldmann's pounding and cursing in three languages—Spanish, German and Yiddish —the ladies inside refused to open and pay their current installments.

Most of the houses were crowded with dirty children, ranging in age from infancy up to seven years. The smaller ones crept around half naked, their brief shirts covering them only to slightly below the navel. One little boy had tied a string around his penis, tugging at it as if he were leading a dog.

The day seemed interminable and futile, and yet by late afternoon Goldmann had sold 250 pesos' worth of merchandise and had collected about 100 pesos due on previous sales. With the new down payments which we had received, we had roughly 150 pesos in cash, a third of which was profit. That meant that each of us had made twenty-five pesos. Conservatively figuring at twenty days a month, this would bring each of us an income of five hundred pesos.

When I quoted the sum to him, Goldmann only laughed bitterly.

"Today was an unusually good day. Sometimes I hardly sell anything. Sometimes nobody wants to pay. You must have brought me luck, Professorlein. You ought to come with me more often!"

At that time I was still inclined to accompany Goldmann on future trips, but I changed my mind on the journey home.

We boarded the bus around five-thirty. Fifteen minutes later it had filled up, but there was no trace of our driver. Finally he emerged out of a tavern, his eyes glittering, his gait unsteady, and his hat at a rakish angle. He straddled the seat behind the wheel with great bravura, and a split second later the bus lurched forward and sputtered out of Tarqui.

Now, in comparison, our morning trip seemed like an idle pleasure cruise. A half hour after our departure darkness fell suddenly, and for the next five hours we raced through pitch-black night. Beyond the weak beam of the headlights stretched an unfathomable void. Sitting behind the driver, I was never sure whether we were really going to round the next curve or were racing straight ahead to overshoot the embankment and plunge to our death.

A few times the engine of the bus became overheated from the uphill climb and we had to stop. The driver got out to put rocks under the rear wheels in order to brace them. "No valen los frenos," he explained laconically. The brakes are no good. Some comfort!

Strangely enough, most of the passengers slept through this ordeal, even Goldmann. When we got home, well past midnight, Frau Goldmann was still up, waiting for her husband. She greeted his arrival with tears of joy, unaware of what good cause she has to be glad every time he returns alive.

I had a quick snack with Goldmann and then I retired. Before I went upstairs, Goldmann told me to let him know any time I wanted to accompany him again. I said I would. Let him know, that is.

*Saturday, July 1, 1939.*    This too has been weathered: Frau Kramer's party is over.

All the people who had been invited—except Josef—arrived on time. The Goldmanns and Horowitz from downstairs, and Levy with his basket of guillotined flowers. For a while Levy talked to Trude about nothing but the new car he bought this week, inciting Horowitz to furious tirades against capitalism behind his back. But all the other men except Levy kept flocking to Eva's side, the way leaves floating on the water will gravitate toward a whirlpool.

Frau Ruth Lipschitz was certainly annoyed by all the attention her sister-in-law was getting, especially since her own husband was right there in the midst of the cheek-pinching, waist-hugging crowd.

"What do they all see in her? She isn't really *that* pretty!"

The Fleischers and the Brauns arrived together; Frau Fleischer in a low-cut, green dress which played up her white skin and her magnificent red hair; Frau Braun heavy with child, but gay and animated as ever. Herr Fleischer quickly said hello to everybody and scuttled over to Eva.

"There he goes," his wife said with resignation. "The older he gets the younger he likes them."

While the men were occupied with Eva, the ladies began to circulate, admiring the new curtains, the new carpets, the china and the silver laid out on the table. The way Frau Kramer talked about "the few things they had been able to save" she made it sound as though she had abandoned the larger and more precious part of her possessions. But she could not resist throwing open the doors of her china cabinet (the doors plus a lock have been added recently, contributing greatly to Frau Kramer's peace of mind) to display whatever silver objects women manage to accumulate in the course of a long marriage.

"Thirty-five kilos of silver!" she announced proudly.

Eva scowled at her mother-in-law, and Walter rushed over and closed the doors of the china cabinet.

"Mama, for heaven's sake, this is not an auction!"

Even Frau Ruth seemed embarrassed, and sidling up to her mother she whispered that they had better start serving.

Frau Kramer looked around at the assembled guests, gave me an accusing glance, and asked why Josef was not here yet. Fortunately he arrived at just this moment, dressed in his black undertaker suit and carrying a small spray of flowers from his garden. He was alone.

Frau Kramer began to flutter like a hen who finds one of her chicks missing.

"But your wife, Herr Blumenthal! We were all looking forward so to meeting your wife!"

"I did not know she was also expected," Josef said stiffly.

"But of course," Frau Kramer said. "When *we* ask a man, we expect him to bring his wife along! We're not yet natives!"

Walter at once led Josef away and introduced him to the other guests. Josef went around mumbling and shaking hands.

Horowitz crept up to me and whispered in my ear:

"Disgusting! I understand he's still keeping slaves!"

"Horowitz, have you taken leave of your senses?"

Frau Kramer gave the signal to begin the informal serving, following her captives around with her cakes.

"Perhaps another piece of Sachertorte, Frau Fleischer?"

"No, thank you, I really can't . . ."

"If you knew how difficult it is to bake in my oven . . ."

"Very well then, just a tiny little piece . . ."

Dr. Lipschitz made the mistake of paying Frau Fleischer a few compliments in the presence of his wife. This incited Frau Ruth to mutter venomously that Frau Fleischer's hair was dyed, a statement which Eva took as a starting point for a violent argument over whether this was so or not. While Walter was trying to stop his wife and his sister from shouting at each other, I noticed that Josef was sending me distress signals with his eyes. He had been cornered by Goldmann and Kramer, who seemed to be badgering him about something. When I came closer I heard Goldmann say:

"Of course we expect your support in all matters concerning our club. In all matters!" he repeated emphatically.

Josef looked puzzled. He could not know that Goldmann had already asked me how much money we could expect from Josef toward whatever expenses we might incur: rental of suitable quarters, purchase of chairs and tables, etc. Josef turned a harassed look upon me.

"I was just explaining to these two gentlemen here that we do have a very fine club in Esperanza, the Club Grampico. I am sure their membership will be most welcome there."

"But who wants to sit in a club with a bunch of Indians!" This from Herr Kramer, with an angry gesture as if he were tapping his cane on the floor.

"I would like to make it clear that the Club Grampico is quite exclusive," Josef said with dignity.

"What Herr Kramer means is that we want to be among our own people," Goldmann said, trying to gloss over Kramer's tactless remark. "You know, a place where we can talk and act as we please!"

"In this country you can talk and act as you please anywhere!"

I motioned to Kramer and Goldmann to let Josef alone for the time being. They retreated reluctantly. Josef glared after them.

"An impossible people, our Jews! They'll flee one country, only to make their own ghetto in another country!"

I said that most people lived in ghettos of their own making. To get his mind off the previous conversation, I steered him out of the corner toward a group which I felt was safe company for him. Hans Braun was talking about his impending trip to the Oriente.

"We're trying to get soil samples," he said. "From what we have so far we're pretty sure that there must be much more oil there. The biggest problem is the accessibility of the deposits. We'll have to go down one of the tributaries of the Amazon by canoe, and then we'll have to hack our way through the jungle. I am sure Herr Blumenthal knows all about the difficulties."

A gleam of adventures remembered came into Josef's jaded eyes and he looked almost young again. He eagerly told about traveling perilous paths on mule back; about sleeping in tents; about chilling attacks of malaria; about being shot at one day when he had refused a drink of the native chicha.

"Do you realize how chicha is made? First the barley is chewed; then it is spit into a large kettle . . ."

Frau Irene retched and her husband put a comforting hand on her shoulder and told her that he would rather be shot at than drink the brew.

For some reason this anecdote was the cue to the inevitable telling of ribald stories which is the curse of every such party. For the next hour or so a number of jokes were exhumed, and then the party began to break up. Josef, the last to arrive, was the first to leave.

"Thank you, it has been delightful. I hope to see you in my house soon."

Frau Kramer, making the most of a mere pleasantry: "We'll be looking forward to your invitation!"

Thank you, thank you. It was nice of you to come. You have to come and see us soon. The cakes were delicious. Yes, I wrapped a piece for you, Dr. Landau. We won't be seeing you before you leave, Dr. Braun? Of course we'll look after your wife! (You know, I was never in *your* house, Frau Irene.) Good-by, thank you very much, Madame Kramer. Don't forget, Fräulein Trude, tomorrow at nine o'clock sharp I'll pick you up in my new car! Come on, Peter, tear yourself away from Eva and let's go. Thank you for coming. No, Ruth, I don't want you to stay; go home to your children. Well, at least *we* don't have to go far; only one flight down. Else will help you with the dishes, Frau Kramer. Go home, Frau Goldmann, you're a guest today. Eva will help. After all it was *her* party too. The hell it was.

And Eva's last words to Walter: "What a waste! What a horrible waste of time and money!"

*Sunday, July 2, 1939.*   This morning Levy came to pick up Trude for a ride. All the members of our household were assembled on the upstairs terrace to watch their departure.

Trude did not look at all like a young girl going on a picnic. She wore a stiff, navy taffeta dress, no doubt forced by Frau Goldmann into this formal attire. Levy danced around excitedly as he helped her into his car. Though Trude must have been aware that we were watching her from upstairs, she did not once turn around as the car drove away.

Eva shook her head and sighed. "Poor Trude."

"Never underestimate the sex appeal of a car," Walter said sagely.

"I don't see that Trude could do better," Frau Kramer commented. "And she could do considerably worse."

"No better foundation for love than a lot of money," Herr Kramer said.

Thus the opinions.

*Wednesday, July 5, 1939.*     Eva has gone into town three days in a row. Before she left this morning she almost had a fight with her father-in-law. He stopped her on the stairs, blocking off her way with his cane.

"Where are you going, Eva?"

"Out."

"Where out?"

"Just out. Now will you let me through, please?"

"Not before you tell me where you're going."

Eva flushed with anger.

"All right," she said softly. "All right. I'll leave after your arm gets tired."

She turned around and walked back to her room, leaving Kramer standing there like a fool with his cane barricading the stairs. I could see that he was shaking with rage. Nothing seems to irritate him more than silent rebellion against which he cannot strike and claw.

"Overbearing," he said to me. "Sometimes she makes me want to slap her face. What is she doing in town, anyway?"

"I wouldn't know," I said.

But I have a good idea of what Eva is doing. I think she is looking for young Aronoff.

*Thursday, July 6, 1939.*     It seems that Eva is not the only one who goes out on secret errands. Today Frau Goldmann complained to me about her daughter.

"I don't know what's got into Trudi. Before, I could hardly get her to leave the house, but last week she got dressed up twice to go into town. I asked her if she had a date with Herr Levy. And you know what she answers: 'Can't I just once have a better reason to get dressed up than a date with Isak Levy?' What better reason, I ask you, can she have? To tell the truth, I'm worried. I tried speaking to her father about it, but he always pooh-poohs my worries about Trudi. Now, tell me honestly, Herr Professor, do you know what Trudi is doing in town?"

I tried to calm Frau Goldmann with the farfetched supposition that Trude was meeting Eva in town.

"But why the secrecy? They could meet right at home!"

"Well, you know how young girls are, Frau Goldmann," I said, feigning a profound, non-existent understanding of young girls.

*Friday, July 7, 1939.*   Once a week, instead of going to the Jungle Café in the afternoon, Dr. Landau, Horowitz and I meet in Horowitz's room to discuss what Dr. Landau calls spiritual matters.

Every time we visit him, Horowitz makes a ritual of brewing tea as if he were a Chinese mandarin. (He has bought a small electric burner and three cups, and has wangled permission from Frau Goldmann to use the electric stove in his room.) According to Horowitz, the tea has to be a deep, golden brown and has to be taken without sugar. Dr. Landau hates tea without sugar, but since the tea as well as the stale, brittle cookies which Horowitz serves with it are free, Dr. Landau cannot pass it up.

Yesterday I finally found out what had been Horowitz' occupation in Vienna. We were sitting in his room—that is, Dr. Landau and I were sitting while Horowitz prowled around, tugging at the curtains, straightening the cover on the bed, sweeping up a few crumbs which I had dropped, and nervously rearranging his books in strict, staggered symmetry. I could not resist teasing him.

"You would have made a wonderful housewife, Horowitz!"

Horowitz blushed at my jest.

"Just an old habit," he said. "My parents died when I was still quite young, and I had to look after the household and be, as the saying goes, father and mother to my two younger sisters."

This was the first I heard of Horowitz' having a family. Why was a

man who had been father and mother to his sisters alone in El Paramo?
I asked Horowitz where his sisters were now. His face became grim.

"After I gave up everything for them . . . my studies . . . I wanted to
be a lawyer . . . they both married Zionists! They're in Palestine now."

"That's gratitude for you," Dr. Landau mocked.

"To me this is not a joking matter, Dr. Landau! Here I was, with two
terms of law at the university, and I had to stop studying and take
over the store to keep us from starving."

"Don't tell me you were a storekeeper, Horowitz!"

"It was just a small store," Horowitz said quickly, as if he wanted
to belittle any capitalistic enterprise in which he had become involved in
order to eat. "Just inexpensive men's clothing. We sold merchandise on
the installment plan."

"Charging a little extra interest for the credit, no doubt?" Dr. Landau
needled. "Comrade Horowitz, sucking the blood of the poor!"

Horowitz seems to bring out a sadistic streak in Dr. Landau. He can
never stop teasing until Horowitz blows up.

"You know, Dr. Landau, I could easily dispense with your visits!"

"Come, come, Horowitz, where is your sense of humor?" Dr. Landau
said amiably.

Horowitz was not yet appeased.

"I'm warning you, Dr. Landau! Don't tease about things which are
sacred to me! You're going to spoil a beautiful friendship."

This would indeed be a pity. I have come to depend on Horowitz
and Dr. Landau for a measure of diversion.


*Saturday, July 8, 1939.*    Eva has had her revenge for Frau Kramer's
party; this morning she spread the news through the house that she
and Walter were going dancing in the evening.

"Dancing!" Frau Kramer said, appalled. "Dancing, in these times!"

"I can't see the difference between dancing and throwing parties," Eva
said acidly.

"At least we don't make a public spectacle of ourselves," Frau Kramer
remonstrated, but with no success whatever.

At noontime Frau Goldmann came upstairs to have a word with
Walter.

"I hear you're going dancing tonight, Herr Walter. Would you take my Trudi along? Of course I'll pay for the expenses!"

By the time Eva and Walter were ready to leave, their party had grown to five people. Horowitz had enthusiastically joined in the venture and had talked me into going along too. To my initial, weak protests he said:

"So you don't dance! So you'll sit and look at the pretty girls! You can still look, can't you?"

As it turned out, there were not too many pretty girls to look at in the Club Casino. We arrived there well after dinner to limit our expenses to a drink or two. It was cold and drafty in the dimly lit main room. A five-man band played loudly but not too well. Only half the tables were occupied, most of them by parties of men.

When we walked in, everybody turned around and stared at us. We were led to a table at the center of the room, near the dance floor. Walter ordered a round of drinks for us, and we sipped cautiously to make them last longer. The band played vigorously and off key, and two couples came out of the shade of the walls and began to dance. The men danced stiffly, the women with exaggerated gyrations of the hips.

Walter nodded to Eva and they got up to dance. As she raised her arms, Eva's dress slipped up. The eyes of the men around the dance floor gravitated toward her legs, as if drawn by a magnet. There were some grins, leers, and whispered remarks.

Horowitz sighed and asked Trude to dance. They made a sorry couple. Trude danced with a pained expression on her face, as if her high-heeled shoes were too tight. The moment the music stopped she fled back to the table ahead of Horowitz.

The waiter removed our empty glasses and glared at us. Walter ordered another round of drinks while we sat waiting for the music to start up again. The next dance Eva danced with Horowitz, who held her unnecessarily close. I felt almost relieved when one of the men rose from his table to cut in on Horowitz and Eva. Horowitz returned to our table, bristling.

"The nerve!" he said.

As if the first man had broken the ice, one after the other came to ask Eva for a dance. They all followed a strict ritual, first bowing to

Walter and asking his permission, and then bowing to Eva. After a while one even came for Trude. He was short and dark, with greasy hair and a gold-toothed grin.

Though none of the other men was much to look at either, Eva seemed to blossom under their attention. She laughed and tossed her head, and I could see that she tried to keep up a Spanish conversation.

Walter was bitter about Eva's flirtatious behavior.

"She's frivolous! Just superficial and frivolous!"

"And very pretty, Walter. Don't forget, very pretty. Don't begrudge her a little flattery!"

But later at night, after Aronoff had walked into the Club Casino, Eva's mood changed perceptibly. He came in with a tall, striking Parameña, and Eva tried vainly to catch his eye as he danced past our table. He danced beautifully, each of his motions a caress. Like most women his partner appeared entirely under his spell, gazing up at him with unconcealed admiration.

Eva became morose and did not object when Walter proposed that we go home. On the way out, Trude kept peeking back over her shoulder at Aronoff, her mouth frozen in a bitter little smile. Noticing her expression, Horowitz suddenly turned venomous:

"A gigolo!" he hissed. "That's all we needed in this town, a Jewish gigolo!"

*Tuesday, July 11, 1939.* Our visit to the Club Casino has brought about some unexpected repercussions. This morning Josef took me violently to task about our innocent evening of entertainment.

"What's the matter with Walter Kramer, taking his wife to a night club?" Josef raged at me.

I was so startled that I had no time to wonder where he had got that information.

"And what, may I ask, is wrong with taking one's wife to a night club?" I countered stiffly.

"It isn't done here!"

"Come now, Josef, our girls were not the only women in the Club Casino. Several other men there were also accompanied by ladies."

"These 'ladies' were not the wives of the men, they were their mistresses! No decent Parameño in his right mind would take his wife to a night club!"

"Other countries, other customs," I said with what I hoped sounded like wry mockery. But Josef took my gibe with a stony face.

"And on top of it all, Walter allows his wife to dance with complete strangers!"

"But, Josef, these men came to our table and asked very politely if they could dance with the girls! It was only civil of Walter to give his permission. What else could he have done?"

"He should have sent them to hell! The impertinence! You didn't see any of the men go to one of the other tables and ask a woman to dance with him?"

I had to admit that Josef was right: our table had been the only one to receive this preferential treatment.

"You know what the Parameños say? Todas las gringas son putas. All the gringas are whores. If you people have to go to night clubs, at least tell Walter to keep the men away from his wife."


*Monday, July 17, 1939.*    A new development: Walter is working for Grushka and Dubrovsky.

As happens frequently, Walter did not have dinner with us. Eva retired immediately after the meal, while I still remained sitting with the Kramers on the veranda. It was almost an hour later when Walter finally walked in. As he absent-mindedly devoured a piece of cake which his mother had kept for him, Frau Kramer mentioned something about another party she wanted to give.

"Mama, we're at the end of our rope. There's no money left."

"What do you mean, no money left? We had five hundred dollars!"

"The rent for the house; furniture; entertaining; and four people eating. . . . On top of everything Alfred came to me today and asked me for a loan. He was quite upset when I told him that we didn't have any money. From what Ruth had told him he thought we were rolling in it. Mama, you wouldn't consider selling some of your silver?"

"Sell my silver! Why don't you sell Eva's silver if you need money!"

"It's bad enough that I can't support my wife properly. I'll be damned if I touch any of her things."

"All right, take her part! Always take her part! But you won't sell my silver either!"

"Very well, Mama, so I'll keep the job," Walter said. "I'm working for Grushka and Dubrovsky."

Frau Kramer caught her breath and began to wail.

"And for that we brought you up! For that we gave you an education, made sacrifices, so you should become a peddler! Woe is me! What did she do to you that you want to become a peddler?"

Walter, furious now, had reached the screaming stage.

"Why do you always have to twist everything so it ends up being Eva's fault? It's not her fault that we have to eat! And we just can't be chewing pieces off my education! Besides, you're the one who wants to entertain, not Eva!"

"Sure, it's all my fault. All your mama's fault. I made you emigrate, I brought Hitler to Austria . . ."

Frau Kramer's hysterical remonstrances were lost in blubbering.

Walter kicked the door open and walked into the other room, where Eva was sitting. (Whenever he is furious he kicks something: a chair, a table leg, a bed, a door.) He was white in the face; not exactly the picture of a happy husband coming home to his pretty little wife. His mother followed him like an enraged Fury.

"Did you hear?" she shouted accusingly at Eva.

"How could I help hearing?" Eva said, masking her agitation with coldness. "High time too. Somebody in this family ought to work!"

Herr Kramer, who had gone in after his wife, froze in the door. I suppose he felt just as guilty as I. The Kramers glared at Eva and Walter. Eva and Walter glared at each other. Everybody hated everybody.

Ah, the joys of family life!


*Tuesday, July 18, 1939.* Today I talked with young Aronoff. Herr Fleischer brought him over to our table in the Jungle Café.

"I don't suppose you remember me, but we have met before," I said when we were being introduced.

"Oh?"

He glanced at me with quick distrust—the distrust, I thought, of the very rich who fear being asked for a handout every time someone claims to know them.

"You were only a boy then. Thirteen, I believe. I was invited to one of your mother's parties."

A glint of ill-concealed mockery appeared in his eyes.

"Ah, yes, my mother used to give those—" I could see him casting about for a polite word—"those highbrow parties."

Clearly he did not think much of those parties, and even less of the people who had attended them. He made me feel foolish for having mentioned the invitation, and I said defensively:

"Professor Einstein also was there."

Young Aronoff's eyes brightened.

"I remember Professor Einstein. He was one of the few famous guests of my mother who did not act as if he expected me to kiss the ground on which he walked."

I thought that an extraordinary man has his own way of making himself unforgettable.

"Do you still want to be a prizefighter, Herr Aronoff?"

I realized too late that this was a silly, condescending question to ask a grown man. But Aronoff only laughed.

"As a matter of fact, I did some amateur fighting. There's a Señor Lopez in Rioverde who offered me six hundred pesos a month if I would train his fighters."

"Six hundred pesos!" Fleischer exclaimed. "Six hundred pesos is a lot of money for doing practically nothing! Why don't you grab the offer?"

"I don't like the climate of Rioverde. Besides, I think I'll be able to manage here. There's plenty of money to be made here."

"There is?" Herr Kramer asked greedily.

"Sure."

With a cheerful, asserting nod Aronoff walked away to join Grushka and Dubrovsky, who were rolling dice in their customary booth.

"I wonder how he's going to make a lot of money in Esperanza," Herr Kramer fretted.

"I'll tell you how," Fleischer said. "By whoring around. I bet you he's being paid by the women. I know my wife would be willing to pay him!"

"You're disgusting, Fleischer," Walter said.

Levy, who had come to our table and had overheard Fleischer's last words, said: "I don't see what a woman can see in Aronoff. A boy not yet dry behind his ears!"

"You should have his looks," Fleischer said maliciously. "And his money too, for that matter."

"How do you know I haven't? How do you know I haven't got more money than he? I'm sure he's only bragging. Those who brag the most usually have the least."

But then Aronoff is not bragging.

A little later I had a chance to have a few words alone with him. I asked him whether his parents were still in Vienna and why they didn't leave while there was still time. He shrugged off my question with an indifference bordering on callousness.

"My father has excellent connections in Vienna. Nothing is going to happen to him. My mother's family has been in Austria for generations. Her father was a major in the Austrian army. They'll both be safe until this thing blows over."

"I think you ought to try to persuade your parents . . ."

"I tried, but they won't listen. If they know better, let them have it their own way!"

He probably did not realize that in spite of his brash demeanor his fine eyes looked troubled. He is just the right age to put up a callous front. Another one of these young men who are ashamed to admit, least of all to themselves, that they too have emotions.


*Thursday, July 20, 1939.*    Herr Kramer has come home with a new rumor, but this one sounds too fantastic to be true. As Kramer would have it, Aronoff has leased the Esperanza bullring for a week from next Sunday. He intends to present a spectacle there, the spectacle being Rudi Brueck, who is supposed to perform several miraculous feats of strength. Just what these feats of strength are supposed to be nobody knows as yet.

*Friday, July 21, 1939.*     This has not been a rumor after all. Aronoff has leased the bullring.

Today posters went up all over town, showing what I consider a grotesque caricature of Rudi Brueck in red tights, with muscles as big as balloons bulging on his arms. The caption above this picture reads:

EL MAGNIFICO GRINGO TARZAN

And below the picture, in smaller print, an account of the feats with which the Gringo Tarzan will delight his distinguidos patrones. He will be chained to a post and break the chain with his muscles. He will bend an iron rod with his bare hands. He will wrestle two opponents at the same time. He will (this in larger print again) let a bus pass over his bare body. And he will fight a bull unarmed, repeating the feat of Ursus by twisting the bull's head by his horns. Tickets were on sale at the box office of the arena. This was a single performance which would not be repeated, so one had better hurry, hurry, hurry and buy tickets.

"Leave it to Aronoff to come up with such an idea," Horowitz said morosely. "Brueck is going to do all the work, and Aronoff is going to rake in all the money."


*Saturday, July 22, 1939.*     We have finally agreed upon a name for our club: Centro Israelita de El Paramo. In conversation the long name is already being shortened to Centro.

More difficult to arrive at than the name of the club was the membership fee. The first proposal called for five pesos a month but was turned down almost unanimously: too much. We have now settled on three pesos a month. Even so, Dr. Landau has refused to become a paying member, a refusal which has earned him a "stingy capitalist" from Horowitz.

Horowitz has joined the new club under protest. He still feels that we would all be safer by joining the Communist party.

Dr. Lipschitz is having himself a field day drafting the club regulations; he keeps constructing interminable sentences of which nobody can make either head or tail.

By now all the aspirants have silently acquiesced in the resolution that Josef is to be the first president of the Centro. Josef himself is so far unaware of the honor that is to befall him. Walter is planning to break the news to him next Saturday, the day we are invited to Josef's house.

Eva remarked that when it rains it pours. First no diversion for weeks, and then one day the invitation to Josef's house and the following day the "bullfight." All the ladies are in a frenzy over what to wear for the visit to the Blumenthals. Frau Goldmann repeatedly asked me whether Levy has also been invited. Horowitz keeps wondering whether the invitation for the Goldmanns includes him too but is firmly resolved not to go even if it does.

"A disgrace that a man, a Jew, should be keeping peones nowadays!" he says about Josef.

He will not be argued out of this crazy notion.

*Monday, July 24, 1939.* "I understand that you're being received by his majesty," Fleischer said to me today.

That means that the Fleischers have not been invited. Neither has Levy. He seemed upset not so much by the slight as by the possibility that Señora Blumenthal's brother might be present.

"That Coronel Jiménez, you better watch out for him! He's after every skirt in Esperanza. He's fathered the children of at least a dozen society ladies. Once he abducted a girl from the convent and the archbishop of Esperanza threatened to have him excommunicated."

Levy must already envision the notorious coronel carrying off his beloved Trude. But from what he told me about the love life of the coronel, he cannot possibly be that hard up.

At any rate, I intend to keep an eye on Eva, though I doubt that she is susceptible just now. She still keeps going into town every other day.

*Monday, July 24, 1939.* The usual session in Josef's loggia this morning. We talked about the party in his house.

"Consuelo is terrified," Josef said. "All these foreigners coming to visit us. I hope they will at least have the decency to speak Spanish in her presence."

Strange how Josef still dissociates himself from us "foreigners." I wonder how he will react when Walter offers him the presidency of the club.

While we were discussing the party, I felt that I ought to clear up Horowitz' status. Was he or was he not invited? (In spite of his protestations to the contrary, I was convinced that he would come if asked.)

"Horowiz invited? I should say not! Do you realize, Norman, that this man is a Bolshevik?"

"You don't know Horowitz, Josef. He is no more a Bolshevik than you and I."

"Well, at least he talks that way. I won't have the man in my house. When are the Jews finally going to learn that it is not for them to be radicals? It's trouble enough being Jewish!"

And on this philosophical note our session ended.

*Tuesday, July 25, 1939.*    More trouble. It started this morning when Herr Kramer was teasing Don.

Eva and I were standing on the terrace, looking down into the garden. The dry sticks which the Indians stuck into the ground four months ago are now beginning to bear roses, and the geraniums are blazing bright red and orange against the white garden wall. It seems like an admonition never to lose hope.

Don was sitting on the gravel walk when Herr Kramer came back from his morning stroll to the tienda around the corner. The dog jumped up and began wagging his tail. Herr Kramer stopped a few paces from him and playfully hit him on the head with his cane. Turning angry, Don yapped and snapped, first for the cane, then for Herr Kramer's hand. Herr Kramer gave him a good whack with the stick and the dog retreated, howling.

Eva, standing beside me, had turned as close to green as her deep tan permitted.

"God damn you," she shouted down at her father-in-law, "why don't you leave the dog alone!"

Herr Kramer was too flabbergasted by her outburst to think of a suitable reply.

Eva turned around, nervously digging her fingers into her cheeks.

"I can't take it any longer," she moaned. "Oh, God, I just can't take it any longer! That stupid, cowardly sadist!"

She ran from the terrace and left me standing alone. By that time Herr Kramer had thought up an answer.

"Impertinent brat," he said to me.

I wonder what makes Eva so testy. Herr Kramer's silly act had by no means merited her outbreak. Perhaps she keeps looking for more faults in her in-laws than are there to find. She must be feeling very guilty because of her frequent trips into town.


*Friday, July 28, 1939.*    Eva certainly keeps us jumping. Today she announced that she would no longer take her meals with us.

This has something to do with Walter's new working schedule. Before he used to be reasonably punctual, at least for lunch. He comes home at odd hours, eating alone while the rest of the family sits around him, badgering him with questions. Usually he leaves again right after lunch, an arrangement which gives Eva no time at all to see him alone.

Today, while Frau Kramer complained about how she had to wait on everybody (stressing "everybody," which probably included me as well as Eva), Eva suddenly came up with the announcement that all this would be different from now on. She would do her own cooking, set her own table in her own room, do her own serving and wash her own dishes.

"I have a right to be alone with my husband for one hour a day."

Frau Kramer was too stunned to make any comment. Nothing was said for the time being, and presently Eva retired to her room to wait for Walter's arrival. Frau Kramer repaired to the kitchen, and there began a furious banging of pots and pans.

Hunched over and despondent looking, Herr Kramer remained in his chair.

"On top of all our troubles we needed *her*," he said.

(Lately he has lost some of his belligerence and is no longer so quick in rapping Eva across the knuckles. Probably he feels that a man idly hanging around the house all day has nothing left on which to base his authority. I suspect that Herr Kramer really resents Eva more than does his wife. Eva makes him feel insignificant—a very irritating state of affairs for an insignificant man.)

Two hours later, when Walter came home for lunch, Eva's recent announcement was rehashed. Throughout this conversation Eva remained secluded in her room.

"So you're not going to eat with us any more," Frau Kramer said to her son, counting on it that a surprise attack would throw Walter off balance.

Walter kept on chewing rapidly, nervously, only half listening to his mother while his mind seemed far away.

"Oh, Eva told you?" he said with a full mouth.

"Then you planned it all out with her!" Frau Kramer exclaimed indignantly. "What's the matter? Are your parents no longer good enough for you to eat with them?"

Walter put down knife and fork and glared at his mother. He was tired and irritated, and he looked ten years older than his age.

"Why do you always have to elevate everything to the status of a major tragedy, Mama? I talked this thing over with Eva, and I think it's a very good idea. You want to lie down and rest after lunch, but if I come home late you can't do it. This way you'll be able to eat when you please, finish up in the kitchen, and take your afternoon nap without being disturbed. Eva never sleeps in the afternoon anyway. It doesn't make any difference to her when I come home for lunch!"

"Have I been complaining?" Frau Kramer asked. "Can you honestly say that I have been complaining?"

"Yes, Mama, you have. Believe me, it will work out better all around this way. At least let's give it a try. It won't do Eva any harm either to learn how to cook."

"Not in *my* kitchen!" Frau Kramer was defending her last stronghold. "You don't have to eat with us if you don't want to, but at least I want to know that you're getting a decent meal every day. I'll do the cooking!"

"All right, Mama, you do the cooking."

Again Walter is compromising all around.


*Saturday, July 29, 1939.*    Since everybody seems to consider our visit to Josef's house a major event, I shall write a full report of it.

We called on the Blumenthals early this afternoon, all dressed up in our best clothes, like Jews about to visit the synagogue on the high holidays. Josef himself was waiting for us at the garden gate and led us up to his house, two in a row, like school children. The ladies praised in a loud voice everything that met their eyes, and I hoped that they would sustain the first good impression on Josef long enough to make him accept the presidency of the Centro.

On the steps of the loggia we were met by Señora Consuelo, still in deep mourning. Her fine Madonna face was pale above the black dress, and the silver crucifix on the thin chain showed up prominently on the dark fabric. I had the uneasy feeling that all my companions were staring at it.

The introductions over, we were herded into the house, Señora Consuelo fluttering nervously ahead of us. Oppressed by the cavernous rooms, the ladies fell silent. The quiet of the house was rent by the mournful singing of one of the muchachas in the servants' quarters. The dogs, locked in the garage, barked furiously.

When we finally stepped into the sun-drenched room where I had first met Señora Consuelo, it was like emerging into the light after a long underwater swim. As upon a signal, all the ladies again broke into loud praise. Señora Consuelo tittered helplessly at the compliments and seemed relieved when we distributed ourselves over the chairs and sofas in the room. She tinkled a silver bell, and an impeccably white-clad Indian appeared to pass around the refreshments, which disappeared with alarming speed.

The conversation was labored, and soon the men separated from the women and formed their own circle close by the open French door. From where I stood I could not follow what the ladies were talking about, but most of the time they talked in German over the head of their hostess. Only Eva and Trude tried to keep up a Spanish conversation.

When Walter noticed that Josef kept throwing worried glances at his wife, he moved in to cut off his view, and as if to forestall any bad impression the ladies might make, he casually informed Josef that we had founded our long-planned club. Josef looked startled, and Walter threw me a quick, annoyed glance to make me understand that I should have prepared Josef.

Josef finally rallied enough to wish us the best of luck.

"There's just one thing we would like to talk over with you, Don José," Walter said with uncalled-for familiarity.

Josef immediately looked alarmed, no doubt expecting to be asked for a sizable contribution. (This, of course, will come later.)

"What we would like to know before we hold elections," Walter said, "is whether you would accept the nomination for president of the Centro."

"Me? Why me? What, my dear Walter, makes you think that I am at all qualified for this . . . distinction?"

"Who would be better qualified than you, Don José? A man deeply respected and well liked among Parameños and immigrants alike . . ."

It was amusing to observe how Josef began to see himself in the light in which Walter was describing him. There is still no better way to make a man do what you would like him to do than by building him up in his own eyes.

"This honor has come so suddenly. Please give me a little while to think it over."

While we stood talking to Josef, the ladies had managed to badger Señora Consuelo into showing them the rest of the house. We followed them upstairs for a tour of the second floor, the ladies curiously swarming ahead, the men trudging behind in forlorn disinterest. I could see that everybody was surprised to find that Josef and his wife occupied separate bedrooms. His was simply furnished, like a study, with heavy bookcases lining the walls. One group of books caught my eye: black bound, with Hebrew letters engraved in gold; Josef's prayer books. As if to strike a proper balance, there was a large wooden crucifix hanging over the bed in Señora Consuelo's room. Clearly, the ladies disapproved.

At the end of the tour of the second floor it seemed a good moment to break up the party. We had seen the house; we had eaten; and on the way down Josef had whispered to me that he would feel very honored to accept the nomination for president of the Centro. Altogether a successful visit.

(Moreover, Señora Consuelo's infamous lady-killing brother had so far failed to make his appearance, and I kept hoping that he would stay away until Eva had safely left the house.)

Instead of returning to the sala, we spilled out onto the loggia and into the garden to say our good-bys. Again Josef accompanied us to the gate, saying with the joviality reserved for unwelcome guests what a pleasure it had been to have us over.

On the way home we discussed Josef's acceptance of the nomination. Everybody seemed pleased (even Herr Kramer, who had flirted with the post himself, and Goldmann, who would rather have seen Levy nominated) except Frau Ruth.

"I think it's a disgrace," she said. "Did you see the crucifix hanging over the bed of his wife? And this man you ask to become president of a Jewish club!"

"I don't see that this has anything to do with Herr Blumenthal's qualifications for the post," Eva said.

"Much you know," Frau Ruth replied. "People just won't stand for it."

But I think Frau Ruth is mistaken. After all, who is better qualified than Josef to become president of the Centro?

*Sunday, July 30, 1939.* This afternoon will go down in our memories as "the day of the bullfight."

Everybody in our house went to see Rudi Brueck. Over vociferous protests from Horowitz—"Why should I put more money into Aronoff's pockets?"—we had obtained the best seats available, in the tenth row in the sombra. We arrived early, but the rows around us filled rapidly with people in a carnival mood. The Indians in their colorful striped ponchos occupied the sections in the sun. Most of the seats in the sombra were taken by immigrants. A few rows in front of us were the Fleischers with a couple I did not know. The woman had a pretty profile, with the turned-up nose and the slanted eyes of a cat. The man beside her, obviously her husband, turned around time and again to stare at Eva. I thought his behavior in very bad taste.

Levy came once to chat with Trude. He seemed hurt that he had not been asked to sit with us. Josef had predicted that the venture would be a shameful debacle and was conspicuously absent.

But so far it did not look like a debacle. The arena was nearly filled, and the crowd began to shout for the Gringo Tarzan. The band struck up what sounded like a march but what, after closer listening, turned out to be "The Blue Danube," and in strutted Rudi Brueck, attired in red tights and nothing else. If anything he looked even more ridiculous than the posters which had graced every wall and fence in Esperanza. He expanded his chest, flexed his arm muscles, clenched his fists, and set his gentle face in a determined grimace of fierceness. The crowd greeted him with shouting and handclapping.

Eva gave Rudi Brueck only a cursory glance. She seemed to be searching for Aronoff, and her face lit up when she discovered him leaning against the fence, an amused grin on his face, as if he had nothing to do with the forthcoming performance.

In the beginning Aronoff had indeed little to worry about. Rudi breezed through his first act—the bending of a steel rod with his bare hands—like an old trouper. His groaning and facial contortions as he wrestled with the rod were all part of the act, and he had no trouble twisting it into the shape of a horseshoe. The crowd applauded wildly and Aronoff nodded to him with the benign smile of a parent watching his child perform a cute trick.

Next two Indians came into the ring and tied Rudi with a heavy chain to a post which had been planted in the center of the arena. Aronoff himself supervised this procedure, tugging here and there at the chain, and Horowitz whispered maliciously that he was, no doubt, loosening up some indented links.

But Horowitz' suspicion notwithstanding, Rudi at first appeared to have some trouble breaking the chain. Though he arched his back, expanded his chest and pushed with his forearms, the chain would not give. At this point providence, in the form of a sudden gust of wind, came to the aid of Rudi Brueck. The wind raised a cloud of dust from the dry ground, which hit Rudi full force in the face. He screwed up his face and let out a mighty sneeze that snapped the chain like so much twine. The crowd laughed and roared their approval all through the next act, which was strictly monkey business.

While Rudi wrestled two diminutive Indians, who alternately tugged at him and threw themselves at him without moving him so much as one inch from where he stood, preparations began for the major act of the show.

The gate which generally admits the bull into the ring was thrown wide open, and an old, rickety bus rolled into the arena. Murmurs of awe ran through the crowd when they saw the bus, and Frau Goldmann declared that she was not going to watch this act, but without so much as taking her eyes off the spectacle for one second.

Brueck lay down on the ground and a broad board was placed across his body. There was some angry muttering in the crowd when they realized that the bus was not going to run smack over Rudi's unprotected body. Again Aronoff came into the ring to supervise the placing of the board. He bent down and reassuringly patted Rudi's shoulder. Horowitz ground his teeth and mumbled something about the bloody capitalists exploiting the underprivileged.

The crowd fell silent as the bus slowly approached the supine Rudi Brueck. The driver kept sticking his head out the window to make sure that the wheel would run over the board and not over the unprotected part of Rudi's body. But even before he reached Rudi, a priest came dashing into the arena, his cassock flapping around his legs and his wide-brimmed hat bobbing on his head.

"My God!" Frau Goldmann shrieked. "He is going to give him the last rites!"

"A disgrace," Horowitz protested. "These priests are even worse than our rabbis!"

And Frau Ruth commented with an air of personal triumph that she had always known that Rudi Brueck was not Jewish.

As it turned out, the priest did not pay the slightest attention to Rudi but posed himself in front of the bus, with both arms outstretched. The driver dismounted and stood hat in hand, rubbing his nose as he listened to the fast and loud remonstrances of the priest. From where we sat we could not understand what he was saying, but soon the word was passed from row to row: the priest said the driver must not take the bus over Rudi. It would be murder.

The driver shrugged and walked off with the priest, leaving the bus in the middle of the arena. The crowd began to look really ugly now, and there were a few shouts of "impostors." Aronoff glanced up at the galleries, throwing his head back like a fine, nervous horse, and then nodded reassuringly to Rudi, who had raised his head off the ground and was trying to see what all the commotion was about.

Before anybody realized what he was going to do, Aronoff himself mounted the bus and sat down in the driver's seat.

"He's going to drive himself," Frau Goldmann gasped. "He'll kill him! Markus, I think I'm going to faint!"

"You do that, Else," said Goldmann, who had jumped up with excitement and was much too keyed up to listen to his wife.

Eva too had jumped up as she watched the bus, driven by Aronoff, inching slowly toward Rudi. Then, just as the wheel touched the board, Aronoff suddenly stepped on the gas and the bus went over Brueck so fast that nobody really had time to realize what had happened. There was a stunned silence while the crowd waited to see if Rudi would come out from under the bus.

Peering through her fingers, Frau Goldmann asked expectantly: "Is he dead?"

For a moment her fear seemed to be borne out. Though the bus had come to a complete stop now, there was no sign of Rudi. Presently a pair of hands appeared from under the bus, desperately clawing the ground. We could only assume that Brueck was hurt, and we stood numb with horror. The next instant we were startled by a string of obscenities in the finest Viennese slang floating up to us on the breeze. These were clearly not the last words of a dying man.

It turned out that the chassis of the bus was too low to permit Rudi to get out. He was trapped and had to wait until the bus could be jacked up. When he finally emerged, dust covered, his face streaked with oil which had dripped on him from the bus, the crowd greeted him with a wild cheer. He raised his hands over his head, shaking them champion fashion, at the same time shouting in German to Aronoff to bring in the damn cow and get it over with.

On the far side of the ring the bull, to whom Rudi had so contemptuously referred as a cow, was being driven into the arena. He was an emaciated animal, hardly more than a calf; sticking his muzzle over the fence, he seemed to take a dim view of the fate that awaited him in the arena. It took three men to coax him out of the pen, but the moment he caught sight of Rudi he realized that he had been grievously overmatched, and headed straight back for the pen.

Slowly approaching the bull Rudi tried to cajole him with promises of such delicacies as a bull might fancy. Now that the gates were closed against him, the bull waited wearily until Rudi was within two paces, and then he turned and fled around the ring. Rudi ran after him in hot pursuit, cheered on by the crowd.

The shouting of the crowd and the wild calls of the man behind him were too much for the bull, and in his fright he released two steaming droppings right in the path of Rudi. Rudi, unable to stop or swerve, stepped into the fresh dung, slipped and fell on his face. He rolled over on his side, his legs smeared, raised his hands like a dying gladiator, and shouted up to our section:

"Jesus Christ, that's all I needed, to get myself full of cow shit!"

The entire refugee section went hysterical.

The bull noticed that his pursurer was no longer behind him, turned around, and came back to the place where Rudi lay prostrate. Lowering his muzzle, he cautiously sniffed at the man, slowly shaking his head from side to side as if trying to figure out the meaning of all this. As the bull stood over him, Rudi inch by inch raised his hands, gripped the bull by the horns, twisted his head, and without too much resistance the animal rolled over on his side and lay down next to Rudi Brueck.

There could have been no better finale to the show than bull and man lying side by side in the dust. The Indians went wild, the men stamping their feet and slapping their thighs, the women doubling over with laughter, some of them crouching down between the benches to relieve themselves after the strain of laughing.

Rudi stood up, filthy beyond recognition, regally bowed to the crowd, and stalked off through the gate which had first admitted him. Outside he was met by Aronoff, who held on to the fence, helpless with laughter. The bull went to nibble on a few blades of grass which he had discovered in one of the cracks in the ground; the crowd, regretful that the show was over, began to file out through the many exits. We too went home.

Ole!

*Tuesday, August 1, 1939.* Frau Ruth Lipschitz is still rehashing our visit to the Blumenthals. What bothers her especially is the position of Señora Consuelo.

"I don't know why he married her," Frau Ruth said, "but I can tell you why she married him. She's only waiting for him to drop dead so she can inherit all his money and marry one of her own kind."

"And where did you get all this confidential information?" Eva mocked.

"It's obvious, isn't it? Why else would a young woman like that want to marry an old Jew?"

"I understand that Herr Blumenthal was married twenty years ago, wasn't he, Professor Bernstein? At that time he wasn't a much older Jew than your husband is now, Ruth."

Frau Ruth drew a deep breath of anger, considered the statement, found no way to refute it, and decided to attack Eva instead.

"So you approve of mixed marriages! I bet you wouldn't hesitate yourself to marry a Gentile!"

"You seem to forget something, Ruth: I'm already married to your brother. But just for the sake of argument; no, I wouldn't hesitate to marry a Gentile if I were in love with him."

"You see!" Frau Ruth exclaimed triumphantly, as if she had made an important point. "You see!"

"I have a very broad-minded wife," Walter said with playful sarcasm.

"Somebody in this family has to be broad-minded," Eva countered belligerently.

"What does she know about these things?" Herr Kramer burst into the conversation. "She just talks to be contrary."

Herr Kramer is not altogether wrong. Eva does have a strong contrary streak. After the rebuke from her father-in-law, she sat tight-lipped and silent. But Frau Ruth had not finished.

"I still don't see why Josef Blumenthal couldn't have married a nice, Jewish girl, with all his money."

The corners of Eva's mouth twitched treacherously, but she swallowed whatever remark was on her tongue. Later, though, when we were alone, she said to me:

"Did you ever notice how harshly Jews condemn a wealthy Jew who marries a Gentile girl? But when a rich Gentile marries a Jewish girl, the same Jews will praise him to high heavens. Where's the logic?"

I would be a wiser man if I knew.

*Wednesday, August 2, 1939.*    Tonight we had a serious discussion concerning the rental of our club quarters. After looking all over Esperanza, we have been unable to find a suitable place which would rent for less than 250 to 300 pesos a month. Our membership is only approximately a hundred, at three pesos a head; that means that the entire membership fees would go toward covering the rent, with nothing left for a fund from which to draw in an emergency. ("What worse emergency could possibly befall us than the one with which we're faced now?" Eva asked, just to be contrary.)

Finally it was Frau Goldmann, the practical-minded one, who came up with a good suggestion. Why not set up a restaurant in the new club quarters and rent out the concession? This might cover, if not the entire rent, at least part of it. It would also provide a livelihood for one family and assorted waiters.

"It ought to be a good business," Goldmann said. "One thing: you got to eat."

Not a very philosophical statement, but true enough. The only question is how much, in our present squeezed financial state, are we willing to spend for food in restaurants?

*Thursday, August 3, 1939.*    Good news!

Josef has made an unexpected, generous gesture: a voluntary contribution of five-hundred pesos toward the purchase of furniture for our club. He was actually a little embarrassed and made light of his gift. But the nomination for club president is already beginning to weigh on him.

*Saturday, August 5, 1939.*    Dr. Lipschitz and Walter have recruited 105 paying members for the Centro. (Married women are admitted free if their husbands are members.) With Josef's donation and the membership dues prepaid for a month, we have collected about eight hundred pesos. Walter has been entrusted with the purchase of furniture, a move which has filled Goldmann with misgivings.

This afternoon he pulled me aside in the Jungle Café and whispered:

"Tell me, Herr Professor, do you think it's wise to entrust Walter Kramer with all that money? After all, he's a gambler! What if he loses it?"

I tried to calm Goldmann, but he has put a flea in my ear now. What if Walter should really lose the money? I shall make it my business to keep reminding him of the furniture. The approaching holidays will offer a good excuse for my sudden interest in the speedy completion of the club facilities.


*Monday, August 7, 1939.*    Today the strangest thing happened to me: I mistook another man for Aronoff.

When I walked into the Jungle Café in the afternoon I saw a young man sitting in one of the booths. His back was toward me, and all I could see was the dark, wavy hair and the handsome profile with the straight nose. As I passed his booth, I put my hand on his shoulder and said:

"Hello, Herr Aronoff. Any news from your parents?"

He looked up at me, and I immediately wondered how I could ever have confused him with Aronoff. Of course there was a resemblance, but it was strictly in the color and the texture of the hair and in the cut of the profile. Now that I saw the young man full face, there could be no mistaking him for Aronoff. His face was much narrower and weaker, with the mouth twisted into a sardonic half-grin. The eyes were a light gray-green, startling beneath the thick brows which almost met on the bridge of his nose. He had been polishing his glasses and now put them back on to look at me.

"Oh, I'm sorry," I said. "I thought you were Herr Aronoff!"

"And now you're disappointed," he said with what almost amounted to a sneer.

"Why should I be disappointed?"

"People are always disappointed when they realize that I'm not Aronoff. Especially the women!"

"Has this happened to you before? I mean, people mistaking you . . ."

"People mistake me for Egon all the time. You see, I'm the proverbial cousin twice removed. My mother and his mother were cousins. No money in my branch of the family, though!"

I did not know why he told me all this. To change the subject, I asked him for his name and how he had happened to come to El Paramo.

He told me that his name was George Klein and that he had come to El Paramo because Aronoff's father had called his mother to tell her that El Paramo was one country which still admitted Jews.

"A regular patriarch, old man Aronoff, always watching over the family."

Again the mysterious sneer. I felt ill at ease with the young man and excused myself, proceeding to my customary booth in the corner.

"We're getting some young blood in now," Fleischer said, pointing his chin in Klein's direction. "This should make the ladies happy."


*Tuesday, August 8, 1939.*     After talking to Aronoff, I am a little less mystified by Herr Klein's behavior.

"That crazy fellow hates me for no good reason," Aronoff said when I spoke to him about his cousin. "He feels he ought to carry on an old family feud."

When I looked at him quizzically, he explained:

"My father once had some difficulties with his father. Because my father would not hear of backing him in a shady business deal, old man Klein forged his name on some papers. When my father found out about it, he had Klein arrested. He was always sorry afterward that he had lost his temper, and he tried to make it up to George's family. You have to understand that my mother had a number of sisters and cousins, and everybody was always sponging on my father. At the same time they all looked down on him because he had less education than they had, so once in a while he just had to blow up. But I don't see what all this has to do with George and me. He seems to think that whatever I achieve I achieve with my father's money."

"It's easy for you to talk, Herr Aronoff. You do have money."

"Oh, I do, do I? I'll let you in on a little secret, Herr Professor. I did not bring the Aronoff fortune with me. In fact I doubt that I have more money with me than George. Let's see what excuse he'll have now for being less successful than I."

(One thing about Aronoff: there was not the slightest doubt in his mind that he would be more successful than his cousin.)


*Thursday, August 10, 1939.*   Today Walter took me along to inspect the progress made in the new quarters of the Centro.

I think the location was a felicitous choice: right in the business center of Esperanza and only a stone's throw from the Jungle Café. Walter pointed out that this would facilitate commuting back and forth between the two places. An advantage, no doubt, for Grushka, Dubrovsky *et al.,* who will want to spread their business activities over both territories.

When we arrived the place was still in a state of complete disarray. Painters were busy giving the walls a fresh coat, and the crude wooden floor was spattered with white paint. Some of the windowpanes were broken, and one could hear the honking of horns in the Calle Miraflores below. All the rooms smelled of turpentine, reminding me of the first night in our new home in Esperanza. It seemed ages ago.

The new furniture was piled into one small room. The chairs and tables were of the most primitive type, bought on the Indian furniture market. Walter said one could not expect much for eight hundred pesos. (Goldmann, of course, has a different theory. He is convinced that Walter has stolen part of the money.)

I asked Walter if the place would be ready for the holidays.

"It has to be ready," Walter said. "We've set the date for the opening ceremonies for next week Saturday, and the Saturday after we will have the ball."

"What ball?"

"The inauguration ball! The ladies feel that if the men want to have a club, they want to have a ball! It's not such a bad idea at that. This way the old-timers will have a chance to get acquainted with the new-comers."

Possibly the ladies are right. Every day there are more newcomers in Esperanza. But does one really have to know them all?

*Friday, August 11, 1939.* A great day. I received my first payment from Goldmann: two hundred pesos. This covers a whole month's rent and board. Disregarding the fact that the payment is profit on my own two hundred dollars, I feel like a millionaire.

*Monday, August 14, 1939.* This morning I had quite a scare: Eva came out of the bathroom and fainted in the hall.

I was on my way to breakfast when I saw Eva groping her way along the wall. I asked her if she was not feeling well; she mumbled something, and the next instant she swayed and keeled over. At first I was too petrified to do anything. Then, I suppose, I started shouting, for the Kramers and Walter came running out of their rooms.

Walter lifted Eva off the floor and carried her inside. I picked up her slippers and ran in after them, with the Kramers crowding in behind me. Walter had put Eva on the bed, a pillow under her feet and her head lowered so as to make the blood return to her head. He was kneeling beside her, massaging her hands and anxiously watching her face.

Frau Kramer looked at her daughter-in-law with alarm.

"Tell me, Walter, is she pregnant?" Frau Kramer whispered.

Walter glanced up with a startled expression, as if the thought had never entered his mind.

"I don't know," he said miserably.

"You don't know!" Frau Kramer was raising her voice now. "How can you even think of having a child! Don't you know we can't afford a baby right now!"

Eva had opened her eyes, and now gave her mother-in-law a look of distaste.

"Don't worry," she said weakly. "We're not going to indulge in any luxuries we can't afford."

Frau Kramer caught the hostility in Eva's voice and silently left the room. I still stood there with the slippers in my hand.

"Are you sure you're not going to have a baby?" Walter asked with a worried face.

"Not unless the stork brings me one," Eva said. Though she was still pale, her voice had come back full strength, and she was her own, testy self again. "Why don't you all go away and leave me alone? Go away!"

She rolled over on her side and turned her back on us.

"Don't you want me to call you a doctor?"

"Just go away. That's all I want."


*Tuesday, August 15, 1939.*    It seems that Eva's fainting was caused by a mild case of food poisoning and that she is really not pregnant. But Walter is still worried about her. After dinner he went for a long walk with me to talk over his problems.

"Perhaps having a baby would help," he mused. "It would give her something to do, something to take her mind off herself. But of course it would be madness, times being what they are. And then we really can't afford it. This peddling business doesn't bring as much as some people say, and I don't want to be tied to it, you know, afraid to look for something else . . ."

"Shouldn't you talk this over with Eva?" I suggested.

"I talked it over with her! She says she doesn't want a baby as long as we're living with my parents. And we just can't move out. We can't afford to!"

(Back to the old excuse. When will Walter Kramer be ready to cut the umbilical cord?)


*Wednesday, August 16, 1939.*    Today Josef bade me go over the speech with him he is to deliver at the opening of the Centro. It was surprisingly similar to the one I intend to make, dwelling in detail upon the tribulations which made us leave Europe and the hospitality which we have met here. I suppose, though, that this was unavoidable: similar circumstances will produce similar thoughts.

In the afternoon Walter broke the news that I have been appointed treasurer of the Centro. He said that it was only an informal appointment so far, but I could be certain I would be elected. I don't know that I am too anxious for the honor. I still haven't forgotten that Kramer and Goldmann thought I made money on the visas.

Walter also brought me a list of the members and an account of dues paid and money spent for furniture and painting. Everything seemed in perfect order. Of course there were no bills for the furniture, and I can already imagine Goldmann's saying that it is just Walter's good fortune that the Indians who sell the furniture don't know how to write.

*Thursday, August 17, 1939.*    With the prospect of the ball in the Centro, a new visitation has struck our house: the problem of what to wear.

Eva, who brought along three evening gowns in her trousseau, is the least affected. Frau Kramer decided to go in a short afternoon dress, but prevailed upon Walter to lend his sister money for the purchase of an evening gown. This comes under the heading of necessities for everyday living.

The biggest battle took place downstairs, at the Goldmanns'. Once more the almost-forgotten loss of Trude's trousseau was bemoaned. But since this was water over the dam—or rather over the lost trunk—Frau Goldmann insisted that Trude had to have a new dress, even if it meant cutting down on food for the rest of the family.

Trude had a real tantrum. She did not want a dress, she said. She did not need a dress because she would not go to the ball. Yes, she would too, Frau Goldmann insisted. Not only would she go, but she would go in a new dress. This went on for a few days: yes, no, yes, no, with everybody taking sides. Of course Frau Goldmann emerged victorious, leading Trude off to Frau Fleischer's fashion salon as if she were lead-

ing a lamb to sacrifice. Nothing but blue lace will do for her Trudi,
Frau Goldmann says.

*Friday, August 18, 1939.*   Eva's fainting had the effect of a stone
dropped into water: rings of rumors have sprung up around it.

I don't know whether Frau Goldmann heard the commotion or
whether Eva talked to Trude. At any rate, the day after Eva had fainted
—I believe it was Tuesday—Goldmann asked me confidentially:

"Tell me, did Eva have an abortion?"

I most indignantly said that she had not been pregnant in the first
place and that her fainting had been caused by food poisoning. I assumed that this was the end of the affair, but to my surprise Herr
Fleischer took me up on it this morning in the Jungle Café.

"Say, I hear the old witch put poison in Eva's food," he said to me. "I
always knew she hated the poor girl's guts!"

"For heaven's sake, how can you say such a thing, Herr Fleischer! Eva
had a case of food poisoning. Frau Kramer had nothing to do with it."

"Well, I wouldn't put it past her," Fleischer said, disappointed.

The third person to take me to task was Frau Irene when I dropped
in on her this afternoon to see how she was getting along while her husband was away.

"What on earth is going on between Eva and Walter, Herr Professor?"
she asked me. "A few days ago Eva paid me a surprise visit. She was
hysterical, sobbing out some story about having a baby or not having a
baby, and that she simply couldn't take it any more. But she would not
say what it was she could not take any more."

I tried to explain as best I could the situation in our household. Frau
Irene shook her head and sighed.

"Eva seems to think that I have the formula for the perfect marriage.
And yet I remember going through everything she is going through
now. I was a few years older and times were more . . . normal perhaps,
but aside from that there was little difference. There were the in-law
troubles and the little jealousies, the fear of not being loved, or rather
of not being loved enough, the competition with my husband's other
interests and hobbies. I think in the end a successful marriage depends

upon one's ability to see the problems in their proper proportions and not to measure them against one's vanity. But how do you explain this to a girl of seventeen?"

I hinted something about Eva and Walter's other difficulties; the ones Walter had mentioned to me.

"The old complaint about the cold virgin," Frau Irene said irritably. "The trouble is that most men are impatient fools. You don't expect a young colt to turn into a race horse overnight! Why expect a girl to turn into a woman at the drop of a blanket?"

I had to concede that Frau Irene was right. Men are impatient fools!

We talked a little while longer, and then I took my leave. I went home to memorize once more the speech I have written for the opening of the Centro tomorrow. But so far I have been unable to commit it to my memory. I will have to read it after all.


*Sunday, August 20, 1939.*    I might as well make a clean breast of it: my speech was a failure, but the opening of the Centro was, nonetheless, a success.

All three rooms were packed with people. The ceremony had been set for the early afternoon, and many had brought children along, their high voices hanging shrilly above the babble of the grownups.

Walter kept circulating among the crowd, chatting and shaking hands with people whom I saw here for the first time. Eva stood in one corner, craning her neck, but if she was looking for Aronoff she was out of luck. He was not there. Trude also was missing. Levy approached me several times to ask me why she had not come. I said that this was probably not the right Sunday afternoon entertainment for a young girl, and Levy looked offended, as if my remark had been directed against him personally.

Frau Kramer, in one of her large-flowered print dresses, kept bringing over ladies to introduce to me. The first one was of impressive proportions, a regular Walkyrie with thick blond braids wound around her head. As I had suspected, she spoke with an atrocious Prussian accent.

"Frau Steinberg, this is my boarder, Professor Bernstein," Frau Kramer said. And then, to me: "Frau Steinberg arrived here two weeks ago. She plans on running a boardinghouse, which ought to be a good business. Frau Steinberg is a widow."

I acknowledged this information with a commiserating nod of my head, and Frau Steinberg was removed from my presence. Five minutes later Frau Kramer was back with another lady. This one was short and square, with very black hair pulled back into a severe knot. Her skin was swarthy, and she had a small mustache and a few black hairs scattered over her chin. (Later Eva said she looked as if she had hair on her teeth—which would not surprise me a bit.)

"Frau Fuchs, meet Professor Bernstein. Professor Bernstein boards with us. He is a widower. Frau Fuchs is looking for a place to live. She is a widow."

After Frau Kramer had put Frau Fuchs back into circulation and approached me with a third lady, a terrible thought began to dawn on me. It seemed that within the past few weeks a flock of elderly widows had descended on Esperanza and that Frau Kramer was busy match-making—for me. As Frau Kramer came near, I fled and sought refuge in the bathroom. I did not dare leave until I heard the shuffling of chairs which told me that people were taking their seats and the ceremony was about to begin.

Returning to the main room, I walked up to one of the seats of honor reserved for me on the platform next to Josef's chair. Josef, as always the last to arrive, came hurrying up the center aisle in his black under-taker's suit, throwing apologetic smiles right and left. Walter rapped the gavel sharply, causing an outbreak of coughing, shuffling and hushing of children, but finally quiet was established.

Herr Kramer read the short prayer designated for the opening of a new house, and then he introduced Josef as the first speaker. Josef rose, went through the ceremony of wiping his reading glasses and clearing his throat, looked at the assembly, and for a moment appeared startled by all the strange faces before him. Then he began in the stumbling manner of one unaccustomed to making speeches. He went into all the details of the misfortune which had brought us to El Paramo and the hospitality with which we had been received here. But, on the whole, he said noth-ing new and original, and though he received considerable applause I thought my speech would be more effective.

I had been under the impression that I was next on the speaker's list, and was taken aback when I saw Dr. Lipschitz, our self-appointed secretary, rise to usurp the dais. He said that he would limit himself to a few, brief words, but this turned out to be an empty promise. After he had hashed over practically everything Josef had said, he went back from our recent persecutions to the Russian and Polish pogroms, the Spanish Inquisition, and so on to the second and first destructions of the temple in Jerusalem. I could already see that he would not be satisfied until he had traced back the story of our vicissitudes to the expulsion from Paradise. All in all, Dr. Lipschitz spoke close to an hour.

By the time my turn came to speak the crowd had become bored and restless. The most sensible action would have been to excuse myself, but I could not resist the lure of the speaker's platform. As soon as I spread my notes before me the written words sprang up from the pages into my mouth and poured out over the defenseless assembly. Though I could see the ennui of repetition descending upon the room, I was unable to stop myself. The only persons hanging rapturously on every one of my words were Frau Fuchs and Frau Steinberg, who had found seats in the first row. Frau Fuchs sat with her legs slightly apart, her skirt riding up on her fat thighs. I could see that she wore long lavender bloomers. I closed by eyes and silently prayed for strength to end my speech. Not enough that I lived through two destructions of the temple today, did I have to have Frau Fuchs's lavender bloomers visited upon me?

When I finished rather abruptly, the applause was of spontaneous gratitude. But the crowd had hardly heaved a big sigh of relief when Horowitz leapt up on the platform and without any introductions began to extol his favorite political ideas. He was hissed and booed, and Walter had to carry him off bodily.

As if to escape any further speechmaking, the people began to file out of the room, but Walter called them back.

"Ladies and gentlemen, please don't leave yet! We will now sing the Hatikvah!"

At first only a few voices rose timidly, but soon the chorus grew in strength. Josef stood on the platform, bewildered by the sudden demonstration. In the street below a few passers-by stopped to stare up at the window. Behind the houses on the opposite side, the Andes rose majestically against the blue sky. I thought that now the Jews had brought their song of hope even to this forsaken corner of the earth. Suddenly I was deeply moved.

On the way out Josef whispered to me that the assembly also should have sung the national anthem. I told him to be patient and give the people time to learn it. Sooner or later Jews always turn into the fiercest patriots of their adopted countries—provided the people there let them.

*Monday, August 21, 1939.*    I am always newly amazed at the callousness that results from a feeling of safety. Though we deplore and bemoan the lack of interest which other nations show in the fate of the Jews under Hitler, we ourselves have given little thought to what has been happening in Europe during the past two months.

Until now we had hoped that the crisis of the Polish Corridor would be settled peacefully, but today we were jolted out of our complacency by the news that Albert Foster, the leading Nazi in Danzig, had publicly announced that the hour of deliverance was near. Still worse was the announcement that the Russians and the Germans have concluded a trade treaty.

The afternoon papers carried a story that Russia and Germany were about to sign a nonaggression pact, but Goldmann insisted that this could not be true. I hope to God he is right this time. If the Germans *and* the Russians should descend on Europe, it would certainly mean the end of Western civilization.

Rumors follow rumors. We hear stories about the French and English making military preparations, and the Germans massing troops in Slovakia near the Polish Corridor. If war *should* break out in Europe, how are the Jews still trapped there going to escape?

*Tuesday, August 22, 1939.*    Today we talked hardly anything but politics at the luncheon in Frau Irene's house (the British have reiterated their pledges to Poland, but at the same time appealed to Germany for a truce in Eastern Europe), a topic which profoundly bores Eva. She seemed more interested in Hans Braun, who has come back from his prospecting tour. Hans looks tanned and virile, and though he has not yet found oil, Walter claims that he reeks of success.

"How can a man be lucky enough to pick the right profession for our times?" Walter said.

"There's nothing wrong with your profession either, Walter," I said.

"You mean being a peddler?"

"I mean being an architect."

In spite of her recent trips into town Eva seemed swayed back again to Hans. He was in high spirits, laughing and joking about the impressive size to which his wife has grown in his absence. (Her baby is due in a few weeks.) But his eyes kept wandering to Eva.

"It's good to come home to civilization," he said.

(This throws a new light upon Esperanza as the seat of civilization. Usually we think of it as just the opposite.)

"I simply had to come back now," Hans said. "I would not miss the ball in the Centro for all the oil in Persia."

Actually, the wisdom of having a ball just now has been questioned. Most of the older people feel that the ball ought to be postponed until we know what is going to happen in Europe. The younger people argue that, after having had their lives ruined by Hitler in Europe, why should they let him spoil their fun in Esperanza?

Trude is the one exception. Though she takes as little interest in politics as Eva, she has been overcome by sudden scruples and has turned into a great advocate of canceling the ball.

"Are you mad?" Frau Goldmann said to her. "Your dress is practically finished!"

Thus global calamities have again been reduced to personal problems.


*Wednesday, August 23, 1939.*   The impossible has happened: Russia and Germany have signed a nonaggression pact. We are all terribly upset, especially Goldmann, who had put so much hope in the Russians. This afternoon was the first time I can recall not seeing Goldmann in the Jungle Café.

When I came home in the evening I learned that there had been some words between Goldmann and Horowitz. Nobody knows exactly what was said, but I understand that Goldmann was holding Horowitz personally responsible for the action of the Russians. The upshot of it is that Horowitz is not on speaking terms with Goldmann. He did not even come in to look at Trude's evening gown, which Frau Goldmann had brought home in the afternoon.

Since everybody from the second floor went downstairs to inspect the dress, I felt I might as well go too. The dress was spread out on the bed before the oohing and aahing ladies, and finally Frau Goldmann pressed Trude into putting it on.

"Let the people see how you look in it, Trudi! I tell you, she looks stunning. But you'll see for yourselves."

Trude was not half so reluctant to put on her dress as I had expected her to be. She retired to the factory and took quite a while before she came out again. When she did, I hardly recognized her.

Not that she really looked stunning. This was strictly an exaggeration brought on by motherly blindness. But she looked taller and thinner in the long gown, and it did bring out the color of her eyes, as Frau Goldmann had said it would. Perhaps the feeling of being well dressed gave Trude a new sense of security, and she moved with more grace and dignity than she usually does. I thought that next to a wedding gown only an evening gown could bring about such a metamorphosis in a young girl.

Eva was enchanted.

"Trude, you look gorgeous, simply gorgeous," she kept repeating.

"Wear it in good health," Frau Kramer said. And in a whispered aside to Frau Goldmann: "I hope the investment pays off."


*Thursday, August 24, 1939.*    The political situation in Europe looks very bad. Talk about it has supplanted all talk about the coming ball at least among us older people. President Roosevelt has appealed to Hitler to maintain the peace; Foster was proclaimed supreme head of the Danzig Free State; and Poland has called up her reserves.

Every hour looks more like war. Walter says that if war should break out before the end of the week, the ball in the Centro would have to be canceled.

"Then we just have to pray for peace until Sunday," Eva said flippantly.

I was really annoyed with her. In my anger I spoke sharply:

"Aren't you ashamed to be talking that way, Eva? Your parents are still in Europe!"

Her eyes filled with quick tears and her lips quivered.

"I won't have my entire life ruined by politics!" she cried, as if her life really depended upon going to the ball on Saturday.

Ah, to be young and naïve again!


*Friday, August 25, 1939.*    Today Hitler renewed his demand for a free hand against Poland, and Roosevelt once more appealed to him to seek a peaceful solution. But in spite of the mounting war threat, preparations for the ball are proceeding at full speed.

Now that Trude has her new dress, even she has entered into the spirit of things. This afternoon she went with Eva to the Centro to help decorate the rooms for the event tomorrow night.

Toward evening I dropped over from the Jungle Café to see how the preparations were progressing. Many of the steady patrons of the café had defected to the newly opened restaurant in the Centro. (The restaurant has been leased by one Fritz Bloch, formerly a forwarding agent in Vienna. Here he works as a self-employed waiter. Though he serves only coffee and cake at present, each order takes an interminable time. But Frau Bloch is said to be a good cook, and perhaps with a more experienced waiter than Herr Bloch—one who manages to spill less than half of each cup of coffee—business should be quite good. People are certainly eager for a variety of eating places.)

The Fleischers were sitting at a table with the couple with whom I had seen them at the "bullfight." Levy came up to have a look around, and later Aronoff's cousin, Herr Klein, accompanied by another young man whom I did not know. Walter dropped in, waved to me and walked to the door of the large assembly hall, calling inside:

"How are you doing, girls?"

I also got up and went to look in through the open door. Eva and

Trude had done quite a job on the room. They had masked the entire wall at the far end with blue and white crepe paper and had mounted a large Mogen David in the center. Now they were busy stringing streamers of the same paper from the corners to the center of the ceiling. In front of the wall with the Mogen David a number of long boards had been placed across some empty crates. Walter explained that this was where the buffet would be set up tomorrow.

Behind the improvised table stood Frau Kramer and Frau Steinberg, wildly gesticulating this way and that. Frau Steinberg's Teutonic features lighted up when she caught sight of me, and I thought it safer to retreat.

Walter walked with me to my table, sat down and chatted for a few minutes, and then left for the Jungle Café to attend either to business or to a dice game with his bosses. After a while Eva came out and joined me.

"Wow," she said, stretching her arms. "I guess I can do with a break now."

She ordered a cup of coffee and a piece of appelstrudel, and Herr Bloch, laboriously scribbling down her order, disappeared for the time which it usually takes to prepare a seven-course gala dinner.

Eva looked around, waved to the Fleischers, asked me if I knew the people who sat with them, but suddenly stopped in the middle of her chatter and stared.

Glancing back over my shoulder, I realized that from where she sat Eva could see George Klein the way I had seen him first: part of his profile, and the dark, wavy hair thickly covering the back of his head. He had taken off his glasses and was polishing them, as seemed to be his habit.

Perhaps Klein felt Eva's glance boring into his back, for he turned around to face her fully. A look of consternation spread over Eva's face. When she noticed that I was observing her, she colored slightly and stammered:

"I thought it was somebody else."

"Yes, there is a resemblance," I said. "Herr Klein is Herr Aronoff's cousin . . . twice removed."

Eva blushed deeply at having given herself away and began to fidget in her chair. Fortunately Herr Bloch came at this moment, slopping coffee all over the table and slamming the appelstrudel down in front of her.

"Here you are, Fräulein. My wife herself baked the appelstrudel. Real Viennese appelstrudel. You're from Vienna, Fräulein?"

"Yes, Frau Kramer is from Vienna," I answered for Eva.

"You mean this young lady here is a Frau! Nowadays even the children get married! There ought to be a law!"

Herr Bloch had spoken loud enough to be heard all over the room, and I could see Klein and his tablemate crane their necks and stare at Eva. Then they put their heads together and whispered. Herr Bloch walked away, muttering to himself. Eva smirked into her coffee and said:

"The opinions are added gratuitously."

All the men in the room were staring at her now, and Eva gulped down the rest of her coffee and rose, saying she had better get back to help Trude. She nearly ran out of the room, conscious that she was being followed by looks. The man at the Fleischers' table sat with his mouth half open and his eyes greedy. I was shocked at the crude expression of desire on his face. I thought that this was one person I did not care to meet, but on my way out Fleischer grabbed me by the sleeve and pulled me over to his table.

"Professor Bernstein, I would like you to meet our friends, Herr and Frau Schwarzkopf."

I shook hands but refused to sit down. My instinctive dislike for Herr Schwarzkopf was still increased by Fleischer's next words:

"Did you see my friend Otto's mouth water when he looked at the little Kramer girl?"

"She is very young, practically a child," Frau Schwarzkopf said. She spoke with a slight accent which I could not place at first. "What use would you have for such a young girl, Otto?"

Frau Schwarzkopf was neither joking nor teasing, but putting the question in deadly seriousness, as if she really expected her husband to explain in detail what he would want with a girl like Eva.

"Such young girls are not much good anyway." Frau Schwarzkopf shrugged her shoulders. "Any man is better off with a mature woman."

I did not like the turn the conversation was taking and excused myself, but for the rest of the day I was haunted by a feeling of queasiness—a queasiness which comes from having said, or having been told, something faintly unpleasant. I cannot quite pin down who said the wrong thing. Fleischer? Frau Schwarzkopf?

But at least I puzzled out Frau Schwarzkopf's accent: Russian.

*Saturday, August 26, 1939.*    Today is the great day.

Eva, who rarely looks at a newspaper, snatched it out of my hand this morning to see if there was still peace in Europe. I keep remembering how she had confided to me aboard ship that her greatest wish had been to go to the Opera Ball when she was eighteen. Does she still dream of meeting Prince Charming at the ball and walking off with him into never-never land?

*Sunday, August 27, 1939.*    Still no war in Europe. In view of this I shall permit myself the frivolity of writing about the ball last night.

I don't know whether to say that Frau Goldmann's investment paid off or that it backfired. Trude has a boy friend now, though not the one of her mother's choosing.

The Goldmanns had decided not to attend the ball for economic reasons. Trude was entrusted to Walter, Horowitz and my safekeeping—not that she really needed that much safekeeping. She looked pretty in her new dress, but faded completely next to Eva. Eva, in a clinging white gown with a deep decolletage and an even lower back, with her golden hair piled up on her head and her golden skin contrasting with the white of the dress, made my throat ache as I looked at her.

Walter too seemed enthralled by her appearance. He could not resist touching her cheek, as if to make sure that she was real. Eva jerked her head away and said testily:

"Don't! You're mussing my hair."

Walter's rapture gave way to disappointment. When he helped her into her wrap, he was careful not to touch her again.

It was almost ten o'clock when we arrived in the Centro. The place was already filled with ladies in their colorful gowns of clinging silk or billowing tulle, and men in tuxedos. There was a sense of excitement in the air, as if this really were the Opera Ball. The buffet at the far end of the hall was laden with food, and arrangements of pink and red carnations in baskets contrasted gaily with the blue and white decoration on the wall.

The smaller rooms and the center section of the large assembly hall had been cleared of furniture, and a number of couples were dancing to the music of a band hired for the evening. Along the walls, tables and chairs had been set up, and people kept filing back and forth between the tables and the buffet.

In one corner an improvised bar had been erected. Dr. Lipschitz was on duty at the crude counter, working like a dervish and, as far as I could tell from the distance, already inebriated and talking incessantly.

As we walked through the hall, Fleischer grabbed Eva from behind and held her fast. He too had had a few drinks too many.

"Isn't she a vision! Tonight's the night, tonight we're going to have fun, girlie! Come on, I'll buy you a drink!"

He headed for the bar, dragging Eva along like a reluctant child. I urged Walter to go along and protect Eva from Fleischer's attention, but he still seemed miffed by her former rebuff and said that she could very well look after herself. Presently Frau Fleischer, dressed in her favorite green, caught sight of Walter, steered toward him, and began to flirt with him.

"Since Peter is off with Eva, we might as well make a night of it, Walter," she suggested with a flirtatious smile.

Walter danced off with her among the other animated couples, and I went to have a look at the bar.

People were jostling each other away from the narrow counter behind which Dr. Lipschitz was in full action. Everybody seemed eager to buy drinks, and for a moment I wondered where all the free-flowing money had suddenly come from. Fleischer had put his left arm around Eva's shoulder, balancing a drink in his right hand. Eva was unsuccessfully trying to squirm out of his grasp.

Raising his glass to her, Fleischer proposed a toast:

"To the most beautiful woman with the most beautiful back in the room!"

He bent over sideways and planted a kiss on Eva's bare back. She jerked away from him as if she had been singed.

"You're drunk," she said soberly.

"Not at all," Fleischer replied in a thick voice. And, raising his glass once more, he spoke over Eva's shoulder: "And also to *your* girl friend, Aronoff! She's pretty too!"

Eva flushed and turned quickly to look behind her.

Aronoff had come up to the bar. He looked extremely handsome in his navy-blue tuxedo. With him was a young girl, about Eva's age, exquisite-looking in her own way, but shorter and not so spectacular as Eva. Aronoff did not even glance at Eva, who stood right in front of him, her eyes wide with longing. He ordered two drinks and handed one to the girl.

"That's the spirit, Aronoff! Get them drunk! You're quite a guy, Aronoff. I like you. My wife likes you too. How about you, Eva? Do you like Aronoff?" Fleischer said.

"You're stinking drunk," Eva said angrily. Her voice shook and she seemed to be trembling all over. She turned quickly and walked away.

"What's the matter with *her?*" Fleischer asked. "Well, never mind, Aronoff. You can't have them all."

We were pushed away from the bar by people battling their way forward, the women emitting high-pitched shrieks of laughter as the men pinched and kissed them in the exuberance of the occasion.

I went to see what had become of Trude. Among the cheerful crowd she sat glumly alone at a table, with Levy solicitously hovering over her.

"Anything else I can get you, Fräulein Trude?" He looked with concern at the plate of untouched food in front of her. "Perhaps a piece of pastry? You like sweets, don't you?"

Without waiting for an answer, Levy rushed off toward the buffet. Trude looked at me with despair in her eyes. I asked her if she wasn't dancing.

"Herr Levy doesn't dance," Trude said miserably.

Just then Walter and Eva danced past. Eva nudged Walter and

whispered something in his ear. Both came over to the table, and Walter asked Trude with false enthusiasm whether she cared to dance. Trude leapt up, eager to get away from her place of captivity, and Eva sat down in her stead.

Hans Braun and his wife made their way through the crowd to our table. Frau Irene was wearing a loose pregnancy blouse of silver material over her long, black satin skirt. She looked enormous.

"Ah, food!" she said when she saw Trude's heaped plate, and sat down. "Whose is it? Who cares! Women and children first, and I'm speaking for both."

She took a fork and began to belabor the food on the plate.

"All she can think of lately is food," Hans said. "You will have to help me out, Eva, and dance with me."

He led Eva off among the dancing couples. Frau Irene was so absorbed in eating that she did not even turn to look after them. But I did not like the way Hans had put his arm around Eva, and I watched them as they weaved their way among the other dancers. And yet, when I saw Hans's lips brush Eva's cheek, I could hardly believe my eyes. Eva stiffened and strained away from him. He looked down at her, puzzled, piqued perhaps, and after another turn around the floor brought her back to the table.

Frau Irene was still eating, and Hans sat down opposite her and patted her hand.

"That's my girl," he said. "If she keeps on eating like that, she'll bust and give birth right here. We'll have to call the baby Centro!"

He looked at his wife with sincere fondness.

Eva looked bewildered, as if trying to figure out how a man could so neatly separate love from desire. She casually began to move away from the table. I followed her to the edge of the dance floor, where she stood gazing longingly at the gaily swaying couples. For once I was sorry that I did not dance. I turned to talk to her, but her eyes had lit up expectantly, and when I followed her glance I could see a dark head cutting toward us through the crowd. I could sense Eva's disappointment when she recognized George Klein.

He stopped a few paces from us, then plunged forward with determination and began to greet me profusely like a long-lost friend. His purpose was transparent enough and I introduced him to Eva. The tip of his tongue flitted across his lips before he said shyly:

"Do you think Herr Kramer would mind if you danced with me, madam?"

Eva could barely hide a smirk. "Herr Kramer isn't anywhere in sight right now," she said.

I could see that she was making fun of Klein, and I knew she would be safe with him. As he danced off with her he held her at a respectful distance, tilting his head back a bit to talk down to her. He seemed neither drunk nor in any way forward in his behavior, and I felt reassured enough to return to the Brauns.

Levy had come back in the meantime and was looking around in consternation.

"Where is Fräulein Goldmann?"

He discovered Trude on the dance floor. She had changed partners and she was dancing with Klein now while Walter danced with Eva.

Levy, in a flurry of excitement, seemed ready to push out on the floor to retrieve her.

"This young man, who is he? Does he know Fräulein Goldmann? Who introduced them? Perhaps I should go and see if she's all right?"

Hans put a restraining hand on Levy's arm.

"Look, Herr Levy, the girl came to dance. That's what a ball is meant for. Let her dance!"

Levy muttered something under his breath and moved to where he could watch Trude more closely. I could see her avoiding his glance every time she danced past him, and Levy returned beaten. When the music stopped, Klein escorted Trude back to the table and thanked her for the dance with stiff formality. Trude looked flushed and animated, and was plainly annoyed by Levy's inquisitiveness. While Levy tried to badger her into eating the piece of cake which he had brought for her, Klein returned with the young man with whom I had seen him once or twice before.

"Fräulein Goldmann, may I introduce my friend Halpern. Kurt and I went to school together."

(Herr Halpern is a gangly youth with very blond hair, a long nose, and an unhealthy complexion. Moreover, he looks as though he had perpetually moist hands.)

In spite of his unattractive appearance, Trude seemed flattered that Halpern wanted to make her acquaintance. She joyfully abandoned her piece of cake to dance with him.

Levy looked crestfallen.

"Where did all these boys come from?" he asked in despair.

He remained sitting by the table, jealously guarding Trude's cake. But from the moment she danced off with Halpern he saw little of her. The dance floor was so crowded now that most of the couples danced in one spot. One of the blue and white streamers overhead had broken and dropped down, trailing on the floor among the long gowns of the women.

Resuming my rounds through the rooms, I caught an occasional glimpse of Trude, now dancing with Klein, now dancing with Horowitz, but most of the time dancing with young Halpern. The sudden rush of attention had put a bloom on her face, and she looked as pretty as she could ever expect to look. Toward the end of the evening she was dancing with Halpern exclusively. Levy sat by the table in a morose mood, filling the ashtray with half-smoked cigarettes.

Eva also had an active evening. She was changing partners so fast that I had trouble keeping track of them. My first chance to speak with her came after midnight, when she collapsed into a chair beside me. But she had hardly sat down when Herr Schwarzkopf came to ask her for a dance. Though she told him that she was very tired, he would not let her alone until she was rude to him. Then he stomped off, his lips set in a thin line.

"God, what a bore," Eva said and yawned.

A few minutes later she was wide awake again. From where we sat we could see Aronoff through the open door, helping his girl into her coat. He lifted her long hair with one hand while he smoothed her coat around her shoulders, his fingers gently brushing the nape of her neck.

Rudi Brueck, who had had himself quite a time, came stumbling out when he noticed that Aronoff was about to leave.

"Hey, wait for me, I'm coming with you!"

"Don't you dare!" the girl called back over her shoulder, laughing gaily. "We're going home!"

Eva's jaw worked as if she were in physical pain.

Feeling his way back into the room, Rudi Brueck bumped into her. "Excuse me, ma'am. Ah, the beautiful statue!"

He bowed clumsily, bumping into me. Then he grasped my lapels to steady himself and whispered with the familiarity which comes with drunkenness:

"You take my advice: you don't want them young and beautiful like her. You want them old and ugly. Them are the only kind who know their business."

He went off, roaring with delight at his own wisdom.

Shortly afterward Walter came to collect us to go home. Horowitz said that he would stay a little while longer, and Trude was not in sight. We finally found her standing in the corner of one room, holding hands with Halpern. When she saw us approach she blushed and dropped his fingers.

"How about going home, Trude?"

"I'll be glad to bring Fräulein Goldmann home," Halpern said.

Levy had crept after us and now spoke up.

"If you want to stay a little longer, Fräulein Trude, I will of course take you home in my car."

"I wouldn't want you to go out of your way, Herr Levy," Trude said sweetly. "I'm sure Herr Halpern won't mind taking me home."

Eva said that Trude was old enough to stay by herself if she wanted to, and we left without her. We were already in the taxi when Walter began voicing some doubts.

"Perhaps we ought to have taken her home. We promised Frau Goldmann."

"Let her be," Eva said. "For once she's having a good time. Maybe she'll even fall in love. Wouldn't it be wonderful?"

"Since when do you think so highly of love?" Walter asked.

"I always have."

I was riding in front beside the driver. When I glanced up into the rear-view mirror, I saw Walter kiss Eva. He was holding her in his arms, and in the dark she seemed to be clinging desperately to him.

I could understand then how Eva had felt when she watched Aronoff caress the neck of another woman. Now she was kissing Walter. But what was she thinking of?

*Monday, August 28, 1939.*   This morning I called on Josef to give him a report on the ball. He had refused to attend, partly because he thought that Señora Consuelo would feel out of place in the Centro, partly because he felt that the ball was ill-timed.

When I arrived at his house he was sitting in the loggia reading the newspaper. He said good morning and motioned to me to sit down beside him, but immediately returned to his reading. While he was busy with the newspaper, I leaned back and gazed out at the ever newly enthralling view: the multitude of flowering rose trees in the garden; the frayed leaves of the palms swinging in the breeze; the green wall of mountains piled up against the sky. I wondered when I had last seen a cloud. We are now in the fourth month of the dry season. Soon the rains will start again.

Finally Josef looked up.

"Any day now," he said without further elaboration.

"You really think so? Perhaps this crisis too will be settled peacefully. So far Hitler has got everything he wanted without firing a shot."

Josef shook his head.

"Not this time. If he attacks Poland, there's going to be a war."

Josef spoke without passion, calmly sucking on his cigar and squinting out into his sun-drenched garden. Zeus, I thought, sublimely sitting on Mount Olympus, deciding the fate of the world.

*Tuesday, August 29, 1939.*   A typical symptom of our severed existence in Esperanza: while most of us are preoccupied with the explosive political situation in Europe—especially those who still have friends and family there—some members of our community are mainly concerned with the approaching holidays.

Today I learned that Herr Levy has generously volunteered to purchase a Torah for us. Everybody is buzzing about Levy's philanthropy, and Frau Goldmann keeps bringing up the subject in front of Trude. But Trude has of late developed a convenient case of deafness.

As always in such matters, not everything is sweetness and light. There are only two planes a week coming in from Panama, from where the Torah is to be delivered—one of the planes arriving on Saturday. An orthodox group, Herr Kramer among them, has already called on Levy, entreating him to make sure that the Torah will not be shipped on the Saturday plane.

"Imagine the holy Torah traveling on the Sabbath!"

Eva and Trude jeer at what they call a bunch of superstitious old Jews. Perhaps thirty years ago I might have jeered with them. But today even I think that the Torah should not arrive on the Sabbath. There is a subtle difference between superstition and tradition. I believe that at my age one has learned to tell the difference.

*Wednesday, August 30, 1939.*    Today Poland decreed partial mobilization.

After dinner Goldmann came upstairs to talk politics with Dr. Lipschitz. When Frau Kramer asked why Frau Goldmann had not come along with her husband, Goldmann told her that his wife was not in a sociable mood.

Frau Goldmann is still cursing the day she bought the new dress for Trude. Ever since the night of the ball Trude has refused to see Herr Levy. He called at the house a few times, but Trude always managed to be out.

"Don't think I don't know what she's up to," Frau Goldmann said bitterly. "She doesn't even have the decency to bring the young man home and introduce him to us. 'I won't have you treat him as my suitor, Mama,' she says to me. Now, I ask you, if he isn't serious, why should she want to waste so much time with him? If I knew him at least! Tell me, Herr Professor, perhaps you know something about him?"

"Well, all I know is that he went to school with Herr Klein."

"Some comfort! At least we know that he went to school," Frau Goldmann said with unusual sarcasm.

*Thursday, August 31, 1939.*    Our feeling of gloom because of the crisis in Europe was heightened by the first rainfall of the season today. At noontime a dark-gray curtain of clouds literally dropped out of the blue and broke in a deluge over the city. For the first time in months I experienced the feeling of being marooned. The world around us was sucked into a gray void, and only our house and the tensions seething in it remained.

In the afternoon Trude put on her raincoat and went out for a "walk." Frau Goldmann cried.

"For that you bring up children," she said.

# Part Three ❧ A Time of Violence

*The earth also was corrupt*
*before God, and the earth was*
*filled with violence.*

GENESIS 6:11

*Friday, September 1, 1939.*    Hitler has attacked Poland!

I think our excitement is increased by the guilty feeling of safety in which we find ourselves. We buzz and dispute, everybody claiming that what happened is exactly what he predicted—even Goldmann, who until the last moment maintained that there would be no war in Europe.

England and France are mobilizing, though still willing to negotiate if Germany withdraws her forces from Poland. The Italians have declared their intention of remaining neutral. For how long, we shall see. Probably until they find out which way lies victory.


*Sunday, September 3, 1939.*    Today England and France declared war on Germany. Now it really looks like the beginning of another world war.

Here, on our safe mountaintop, a war between the optimists and the pessimists has broken out. The optimists, vociferously led by Goldmann, predict that Hitler will be annihilated within three months—half a year at the most. The pessimists, and I am afraid that I am one of them, realize that Hitler is too well prepared for a fast defeat. Even if he does not win—which God forbid!—the war is bound to last for a long time.

We don't dare talk about it, but there is one thought uppermost in our minds now: what will become of the Jews left in Europe?


*Monday, September 4, 1939.*    All our conversations are monopolized by the war. In the general excitement the arrival of the Torah has gone almost unnoticed and poor Levy has been cheated out of the share of gratitude still due him.


*Wednesday, September 6, 1939.*    The war in Europe is going very badly. Hitler is advancing at a frightening pace. His panzer divisions and his Luftwaffe are simply smashing the Polish defenses.

Contrary to her frivolous behavior a week ago, Eva has been frantic about the fate of her parents ever since the outbreak of the war. Today she received a letter which brought her some relief. "We are going to see Arnold," her parents write in the cryptic manner in which Jews nowadays transmit information. Eva says this means that they are joining an illegal transport to Palestine.

"They still can get out through Italy," Eva said, politics-conscious for the first time in her life. "I begged them to come here. They would be safe here, but they want to join my brother and his wife in Palestine. Until now I was the little one, but in the meantime my brother and his wife have had a baby, so there's one even younger. Sometimes I wonder if parents ever love their children as much as they love their grandchildren."

*Thursday, September 7, 1939.* Among all the disastrous news from Europe, a joyful event here in Esperanza: Frau Irene had her baby today, a little boy.

Eva is as excited as if it were her own. After his father, she was the first person allowed to see the infant. Her eyes shine every time she describes the baby, and Walter looks worried.

Something else I didn't know: Dr. Landau delivered the baby. He never breathed a word about it at Horowitz' last tea party. No doubt he does not want it talked about. He has no license to practice medicine in El Paramo.

*Saturday, September 9, 1939.* In spite of the continuing bad war news, talk about the approaching holidays has now taken precedence in our conversations. Since we have no rabbi here, Herr Kramer has been selected as the only one fit to conduct holiday services. Levy, who as the donor of the Torah rates the honor, will assist.

Of course Herr Kramer is overjoyed. He has led an idle life for months now and needed a boost for his deflated ego. His new, semiofficial standing as Rosh Hakol has fanned his old despotism, bringing on a falling out with Eva over her synagogue attendance.

This evening, after dinner, Eva and Walter joined the Kramers in their room. Ever since Eva and Walter started eating by themselves, these visits have become less and less frequent. The Lipschitzes had arrived earlier, and Frau Ruth greeted her brother and sister-in-law with a sarcastic: "Well, well, rare guests!"

Eva's face immediately stiffened into hostility, and she sat down on Frau Kramer's couch, as far away as possible from the rest of the company. Walter flopped down beside her and put his head in her lap.

"For this you could have stayed in your own room," Dr. Lipschitz teased.

"You're just jealous," Walter said.

It all sounded like the amiable banter of any family circle. Realizing that this might go on for a while, if not checked, Frau Kramer broke in:

"So how do you like the new Rosh Hakol? Aren't you proud of your father? Finally people are beginning to appreciate him! Tell me, how many Jewish men in Esperanza would be able to conduct services?"

Through this eulogy Herr Kramer sat filled with silent pride, his hands folded over his belly, resting on the knob of an imaginary cane. Everyone had a word of flattery for him—everyone but Eva, who sat absent-mindedly twisting horns of Walter's hair.

"I have already taken seats for all of us," Herr Kramer said, pleased with the prospect of bringing such a large, favorably inclined audience with him.

Eva snapped back into reality and sat up straight.

"I hope you didn't take a ticket for me," she said. "I'm not going."

"What nonsense is this?" Herr Kramer asked sharply.

"I'm not going."

Walter raised his head out of Eva's lap and looked at her.

"What's got into you, Eva? We're all going. Everybody will be there."

"Everybody except me."

"Why do you always have to be so contrary?" Frau Kramer said. "Can't you just once do what everybody else does?"

"I don't like doing what everybody else does. I like to have a good reason for what I'm doing."

"May I ask then," Dr. Lipschitz said in his most legal manner, "if you like to have a good reason for what you're doing, what is the good reason for not wanting to come to the synagogue if surely every other Jewish soul in this city will come?"

Even in her anger Eva had to grin.

"Look, Alfred, I just don't believe in all this breast-beating and once-yearly repenting. People think they can automatically turn into saints by attending services on Rosh Hashana and Yom Kippur, when actually not one among them could keep the Ten Commandments for three days in a row."

Everybody in the room looked guilty, a feeling which only increased the already prevalent hostility.

"Now, look here, Miss Smart," Herr Kramer said in his no-nonsense manner, "nobody here gives a damn about what you think. You're going to come!"

"I'm sorry, but I won't."

"Be sensible, Eva," Frau Ruth said. "What difference does it make to you if you come? Why make an issue of it? And if you don't come, what are people going to say with Papa praying before the congregation?"

"So that's what it boils down to," Eva said maliciously. "Not how displeased God will be with me if I don't go, but what people are going to say. Well, I don't care what people are going to say! My parents won't be going to temple this year, and I don't see why I should."

This gave the argument a new, hard-to-refute turn. Eva had played on the guilt feelings of all of us who were safe here. A great many Jews would be unable to attend services this year. Eva made it appear that she would rather show solidarity with them than with us.

But I knew that this was only trickery on her part; that she was not really principled but stubborn. Still, she had achieved a temporary victory and the topic was dropped for the moment.

*Wednesday, September 13, 1939.*    The Germans are still advancing in Poland. It seems that everybody underestimated their military power and that none of the other nations is even half prepared to meet them. Lately the newspapers here have been printing a new word: guerra relámpago—Blitzkrieg.

Tomorrow evening begins Rosh Hashana. We are approaching the holidays in a very somber mood. Eva says that now at least we will have something to pray for. She is incorrigible.

*Saturday, September 16, 1939.* As was to be expected, the holiday services passed without Eva's attendance. Once an issue had been made of it, she could not go back on what she had said. But I believe that in the end she regretted her decision.

The large assembly hall of the Centro had been converted into a makeshift synagogue, with the rows of chairs arranged at an awkward angle so as to face east toward the crude ark which contained the new Torah. Herr Kramer acquitted himself splendidly, chanting the ancient prayers as if he had done so for years. Levy vigorously joined in the choruses, at the same time throwing furtive, impious glances at the women's section. But, according to the wishes of some orthodox members of the congregation, a curtain had been draped before the rows of chairs where the ladies sat, and if Trude was among them she was concealed from Levy's view.

I never saw so many men crying at services. Doubtless they were moved not so much by the prayers as by the thoughts and memories which they evoked.

My biggest surprise was to come across Horowitz. He was sitting in the last row, wrapped to his teeth in his prayer shawl. I violated the holiday spirit by sneaking up to him and whispering in his ear:

"So, Horowitz, the Communist party has given you leave of absence to attend the holiday services?"

The result: Horowitz does not speak to me.

*Monday, September 18, 1939.* Saturday I was still joking about Horowitz, but yesterday something happened which has brought near ostracism to him: the Russians have invaded Poland from the east!

Apparently the Soviet government was alarmed by the progress of the Germans and decided to act before they had them at their own border. Our only comfort is that the Polish Jews who will come under Russian domination will be comparatively safe.

*Thursday, September 21, 1939.* Two days ago, the Russian and German armies met at Brest-Litovsk.

"What do you think of your comrades now?" Dr. Landau taunted Horowitz at our tea party this afternoon. And as if this were not enough, he had to tease him about his visit to the synagogue. Now that Horowitz had begun to mellow toward me, Dr. Landau got his hackles up again.

"If you weren't so stingy you would have bought a seat yourself!" Horowitz screeched.

"The communications I have with God I can manage without the intercession of Herr Kramer," Dr. Landau replied with asperity. "By the way, Horowitz, which side were you praying for? The Jews or the allies of your Russian comrades?"

Horowitz has forbidden Dr. Landau to visit him again.

*Friday, September 22, 1939.*     Tomorrow is Yom Kippur.

Frau Kramer is already cooking as if we were embarking upon a fasting feat comparable to Gandhi's. The smell of food in the house alone will be enough to make us hungry.

I asked Eva if she was going to fast.

"Of course," she said. "I've been fasting since I was twelve."

Frau Ruth, who had come over to help her mother with the cooking, made a remark about Eva's inconsistency.

"No inconsistency at all," Eva said coolly. "The Jews in Europe might not be able to go to temple, but you can bet that nobody will try to keep them from fasting."

For one so young she has a remarkably sharp wit. If she weren't so pretty, I would say that she has the makings of a shrew.

*Monday, September 25, 1939.*     There had been some grumbling about Josef's absence from the Rosh Hashana services ("The president of the Centro of all people! Naturally, what can you expect of a man whose wife is not Jewish . . .") but he made up for it by spending the entire Yom Kippur in the temple.

Afterward we walked home together. The weather was spendid—the proverbial good weather for the Jewish holidays, even here in the middle of the rainy season. After the long fast the thin, crisp mountain air made my head spin and my ears buzz. I suppose Josef must have felt the same effect, for he said to me:

"I haven't been fasting for years. First, when I was alone here, it seemed like such a futile gesture. And later, after I had lost the habit, it struck me as an insurmountable task every time I thought of it. I believe one needs the psychological backing of a crowd to go through with what one considers unnecessary and impossible."

This may be putting it too patly. There is always the question of tradition; or, for those who have it, faith.

*Sunday, September 30, 1939.*    After less than four weeks, it seems that the war in Poland is over. On Wednesday Warsaw surrendered, and by now Germany and Russia have divided Poland between them. The Soviet government also concluded a treaty with Estonia which gives them naval bases on Estonian territory.

"Imperialistic designs!" Goldmann screams.

"Better the Russians than the Germans," Horowitz says, echoing the secret thoughts of most of us.

*Sunday, October 1, 1939.*    Today the Braun boy was circumcised.

The ceremony had been postponed until after the traditional seven days because the baby had contracted jaundice. But he is fine now and a Jew. Or is this a contradiction?

I had been offered the honor of holding the boy during the operation. I wonder whether I am becoming senile that I am so affected by religious ceremonies. While Dr. Landau performed his new duty as our mohel, the memory of Arthur's circumcision came back to me, bringing a surge of sharp, unexpected pain. But soon I was brought back to reality by the baby's wailing upon becoming a Jew, and an instant later Frau Irene snatched her son away from me. While she and Frau Steinberg cooed over the child, the men who had been present at the circumcision went downstairs to join the other guests in the sala.

A large, cold buffet had been set up, and Hans Braun urged everybody to eat and drink.

As so often, Eva was the center of a group of men, her golden head gleaming among the graying and balding ones. Some amiable bantering was going on as I joined the group.

"So, when will we be able to congratulate you?" Fleischer teased and Eva blushed guiltily. "Isn't she sweet the way she blushes?"

He sneaked his arm around Eva's waist. Her lips quivered into the wretched smile with which she generally tried to conceal her disgust at physical contact.

Walter came and peeled Fleischer's arm from Eva's waist. "Kindly unhand my wife!"

For once Eva looked at him with gratitude. He caught her glance, and his eyes lit up with the sudden desire which she seems to instill in him in spite of what he told me about her. I could see that the mood of the circumcision was upon us. In the mind there was only one step from the circumcision to the birth to the act of procreation.

Everybody began to clamor for Frau Irene, and finally she came downstairs to accept the congratulations. Now that the circumcision was over, people wanted to know what the Brauns were going to call their son.

"We're going to call him Enrique Carlos," Frau Irene said.

It was strange to hear a Spanish name for a Jewish baby. Herr Fleischer, already affected by alcohol, raised his glass and shouted:

"To Enrique Carlos Braun, citizen of El Paramo!"

There was a moment of surprise as we contemplated the toast, and then we all raised our glasses and chimed in:

"To the Citizen!"

And Hans added quietly and fervently under his breath:

"May he never have a J stamped in his passport."

*Wednesday, October 4, 1939.* The resolutions of the Pan-American conference in Panama have now become official. It seems that the American republics—and that includes El Paramo as well as the United States—will remain neutral.

Again we look at the results from two different viewpoints: On the one hand, we are disappointed that the United States will not join forces with Britain and France. On the other hand, we are glad that our young men here will not be drafted into the army. Not very idealistic perhaps, but what man in his right mind ever *wanted* to be drafted?

*Friday, October 6, 1939.* Now that the holidays are over—and this includes the circumcision of the Citizen—life seems doubly humdrum.

The rainy season again weighs heavily upon us. The air is leaden; the afternoons are one long twilight; evening seems to come earlier even though the length of the days does not vary here, and the frogs, which were quiet all summer, have resumed their croaking.

What adds to my melancholy mood is that Eva and Walter have gone back to eating by themselves. The holiday meals were brightened by Eva's presence at the table and the cantankerous stimulation which she brought to the conversation. Now the Kramers and I are back to re-hashing the past, with an occasional verbose assist from Dr. Lipschitz.

The only time I see Eva and Walter—if at all—is at night after dinner. Now and then I meet Walter on the stairs when he comes home. He carries his two grips which contain the merchandise he peddles from door to door. His shoulders droop, his suit is crumpled, and he looks spiritless and beaten. I cannot help thinking of him as a man cheated out of his youth. At twenty-five he should be taking care of a wife—a baby perhaps—but not a family of five adults and two children. In spite of all his wild schemes, I know that Dr. Lipschitz is still without an income. Walter is regularly helping him out with "loans." They may still have some of the money left which they brought with them, but what if it runs out?

Strange that these thoughts did not bother me during the dry season. Why does everything seem so much worse when it rains?

*Monday, October 9, 1939.* During a long, private chat with young Aronoff this afternoon, I made the surprising discovery that, in a far-fetched way, I am also responsible for his coming to El Paramo.

It was raining hard when I came to the Jungle Café. I found Aronoff sitting alone in a booth, idly rattling a tumbler with dice in his hand. My eyes were caught by his strong long fingers, and remembering his mother's Bechstein grand I thought of what a wonderful pianist he would have made if he had had any talent. As it seems, his talent lies elsewhere. He has gone into business with Rudi Brueck—producing soap, of all things. People say that he is making quite a bit of money, a rumor which throws Horowitz into fits of fury.

When I passed his booth Aronoff smiled at me. I took this as an invitation and sat down opposite him.

"All alone today? Where is your bodyguard?" I asked.

Aronoff grinned.

"He's home minding the factory."

(His factory, like most of the others run by refugees, is set up in an empty garage.)

"Tell me, Herr Aronoff, this is something which has puzzled me for a long time: how did you ever happen to pick out such an unlikely companion as Rudi Brueck?"

Aronoff thoughtfully rattled the tumbler and threw the dice out on the table. He rolled two sixes and three twos.

"Full house," he said. "Well, for one, without Rudi I would never have come to El Paramo. You see, I was supposed to wait in Vienna for my visa to the United States. But the quota number took some time, and then one day I was cornered in the corridor of the house where I lived by a fellow with whom I had gone to school. He wore an SA uniform and he hit me and I couldn't hit back. Next day I went illegally over the Yugoslav border. I told my father he could pull all the strings he wanted to get me a visa somewhere, but I was not staying one day longer. I lived a couple of weeks in Yugoslavia, even spent a few days in jail, and then my father sent me a visitor's visa to Italy. That's where I met Rudi."

Aronoff paused and chuckled.

"That is one encounter I'll never forget. I met Rudi in Rome at three o'clock in the morning, just as he was taking a bath in the Fontana del Rutelli right behind the Grand Hotel. He was fully clothed, and he was singing a Viennese drinking song at the top of his voice. "Es wird a Wein sein, und mir wern nimmer sein." With the little Italian I speak and a few lire I got him away from the two carbinieri who wanted to arrest him and brought him to the pensione where he told me he was living. He was dead drunk, and he kept embracing me and thanking me for having saved him from drowning. Next day I dropped in to see how he was, and he talked me into moving in and sharing his room.

"I lived there for a month with Rudi. Naturally, if you live with somebody you find out a lot about him. For instance, Rudi had some beautiful pigskin luggage. He said he had it from his estranged wife, but when I took a good look I saw that the gold initials on it read A.v.H. Well, the lady hadn't quite been his wife, Rudi admitted. But she had been a very dear friend and she had given him the luggage for a going-away present. Rudi was quite proud of it that his lady friend had been a von—a Frau von Heggern, if I recall correctly."

(At the mention of the familiar name I felt my stomach contract with frightful, joyful recognition. And almost instantly I remembered Christine's telling me that a middle-aged, widowed aunt of hers had got involved with a young wrestler, a Jew. "It seems that all the Heggern women have a weakness for Jews," she had said in a bitter jest.)

"It was Frau von Heggern who advised Rudi to try for a visa to El Paramo," Aronoff said. "She had a niece who had a friend who had gone there. And when my quota number for the States did not come through after a month and my Italian visa expired, I decided to join Rudi. So here I am."

Should one call it destiny? Or what would one call the last-minute impulse of telephoning Christine to say good-by to her? After all, our affair had come to an end a year before Hitler, and she had always seemed relieved afterward that the breakup could not be blamed on ulterior motives on her part. I had not spoken with her since I had asked for her brother's help in my search for Arthur, and we talked stiffly, like strangers.

"I am leaving for El Paramo tomorrow."

"Good-by. Good luck."

This was all our affair had come down to in the end. This—and Aronoff and Rudi Brueck in El Paramo.

*Thursday, October 12, 1939.* The Centro has drawn away quite a bit of business from the Jungle Café. This has little effect on the busy morning hours when the peddlers make their transactions there, but toward evening, especially around dinnertime, the crowd in the Jungle Café thins out noticeably.

Now that Herr Bloch has added dining facilities, many of the bachelors and even some of the married couples have their dinner in the Centro. (Since I am paying for my board, I usually arrive after dinner. Though Goldmann assures me that business is good, I feel that I cannot afford to be wasteful.)

The service also has improved, mainly because Herr Bloch has hired a waiter to help out during the busy dinner hour, none other than young Kurt Halpern, making his tray-laden way among the tables in his gangly fashion. It is obvious that this was not what his mother had brought him up for. Still, he gets a free meal, some tips, and what little Herr Bloch pays him. At least an income.

Goldmann, who by now has found out that Halpern is his daughter's secret love, makes it clear that he does not consider waiting on tables a respectable occupation. Whenever he eats in the Centro he takes malicious pleasure in harassing poor Halpern with a million contradictory requests. To Trude he never speaks of him in any way other than "that waiter of yours." If he is particularly annoyed by the quiet arrogance with which she ignores his baiting, he adds: "And not even a good waiter!"


*Sunday, October 15, 1939.* Trude and Eva have become steady habitués of the Centro. In a way this is ironical, for neither of them had a good word for the club when it was first proposed.

I suppose that Trude wants to be close to her beloved Halpern, but I can't see what should draw Eva into the club. Perhaps Walter encourages her to come along. Of late he has become an afficionado of the card room in the Centro. Eva's presence in the next room might make him feel less guilty for gambling late into the night.

(I for one consider it unfortunate that the Centro has turned into a gambling den. Aside from the nightly poker and dice games going on among the men, the ladies have taken to the tables, playing interminable games of gin rummy. They all use the argument that there is little other diversion in Esperanza.)

Eva is one of the few who do not like to gamble. She will drop in at the card room, watch Walter for a while, and then leave again to sit with Trude by a table in the next room. Often they sit there until late at night, when Walter finally gets up from the poker table to take them home. This is the only way Trude is able to stay out that late.

As soon as the dinner rush eases off, Halpern sheds his white waiter's jacket and comes to sit with her, while Eva acts as a discreet chaperon. Not even Frau Goldmann could find fault with this arrangement. There must be occasions when Trude and Halpern meet alone, but as long as these meetings take place during the daylight hours, Frau Goldmann, like most mothers, seems to feel that her daughter can come to no harm.

Still, I don't see what pleasure Eva can derive from watching Trude and Halpern holding hands under the table and looking at each other with calves' eyes.

*Monday, October 16, 1939.*    My monthly accounting with Goldmann. He seems pleased with the way business has been coming along lately.

"Levy has given us twice as much credit this time," he bragged. "He can see his merchandise is in good hands. And under the circumstances it's very nice of him to help us along."

I did not inquire into the "circumstances," but this was not enough to dissuade Goldmann from pouring out his heart to me.

"God sees to it that the trees don't grow into the sky," he said. "Here I am, doing pretty well. Else's slips are getting better every day and there is some real demand for them now. But my Fräulein daughter, she has to run around with this Lausbub instead of paying a little attention to a solid businessman who is seriously interested in her."

"Look, Herr Goldmann, Trude is a young girl. It's only natural that she should prefer a younger man to . . . well . . . "

Since Goldmann had not mentioned Levy's name outright, I did not see how I could spoil his little game of discretion.

"Natural, natural," Goldmann said contritely. "Trude isn't the girl who can afford to play around. Look at her! Would you honestly say she's pretty? Well, she has been looking better lately. She's lost some

weight and she's taking care of herself now, but that's only one more reason why she should do her grabbing while the grabbing is good!"

In other words, Goldmann suggested that Trude ought to use the
deceptive bloom the love for Halpern had brought her for snaring Isak
Levy.

"Now tell me," Goldmann continued his monologue, "what can possibly come of her running around with this Lausbub? Who is he? What
does he have? Is he going to marry her? Of course not! The moment
he finds a prettier girl he'll run out on her. And then what? Trude
hasn't got half a dozen men lined up willing to marry her! The little
Kramer girl can do all the fooling around she wants to. She'll always
have some moron drooling over her. But not my Trude!"

I did not quite grasp how Eva had found her way into Goldmann's
accusations. And what was that "fooling around" Goldmann had mentioned in connection with her?

"I think you're doing Eva an injustice," I said. "She only goes along
to keep Trude company."

"Oh, she does, does she?" Goldmann sneered. "And what about
Klein?"

"What about him?"

"Don't tell me you haven't noticed anything!"

"Of course I have seen Herr Klein come up to the Centro once in a
while. And it is only natural that if his friend Halpern is sitting with
the girls, he should sit down with them too."

"Here you go again: natural, natural! You take a good look and you'll
see that Herr Klein is doing the natural thing. He can't take his eyes
off Eva!"

Perhaps Goldmann is mistaken and just transfers his suspicion from
Trude to Eva. Next time I see Klein sitting with the girls I will certainly take a closer look at him.


*Wednesday, October 18, 1939.*　　This morning when I came out on
the terrace I found Trude and Eva bent over a sheet of paper, reading.
Their heads were close together, with the sun glinting in their hair and

the rectangular, green fields on the slopes of the Grampico forming a peaceful backdrop.

Trude was the first to notice me. She glanced up, blushed violently, and hastily snatched the sheet of paper and folded it, written side inward. I suspected that she was trying to hide some of her writing because she had once told me that she would never write another word in German.

I also realized that Goldmann was right about her. She had become prettier within the past weeks. Her clothes, which formerly had strained at all the seams, now fitted her again. Her once lifeless hair was brushed and curled, and in some miraculous way she had even managed to acquire a tan. Altogether she looked the way she was meant to look—like a young girl in love.

Well, I thought, bravo for Halpern!

I seemed to have interrupted a secret discussion between the girls. They stopped talking but kept on looking at each other, barely suppressing their giggles. After a while Trude said that she had to go downstairs now and left, holding the paper awkwardly behind her back.

Eva and I sat quiet for a few minutes, gazing out at the Andes and enjoying the short, sunny respite before the rains would start again. I was sorely tempted to lead Eva into a conversation in which I could sound her out about Klein, but I managed to hold my tongue and it was she who broke the silence.

"Did you notice how pretty Trude has been looking lately?"

I said that I had indeed noticed. Eva thoughtfully looked at me, as if appraising me, and then burst out in sudden anger:

"I think it's mean the way the Goldmanns are treating Trude! The way they're always teasing her about Kurt! Why can't they just leave her alone? She isn't doing anything wrong."

"Look, Eva, I suppose the Goldmanns are no different from other parents. They just want what's best for their children."

"And why do parents always think *they* know what's best for their children? Half the time they don't even know their children! Trude is happy now, she's even done some writing again . . ."

Realizing that she had betrayed a confidence, Eva clapped her hand over her mouth.

"Don't feel bad, Eva, I know about Trude's writing. And I am glad that she has resumed it. It's always wrong to direct the grudge that you hold against the world against yourself and your talents. If you've been hurt you don't heal yourself by hurting yourself more."

Eva looked at me sharply, wondering perhaps how much I knew about Trude—or about her. Wasn't she too hurt and trying, possibly, to hurt herself more?

"Eva," I said spontaneously, "you and Trude . . . you're both so young . . . try to understand that if an older person takes an interest in what you're doing it isn't always to spoil your fun in life."

I could sense Eva retreating into her shell. She put on her five-hundred-year-old face and spoke with a tired voice:

"Look, Professor Bernstein, all we want is to be left alone to live our own lives. Is that so much to ask?"

I had to smile inwardly. How naïve she was beneath her mask of sophistication! She really thought that she was asking for little. But is anybody ever left alone to live his own life?

*Sunday, October 22, 1939.*     Some cheerful news today: at dinner Dr. Lipschitz announced that he was going into the dry-cleaning business.

The idea sounds marvelous and I just don't understand why nobody hit upon it before. There is not one single dry cleaner in Esperanza! Of course we all wondered how Dr. Lipschitz was going to overcome his lack of experience.

His answer was simple: he had already found a business partner, one who ought to understand about spots and their removal; a doctor of chemistry no less, Vogel by name.

Eva, with her own wry humor, said that an experienced dry cleaner might have been preferable. But Dr. Lipschitz was outraged at her gibe. What was there so difficult about the business, he said, that a man who knew about spots and cleaning solutions should not be perfectly able to handle it? Besides, they had already written to the United States for a manual on dry cleaning. And even though the work would be done by hand at first, they would eventually purchase the necessary machinery.

Eva would see! We all would see! Dr. Lipschitz was going to be the first one to get rich in Esperanza!

He has my blessing, and more power to him.

*Monday, October 23, 1939.*   Today we met Dr. Vogel. Frau Kramer had told her son-in-law to bring him along for the inevitable feeding ritual with which every near-member is initiated into the family.

After dinner Eva and Walter came over to get acquainted with the future business tycoon. I noticed Eva watching Dr. Vogel and his wife with a malicious glint in her eye. Even I, with the best of intentions, could not say that the Vogels are an attractive couple.

Frau Vogel is a small, stout woman with mousy hair and the face of a passport photo. She wears no make-up and no nail polish and sticks faithfully to the role of the humorless German housewife. I could see that she was irritated by what she must consider Eva's flippancy and her flashy way of dressing. Also by the fact that now and then her husband stared unblinkingly at Eva, as if he were afraid to blot out her image by a movement of his lids.

Compared to his wife, Dr. Vogel is a man of striking appearance, though not striking in the sense of handsome. He is very thin and tall, with a long head, a short neck, and shoulders which rise on either side of his neck like stunted wings. His pale-blue eyes are set close together, and he speaks in a high, rasping voice which sounds incongruous emanating from such a tall man. He looked like a large, scraggy bird as he stalked around armed with a magnifying glass to search our clothing for spots.

Watching him, Eva was so delighted that she almost burst out laughing. I could tell by her gleeful expression that she had already made up a nickname for him. She was a little startled when I asked her what it was, but readily admitted to the misdemeanor. After all, it was she who had compared Dr. Landau to a miniature bulldog and Horowitz to a porcupine.

And who is to say that whooping crane does not fit Dr. Vogel perfectly?

*Thursday, October 26, 1939.* I can no longer put off writing about Eva and Klein.

It seems that Goldmann was right about them. If anything, he understated rather than exaggerated the case. He made it sound as though Klein were the aggressor while Eva was the inactive, though willing, bystander. Actually she keeps provoking Klein.

With my inbred naïveté I refused to believe my own eyes at first. Moreover, I felt rather ridiculous as I sat in the Centro, watching Eva and Klein from behind my newspaper like some third-rate detective. But after a few nights of spying I found that there was already a fixed pattern to their meetings.

Eva and Trude would usually come to the Centro after dinner, around eight o'clock. Walter would deposit them at a table and then retire to his calling in the card room. The girls would sit alone until ten o'clock, when Halpern would slip out of his waiter's jacket to join them. A few minutes later Herr Klein would suddenly materialize out of nowhere, feign surprise at discovering his friend sitting with Trude and Eva, and join them at their table.

I never sat close enough to hear what the four were talking about— a lot of nonsense no doubt to gather from their giggling—but I could plainly see how Eva smiled at Klein, holding his gaze with a teasing, secret intimacy. In his consternation he kept taking off his glasses to polish them with fierce ardor. Without his glasses his face looked naked and vulnerable, and in spite of his light eyes the resemblance to Aronoff became more marked.

A dismaying suspicion began to dawn on me: the longer I looked at Klein the more certain I became that Eva's interest in him was mostly misdirected interest in his cousin. She seemed to be willing to settle for second best. If she could not have Aronoff she would take Klein. And there was no doubt that she could have Klein. Whereas Aronoff had ignored her, she would only have to snap her fingers and his cousin would jump.

I was shocked by the thought that, though Eva never went near a card table, she was really gambling for higher stakes than any of the people inside the card room. For how long could these secret games of smiling at each other, the accidental touching of hands, and collision of knees under the table go on without coming to a head? If Klein was a normal young man he would sooner or later want to come to a normal conclusion.

What bothered me most was that Walter had no inkling of what went on between Klein and his wife. Oblivious of the danger to Eva, he kept whiling away his evenings at the poker table. Several times I found myself on the verge of speaking to him. I would drop in at the card room, where he was sitting in the peculiarly disheveled attire which card players attain late at night. While he furiously shuffled and dealt, I would carry on an imaginary conversation with him. I would tell him not to be a fool; not to risk the possession of his wife for what little he stood to win at the poker table; to compare her attractions to the attractions of the unshaven Grushka, Dubrovsky, *et al.*

I tried to suggest these thoughts to Walter with all my might, but he is a poor medium. Or perhaps he has no reason to worry and I am really the one who is seeing ghosts. Perhaps I am only jealous because, instead of picking me, Eva picked a boy more suitable in age for her harmless flirtations.

*Monday, October 30, 1939.*    This afternoon Goldmann called me downstairs to inspect the new batch of merchandise which he had brought home from Levy. Out of courtesy he wants to make me feel an active partner in the business.

Levy has really overextended himself this time, possibly in a last effort to impress Trude. There were bolts of fabric stacked against one wall of the "factory," boxes with stockings and men's shirts against the other. Frau Goldmann's working area is shrinking continually, and Frau Gruen's bed (the forgotten member of the family still sleeps in the factory) is almost buried under a heap of merchandise.

The accumulation of goods in which I am a partner gave me a fleeting sense of wealth. This in spite of Frau Gruen perching on the bed, blinking her eyes like a night owl aroused in the middle of the day.

*Thursday, November 2, 1939.*    Goldmann, never one to rest upon his accomplishments, has taken it out of my hands to warn Walter about Eva and Klein.

It happened last night in the Centro. A club meeting was scheduled in the large assembly room for nine o'clock. The main purpose was to draw up a joint petition to the Jefe de Inmigración, Señor Moran, requesting permission for new immigrants to engage in businesses other than industry and agriculture. It was an important meeting and I had been warned to attend "even if your friend, Herr Blumenthal, does not honor us with his presence." (Josef really serves as a figurehead rather than an active president of the Centro.)

I arrived at the Centro with the best intentions of sitting in on the meeting, but when I saw Dr. Lipschitz entering the assembly hall with a sheaf of pages in his hand and an orator's gleam in his eye I thought better of it and hastily excused myself on the transparent grounds of a splitting headache.

The next hour and a half I spent browsing through a newspaper in the adjacent room, while I listened with guilty relief to the monotonous, endless gargling of Dr. Lipschitz' voice floating out through the open door. Luckily, the acoustics were such that I could not understand his words and therefore was not turned into a captive audience against my will.

Trude and Eva were sitting at their customary table, close by the window. By the time the meeting was over and the members came filing out of the assembly hall, shouting back and forth like children who had just been dismissed from school, Halpern and Klein had already joined the girls by the table. Trude, who apparently had not known that her father was in the Centro, looked surprised and flushed when she saw him come through the door with Levy. But instead of approaching her, as Trude had anticipated, Goldmann steered Levy toward the far end of the room and maneuvered him into a chair with his back to Trude. Goldmann himself sat down without a second look at his daughter, pretending to ignore her.

After about ten minutes which must have seemed an eternity to Trude

—she fidgeted in her chair and looked unhappy—Levy got up and left. Goldmann came over and sat down by the table with me.

"Look at her," he said, glowering at his daughter. "Sitting there with her waiter! A girl shouldn't have a little pride! And Eva also ought to have more sense than to play footsy with Klein right in front of everybody."

Goldmann was observing the girls through the distorting lens of suspicion, for at the moment they could not have acted more decorously. They sat rigid, barely talking, with the alertness of birds who know themselves watched by a cat.

"I ought to speak to Walter, that's what I ought to do," Goldmann mused. "Yes, I guess I will speak to Walter!"

"Herr Goldmann, do you realize that this is none of your business?" I said mildly enough so as not to dissuade him.

"None of my business! Why, Eva is practically a child! I couldn't feel more responsible for her if she were my own daughter."

Just then Walter came through on his way to the card room. He stopped by Eva's table, spoke a few words with her, benignly patted her head, and continued on his inevitable course. When he passed our table Goldmann reached out and grabbed his coat. Walter looked back, plainly annoyed at having been delayed.

"Yes, Herr Goldmann, what is it?"

"I would like to have just one word with you, Walter," Goldmann began with a winning smile. "It's about Eva . . ."

"What about Eva?"

"Well, I think it's not wise for you to play cards every night . . ."

"Now see here, Herr Goldmann . . ."

"What I mean is, how does it look, she sitting here every night with a young man until all hours while you play cards? You know what I mean . . ."

"No, I don't," Walter said.

"Well, what are people going to say . . ."

"Has anybody been making remarks?" Walter's face had grown a trifle alarmed.

"No, not yet," Goldmann said quickly. "But you know how people talk right away even if there's nothing behind it."

Walter looked thoughtfully at the table where his wife sat with Trude and the two young men. When he spoke to Goldmann, his voice was beginning to sound irritated.

"Now look here, Herr Goldmann, my wife isn't sitting there alone with a young man. She's sitting with your daughter and her boy friend, and I don't see how anybody can find fault with that!"

"If Eva wasn't sitting there, Trude wouldn't be either!" Goldmann shouted.

Without knowing it, he had laid bare what was behind his concern for Eva's virtue.

Walter caught on to his transparent maneuver.

"Look, Herr Goldmann, if you don't want your daughter to go out with Eva, you tell her so. But leave my wife out of your intrigues!"

Walter brushed off Goldmann's hand, which still clung to his coat, and proceeded toward his original destination. At the door of the card room he stopped and glanced back at Eva. For a moment he seemed to vacillate, then he shrugged and disappeared through the door.

"Just try to do a man a good turn," Goldmann mumbled with bitter piousness. "You mark my word, Walter will still be sorry for not listening to me! Well, no use sitting around any longer. The countess won't come home with me anyway."

Looking grim, Goldmann finally stomped out in defeat. All he had accomplished was to irk Walter.

But perhaps even this is more of an accomplishment than appears at first sight.


*Saturday, November 4, 1939.*    On his way out this morning Walter accosted me in the street, ostensibly to talk with me about politics (the United States has repealed its Neutrality Act and is now selling arms to England and France), actually to set me straight on what Goldmann had said about Eva and Klein.

I was walking to the tienda to purchase some rolls for Frau Kramer. Don was running behind me, carrying an old rag in his mouth and barking for my attention. He loves to pick up things from the gutter. The morning air was pure and scented with the smell of eucalyptus wafting down from the mountain slopes. It had been cold the previous night, and the peak of the Grampico wore a jaunty cap of snow.

I stopped when Walter called out to me, and for a while we stood discussing the news before Walter came out with what was on his mind.

"You don't really believe Goldmann's insinuations, Professor Bernstein? I mean, what he said about Eva. There's absolutely nothing to it. I asked her myself."

"You did!" I exclaimed, unable to hide my surprise.

"Why, sure," Walter said. "It seemed like the most reasonable thing to do. If there was anything going on between her and Klein, I would want her to know that I know and don't approve of it."

"And what did Eva say?"

"She just laughed! As a matter of fact, she was quite frank about the whole business. She said it was true that Klein had a crush on her, you know, the way a young boy would admire a married woman. Naturally she was flattered, but she did nothing to encourage him."

"She told you all that!"

"You know Eva, she's not one to beat around the bush," Walter called back cheerfully as he jumped on the passing bus.

This is bad. This is much worse than I had anticipated. Eva putting on the act of disarming frankness, telling Walter that Klein had a crush on her to forestall any ideas which Walter might get by himself.

I had done that myself ages ago. Always hinting that some of my students had a crush on me. Just in case—just in case I should ever be seen with Christine. (Only now am I beginning to wonder why I had to look for a subterfuge when I didn't much care what Alma thought of me. Misguided concern for her feelings, or rather fear of a scandal?)

But somehow such slyness seems out of character for Eva. It would have been much more like her to deny violently any accusations. And why are husbands always so blind that they are the last ones to realize what is going on?


*Tuesday, November 7, 1939.*    For the past few days the weather has been so bad that, except for the most urgent business, none of us has ventured out. It has been raining day and night, and even the mornings are gray and dripping. The clouds keep whirling around the mountains like steam rising out of a witch's caldron.

Eva and Trude sit alternately downstairs in the Goldmanns' sala or upstairs in Eva's room and sulk. I am grateful for Horowitz' presence in the house, though his preaching of the gospel of equality is beginning to get on my nerves.

Dr. Landau, who beat his way through the rain in order not to miss our twice-weekly session, has more patience with Horowitz, in spite of all the heckling to which he subjects him. Today, after he had silently listened to one of Horowitz' repetitious tirades on the merits of Communism, he simply said:

"Why don't you stop trying to convert us, Horowitz? This is much too dreary a day to talk about politics anyway. Can't we talk about something more cheerful? Women, for instance?"

So we did.


*Friday, November 10, 1939.*    It seems that the continuous bad weather and the mounting bad tempers had to reach a culmination in some sort of catastrophe.

At dinnertime Dr. Lipschitz and his wife came over, both white-faced and distraught. There had been an accident in the garage where they do their dry cleaning. Nobody had been injured, but under the financial circumstances they had suffered a crushing loss.

This is what happened:

The girl whom they had hired to do the coarse, manual cleaning had been washing a number of suits in benzine. When the rains began to come down particularly hard this afternoon, she had, in spite of repeated previous warnings, closed the garage door and built a fire in the corner to warm herself.

Inevitably, a spark had drifted across the garage and had set all the benzine-soaked suits ablaze. The girl had escaped unharmed and the fire was eventually put out, but the suits were damaged beyond repair and would have to be replaced. The question was, where would the money for this purpose come from?

The moment money was mentioned, Eva put on her most hostile expression.

"Don't look at Walter," she said to Frau Ruth, who was doing just that, "he hasn't got any money."

"Perhaps if you'd see to it that he didn't gamble it all away in the Centro, he might have some now to help us out," Frau Ruth countered with venom.

"I am the last person in the world to whom Walter would listen."

"Look, Ruth, all this bickering won't get you any money," Walter said tiredly. "You'll have to borrow it from someone else. Or perhaps you could sell something . . ."

"What could we sell?" Dr. Lipschitz asked, palms turned upward as if to show that he held nothing worth selling.

Frau Ruth's eyes had wandered to her mother's locked silver cabinet.

"Mama . . ." she said uncertainly.

A look of alarm spread over Frau Kramer's face and she went to stand before the cabinet, determined to fight off a hostile army if need be.

"We cannot sell the silver!" Herr Kramer cried, slamming his hand on the table and jumping up to make his point. "The silver is our last resort for an emergency!"

"This *is* an emergency!" Dr. Lipschitz wailed.

"I mean a serious emergency, like a sickness or an operation, God forbid. As Walter said, you'll have to get the money elsewhere. What about your partner?"

"He's liable for only half the loss. And he has no money either."

All this talk about borrowing money had reached a dangerous point, and I thought it best to steal unobtrusively out of the room. Once or twice Dr. Lipschitz had looked in my direction, and I did not like what went on in his mind. I tried to build up a good, protective resource of anger. What did all these people think? That I was a bank?

But apparently Dr. Lipschitz misconstrued the motive for my leaving. He seemed to think that I had only left to spare him the embarrassment of having to ask me for a loan in front of all the others. He followed me out of the room and shouted after me in a hoarse whisper:

"Could I talk to you for a minute, Herr Professor?"

What could I do? Refuse to listen to him?

"It's not so much I want," Dr. Lipschitz said in a wheedling tone. "Only three hundred pesos. Just enough to give each of the owners of the suits something to appease him. A hundred pesos for me, a hundred pesos from Dr. Vogel. It doesn't nearly cover the cost of a suit. And what are three hundred pesos to you?"

"You know I'd like to help, Dr. Lipschitz, but . . ."

"Of course I know you'd like to help! Believe me, I wouldn't ask you if I knew of any other possibility! You already did so much for us when you got us the visas."

Here he was, like Goldmann before him, trying to impress me with the obligation which arises out of saving people.

"Well, I don't know," I said. "Some of my money is tied up (by now everybody knows about my partnership with Goldmann), I'm not sure I can spare that much. Two hundred perhaps . . ."

"Anything, anything at all will help!" Dr. Lipschitz said, with the desperation of the mendicant.

"I'll have to get it out of the bank, though. Will tomorrow be all right?"

"Sure, sure, tomorrow will be fine."

I was shamed by the relief on his face when he returned to the room to tell, no doubt, of his success.

And why had I chiseled a hundred pesos off the amount he had asked from me? What difference did it make whether I let him have two hundred or three hundred pesos? Was I trying to play God, or what, if anything, was I trying to prove? That although I was not a philanthropist I wasn't a miser either?


*Monday, November 13, 1939.*    Today we received an answer from Señor Moran, the Jefe de Inmigración, concerning our petition for loosening business restrictions. The answer was passed on via Brody, the owner of the Jungle Café, who has his own mysterious connections with government officials.

Señor Moran let us know that, though it was, alas, not in his power to change the immigration laws, he was willing, for a nominal remuneration, to keep one eye shut; if necessary, both.

This has given rise to great hopes and much wild planning. Everybody wants to get into some sort of business, the majority into the line which until now has been the prerogative of the old immigration, namely, import. Levy, who does mainly legal business, seems unperturbed, but Grushka and Dubrovsky take a dim view of the new development. Walter says they anticipate a lot of competition and price cutting in the future. But they also hope that many of the new importers will fail because of their poor knowledge of the market. Not a very philanthropical attitude either.

*Thursday, November 16, 1939.*    The bad weather is definitely irritating. It affects even people whom I would have thought immune to such vicissitudes.

This evening Grushka appeared in the Centro for his nightly poker game, wearing dark glasses. He said he was suffering from eyestrain and did not remove them until late at night, when he absent-mindedly took them off to rub his eyes. It became apparent then that he sported what is generally referred to as a beautiful shiner. When he noticed that everybody was looking at him with interest, he quickly put the glasses on again.

"An accident," he explained, without anybody's having asked him. "I walked into a door."

We all wondered at what odd angle. Of course nobody believes Grushka's explanation, and the wild guesses range from his having had a fight with his partner to his having been hit by his mistress. No doubt the truth will come out sooner or later. In the long run nothing ever remains concealed in Esperanza.

*Saturday, November 18, 1939.*    By now we know the origin of Grushka's black eye, which still harmonizes beautifully with his black beard. It was administered by none other than young Aronoff.

As is frequently the case, I have the story at second hand, from Fleischer, who claims he was present in the Jungle Café, where the argument between Grushka and Aronoff is said to have taken place. But Fleischer's reports are never one hundred per cent reliable. This is what he told me:

The fight took place Wednesday afternoon. It was pouring hard outside and the Jungle Café was virtually deserted except for a few diehards, Grushka, Aronoff, and Fleischer among them. Fleischer says he was sitting alone, reading a newspaper and having a tinto, when Aronoff came in. Grushka and Dubrovsky were sitting in their customary booth, rolling dice. Fleischer smiled at Aronoff and motioned to him to join him. Aronoff shook his head and silently pointed at his bulging briefcase: he had work to do.

He sat down in another booth, ordered a tinto and spread his papers before him. Fleischer claims he could see Aronoff pick up some fabric samples, and then a single silk stocking as if he were appraising its color and quality.

Grushka and Co. had stopped rolling dice when Aronoff came in and had started whispering. Grushka kept sticking his head out of the booth to see what Aronoff was doing. When he saw him lift up the stocking he rose and walked over to the booth.

"You're not planning to import stockings?" Fleischer says Grushka said to Aronoff.

"Maybe I will, maybe I won't," Aronoff replied calmly. "That depends entirely on how much money there's in it."

"There won't be any money in it, believe me!" Grushka was getting excited. "There won't be any money in it because you won't bring in any stockings!"

"Well, I happen to have an import license," Aronoff said in a friendly tone. "It says on it that I can bring in a certain quota."

"I don't care what it says on your import license! I tell you you won't bring in any stockings!"

"Now, Grushka," Aronoff said (in Fleischer's words), smiling up at Grushka, "if I should want your valuable opinion on my business ventures I'll consult you. But I don't recall having consulted you now. As a matter of fact I'm busy. So why don't you go back to your booth and shoot craps?"

All this, Fleischer said, was delivered with beautifully studied insolence.

The effect was explosive: Grushka blew his top. He began to scream, addressing the practically empty room:

"You foreigners come here," Grushka shouted, using his fluent Spanish instead of the Yiddish, which he knew would be lost on Aronoff, "you foreigners come here and you think you can take our business away from us. We worked hard here, we gained the respect of the natives" (Fleischer says Aronoff laughed heartily at this point) "and you come with your doctor's titles and your education and you speak German and you mock our Yiddish and you make believe you can't understand, especially you, with your name, your father was a Russian Jew, you should be ashamed, but I'll show you! Not with me, you won't! I've been here over twenty years! I have my connections! You bring in stockings and I'll have you deported! I'm warning you, I'll have you deported!"

Fleischer says Aronoff stopped laughing and grew pale. "Come again," he said softly.

"Deported, you hear me, deported!" Grushka shrieked.

"Are you threatening me, Grushka?" Aronoff asked. He had put the stocking away and was very pale now.

"You bet I'm threatening you," Grushka said, faltering a little and backing away when he saw Aronoff rise slowly from the bench in his booth.

"Now look here, Grushka," Aronoff said, deliberately approaching Grushka, who all the time kept backing away from him, "I haven't come over five thousand miles to run into you! I don't happen to like gangsters whether they're Aryan or Jewish. As a matter of fact I dislike Jewish gangsters even more because they make me ashamed of myself."

Aronoff was clenching his fists as he advanced on Grushka.

"Don't you dare touch me!"

Grushka had backed all the way against the wall and was openly afraid now.

"Don't you dare touch me, I'm warning you. You're a nobody here. I know about your rich father. Maybe over there you had influence, you were a rich man's son . . ."

It was at this point that Aronoff struck him.

Fleischer says his arm just shot forward as if by an uncontrollable reflex, and he landed a beautiful blow on Grushka's eye. Grushka doubled over, clamping his hands over his face, and Dubrovsky in his booth squealed as though he had been hit.

Aronoff, Fleischer says, caught Grushka under the arms and propped him up on a chair. He wet a handkerchief in a glass of water and handed it to Grushka.

"I'm sorry I had to do that, Grushka. Especially since you're old enough to be my father," Aronoff said.

(This was adding insult to injury. Grushka is in his late thirties and prides himself on looking younger.)

Leaving his handkerchief with Grushka, Aronoff walked back to his booth and resumed his work. Grushka stumbled out of the Jungle Café, leaning on the shoulder of his partner. Fleischer says he heard him mumble under his breath that he would get Aronoff for this.

But of course Fleischer's reports are never to be trusted.

*Tuesday, November 21, 1939.*　　Aronoff has confirmed Fleischer's story.

"Aren't you afraid of Grushka's retaliation?" I asked him when I spoke to him today in the Centro. "You know he does have connections here."

"So have I," Aronoff said, making the age-old gesture of counting money. "How do you think I got an import license?"

"There's something else I want you to know, Herr Aronoff," I said. "Some people haven't taken it kindly that you beat up a Jew."

"Hah!" Aronoff threw his head back in a mirthful imitation of laughter. "In the first place, I didn't beat up Grushka. If I had, he would still be in the hospital. In the second place, I don't see what his being Jewish has to do with our private differences. The man is a gangster. He threatened me. There's no point in arguing with that kind of people. The only language they understand is physical violence. All those men who go around threatening others are really cowards. Touch them once and they cry like babies. Anyway, I didn't strike Grushka until he drew my father into the argument."

"And why should that have upset you so? Surely you must have heard similar remarks before."

"Exactly! Please, don't misunderstand me. I have the greatest respect for the achievements of my father. He came to Vienna a Russian prisoner of war without any money, and what he has he built up himself. Unfortunately, he's still sitting there, guarding it like a fool. But I never had to fall back on my father for what I wanted. I won my collection of sports trophies. My father didn't buy them for me. The same goes for women; I never paid, in any form. The same is going to hold for business. I just don't like any cracks about my rich father, not from Grushka or anyone else."

I took the hint and stopped talking about the incident. But I cannot help thinking that with all his endowments Aronoff could do with a little sense of humor. He is taking himself far too seriously. But then he is perhaps too young to have found out that man, even at his best, is a rather ridiculous creature.


*Saturday, November 25, 1939.*   Yesterday evening we had dinner at the Brauns'. Hans had invited his boss, Dr. Zwingli, director of the Panamerican Oil Company in El Paramo, a charming, cultivated Swiss gentleman, and his wife. We talked about music, painting, literature; very little about politics. It seemed like old times.

Later, over a cordial in the sala, we discussed the future of the Panamerican Oil Company in El Paramo. Hans said he was due to leave on another prospecting trip in a fortnight.

"We know there's more oil there! If we could just get at it!"

Dr. Zwingli explained what a boon it would be to the economy of El Paramo if a really rich strike of oil could be made in the jungle. The trouble was that most locations were simply inaccessible.

"You ought to go along with Dr. Braun some day, Professor Bernstein," he said to me. "It's a trip you'll never forget. Of course it might be too strenuous for you just now since most of the trip has to be made on muleback. But we're building a road past Aguas Calientes now and we ordered prefabricated huts from the United States for setting up a camp in the jungle. It might take us a couple of years though before we're done. You know the speed with which work is accomplished here. Once we've finished you'll be welcome to visit the camp as a guest of the company. And the same goes for you, madam," he said with a grave bow in Eva's direction.

"Why, thank you, I'll be looking forward to it," Eva said archly. "Of course two years is such a long time!"

Dr. Zwingli looked at me and we smiled at each other with the sad knowledge of age.

"Is it really?" he said.


*Tuesday, November 28, 1939.*   I am writing this before a business conference Goldmann and I are to have with Levy. Something terrible has happened. Last night our entire merchandise was stolen from Goldmann's factory.

The theft was not discovered until this morning, when Frau Goldmann came into the room to wake her sister-in-law. I should have known that something was wrong when I heard Frau Goldmann's piercing shriek all the way up to the second floor. But I still remembered her encounter with the mouse aboard ship, and I assumed that one had wandered in from the garden and had surprised Frau Goldmann in her kitchen.

Five minutes later Goldmann came upstairs, white to his shaven skull.

"We're ruined," he moaned. "We might as well kill ourselves! We're ruined!"

Since I still did not know about the theft, I jumped to the first conclusion which came to my mind: Trude had told her parents that she was pregnant and that Halpern would not marry her.

"Calm yourself, Herr Goldmann! It can't be as bad as all that. There are worse things in life . . ."

"Worse things! Everything is lost! Every last piece of goods is gone, I'm telling you! You should be tearing your hair instead of mouthing platitudes to me!"

Though Goldmann had still not told me what had happened, the truth suddenly hit me like an unexpected blow of the fist. For why should I be tearing my hair if the stolen goods he had mentioned were not our goods, the merchandise Levy had so generously sold us on ninety-day credit?

Immediately I was seized by the numbness which overcomes me in every crisis; the unwillingness to tackle reality.

"Don't make silly jokes, Herr Goldmann, this isn't April Fools' Day," I said weakly.

"Jokes, jokes!" Goldmann shrieked in a desperate falsetto, clawing at his bald head and baring his row of broken front teeth. "Come downstairs if you think I'm joking and have a good laugh yourself!"

This was a command rather than an invitation, and though the last thing in the world I wanted was to convince myself that Goldmann had told the truth I had to follow him downstairs and accept my share of the misfortune.

In the Goldmann apartment the mood had already changed from the desperately hysterical to the macabre. Frau Goldmann sat slumped in a chair, for once too stricken to assuage her mind with feverish work. Trude stood by the window, with her back toward the room. She did not turn around when we came in. Frau Gruen was nowhere to be seen. Presumably she was perching on her roost in the factory, staring with unseeing eyes at the empty room.

The thought of Frau Gruen brought a question to my mind: since she slept in the factory, how was it possible that all the merchandise should have been stolen without her hearing anything? But before I could ask him, Goldmann said harshly:

"You wanted to laugh? Come on, laugh!"

He escorted me to the factory, grim-faced, like a guard leading a prisoner to his doom. Pushing the door open, he stood behind me to cut off any attempt at retreat.

"Here, take a look!"

Just as I had imagined, Frau Gruen was crouching on her bed. She smiled vacantly when she saw me, but she seemed frightened. Except for the bed on which she sat and Frau Goldmann's sewing machine, which mercifully had proved too heavy for removal, the room was bare. Gone were the stacks of boxes containing men's shirts and ladies' stockings; gone were the bolts of goods, the cheap handbags, the crude sweaters; gone were Frau Goldmann's gowns and slips, finished and unfinished.

"Why, they even took the scissors and threads!" Goldmann exclaimed.

Gazing about me for a minute or so, I felt nothing but the sensation of absolute numbness and some amazement that this terrible loss should affect *me*. But I knew that I was expected to show some proof of feeling stricken and I muttered:

"How horrible. How horrible."

I stepped back and Goldmann slammed the door viciously. Silently, like mourners in a funeral procession, we walked back to the living room. Frau Goldmann still sat hunched in her chair and Trude was still staring out the window.

"But how was all this possible with Frau Gruen sleeping in the room?" I finally asked.

"Because," Goldmann replied, gazing ominously at the back of his daughter, "she *wasn't* sleeping in her room! And why wasn't she sleeping in her room? Because she was listening to the radio in the living room! And why was she listening to the radio? Because Else and I were not at home! And why weren't we home? Because we have to run after our daughter, the princess, to keep her out of mischief!"

While Goldmann was asking all those questions and supplying his own answers, as if he were conducting a weirdly rearranged Seder, the memory of the night before came back to me. I had indeed been surprised to see Frau Goldmann in the Centro; Frau Goldmann, who during the day usually was too busy to leave the house and at night was too tired or too concerned with saving money to frequent any place of entertainment—even one so humble as the restaurant of the Centro. And I also remembered that this morning at the breakfast table Frau Kramer had complained about the noise the radio had made downstairs the night before "so loud you could not hear yourself think" (nor, for that matter, hear anybody getting in through the window and carrying off all our merchandise).

I could only surmise why Frau Goldmann had gone to the Centro. She had once complained to me that Trude refused to bring Halpern home and that she had never seen the young man. Perhaps Frau Goldmann had wanted to find out for herself what brilliant qualities Halpern had to make Trude favor him over a catch like Levy. I could also see that both Herr and Frau Goldmann were indirectly blaming Trude for the loss of the merchandise.

"You bring a child into the world," Herr Goldmann said, in his anxiety usurping the act which is the prerogative of the mother, "you feed it, you clothe it, you nurse it through sicknesses, you make sacrifices to give it a good education, but the moment *you* need something it turns its back on you!"

Enumerating all the reasons why Trude ought to be beholden, Goldmann seemed to resume a conversation which had begun before I came downstairs and had only been interrupted while he went to fetch me.

Trude, who up until now had stood mute, whirled around. Her eyes were red and her nose swollen, disfigured beyond its natural misshapenness. She screamed back at her father in a hysterical voice:

"What do you want me to do? Go throw myself at Herr Levy's feet? It isn't my fault that the merchandise was stolen!"

"If you had been where you should be at night and your mother and I had not had to go running after you . . ."

"Oh, leave me alone!" Trude cried, turning back to the window.

"You see what I mean." Goldmann spoke to me in a mournful voice. "All I ask her is to be civil to a business relation, and that's how she acts! I used to think she was smart. But she's stupid, I'm telling you, stupid! I explained to her what Herr Levy can do to me if I don't pay for his merchandise in ninety days: he can have me thrown in jail! Me and the Herr Professor here! And how am I ever going to make the money to pay Levy if he doesn't give me more merchandise to sell? Isn't that enough reason to be just a little civil to a man?"

(I must say this about Goldmann: even under the first shock of the loss he had already figured out a way to extricate himself from his predicament. I could imagine him explaining his point to Levy. What would Levy gain by having him—and me—thrown in jail? Was he Moses to get water out of a stone? On the other hand, if he gave Goldmann more merchandise, if he gave him a chance to make some money, Goldmann could always try to make good the loss. One could not blame Goldmann for feeling irked because Trude would do nothing to help along this ingenious plan.)

"I'm going into town now," Goldmann said. "I'm going to tell Herr Levy what happened and I'm going to ask him to have lunch with us. I want you to be here when he comes, Trude. And about tonight: if you dare leave the house, I'll come to the Centro and slap your face in front of everybody, so help me!"

"What are you trying to do!" Trude screamed. "Not enough that Aunt Paula is crazy, do you want to drive *me* crazy too?"

She stopped, her mouth agape, her lips quivering as he stared in the direction of the door. None of us had heard Frau Gruen come into the room. She stood there, blinking rapidly, like an animal that had crawled out of its cave into the sunlight. Had she heard—and had she understood—what Trude had said about her? She gave no sign of having heard anything.

"Can I help you in the kitchen, Else?" she asked humbly.

Frau Goldmann scrambled to her feet. "Yes, yes, I'd better start cooking if you want to bring Herr Levy along. Trude, I'll want you to get me a few things from the tienda."

"All right, Mama," Trude said dejectedly, and all three women left the room.

Goldmann looked very bitter.

"Women," he said. "They're born with their business and they sit on it. That's all they do: sit on it! But whenever there's a real crisis, who's got to drink the bitter portion? The man of the family! But I'll show them, my Fräulein daughter included. I'll get us out of this one too! By the way, you'll eat with us, Professor Bernstein. If we hang, we'll hang together."

No doubt we will. Not only financially, but also emotionally. Half the merchandise for whose loss Trude is being persecuted is mine.


*Wednesday, November 29, 1939.*    The luncheon with Levy went better than either Goldmann or I had expected. Levy agreed almost immediately to let Goldmann have another batch of merchandise. I doubt that his willingness to help us had anything to do with Trude, whom he treated with cool, impersonal courtesy all through the meal. As Goldmann pointed out to me, Levy is too shrewd a businessman to lose all rather than regain the loss at a small, additional risk. And possibly the sums involved, though huge to us, might appear small to Levy. With the stolen merchandise, which amounted to about eight hundred dollars' worth of goods, and what Levy is willing to give us now, we owe him nearly twelve hundred dollars. The sum of money this represents to either of us is relative to our fortunes: more than four times what I still have in the bank. And probably only a small fraction of what Levy owns.

For the moment we are safe from jail and starvation. And somehow a debt for which one is not pressed seems like an abstract obligation, something that exists on paper rather than in reality. This makes the humiliation through which Goldmann put Trude all the more absurd.

Still, he remained adamant and would not let her go to the Centro. She went to talk with Eva in the afternoon, and I could hear her wild sobbing all the way out into the corridor. Eva came to the kitchen to get Trude a glass of water.

"What a beast that Goldmann is," she said.

In the evening Eva sat alone by the table which both girls usually occupied. Halpern joined her after his work. She spoke to him and he looked despondent. After a while Klein sat down with them with his studied nonchalance. Halpern stayed for another ten minutes or so; then he rose and left, abandoning Eva and Klein to their own devices.

I watched them warily. Once or twice I was certain that I saw their hands touch. Perhaps they were secretly glad to be rid of Trude and Halpern. I would have joined them if Fleischer had not previously invited me to sit with him and the Schwarzkopfs. While I kept my eyes on Eva and Klein, I listened with half an ear to Frau Schwarzkopf telling the story of her life.

"Emigration," she said. "I was a refugee long before any of you even knew what it meant to leave his home. I lost my mother in the Revolution . . . the swine shot her . . . my father was rich . . . furniture factory, more than two hundred workers . . . ballet lessons . . . I was one of the youngest stars in the Imperial Russian Ballet . . ."

The last came through to me clearly, and I shot a quick glance at Frau Schwarzkopf, trying to guess her age. She must have been at least thirteen at the time of the Russian Revolution. That would make her about thirty-five now. She looked younger with her green, Slavic eyes, slanted and crinkled at the corners, and the upturned nose of a cat.

". . . we drove all night after they killed my mother . . . I was the oldest, I was holding the reins . . ."

As her voice drifted past my ear I thought drowsily how we love to gorge ourselves on stories of emigrations past and present. If one of us stopped speaking and the next one took up the narrative, you could hardly tell that there had been a change.

I went through the usual motions of attentive listening, nodding and mumbling while my interest remained with Eva. Suddenly I realized that I was not the only one watching her. Herr Schwarzkopf also kept staring at her. As once before, I was repulsed by the naked desire in his eyes.

"I don't know what sort of man this Kramer is," he said when he saw me looking at him. "I wouldn't allow my wife to sit alone with another man night after night. Such a beautiful woman too!"

I thought Schwarzkopf's concern for Eva's virtue touching, especially since he was stripping her with his eyes. But perhaps I was too hard on him. Wasn't I also angry with Walter for exposing Eva to temptation? If he did not want to keep her pure for himself, he ought at least to keep her pure for me—and Schwarzkopf. What hypocrites we all are!

Still, I shall see whether I can't prevail upon Goldmann to let Trude go out again at night. I have come to the conclusion that it is Eva and not Trude who needs a chaperon.

*Friday, December 8, 1939.*     Last night was the first evening of Hanukkah. We all got together for a little informal celebration, and I used the opportunity to draw Goldmann aside and put in a word for Trude. But my pleading was to no avail.

"The only way she can leave the house at night is over my dead body," Goldmann declared dramatically.

This attitude is doubly idiotic because there is no doubt that Trude continues to see Halpern in the daytime. Goldmann simply cannot keep tabs on his daughter twenty-four hours a day. Besides, he has stepped up his trips into the provinces to three times a week in order to make good our debts to Levy. And though he has impressed upon Frau Goldmann the need for utter vigilance, how is she to know what Trude does on her marketing trips into town?

In the meantime, Eva is left to her daily tête-à-tête with Klein.

If Walter has not been suspicious until now, it is high time for him to take notice. Herr Schwarzkopf and I are no longer the only ones who realize what is going on. Fleischer, of course, has already made one of his apt little dirty remarks. And a couple of days ago Herr Kramer asked me if this young man who was sitting with his daughter-in-law was not supposed to be Trude's boy friend. I had to set him straight, pointing out Halpern, who was still waiting on tables at this late hour. Now that Trude no longer comes here, he willingly works overtime.

Herr Kramer watched Eva all evening, looking thoughtful and suspicious. But he did not say anything, and I wonder what goes on in his mind.

*Monday, December 11, 1939.* Another comment about Eva and Klein came from the least expected quarters. Yesterday evening Aronoff sat down at my table for a few minutes. He does that sometimes; out of courtesy perhaps, or perhaps because I knew his mother. Pointing with his chin in the direction of Eva and Klein, he crooked his full, sensuous mouth into an amused grin.

"Cousin Georgie's biting off more than he can chew," he said. "Getting involved with a married woman!"

"What do you mean 'getting involved'?" I asked with uncalled-for indignation.

"You don't think he's just sitting there to keep her company, Herr Professor?"

In the anger which he had aroused in me (and what had he done except called a spade a spade?) I tried to get back at him:

"Now don't tell me *you* have any moral scruples when it comes to courting a married woman?"

He threw back his head and laughed his short, peculiar laugh which he stifles the moment it escapes his lips.

"Not at all," he said. "I'm just more careful than George. I get involved only with happily married women."

"What?" I don't know whether I looked horrified or just dumfounded.

"Look, it's simple," Aronoff said patiently. "A happily married woman, preferably one who has children, doesn't want to leave her husband and her children to marry you. All she wants is a little fun, and that's fine with me. But take an unhappily married woman, and before you know it she'll be trying to badger you into marrying her. She's not out for fun; she's prowling for a new husband."

"And what makes you think that Frau Kramer is unhappily married?" I asked tartly.

He looked at me, his eyebrows slightly raised, as if he questioned my intelligence.

"Isn't it obvious? I understand the Kramers have been married a year or less. Still, he is always in there" (jerking his head in the direction of the card room) "while she is sitting out here with George. And even the few times I have seen them together they didn't strike me as deliriously happy . . ."

And I had always thought that Aronoff had not even noticed Eva!

At the moment I did not know whether I was most disturbed by his perception, his coldly calculating mind, or the fact that he was as near the truth as one could get without knowing Eva and Walter.

"Tell me, Herr Aronoff, how old are you?"

He seemed perplexed by the question and thought for a second as though he could not recall his age.

"Twenty-two," he said. "Why?"

"Oh, I just wondered."

He shrugged and shook his head, possibly thinking me a little queer, and then went to have a look into the card room.


*Thursday, December 14, 1939.*    Today Frau Goldmann provided a little comic relief with which we can all do once in a while.

"We are not safe here!" she wailed this morning. "If the Nazis can sail a ship right into the harbor of Montevideo, we are not safe here!"

"Don't be silly, Mama," Trude said indignantly. "Montevideo is almost as far from Esperanza as Paris is from Moscow."

Of course we are all excited about the sinking of the *Graf Spee,* but nobody has attached the same implications to it as Frau Goldmann.


*Friday, December 15, 1939.*    Yesterday Russia was expelled from the League of Nations because of the act of aggression against Finland. It

is all one big farce, and people here are beginning to get so disgusted
with the Russians that they don't even heckle Horowitz any longer.


*Tuesday, December 19, 1939.*    As part of the cycle of catastrophes
upon which we seem to have embarked, Walter has lost his job. He was
publicly fired in the card room of the Centro.

I only saw Walter when he came out of the card room, pale and
glassy-eyed with fury. He passed my table without seeing me, got his
coat and left. The rest of the report I have, as usual, from Fleischer, who
knows the details of every incident—even of those he never witnessed.
According to him, this is what happened:

Grushka, Dubrovsky, Walter, and Brody, the master of the Jungle
Café, were playing poker. Fleischer was kibitzing. After Grushka had
had a straight losing streak for about two hours, he excused himself and
went to the bathroom. When he returned he had a new pack of cards
with him. He insisted that they start playing with the new cards to
change his luck. Walter asked to have a look at the new pack in order
to ascertain that it had not been opened. Grushka refused, pointedly
asking Walter if he did not trust him. Walter said he was sure that the
other players also would like to inspect the pack—a request in which
they did not back him up. Nevertheless, he kept insisting.

"You don't think I marked the cards?" Grushka challenged Walter.

"I didn't say you marked the cards. All I said was that I wanted to look
at them. Of course I can't force you to show them to me. But if you
won't, I can't go on playing."

Walter picked up his money (he had been winning for a change) and
rose.

"You hear this," Grushka began in a dangerously low voice, addressing
the other players at the table and whoever was willing to listen in the
card room, "you hear this, he calls me a crook! I treat him like a brother,
I give him a chance to make a living, and he calls me a crook! All right!"
Grushka suddenly screamed, slamming the pack of cards down on the
table but cautiously keeping his hand cupped over it, Fleischer says, "all
right, if you think I'm a crook you don't have to work for me! I don't
have to take this from you or anybody else! You come here without a

penny in your pocket and you call me a crook! Go see if you can make a living off your fine doctor friends!"

Fleischer says Walter angrily stuffed the money into his pocket and turned to leave.

"I'll return whatever merchandise I still have, tomorrow," he said with a trembling voice.

"Return it, keep it!" Grushka cried, enraged beyond reason. "What do I care! Calling me a crook!"

It was after this exchange that I saw Walter coming out of the card room. He was followed by Fleischer, who came to spread the news. Personally, Fleischer said, he believed that Grushka had marked the cards. Why else should he have refused to show them to Walter?

*Friday, December 22, 1939.*    Some unexpected good has come out of Walter's quarrel with Grushka: Eva's idyl with young Klein has been terminated for the moment.

Walter has not been in the Centro for days. I don't think his absence is so much due to lack of money—he used to gamble even before he had his job—but rather to the desire to avoid his former boss. He might also feel embarrassed meeting the people who witnessed his firing.

Since Eva cannot very well go to the Centro alone at night, and Trude is still under house arrest, Eva has been unable to meet with Klein. As the Spanish saying goes: No hay mal que bien no venga. There's nothing so bad that it wouldn't bring some good.

*Monday, December 25, 1939.*    Whatever made me think that I could see through the wiles of young girls? I was sure that Eva had all but forgotten about young Klein. But yesterday I saw them strolling together in the street in broad daylight. Trude and Halpern were with them.

The girls had obviously been to the market, for two little Indian boys came trotting behind them with baskets loaded with purchases. They might have just run into Halpern and Klein, but their clothes belied an accidental meeting. Eva wore her favorite white dress, and Trude the pink silk which Frau Goldmann can never get her to wear when Levy comes to the house. Neither of the dresses seemed the proper attire for a trip to the market, confirming me in my suspicion that the meeting had been a carefully planned accident.

For my part, I would have hushed up the incident. Perhaps a hint to Eva that I had seen her—but why speculate? Unfortunately, Herr Kramer and Herr Goldmann also saw the girls.

We were riding the bus home after a casual morning get-together in the Jungle Café. In spite of the speed with which we passed, we could clearly see the young people as they walked along together, looking gay and animated.

"Just wait till I get my hands on Trude!" Goldmann threatened. "And your daughter-in-law too! She's the one who puts her up to it!" he said to Kramer.

"That's a lie," Herr Kramer said with his particular gift for diplomacy.

"Don't you call me a liar! Just ask Professor Bernstein if Eva hasn't been sitting with Klein night after night! If Walter were my son, I'd have a good talk with him!"

"You run your family, I'll run mine," Kramer said haughtily.

But I am sure that this time he will talk to Walter. Now I am doubly sorry that I did not speak to Walter myself. Herr Kramer, with his delicate way of putting things, can only cause discord.


*Tuesday, December 26, 1939.*     I am still trembling as I write this. The only reason I try to write at all is to keep my mind occupied until I hear Eva come in. She has to come in sooner or later.

I should never have left her alone out there in that dark, solitary place. But what could I do? She said she would hurl herself off the ledge if I did not go away!

Again I am trying to turn time back to a point when I could have warned Walter about Eva and Klein instead of letting Herr Kramer stir up a quarrel.

The quarrel started shortly after Walter had had his nightly chat with his parents. While I sat on the veranda with Frau Kramer, Herr Kramer called his son into the other room. I could hear his conspiratorial whispers without understanding what he said, and once or twice what sounded like an angry bark from Walter. Frau Kramer kept smiling at me innocently, but I am sure she knew what was going on. When Herr Kramer returned to the veranda without Walter, she did not ask where her son had gone.

A few minutes later the first loud words of the argument between Eva and Walter came through the closed door of their room. They had already worked themselves into a fury, for what I heard no longer sounded like the beginning of the quarrel.

"I won't have anybody tell me with whom to associate!" Eva shouted. "I'm a grown woman! I can talk with anybody I want to!"

"Talk!" Walter screamed back. "You had a date with him!"

"That's not true! We just ran into each other!"

"Really? All dressed up?"

"I always dress up! I don't believe in running around sloppy, like some other people in this house!"

Frau Kramer had been listening intently. Now she flushed, understanding against whom Eva's remark was directed. She had only recently criticized Eva's predilection for pretty clothes. But can an ugly woman ever understand the pleasures of Narcissus?

"I don't want you to speak to him again!" Walter shouted.

"While you were playing cards every night, he was good enough to keep me company. Now you don't want me to speak to him! I won't turn my friendships on and off at your convenience!"

"Eva, I'm warning you!"

At this point I excused myself and left the veranda with the feeble pretext that I wanted to do some reading in my room. The truth is that I was too embarrassed to go on listening to the argument in the presence of the Kramers. I don't know what was said between that moment and a little later, when Eva came bursting out of the room just after I had passed her door.

"I'm not staying one minute longer in this house!" she screamed. Her voice sounded choked as if she were on the brink of tears. She ran down the stairs and out of the house, leaving the front door open behind her.

Walter came out of his room and bent over the banister of the upstairs gallery. His face was white and he too seemed close to tears.

"Go to hell!" he shouted after Eva.

There was no reply, and we both stood for a few seconds listening for some sound from Eva. When it became clear that she had really run out into the night, I turned on Walter:

"Walter, you can't let her go out there alone! It's cold and dark, and she hasn't even got a coat on. What if it starts to rain? She can catch her death in this damp weather. She's hysterical, who knows what she'll do!"

"I don't care!" Walter screamed with the rage of one who does. He ran back into his room and slammed the door behind him.

I vacillated between reasoning with him and running after Eva. Finally I decided to follow her. While I was talking to Walter, she might have got too far away.

As soon as I realized her head start I went after her without first getting my coat. The air outside was damp and cold, but it had stopped raining. A caravan of ragged clouds was scurrying across the moon. In a moment of brightness I saw Eva running ahead of me at the end of the street.

I followed her, unable to diminish the distance between us and afraid to call out to her. Since I completely lose my sense of direction in the dark, I did not realize that we were heading for Irene Braun's house until we stood before it. Eva pushed open the garden gate and walked up to the house, while I remained hidden in the deep shadow of a garden wall. I felt relieved by the thought that she was only going to cry on Frau Irene's shoulder.

A moment later I saw Eva's silhouette outlined against the lighted window of the ground floor as she peered inside. Through the sheer curtains I could see a number of people moving about in the room. Frau Irene was having company. Eva stood outside the window, longingly gazing in with her mouth half open like a hungry child. Then she turned and walked back through the garden gate.

Again we resumed our wandering through the streets, Eva too deeply involved in her pain to notice that she was being followed. Her pace was slower now and I thought that she was heading toward home when she suddenly made a sharp turn to the left and began to walk faster again, as though toward some well-known destination. Some devil inside of me made my curiosity overpower my common sense so that, instead of stopping Eva, I cautiously kept on following her.

We climbed a steep street which led toward the woods. Soon there were no houses and the road narrowed and ran on between empty lots, squared off by adobe walls. In the end the street turned into a path, and I began to have serious qualms when I saw Eva disappear into the woods. But she never stopped to get her bearings, as though she had used this path before.

I kept behind her like a clumsy shadow. Once I was frightened when I made out the white pants and blouses of a group of Indians clustering by the side of the path. One of the men, dead drunk, was howling like a wounded animal. The women were looking after Eva and giggling. For a while I could hear the tinkling of their cheap glass beads behind me.

The road had become steeper and I could feel my breath hurt in my chest. I could not have called out to Eva now even if I wanted to.

Suddenly the woods ended and we stepped out on a clearing. The moon had come out full, and in spite of the pain in my chest I felt entranced by what I saw. In the luminous blue of the night stretched range after range of mountains—ranges which I had never known lay beyond the woods. Here and there a peak gleamed bluish with freshly fallen snow. I was so enthralled that I did not notice that Eva had gone dangerously near to where the clearing broke off into a deep abyss. When I saw her standing far out on a protruding cliff, my heart contracted with fright and I unthinkingly called out to her:

"Eva!"

She turned, and in the blue moonlight her face looked half hopeful, as if she thought that Walter had followed her after all.

"It's me, Professor Bernstein! Eva, come away from there!"

I slowly began approaching her, the way one might approach a shy, wild animal. She watched me warily and suddenly she screamed:

"Don't come near me! If you come one step nearer I'll . . . I'll throw myself off the cliff!"

"Eva, come with me," I pleaded. "Don't act like a silly child."

"What do you all want from me? Don't do this, don't do that! Don't go here, don't go there! Leave me alone! Leave me the hell alone! Go away, you hear me!"

She stamped her foot like a naughty child. I did not know what to do with her. Now that we had stopped walking, I was beginning to feel the cold, and the pain in my chest had become alarmingly strong. Suddenly I was frightened.

What was I doing here, a man of my age, climbing hills at this altitude in the stinging night air? Wasn't it Walter's job to look after his wife? Had I gone insane? Was the emigration affecting my mind the way Frau Goldmann claimed it affected the mind of her husband?

I realize only now that I was looking for an excuse to abandon Eva and run home. The pain in my chest was excruciating. I had become more frightened for myself than for her.

"Go on! Go home and leave me alone!" she screeched. Her voice sounded harsh and ugly, and I went.

I went back the way I had come, groping along in the dark, which seemed denser now that Eva was not leading me, stumbling over the ruts in the road, anxiously listening to the beating of my heart. The Indians were still sitting in the same spot, the drunken man howling as before. Now that I was alone the huddling group seemed sinister and I was afraid of them. I walked as fast as I dared in the dark until I reached home. The front door still stood open. I shut it, but opened it again, remembering that Eva had no keys.

As I climbed the stairs, half pulling myself up by the banister, I heard a door softly open and close. Walter must have looked out to see whether Eva was coming in.

Once in my room I threw myself on the bed. The beating of my heart abated slowly and the pain grew weaker. As I recovered, I was freshly assailed by my conscience for having abandoned Eva. I closed my eyes, but sleep would not come and I got up again and began to write.

My God, it is nearly midnight! What if something has happened to Eva! Those Indians were drunk. They are harmless people, but still . . . Was that the front door? Yes, thank God! I can hear her steps on the stairs. She must have gone to the bathroom. I can hear the water running.

I think I will be able to sleep now.

*Wednesday, December 27, 1939.* There is no better way to lose a friend than to surprise him in his moment of weakness.

Both Eva and Walter avoid me, as if I were to blame for their difficulties. Walter barely gave me a civil good morning today, and when Eva saw me on the terrace she recoiled as if I were an evil spirit.

Still, I took it for a good sign that she had recovered enough to want her daily sun bath, and I left in order to give her some privacy. As she spread her large towel on the concrete floor, I noticed that one of her wrists was bandaged. My conscience pricked me and I asked her if she had hurt herself.

"I sprained my wrist," she said sullenly.

What if she had broken a leg? She might have lain in the woods all night with nobody coming to her rescue!

Why does the imagination insist on piling troubles on those already existing?

*Monday, January 1, 1940.*     A new year has begun.

If I were suspicious enough to look for omens, I would say that it has not begun propitiously.

Last evening we were invited to the Brauns' for an informal New Year's Eve party. The crowd consisted mostly of younger people, the Fleischers and Schwarzkopfs among them. Herr Fleischer got so drunk that he ripped the strap of Eva's low-cut gown, which fell down to reveal most of her breast. Schwarzkopf made a big display of indignation but nearly choked on his own saliva.

Eva and Walter are still not on speaking terms, and even Frau Irene noticed that something was wrong. When she asked me what had happened, I told her that Eva and Walter just had the common troubles of newlyweds.

But do all newlyweds have such troubles?

*Wednesday, January 3, 1940.*     In our house one quarrel seems to beget another. At times I think that the entire layout of the house has been so conceived as to render any argument clearly audible.

Tonight it was Trude's turn to run away.

I came home early from the Centro, around ten o'clock. The rain was light and I had gone without an umbrella, but I had pulled down the brim of my hat over my eyes so that I did not see the figure huddled on the front steps until the last moment. My first guess was that Eva had stormed out in another tantrum. Therefore I was doubly surprised when I recognized Frau Gruen's voice.

"Good evening. More rain tonight," she said sensibly.

I could not have been more startled if one of the palm trees in the front yard had suddenly addressed me. I believe I even forgot to return the greeting.

"You're home early tonight," Frau Gruen said, adding with a note of apology in her voice: "Sometimes I hear you come in at night."

To hear Frau Gruen talk normally was an unsettling experience. I had never considered the possibility of having a conversation with her, and I was at a loss as to what to say. Finally I said lamely that she shouldn't be sitting out here in the rain.

"I can't go in," she said. "I can't listen to them harassing the poor child. If only my husband were alive, he would know what to do, how to help. But you go on in. You don't have to stand here, keeping me company."

I stepped around her and entered the hall. The shrill voices of Goldmann and Trude assaulted my ear the way pungent odors of cooking sometimes assault the nose as one walks into a house. I could see Trude through the sheer curtains of the large glass door which connects the Goldmanns' living room with the hall. She was wearing her coat.

"I tell you I'm going out!" Trude screamed.

"And I tell you you're staying home!" Goldmann outshouted her in his falsetto.

"You can't force me to stay home! I'm not a prisoner here!"

"I'll show you what I can do to you!" Goldmann took one menacing step forward, but that was as far as he went.

"All you can do is let me starve to death," Trude said with the defiance of one who knows herself safe from such a fate.

"If you leave this house tonight, I might do just that!"

"You'd be doing me a favor!" Trude screamed.

Her hand was on the doorknob, and I quickly scrambled up the stairs to keep her from seeing me. Bad enough that Walter and Eva are avoiding me, should I also jeopardize my friendly relations with the Goldmanns?

*Thursday, January 4, 1940.*    "Why does everything have to happen to us?"

Frau Goldmann's wail is still ringing in my ears.

This morning Frau Gruen did not appear at the breakfast table. When Frau Goldmann went looking for her, she found that her bed had not been slept in. There was no trace of her around the house and the garden, and even a search through the neighboring streets proved futile.

As soon as the news of Frau Gruen's disappearance spread to the second floor, I felt my familiar twinges of guilt. Shouldn't I have gone in and warned the Goldmanns when I found Frau Gruen sitting on the front stoop last night? But then it was Trude who had threatened to run away, not her aunt.

Why would the old woman want to do such a thing?

This is exactly what everybody is trying to figure out. Did she know what she was doing or did she just wander away and fail to find her way home?

I felt it my duty to tell the Goldmanns that I had seen Frau Gruen outside and that I was sorry not to have warned them earlier.

"Don't worry about it," Goldmann said glumly. "It's not your fault. *She* should have told us. *She* saw her too when she went out!"

She—Trude—sat hunched on the living-room sofa, a glazed expression on her face. Obviously she was too stunned to say anything in her own defense.

"It's all my fault, it's all my fault," she kept mumbling.

"Of course it's your fault, you stupid goose," Goldmann said viciously. "You should have known better than to walk away and leave her sitting there!"

Frau Goldmann suddenly raised her voice.

"Now stop accusing the child, Markus! All morning long you've been accusing her! How do you know it isn't your fault that Paula ran away? She heard you say often enough how hard it was to feed so many mouths."

"And what about you?" Goldmann said to his wife. "Haven't you often said she was driving you crazy too, right in front of her? If she could understand what I was saying, she could also understand you!"

They were tossing guilt back and forth like a ball, first each blaming the other, the next moment reversing themselves and each admitting himself the guilty one. They nearly had me claiming the fault for Frau Gruen's disappearance when Eva and Walter came downstairs.

As if their sight made Frau Goldmann doubly aware of her bereavement, she immediately burst into tears.

"Oh, Herr Walter, just what are we going to do?"

"That's what I came to talk to you about," Walter said. "You have to face this thing realistically. We all know that Frau Gruen is in no condition to find her way home alone. We'll have to depend on somebody to bring her home."

"But how, how?" Goldmann asked.

"Well," Walter said slowly, "I thought you might put a notice in the newspaper with her description and the offer of a reward to whoever brought her back."

"Yes, yes, reward," Goldmann repeated vacantly, as if this were a foreign word which he was hearing for the first time.

Frau Goldmann, in spite of her histrionics always the one more willing to tackle reality, exclaimed:

"But where are we going to get the money for a reward!" And then, looking half hopefully at Walter: "Perhaps you could . . ."

Walter shook his head.

"No, no! Under the circumstances I would offer you my last peso, but I'm hard pressed myself. In fact I don't know where this month's rent is going to come from."

Everybody was looking at me now. I felt the tight knot in my stomach which always forms there when people talk of their need for money and look at me. Not this time, I thought. Not a penny more to Goldmann. Hadn't I lost enough with him? And what about the money Dr. Lipschitz still owed me? And why was Walter looking at me when he spoke of being unable to pay the rent?

Though I felt contemptible, I did not make the offer which everybody seemed to be expecting of me. Suppose I should need help tomorrow, who would look out for me?

Trude, who had sat silent, suddenly spoke up:

"I'll get the money."

"You, Trudi? Where would you get the money?" Frau Goldmann

asked. And then, horrified: "You wouldn't do anything . . . foolish!"

"Oh, Mama, who would pay *me?*" Trude said in a tired voice. "Don't worry, I'll get the money in a nice, decent manner. You'll be sure to approve. How much do you think we ought to offer, Walter?"

"Two, three hundred pesos perhaps?"

"Trudi, I insist . . ." Frau Goldmann said.

"Think, Mama. Who's the only person in Esperanza who would lend me money?"

"Herr Levy?" Frau Goldmann suggested, not quite believing.

"Yes, Herr Levy."

Eva was even more surprised than Frau Goldmann. She quickly glanced from Trude to me as if to say: Now what have you done! If Levy lent Trude the money, there would be strings attached. Eva's accusing glance forced me into action.

"Trude, perhaps I . . ." I began.

"No, Professor Bernstein, my mind is made up. I'm going to ask Herr Levy for the money."

Poor girl, she must have thought I was going to offer her the loan after all, when all I meant to say was that perhaps I could talk to Levy. This way she would not have to humiliate herself. Her insistence on speaking to Levy made me suspect that she wanted to do it as a sort of penance. I, with my varied guilt feelings, ought to be the first to understand her motives.

Goldmann forgot that he had berated Trude only a few minutes earlier and went to throw his arms around her. Trude impatiently squirmed out of his embrace and left the room without another word. Eva signaled that we too ought to leave. We walked up the stairs together. Eva looked grim and avoided my eyes.

"They're going to find Frau Gruen," I said in a weak attempt to break through her angry silence.

"I hope to God she comes back by herself," Eva said fiercely. This, of course, would mean that Trude need not accept the reward money from Levy.

Walter took an even dimmer view of the whole affair.

"Under normal circumstances, a woman like Frau Gruen would be in an institution. The Goldmanns will be lucky if they find her alive."

*Friday, January 5, 1940.*      Second day of waiting. Still no trace of Frau Gruen.

This morning the offer of a reward for her return appeared in the *Día*. Trude must have gone directly to Levy yesterday afternoon. He came to the house this morning and has been sitting with the Goldmanns ever since, like a member of the family. Perhaps Trude refused to accept the money before it was needed and Levy wants to be on hand when Frau Gruen is brought back.

The shocking part is that now the search for the old woman has turned into a treasure hunt. Everybody in Esperanza who can read a newspaper and can use three hundred pesos—and who cannot?—is out to find Frau Gruen. Half the population is in a holiday mood as they start out, laughing and jesting, to search for her in the woods and the ravines. Several callers even came to the house for more particulars about her.

Levy, with his fluent Spanish, handles all comers, while the Goldmanns and Trude sit in the sala in utter dejection. Everybody in the house and many of our outside acquaintances filed in and out of the Goldmanns' apartment. Frau Goldmann was too stricken to show any hospitality, but Horowitz threw open the doors of his room and served tea, though generally he hates having people track mud into his sanctuary.

Several times Eva came downstairs, her face screwed up in disgust.

"They all put on a tragic air, but deep inside they think of it as a circus," she said.

Whenever a new caller knocked, Trude started and stared at the door.

"Don't worry, Fräulein Trude, they're sure to find her," Levy consoled her.

"Perhaps she's dead."

I thought I detected a hopeful note in Trude's voice. But I might have been mistaken.


*Saturday, January 6, 1940.*      Afternoon of the third day. Still no news. This morning Josef came to call. He said he had personally spoken to the Jefe de Policía, and all carabineros had been alerted to be on the lookout for Frau Gruen. Privately he said to me:

"A very embarrassing incident. If they had a madwoman in the house, they should have kept her under better vigilance. Fortunately the natives here are gentle and nobody will harm her. But with the rain and the cold we've been having, it will be a miracle if they find her alive."

*Sunday, January 7, 1940.*   She is back! Frau Gruen is back!

Shortly before nightfall a small Indian shepherd boy brought her home. It was a strange procession: the Indian boy leading the way; behind him, holding on to his staff, Frau Gruen, filthy and bedraggled but following meekly; last the baaing, skipping herd of sheep.

Goldmann broke down and cried when he saw his sister.

"Paula, Paula, where have you been? Why did you do this to us?"

Frau Gruen looked bewildered at her brother crying and at all the people milling about the house.

"I had to talk to Aaron because of the money," she said.

When Levy heard the word "money" and the name "Aaron," he looked around nervously and whispered to Frau Goldmann:

"Who is this Aaron?"

"Her husband," Frau Goldmann whispered back. "He's been dead for over twenty years." Then she raised her voice: "Paula, aren't you hungry, Paula? You haven't eaten in three days!"

Frau Gruen blinked her eyes and shook her head.

"Aaron took me to a restaurant," she said. "A lovely place in the Stadtpark. All the trees were in bloom and it smelled good. But then it started to rain and I got wet. See how wet I am?" she said, pointing to her bedraggled clothes as if to prove that she was not lying.

Frau Goldmann sniffled and quickly led her sister-in-law out of the room. Trude put her head on the table and cried soundlessly. Levy shyly patted her hair.

"It's all right, Fräulein Trude. It's all right. She's home now."

The little Indian, who stood in the door looking about him with wide eyes, turned to leave.

"Wait, wait!" Levy called, running after him. He pulled a few bills out of his pocket and pressed them into the hand of the boy. The little

Indian looked stunned, obviously at a loss to understand what the money was for. When he spoke to Levy, it first became clear why he had brought Frau Gruen home.

He knew all the people in our house, for he sometimes grazed his sheep in our street. This morning he had recognized "la señora vieja" lying in a quebrada adjacent to the meadow where he had driven his sheep. He had thought she was lost and had led her back. No, he had not read about the reward in the newspaper. He could not read.

As he spoke, Trude raised her tear-stained face from the table. The corners of her mouth began to twitch; she smirked and then she began to laugh like a madwoman. Levy ran back to her and put his hand on her shoulder.

Eva, who had also jumped to Trude's side when she started her fit of laughter, slapped his hand viciously. He drew it back, too perplexed to say anything.

"Leave her alone!" Eva shouted. "Can't you see she's hysterical? It's just been too much for her. This whole miserable thing has been too much for her!"


*Wednesday, January 10, 1940.*    After all the excitement in our house, the last few days seemed eerily quiet. Nobody argued. Nobody screamed, ran away, or disappeared.

Frau Gruen has again retired to her perch in the factory, oblivious of all the heartache she caused. Trude stays at home all the time and Levy is a daily caller. Sort of an ambulant boarder, Horowitz says. Just that he does not sleep over—yet.

Eva and Walter are on better terms again. They even went to the Centro a few times. Walter stayed out of the card room and Eva kept away from her former friends, except for a brief talk with Halpern. After she had spoken with him, he remained sitting by his table with the pinched, long-nosed look of a dejected greyhound. His pimples stood out red on his pallid skin. Later Klein came and tried to cheer up his friend, throwing surreptitious glances at Eva, who had gone back to sit with Walter. Eva tried to keep her face averted, but once or twice she darted Klein a quick look, belying her feigned disinterest.

Thus on the surface everything appears normal, except for one slight deviation: instead of taking her daily sun bath, Eva now goes for a long walk with Don every morning.

*Saturday, January 13, 1940.*   Eva has trained Don to become a retriever. Now he goes after everything that moves: unsuspecting chickens and pigs, or sticks and stones hurled for his entertainment. Today he raced after a whirling piece of white paper and brought it back, placing it at my feet. I picked it up, ready to toss it away again, when my eye was caught by part of a verse written in German:

> They say to us these are no times for love
> They speak to us of more important matters

The rest was torn off, as if the page had been ripped to pieces. I could see that Trude was destroying her poetry. They say to us. I hope she does not think of me as one of "them." There is always a time to love.

*Tuesday, January 16, 1940.*   Walter has approached me for a loan. I had been fearing this for a while now, but I did not see how I could turn him down. Especially since he was sly enough to frame his request as an advance payment on the rent I am paying him. I made only a feeble attempt to fend him off.

"And what about next month, Walter?"

"Look, Herr Professor, I've got enough worries for now. Next month I'll think about next month."

I was reminded of what Arthur once said about Walter Kramer: he hates to plan ahead; he confuses living haphazardly with living adventurously.

*Friday, January 19, 1940.*   An unexpected stroke of luck: as I was about to approach Josef on Walter's behalf, Josef himself broached the subject.

"I understand Walter has stopped working for those two crooks," he said to me.

(He always speaks of Grushka and Dubrovsky as "those two crooks," as if this were their registered firm name.)

"Yes, Walter has been out of work for over a month now."

"Listen, Norman, I don't have to beat about the bush with you. Architect Carillo has asked me again if I know a reliable gringo for him. He's willing to pay 350 pesos a month now. I don't know why I should be doing this for Walter. God knows he didn't appreciate the offer the last time! But perhaps he'll have more sense now."

We talked for a while about Walter's failure to make use of his training.

"I know what's wrong with him," Josef said. "Lack of confidence in himself. He would rather fail at an odd job than in his chosen profession. What cowards these young people are nowadays!"

But soon our conversation veered from Walter to the usual topics: politics, the weather, and our health.

I remarked that Josef had lost some of his ruddy color. He also looked thinner.

Josef said it was his liver: sooner or later everybody in Esperanza got liver trouble. Something to do with the food. He showed me some pills which the doctor had prescribed for him. I asked if they helped.

He shrugged. "I take them to calm my conscience."


*Tuesday, January 23, 1940.*     Walter has accepted the new job, though not with the enthusiasm I had expected.

"What are 350 pesos a month?" he said.

"More than nothing," Eva retorted.

Whenever money matters are being discussed, she shows her most shrewish side. Somehow it seems incongruous that a young, beautiful creature like Eva should be at all concerned with money. I wonder whether she could be happy with a rich husband, one who could shelter her from all care? But I doubt that pecuniary security would be enough for her.


*Saturday, January 27, 1940.*     I have noticed a business upswing in our community.

First, there is Walter's steady job. Now that he has actually begun to work he seems much happier than during the past months. His hours are regular, from nine to one and from two to six, and if he does not get sidetracked into the Jungle Café he even comes home on time.

Dr. Lipschitz also brags about his expanding business, knocking on wood at the same time. He has ordered some noninflammable cleaning fluid from the United States and has hired a second muchacha to help with the cleaning. His only complaint: what did he need Dr. Vogel for?

Our string of importers is getting longer every day. In addition to the old guard, Walter's former bosses and Levy, we have Aronoff, recently Klein (either because he promises himself great profits or to emulate his envied cousin), Fleischer, who brings in American dresses and costume jewelry for his wife's fashion salon, and none other than the voice of the proletariat, Leo Horowitz.

Horowitz first mentioned the project at our last tea party.

"I'll stick to merchandise I know: men's wear," he said, adding as an afterthought: "Better men's wear. Who knows, perhaps I'll even open a little store, Señor Moran permitting."

"Better men's wear," Dr. Landau mused aloud, and I could tell by the glint in his eye that he had a barb up his sleeve. "Nothing but the finest for the proletariat. I suppose your stuff will be quite expensive, Horowitz?"

"I wouldn't count on you for a customer," Horowitz parried. "The kind of necktie you're wearing I would be ashamed to use for a floor rag."

Dr. Landau squinted down at his necktie. It was of a nondescript color, a gray that had gone green with age, frayed at the knot and decorated with a few stains.

"I've had this tie for close to twenty years," Dr. Landau said with wry dignity. "Longer than some men keep their wives. I'm very fond of it."

Even if he were not as wealthy as Horowitz claims he is, Dr. Landau could well afford to buy a new necktie. His business too has improved. After it became known that he had delivered Frau Braun's baby, he began to receive what he called "invitations." People would invite him to spend the day in their homes, have lunch and dinner with them, and while he was there submit to a casual examination. Was it a crime to consult a doctor who happened to be one's house guest? Since he had not been called for a visit and was not being paid, who could say that he was practicing medicine illegally?

Although all these transactions appear to be on the basis of barter, there actually is money involved. Dr. Landau, who has moved into Frau Steinberg's pensión, has an arrangement with her under which he is refunded the money for the meals he skips. The more often he eats out the more he saves on his rent. But lately a few of his patients have insisted on paying rather than feeding him. It seems that not everybody can stomach Dr. Landau for a whole day just because he has to attend to a case of grippe.

Dr. Landau takes this ingratitude wistfully but stoically.

"Just wait till the young people start having babies! Then they'll want me around all the time."

This led us into speculations about all the likely prospects. The list was not too long, but Horowitz said that any day now Dr. Landau would be able to add Trude to his list of possible patients.

*Thursday, February 1, 1940.* Horowitz was right about Trude and Levy. At lunch today Goldmann announced the engagement of his daughter.

I had become suspicious right away when Frau Goldmann asked me to eat with them. And when I saw the table she had set I was sure of what was in store. This was not a table prepared for a business luncheon, although Frau Goldmann had tried to pass it off as such. Not with the yellow damask tablecloth, the crystal bowl filled with roses in the center of the table, the good, "saved" silver and china, nor the bottle of champagne which Herr Levy produced upon his arrival instead of the customary basket of flowers.

(Besides, Frau Goldmann had asked Horowitz if he would mind very much not to eat with them today.)

I kept wondering why I, of all the people in the house, had been asked to attend. Was this some kind of deferred punishment because I had failed to offer Trude the reward money for her lost aunt? Was it to make me feel responsible for this match and whatever the results of it might be?

As soon as we had sat down at the table, Goldmann relieved me of my doubts.

"Professor Bernstein," he began solemnly, clearing his throat as if he were too moved to speak, "since neither we nor Herr Levy have any family here and you have helped us in so many ways that you have become more than family to us, I want you to be the first one to hear about the engagement of our Trude to our much-esteemed Herr Levy."

Trude sat through the entire speech looking almost defiant, but she winced when her father swung into the last flourish. As for me, what could I say but that I was honored and flattered to have been invited for the occasion?

Herr Levy, in a dark-blue suit with natty white stripes, stood up, his homely face flushed with pleasure, and said:

"Please permit me to open the bottle of champagne so that we may all drink a toast to my lovely bride!"

Trude blushed and stared into her empty plate as if it contained some invisible formula on how to live through this embarrassing moment, while Herr Levy started on his struggle to uncork the bottle. The procedure was accompanied by all the customary mishaps, and when the long-expected pop was finally heard, some of the champagne gushed out and spilled on Trude's new, brown taffeta dress.

After Frau Goldmann had blotted Trude dry with a towel, assuring Levy with an agonized face that it "really didn't matter, just a few drops on this old dress," we finally got around to drinking the toast to Levy's lovely bride.

We had hardly set down our glasses when Frau Goldmann rushed out into the kitchen and began serving the meal. She had spared no expense and it was, to use a cliché, a meal fit for a king. Levy certainly seemed to feel like one, even if Trude did not appear proud as a queen.

I doubt that she said more than ten words during the entire meal, but she ate with voracious appetite. I noticed that she had gained back all the weight she had taken off during her brief love affair with Halpern, but aside from that she looked neat and scrubbed, with her hair set and a new pair of glasses attractively framed to soften the look of a homely spinster. I thought that if Levy kept telling her long enough how pretty she was she might in the end really become pretty.

Most of the talking during the meal was done by Levy, punctuated by appropriate interjections from Herr and Frau Goldmann. Business was good, thank God, better than ever before. The arrival of so many gringos had greatly contributed to the raising of the standard of living: the good people of Esperanza had had their eyes opened to all sorts of luxuries and were buying like crazy. The dollars brought into the country with the required landing money also had helped the economy.

Herr Goldmann said that he had also noticed a stronger urge to buy among his customers. Before long he would be able to pay off our debt to Herr Levy, and then, who knows, he might give up traveling and open a small store in Esperanza.

(This was news to me, and I suspected that Levy was behind the plan. How would it look, the father-in-law of the richest merchant in town peddling in the provinces?)

Between the soup and the meat course, Levy extracted a small box from his pocket and presented Trude with the most startlingly big diamond I have ever seen. This act would have been more appropriate with the toast, but in the excitement of uncorking the bottle Levy had clearly forgotten about it. The effect the stone had on the Goldmanns was effective despite the faux pas.

"My God!" Frau Goldmann gasped. "What a magnificent gem! What color, what fire, so put it on, Trudi, oh Herr Levy, oh, Isak . . ." and she ran around the table and kissed Levy as if she and not Trude had been the recipient of the ring.

"Very beautiful, must have cost a fortune," Goldmann said, motioning to Trude to show her appreciation.

Trude had put on the ring and was holding her hand at a distance to admire the fire of the stone. The ring looked very well on her long, tapered fingers. Gradually a glow rose to her face, as if the feeling of preciousness originating from the jewel had flooded her all over. She was discovering an unknown weakness in herself: a weakness for precious stones.

"Thank you," she said huskily. "Thank you very much. It is gorgeous."

I noticed that even in her surge of gratefulness she did not address

Levy by his first name, as if such a familiarity were still out of the question.

The rest of the meal passed much as had the first half, with Levy lauding his prosperity.

After we had finished the dessert, Frau Goldmann carefully removed the cookies from the crystal platter on which she had served them, dramatically raised the platter with both hands and, gathering us all in in one look, exclaimed:

"Here's to good luck!"

Then she smashed the platter to the floor, where it broke into many glittering pieces.

"Mama, your good platter!" Trude gasped.

"What is a platter compared to your happiness?" Frau Goldmann said, tears streaming down her face.

Did Frau Goldmann really believe that the evil spirits could be appeased by the sacrifice of a treasured possession? Or had her exclamation been ambiguous? Perhaps she was trying to do penance for sacrificing Trude's happiness by sacrificing her favorite piece of crystal.

*Sunday, February 4, 1940.* The size of the stone in Trude's engagement ring has caused a number of comments upstairs, especially among the ladies. Frau Lipschitz acidly remarked that it was indeed enormous, but no doubt full of flaws. Frau Kramer said that Trude had made a good catch, adding with an accusing look at Eva that not every mother's child was so lucky.

"I certainly wasn't," Eva retorted, looking her mother-in-law straight in the eye.

*Thursday, February 8, 1940.* Some political news: yesterday British ships entered Norwegian waters to rescue more than three hundred prisoners of war from the German ship *Altmark*. The Norwegian government protested the violation of its waters. Will the small nations never learn?

*Monday, February 12, 1940.*    This afternoon Trude and Eva came up to the Centro, the first time since Trude broke with Halpern. Apparently Trude decided that she could not remain a recluse for the rest of her life.

Halpern turned a beet-red when he saw the two girls come in, but did not go near their table to take their order. In a moment of insight and tact, Herr Bloch himself attended to them while Halpern remained in the background, glaring at Trude with scorn mingled with hurt.

Trude placed her left hand on the table as if she wanted to taunt the poor boy. Try to understand women! I had always thought she was in love with him.

*Friday, February 16, 1940.*    Today Eva made the surprising announcement that Trude is to be married some time next month.

"Why the hurry?" Frau Lipschitz asked, with titillated curiosity. "Maybe a happy event coming up . . . too soon?"

"You idiot," Eva said rudely. "They don't want to wait until April because Passover falls in April and then they couldn't get married for forty days. At least they couldn't have a religious ceremony, and this is what Levy and the Goldmanns want."

"And what about Trude?" I asked.

Eva shrugged.

"Trude? She doesn't care much one way or the other. It isn't her wedding."

"So whose wedding is it?" Frau Kramer asked indignantly. "Have you ever heard such nonsense!"

*Friday, February 23, 1940.*    The preparations for her daughter's wedding have thrown Frau Goldmann into a tizzy. The entire past week she neglected her factory, shopping for a new trousseau for Trude to replace the one lost in the Rio Verde.

"Levy should not say he's taking my Trude without a shirt on her back," she keeps justifying her spending spree to anyone who cares to listen. But this is only an excuse. She really enjoys ransacking the stores of Esperanza for fabrics and linens. Most of the time, though, she ends up making her purchases in Levy's store, where she can buy on credit. Thus everybody saves face: Herr Levy by pretending that he believes in such future payments. Trude by not having to jump into her marriage bed without a shirt on her back.

"The nightgowns, of course, I'll make myself," Frau Goldmann says with a pretty little titter.

*Thursday, February 29, 1940.* Trude and Levy are now officially accepted as a couple. The first novelty of their engagement has worn off and they are invited everywhere together as if it had never been otherwise.

Yesterday we all went to the Brauns' for lunch. Even after a year here, entering the house of the Brauns seems like entering a magic world of security where nothing was altered by such events as Hitler and the war.

For a change Hans was at home to entertain his guests. The Panamerican Oil Company has temporarily abandoned the search for oil in the selva, and Hans is idling in Esperanza. The difference between his idling and our idling is that he is being paid for it.

*Monday, March 4, 1940.* After working for only a month at his new job, Walter is already up for a raise. I received the good news from Josef, who confided it to me under strict secrecy.

"It's just as I told you, Norman. There's nothing a gringo can't achieve in Esperanza. Jaime Carillo is extremely pleased with the work Walter has been doing for him. 'Que trabajadór este gringo,' he said to me. What a worker this gringo. Now he is afraid that Walter might be snatched up by one of his competitors. He told me confidentially that he is going to raise his salary next month. But don't mention anything to Walter yet. With my friend Jaime you never know. He might change his mind tomorrow."

We went on to talk about the building industry in general, and

Josef told me that there was a big building boom in the making.

"What you ought to do is buy some lots in the north of the city, Norman. They can still be had for a song, but five years from now they'll be worth a fortune. Esperanza is growing all the time. Did I ever show you the property I own? When I bought it, it was nothing but a wilderness. Now they've already built a road up there, and a few houses. But you can still get a good idea of how it looked years ago."

Suddenly taken with the idea, Josef ordered his car to show me his land. We drove a few blocks and then turned left into a street which ran steeply uphill. My heart gave a sharp leap when I recognized it as the street through which I had followed Eva the night she ran away. We passed the few, straggling houses and stopped where the road turned into a path amidst the empty lots.

Josef got out of the car and beckoned me to follow him. Now, in the broad daylight, I saw what I had not noticed the night I went after Eva: from where we stood we could see the entire city of Esperanza stretched out in the valley below, long and narrow like a lazy, reddish-brown worm basking in the sun. The chimes of a bell floated up to us on the still morning air. Opposite us, on the slopes of the Grampico, a white herd of sheep moved across the green rectangles of the fields. The mournful cry of a mule was followed by the yapping protest of a dog, and then all was quiet again. It was a picture of such peace that it made my heart ache.

How had we come so soon to take all this for granted? No war, no famine, no concentration camps. Here we were gringos, not Jews. For the first time since we had come here—and it was over a year now—I felt grateful. Was this what Josef had really brought me up here for?

I glanced at him sideways. He stood proud like a sovereign, pointing out over the lots before us.

"All this, mine," he said, including the city and the mountains in his sweeping gesture. "Soon this land will be part of the city too."

"Very beautiful," I said. "Such a beautiful view. One should build a house here."

"Yes, it is very beautiful. But if I were to build another house I would not build it here. I would build it on the other side of the slope. Come, let me show you where."

He began walking toward the woods, taking the same footpath which Eva had taken. In the daylight I saw that the trees which had seemed so sinister and menacing at night were little more than saplings, tender, young eucalyptus trees whose leaves ranged in color from blue to silver.

At the end of the footpath we stepped out onto the familiar clearing where Eva had threatened to hurl herself off the cliff. The sloping meadow was golden with bright yellow buttercups, as if it had absorbed the glow of the sun. Beyond the abyss at the edge of the clearing the blue of the farthest mountain range dissolved into the blue of the distance. In the glass-clear air we could see five snow-covered mountain peaks rising above the granite of the cordilleras.

"Here," Josef said, "I would build another house if I live long enough."

His remark startled me and I threw a quick glance at him, guiltily aware that I had forgotten to inquire after his health. I thought that the once full line of his cheeks had become even more flaccid—but perhaps the bright light of the noonday sun was not the most flattering for men our age.

"And how is your liver?" I asked.

"Not too good," he said with a shrug.

After we had climbed back up the slope we both had to stop to catch our breath. As we stood panting I thought to hear a whispering above the rustle of leaves, and when I looked around I saw two pairs of feet—one a woman's, the other a man's—sticking out from behind a bush not too far from where we stood. The man's feet were pointed toes down, the woman's feet toes up, in the traditional position of lovers.

Josef followed the direction of my glance and frowned. He took a step as if to walk toward the bush, but changed his mind and headed back to the car. For a few minutes we walked in silence, one behind the other, on the narrow footpath. When we reached the road where we could walk abreast again, Josef said to me:

"It's a disgrace. They shouldn't do that. It doesn't look good in front of the Parameños."

"What makes you so sure that those two were our people? Is love-making restricted to gringos?"

"No, but the Parameños are very conservative in this respect. They feel that there is a time and a place for such things. And midmorning on a mountain slope is neither."


*Wednesday, March 6, 1940.*    I wonder whether there is a connection between the two pairs of feet which I saw sticking out from behind the bush and what happened today after lunch.

Dr. Lipschitz had dropped in to discuss some club matters with his father-in-law. Frau Kramer had cleared the dishes from the table and retired to the kitchen. We men were sitting on the veranda. Eva was outside on the terrace, waiting for Walter. I saw her repeatedly approach the door which connects the terrace with the veranda, but every time she turned away again. Finally she knocked and came in. Herr Kramer looked up, annoyed by the interruption.

"Yes, what is it?"

"I'll take up only a minute," Eva said hastily. "I'd just like Alfred to ask Dr. Vogel if he knows how to remove a grass stain. I got one on my skirt and it won't come out."

Dr. Lipschitz promised to get her the information and Eva left. But I cannot stop thinking about the grass stain on her skirt.

What is the matter with me? She might easily have soiled her skirt by sitting on the lawn in our very own backyard!


*Monday, March 11, 1940.*    If downstairs the preparations for Trude's wedding are in full swing, upstairs plans for the Passover holidays next month are also beginning to take shape. Encouraged by her recent prosperity (Walter's raise has indeed come through and Dr. Lipschitz also makes regular monthly contributions to his in-laws now), Frau Kramer has proposed to buy an extra set of dishes for Passover. This idea has met with violent opposition from Eva. She claims that the whole idea of a second set of dishes is foolish since one cannot get kosher food in Esperanza, let alone food kosher for Passover.

"It's nothing but a devious way of wanting to bribe God by half measures," Eva says precociously.

This will not stop Frau Kramer from buying the dishes, especially since she has no idea what Eva is talking about.

*Thursday, March 14, 1940.*　　The war in Finland is over. The Finns have ceded quite a bit of their territory to the Russians and have also given them a naval base at Hangö.

Goldmann has voiced grave doubts as to whether he ought to keep Horowitz on as a boarder, and even if he does, whether he ought to invite him to Trude's wedding. Sometimes I think Goldmann is even more of a fool than Horowitz.

*Sunday, March 24, 1940.*　　Two events to record, one political, the other local.

First: Daladier has resigned and Paul Reynaud has formed a new French government. Perhaps there is still hope for France.

Second: Yesterday evening there was an informal Purim dance in the Centro. Trude claimed that she was too exhausted from the preparations for her wedding and refused to attend the dance. No doubt she does not wish to stir up old memories. Even Eva was reluctant to go and Walter had to press her.

I noticed that Herr Klein was conspicuously absent from the festivities, but Eva had her usual bevy of admirers to dance with. Most of the evening passed decorously. The only one to add a flurry of excitement was Aronoff, who came to the dance with one lady but left with another.

By the way, Eva seems to have got over her crush on Aronoff. She observed him with amused detachment rather than with the jealousy which his carousing with other women used to bring out in her. I even feel inclined to interpret Klein's absence from the dance as a good sign. Perhaps now that Walter has a steady job, Eva will be more willing to settle down.

*Tuesday, March 26, 1940.*　　The signs of Trude's wedding drawing near (only five days left now) are multiplying like bad omens before the

Ides of March. Today Frau Goldmann brought Trude's wedding gown home. Levy had especially ordered the material for it from Panama. Only the finest silk and lace for his bride. Eva went downstairs to help unwrap the dress. When she came upstairs again, she looked wistful and depressed.

"Such a gorgeous gown," she said. "And for what?"

For one who begrudges Frau Kramer a second set of dishes for Passover, she seems unduly impressed by the symbolism of a white wedding gown.

Levy also seems to be having his premarriage troubles. Today Walter told me with mock indignation that Levy had questioned him about the most reliable ways of contraception. Something safe that would not offend the sensibilities of his bride. Imagine a man Levy's age not knowing how to go about that, Walter said.

But then, I suppose, in his career as a lover Levy was rarely in a situation in which he had to consider the feelings of the lady; in this case a nice girl, and a virgin to boot.

*Friday, March 29, 1940.* "Tomorrow is the day of wrath," Eva says.

All the preparations for the wedding are finished. The guests have been invited; the food for the occasion has been ordered from Frau Steinberg ("Who wants to bother on a day like that?" Frau Goldmann said tearfully); only the baking was done at home.

Frau Kramer contributed liberally of her time and labor, turning out cakes as if it were the wedding of one of her own children. Possibly because there are no emotional strings attached, she enjoys Trude's wedding more than she could ever have enjoyed those of her own offspring— especially Walter's wedding. If she assists Frau Goldmann in shedding tears every time they meet on the stairs, she does so strictly as a gesture of comradeship.

The canopy has been erected in the hall below, and Frau Kramer has filled pails with flowers with which she will decorate the banister of the stairs tomorrow in another bacchanalian outburst. Herr Kramer, who will perform the ceremony, spent most of the day secluded on the veranda, rocking over his prayer book in anxious rehearsal for the event.

For the past few days I hardly get to see Eva. Now that she stands to lose the only other young girl in the house, she does not budge from Trude's side. I suspect that she is lending her moral support as the hour approaches.

When questioned how he feels about the wedding of his daughter, Goldmann says with forced cheer:

"Can a man ask for a better son-in-law than the one I'm getting?"

But underneath he seems glum and moody. In the last analysis it is always the father who suffers most from the physical aspect of delivering his daughter to another man.

*Saturday, March 30, 1940.*　　The house is quiet now. All the guests have left. We have retired to our rooms, and Trude and Levy have gone to spend their wedding night in a hotel before leaving tomorrow morning for their honeymoon in Miami.

"Nothing too good for my Trude," Levy says of his bride, who now has changed from Frau Goldmann's Trudi into his Trude. Frau Goldmann is probably lying in bed now, still crying over her loss.

The day began with tears. Seized by a last-minute panic, Trude came upstairs to cry on Eva's shoulder. Her hair was put up in curlers; her eyes were slightly out of focus without her glasses, the dark circles beneath them telltale signs of a sleepless night.

After Trude had calmed herself and gone down again, the house came alive with women dressing and running to and fro. Frau Kramer, still in her robe, was busily winding garlands around the banister. Eva had decided against wearing her white dress—white was for the bride—and wore blue instead, a blue that made her eyes look almost violet. She finished dressing much faster than is her habit and ran downstairs to assist Trude.

Around ten o'clock we all went downstairs. Frau Goldmann had asked us to be on hand to help receive the guests. She herself was dissolved in tears and unable to attend to the amenities.

"Else, for God's sake, control yourself, Else," Goldmann kept begging her. "People will think we're sending Trude to her death, God forbid."

Frau Goldmann finally collected herself enough to propose that we all go and have a peek at the bride, who was dressing in her parents' bedroom. Just then Levy walked in, very elegant in a dark tuxedo with a white chrysanthemum in his lapel, and a new black hat sitting straight on his head. Frau Goldmann shooed him away when he wanted to join us.

"No, no! It is bad luck for the groom to see the bride before the wedding!"

Levy retired to the sala to sulk, walk in circles, and bite his fingernails, while we went to look at Trude.

Frau Goldmann's knocking brought Eva to the door.

"Go away, Frau Goldmann, you're only making her nervous."

"I, her own mother!"

"Please, Mama." Trude had come up behind Eva and we got a glimpse of white silk and lace, real French Chantilly lace, Goldmann explained reverently.

"Trudi, darling," Frau Goldmann spoke over Eva's shoulder, "perhaps you'll still change your mind. Perhaps you won't wear your glasses . . . Just for the ceremony, Trudi!"

"Mama, you know I'm blind as a bat without my glasses! I might break a leg . . ." There was a short pause before Trude continued: "Maybe I won't wear my glasses at that."

Eva shut the door in our faces and we trudged back to the hall. Levy had come out of the sala to assist Herr Kramer with the inspection of the huppah. ("Just to make sure it won't collapse on our heads, God forbid!") Frau Goldmann went to check in the kitchen and broke into loud laments when she discovered that Frau Steinberg had not yet arrived with the food.

"You mark my word, Markus! You'll see! The guests will be here any minute and there won't be a bite to eat in the house! I should have done everything myself!"

Five minutes later these predictions of catastrophe were proved untrue by Frau Steinberg, who arrived puffing and sweating, showering German curses over an Indian boy and girl who carried large, covered baskets from which rose a delicious scent. While the women repaired to the kitchen to help Frau Steinberg, I joined the men in the inspection of wedding presents which were lined up on a table in one corner of the hall.

It appeared that an entire silver store had been sacked for the occasion. There were silver bowls and silver platters, silver cups and silver ashtrays, silver candlesticks, silver cake knives, and a multitude of silver salt cellars: little silver Indians carrying barrels for salt on their backs; silver llamas with silver barrels; silver pesos hammered into salt cellars; several silver pesos welded together into salt cellars. Truly, the wedding guests must have wished Trude and Levy a spiced marriage. Or else they had bought the salt cellars because they were the least expensive items obtainable.

There were also a few crystal bowls, crystal vases, crystal platters. A sensible set of aluminum pots. And several unidentifiable objects of mysterious purpose.

Horowitz had joined us in the survey of this capitalistic display, but before he could launch into an attack on the vices produced by too much wealth, the wedding guests began to arrive. By and by all the people with whom the Goldmanns had social contact—and some with whom they had not had until this day—walked in. Even Grushka, for once clean-shaven, was present. The Fleischers, the Lipschitzes, the Vogels, Dr. Landau ("His was the tiny one-peso silver salt cellar, you may be sure," Horowitz said), a number of newcomers with whom Goldmann must have struck up an acquaintance for the sole purpose of adding to the number of wedding guests.

Josef walked in with a very pretty lady. I had to look twice before I recognized Señora Blumenthal. This was the first time I had seen her out of mourning. She wore a yellow silk dress and a yellow straw hat, and she looked delicate and exotic among our plumper, pinker ladies.

When the room was almost filled I saw George Klein slip in through the open door. I could not help wondering who had asked him. Certainly not the Goldmanns or Levy. And why would Trude ask a member of the former foursome which she had deserted? A last gesture of defiance? Or was she trying to further the romance between Eva and Klein?

I did not have much time to ponder the question, for Herr Kramer had already taken up his position under the canopy and was trying to shush the crowd.

"Shah! Shah! Quiet please!" And when the murmuring, laughing and shuffling continued, in an attempt at wit: "Herr Levy here is most anxious to get married!"

Gradually the noise abated; the people cleared a path between the huppah and the door from which the bride would emerge and the men, who had held their hats in their hands, put them on. Herr Kramer cleared his voice and began to sway back and forth over his prayer book. Levy had donned his prayer shawl and stepped up under the canopy. He stood there, nervously tugging at his collar, his cuffs, and his chin as he automatically swayed to Herr Kramer's chanting. It was quiet now except for Herr Kramer's singsong and the sobbing of Frau Goldmann, which could be heard even before the door opened and Trude appeared on the arm of her father.

An aahh of surprise rustled through the ranks of the guests. In spite of herself Trude looked as pretty as any bride in traditional white. The long dress with the full skirt made her look tall and thin-waisted, and the several layers of veil over her face lent her features a softening vagueness. She was not wearing her glasses.

As Trude groped blindly toward the huppah, I could see Levy's Adam's apple pop up above his collar and disappear again. What was uppermost in his mind now? Love, desire, last-minute qualms, or still worry over the right kind of contraceptive? No doubt Trude looked very beautiful to him under her heavy veil.

Perhaps Trude's nearsightedness did for Levy what the veil did for her. Perhaps she saw him only as a blur, the mere outline of a man who could be any man she wished him to be at this moment.

While Trude took her place by Levy's side and Herr Kramer's chanting grew louder, I saw Klein slowly edging toward Eva until he stood right behind her. The room was quite crowded and I was sure their bodies were touching. Instead of watching the bridal couple, I continued observing Eva and Klein.

Something about Klein looked strange, and then I realized that he also had taken off his glasses. From the side he looked almost like Aronoff now. As I watched him breathing down on Eva's hair I cursed his profile and my suspicious mind and the day I had not offered Trude the reward money for her aunt. Of course Walter, who should have been near his wife, was standing way off in the first row between his mother and Frau Goldmann.

I was so preoccupied with Eva and Klein that my attention was returned to the bridal couple only when I heard the grinding of glass under Levy's heel and I knew that the marriage had been sealed. Then Trude's veils were raised for the kiss and the guests surged forward.

I could no longer see whether Levy really got a chance to kiss his bride before Frau Goldmann hurled herself on her daughter. But while I did not see Trude being kissed by her groom, I am quite certain that I saw Klein's mouth brush Eva's hair before he moved away and mingled with the other guests.

Walter first noticed Klein when he came over to congratulate Trude. He looked at the man sharply and then turned around to search for Eva, who by now was innocently chatting with Frau Fleischer. Walter was fooled into looking relieved.

I tried to get near Trude myself but could not reach her. She was swept by the wave of guests into the sala where, behind closed doors, Frau Steinberg had silently set up the buffet during the ceremony. The guests threw themselves on the food as if they and not Trude had been keeping the traditional fast before the wedding.

Fighting his way to Trude's side with flailing arms, Levy instantly began heaping a plate for her.

"Eat, darling, eat, you must be hungry!"

"Go ahead, eat, you'll need all your strength, Frau Levy," Fleischer teased.

Trude looked startled at the sound of her new name. She had thrown back her veil and put on her glasses, and she avoided looking at Levy, who followed her around like a faithful dog.

As if the food had given the guests new strength, the voices began to rise and soon it was impossible to converse without shouting. Levy had provided a liberal amount of spirits and everybody seemed to be having a good time, even Frau Goldmann, who sat on the sofa and let Frau Kramer feed and comfort her. But much as I craned my neck I could not find a trace of Goldmann.

I went back out in the hall, which was almost deserted now, and from there into the corridor. Through the open door of his bedroom I could see Goldmann sitting on the bed, a handkerchief pressed over his eyes. He was crying silently, and I stole away without a sound.

Later Goldmann returned to the sala, where Trude managed to hold out until after the last guest had left and we had gone upstairs. Shortly afterward we heard Frau Goldmann's wailing rise once more to a crescendo, and then Eva came in from the terrace and said that Trude and Levy had driven away in his car.

"Poor Trude," she said. "I always wanted to get married in white. But then I suppose it doesn't matter what you get married in but whom you get married to."

*Wednesday, April 3, 1940.*   Aside from Eva, nobody seems to be thinking of Trude as "poor Trude."

"Tell me, can a girl do better than be taken on her honeymoon to Miami?" Frau Lipschitz asked. "A little over a year ago when the Goldmanns were still in Vienna and Herr Goldmann was in a concentration camp, would they ever in their wildest dreams have thought of such a thing?"

"Miami," Frau Kramer said, letting the word melt on her tongue like a rare confection. "Miami. It sounds so romantic."

She sighed and looked nostalgic for all the romance she had missed in life. Trude was lucky; she did not realize how lucky. But Frau Kramer, who also had been an ugly girl, knew.

Horowitz is unexpectedly wistful.

"Now that I have finally got used to her face she has to go and get herself married," he complained.

"You should have thought of that sooner, Horowitz," Dr. Landau said. "She might still have preferred your offer of equality to Levy's wealth. Anyway, you are a few years younger than Levy."

"I am," Horowitz said, with great dignity, "considerably younger than Herr Levy."

(There are two things Horowitz is extremely vain about: his hands and his youthful looks. But what he thinks of as his youthfulness is really nothing but the agelessness of a gnome. I cannot imagine him looking any younger and I doubt that he will ever look older than now.)

Walter, in his own way, also is disturbed by Trude's marriage. He says that Eva's pitying her is only an act; that she really envies her the glamour of being rich.

"If I could offer her some of that, she wouldn't be so restless, running off every morning like a stray dog."

I think this is another case of transferred feelings. It is really Walter who wants the glamour of being rich. Eva would settle for security and a little more attention.


*Saturday, April 6, 1940.*　　Horowitz, still prowling for an attractive woman within his reach, asked me this afternoon to introduce him to Frau Schwarzkopf. I tried to comply that evening in the Centro, but forgetting that I am no wit felt called upon to introduce Horowitz with a joke.

"Frau Schwarzkopf," I said, "my friend Horowitz has been wanting to meet you for the longest time. Being a Communist, he is fascinated by anything Russian."

Frau Schwarzkopf turned white.

"How dare you come to my table?" she said to Horowitz. "You killed my sweet mother! I spit on you!"

And she did spit in the general direction of Horowitz.

Horowitz beat a hasty retreat into the card room and I followed him to apologize for my faux pas. But he only kept shaking his head, barely listening to my explanations.

"She spat at me," he said, with wonder bordering on awe. "That crazy woman actually spat at me!"


*Wednesday, April 10, 1940.*　　The Germans have attacked Norway and occupied Denmark!

Only one day after the French and British governments announced that the waters around Norway had been mined to prevent the passage of German ships, the Nazis descended on Norway. The newspapers say that they took Oslo, Bergen, Trondheim, Stavanger and Narvik. Denmark fell without any formal resistance.

Frau Goldmann, who likes to look for farfetched trouble, is frantic lest the United States should enter the war and the "children" should encounter difficulties in returning to El Paramo. The rest of us are not—shall I call it as optimistic as Frau Goldmann?—to hope for such an early entry of the Americans into the war. What preoccupies us most is whether there are many Jews in Denmark and Norway and how safe they will be there under Nazi rule.

*Sunday, April 14, 1940.*    Today the news is a little more reassuring. The Norwegians have rallied from the surprise attack and have driven the Germans out of Bergen and Trondheim. And yesterday the British attacked Narvik, sank all the enemy ships in the harbor, and occupied the town. Perhaps the tide is turning after all.

*Thursday, April 18, 1940.*    Amidst all the war news, Frau Kramer today won a strategic victory for herself. With Passover only a few days away, she finally prevailed upon Walter and Dr. Lipschitz to give her the money for an extra set of dishes. Eva was irate.

"If I buy myself a much-needed pair of shoes, all hell breaks loose," she said. "But to spend a lot of money for some dishes which are used only once a year, that's all right!"

*Sunday, April 21, 1940.*    More good news! English and French troops have landed in southern Norway. At least now we can look forward to the Passover holidays in a more cheerful frame of mind.

*Wednesday, April 24, 1940.*    Our second Seder in Esperanza.
It seems incredible that a full year should have elapsed since we last sat down to the holiday meal. This year the matzoth arrived on time and Frau Kramer's new set of dishes lent a festive air to the Seder, even

if Eva kept pointing out maliciously that the food on them was not kosher.

Trude and Levy are still in Miami (they were supposed to come home last Saturday but postponed their return for another week) and Frau Kramer asked the Goldmanns to celebrate with us. Our company failed to keep Frau Goldmann from having several good cries. She said she missed the "children." But soon her mournful mood was swept away by the commotion of the festivities, the smell of fish and chicken from the kitchen, the bustling of Frau Kramer and Frau Lipschitz, the clinking of glasses and the crackling of matzoths being broken.

Horowitz had been asked up with the Goldmanns. As on all religious occasions he momentarily put aside his political convictions and joined wholeheartedly in the feast. Herr Kramer read the Haggadah, and whenever he reached a passage which is usually sung by all the males present, Dr. Lipschitz, Goldmann, Horowitz, and I chimed in. Since by tradition every family uses different melodies for the different songs, we sounded about as harmonious as a Hindemith symphony.

Little Kurt acquitted himself well in asking the four questions; was beamed upon by his proud parents, applauded by his grandmother, and rewarded by his grandfather and his uncle Walter with a peso apiece. This so enraged the smaller boy that he began to howl at the top of his voice. He would not be calmed until he was allowed to stand up on one of the chairs and sing "Ay Jalisco no te rajes." After he too had received his pesos and his applause, quiet was established and the ceremony could continue. But the peace did not last long, and soon the children were running around the table again or crawling under it, bumping into the legs of the grownups.

In other words, a real, traditional Seder. I would not have it any other way.

*Saturday, April 27, 1940.* One sign of our isolation in Esperanza is that little things have become events to us. For instance the return of Levy and Trude. (I still cannot get myself to refer to them as the Levys.)

The preparations for their welcome could not have been more feverish if they had spent a three-year sojourn at the South Pole rather than a three-week honeymoon in Miami. Only a feat of will power kept Frau Kramer from winding garlands around the banister.

In the morning Levy's car with the chauffeur came to take the Goldmanns to the airport. None of us was asked to come along. There was room for only six in the car, Frau Goldmann explained apologetically, and where, with all the luggage, would the "children" sit?

At about one o'clock the "children" were brought home in triumph. Levy jumped out first, opening the doors ahead of his chauffeur to help his wife and his mother-in-law out of the car. He looked healthy, with a nice tan, and marriage seemed to have miraculously rejuvenated him to the point where he even appeared to have more hair.

Trude also looked surprisingly well. She wore a new suit which Levy had bought for her in Miami, a real American suit, which was immediately acknowledged by the other ladies with an admiring ahh. Her hair was done in a novel, becoming way, and she had acquired a pair of oddly shaped, horn-rimmed glasses, which made them look an asset rather than a liability. A scant three weeks of marriage to Levy had done a lot for her. Perhaps all those cynics who had sneeringly said that Trude had made her luck had been right in spite of themselves.

The Goldmanns and the "children" retired for a private family meal (Frau Kramer had kept the food warm for them) and afterward we were called down for the distribution of presents which Trude had brought for all of us.

There were neckties for Walter and Herr Kramer; a beautiful handbag for Eva ("I never had anything so beautiful in all my life!"); a frilly silk dress for Frau Goldmann ("What's the matter with you, Trudi, you think I am a young girl perhaps?" but all this with pleasure in her voice); a sweater for Herr Goldmann; a large pigskin billfold for me ("To hold all the money you and Papa are going to make.")

Trude obviously enjoyed the new luxury of being able to be generous.

"I'm only sorry you couldn't eat with us," she said. "But as soon as we're through furnishing our house, I want you all to come over for dinner."

This was the first we had heard of the Levys' having rented (or bought?) a house. Trude explained with a laugh that her mother had forbidden her to mention anything about it for fear of the evil eye, a precaution for which she was greatly commended by Frau Kramer.

The Levys soon left with the excuse that they were tired from the trip.

Upstairs, Eva put her new handbag on the dining-room table and gazed at it rapturously.

"United States," she said, as if all the symbolism of the word were contained in the large, shiny, red bag.

Perhaps she was thinking that if she had gone to the States instead of coming to El Paramo, all her dreams—whatever dreams she might be having now—would have come true.

"You see," Walter said, with the quick, bitter misunderstanding of the insecure husband, "all she really thinks about is clothes!"

*Wednesday, May 1, 1940.*    Yesterday was the last evening of Passover.

With the end of the holidays the respite in Europe also seems to have come to an end. Norwegian resistance, in which we had placed so much hope, is broken, and King Haakon and his cabinet have fled to London. We all feel that it is only a matter of days now before the English and the French will retreat from Norway.

*Monday, May 6, 1940.*    We seem to be leading a double life here, half of which is taken up by worries over the war in Europe (Anglo-French forces retreated from Norway a few days ago) and the other half given over to such frivolities as attending parties, visiting the Centro or some of the other clubs which have sprung up, and spreading gossip.

With the constant influx of refugees several new clubs have been founded. Besides the Centro we now have a Czech, Polish, Austrian, and German Club, a B'nai B'rith, and a budding Zionist movement. Being a member of one club does not exclude one from sitting on the board of another. I have myself been approached to become a member of the Polish Club because I was born in Poland; of the Austrian Club because I spent most of my life in Austria; of the B'nai B'rith because obviously I am Jewish. Not to mention my standing invitation to join

Horowitz' Communist party. It was also suggested that I enlist the proper efforts to found a Hevrah Kadishah. (Sooner or later somebody is going to die, and what then?)

In trying to get my political support, people generally appeal to my superior intellect, but the moment I disagree with them they pronounce me the biggest fool alive. What strikes me as particularly ludicrous are the internal strifes and feuds between the clubs. But if we did not create some sort of friction in our haven of safety, I think we would all die of boredom.

*Saturday, May 11, 1940.*    Without any warning the Nazis have invaded the Netherlands, Belgium, and Luxembourg!

We stay glued to the radio and snatch up extra editions of the *Día* to find out what is happening in Europe, but nothing much is known yet. One thing we learned was that Winston Churchill has replaced Neville Chamberlain as British prime minister.

"High time too that they got rid of the old moron with the umbrella, may he rot in hell," Goldmann said. "If the English had sent somebody with brains to Munich, perhaps all this would never have happened."

Again we think of the Jews in the attacked countries before we can worry about the fate of the rest of the population. Everybody seems to have a friend, brother, sister, uncle, or uncle's uncle who fled either to Belgium or to Holland. Time and again one hears the refrain: "I told them to come here . . . I wrote to them . . . I warned them . . ." (I had to think of the letter which Josef had written me ages ago. Who ever heeds such warnings?) "They laughed at me when I told them that I was emigrating to El Paramo!"

The worst thing is that beneath our anxiety we feel smug, as if it were our personal accomplishment that we are safe here. Actually it is nothing but a stroke of blind luck. But for the grace of God any of us might be in Belgium or Holland today.

*Wednesday, May 15, 1940.*    Again we talk and think nothing but war.

The Germans are repeating the Blitzkrieg methods which they used in Poland. While the British and French sent expeditionary forces into Belgium to assist the Belgian army, the Germans crossed the Meuse at Sedan. Day before yesterday Rotterdam surrendered and Queen Wilhelmina and her government fled to London. Soon the kings in exile will outnumber the commoners there.

But this is no time for jokes. Yesterday the Dutch army capitulated and the war in Holland is over. We hope that the Dutch, who have always been friends of the Jews, will help the unfortunate ones who are trapped there to escape or hide out.


*Friday, May 17, 1940.* With the excitement over the war, none of us has really taken notice of the fact that the rainy season has come to an end. Today I was reminded of the change of seasons when Eva came outside on the terrace to take a sunbath.

From behind my newspaper I watched her spread her towel on the concrete floor, peel off her robe, and stretch out in the sun. It was like old times (Old times, just a year ago!), except that her skin was not so dark as it used to be, no longer a deep bronze but rather a fawn color, faded from the mornings when she goes off to I don't know where nor do I want to know.

She lay quiet until we heard a car come to a stop in front of the house. Raising herself on her knees, Eva peeked down between the grating of the iron railing.

"It's Trude's car," she said.

She called down a greeting, and Trude called back that she would come upstairs right after dropping in on her mother. Eva went back to sunning herself. More than half an hour passed without Trude's making her appearance.

Suddenly the air was rent by a scream—one of Frau Goldmann's piercing shrieks which may announce anything from the intrusion of a mouse to a serious disaster. Eva sat up abruptly, her face taut and her nostrils quivering, as if she were trying to scent the trouble over the wind. A few seconds later we heard Frau Goldmann's wild sobbing coming through the open window below, and Eva turned to me and said:

"Trude is going to have a baby."

She made the statement in such a positive manner that I did not question it for a moment. Now, in retrospect, I realize that Frau Goldmann might have had a multitude of other reasons for crying. Trude could have told her that Levy was beating her. (Unlikely, I admit.) That she was about to leave him. That he had lost all his money. Or that he had syphilis.

But of course Eva was right.

When Trude finally came upstairs Eva greeted her with the words: "Congratulations! When do we expect the happy event?"

Trude looked stunned. "How did you know?" she asked. "I'm not showing yet!"

She squinted down her figure, as ample as ever but certainly not ampler.

"With your mother, God bless her, you don't need a town crier," Eva said. "I bet they could hear her all over Esperanza!"

*Saturday, May 18, 1940.* The news of Trude's pregnancy has temporarily pushed the war talk into the background. Here is an assorted selection of comments:

Frau Lipschitz: "Well, they were in a hurry, weren't they? Perhaps this was the reason why they couldn't wait to get married after Passover!"

Dr. Lipschitz: "At least Levy proved he's still up to it."

Herr Kramer: "Good! Nothing like a baby to keep a woman from getting ideas!"

Frau Kramer: "I always say people should have children right away."

The last remark drew a sneer from Eva. No doubt she still remembers the cries of horror Frau Kramer had raised at the suspicion that Eva might be pregnant.

Walter said with mock indignation that all the good advice he had given Levy had gone for naught. Eva was not critical of Trude or Levy, but of Frau Goldmann.

"I don't know why she goes around hanging her head," Eva said.

"After she moved heaven and earth to get Trude married, what did she expect? That Levy would not" (out of consideration for me she refrained from using the crude word that was on her lips) "make use of his marital rights?"

To everyone's surprise, Herr Goldmann is absolutely delighted. He struts around with his chest sticking out, telling anyone who cares to listen (and not sparing those who don't):

"I'm going to be a grandfather! *I* am going to be a *grandfather!*"

*Monday, May 20, 1940.*    Now that the excitement over Trude's pregnancy has worn off, we are back to our war worries.

The Germans have penetrated deep into France along the Somme valley, cutting off the British and Belgian forces in Flanders from the main French armies. General Weygand has replaced General Gamelin as French commander in chief, but this change has not done the French much good. Brussels and Namur have fallen, and the British and Belgian armies are retreating toward Ostend and Dunkirk.

"How much longer can they retreat?" Goldmann asks. "There's only the ocean beyond Ostend!"

*Friday, May 24, 1940.*    When I called on Josef this morning I did not find him in his wicker chair in the loggia. Instead I was greeted by Señora Consuelo, who told me with a worried face that Josef was in bed; his liver was troubling him.

I said that I would call some other day if Josef was resting, but she insisted that I go upstairs with her to see him.

Josef was lying in bed in his austere room. The light from the chalk-white walls reflected greenish on his cheeks. His jowls were drooping as he rested on his pillow, and I realized with a shock that he had lost a lot of weight. I suppose my worry showed on my face, for Josef raised his hand in a belittling gesture and said:

"Es nada. It is nothing."

Señora Consuelo sat down on the edge of the bed and caught his hand in her two slender ones. She looked anxiously at him and then at me, as if she expected some sort of reassurance from me. Josef withdrew his hand with that peculiar male embarrassment resulting from a public display of affection, patted her fingers and said to me:

"Consuelo is worried. I was never sick in all the years of our marriage. She can't understand that at our age one has to expect a gradual setting in of decay."

He smiled wanly, leaving me with a queer feeling of uneasiness because he had included me in the age of decay. I asked him what his doctor had to say. He shrugged.

"The same old thing. It's my liver. Rest, hot-water bottles, careful diet. I'll be up and around in a couple of days."

As usual he was speaking to me in German. Señora Consuelo sat with her mouth a little open, reading the words from his lips. Suddenly she turned to me and said in rapid Spanish:

"Don't believe him, Señor Professor! He's in pain all the time. He won't admit it, but I know he's in pain! I can feel it right here!"

She pressed her fist into her body where she surmised the liver might be, as if to indicate that the mystical bond of marriage had empowered her to feel all the ailments of her husband. Some of her anxiety transmitted itself to me and I asked Josef a rash question:

"Won't you let Dr. Landau take a look at you?"

"Absolutely not! He has no license to practice medicine in El Paramo. Besides, I'm perfectly satisfied with Dr. Ramirez. He is a fine doctor. He studied in France."

The flicker of hope which had crept into Señora Consuelo's eyes when I mentioned Dr. Landau's name disappeared. She sighed and stood up.

Josef slapped his hand impatiently on his silk quilt cover.

"You all worry too much," he said. "I tell you it is nothing. I can't even sneeze in this house without my wife being afraid that I am at the brink of death!"

Señora Consuelo walked to the door. "I'll tell cook to make a nice, strong broth for you." ("Una sopita fuerte," she said.) "It will give you strength."

"A wonderful woman," Josef said after she had left. "I'm afraid I am a difficult patient. But don't worry, I'll be up in no time!"

*Monday, May 27, 1940.*    Another black day yesterday. Boulogne has fallen to the Germans and King Leopold of Belgium has ordered his troops to capitulate.

There are so many Jews in Belgium!

*Wednesday, May 29, 1940.*    The British have withdrawn their troops all the way to Dunkirk. The newspapers say they will attempt to evacuate them from there. It seems like an impossible task.

In contrast to this news, an example of how divorced we are from the political turmoil: Trude has insisted that we come to her house on Saturday for a party.

"We are fiddling while Rome is burning," Horowitz says glumly.

*Sunday, June 2, 1940.*    Now that we have been to Trude's new home, I feel that a sense of permanence has settled upon us. It was strange but reassuring to look around without seeing one single piece of furniture knocked together from a dismantled crate.

Trude's house is furnished with somber elegance: mahogany furniture with wine-colored upholstery in the sala; ornate, carved chairs and tables in the dining room. Only the bright, colorful carpets and the sheer curtains on the windows add a note of gaiety. Trude was delighted with the compliments she drew from her guests.

"Eva helped select the furniture. She came over every single morning," Trude said, stressing "every single morning."

With the help of Frau Goldmann, Trude had prepared a lavish repast for her guests. But she was still uncertain in the handling of the two muchachas who served the meal—servants are a novel luxury to her—and half the time she had to restrain her mother from leaving the table and running into the kitchen.

"Mama, please! Mama, you're a guest in my house!"

With ever so slight an emphasis on *my* house. And then, angrily turning on her father when she saw him cutting up his meat into small pieces:

"Papa, where are your new teeth?"

The heads of all the guests simultaneously swiveled toward Goldmann, like the heads of spectators at a tennis match following the course of the ball.

"Do you really have new teeth, Herr Goldmann?" Eva asked incredulously.

"Of course I have new teeth!" Goldmann reached into the breast pocket of his suit and extracted a partial denture, which he playfully snapped at us. "See!"

"Markus, this is disgusting!" Frau Goldmann screeched. "Either put the teeth in your mouth or put them back in your pocket!"

"I prefer to put them in my pocket. They cause me less discomfort there."

I recalled how Goldmann had vowed never to replace his knocked-out teeth. But time passes, one forgets, and Goldmann has acquired a denture.

A new era has indeed begun.

# Part Four ❧ Prosperity

*And God blessed Noah and his*
*sons, and said unto them,*
*Be fruitful, and multiply,*
*and replenish the earth.*

GENESIS 9:1

*Thursday, June 6, 1940.*    While the war in Europe is going from bad to worse (we have learned only now of the terrible British losses at Dunkirk), our lives in Esperanza seem to follow an upward trend which was symbolically inaugurated by the acquisition of Goldmann's new teeth.

"I tell you, my son-in-law is a golden person," Goldmann said to me today. "He got me a permit to open a store in Esperanza."

Then he announced casually that he had already rented a place and that I would, of course, remain his partner. I did not know whether to be annoyed or delighted by the manner in which Goldmann disposes of my business ambitions.

He insisted that I go with him to take a look at our new place of business. By sheer coincidence ("After all, can *you* think of a better location?" Goldmann asked) our store is adjacent to Levy's and located in a building owned by Levy.

"But don't think that we're not going to pay rent," Goldmann said to forestall any such suspicion on my part. "I'll pay Levy rent" (reverting to the first person singular), "I'll pay him every last cent for his merchandise. I'll pay him interest on the credit! Nobody is going to say that Markus Goldmann lives off his son-in-law!"

Nevertheless, this is exactly what people are saying. Especially Herr Kramer, who still leads an idle life after more than a year here, is green with envy.

"Why can't I have such luck?" he complains. "My son-in-law wouldn't set me up in business!"

In fact, Dr. Lipschitz goes to every length to discourage Herr Kramer from visiting his dry-cleaning plant, as he calls the garage housing his establishment. ("I've got one partner, who needed him! Do I need another one to come in and drive me crazy?")

Herr Fleischer stands almost alone in his opinion that Levy is anything but a philanthropist.

"A shrewd businessman, that's all he is. Instead of supporting Goldmann, he lets him work for his money! And whatever Goldmann earns above his needs will eventually go to Trude. This way Levy can never be the loser, provided Goldmann doesn't outlive him, which is very well possible. After all, they're practically the same age!"

*Tuesday, June 11, 1940.*　　Now that the Germans have penetrated deep into France, Italy has declared war on the British and the French and has invaded France from the south. This move is no surprise to any of us who remember the treachery of the Italians from the First World War. They always turn with the wind to join the victor.

*Thursday, June 13, 1940.*　　A black thirteenth today. We learned over the radio that Paris has been evacuated before the German advance. *We have lost Paris!*

There is such a magic sound to the name of that city that even people who have never been there think of it with sentimentality. The mood in the Jungle Café and in the Centro was unusually somber, and people talked in whispers as if a dear friend had died. It seems that we needed the symbolism of the fall of Paris to impress upon us the gravity of the situation.

*Sunday, June 16, 1940.*　　Another black day yesterday. The Nazis captured Verdun and the Russians moved into Estonia, Latvia, and Lithuania. At least where the Russians are concerned we find some solace in blaming Horowitz for their actions.

*Tuesday, June 18, 1940.*　　Marshal Pétain has replaced Paul Reynaud as the head of the French government and has asked the Germans for an armistice.

The war in France is as good as over.

*Saturday, June 22, 1940.*　　An incident, amusing in retrospect now that the fright has been forgotten, to shake us out of our repetitive speculations about the war: one might say that yesterday God took a hand in one of our internal strifes. The place was the card room of the Centro, where the Zionists hold their meetings; the issue, an exchange between Horowitz and Walter Kramer.

(Of course Horowitz is not a member of the Zionist organization, a circumstance which does not deter him from attending their meetings. Now and then he will jump up to interrupt the proceedings with fervent pleas to all present to join the only party which can bring the Jews equality.)

Dr. Lipschitz, who by now should be used to these outbursts, still gets riled every time Horowitz makes an impromptu speech. Yesterday he cut Horowitz short, saying:

"Herr Horowitz, please! To the best of my recollection if my memory does not trick me, and it does not, you are not a paying member of the Zionist organization. Should you wish to join and pay the back dues, we will gladly listen to your opinions on whatever matters you happen to have opinions on."

Horowitz' face turned a lovely purple.

"This room belongs to the Centro! I am a member of the Centro! I have as much right to be in this room as you have!"

"Nobody questions your right to be in this room, Horowitz," Walter Kramer joined in the debate, "if you will do so quietly."

"You!" Horowitz screeched at Walter. "You! It's because of people like you that the Jews have never found acceptance. You always urge them to separate, to make a showpiece and a fetish of their Jewishness! Now you would put them in a country of their own so that they would make an even easier target for their enemies, instead of letting them do what they should have done long ago, join the masses of the proletariat and dissolve into the brotherhood of common men."

"Look, Horowitz, if you were so eager to dissolve into the brotherhood of common men, why did you come to El Paramo instead of going to Russia?"

Horowitz' face darkened by two shades.

"For the same reason that you did not go to Palestine!"

It was at this point that God took a hand in the discussion.

No sooner had Walter and Horowitz stopped shouting than a distant grumbling became audible, as if a heavy truck had passed in the street below. Gradually the noise became louder, like a big wind coming up or an airplane flying close enough over the house to make the roof shake. We looked at each other, too stunned momentarily to realize what was going on. Goldmann was the first to glance up at the ceiling. He raised a pointing finger, his lips forming words while his throat seemed unable to produce sounds. The light fixtures, suspended from the ceiling on long wires, were gently swaying back and forth as if they had a life of their own. The floor beneath our feet vibrated like a sleeping animal angrily come to life. Goldmann's voice finally returned with a vengeance and he screamed in his high falsetto:

"Earthquake!"

I am trying to recapture my feelings of the moment. First of all I experienced the utter helplessness which Josef once had described to me. I believe I remained petrified in my seat, waiting for the ceiling to collapse on my head or the floor to open beneath me—as God would see fit to dispose of me. I clearly remember thinking of God. Possibly I was even praying. Through the window I could see the light posts in the street drunkenly weaving back and forth. In the house on the opposite side, a woman was frantically running around in a room, pulling her hair with one hand and clutching the image of a saint to her breast with the other. Not for one second did I think of Eva, who was in the next room, or of the possibility of saving her. This goes to show how much one can rely on one's daydreams!

The reaction of each of the men was different. Goldmann gingerly jumped over the conference table and ran for the exit, where Horowitz had already sought salvation. (He later explained that he had heard a doorjamb was the safest place under which to stand during an earthquake.) While Dr. Lipschitz pleaded with Horowitz to let him through, Goldmann fiercely tried to jostle both men aside. Walter Kramer had jumped up when the ground began to heave under us, but remained glued to the spot, repeating over and over again that Eva must be terrified.

The whole thing was over in a few seconds. The silence after the eerie grumbling came like a quiet thunderclap. Ceiling and floor had remained intact and only a couple of chairs had toppled over, a consequence of the panic rather than the earthquake. The men struggling in the doorway grinned sheepishly at each other and, with an air of feigned nonchalance, came back to the table.

No sooner had they cleared the door than Eva appeared there. I was surprised to see that she seemed not the least bit frightened. Quite the contrary, she looked exhilarated as if she had actually enjoyed the experience. Glancing around, she burst out laughing.

"Well, gentlemen, I can see *you* didn't relish the diversion!"

Dr. Lipschitz, still pale and with little beads of perspiration on his forehead, turned to Walter Kramer and said angrily:

"That wife of yours, doesn't she have any fear of God?"

*Friday, June 28, 1940.* Goldmann has found himself a new hero: he is General Charles de Gaulle. Although France has by now signed an armistice with Germany and Italy, General de Gaulle, at the head of the French National Committee in London, has pledged continued French opposition to Germany.

"This de Gaulle, you mark my word, he's a great man! All the French are cowards, but de Gaulle will manage to pull them out of the . . . !"

I cannot help remembering the times when Goldmann put his trust in the Russians and I shudder.

Thinking of the Russians reminds me that troubled times have come for Horowitz. Not only because he is held personally responsible for the Russian occupation of Bessarabia but because the Goldmanns have decided to move out of the house.

Now that Trude is getting along in her pregnancy, Frau Goldmann feels that she would like to live near her. Obviously Levy has not asked his in-laws to move in with him ("Very smart of Levy," Eva says. "A very smart man. I get to like him better every day!"), for Frau Goldmann is looking for a small house in the vicinity of Trude's home.

"Should we find a large house within our means, we'll gladly take Herr Horowitz along," Frau Goldmann says. "If not, we will regretfully have to leave him behind."

Horowitz is vacillating whether to offer Frau Goldmann a raise in his rent.

"Much she needs *my* money now," he complains, adding bitterly that all his troubles were, of course, caused by a capitalist. "Here I am, comfortable, happy, living in a clean house with good food, so Levy has to come along and spoil everything! If only my business were going a little better I'd show him! I'd rent a house of my own!"

(As if Levy had married Trude for the sole purpose of evicting Horowitz from his home!)

Horowitz' tiny store—a mere hole in the wall which in proportions fits nicely around his minute body—has come off to a slow start. I think that people pass it by because they fail to notice it. Horowitz has now hit upon a remedy and has ordered an enormous sign to be hung up over the entrance:

CASA LEÓN
(for Leo Horowitz)
ARTICULOS FINOS PARA EL CABALLERO DISTINGUIDO

If this does not draw the customers, Horowitz says, he will have to hire Rudi Brueck to do handsprings outside his store in order to attract attention.

*Wednesday, July 3, 1940.*    I had thought that Walter would be disturbed over losing the Goldmanns as tenants, but their plan to move has actually proved agreeable to him.

"If Carillo wants to go off chasing women and leaves the running of the business to me, he'll have to give me another raise," Walter said. "And with an additional hundred pesos a month I can afford to rent the downstairs apartment myself. This will give Eva a home of her own, especially the kitchen she keeps bothering me about. The Goldmanns couldn't have done me a bigger favor."

*Wednesday, July 10, 1940.*    Today I paid Josef the second visit this week. When I called on Monday, Señora Consuelo had whispered that I must come see him more often.

Josef is out of bed now, but he still looks bad. The skin of his face is yellow, with little red veins in it, and his eyes are bloodshot. Although the sun was bright this morning and it was warm even in the shade, Josef shivered as he sat in his customary wicker chair in the loggia.

Considering that we are such old friends, it is strange that I should find it so difficult to keep a conversation going with him. We rarely talk about personal matters and most of the time stick to rehashing the war news: the recent battle of Oran; the ironic fact that the French government in Vichy has severed relations with Britain; the sorry news that Laval is back in power.

Josef seemed listless and talked without his usual keen interest in politics.

*Monday, July 15, 1940.*    Today was moving day for the Goldmanns —a day which Frau Goldmann cursed from dawn to dusk. Though there was no river to cross in which her precious possessions might be lost forever, she relived all the agonies of our debarkation in Rioverde.

"Beasts!" she said to the Indians who carried out her treasures and dumped them on the truck that was to take them to her new home. "Nothing but wild beasts! You'd think they'd never been inside a human habitation before!"

The Indians took her shouting stoically, a vacant grin on their olive faces. "Gringa loca," they said. Crazy foreigner. Did it really matter if a table was scratched and a pane of glass in the china cabinet broken?

"And not only that they're clumsy, they steal with their eyes!" Frau Goldmann wailed. "I tell you, Markus, one can't watch them enough! They steal with their eyes!"

Finally Herr Goldmann threw up his hands and said that her complaints were more than he could bear; that moving was a woman's business; that he was indispensable in the store; and he cowardly fled the scene of the holocaust.

Only Horowitz remained as Frau Goldmann's mainstay. As a last-minute reprieve he had been allowed to move with the Goldmanns into their new home. There was no menial task which he would not have done gladly for Frau Goldmann today.

A little later Trude came over to offer her help, only to throw her mother into another fit of histrionics.

"Don't you dare touch anything! A woman in your condition!"

"Mama, don't be childish! Dr. Landau says I'm perfectly able to do anything I want to do—except horseback riding. And I have no such ambitions."

*Friday, July 19, 1940.*     Eva and Walter have moved downstairs—over Frau Kramer's protest.

"What do you want, Mama?" Walter said irritably when his mother would not cease her remonstrances. "All the time you kept saying that you could use an additional room. Well, you've got one now!"

"*I* said such a thing?" Frau Kramer protested, completely forgetting how she had fought to keep the entrance to Eva's room open. "What do I need such a large apartment for? And what, I ask you, does your wife need an apartment for? Half the day she isn't home anyway!"

"Is that true, Eva?" Walter asked.

"You don't think your mother is lying to you?" Eva replied with her gentle gift for antagonizing everybody.

"Well, where the hell do you go every day?"

Eva put on her superior face—another maddening habit of hers.

"Where do I go? I go for walks with Trude! A pregnant woman is supposed to exercise, and Trude is much too lazy to go walking by herself!"

*Tuesday, July 23, 1940.*     Our tea parties have moved to a new location.

Horowitz spends most of his time in his store now. He has transferred his electric stove, his tea kettle, his cups and saucers, and two rickety chairs into the small room behind his store. This room doubles as a bodega and a social gathering place, sort of a private club run by Leo Horowitz. Everybody who passes the Casa León drops in. This popularity gives him a chance to extol his political views more widely—not that he ever makes any proselytes. Most adults are as firmly embedded in their political convictions as crustaceans in so many layers of rock.

Dr. Landau and I have to hurry now and come right after the midday siesta if we want to find an unoccupied chair in Horowitz' back room. Sitting there, we can look across the street to Levy's Casa Universal, Goldmann's Casa Elsa, and a little farther down the Avenida Bolívar, Frau Fleischer's fashion salon, Vogue. What makes this view even more pleasant is the sight of the ladies strolling from store to store as they make their purchases. (A few days ago Frau Fuchs stepped into the Casa Elsa, after ogling a nightgown in the window. Presently the nightgown was removed from the showcase, and Dr. Landau, watching from Horowitz' back room like a spider, proceeded to such a graphic description of Frau Fuchs in the nightgown as could make a man shun women forever.)

Horowitz said wistfully that he should also have gone into ladies' wear.

"Women buy. Men sell. Do you ever see Aronoff, with all his money, buy anything? But selling, that's another story! Even Levy has become his customer!"

And, says Horowitz, there are certain items Aronoff can get which nobody else can get.

"I tell you, he comes in here and shows me silk ties . . . such silk, such patterns! Nobody else in Esperanza has such ties! So what can I do? I order from him!"

"You, Horowitz, ordering merchandise from Aronoff!"

"Well, should I wait until he sells the ties to my competitors? You think I like buying from Aronoff? You think I wouldn't rather buy from his cousin, what's his name, Klein? He sells cheaper too than Aronoff! But then, if you buy from Aronoff, you know you'll get what you ordered."

"Tell me, Horowitz, what have you got against Aronoff?" I asked.

"I don't know. He's so . . . he's so . . . ."

"Capitalistic," Dr. Landau offered helpfully.

At this point in the conversation, Aronoff came out of Levy's store. The afternoon sun was full upon him, painting dark shadows around his deep-set eyes and throwing his sensuous mouth into sharp relief. As so often before, I was struck by the air of effortless virility about him. A woman walked by, stopped by the window of the Almacén Vogue and glanced slyly back at him. The corners of his lips curled slightly but he did not follow her.

Horowitz, who had observed this little scene, said bitterly:

"Women! He's got all the women! On me he's making money, so no wonder he's got all the women. Would they look at him twice without his money? The only woman who doesn't pay the slightest attention to him is Eva Kramer. She's not like the others. She's different," he added, almost with reverence.

"Funny person that Eva Kramer," Dr. Landau said. "Such a beautiful girl and not interested in men."

That's what he thinks!

*Saturday, July 27, 1940.* A little thought-provoking incident this morning:

I was sitting on the terrace, reading the morning paper. Eva had gone off half an hour earlier on one of her strolls, accompanied by Don, who ran after her with wild, cheerful barks. Through the open door to the apartment I could hear Frau Kramer vigorously belaboring her carpets with a palmetto broom. Presently she came out on the terrace in her national costume—slippers, robe, and a scarf wound around her hair—to shake out a dustcloth.

As she stood leaning over the banister, Levy's chauffeur-driven car pulled up in front of the house and Trude clumsily got out of it. She looked heavy and amorphous as she stood in the garden below, her maternity dress floating around her, her feet in the flat-heeled shoes planted slightly apart, her upturned face freckled and bloated.

"Good morning!" she called up to Frau Kramer. "Is Eva home?"

"Eva?" Frau Kramer said. "Of course she isn't home! Didn't she go to your house?"

Trude's mouth opened and for a moment she looked confused. Then she quickly slapped her hand to her forehead and exclaimed:

"How stupid of me! I had Ramón drive me to the market and I forgot all about Eva! I guess I'd better hurry home!"

She walked heavily back to the car and got in, head first and massive rear last. Frau Kramer watched scornfully as the car drove away. Then she turned to me:

"Featherbrains, those girls. Give them a household to run and they lose their heads completely!"

Frau Kramer went inside to finish tidying up her realm in righteous indignation. In a way I was glad that it had not occurred to her that Trude might not be a featherbrain so much as a liar.

*Tuesday, July 30, 1940.*     Josef is worse again.

When I called on him today he was in his room, sitting in an easy chair by the window. Señora Consuelo had tucked a blanket around him, but one of his slippered feet stuck out below. Between the pajamas and the slippers the skin across his ankle was bluish-white and flaky. He talked listlessly about the political situation in Europe and about the weather in Esperanza, now in the glory of the dry season.

I cautiously brought up Dr. Landau's name again, but Josef was still firm about not wanting to consult him.

"It is nothing," he said again.

But his face looked even more drawn than the last time I had seen him, and now and then he shut his eyes and compressed his lips as if he were trying to stave off a surge of pain.

Frankly, I am frightened. I shall try to describe his symptoms to Dr. Landau and hear what he has to say.

*Saturday, August 3, 1940.*     Today Don followed me to the Centro.

When I left home he accompanied me to the corner as is his habit, but this time, instead of trotting home after I had boarded the bus, he jumped in after me. He got off with me at the station near the Centro and continued to follow me, always pretending that he was more interested in the novel scents along the way than in where I was going. But when I entered the Centro he was still behind me. It was about four o'clock in the afternoon and virtually everybody was there for a cup of coffee: the Goldmanns; the Lipschitzes; the Fleischers; Horowitz; Levy and Trude. Don's joy in meeting so many of his acquaintances—some of whom he had not seen in quite a while—was beyond description. He, in turn, was greeted by all who knew him like an honorary member of the club.

After he had said hello to all his friends he came back and lay down beside me. I was in the middle of a conversation with Horowitz when Don got up quietly and walked over to another table.

Looking around, I saw that Klein had come in. Don sat down beside him and put his muzzle on his knee. Klein stroked the dog's head until he realized that I was staring at him. Belatedly he tried to shoo Don away but the dog would not budge.

Frau Lipschitz noticed that Klein was trying to get rid of Don and called out:

"Don! Here, Don! Don't bother the gentleman, you don't even know him!"

Don looked back at her, flicked his tail twice, and lay down under Klein's chair.

Frau Lipschitz shook her head.

"I don't know what's got into the dog," she said. "He usually doesn't take to strangers."

My eyes met Trude's for a brief second, but we quickly looked away from each other, like thieves.

*Wednesday, August 7, 1940.* Today Señora Consuelo finally prevailed upon me to call Dr. Landau. Josef had passed out during the night on his way to the bathroom—after his own doctor had prescribed a laxative to "clean out the patient."

A sign of how worn out Josef was: he did not even have the strength to protest Dr. Landau's visit and meekly submitted to an examination.

Dr. Landau was shaking with fury and frustration when he came downstairs to the room where Señora Consuelo and I were waiting. Señora Consuelo immediately questioned him whether Josef's trouble was indeed caused by an enlarged liver. Dr. Landau replied with bitter mockery in German, directing the answer at me and leaving me with the unpleasant task of translating it for Señora Consuelo:

"Enlarged liver, my foot! Herr Blumenthal's got a growth there so big you can already feel it with your fingers! He ought to be taken to a hospital immediately for X rays and an operation!"

*Sunday, August 11, 1940.*    Josef is to be operated on tomorrow, early in the morning. The X rays taken two days ago clearly showed a tumor on his liver. By appealing directly to the president of El Paramo, his boyhood friend, Señora Consuelo's brother obtained permission for Dr. Landau to assist Dr. Guerrera at the operation.

This afternoon I went to visit Josef. He had had a number of visitors before me. His wife's family had been to see him in the morning, and later in the day Kramer, Goldmann, and Levy to bring the best wishes of the Jewish community. ("After all, if not for Señor Blumenthal, many of us would not be here today!")

Señora Consuelo had been in the hospital since daybreak, silently praying as she sat in the huge easy chair beneath the crucifix in the corner of the room. Her eyes never left Josef's bed.

Dr. Landau had spread word around that blood would be needed for a transfusion, and shortly after I had arrived in the hospital Eva, Walter, Dr. Lipschitz, Herr Fleischer and, surprisingly, Horowitz came to be tested. ("So what," Horowitz said when Fleischer teased him about having his blood transfused into capitalistic veins, "to save a Jewish life I can spare a pint of blood!" Proving again that when it comes to dying people revert from politics to religion.)

Eva was the only one who qualified and was told to hold herself in readiness for tomorrow.

The coming and going proved a diversion to Josef, but after everybody had left and he was alone with his wife and me, I could see that beneath his outward optimism he was terribly frightened. When I said good-by to him he did something he had not done since the day of my arrival: he embraced me.

I wish it were twenty-four hours later. Josef has begged me to stay with Señora Consuelo tomorrow and give her strength.

Where am I supposed to get strength? I feel frightened and guilty. Dr. Landau says the X rays look very bad.

*Monday, August 12, 1940.*     We all know that death is inevitable, yet every time this fact is brought home to us it is a renewed shock. Josef is beyond help.

Dr. Landau says he may have another month to live, perhaps two months; perhaps half a year. "Sometimes they hang onto life a long time, especially if they have a strong heart like Herr Blumenthal's."

Señora Consuelo is still frozen in rigid disbelief.

"Of course he will get well," she says. "Didn't he live through the operation? He will get well as soon as he comes home!"

I spoke to Dr. Landau after he came out of the operating room. White-faced, in his white coat and white cap, he looked like a ghost.

"I never liked operations," he said. "The human body is frail and we know so little."

"Will he be all right?" I asked, aware that Dr. Landau would have told me so immediately if this were the case.

"If he dies fast he will be all right. He is too far gone for help. And why? Because of neglect, stupidity, ignorance, superstition."

Dr. Landau sounded as if he were enumerating the plagues.

"I cannot believe that he is going to die," I said.

I cannot believe it, for we were boys and young men together, and if his time to die has come mine cannot be far off.

*Tuesday, August 13, 1940.*     This morning Herr Kramer reminded me that today was Tisha B'ab, the great day of mourning for the destruction of the temple. It could not have fallen in a grimmer period of the year. For days the Nazis have been bombing England heavily; we are beginning to wonder when they will attempt an invasion. And the Italians, always ready to take advantage of a weakened enemy, have invaded British Somaliland.

In the afternoon Josef had a relapse and Eva was hurriedly called in for a transfusion. When she came out of his room she looked white and shaky, and a sister had to help her to one of the stone benches beneath the colonnades which run around the inside patio of the hospital.

Eva closed her eyes and leaned her head against a pillar. She appeared strained and her face had lost some of its childish roundness.

"I never knew anybody who was dying," she said, opening her eyes again. "It's hard to imagine, especially in this place. It doesn't look like a hospital at all. It looks like a convent."

Eva is right. This is nothing like our hospitals in Europe with their long, shiny corridors, and nurses and interns scurrying back and forth. Dr. Guerrera's hospital is a flat structure built around an inside patio. Beneath the pillared archway, Catholic sisters in long white habits pass from room to room. There are rose trees and beds of blue irises between the tiled walks of the patio, and in the center a fountain, dry now because of the season. Instead of the soft trickling of water one hears the groaning of the postoperative cases, a grim reminder that one is in a hospital after all.

After a while Señora Consuelo came out of Josef's room to thank Eva. She embraced her, patting her back in the native fashion.

"Que Dios le pague," she said. "May God reward you."

Eva winced, whether because of the physical contact or because of what Señora Consuelo had said, I don't know. I doubt that she believes in such rewards. But perhaps she should. We can all stand a credit account with God.


*Thursday, August 15, 1940.*    "Where will we bury him when he dies?" Herr Kramer said to me today. "There is no Jewish cemetery in Esperanza!"

"He isn't going to die yet," I replied testily. "Besides, I don't think it will make much difference to Josef where he is buried."

"But he ought to be buried in a Jewish cemetery," Herr Kramer insisted. "You will have to talk to him about it!"

I felt anger rising up inside of me like a surge of bile.

"See here, Herr Kramer, I refuse to bury a man while he is still alive! He has no idea yet that he is going to die. And if you value my friendship at all, don't go sneaking in behind my back to talk with him about cemeteries."

I could tell from Herr Kramer's guilty face that this was exactly what he had had in mind.

"Besides, Josef's burial place is something to be decided on by him and Señora Blumenthal."

Frau Lipschitz, who had been present during the argument, wrinkled her nose.

"Much she'll care where he is buried! If you want my opinion, he won't be cold in his grave before she'll get married to one of her own kind!"


*Saturday, August 17, 1940.*    Surprisingly, Walter is a daily visitor to Josef. He never stays long, just drops in, speaks a few words with Josef and leaves again. Today he was very excited about the recent German bombing raids which ranged as far as Scotland, but he kept his accounts down to a minimum. Josef is still too listless and weak for long conversations, but he appreciates Walter's visits.

"It's very good of him to come. Really a nice young man, that Walter Kramer. He has his weaknesses . . . but then he's still young."

I made a remark to Walter about his faithful attendance.

"Look, I owe Herr Blumenthal my job," he said. "I didn't think too much of it at first, but it turned out all right. Next week I'm going down to Aguas Calientes for Carillo to look over the territory and make some initial sketches for a hotel and a couple of private homes which he's to build there. There is an extra bonus in it for me. But what's more important, people are beginning to realize that I am doing most of Carillo's building. I get a chance to make a reputation for myself. I've already had a few offers to build houses for some prominent citizens— and the hell with Carillo."


*Monday, August 19, 1940.*    Another anniversary: it is a year today that the Centro was opened.

Still, I was shocked when Walter told me that an anniversary ball had been planned for the coming Saturday. I had been so preoccupied with Josef's sickness that the news reached me only now. I tried to remonstrate with Walter.

"How will it look, with the president of the Centro sick in the hospital and the situation in Europe as bad as it is just now?" (Two days ago the Germans proclaimed a total blockade of British waters.)

Walter shrugged.

"Herr Blumenthal will be out of the hospital before the end of the week," he said. "And there isn't a thing we can do about the situation in Europe. Life just goes on."

*Tuesday, August 20, 1940.* Today Aronoff stopped me in the street and inquired after Josef. I was surprised that he should be interested. I doubt that he has ever talked with Josef.

"Too bad," he said when I told him the sad truth. "A very remarkable old man."

"Remarkable, why?"

"Well, it took guts to come here twenty-five years ago, when he did not have to come. It's always easier to stay put where you are and be satisfied with what you can make there. How many of us would have come to El Paramo had we had a choice?"

*Thursday, August 22, 1940.* Josef is going home tomorrow.

For the past two days he has intermittently been out of bed, taking short walks, supported on one side by a sister and on the other by Señora Consuelo. It is sad to see how little is left of the once robust man. Though his abdomen is still extended with the dressing, his chest is sunken and his legs and arms are spindly. He walks haltingly and hunched over, like an invalid learning to walk again. The sisters pass, smile and whisper to Señora Consuelo that he is doing very well. It is all part of an old ritual in which lying is not a sin. Perhaps they also believe in miracles.

Josef himself never discusses his sickness. He inquires after everyday events; his household; his dogs; and even affairs of the Centro. Some fool told him that there is to be a ball Saturday, and today I was touched when he urged me to attend.

"Look, Norman, men our age must grab all the little pleasures that are left us."

Perhaps he is right. Perhaps I ought to go to the ball.

*Friday, August 23, 1940.* Walter assisted in bringing Josef home today. While Señora Consuelo exchanged farewell embraces with the sisters, Walter gently helped Josef ease himself into his car. We rode back, Señora Consuelo and I sitting in the back with Josef, Walter in front with the chauffeur.

Josef's entire staff—the cook, the muchachas, the Indian who waits on the table, and the two Indians who tend the garden—were waiting by the gate to welcome him.

"Bienvenído patrón!" they shouted.

The cook, who has been with the Blumenthals ever since they were married, cried bitterly when she saw how thin he had become.

"We will feed him well, señora, and he will soon be his old self again," she assured her mistress.

Together with the chauffeur, Walter carried Josef upstairs and helped place him in his easy chair by the window. While Señora Consuelo rushed for additional blankets and the servants retired to attend to their duties, Walter briefly mentioned that he was going to Aguas Calientes next week.

A flicker of interest crept into Josef's eyes when he heard the name of the place. "You know, I built the road from Esperanza to Aguas Calientes," he said.

"I know," Walter said.

In the afternoon the entire colony knew that Walter had helped to bring Josef home.

"What's the matter with Walter Kramer?" Herr Fleischer asked suspiciously. "Does he want Herr Blumenthal to mention him in his will?"

Thus people will question even the most honest intentions.

*Sunday, August 25, 1940.*     Calming my conscience with the excuse that Josef himself had urged me to, I attended the anniversary ball in the Centro last night.

It was distinguished from the inauguration ball by its name only. The buffet was set up in the same spot, under the same blue and white banner, as the last time. The same ladies donated the identical dishes which they had given for the previous event. The same men acted as bartenders and the same people got drunk. And a few unfortunate women even wore the same dresses.

Eva wore a pale-pink silk gown which gave her an ethereal quality. The men with whom she danced held her with a certain tenderness, as if she were a fragile object. Only Fleischer kept forcing her into his embrace until she threatened to slap him. He took it as a joke, but I think she was serious.

Though Herr Klein was present this time he did not dance with Eva and became conspicuous through the omission. I don't know whether Eva avoided him to keep Walter off guard, or whether she did not trust Klein to put his arms around her. He spent the whole evening near the bar, dancing only once or twice with the girl Halpern had brought to the ball.

(By the way, Halpern has quit his job in the Centro and has gone into partnership with Klein. This may not bring him a larger income, but at least it spares him the embarrassment of having to wait on Trude and Levy.)

At the dance Halpern seemed to find solace in the company of another homely girl who must be one of the new arrivals. He kept taking her past Trude's table as if to impress her with the fact that she was expendable.

If Halpern was able to do without Trude, Levy clearly was not. He did not budge from her side, turning away the few who, out of courtesy, came to ask her for a dance with the words:

"You must excuse us, but we're expecting!"

"You know," Fleischer whispered drunkenly, "he's guarding her like a signed blank check. Anybody can fill in now!"

He was so delighted with his wit that he began threading his way from table to table to spread the joke. When Eva saw him approach she fled and came to sit with me.

"If drunks were able to see themselves, they would never touch another drop of alcohol," she said.

Out on the dance floor Walter was dancing cheek to cheek with Frau Fleischer. Her red hair brushed across his face and he kept his eyes half closed.

As she watched Walter, a contemptuous little sneer appeared around Eva's mouth. Cautiously her eyes moved away to where Klein was sitting near the bar. He had taken off his glasses and was staring at her with his eyes naked and hungry. When their eyes met he squirmed as if to get up, but Eva slowly turned her face away without changing her expression and he sank back onto his chair.

Later Herr Schwarzkopf came to wheedle a dance from Eva, but she curtly turned him away.

"That is one man I can't stand," she said. "The worst part is that I have already turned him down three times tonight and he still comes back for more!"

The most talked-about contretemps of the evening—which otherwise passed uneventfully—was provided by Aronoff. Shortly after midnight he was found making love to a lady in the bathroom.

When Eva heard about it she broke into sincere laughter, untinged by wistfulness. Perhaps she has really outgrown Aronoff. Or perhaps he has been entirely supplanted by Klein. I don't know that this is the better alternative. Aronoff at least is a man.


*Monday, August 26, 1940.*    Walter has left for Aguas Calientes.

This morning, just before he was picked up by the car which Señor Carillo had put at his disposal for the trip, he made a jesting remark to me:

"You'll keep an eye on Eva while I'm gone, Herr Professor!"

Eva flushed violently at the joke.

"I don't need watching," she said in a sharp voice.

"You see," Walter said, "she takes every innocent remark as an insult! Or do you have a bad conscience?"

"Why should I have a bad conscience?"

"Well, I don't know. You see, I asked her to come along," Walter explained to me. "There's plenty of room in the car. But she wouldn't come. Not interested, the lady said."

"What am I to do for four days in a god-forsaken place like Aguas Calientes?"

"It's supposed to be a very beautiful place. That's why they want to put up a hotel there."

"I'll go when the hotel is finished," Eva said.

We were talking in our front yard where we stood waiting for the car to come for Walter. The sun was hot and high, even in the forenoon, and we threw short, squat shadows on the white gravel walk. There was not a cloud in the sky, and the ridge of the Andes had a plastic, three-dimensional clearness. It was a beautiful day and I thought Eva a fool for not going along with Walter.

On the terrace above Frau Kramer appeared in turban and robe to shake out a dustcloth. Walter had been up to say good-by to his parents earlier, and when Frau Kramer saw him standing in the garden below she bent over the banister to utter the old, self-answering inquiry:

"You're still here?" And then, as an afterthought: "Did you tell her?"

"Oh, yes, Eva, I almost forgot," Walter said. "Mama told me you could eat with them while I'm gone. And if you're afraid to sleep alone downstairs you can sleep upstairs in our old room."

Eva recoiled; her face became flat and hard and she said quickly, addressing herself to Walter rather than to Frau Kramer, who stood directly above us:

"That's very kind of your mother, but no, thank you. I've already been invited by Trude and Irene Braun, and I'm not at all afraid to sleep alone."

"Eva has already been invited," Walter transmitted the answer upstairs.

Frau Kramer retreated from the terrace, her face screwed up in a grimace of hurt feelings mixed with relief.

Outside the gate the car arrived, forty-five minutes late but with the horn wildly blowing as if it had come for a tardy passenger.

"Well, good-by again!" Walter called, snatched up his suitcase, pressed a quick kiss on Eva's cheek (she had cleverly managed to turn away her mouth), and dashed out to the car, which departed honking in a gray cloud of dust.

"Four days," Eva said with a little sigh.

I still wonder whether it was a sigh of sorrow or of relief.

*Wednesday, August 28, 1940.*     A frightening occurrence last night: we had a prowler around the house.

Ever since Josef became sick I have been sleeping very poorly. I usually make my entries at night and then try to read myself to sleep. But last evening even reading failed to make me drowsy, and after I had turned out the light I got up once more and stood looking out the window into our back yard.

The night was cold and moonlit, and the air eerily luminous and dark blue. The shadows in the garden were thick and black, like shreds of velvet cast upon the lawn. There was not a breeze, and I was marveling at the rigid silhouettes of the palm trees which the moonlight traced upon the ground when I suddenly saw one of the shadows move. It took me a second to realize that what I had seen was not the swaying of a palm leaf but a figure gliding over the wall which separates our garden from the empty lot behind it. The figure was temporarily swallowed by the heavy shadow of the garden wall and I thought I had been tricked by my vision. But the next instant a man emerged from the shadow and bounded across the lawn toward the house.

I wonder whether all people act stupidly in an emergency. At first I stood petrified, not knowing what to do. Next I thought of Eva sleeping alone downstairs. I turned on the light, slipped into my robe and ran out onto the gallery above the hall. I had already begun to descend the stairs when it occurred to me that I ought to have some sort of weapon. The only thing I could think of was a kitchen knife, so I turned around and rushed back into Frau Kramer's kitchen. She had been putting up some new curtains in the afternoon and there was a hammer lying on the kitchen table. I forgot about the knife, grabbed the hammer and ran downstairs.

Without much thinking, I first approached the door connecting the hall with the corridor which leads to Eva's bedroom at the back of the house. I tried the door, but it was locked.

I thought of knocking, but was afraid that this might frighten Eva if she was asleep. Instead I decided to venture outside and take a look around the house. I don't know whether I felt more scared or silly as I sneaked out, holding my robe together with one hand and clutching the hammer with the other. If anybody had surprised me, he would undoubtedly have taken me for a lunatic.

As it turned out, there was not a soul around the house. I walked all the way toward the back, first listening at Eva's kitchen door, which leads into the garden, and then under her bedroom window. But both door and window were securely locked and there was not a sound within.

As I threaded my way back along the house, it dawned on me that the prowler had probably been scared away when I turned on the light in my room.

The first thing I did this morning was to go downstairs and ask Eva if she had heard anything suspicious the previous night. The door to her corridor was still locked and only after I had knocked repeatedly did she come to open it. She was sleepy-eyed, wearing her robe, and she yawned in my face. She said she had read late and had overslept now that Walter was not at home to wake her. But she had heard nothing. Possibly I might have been mistaken.

I went upstairs again and talked over the incident with the Kramers at the breakfast table. Notwithstanding my report that the prowler had come over the back wall, Herr Kramer maintained that it was all Eva's fault because she never locked the front gate at night. In the future he would personally see to it. Frau Kramer wondered why Don had not barked. But then Don has a habit of sleeping at the most inopportune times.


*Thursday, August 29, 1940.*    The nightly intruder has repeated his visit—but I know better now than to take him for a prowler.

This time I saw him by mere chance. Exhausted from my adventure the night before I had gone to bed right after finishing my entry and had fallen asleep almost instantly. When I was awakened by drunken singing and shouting I thought at first that it was close to morning, but when I reluctantly opened my eyes I found that it was still dark.

For a while I lay motionless, hoping that the noise would stop and that I would fall asleep again. The drunken singing and the playing of the reed pipe only became louder, and then I remembered that the previous day had been San Pablo and that the Indian who lives in the cornfield behind our house was probably celebrating the day of his patron saint.

I was loath to get up and shut the window, which I had left open, sure that once I rose I would be unable to fall asleep again. But the party in the adobe hut of our neighbor might go on for hours, so I decided that I had better get up and close the window after all.

The night was clear and calm like the one before, the blue tinged with the red glow of the fire which the Indian had lit in his back yard. Against the fire I could see a number of figures crouching in a circle around a man and a woman who were dancing. The woman was holding her skirt with both hands, swishing it from side to side as she turned. The man had lowered himself on one knee, twirling a handkerchief above his head as the woman slowly, ceremoniously circled around him.

Don was loose in the garden, barking furiously at the wall from behind which the singing and shouting emanated. Once or twice he tried to scale the wall but it proved too high for him. Suddenly he lost interest in the wall and dashed across the garden. Looking after Don, I saw a man standing in the middle of our lawn.

I had not seen him enter, but he must have come in the same manner as on the previous night. I held my breath as I waited for his scream when Don attacked him—but nothing of the sort happened. Don gave one little yelp and started to jump around him like a puppy. The man bent down and patted his head. When he straightened up again the moonlight hit his face and I could see a glint of glasses. Accompanied by Don he walked toward the house and vanished into its dark shadow. I bent forward in the open window and thought to hear the soft opening and closing of a door below. Then it was quiet again and Don returned to barking at the wall and chasing his own shadow.

I don't know how long I remained standing by the window, trying to arrange and rearrange in my mind what had happened the past two nights. I knew now why Eva had locked the door to her corridor and why she had looked tired and sleepy in the morning. I also knew why Don had not barked. I felt a deep, churning hurt, not unlike the one I had felt when Christine told me that it was over between us. Despairing of being able to fall asleep I went back to bed, but I must have slept, for I remember dreaming of Eva dancing with the Indian to the lament of the reed pipe.

This morning Eva came up on the terrace to take her sun bath. It was the third morning in a row that she had not gone for a long walk. She lay there with her almost-bare body, her palms turned upward and her lips slightly parted, breathing evenly. Her hair was spread around her on the towel and her face looked smooth and innocent.

The slut, I thought furiously. Oh, God, the slut! But cursing her in my mind did not make me feel better. One does not restore a dream by sullying it.

When Eva opened her eyes I said to her:

"You're a sound sleeper. You ought to make sure to lock your kitchen door securely at night. I heard noises again yesterday. I am convinced that somebody knows that Walter is away and is trying to break in."

Eva looked startled and then asked resentfully:

"What's the matter with you? Don't you sleep at night?"

In the afternoon she came up to the Centro and looked around. She blushed when she saw me—something she has never done before—and went to join Trude, who sat separated from the table by her massive belly.

Before I left I asked Eva if she wanted to come home with me. She shook her head and told me that Trude had invited her for dinner. Trude smiled a conspiratorial smile.

I wonder whether Eva was waiting to warn Klein off.


*Friday, August 30, 1940.*     Nothing last night.

I was so worn out from my two sleepless nights that I kept myself awake by sheer will power until eleven o'clock. I sat looking out the window from my darkened room until a quarter past eleven, but nobody came. Perhaps Klein used a new approach to the house and I did not see him. Perhaps he came after I went to sleep. I can't be sure and I keep telling myself that I don't care. This is Walter's affair. Thank God, he is coming home tonight.

*Tuesday, September 3, 1940.*     Every day I spend two hours with Josef. I try to remember how it was when I used to enjoy my visits to his house; our quiet sessions in the loggia, with the dogs lying at our feet and the palms swaying before the backdrop of the mountains.

Now every hour I spend with Josef is purgatory. I cannot forget for one moment that he is dying—even on the days when he feels better and leaves the bed to sit in his chair by the window. It is almost impossible for me to think of something to say to him. Outside of the great upheaval in Europe (day before yesterday it was one year since the war began!), every topic seems too trivial to be discussed with a dying man. Strangely, Josef now seems to crave the trivial. Today he asked me how Horowitz was doing. He smiled contentedly when I told him that Horowitz' business had picked up quite a bit after Aronoff had talked him into importing raincoats.

"Just let the man make a little money and he will soon forget about Communism," Josef said.

*Sunday, September 8, 1940.*     Yesterday I went to a birthday party: the Citizen was one year old.

He is a handsome boy with the bright eyes of his mother, but I doubt that he was old enough to enjoy the party, especially the conversation. We talked of nothing but war and Josef's sickness.

Last week Antonescu became premier of Rumania and King Carol fled and was replaced by his son Michael. The heavy bombardments on London continue.

As for Josef—there is little change.

*Wednesday, September 11, 1940.*     Today I told Horowitz what Josef had said about him last week. Horowitz exploded in anger—not against Josef but against Aronoff.

"He wants to corrupt me!" he said. "That's why he comes to me with these ideas. He wants to corrupt me!"

But I doubt that Aronoff is moved by any ideological motives to make Horowitz prosperous. I believe that his reasons are purely materialistic. He made as much money on the raincoat deal as Horowitz did.

I remember when he first proposed the business to Horowitz. I happened to be sitting with Dr. Landau in the back room while Horowitz was standing near his entrance, guarding his store against would-be shoplifters. Outside, a torrential rain was peppering the sidewalk. Suddenly a tall, broad-shouldered figure ducked into the Casa León. It was Aronoff. Shaking himself like a wet dog, he asked Horowitz:

"Do you mind if I wait out the rain here?"

Horowitz gave his consent with a minimum of civility. If he could have thought of an excuse he would have loved to turn Aronoff out. Aronoff remained close by the entrance, slapping his wet hat against his thigh while he glanced from the street to Horowitz and back to the street.

"Tell me, Herr Horowitz," he finally asked, "have you ever noticed what the men in Esperanza wear on a rainy day?"

Horowitz peeked outside suspiciously, as if the familiar street were suddenly crawling with dangerous enemies.

"What are they wearing!" he exclaimed indignantly. "They're wearing suits! What else should they be wearing?"

"Shouldn't they be wearing something else?" Aronoff asked.

"What is this, a riddle?" Horowitz fumed. "You think you can come in here and play games with me just because your name is Aronoff!"

"Don't be a fool, Herr Horowitz," Aronoff said with resignation. "If you're too blind to see for yourself, I'll tell you what the men are not wearing: not one of them is wearing a raincoat. And why aren't they wearing raincoats? Because there are none to be had in Esperanza! A city in which it rains six months out of the year, and not one store carrying raincoats! How would you like to sell raincoats, hundreds of raincoats, Herr Horowitz?"

Horowitz gaped at Aronoff and cautiously retreated a step or two, as if Aronoff were the evil one come to bargain for his soul.

The result was that Aronoff talked Horowitz into ordering, not hundreds, but two dozen raincoats for a trial.

One might say that the rest is history.

An hour after Horowitz had displayed the first raincoat in his tiny window, with the legend beneath it: "Impermeable Fino Importado," the coat was sold. Within the next two days he sold the rest of the coats. The news that the gringo in the Casa León had raincoats spread like wildfire and for days Horowitz was sieged by frustrated would-be buyers. He turned to Aronoff in a frenzy, throwing all scruples and ideology to the wind.

"Get me twenty dozen coats," he begged. "And get them for me before one of my competitors starts horning in on the business. Why should they make money on my idea?"

And thus Horowitz was started on his way to becoming a capitalist. It was only after he had sold the raincoats and had counted the profit that he came to the conclusion that Aronoff had set out, a priori, to corrupt him. But by then it was too late to turn back the tide of prosperity.

*Sunday, September 15, 1940.*    Today Walter accompanied me on my visit to Josef.

In a procedure that now has become a ritual, we first talked about the war. (A few days ago the British bombed several Continental ports in an effort to keep the Germans from attempting an invasion. In view of the fact that the Italians have invaded Egypt, this small British gain is a minor consolation to us.) But only when Walter began to talk about his recent trip to Aguas Calientes did Josef show real interest in the conversation. Walter said that with the road from Esperanza making it easily accessible, the new hotel in Aguas Calientes should be doing brisk business during the dry season.

Josef's eyes brightened at the mention of the road—*his* road. Walter had told me earlier that the road would need considerable widening and improving to become serviceable, but he said nothing about this to Josef. What always amazes me anew is that Walter can be the most thoughtless person one moment, the next the most tactful.

Much as Josef seemed to enjoy Walter's visit, he soon began to show signs of weariness and we left. Walter asked me if I would like to come along and see the site where the firm Carillo was to build a low-cost housing project for the city. He said Eva had promised to come along too.

Ever since Walter's return, I have been baffled by a new closeness between Walter and Eva. This is the first time that Eva has displayed any real interest in Walter's work. She has repeatedly accompanied him to his local building projects and has drastically curtailed her morning strolls. I cannot fathom what caused this change of attitude. Perhaps she is haunted by a guilty conscience. Perhaps all this is just part of her pattern of deceit.

But how deceitful can a woman get?

*Thursday, September 19, 1940.*　　This morning Herr Kramer joined me on the terrace to discuss the news. It was heartening inasmuch as the British, now that they are receiving arms from the United States, have inflicted heavy losses on the German air raiders.

Eva lay sunning herself on her towel, listening to us with closed eyes and a bored face. After a while Frau Kramer appeared in her working clothes, glanced disapprovingly at the lounging Eva, and pointedly asked what had become of her daily walks with Trude.

Without opening her eyes, Eva brazenly replied that Trude was so heavy now that she simply refused to move.

She *is* deceitful!

*Monday, September 23, 1940.*　　Lately Josef's mind has been wandering. One moment he will talk about the present, the next he will slip back into the past with no transition whatsoever. Yesterday he suddenly asked me what had become of my sister Reisel, the one who ran away with the cavalry officer.

I was so startled by the unexpected question that it took me a while to gather my wits. I had not thought of my sister Reisel for years, mostly, I suppose, because of some leftover childhood fear. I had been only ten when Reisel ran away, and the picture of my father tearing his clothes, sprinkling ashes on his head, and sitting shibah in his stockinged feet had made an overpowering impression on me. Perhaps what had made me feel so guilty during my affair with Christine had not been so much the thought of my wife but the memory of my father, mourning for dead his daughter who had run away with a Gentile.

As for Reisel—I could not answer Josef's question. I only hope that wherever she may be today people know her as the wife of an officer and nobody remembers that her maiden name was Bernstein.

*Saturday, September 28, 1940.*    Yesterday Italy and Germany concluded a ten-year military and economic treaty with Japan. We all laugh that the Japanese have suddenly turned into acceptable Aryans. But on the whole the reports from the war do not tickle our risibility. Early this week British and French troops under General de Gaulle attempted to occupy Dakar. Unfortunately, by the middle of the week they had to abandon their attempt.

There is not much news here. Josef's condition seems stationary now. Tonight I will have a welcome respite from my daily visits to him: a party at the Brauns'.

*Sunday, September 29, 1940.*    Eva has again managed to baffle me completely. She is beginning to encourage the attention of Herr Schwarzkopf, whom she has always professed to loath.

I was surprised to find that the Schwarzkopfs had been invited to the party at the Brauns' last night. Somehow they seemed to fit in oddly among the other guests. Outside of Eva and Walter, the Lipschitzes had been asked; also the Fleischers, Trude and Levy, and Horowitz, who, with his recent business success, is beginning to crash the more capitalistic circles.

As always at the Brauns', we had a delicious meal, which Herr Fleischer spiced (or should I say spoiled?) with a barrage of off-color stories. After dinner we broke up into smaller groups and sat around in the sala, sipping cordials and listening to some of Hans Braun's fine classical records.

Eva and Trude retired into a corner and stood there whispering together. Eva kept shaking her head and Trude looked worried. Presently Levy broke up the twosome by fetching his wife away and escorting her to a huge easy chair which he had pulled up for her by the fireplace.

(Trude has grown to monstrous size and her legs are pitifully swollen. Contrary to Dr. Landau's instructions that she keep moving, Levy insists that she ought to keep off her feet. Lazy Trude is only too glad to take her husband's advice.)

For the rest of the evening Trude remained in the chair, permitting Levy to prop a cushion under her feet, stuff her with sweets, and fan her flushed face. Eva said that Levy was behaving like a complete fool even before the baby was born, but I suspect that she was just envying Trude.

Not that Eva was not getting her usual quota of attention from the men. As always, Fleischer was showering her with flattery; Dr. Lipschitz sneaked an occasional affectionate pinch behind the back of his wife; and Schwarzkopf literally smothered her with what he considers his charm.

In spite of her rude behavior toward him, Eva seems to attract Schwarzkopf like a magnet. Last night his persistent pursuit of her was briefly rewarded. Eva had sat down to listen to the music. Before anybody could beat him to it, Schwarzkopf sat down beside her, bending forward and gazing at her with an ingratiating, silly grin on his face. But Eva's eyes were closed as she surrendered herself to the music. When Schwarzkopf realized that she was too absorbed to acknowledge his presence, he put his hand on her arm to draw her attention.

Eva reached across with her other hand and brushed off Schwarzkopf's fingers. He looked hurt, but two minutes later his hand crept back to her arm. Again she brushed him off. When he touched her a third time she opened her eyes and looked up angrily. Then, just before she turned her face to Schwarzkopf, she caught sight of Walter and Frau Schwarzkopf standing by the bar at the opposite end of the room. Frau Schwarzkopf was fluttering her eyes at Walter, and where they leaned on the bar their arms were touching tightly from shoulder to elbow.

Eva's expression of anger changed to interest. Walter looked confused when he saw his wife watching him but was arrested halfway in the act of moving away from Frau Schwarzkopf when he noticed Schwarzkopf's hand on Eva's arm. He grinned at Eva in a half-hopeful, half-conspiratorial manner. Eva smiled back at him, closed her eyes, and permitted Schwarzkopf's hand to remain where it was.

I was really vexed by Eva's behavior. What she expects from further-ing an alliance between Walter and Frau Schwarzkopf (and I cannot think of another explanation for her odd attitude) is beyond me. I doubt that Eva has any idea of how much trouble an older woman can stir up when she gets involved with a younger man.

Before I could think of a discreet way to warn Eva, Frau Lipschitz relieved me of the delicate task by pulling Eva aside and saying quite bluntly:

"You'd better watch out for your husband and that Schwarzkopf woman. She's making a play for him!"

"Let's make a deal, Ruth: you watch out for your husband and I watch out for mine."

"All right, if you don't want some friendly advice! But mark my word, she's a vulgar and dangerous person!"

Frau Ruth stalked off and sat down beside Trude, presumably en-tertaining her for the rest of the evening with horror stories about the pains and dangers accompanying childbirth.

But she can hardly have created a greater feeling of uneasiness in Trude than Eva roused in me by submitting to Schwarzkopf's touch.

*Wednesday, October 2, 1940.*     Tomorrow is Rosh Hashana. Once again the house smells of baking and gefüllte fish. Another year of our lives has become a drop in eternity.

Life goes too fast.

*Sunday, October 6, 1940.*     The holidays passed uneventfully. As last year, Herr Kramer prayed before the congregation. Eva was again con-spicuously absent from the services. But this time Levy did not have to crane his neck for a glimpse of Trude. He knew that she was there, her bloated belly testifying to his proud ownership.

During the intermissions people talked less about politics and more about the need for a Hevrah Kadishah. Everybody seems to be waiting for Josef's death. Herr Kramer is still badgering me about a proper burial place for Josef. Frau Fuchs of the hairy teeth has offered herself for the pious job of washing the departed, thus adding a new dimension to the horror of dying.

*Friday, October 11, 1940.*    Politically a very active week in Europe. A few days ago Hitler and Mussolini conferred at the Brenner Pass. ("May they both rot in hell and the rest of the gangsters with them," Goldmann said.) Tuesday German troops entered Rumania, presumably to "protect" the oilfields there. To us this means more Jews under Nazi domination. Yesterday the Nazis made another heavy air raid on London. Even those among us who never had much liking for the English are beginning to feel great admiration for their courage. The only comforting news is that the French have taken possession of Duala in West Africa. It seems that for once Goldmann picked a winner in General de Gaulle.

In the afternoon I called on Josef and we reminisced about our walk home together after the Yom Kippur services last year, as if this were an event which had taken place in the remote past.

"Tomorrow you will have to do without me," Josef said sadly.

Before I left he pressed my hand and asked me to pray for him. I am not sure in just which way he meant it.

*Wednesday, October 16, 1940.*    Today Josef himself brought up the question of where he is to be buried.

"You're not dying yet," I said lamely when he broached the subject.

His yellow lips twisted into a sad smile.

"You don't have to tell a man when he is rotting alive," he said. "You and Dr. Landau, always coming here with your sanctimonious faces . . ."

He closed his eyes and for a few minutes lay silent, the blanket above his body rising and falling as if he were asleep. I thought his mind had wandered as it does so often now, but soon he began to speak again.

"Have you ever seen the cemetery in Esperanza?" he asked.

I told him that I had not.

"I don't want to be buried there. It is a barren and desolate place at the other end of the city. There are no graves there. The coffins are stacked up vertically, one above the other, in niches carved out of the rock like postal boxes. You lie there like an unclaimed letter for the rest of eternity. I want to be buried in the ground. I want a stone on my grave and some flowers."

He paused and dozed off again. Or his mind had taken some devious detour only to return to the same topic.

"You remember the land I showed you once? The land up in the woods. I want to give it to the Centro for a Jewish cemetery."

"The land where you wanted to build your house?" I asked incredulously.

Again his lips curled into a bitter smile.

"The dreams one has," he said. "There were so many things I was going to do. For years I promised Consuelo to take her on a trip to Europe. But there was always something . . . a building to be finished . . . an investment to be made . . . now the war. All excuses. You know why most men never realize their dreams? Not for lack of opportunity but because of sloth."

*Sunday, October 20, 1940.*  The news that Josef wants to donate his land for a Jewish cemetery has created quite a stir in the Centro.

"Just let a man reach the threshold of death and he wants to return to the fold of his own people," Dr. Landau said thoughtfully. "We are never as emancipated as we think we are."

*Tuesday, October 22, 1940.*  The past few days Josef has become increasingly preoccupied with death.

"Who is going to say Kaddish for me?" he asked. "I should have had a son . . . But this was one thing I decided when I married Consuelo: we would not have children."

Incongruously, he began to chuckle to himself.

"Consuelo was baffled when I told her before we were married that I did not want children. 'But aren't we going to live as man and wife?' she asked. Poor Consuelo, she was so naïve!"

Again he lay quiet, breathing heavily. In the stillness of the room the smell of decay was oppressive. I wished Señora Consuelo would come to keep us company, but she never disturbs Josef when I am with him.

"Still, a man should have a son." Josef took up the thread of his former thought. "A son to say Kaddish for him. That's what my father always called me: his Kaddish. It was one of the first prayers we learned in cheder. The prayer for the dead. But when my father died I was already in South America."

He stopped speaking. I wondered whether he had said Kaddish for his father. There had been no Jewish congregation in Esperanza at that time.

What was he thinking of now? He lay with his eyes closed, the skin of his wasted face flaccid, his brow furrowed.

"The stench," he said, and for an instant I thought he had noticed the stench in the room. "The stench in the cheder. Do you remember the rabbi? He used to seal all the windows with wax for the winter. Winter and cheder always seemed to last eternally. We had a servant girl who used to carry me there when I was only three. She had high sheepskin boots and the snow crunched under her soles when she walked. I can still hear the crunching of the snow. . . . Do you remember how the rabbi used to hit you with his stick and how I told him one day if he did not stop hitting you there would be no more free chickens for him? You were like a brother to me. Do you remember how we cut off our sidelocks when the boys in the Gymnasium were teasing us . . . and the beating we got from our fathers when they found out? Do you remember . . ."

He went on like that for a while, digging up incidents which I had long forgotten. Perhaps this return to childhood was just another way of denying the approach of death.

One thing Josef accomplished with his reminiscing: he has started me on a macabre train of thought. He was always the trail blazer for the two of us. He was the first to go to the Gymnasium in Lemberg. I followed after him. He was the first to cut his sidelocks. I only aped him.

The first to visit a brothel; to enroll at the University of Vienna; to go to South America.

Now he is the first to die.

I am only sixty-two. Some people live to be ninety.

*Saturday, October 26, 1940.*   Today Goldmann cornered me and insisted that I come to inspect his books.

"A fine partner you are!" he said to me. "Not even interested in our business!"

I told Goldmann that I had no head for business just now and that I had complete confidence in him. (As if I had a choice!) But Goldmann remained adamant. If I did not check the books occasionally, people would soon be saying that he was stealing from me, what with business prospering, thank God!

Finally I permitted him to drag me into the Casa Elsa.

The store had changed considerably since I had last visited it. The glass-covered showcases which Frau Goldmann had ordered had arrived in the meantime, and the merchandise was displayed in such a way as to make each item look better than it was. I thought I could discern Frau Goldmann's artful hand. The shelves on the walls were laden with merchandise (obtained from Levy on long-term credit) and in the back room two sewing machines were humming busily.

Frau Goldmann proudly ushered me into her new factory, where she does the cutting while two girls do the sewing. Glad as she was to have help, she still had one complaint.

"You can't leave them alone for one minute," Frau Goldmann said. "They steal anything they can lay their hands on."

One corner of the factory had been set aside as an office for Goldmann. It was there that he piled his books before me on the battered, secondhand desk.

"Here, see for yourself how things are going!"

He stood gloating over my shoulder as I exclaimed with surprise at the upswing business had taken. According to the books, Goldmann had already paid off our entire debt to Levy and had obtained an even larger credit from him—merchandise somewhere in the neighborhood of five thousand dollars—a forbidding-looking sum. The turnover seemed to be getting better every month.

"You're making five hundred pesos a month now instead of two hundred," Goldmann revealed to me. "But if you would take out only two hundred fifty and leave the rest in the business, we could use it for increasing our capital. Of course I'll match you peso for peso!"

I told Goldmann to proceed any way he saw fit. He is the business brain among us.


*Thursday, October 31, 1940.*     The war in Europe keeps spreading. Two days ago the Italians invaded Greece from Albania. Yesterday British reinforcements were landed on Crete and other Greek islands, and in accordance with a treaty the Russians delivered a considerable number of fighter planes to Greece. The planes of the Russian allies of the Germans will, no doubt, be used to fight off the Italian allies of the Germans. Thus the irony of politics.


*Monday, November 4, 1940.*     We have run into some trouble with the land which Josef wants to donate for a Jewish cemetery. It seems that the zoning laws of Esperanza do not permit a cemetery inside the city limits; and this particular piece of land lies within the limits.

Today Josef's lawyer, a Dr. Gutiérrez, called on Josef, all apologies. He tiptoed into the room and stood hat in hand, gazing at Josef's wasted form in the bed with awe and curiosity.

When Josef heard the bad news he rallied and almost sat up in bed, a feat he had been unable to accomplish by himself for days.

"I don't care what the zoning laws say!" he shouted hoarsely. "You're a lawyer! You get us a permit for a cemetery!"

Dr. Gutiérrez promised to do what he could. If necessary he would call on the president. But Josef must be patient; it would take a while.

"Well, hurry it up," Josef said gruffly. He had sunk back on his pillow and closed his eyes. "I haven't got much time left and I want a Jewish burial."

I am not at all sure Josef realized that he had said the last words in Yiddish: a yiddishe levaye.

*Friday, November 8, 1940.*    Josef died this afternoon.

I had called on him in the morning, but he was already in a coma and did not recognize me. The house was eerily quiet and only the rattling breath of the dying man was audible all the way down into the hall. The Indians, always moving about soundlessly, were mere shadows; the women were ready to break into wailing the moment the rattling of the breath stopped.

I went home without speaking to Señora Consuelo. In the afternoon she sent over the Indian to tell me that Josef had died.

I was sitting on the terrace when the boy called up the message to me. It had been a cloudy morning but had cleared up later in the day, and Eva was sunning herself. Her skin has again turned a deep, golden brown. When she heard the news she drew her robe around her, as if death called for a chaste gesture on her part.

I took my hat and hurried over to Josef's house. The cook was cowering beneath the loggia, sobbing loudly. The other Indians stood around with vacant expressions on their faces, for all I know depicting grief. I hesitated a moment before I stepped inside, afraid of having to face Josef's widow.

In the hall inside I found Dr. Landau and Señora Consuelo, who had already changed into black. I doubt that Josef's face looked deader than hers, but she did not cry. None of her family had as yet arrived, and she was alone with Dr. Landau and me.

She looked up when I came in and said:

"He wanted a Jewish burial. These were the last words he said to me."

I was surprised at her composure, but from behind her Dr. Landau motioned to me, indicating that she was still in a state of shock. She did not break down until her sisters swept into the house, weeping. Then she fainted and had to be carried upstairs.

In the meantime the news of Josef's death had spread in the town. Before I had a chance to go upstairs and have a last look at him, Herr Kramer and Herr Levy arrived, both with the stiff expression of artificial sorrow on their faces. Josef's death had been anticipated for so long that now it had come as an anticlimax. For a moment I hoped fervently that my death would be sudden enough to leave an impact of loss.

Shortly after Kramer and Levy, Señora Consuelo's brother, Coronel Jiménez, came clanging into the house, resplendent in boots and dazzling uniform, but already with the Parameño's ever-ready black band of mourning on his sleeve. The only one who had met him previously was Dr. Landau, and he introduced him to us in the absence of Señora Consuelo.

Next ensued some embarrassing wrangling over Josef's funeral. Coronel Jiménez led off by informing us that he had already ordered a coffin covered in purple velvet, and that shortly flowers from the vast family would begin to arrive. Herr Kramer insisted heatedly that, according to orthodox Jewish laws, Josef must have a plain, wooden coffin and no flowers—absolutely no flowers. ("This is a funeral, not a wedding!") Moreover, Josef could not be buried tomorrow as planned by the family, for tomorrow was Saturday and no Jew may be buried on the Sabbath. Coronel Jiménez countered that the sanitary laws of El Paramo required immediate burial, but was persuaded, after much hand-wringing and entreaties, to call on the proper authorities to request permission for the postponement of the funeral.

No sooner had he left than Dr. Gutiérrez came with the disappointing news that it would still take weeks—months perhaps—before the city would grant us rights to a cemetery within its limits. Josef would have to be buried, if only temporarily, in the cemetery of Esperanza.

In the meantime Frau Fuchs had come stomping in and demanded in martial tones to be shown to the room of the departed. Dr. Landau whispered to me that she had probably spent the last days perching on the roof of a neighboring house, like a vulture.

After Walter Kramer arrived we all went upstairs to have a last look at Josef. He was stretched out on his bed, his eyes closed, his hands folded over his chest. His face was waxen but no longer yellow. It was white and almost smooth now that the pain that had racked him had ceased forever. I felt a great sadness looking at him—not so much because he was dead as because I was alone now and there would be no more reunions after the one at the railroad station of Esperanz

In one corner of the room sat the Catholic sister who had taken care of Josef during the last days of his illness, silently moving her lips as she ran the beads of her rosary through her fingers. Frau Fuchs was standing by Josef's bed, still with her hat and coat on, casting poisonous glances at the sister.

"She will have to go," Frau Fuchs said to us in German.

The sister threw a brief glance at the men who had crowded into the room and silently went on praying. There was again a whispered discussion among the men, one trying to pass on to the other the task of dismissing the sister. The shuffling and whispering attracted Señora Consuelo, who, blind with tears, came groping her way into the room to ask what was going on.

Walter looked uncomfortably from Señora Consuelo to Frau Fuchs to the sister praying in the corner.

"Let her stay, Frau Fuchs," he said, adding with the impiousness which does not desert youth even in the face of death: "He will go well insured to whatever part of heaven he's going to."

On the way home, though, Walter struck a more somber note.

"You know," he said, "Herr Blumenthal's death leaves me with the feeling that a limb has been cut off our community here. The only organic link connecting us with the people of Esperanza. Now we are on our own."


*Sunday, November 10, 1940.* I am still depressed by the memory of the morning. There is so little solace in a Jewish funeral.

Josef's coffin, placed on a bier in the center of the hall of his house, had been draped with a simple, black cloth. All the flowers which had been sent by his Parameño relatives and friends had been piled into the garage. Señora Consuelo's brother and sisters scurried around, explaining in apologetic whispers that the wreaths had been received but that, alas, the religion of the late Don José forbade the use of funeral decorations. People kept throwing shocked glances at us, as though we were barbarians.

Señora Consuelo came down from her room only after all the people who were to ride in the funeral procession had assembled in the hall below. The crowd was so great that it overflowed onto the loggia and into the garden. I had been appointed one of the pallbearers, and after I had helped place the coffin in the hearse, I got into the car with Señora Consuelo and the nearest of her kin. All the long, slow way to the cemetery we rode in silence. Señora Consuelo's sisters wept and held her hands. Coronel Jiménez sat beside me, looking grim and, as it appeared to me, embarrassed by the sight of the bare hearse before us.

The cemetery was not far from the railroad station where we had first arrived in Esperanza. There we had to wait a long time until the last car had disgorged the last member of the funeral procession. I could see Señora Consuelo, black veil over her face, wavering in the heat of forenoon as she leaned on the arm of her brother.

Now, as we stood waiting, I realized that practically the entire Jewish community had come to Josef's funeral, even such unlikely mourners as Grushka, Dubrovsky, and Brody. Only Trude and Frau Goldmann were missing. (Goldmann whispered to me that his wife had stayed home to keep a vigil over Trude.) A little distance from me Eva stood next to Walter, looking somber in a black dress which I had never seen her wear in the morning.

When all the people were assembled, the coffin was again placed on the shoulders of the pallbearers and, with Señora Consuelo and her family behind us, we led the way through the narrow gate into the cemetery.

The place was as desolate as Josef had described it to me. We passed rows and rows of graves, hewn out of the rock one above the other, until we arrived at an empty niche, the third from the ground above two sealed ones. There we lowered the coffin to the ground and Herr Kramer stepped forward to intone the prayers.

While he chanted my eye kept skimming over the crowd. I caught a glimpse of the Fleischers and the Schwarzkopfs, and of Horowitz' sheepish face among the others. And then I saw Eva's blond head moving around restlessly. She had become separated from Walter and now she seemed anxious to get close to him again. Presently I noticed that Klein was trying to catch up with her. That he had come to search her out at Josef's funeral only strengthened me in my suspicion that Eva had been avoiding him since Walter's return from Aguas Calientes. He looked desperate when she reached Walter's side before he could catch up with her. After lingering in the crowd for another few minutes, Klein dropped out of sight and disappeared.

Meanwhile Herr Kramer had finished with the prayers, and we lifted the coffin from the ground and pushed it into the niche, which seemed to close tightly around it. Señora Consuelo stood rigid while a heavy iron plaque with Josef's name and the dates of his birth and death was fastened over the opening.

She remained standing before the rocky grave even after the crowd had dispersed and headed for the gate. I hesitated whether to wait for her, but then decided to join Levy, who had offered me a ride home in his car. By the gate Levy's chauffeur came running with Frau Goldmann's message that Trude had started on her labor, and Levy grabbed Dr. Landau and sped off without any apologies or good-bys to me. (As it turned out later, the call for Dr. Landau had been a false alarm, brought on by Frau Goldmann's hysteria.)

In the end I rode home with Walter and Eva. We discussed death in general, as one will after a funeral, and Walter made a remark which I seem unable to get out of my mind. He said that Esperanza was a good place in which to wait out the war, but he would not want to die here.

I don't want to die here either!

*Thursday, November 14, 1940.*    I would never have believed it possible, but now that Josef is dead the hours which I used to spend with him every day weigh heavy on me. I try to fill up the idle time by reading the newspapers more thoroughly. The German air raids on England seem to be tapering off now that winter and bad weather are closing in on the island. The English themselves destroyed half the Italian fleet in the harbor of Taranto yesterday. Again we permit ourselves the faint hope that the fortunes of war might be changing.

Of course there is always news to spoil what little elation we might feel. Day before yesterday Molotov conferred with Hitler in Berlin, and the papers say that Russian troops are massing on the Rumanian border. We have learned enough during the past year of war to know what that means.

Here in Esperanza Levy has quietly ascended to the post of president of the Centro. One of his first moves was to propose a raising of the membership fee. He claims that everybody is making enough money now to contribute a little more toward the fund of the community. Dr. Landau, who was on the verge of joining the club, changed his mind when he learned of the proposed increase in dues. Horowitz called him stingy, but not a stingy capitalist, as in olden times. "Capitalist" is one word that is gradually fading from Horowitz' vocabulary.

*Friday, November 22, 1940.* Yesterday I remarked at our tea party that I had not seen Señora Consuelo since Josef's funeral. As though she had learned through some sixth sense of what I had said, Señora Consuelo sent the Indian over this morning to ask me to lunch.

We ate in the large, formal dining room, just the two of us. Señora Consuelo, in deep black, sitting at one end of the table, I at the broad side in the chair of the guest. The place where Josef used to sit was empty, but the china and silver had been laid out for him as if he were expected momentarily.

It was all very depressing, and the conversation between Señora Consuelo and me was most awkward. My mind seemed to draw a complete blank and I forgot most of the Spanish I had acquired in the past two years. Half the time I felt as if I had arrived poorly prepared to take an important test. I still wonder whether Señora Consuelo expected some sort of solace from me or whether she just wanted to see me sit where I used to sit on the rare occasions when she had lunch with Josef and me.

Another thing that kept distracting me: one of the dogs had wandered into the dining room and had stretched out under Josef's chair, his head upon his paws, his eyes upon me with what I thought a look of accusation.

Do I feel guilty for being alive while Josef is dead?

*Monday, November 25, 1940.* This time it is not a false alarm: Trude has started on her labor pains!

Dr. Lipschitz and I were sitting on the Kramers' veranda, discussing the war news of the past week (Hungary and Rumania have joined the Berlin-Rome-Tokyo Pact) when Eva burst in, shouting excitedly that Trude had begun her labor while she was visiting her this afternoon.

"Frau Goldmann is half insane with fear," Eva said. "Trude is still in her seventh month and Frau Goldmann says she knew all the time that something would go wrong."

I asked Eva what Dr. Landau had said, and she told us that he could see no reason why a seven-month baby should not live, especially since this one seemed to be a big child.

"Seven-month baby, humph," said Frau Lipschitz, who had come in from the kitchen just as Eva related the news. "The way Trude looks, she might be in the tenth month! If you ask me, I always thought there was something fishy about her hasty marriage."

"Nobody asked you, so why don't you keep your filthy thoughts to yourself?" Eva said rudely.

While Frau Lipschitz still struggled for a suitable reply, Eva left the room, slamming the door behind her.


*Tuesday, November 26, 1940.*    It is over twenty-four hours now since Trude started on her labor pains.

Eva came back from her house a short while ago, looking weary and frightened; quite different from her gay state this morning. (Then she had described to us how Goldmann and Levy kept walking circles on the living-room carpet, interrupting their pacing to argue whether to name *him* for Goldmann's father or for Levy's father. As if it did not even enter their minds that the baby could be a girl.)

In the afternoon the mood had been completely altered, Eva said. She had entered the house, expecting to be greeted by the crying of the newborn infant. Instead she had found Levy sitting in a chair, holding his head in his hands and moaning:

"Oh, God, if she would only have the baby already! I don't care even if it is a girl!"

Goldmann stood in one corner of the room, swaying back and forth and saying (as Eva later learned) Tillim, the prayer to be said in time of great danger. When he was through he turned on Levy and hissed: "She didn't have to have a baby right away!"

Frau Goldmann carried on the worst.

"You'll never believe this," Eva said, "but she actually stood banging her head against the wall, wailing that if anything should happen to Trude she would kill herself."

Even Dr. Landau seemed worried. He said that if Trude did not have the baby by midnight he would have to take her to the hospital for a Caesarean. At the mention of such a possibility Frau Goldmann began to scream at the top of her voice.

Trude, though, was very brave, Eva said. There was not a sound out of her. Even Frau Steinberg, who had come to help Dr. Landau with the delivery, could not praise her enough.


*Wednesday, November 27, 1940.*    Good news! Trude has given birth to a baby girl! She had steadfastly refused to be taken to the hospital and at about four o'clock in the morning had borne the baby under her own power.

Eva told us she could sense the immense relief even before she stepped into Trude's house this morning. The door stood ajar and the center hall was deserted. Everybody, including the servants, seemed to have run upstairs. From the second floor came a babble of voices, dominated by the loud weeping of Frau Goldmann. But it was obvious that she was crying for joy.

Presently Levy appeared on the upstairs landing, beside himself with pride and foolishness, Eva said, to call down to her that he had just become the father of the most beautiful baby daughter. Next Herr Goldmann came to announce in his turn that he had become grandfather of the most beautiful grandchild. In spite of the tears streaming down his cheeks he grinned like a loon. Finally Frau Goldmann swept downstairs and folded Eva into her arms, crying and whispering into her ear:

"God willing, you next."

(This Eva told with a wry smile.)

The last one to come out of Trude's bedroom was Dr. Landau. He drove everybody away to give the new mother her hard-earned rest. Eva

asked if she could see the baby, if not Trude, and Frau Steinberg took
her into the newly furnished nursery and let her peek into the crib.

At this point Eva inexplicably broke off her report.

"Nu, so how does it look?" Frau Kramer prompted.

Eva sighed a little and shook her head.

"Poor little thing. She's the image of her mother."


*Saturday, November 30, 1940.*     Ever since the baby was born, Eva has
been a daily visitor at Trude's house. And this time she really goes to
visit Trude. I am reminded of the fascination the Citizen held for her
when he was newly born. Sometimes I think that most of her sassiness
is nothing but a mask for her frustration.


*Wednesday, December 4, 1940.*     Yesterday the Greeks broke through
the Italian defenses in Albania. They captured Porto Edda and took
close to thirty thousand prisoners. This has given rise to much jubilation
among our people and even makes the plans for a combination Hanuk-
kah-New Year's Eve ball in the Centro seem less frivolous.


*Monday, December 9, 1940.*     This morning Eva told me that Trude
was well enough now to receive visitors—male visitors, that is. All her
female acquaintances called on her long ago, not so much to extend
their good wishes, I suspect, as to rehash all the agonizing details of
the birth.

Before I visited Trude this afternoon I passed through the flower
market and bought a large bouquet of pink roses—all with stems. Eva
had gone over to Trude's house earlier, and I had asked her to announce
me for later in the afternoon.

The muchacha let me in when I rang the doorbell, and the silence in
the house told me that life had gone back to normal. Levy was away
tending his store. Frau Goldmann, who for the first week after the birth
had not budged from Trude's side, had returned to her neglected factory. Herr Goldmann had gone back to keep his books and insult his
customers.

I looked about me cautiously, afraid of falling into the clutches of Frau Steinberg, but even she was no longer around. The muchacha told me to go upstairs: Señora Trude was resting in her bedroom and Señora Eva was with her.

Holding the big bunch of roses, I slowly heaved myself up the stairs. (Lately I have noticed that climbing stairs is becoming increasingly harder for me.) I had almost reached the top when I heard Trude's voice coming out of the open bedroom door. She seemed upset over something, for she almost shouted, and I could clearly hear her mention the name of George Klein.

Just then my head must have appeared above the landing. From where she was sitting on the bed, Trude could see me. She stopped in the middle of the sentence and looked guilty. Eva, who had stood with her back to the door, turned around and blushed. I thought—too late—that I should have coughed or made my approach known in some other way. Probably the girls thought I had been eavesdropping.

I tried to divert them with a particularly cheerful demeanor, thrusting the roses into Trude's arms and telling her how marvelous she looked. But all the time I kept wondering about what she had said, or was going to say, about Klein.

With my flowers in her arm, Trude rose from the bed. She wore a long, lavender silk robe, and her girth was still formidable. If the baby had not started wailing in the next room at this precise moment, I should have thought Trude was still pregnant.

"She's awake. Come take a look at my little doll," Trude said tenderly.

She led the way into the nursery, which was furnished with the extravagance which only a wealthy man who had become a father late in life would lavish on a child's room. There were ruffles and laces everywhere, and even my indifferent eyes were captured by the precious Oriental rug on the floor. ("Nothing too good for my daughter," I could hear Levy say.)

Trude pulled back the curtains of the cradle and began to coo inside. After a while the baby stopped crying, and Trude moved over to let me take a look.

The baby's face was still red from crying, and she looked like Trude in one of her more unfortunate moments, after she had acquired a severe sunburn. I broke into sounds of false enthusiasm and told Trude that her daughter was very pretty. Trude let me go on for a while and then she burst out laughing.

"I know she's hideous," she said. "The image of her mama. But that makes no difference to me. I still love her. The only two people who seriously insist that they never saw a more beautiful baby are my father and my husband. But then Isak has never seen a newborn baby before, and the only baby Papa ever looked at closely was me. So there!"

I thought Trude was a very smart, sensible girl not to be blinded by her sentiments. At least I thought so until she told me how she planned to name the baby.

"Her middle name will be Sarah, for my husband's late mother. But what I really want to call her . . . I want to call her Norma, for you."

I was so touched that I did not know what to say, and I could not quite master my emotions until I walked home with Eva. It was only then that I remembered again the argument the girls had been having at my arrival. But we were still talking about Trude and little Norma, and I did not see how I could shift the conversation to Klein without being obvious. So I kept quiet and worried secretly.

When I came upstairs Frau Lipschitz, who was visiting with her mother (she is always visiting with her mother) cornered me in the corridor.

"Did you see the pearls?" she asked.

"What pearls?"

"The string of pearls Levy gave Trude for the birth of the baby!"

I tried to think back and seemed to recall that Trude had worn a string of pearls around her neck, small, white pearls such as one might see every day.

"What about the pearls?" I asked.

Frau Lipschitz screwed up her face in disgust.

"They're real! Real, genuine pearls! And she didn't even have a boy!" said Frau Lipschitz, who has two boys but no pearls.

*Friday, December 13, 1940.*   Nothing particularly disastrous about this Friday the 13th except that for the past few days the weather has been abominable. With short interruptions it has been pouring day and night, and the chorus of the frogs is deafening, even during the daytime.

Moreover, I have caught a cold and cannot go out. Thus I am delivered helplessly to Herr Kramer's reminiscences about the drygoods business. I hope that one of these days the sun will come out again and that I will be cured of my cold and relieved of having to hear about the pleasures of selling odds and ends of textiles.

My only diversion is reading the papers. I am warming my heart on the news of the recent surprise attack by the British on the Italians in North Africa. By now the British have captured one thousand prisoners and have advanced as far as Sidi Barrâni.

*Tuesday, December 17, 1940.* Today the sun was shining, my cold was better, and I decided to visit the Centro, only to have my first outing in days spoiled by Trude. She has finally learned the bitter lesson of what it means to meddle in other people's affairs. Today she was in tears, appealing to me for help.

"I tell you, he's going to kill himself!" she said.

Not that I see how I could possibly help in this affair.

The trouble started when Klein came up to the Centro this afternoon and found Eva and Walter sitting at a table with the Schwarzkopfs. (Unfortunately, this foursome is no longer a rare combination. They have been seen together in nightclubs, at the movies, and in the Centro.)

They were already sitting around a table when I came in, and since they did not ask me to join them I went and sat down with Levy and Trude. Levy soon excused himself and returned to his store.

Chatting with Trude, I remarked that I found the friendship between Eva and Walter and the Schwarzkopfs rather strange.

"I don't see what Eva can have in common with Frau Schwarzkopf," Trude said, her voice sounding harsh with the jealousy of the neglected friend.

Poor Trude was too concerned with her own hurt feelings to see that it was not Eva but Walter who had things in common with Frau Schwarzkopf. She sat close to him, fluttering her lashes as she gazed up at him. And under the table I could see her arched, perfect legs pressing against Walter's thighs.

Eva sat between Walter and Schwarzkopf, observing her husband and

Frau Schwarzkopf with a detached, faintly amused air. Again I had the distinct impression that she condoned what was going on. But her tolerance did not extend to Schwarzkopf. Whenever he tried to pull closer to her, she shrank from his touch.

It was just in one of those moments when Schwarzkopf bent close to her that Klein walked in. He stopped and reared back like a frightened horse. Without his glasses his face looked particularly naked and vulnerable.

Eva noticed him out of the corner of her eye and shifted her position until she sat with her back to him. Though she went on talking to Schwarzkopf, she looked as if she had tensed all the muscles in her back to fend off an attack.

Trude squirmed in her chair and tried to catch Klein's eye. He stood with his arms hanging down, his fists clenching and unclenching, the tip of his tongue nervously moistening his lips. When he took one step forward, Trude jumped up and muttered without looking at me:

"Excuse me, I'll be back in a minute."

She walked over to Klein, cutting off his path and crowding him out through the door. When she came back—after not one but after nearly fifteen minutes—she was close to tears. She laboriously blew her nose before she trusted herself to speak.

"Herr Professor," she whispered across the table, "you have to help me. I have to talk with you, but not here. Could we walk home together?"

For Trude to propose a long walk was a sure sign that something serious must have happened. She was very nervous even after we had left the Centro and kept glancing behind her. When she had finally satisfied herself that we were unobserved, she blurted out:

"I tell you, he's going to kill himself!"

There was no need for me to ask who was going to kill himself.

Again Trude tried to regain her poise by blowing her nose.

"I don't know what to do!" she said. "He says I have to talk to Eva. I have to convince her that she must marry him!"

I stopped Trude and caught her by the arm.

"Trude, did you know all the time that things had gone so far?"

She shook her head indignantly.

"Of course not! Oh, I knew that he had a crush on her and that they were meeting secretly, but I never thought that anything *serious* was going on between them. And now he says he's going to kill himself!"

She looked at me with remorse—for we both knew that she had abetted this relationship—and yet, I thought, in secret delight, for here was a man threatening to kill himself for a woman, something no man would ever do for the love of Trude.

I asked Trude to tell me exactly what Klein had said.

"But I told you: he said he's going to kill himself! He said that ever since Walter has been making more money, Eva has refused to see him."

This, I knew, was not so. Walter's financial situation had bettered itself some time before he and Eva had moved downstairs; before he had made his trip to Aguas Calientes; before Klein's nightly visits. It was after these visits that Eva had begun to curtail her morning strolls.

"And he said," Trude went on, "that now that Walter has her back, he wants to trade her for Frau Schwarzkopf. You know, exchange sort of . . ."

Trude seemed embarrassed as she tried to imply what had crossed my mind more than once during the past few weeks.

"And if Klein ever finds out that Schwarzkopf has touched Eva," Trude said, "he's going to kill Schwarzkopf and Eva and himself!"

"Now, Trude, you're too sensible to believe in all these threats of mass murder!" I said. (Besides, the idea of Schwarzkopf touching Eva was unthinkable. I was positive that she considered him repulsive.) "What Klein wants is to have you frighten Eva into another meeting with him."

"Well, I think she should talk to him," Trude said. "It isn't fair to let him suffer and just laugh about him."

"I don't think that Eva is laughing about Herr Klein. I think she has just grown indifferent to him. That is something a gentleman ought to accept quietly."

(Why was I so self-righteous? Had I accepted it quietly when Christine had called an end to our affair?)

"But he isn't going to accept it quietly! You'll see, he'll do something terrible! I've already warned Eva but she won't listen to me. Now it's your turn to speak to her. We just can't take this responsibility upon ourselves and not do anything."

I resented the way Trude kept shifting the responsibility over on me—

especially since I was as guilty as she in permitting this affair to get out of hand. But if I was going to talk to Eva, what was I going to tell her? That she must leave her husband and marry her lover?

A man is said to have a moral obligation in such a case. But does a woman?

*Friday, December 20, 1940.*    On treacherous terrain, a loose pebble skidding down may well mean the beginning of an avalanche.

I had not attributed too much significance to what Trude had told me about Klein's threats a few days ago, but this afternoon, on my way out, I came across him in the downstairs hall of our house. To find him rattling Eva's bolted door in broad daylight left me speechless. After I had recovered from the initial shock, I walked up behind him and grabbed him by the shoulders.

"What the devil do you think you're doing here?"

He whirled around, and beneath his hostile mien I could see that he was relieved to face just me.

"I know she's in there," he said. "She locked herself in and won't talk to me."

"Haven't you got sense and pride enough to go home and leave her alone if she doesn't want to see you?" I asked.

"No."

"Just imagine if somebody else had caught you rattling her door, do you realize what embarrassment you might have caused Eva?"

"I don't care. She doesn't care either how much she hurts me."

I had never spoken more than a few words with Klein before, and I saw only now how childish and immature he was.

"Don't you think that at your age you ought to act like a gentleman?" I asked.

"I love her," he replied sullenly.

I could see that I would have a hard time reasoning with him, and the downstairs hall where we might be surprised by the Kramers as soon as they rose from their afternoon nap was certainly not the place for it. I suggested that since Eva seemed unwilling to let him in he might come upstairs to my room.

He looked at me with open distrust.

"Why should you want me to come to your room?"

"I think Eva values my advice. Perhaps I could straighten out things between you."

These were certainly not my true motives for wanting to get Klein away from Eva's bolted door. All I wanted was to protect her reputation for what it was still worth. Wasn't she like a daughter to me—or so I told myself?

While Klein reluctantly followed me up the stairs and I led him past the room of the Kramers as quietly as possible, I kept cursing myself for having put off the talk with Eva. By acting sooner I might have prevented Klein's visit to the house. I tried to make the best of the present situation by ushering him quickly into my room and tightly shutting the door behind us.

"Sit down!"

He sat down obediently on my couch. Looking at him I could see that he really appeared as if he had suffered a great deal. His face was white and strained, and there were sharp lines around his mouth. He had lost some weight and his clothes hung loosely about him. Even his nose had become thinner and his glasses kept slipping down the bridge. Finally he took them off and began to polish them nervously. His eyes were large, green, hurt, and slightly out of focus.

"All right then, tell me all about it," I prodded with false benevolence. Inwardly I was annoyed that he had made me feel pity for him when I knew that I ought to be angry.

"There's nothing to tell," he said. "I love her. I can't live without her."

How often, I thought, had that trite phrase been repeated? How often had people claimed to be unable to go on living without a certain person, only to go on living in the end?

Still, I was surprised when he told me that he had tried to kill himself.

"Yes, it's true," he said when he saw me glance sharply at him. "I was so upset that I got sick. The doctor gave me some sleeping pills and I took them all. I thought I was going to die, but I didn't. I'm too tough."

I had to hide a smile. He had not wanted to die, or he would have managed to take the proper dose. In a way I felt sorry for all his wasted dramatics.

"But I've changed my mind now," he said. "I don't want to kill myself any longer. All I want is to get Eva to talk with me. I could make her understand that she's got to marry me! I just won't let Walter take her back now that he needs her for his own shady purposes. I have a right to her!"

"And what do you think gives you a right to her?"

"What gives me a *right* to her? What gives me a right to her! She was my mistress for nine months—*that* gives me a right to her!"

All my sympathy for him vanished. He was childish and stupid and indiscreet, and I felt like striking him hard across the mouth.

"You might have thought of marrying her before you let her become your mistress," I said coldly. It was so easy to be righteous when your own actions were not on trial!

"I didn't know then," Klein said miserably. "I didn't know then how it would be. I never really wanted to get married. But now I love her."

"And you think that by marrying her you can keep her."

He nodded before he realized that I had trapped him.

"Look at Eva and Walter! Do you really think a wedding band is all it takes to make a marriage last? What good would it do you to bully Eva into marrying you if she didn't love you?"

"But she does!"

"She certainly doesn't act as if she did. Did she ever tell you that she loved you?"

His look wavered, and finally he turned his head toward the wall. Without his saying so, I knew that Eva had never told him that she loved him. He had persuaded himself to believe that she did, but clearly she had never told him so.

I was jubilant over my discovery.

"Suppose Eva would tell you herself that she didn't love you, would you leave her alone afterward?" I asked.

He looked at me suspiciously, trying to see where I had laid the trap for him.

"You would persuade her to speak with me?"

I said I would try, provided he would promise to abide by her decision.

There was a glimmer of hope in his eyes, the pitiful, false hope of all abandoned lovers that they might still sway the feelings of the deserter with the right words. I knew differently from bitter experience.

I promised to arrange a meeting for him. In a sudden rush of gratitude Klein thanked me profusely as I showed him down the stairs and out of the house. I stood by the garden gate until he had disappeared around the corner and I was certain that he would not turn back.

Then I went inside and knocked on Eva's door, but she would not open. Once or twice I called in a hoarse whisper, "It's me, Professor Bernstein," without any success. I did not want to attract the attention of the Kramers and decided that the message would keep until tomorrow.

When I went upstairs to get my hat Frau Kramer, who had been standing on the terrace, came into the corridor.

"Wasn't that Herr Klein who just walked out of the house?" she asked.

"Yes."

"What did he want?"

"He came to borrow a book from me," I lied blandly.

"Oh?" Frau Kramer said, raising her eyebrows.

I could see that she did not believe me, but fortunately I don't have to answer to her for my activities.


*Saturday, December 21, 1940.*    This morning I cornered Eva on the terrace and told her that I had to have a word with her. She had already stripped for her sun bath and seemed annoyed when I suggested that we had better talk in my room.

"Well, what is it? You sound so mysterious," she said as she began to wrap herself in her robe again, covering her golden skin. "What have I done now?"

Perhaps she expected me to forward some complaint from her mother-in-law. I waited until we were securely shut into my room before I told her that the message I had for her was from Klein.

Eva just sat down on my couch in stunned silence, looking at me with lips slightly parted in surprise. I could see that I was the last person she had expected to act as an intermediary on Klein's behalf.

"Eva, Herr Klein is very desperate," I said. "You'll have to talk with him."

"Did he have the nerve to approach you?" Eva asked angrily, avoiding the issue.

I shook my head.

"I caught him yesterday when he was rattling your door and took him upstairs to spare you embarrassment. But you did hear him, didn't you?"

She averted her gaze and I knew that she had heard him.

"Eva, this isn't the way to act. You can't lead a man on and then simply cast him aside without an explanation. He told me he wanted to kill himself!"

"Don't worry, he won't," Eva said callously, and I knew that she was right.

"He wants to marry you."

"Well, I don't want to marry him."

"Then you don't love him?"

"No, I don't," she said without a moment's hesitation.

"And you never did love him?"

She looked thoughtful. "I don't know. For a while perhaps I was infatuated with him. Oh, not really with him" (and I instantly thought of Aronoff, but it turned out that that was not what she meant) "but with the way he felt about me. He wanted me as a woman. You don't know what it means to be wanted. I thought if he only wanted me badly enough . . ."

Her voice trailed off. I tried to puzzle out what she had meant. Had Walter stopped wanting her as a woman (after all, there had been their bedroom troubles) and had she hoped to find with Klein what she had not found with Walter? Or had Klein meant the same disappointment for her? I could not ask her any of these questions, but I could probe.

"Herr Klein wants you very badly, Eva. He says he has a right to you."

"A right to me!"

I had to tell her what Klein had said, for if she did not stop him he might go on saying the same thing to other people.

"He says you were his mistress for nine months."

She colored deeply, not with the blush of embarrassed modesty but with the ugly red of anger.

"Why, the miserable bastard!" she exclaimed in one of her rare, shocking outbursts of profanity. "To tell such a lie just because once or twice . . ."

She broke off in confusion, realizing that she had admitted more than she had intended to admit.

Once or twice, I thought. Once or twice, when?

How I wished that I could ask Eva! Instead I said to her:

"You'll have to speak with him, Eva. You'll have to tell him that you don't love him. He won't leave you alone unless you do."

"But we never talked about love," Eva said angrily. "We never talked about love and we never talked about marriage. It was understood that he did not want to get married yet. It's only since we broke off that he wants to marry me. He thinks all he has to do is propose. It doesn't work that way."

"I'll arrange a meeting for you," I said.

"I don't want to talk with him in private. I know him, he'll make a scene. He'll appeal to my pity. I can't stand men who appeal to my pity. I don't want him to humiliate himself. If he wants to, I'll talk with him in the Centro. He can sit at a table with you, and I'll join you. Then you can go away for a while—a short while—and I'll tell him that I don't love him and that I won't marry him. And then I want you to come back and keep him from making a fool of himself."

"All right," I said, "I'll arrange the meeting the way you want it. Try to be kind to him."

Eva frowned but refrained from making a sarcastic remark. Then she rose and left. I congratulated myself on having proceeded as discreetly as possible, but I had not counted on Frau Kramer's eagle eye.

"What was Eva doing in your room this morning?" she asked me at lunch.

Forgetting that I had used the same excuse the day before, I said that Eva had come to borrow a book.

"What's the matter? Are you opening a lending library?" Frau Kramer asked.

*Wednesday, December 25, 1940.* Today I lunched again with Señora Consuelo. She told me that finally permission for a cemetery within the confines of the city had been granted. As soon as the ground is broken we will be able to transfer Josef's remains to a proper grave in the earth.

In the afternoon I searched out Klein in the Centro (I had avoided going there for several days) and told him under what conditions Eva was willing to meet him. He was angry and disappointed, and in his resentment he kicked Don, who had come to the Centro with me and was nuzzling Klein's knee. Don yelped in surprise and escaped, tail between his legs, to hide under another table.

"Shame on you!" Frau Lipschitz called across the room. "Kicking a friendly puppy!"

(Don has grown to an awe-inspiring size.)

In the end Klein agreed to Eva's proposal and angrily stalked out of the Centro, whereupon Don crept from his hiding place and lay down under my chair. Poor dog, how was he to know that the kick in the ribs was not meant for him but for his mistress!

In the evening Eva came upstairs briefly to watch Herr Kramer light the first candle of Hanukkah. I managed to pull her aside and ask her casually if she was coming to the Centro tomorrow. She understood.


*Thursday, December 26, 1940.*    The role of intermediary is not a pleasant one. I am sure that of the three of us I felt the most awkward this afternoon.

As had been agreed, I was sitting with Klein at a table when Eva walked in. We had both arrived fifteen minutes earlier and had drifted into a far corner of the large assembly room so as not to arouse suspicion. Our conversation was labored, and time and again Klein asked if I was sure that Eva would really come.

When she finally came in, Klein grew extremely tense and I could see that his hands were shaking badly as he polished his glasses.

He half rose from his chair when Eva sat down with us and looked at her with the sickening, pleading expression of a mendicant. I felt embarrassed for him. Eva gave him a short glance and quickly turned her face to me, smiling brightly and insincerely:

"Well, here I am," she said.

Then we sat around for one full minute without saying a single word. Herr Bloch came to take Eva's order and to discuss with us the world-

333 · <i>Part Four—Prosperity</i>

shaking aspects of the weather. After he had delivered Eva's coffee and cake, I excused myself.

Afraid that Klein might lose control of himself, I lingered near the door to the card room.

I don't really know what was said verbatim, but I could see on Klein's face that Eva was telling him exactly what she had said she would tell him. Once he reached across the table and tried to take her hand. Eva rose and walked away from him without looking back. As she passed me she whispered:

"You'd better go to him, Herr Professor, I don't want him to come after me."

When I got to the table I realized that Klein was in no condition to follow her. He was rocking back and forth in his chair, clutching his hand over his chest as if trying to assuage some physical pain.

"My heart," he moaned. "I think I'm going to have a heart attack."

I felt a cruel urge to laugh.

"So she will not marry you," I said.

"No, she won't. She says she doesn't love me. But that's not true. If I were rich, she would come with me. She's no better than Trude. But someday she'll be sorry. I would have taken her to the United States with me. You're surprised, aren't you? I got my visa a few days ago. Nobody even knew that I had applied for a visa! I could have taken her out of this hellhole of a city. Now she can rot here for all I care!"

Suddenly he rose and walked away without saying good-by. Stumbling over the doorstep as he rushed out, he nearly collided with his cousin.

Aronoff was still shaking his head when he passed my table.

"Have you ever said hello to a guy and he answered you 'go to hell'?" he asked. "My cousin George must be going crazy. He wasn't quite right in the head even as a kid."

I was tempted to tell Aronoff that he had little reason to scoff at Klein. But for the confounded family resemblance, who knows if Eva would ever have noticed him?

Saturday, December 28, 1940.     The curse of a small town is that there can be no secrecy.

I had hoped it would go unobserved that Eva and Klein had sat to-gether alone for a few minutes, but somebody must have spoken to Walter about it. This morning he came upstairs to question me before he left for work. He tried to sound casual but he seemed worried.

"What is this I hear about your arranging meetings between my wife and Klein?" he asked.

It took his grin to reassure me that he was joking and that he really had no idea of how close he had hit to the truth.

"I happened to be sitting at a table with Herr Klein. When Eva came in I invited her to join us. Anything wrong with that?" I asked with all the hurt dignity I could muster.

"Well, the way I heard it, you left Eva and Klein sitting there alone."

(I wondered briefly who his informant might be. Goldmann; Levy; Fleischer; possibly Herr Bloch? Any little deviation from the norm was newsworthy in Esperanza.)

"Can't a man so much as go to the bathroom for one minute without giving people cause for gossip?" I said, with indignation.

Now let Walter inquire if I had indeed gone to the bathroom!


*Wednesday, January 1, 1941.*　　Last night was the New Year's Eve ball in the Centro.

As time passes we seem to be putting more and more distance be-tween ourselves and Europe. Everybody was in an exuberant mood, as though the state of the world around us did not concern us the least bit.

I hardly remember seeing Eva in such high spirits before. Perhaps she has a new sense of freedom now that the affair Klein is ended. She was friendly and courteous to all the men who came to ask her for dances, even to Schwarzkopf—not that I condone such friendliness.

Walter danced almost exclusively with Frau Schwarzkopf, and people were saying what people usually say in such a case.

Herr Klein remained absent from the festivities, and for the first time Aronoff too was missing. When Frau Fleischer remarked upon this, her husband said wittily:

"Don't worry about Aronoff! Why should he bring his women here if he can take a short cut right into bed?"

As for me, I spent most of the evening sitting at a table with the Brauns. Hans Braun said something about the frequency with which Walter danced with Frau Schwarzkopf, but with the innocence of so many sophisticated people, attributed this simply to Walter's desire to have a good time.

By the way, speaking of having a good time, we are invited to the Brauns' for the coming Saturday.

*Sunday, January 5, 1941.*     Suddenly a note of anticipation and excitement has entered my life: I am going on a trip to the camp of the Panamerican Oil Company in the jungle!

When we had dinner at the Brauns' yesterday evening, Dr. Zwingli, whom I had met there once before, issued the invitation. He said that with the war and the current need for oil the budget of the company has been augmented, and the road leading to the camp will be finished ahead of schedule. At present it extends about a hundred miles beyond Aguas Calientes. From there on we will have to travel another five hours on muleback—provided we feel up to such an adventure.

Eva was all in favor of the trip, in fact enthusiastic, quite unlike the time she refused to accompany Walter to Aguas Calientes. (But then there is nothing now to keep her in Esperanza.)

Perhaps this invitation is really a godsend. Perhaps what Eva and Walter need is a few days together in the jungle, cut off from all other people, to find each other again. Hans will be too busy to bother with them, and I certainly won't intrude on them.

*Wednesday, January 8, 1941.*     Today I was sorely disabused of my dream as a benevolent guardian angel. Walter casually informed me that the Schwarzkopfs had been included in our safari. He had spoken to Dr. Zwingli and had obtained permission to bring them along.

In the afternoon I met Hans Braun in the street. He seemed annoyed.

"Did Walter tell you about the Schwarzkopfs? Frankly, I don't like the way he's trying to stretch Dr. Zwingli's hospitality. Why does he want them along?"

Even if I did not hint at Walter's motives, I'm afraid Hans will catch on soon enough. For me some of the froth has been skimmed off the anticipation.

We are to start out Monday morning.

*Monday, January 13, 1941.*    I shall write as much as my exhaustion permits. Five hours on muleback do not sound nearly so grueling as they feel. I am lying in bed (on my side) as I make this entry.

This morning at five-thirty the station wagon of the Panamerican Oil Company came to pick us up. Walter was still half asleep, but Eva looked fresh and pretty in spite of the early hour. She wore boots, riding pants and a tight-fitting, white sweater which emphasized her breasts. I could not help wishing that she had chosen a less-revealing attire. Hans Braun gave her a look of appreciation as she got into the car, and Schwarzkopf practically devoured her with his eyes.

After we had distributed ourselves (Hans next to the driver, I beside Eva, much to Schwarzkopf's chagrin, and Frau Schwarzkopf next to Walter) we crossed the sleeping city and soon hit the open road. The car jolted merrily forward over the ruts and holes which the rainy season had left in the road, but after a while my system became adjusted to the constant shaking.

At first the road did not appear too dangerous. For the most part we rode through level fields as we approached the snow-covered mountains in the distance. It was still too early in the morning for a conversation, but this did not keep Frau Schwarzkopf from regaling us with another version of how she had escaped from the Bolsheviks. This time, instead of holding the reins of the cart which had transported her family across the border, she traveled in the arms of her wet nurse.

I calculated that this little switch neatly chopped some ten to twelve years off Frau Schwarzkopf's age. It took a sarcastic remark from Eva to silence her.

Looking into the rear-view mirror, I saw that Frau Schwarzkopf had snuggled closer to Walter, who slept leaning against the window. Schwarzkopf sat in the last row of the car and looked worried, possibly afraid that Eva might finally manage to bait his wife into a fight.

Again we rode in silence. After an hour or so we reached the foot of the mountains and the road became steep and winding. The valley beneath us sank lower and lower, until it looked like the clumsy drawing of a child with the irregular fields of many greens and browns cutting into each other. The air became thin and cold, and strong blasts of wind carried clouds of dust from the naked mountains. We had to roll up the windows of the car, and soon it became hot and stuffy inside. Hans Braun comforted us with the information that we should soon begin our descent.

Frau Schwarzkopf did her good deed for the day by passing around sandwiches, with the gleeful remark that Eva had not thought of providing food for her husband. As I listened to the chomping of Walter's teeth behind me, I thought that half the battle for a man's affection was the battle for his stomach.

After the next bend the road dipped steeply, and we could see below us a lush green valley crisscrossed by the sparkle of water. As we descended the air became warmer and damper, reminding me of Rioverde. Hans told us that we were approaching the subtropical line and that the earth in the valley below was still as alive as it was millions of years ago.

"Can you see the steeple of the church down there?" Walter said. "That's Aguas Calientes, where I built my hotel!"

The road to Aguas Calientes led through fields of light green, swaying stalks of sugar cane, and past houses with thatched roofs built on stilts high above the damp ground.

Aguas Calientes turned out to be an ancient, dilapidated village, its only new structure the hotel built by Walter. Even before our car pulled up in front of it, Frau Schwarzkopf broke into loud sounds of enthusiasm and Walter looked gratified.

We stopped for a brief lunch in the hotel. The dining room was not yet finished and we were the only guests in it. Through the window we could see the mountains that enclosed the valley in an almost unbroken circle. It was very warm and damp and we were all eager to leave, but the man who runs the hotel, a German refugee by the name of Mayer, would not let us depart before he had shown us the pride of Aguas Calientes: the two swimming pools.

The one pool opposite the hotel held icy mineral water. The other pool, which was reached via a hilly street, was smaller than the first one, filled with a thick, revolting-looking yellow liquid which explained the odor that hung all over the valley: sulphur.

"Let's get out of here," Eva whispered behind Herr Mayer's back. "This place stinks like the gateway to hell!"

Now, looking back, Aguas Calientes turned out to be just that: the gateway to hell. And on this note, I believe, I shall finish my entry for today.

*Tuesday, January 14, 1941.*   I have had a good night's sleep and an excellent breakfast. Hans got up long before the rest of us and left on some errand in the jungle, accompanied by several Indians. We were entrusted to the man who runs the camp, a big, humorless Swede with enormous hands and feet. He acts like a housewife on whom a horde of unwelcome guests have descended: polite, but leaving no doubt that he cannot wait to see us depart. Now he has taken my companions out on the shooting range behind the long, low-slung building in which we have been quartered. As I sit writing I can hear the crack of shots at irregular intervals. Perhaps our Swedish friend hopes that a fortunate accident might reduce our number.

Now back to where I left off yesterday.

After we had inspected the sulphur pool we took our leave of Herr Mayer and piled into the car. As we left Aguas Calientes behind us the trip became as perilous as the one with Goldmann to Tarqui. On the left the steep wall of mountains overhung the road like a threat. On the right chasms too frightening for the eye to explore opened up beneath us. The road was wide enough for only one car, with small platforms built out above the abyss every two hundred and fifty yards or so to allow for the passage of two vehicles.

We had to back into these platforms several times to make room for cars—or, worse yet, for buses—approaching from the opposite direction. In this perilous fashion we proceeded for about a hundred miles.

It was four o'clock in the afternoon when the road before us suddenly turned into a narrow path, running almost like a tunnel between the rocks. Where the pavement of the road came to an end there stood a ragged Indian with a group of sullen-looking, emaciated mules—our riding animals.

"This is where we get off," Hans said.

We clambered out of the car and stretched our stiff legs. Advancing a few steps, I found myself at the entrance to a short bridge. At a drop of perhaps a hundred feet beneath the bridge, the trickle of a shallow river was winding its way among the rocks. To the right, across the chasm, a waterfall cascaded downward into the river in a white splash of foam.

"El Velo de Novia. The Bridal Veil," Hans said, pointing at the water dropping white and virginal from the barren, gray shoulder of the mountain.

While we stood looking the chauffeur had unloaded our baggage. Now he swung the car around and departed, wildly honking his horn. We were left alone in the wilderness with nothing but the mules for transportation.

Two of the beasts were used for pack animals, the rest for riding. Whereas my companions seemed to encounter little difficulty in heaving themselves into the saddle, I found it impossible to swing my leg over the animal's rear. Once, when I had almost succeeded, the entire saddle gave way and, with my foot still in the stirrup, I came to land under the mule. Finally Hans and the Indian half pulled, half pushed me into the saddle.

Then we headed into the trail, a caravan consisting of seven people, including the Indian, and nine mules. The path was so narrow that it hardly allowed for the width of mule and rider. As we moved along, one of my legs kept grazing the side of the mountain while the other dangled above the deep quebrada, now on our left. Since we rode in single file, the only way to keep up a conversation was by shouting back and forth, and we soon gave it up. We proceeded in silence for another two hours, edging forward on the narrow mountain path.

The sun was setting and the air around us became tinted with the blue of twilight when the path, which had wound its tortuous way around the mountains, suddenly became wider.

It seemed that we had crossed one range of the cordillera. Now, as we neared the end of the path, my eyes met a breath-taking sight. I could see that we were severed from the next range by a gulf whose depth and width I preferred not to contemplate. The river, which we had first seen when it was nourished by the Velo de Novia, had since our last encounter spread to an impressive breadth. It now flowed beneath us, a many-armed monster embracing a myriad of small islands—some nothing but a heap of gray pebbles, others green with vegetation—as it sluggishly pursued its way toward the west.

"I know what the sight does to you," Hans said as we stood gaping. "But we can't afford to waste any time if we want to get across before it gets any darker."

"Across where?" I asked, with profound misgivings.

"Across the river, of course," Hans said matter-of-factly.

With the cracking of his whip the Indian started our caravan moving again, and after the next bend I saw what I had not anticipated and what, considering that I will have to cross it again on my way back, I wish I had never seen.

Suspended across the abyss between cordillera and cordillera was a bridge. But not the kind of bridge to which we have become conditioned in Western civilization. This bridge was made of slender, wooden boards, not wider than three or four feet, swaying gently from supporting hemp ropes. The span it covered was at least a hundred feet, and the only protection for whoever was foolhardy enough to cross it consisted of hemp ropes running on either side in lieu of a sturdier railing.

"Is this where we are supposed to cross?" I asked incredulously.

"This is where we're going to cross," Hans said.

"Holy Mary, Mother of God!" Frau Schwarzkopf exclaimed.

Her husband's eyes became large and worried and his lower lip sagged a little, giving him the expression of a little boy about to cry. Walter said querulously that if Hans had warned us we might not have brought the women along. Only Eva insisted that the bridge looked like fun, and offered to cross first.

"Look, the bridge is perfectly safe," Hans said impatiently. "It has been in use for hundreds of years." (Some comfort!) And to prove it he sent the pack animals across first.

Their hoofs clattered on the wooden boards as the whole structure gently swayed from side to side. Next came the Indian, Walter, and then Schwarzkopf. When Frau Schwarzkopf's turn came she quickly crossed herself before she started on the dangerous journey.

Eva was next. She dug her heels into the flanks of the animal and the mule started across at a halting trot. Hans called sharply out to her to stop that nonsense.

But even after Eva had safely reached the other side the bridge was still swaying more than I cared for. For once my mule displayed some unexpected horse sense, and refused to set foot on the shaking contraption. Hans tried to prod him from behind with a twig, and when this persuasion failed he dug into the vocabulary of the muledriver. This use of obscenity so shocked the mule that it bounded forward and started on its trek across.

Now that the shivering boards were beneath me, I noticed that they were not tightly joined together but that there were open spaces of more than an inch between them. My eyes kept veering toward these gaps, drawn by a morbid fascination. Three quarters of the way across the bridge, my graceless mule stumbled and one of his front legs was caught for a brief second in one of the gaps. I felt my not inconsiderable weight slipping forward in the saddle, and hanging onto the knob for dear life, I wondered whether I ought to say good-by to this world and prepare for my trip into the next. In the meantime my mule had disengaged its leg and calmly proceeded as if it had not just given me the scare of my life.

When I reached the other side I found Eva half lying in the saddle, convulsed with laughter.

"Your face looked so funny when you came off the bridge!"

How was the face of a man to look when he had nearly befouled himself from fright?

Hans was the last one to come across, and presently we were on our way again. I suppose I acted rather morose for the rest of the journey. Now and then Eva cast a glance at me over her shoulder, followed by the shaking of her back, as if she were giggling silently. But soon it became so dark that I was spared this mortifying sight.

By then we had left the steep, crooked mountain path and were proceeding along a narrow road which ran along an irrigation ditch. The jungle had crept close on either side, and we were riding along between two dense, black walls, with only the narrow strip of the road to guide us. In the night the jungle came alive with the weird cries of birds and other wild creatures. I had been in the saddle for more than four hours now, and my seat ached like a heel being chafed raw by the stiff leather of a new shoe. As I gave myself over to the stinging pain, I wondered dully what devil had possessed me—a man my age—to come on such a trip.

Just as I had reached the lowest depth of despair I heard Hans urging on his mule behind me, and passing me on his way toward the head of the line he called out that we would be at the camp in ten minutes. When finally the lights of the camp came in sight and I was allowed to dismount, my legs remained bowed like those of a jockey and refused to return to their normal shape for quite a while.

Through the fog of exhaustion I perceived people rushing out of the sheds which surrounded a long, low building to take care of our mules, while Hans herded us inside the house that was to be our home for the next few days. We were introduced to Herr Knudsen, the Swede, but were all too tired for amenities—a circumstance which only seemed to please our host.

In spite of my aching backside I slept like a log, and this morning when I looked out my window and saw the strange landscape around me, the fleshy green of the jungle blazing with the sudden glow of orchids among the leaves, and smelled the rich steam of the black earth, I was not sorry that I had made the trip.


*Wednesday, January 15, 1941.*     This is our second day here. I am not sure whether I am sorry that our stay will be so brief. There is really not much to do except absorb the strangeness around us.

Seen in broad daylight the camp is a rather primitive affair, erected on a clearing in the jungle. The main building in which we are quartered is a low one-story structure made of redwood boards which don't rot with the dampness. It is covered with a silvery, corrugated tin roof on which the rain last night sounded like an angry fusillade. Like all the smaller sheds around it, the main building is set on stilts above the ground.

The food here is simple but surprisingly good. Most of it comes from cans, except for the chickens which, before they are turned into meals, wander all over the clearing and in and out among the stilts of the buildings. Hans says that the chickens are the only fresh meat they can get in the jungle. Now and then a fish from the river, but that is all.

The help here is all male: short, white-clad Indians, their black hair twisted into pigtails around a length of red or white ribbon. The servants move around soundlessly on rope-soled shoes to clean our rooms and serve our meals. Work is performed at a leisurely pace, and time crawls even more slowly than in Esperanza.

So far I have not ventured much beyond the limits of the compound. This is not so much due to lack of curiosity as to the fact that Eva has decided to spend the first two days loafing around the house. Schwarz-kopf does not budge from her side. In spite of my aversion, I have attached myself to him like a fly to flypaper. He in turn regards me with the affection one might show the carrier of a strange, contagious disease.

Hans has promised to take us on a short trek through the jungle tomorrow, down to where the Rio Verde flows along the border of the camp. Until now we have seen Hans only at the evening meal. During the day he is off prospecting, and occasionally we can hear the dull blast of dynamiting as he probes the ground for mineral samples.

The only ones who so far have shown some spirit of adventure are Walter and Frau Schwarzkopf. They have repeatedly ventured off among the dense trees—whether to explore the fauna and flora or some other possibilities is anybody's guess. I have been waiting in vain for some protest from Eva or Schwarzkopf against these private excursions, but neither has voiced any objections. One consolation: Eva is still keeping her distance from Schwarzkopf, aided and abetted in this laudable behavior by my constant presence.

But the odd pairing off has caused some confusion to Herr Knudsen. He keeps addressing Eva as Frau Schwarzkopf and Frau Schwarzkopf as Frau Kramer. Not that I can blame him. Even a more sophisticated person than he might become confused.


*Thursday, January 16, 1941.* This morning Hans interrupted his work to take us on the promised excursion. The taciturn Swede came along, wearing a white tropical helmet and carrying a dangerous-looking machete. The purpose of the machete soon became apparent. In the few days during which the narrow footpath leading down to the river had not been used, the jungle had begun to reclaim it. Strands of twisting greenery reached across it, ready to snare and trip any rash intruder.

Again we walked one behind the other, in a single file like ducks. The raucous cackling of birds resounded in the domelike branches of the trees, which shut out most of the daylight. Now and then there was an exotic streak of red or yellow feathers as a bird dived from one branch to another, accompanied by the delighted cries of the women.

Among the dark, heavy leaves the spotted mouths of fiery orchids looked vicious in their beauty as they strangled their hosts. All the time we were descending, with Herr Knudsen clearing the path before us. At one point we had to cross a stagnant pool of water, with only a fallen, rotting tree trunk for a bridge. As we inched across one by one, I noticed some slithering motion on the bottom of the muddy water. Arriving on the other side, Eva asked Hans if the ripples we had seen had been caused by alligators.

"Very likely," Hans said, unperturbed.

After that we all seemed to step more cautiously. We had walked for about half an hour when we emerged from under the dome of the trees. The bright sunlight smote us with a blinding glare that was intensified by the reflection from the slate-gray field of pebbles on which we found ourselves. The vegetation stopped behind us in a wavering line against the field of pebbles. At the edge of the gently sloping incline we saw the river, wide and swift now, rushing over the rocks toward its final destination, the Pacific.

We picked our way over the shifting pebbles and climbed down to the river's edge. There we sat on some protruding rocks to watch the clear water churling in a multitude of eddies. It was very hot now and the midday sun was standing directly overhead.

I don't know who came up first with the idea of a swim but before long Hans, Walter, and Schwarzkopf had retired behind a large rock to strip. I decided not to indulge but to stick to the safety of a bathtub.

After a while the three men emerged, waist deep in water. Schwarzkopf came to splash beneath the boulder on which I was sitting with the two women. I could see the dancing reflection of the water play over his bare buttocks. I was sure that he had come close in order to show himself to Eva.

"How about you, Eva?" he called up to her. "Won't you come in for a swim? Just take off your clothes and come on in! We've all seen a naked woman before!"

"No," Eva said. Her mouth had become set and hard, and she did not look at him.

To my surprise Frau Schwarzkopf now turned on Eva. "What do you think you have to hide which another woman hasn't got?"

"Nothing. I just don't like to swim in the nude. Why don't you?"

Frau Schwarzkopf abruptly turned away. I wondered whether she was jealous because Eva had a younger body than she.

After a while the men came out of the water, dressed behind a rock, and we traced our way back to the camp.

Walter and Frau Schwarzkopf were the last in line. Looking back after I had crossed the muddy pool on the tree trunk, I just caught sight of Frau Schwarzkopf slipping along the last steps on the slimy trunk and landing in Walter's outstretched arms. She remained leaning against him, her face uptilted as if she expected him to kiss her. He was already bending down when he saw me looking at him; he flushed and let her go.

I turned around quickly, only to see Schwarzkopf, his hands on Eva's hips, pushing her up the incline of the path. I told myself that it was the sodden, damp heat of midday which made me feel a sudden wave of nausea. When we reached the camp I had a splitting headache.

At lunch the sensuous mood of the jungle seemed to catch up even with Hans. I caught him looking at Eva in a way he had not looked at her since the night of the ball when he had kissed her cheek.

"Damn her," he said irritably when he saw me staring at him. "Why does she have to be so . . . tempting?"

*Friday, January 17, 1941.*   Today we had rain all day long. It was impossible to set foot outside, and the heat and humidity inside the house were almost unbearable. Not a breeze stirred, and the Indian blankets beside the window hung motionless, limp and damp. Our seclusion and the way we were thrown together reminded me of our passage from Europe to South America.

As aboard ship, the urge for self-revelation became strong in some of my companions, particularly in Frau Schwarzkopf. She began by challenging me at the breakfast table to call her by her first name.

"You call Eva by her first name. I'm not so old that you should keep calling me Frau Schwarzkopf all the time."

I assured her that she was very young, which was what she had wanted to hear in the first place. I added that I had simply felt we were not well enough acquainted for me to call her by her first name. This excuse was clearly a mistake, for it started Frau Katja again on her life story. Eva stopped her with a rude remark from giving us another rendition of her escape from Russia, but this did not spare us the next installment of Frau Katja's adventures.

Taking up the stance of an orator before me, she began:

"Did I ever tell you that my family ended up in Berlin? That's where I grew up. My father never married again, but we had a Russian nurse all through the years. We were five children, two boys and three girls. I was the youngest. At home and in the ballet school we always spoke Russian, that's how I got my accent. My father did not want us to forget the language of our sainted mother. 'Someday, God willing,' he used to say, 'the devils will cut each other's throats and we will be able to go back.' Of course we never did. In the meantime my father got rich again manufacturing furniture, and I was getting to be a famous dancer. Then I met Otto and that was the end of it."

"The end of what? Of your being a famous dancer or of your father's wealth?" Eva taunted.

"You're stupid," Frau Katja said. "I wouldn't expect you to understand. Of course Otto didn't want me to go on dancing! He could not stand another man looking at me. How often did he tell me that he had never met a woman with legs like mine . . ."

Frau Katja unexpectedly bent over and with one graceful sweep raised her wide skirt almost up to her thighs to show her shapely legs.

". . . with breasts like mine." Her hands dropped the skirt and shot up, cupping her breasts. "No two people ever loved each other as Otto and I loved each other!"

Schwarzkopf had slid down in his chair, his eyes lowered on the remnants of his breakfast on the plate before him, his face crimson. He did not dare look left or right for fear of meeting somebody's eyes.

Squinting up at the electric fixture on the ceiling, Herr Knudsen muttered that he thought there was something wrong with the electric generator and he had better see to it. Hans was staring at Frau Katja as though he did not quite believe that he had seen and heard what he had seen and heard. At the other end of the table, Eva could not have looked more disgusted if Frau Katja had stripped in public. Only Walter seemed utterly captivated.

This was the effect for which Frau Katja had striven all along. Now she rushed through the rest of her account like a person who had made her one important point.

"Otto and I were married, and for five years we were the happiest people in the world. Every day he brought me flowers. Every single day. Then Hitler came and we had to run again and it was all over."

Her hands dropped from her breasts and her features went through a swift transformation from utmost joy to deepest sadness, such as only a Slav can accomplish. In one quick movement she had shown how, with the stoppage of the daily delivery of flowers, their love had come to an end.

"Katja darling, I think these people are really not very interested in our private affairs," Herr Schwarzkopf said unhappily. He looked at Eva with pleading eyes, trying to make her understand that all this had taken place long ago.

Eva did not look at him. With the familiar, malicious glint in her eyes she said to Frau Katja:

"Tell me, Katja, how long have you been married to Otto?"

"Thirteen years."

"You mean to say that if he had brought you flowers every single day for thirteen years, you would be just as much in love with him today as you were then?"

Frau Katja looked startled. Even she could see that this question was tricky. Yet it called for an answer, and answer it she did—in her way.

"You," she said. "You're stupid. What would you know about love?"

*Saturday, January 18, 1941.* This is remarkable: today Frau Katja treated us to a display of witchcraft.

Of course Eva is pooh-poohing the whole thing, offering a number of quite reasonable explanations for what happened. Still, I cannot shake the eerie feeling that I had an encounter with the supernatural. This is what happened:

Shortly after breakfast, when I began to grope for a cigarette, I noticed that I had left my cigarette case in the room. Returning there, I was dismayed to discover that the case was gone. I seemed to remember that I had put it in the top drawer of my dresser the night before, but much as I rummaged in the drawer I could not locate it.

Normally such a loss would not have distressed me. But the cigarette case was made of solid gold and had been a gift from Christine for my fiftieth birthday.

After searching for a minute or so I became frantic and sick with an entirely unreasonable grief. My first thought was that the case had been stolen, but Herr Knudsen had told us that he personally vouched for the honesty of his Indians.

He was still vouching for their honesty when I returned to the dining room to report my loss.

"Well," Frau Katja said, "then there's only one explanation: the cigarette case was stolen by the devil."

I was on the verge of making a sharp reply when I realized that she had spoken in perfect seriousness.

"The devil just loves stealing objects which are precious to people! But there are ways of getting them back," Frau Katja added craftily.

"And you're the one who knows how," Eva said dryly, but her tone of derision was lost on Frau Katja.

"Naturally."

"Katja darling, not here!" her husband pleaded. He looked extremely unhappy, the way he usually looked when he expected his wife to do something embarrassing.

"Well, if the Herr Professor does not want his cigarette case back . . ." Frau Katja said, offended.

I said eagerly that I did want it back.

"Then the only thing to do is to tie the devil's feet before he gets away," Frau Katja said. "Would you like me to do it for you?"

I thought I had nothing to lose and gave her permission to proceed.

Frau Katja asked that two chairs be placed back to back. Walter and Hans rose to fill her request, both working with the half-amused, half-embarrassed grin of people who had been called out of the audience to assist with some magic act on stage.

After the two chairs had been placed back to back, Frau Katja asked me for a handkerchief.

"A clean handkerchief," she added as an afterthought.

Possibly anticipating this fastidious streak in the devil, I had provided myself with a clean handkerchief this morning. I handed it to her and stepped back to watch as she seriously and meticulously tied the hind legs of the two chairs together.

"There," she said, "that should hold him good and tight!"

"And now this silly hocus-pocus is supposed to work," Eva mocked.

"This is no silly hocus-pocus! I learned it from my nurse who learned it from her grandmother who learned it from *her* grandmother. It always works, you'll see!"

Hans and Walter smiled gently at each other, like two adults who would not destroy a child's belief in Santa Claus. Herr Schwarzkopf stood by the window, staring outside and washing his hands of the whole matter. Eva just looked outraged. As for me, I did not know what to think.

Just then one of the Indians came in to clean up the room after breakfast. When he began tugging at the two chairs, Frau Katja let out a hysterical shriek.

"No toque!" she yelled. "Don't touch it!"

Then she went on to explain to the Indian in broken Spanish that she had tied the devil's feet and that he must remain this way until he returned the stolen cigarette case of the Señor Professor.

The Indian backed away from the chairs as if he expected them to turn momentarily into a cloven-footed, horned creature. He finished the cleaning of the room with unusual speed.

Frau Katja said that there was no need to keep an eye on the devil as long as he was chained, and we went outside to sit in the sun and do some shooting on the range behind the house. About an hour later we went inside again. The two chairs still stood as we had left them, back to back, with their legs tied together.

As we came into the cool of the house from out of the sun, my nose, which is very sensitive to changes of temperature, began to run. I excused myself and went to get a replacement for the handkerchief which temporarily shackled the devil. While I was in my room, I decided to look once more for my cigarette case.

I opened the top drawer of my chest, reached inside and began to feel around in all the corners. In the left back corner something felt bulky beneath the paper which lined the bottom of the drawer, and lifting the paper I saw the golden gleam of my cigarette case.

To say that I was shaken would be an understatement. I was still speechless when I returned to the dining room, cigarette case in hand.

"I told you so!" Frau Katja exclaimed triumphantly when she saw me. "It always works!"

There was considerable surprise among the others, and even Herr Schwarzkopf looked startled.

"How did you do it, Katja darling?" he asked.

"Don't you see she didn't do a damned thing?" Eva said angrily. "All she did was frighten the Indian with her story, and he or whoever took the case went and put it back while we were outside."

"Now see here, Frau Schwarzkopf," the Swede said to Eva, "all these boys have been with me for years and they don't steal!"

"All right, so they don't steal. Tell me, Herr Professor, when you first looked for your cigarette case, did you really look thoroughly? I mean, did you take out everything from the drawer and look under the paper before?"

I had to admit that I had not done that, but still I was quite sure that I had passed my hand around in all the corners and had not felt a thing.

"So there," Eva said. "That explains it!"

"*You* are the only one who believes *that!*" Frau Katja shouted. "Everybody else knows what really happened!"

Later in the afternoon Eva confessed that she really thought Frau Katja herself had taken the cigarette case. She knew that I was sure to miss it, for I always took it out right after breakfast. She could have removed it from my room after I had left for breakfast and replaced it when we were out on the shooting range and she had excused herself to go to the bathroom.

"And why would Frau Katja do such a thing?" I asked.

"I'm afraid the whole maneuver is aimed to impress me. Katja wants to prove that she has some special powers and that people had better do what she wants, or else."

"Do you know what she wants you to do?"

"No, I have no idea," Eva said.

But from the look on her face I could tell that she was lying.

*Sunday, January 19, 1941.*    Today I learned what Frau Katja wants from Eva: she wants Eva's support in getting Walter to resign from his job with Carillo and go into business for himself, forming a partnership with the Schwarzkopfs.

Much against my will, I was drawn into an argument about the pros and cons of this proposition. The topic came up without warning in the afternoon, while we were sitting in the house to wait out a short thunder-shower. Hans was somewhere off in the jungle. I was alone with Eva, Walter, and the Schwarzkopfs when Frau Katja said suddenly:

"And I still think it's a very good idea. I'm sure the Herr Professor here is going to agree."

I am by nature a man who becomes wary if people take it for granted that he will approve of an idea he has not heard yet—especially if these people happen to be Katja Schwarzkopf.

"I would not bank on that, Frau Katja," I warned her jestingly.

"Just wait till you hear it," she said. "Take Walter here. He has talent, he works hard, and what has he got to show for it? Nothing! Why should a man with his talent and his ambition work his fingers to the bone for somebody else if he can make a fortune working for himself? I ask you, Herr Professor, and you tell me why."

It was typical of Frau Katja to end her question on such a dramatic note, as if my opinion could really swerve Walter this way or that.

Looking from one to the other to see how they were reacting, I could tell that they had talked the matter over before. Herr Schwarzkopf looked eager, his round eyes flitting from Walter to Eva, as though he were a puppy not quite sure of who would throw him a bone. Walter seemed hesitant and thoughtful, tugging at his forelock the way he is wont to do when something troubles him. Eva's face was antagonistic as she glared across the room at Frau Katja who, in her riding habit, looked like a ringmaster trying to whip sluggish beasts into a performance.

"What if it doesn't work out?" Eva said. "What if Walter gives up his job and it doesn't work out?"

"And why shouldn't it work out? You tell me, Herr Professor, you're impartial, you have nothing to gain or lose, why shouldn't it work out?" Frau Katja demanded. "Now, our idea is that Walter ought to give up his job and go into partnership with Otto and me. He could go on building and we would furnish the houses he builds. Walter has enough of a reputation now to draw plenty of customers, and we have a little money to start a furniture factory. Besides, I'm sure we can get a bank to finance us if we need more."

Clearly Frau Katja had given the idea a lot of thought and seemed bent on drawing Walter into a partnership, even if not for materialistic reasons alone. She went on at great length about how much she knew about the furniture business—why, she had practically grown up in a furniture factory, and her husband had had a furniture store back in Berlin, so there! But she failed to stir Eva's interest until she mentioned that there might be room for Eva in the plan.

"I learned to make curtains and draperies before we left Berlin," Frau Katja said. "This will come in handy with decorating interiors, and I could teach Eva to help me."

"I don't want Eva to work," Walter said sharply, showing that he was an old-fashioned husband at heart.

Frau Katja flinched as though she had received a slap.

"And why shouldn't our precious Eva work? Would it do her any harm if she learned a trade? We would pay her, and she would have all the money she wanted for clothes and things, and nobody could tell her what to do and not to do." And then, turning directly to Eva, she added: "You don't know what it means for a woman to have money of her own!"

I could see Eva softening under Frau Katja's siren song. She was just emancipated enough to be lured by the offer of the older woman and still young enough to confuse financial independence with the sort of moral independence she seemed to crave.

"I'd love to work," Eva said, her eyes shining.

"Of course you'll love to work," Frau Katja crooned. "You just have to help me convince your stubborn husband! How about it, Walter?"

"We'll see," Walter said soberly, shooting a worried glance at Eva's glowing face. "We'll see." And, turning to me as a last refuge: "What do you say, Professor Bernstein?"

I threw up my hands.

"What do you want me to say? This is one thing about which you have to make up your own mind!"


*Monday, January 20, 1941.*   This morning we went down to the river again. It was bright and sunny, and the ladies brought along their bathing suits to join the men for a swim. Afterward, when Eva stood on a rock drying herself, Walter said innocently:

"Nothing as beautiful as a wet, young body!"

Sitting on a boulder beside me, Frau Katja flinched and quickly spread her fingers to cover the tiny, dark-blue spider veins which mar the skin of her solid, shapely legs. She looked up at Eva with a loathing that frightened me.

I thought of her look of hatred again in the afternoon, when Walter pulled me aside to ask me once more what I thought of his going into partnership with the Schwarzkopfs.

"As far as the business aspect is concerned, I don't think it's a bad idea," I said cautiously.

Walter looked at me as though trying to read from my face just what were my reservations. A slight deepening of his color seemed to indicate that he had caught on to what I was thinking.

"Well, I would rather keep Eva out of it too," he said slowly, as if I had actually voiced my objections. "Regardless of how things might be between us, I feel responsible for her. I mean, she's my wife, after all. I just don't know what's got into her! At first she was so opposed to the idea, and now she's all for it. I just can't see her going to work every day, spending in a dusty shop the hours she used to spend in the sun. Especially if there is no need for it!"

Suddenly Walter stopped in what he was saying and looked up. (We were standing on the shooting range behind the house.) Following his glance, I saw Eva reclining against one of the stilts which support the house. Leaning over her, his hands planted on a stilt at either side of her body, was Schwarzkopf. From where we stood it looked as though he would lower his weight on her at any moment.

To me this was a revolting sight and, glancing sideways at Walter, I saw that he was not pleased either. I began to understand that he did not so much want to spare Eva the exertion of work as the daily contact with Schwarzkopf.

Calculating Schwarzkopf's age for the first time, I realized that he must be old enough to be Eva's father. I had always felt impeded by my age from making advances to Eva, and it infuriated me that Schwarzkopf lacked the same delicacy.

Similar thoughts must have crossed Walter's mind as he stood gazing up at his wife.

"I don't know. I just don't know," he said unhappily.

Just then Frau Katja came out of the house. She stopped to look around, located Walter on the shooting range below and walked past Eva and Schwarzkopf without giving them a glance. Before scampering down the bank toward us, she turned her profile and raised her hand over her eyes under the pretext of scanning the sky for clouds.

Her body in the white sweater and the tight riding breeches was in perfect outline against the dark wood of the house, and her upraised chin had a clean, young line which it lacks when she forgets to hold her head high. I knew that she was posing for Walter.

I heard Walter swallow hard. Sneaking a glance at him I saw that the veins in his neck were throbbing and that he was taut with desire. With my knowledge of how things were between him and Eva I could understand the temptation Frau Katja offered him, and for a moment I respected him for what I thought were his moral scruples about involving Eva. The next instant he shattered this illusion with a question. Staring up at Frau Katja with an unchanged expression, Walter asked softly:

"Tell me, Professor Bernstein, was there ever anything between Eva and Klein?"

I was so dumfounded that I asked him to repeat the question.

"I said, do you know if my wife had an affair with George Klein?"

"Why ask me?"

"Because sometimes I think you know more about Eva than anybody else. Did she?"

I knew now what he wanted from me. If I confirmed his suspicion, I would automatically give Walter absolution. He would be free to go ahead and do what he wanted; free to throw Eva to Schwarzkopf; free of what he called his responsibility.

Well, I thought, I would not make it that easy for Walter Kramer. No man can be absolved by another man from what his conscience tells him is wrong to do.

Mustering all my sarcasm, I said:

"My dear Walter, you greatly overestimate my omniscience."

Walter's face slackened and he looked disappointed. He smiled only a feeble smile when Frau Katja came bounding down the bank toward us. The responsibility was back with him.

"What have you two been talking about?" Frau Katja demanded, sensing Walter's dark mood. "You haven't been advising Walter against our business deal, Herr Professor?"

"I haven't been advising Walter on anything," I said.

I suppose Frau Katja still wonders why I was so angry.


*Tuesday, January 21, 1941.* I slept very poorly last night. It had been an unusually hot and damp evening, and before retiring I had gone for a stroll on the dark shooting range to cool off. At the edge of the jungle I unexpectedly ran into Knudsen—he gave me quite a start, suddenly addressing me out of the dense blackness—and we stood talking for a while. He mentioned casually that there were still headhunters loose in this part of the jungle, and after that announcement I felt grateful when he offered to walk me back to the house.

I don't know what it was—the heat or my conversation with Knudsen

—but I slept fitfully. I kept waking up, and at one time I seemed to hear some walking back and forth in the corridor, but I might have been dreaming.

This morning Herr Knudsen further added to my feeling of irritation by addressing Eva as Frau Schwarzkopf at the breakfast table. Even Hans was exasperated.

"For heaven's sake, Knudsen," he said, "can't you remember after one week that this lady is Frau Kramer!"

Herr Knudsen gave Eva a long, somber stare.

"So," he said, without adding any apology to his brief statement.

Ever since my talk with Walter yesterday I have an odd feeling in the pit of my stomach, the undefinable, torturing sensation that something is not quite as it ought to be. I remember having a very similar feeling shortly before Christine told me that it was all over between us.

The thought that we are leaving tomorrow is a relief. Even the memory of the swaying bridge has lost its horror for me.

# Part Five  ❧  The Imagination of Man

*For the imagination of man's heart*
*is evil from his youth.*

GENESIS 8:21

*Wednesday, January 29, 1941.* We have been back in Esperanza almost a week now. In all this time I have not once talked with Eva and Walter. I don't know whether I am avoiding them or they are avoiding me.

I had hoped that no rumors would follow our trip to the jungle, but any such hope is futile in a small town like Esperanza. Yesterday Fleischer accosted me in the Centro.

"Tell me, Professor Bernstein, is it true what they say happened on your little excursion?" he asked me with a confidential smirk.

"And what is supposed to have happened?" I said stiffly.

"You know, sort of a switcheroo," Fleischer said, winking broadly.

The word so offended me that I could hardly control the urge to make a rude reply. Besides, I could not understand who might be spreading this rumor.

"Look, Herr Fleischer," I said with difficulty, "the only people on the trip were the Kramers, the Schwarzkopfs, Dr. Braun and I. Dr. Braun is still in the jungle. That leaves the five of us who came back. Now don't tell me that one of us has been making up this story!"

"Don't get angry with me!" Fleischer protested. "I'm not saying that these rumors are true. I'm just asking you if they are. As you pointed out yourself, you're one of the few who ought to know."

"Well, it's an out-and-out lie," I said.

Fleischer walked away from me with a little, skeptical smile on his face. I knew that he did not believe me. He had probably not come to me for information but rather to let me know what people were saying.

But who could have spread the rumor? I doubt that Walter and Eva are interested in undermining their own reputations. I myself have not spoken about our trip to anybody. That leaves only the Schwarzkopfs. Otto Schwarzkopf might be a boor in my book, but on the whole he tries to act like a gentleman.

Frau Katja? I would not put it past her. There is always the urge of the older woman to brag about having caught herself a younger lover. When it comes to proving how desirable she is, I suppose many a woman will sacrifice her good name to her vanity.

*Monday, February 3, 1941.* Eva and Walter are acting anything but discreetly.

Instead of making an effort to discourage the rumors about them, they are seen everywhere with the Schwarzkopfs. A few nights last week the Schwarzkopfs called on them in their apartment downstairs. I could hear their voices and laughter floating up to me through the open window of the dining room. But this did not bother me. What bothered me were the long silences later on, before the Schwarzkopfs sneaked out some time after midnight.

*Saturday, February 8, 1941.* Today Goldmann took me to task about the rumors which I am still denying with stubborn foolishness.

I had dropped in at the Casa Elsa this afternoon for our monthly accounting. Frau Goldmann was in the front store, wrapping a package for a customer. Trude, who was calling on her mother, sat on a chair beside the counter. Her face looked green and bloated as though she were not feeling well, but her eyes lit up when she saw me.

"You know, Professor Bernstein, you never come to look at my Norma," she said reproachfully.

I promised that I would soon make good my neglect. In the meantime Frau Goldmann had finished with her customer, and Goldmann, who had heard our voices from the back room, had come outside to join us. Rubbing his hands, he said to me:

"Just wait till you see the books. Business has been excellent, knock on wood. I tell you, the smartest thing we ever did was going into business for ourselves."

"Talking about business," Frau Goldmann said, "is it true what they say about Walter Kramer and the Schwarzkopfs? I mean, that they are going into business together," she added quickly.

"Come now, Else," Goldmann sneered, "the Herr Professor knows about the other business too. You know, the exchange business . . ."

"Markus, how you do talk in front of the child," Frau Goldmann said sharply.

"Mama, for heaven's sake, I'm a married woman now. Besides, not a word of what they say about Eva is true!" Trude said.

She looked at me pleadingly.

"Of course it isn't true," I said, with an indignation that is beginning to wear thin.

A little later, while I was trying to concentrate on the books in Goldmann's office, he brought up the subject again.

"Look, I can understand a man wanting a little change," he said. "A man can get tired even of the most beautiful wife. But why does he have to exchange her, throw her to Schwarzkopf, a nobody, a man who's being supported by his wife . . ."

(Goldmann is forgetting the times when he was being supported by his wife.)

"Not a word true," I said tiredly.

"Besides," Goldmann continued, my remark impressing him no more than the bark of a dog, "why of all the women in Esperanza does Walter Kramer have to get involved with Frau Schwarzkopf? He might remember that his father is Rosh Hakol and the president of the Hevrah Kadishah before he starts something up with a shickseh! And what, may I ask, are you laughing about?"

I could not explain to Goldmann why I was laughing. He would never understand what I could find amusing about a man who approved of adultery as long as it took place between the members of the same religion. So I kept quiet and concentrated on my work, hoping that the interesting theme was closed for the day. But I had not counted on Levy, who had dropped in to pick up his wife.

He stopped me on my way out of the Casa Elsa.

"You're living in the same house with them," Levy said to me without specifying whom he meant by "them." "You tell my wife what's going on there every night!"

I tried to disengage myself from Levy's clutch on my sleeve.

"I have nothing to tell Trude."

Levy took my protests with the same good faith with which Goldmann had taken them.

"I'm telling you in front of witnesses, Trude, I won't have you associating with that woman any more!"

"You can't tell me with whom to associate!" Trude screeched in sudden anger, tears welling up in her eyes. "Eva is my friend! The only friend I've got here!"

Frau Goldmann turned viciously on her son-in-law.

"Don't upset her in her condition!"

I glanced at Trude. She was staring down into her lap, wiping the corners of her eyes with the back of her hand. Her head bowed, she smiled wanly up at me.

"Yes. I'm pregnant again," she said.

*Tuesday, February 11, 1941.* I have been so preoccupied with the unsavory Schwarzkopf affair that I have forgotten to make mention of more cheerful news: at just about the time of our trip to the jungle the British forces opened a drive into Italian East Africa. By now they have penetrated into Ethiopia and have taken Eritrea, Tobruk, Derna, Bengasi, and El Agheila. They are said to have captured over 100,000 Italian prisoners at a cost of only 3,000 casualties. We have become so unused to good news that we cannot quite believe these numbers.

*Thursday, February 13, 1941.* It is amazing how long a rumor has to travel before it reaches the point closest to home. Herr Kramer has got wind of the widely discussed scandal only now, after the novelty has worn off.

There was an extraordinary session of the board of the Centro this afternoon from which Herr Kramer returned in a highly morose mood. He hardly picked at his dinner, finding fault with everything Frau Kramer set before him, until, in a fury, she snatched up the dishes from the table and repaired to the kitchen to brood about the sufferings which a husband can inflict upon his wife.

As always after witnessing a family scene I was too embarrassed to get up and leave, so I remained at the table in the hope that Herr Kramer would say something to dispel the aftertaste of the silly quarrel. But instead of making some jesting remark about his wife's cooking he said:

"Schapiro. You know Schapiro?"

This question was strictly rhetorical, for who did not know Schapiro? Schapiro, who had come only recently from Argentina to El Paramo (And why, I ask you, would a man come from Argentina to El Paramo?), was the only really orthodox Jew in Esperanza. He wore a short beard and sidelocks, pinned up and hidden under his black felt hat; he strictly observed the Sabbath; he ate only chickens which he himself killed ritually; in brief, as the Jewish saying has it, he was grabbing God by the feet every day.

"They want to make him Rosh Hakol," Herr Kramer said.

I began to understand now why Herr Kramer had been so irritable at mealtime. A man who has little left in life except his honorary functions would certainly resent losing one of them. On the other hand, Schapiro was probably better qualified for the post of religious head of the community than Herr Kramer.

"Well, perhaps they want a Rosh Hakol with sidelocks," I said in an attempt to joke. "If bad comes to worse, you can always grow sidelocks too."

"It has nothing to do with sidelocks!" Herr Kramer said, raising his voice.

I immediately regretted that I had overestimated his sense of humor and feared that he would break into renewed vituperations, but he sank back into morose thoughts.

"Tell me, you know these Schwarzkopfs?" Herr Kramer asked suddenly.

"Why, yes."

"What sort of people are they?"

In order to avoid answering such a general question I replied with a question:

"How do you mean that?"

"The woman, they say, is not Jewish."

I began to see light.

"No, Frau Schwarzkopf is not Jewish."

"Then what business has my son running around with them?"

"Now look here, Herr Kramer, you can't expect Walter not to associate with a couple just because one of the partners happens to be a Gentile!"

"Associate! Who's talking about associating! That's not what people tell me they're doing together!"

Who had whispered the rumor to him? Goldmann? Levy? Dr. Lipschitz in an attempt to salvage the family honor? Or perhaps Schapiro himself in the heat of the competition for the post of Rosh Hakol?

"I don't know if what you heard is true" (I have by now abandoned all positive denials)—"all I know is that Walter wants to go into business partnership with the Schwarzkopfs."

"Over my dead body," Herr Kramer said emphatically. "Go into partnership with goyim! That's all I need! After all, he's got to think of my position in the community. You just leave it to me. Tonight I'll have a word with him!"


*Friday, February 14, 1941.*    Herr Kramer came back from his visit downstairs last night a beaten man.

"He won't listen to me," he told me, more in wonder than in anger. "He won't listen to me. You bring up a son; you put him through school and university, and then, when you want to advise him he tells you he's going to do so and so and if you don't like it, you can go to hell!"

I doubt that Walter had used those exact words.

"And his wife right there too, assisting him! Throwing in her two cents' worth of wisdom! Giving me a lecture on tolerance! 'A Gentile woman who has followed her husband into the emigration deserves some respect,' she tells me. A big speech she makes. Well, at least I know now that it wasn't Walter's idea, this partnership and association. Eva put him up to it. I always said this girl would be our ruin!"

He went on raving and ranting like that for a while, and I saw no point in arguing with him. There was a grain of justice in what he said. If Eva had not wanted to further this friendship with the Schwarzkopfs she could—and would—have stifled it in the very beginning.


*Wednesday, February 19, 1941.*    I doubt that Frau Katja ever heard about the ruse of carrying the battle into the camp of the enemy, but that is exactly what she did. This afternoon she appeared at our house with a cake for Frau Kramer.

I do not know if Walter had told her about the argument with his father or if he had mentioned that all was not sweetness and light between his mother and Eva. At any rate, Frau Katja seemed to have come to the conclusion that her only possible ally in the Kramer household could be Walter's mother.

When I came upon Frau Katja on our upstairs landing this afternoon I could hardly believe my eyes, and in my surprise I blurted out:

"What are *you* doing here?"

"I have come to bring a cake for Frau Kramer," Frau Katja replied calmly. "I baked it myself from an old Russian recipe. You will be so kind as to introduce me."

I was too stunned by her boldness to protest. She had certainly timed her visit cleverly. Walter was away supervising one of his building projects. Herr Kramer had gone to another session in the Centro. Eva, who had learned of Trude's pregnancy, was calling on her neglected friend. I had just been on my way out, and if she had not met me in the corridor Frau Katja would, no doubt, have introduced herself.

I knocked on the door of Frau Kramer's room and called out:

"May I come in? I have a visitor for you!"

"A visitor?" came Frau Kramer's surprised voice. "Just a minute please!"

I could hear the rapid shuffling of feet and the hasty little noises of pillows being fluffed and ashtrays being emptied.

"All right, so come in!"

I opened the door and beckoned to Frau Katja to step inside ahead of me. Frau Kramer looked a little startled when she saw an unknown face and quickly stuffed the hair net, which she still wore after her afternoon nap, into the pocket of her robe.

I was clearing my throat and searching for a proper introduction when Frau Kramer anticipated me, saying:

"I believe I don't know this lady."

"Allow me to introduce Frau Schwarzkopf," I said bravely, expecting the worst. But Frau Kramer was so surprised that she could not even work up a hostile expression.

"Yes?"

"I have come to bring you a cake, madam," Frau Katja said brazenly. "I baked it myself. An old Russian recipe."

She whipped the wrapping off a large tray to unveil a huge, round cake, glistening with pink and white icing. "Walter tells me you love cakes and are interested in new recipes. You wouldn't believe how often Walter talks to me of his mother. I just had to come and meet you. You see, I never had a mother myself."

"What?" Frau Kramer said, still stunned.

"My mother was killed in the Russian Revolution while I was still an infant."

"I'm very sorry to hear that," Frau Kramer said helplessly, as if the Russian Revolution had taken place only yesterday.

"We will taste the cake right away, yes? I can't wait to see how it turned out. Let me get a knife! Where is the kitchen?"

And Frau Katja rushed off in the direction where she assumed the kitchen lay.

Raising her hands in a gesture of utter despair, Frau Kramer whispered to me across the room:

"This crazy woman, what does she want from me?"

"She wants you to taste her cake," I said, backing out through the door and making my escape.

The real fireworks started only in the evening after Herr Kramer came home and learned of the visit.

"The nerve!" he screamed. "The nerve of that woman to come to my house! And you"—turning on his wife—"you haven't even got brains enough to throw her out! Her and her cake! How long did she stay here?"

"Over an hour," Frau Kramer said meekly.

"Over an hour! What did she do here for over an hour?"

"Well, after she had brought me the cake I had to make coffee for her. So we sat down and tasted the cake and had coffee and she told me all about how she escaped from the Bolsheviks and about her mother and her father and the ballet and all that."

Herr Kramer was so furious that he only gasped like a fish that had been out of the water for too long. But by the time Dr. Lipschitz and his wife came over for their evening visit he had recaptured enough breath to launch into another tirade.

"So what do you say to your mother, entertaining the shickseh in our house?" he concluded.

"You're joking, Papa. Mama, he's making a silly joke!" Frau Ruth said.

"I'm joking? Look at the cake! Does the cake look like a joke to you?"

"Mama, really!" Frau Ruth looked horrified. "What are people going to say when they find out?"

"How are they going to find out?" Frau Kramer protested.

"The woman, you don't think she isn't going to spread the news all over town!" Herr Kramer shouted. "That's what she came here for in the first place! To prove to everybody that we're all right behind Walter in this disgraceful affair!"

"That's not true, Jakob," Frau Kramer said. "She seemed like a very nice woman. Not like some other women who always make trouble." (I was sure she had Eva in mind.) "She spoke very nicely about how talented Walter is and she treated me with the greatest respect."

I could see that Frau Katja had not wasted her hour here. Frau Kramer turned to me with a hopeful face.

"Tell me, Herr Professor, her mother, you know, the one who was killed in the Russian Revolution" (as if Frau Katja had had several mothers)—"perhaps she was Jewish?"

"I doubt it. Frau Schwarzkopf showed me a little ikon that had belonged to her mother."

Frau Kramer sighed. "Still, a very nice woman," she said.


*Monday, February 24, 1941.*    Today we transferred Josef's coffin to the new Jewish cemetery.

Unlike the funeral it was a quiet affair, attended only by Señora Consuelo, her brother the coronel, Herr Kramer, representing the Hevrah Kadishah; Levy, representing the Centro; Schapiro, the new Rosh Hakol; Walter and myself.

The coronel had made all the legal arrangements for the release of the coffin, and we rode out to the cemetery early in the morning to pick up Josef's remains. The place was even more desolate than I remembered it.

After the coronel had shown the gatekeeper a large, official-looking sheet of parchment, the man came with us to open the grave and help us carry the coffin out to the hearse. In order to reach the Jewish cemetery at the opposite outskirts of Esperanza we had to recross the entire city, a ride we made at an impiously fast pace for a funeral procession.

Once we reached the suburbs I completely lost the feeling that I was about to attend a burial. Everything around me seemed gay and familiar: the brightly painted villas surrounded by large gardens in full bloom; the undulating, green ridge of the Andes against the blue sky, with the jagged peak of the Grampico obscenely towering above it. When the hearse began to climb the steep street through which I had followed Eva the night she ran away, I even experienced a passing fear that we might run into a couple of secret lovers in the woods.

But my fears had been premature. If I had envisioned us stumbling along the narrow path under the weight of the coffin I was disappointed. What had previously been the path had been expanded into a road wide enough to accommodate one car. And the former lovers' rendezvous had been fenced in by a high adobe wall which, though still new, already showed signs of disintegration.

Except for the wall which fenced it off on three sides, the clearing still looked as I remembered it from my last visit there with Josef: the meadow, covered with bright yellow buttercups, gently sloping toward the cliff from which Eva had threatened to hurl herself; and beyond it the blue ranges of the mountains dissolving into the hazy distance.

The men carrying the coffin headed toward a heap of brown earth in the highest part of the meadow where a grave had already been dug. The coffin was lowered into it, and after Schapiro had said the prayers (Herr Kramer all the while looking arrogantly off into the distance) the three chauffeurs began piling in the earth until it formed a small mound above the ground.

We stepped back for a moment to give Señora Consuelo privacy to say her own prayers. She stood with her hands clasped and her head bowed, a slender, black figure beside the damp mound of earth which looked like an open wound in the green of the meadow. When she turned around there was a sad smile about her lips. She said softly that Josef would be happy here.

We walked back to the cars, Walter and I trailing along last. Glancing back over his shoulder, Walter said:

"And to think that this used to be a lovers' rendezvous!"

"Was it?" I asked, surprised that Walter should know about it.

Walter gave me a pitying look.

"You know, Professor Bernstein, you're the one person who has no idea of what's going on in Esperanza."

Sometimes I wish I were.

*Wednesday, February 26, 1941.* The transfer of Josef's coffin has posed a new problem: should the setting of the stone take place a year after the first or after the second burial? Nobody seems to be sure of the answer, and after much shouting and argument we have decided to write to the United States for rabbinical advice.

*Sunday, March 2, 1941.* There seems to have been a lull in the war activities during the winter months. Now, with the coming of spring, the Germans are beginning to stir again. Yesterday Bulgaria joined the Rome-Berlin axis and German troops entered Sofia. The British delegation had left about a week ago ("Rats abandoning the sinking ship," Goldmann had said) and the Russians have warned the Bulgarian government not to expect any Soviet aid. ("More rats," says our strategist Goldmann.)

Everybody is talking war again and the affair Schwarzkopf-Kramer has been pushed into the background.

*Friday, March 7, 1941.* "So we're no longer good enough for him to live in the same house with us," Herr Kramer said to me this morning.

I only raised my eyebrows at this cryptic remark, and he finally volunteered the information that Walter had rented a house for himself and was planning to move out in another week.

In the afternoon I met Walter in the Centro. He verified the news.

"Yes, it's true. I quit my job with Carillo and our furniture factory will begin to operate this month. I also have some prospects lined up for building and furnishing a few private homes. We can afford a house of our own now. Eva likes the idea of more room, and besides we can do with a little privacy."

This is the first I have heard of Walter's need for privacy. But then he has more to hide now than he had before.

What surprises me is that I am upset by the thought of losing Walter and Eva as the downstairs tenants. The way I have felt about them lately, I should have expected to welcome such a change. But the truth is that I simply cannot imagine the terrace and the garden without Eva taking her daily sun bath there.

Another worry: who is going to move in downstairs?


*Sunday, March 9, 1941.*     I have learned that the Lipschitzes are going to be our new downstairs tenants.

Dr. Lipschitz has moved his expanding dry-cleaning business out of the original garage into larger quarters. Now he claims that he no longer needs the house that went with the garage. Of course he might have found another suitable house for his family, but Frau Kramer revealed what was really at the bottom of the matter.

"If the grandparents are living in the same house," Frau Kramer said, "Ruth and Alfred won't have to worry about leaving the children alone with a muchacha when they go out in the evening."

It also occurred to me that after some shrewd calculations Dr. Lipschitz might have concluded that sharing the house with his in-laws would be to his advantage. Since he has to contribute to their support he might as well avail himself of their services.

I only hope he does not consider me an honorary grandparent. The two Lipschitz boys have a reputation for not being entirely domesticated.


*Wednesday, March 12, 1941.*     The United States is beginning to wake up!

Yesterday the Congress passed what they call the Lend-Lease Act, which empowers the president to provide goods and services to those nations whose defense seems vital to the defense of the United States. Goldmann argued that there was little idealism in the motive for such help, but I think we ought to be concerned with results rather than with idealism.

Tonight is a Purim dance in the Centro. After some deliberation I have decided not to attend. If the Schwarzkopfs come with Walter and Eva, it can only be embarrassing. If Eva and Walter don't come at all, there is little reason for me to go.

*Monday, March 17, 1941.* The bedlam this morning was reminiscent of the day the Goldmanns moved out. Furniture was being carried outside, open doors were slammed shut by the wind, and Don, chained to his hut, barked like a demon.

The small truck which Walter had hired had to make several trips before everything was carted away. Frau Schwarzkopf had come over to give orders, shout at the cargadores, and in general comport herself as if she and not Eva were moving.

After everybody had left Eva came back in the afternoon with a broom to give all the rooms another sweeping.

"With my sister-in-law moving in after me, I can't be too thorough," she said. "She'll go looking for dust in every corner with a microscope."

Whenever I'm worried about somebody trying to take advantage of Eva, I must remind myself that she has a healthy streak of shrewishness in her.

*Saturday, March 22, 1941.* This is worse than I had expected. I had thought the Lipschitzes were just another couple with two unmanageable children. Unfortunately, they are also relatives of the Kramers. The two boys spend most of their time upstairs—or so it seems to me—running in one door and out the other in a never-ending chase. This afternoon they decided to play in the corridor, bouncing a ball off my door just as I was taking a nap. When I complained to Frau Kramer, she said to me:

"What do you want? Children!"

But even when the boys are quiet, which does not happen often, Frau Ruth's clear, metallic voice sounds through the house as she stands in the hall below communicating with her mother upstairs. Apparently no one has as yet told Frau Ruth that the stairs in this house were constructed in order to be mounted by people from downstairs who wish to speak to people upstairs. All day long I have to listen to such world-shaking problems as: "Mama, do you think I should wax the floors first or hang the curtains first?" and Frau Kramer advising her daughter that her sons are dressed too warmly or not warmly enough.

Today I felt weak and nauseous all morning long—and this after only three days of sharing the house with the Lipschitzes. The only other creature who suffers as much is Don. The children constantly tease him, pulling his tail or throwing stones at him, and he has taken refuge in his hut and only comes out when the coast is clear.

I wish Don were not such a good-natured dog and would take a bite out of one of the little monsters. I would even be willing to hold them for him!


*Thursday, March 27, 1941.*    Yugoslavia has veered toward the axis. Two days ago its envoy signed the Rome-Tokyo-Berlin Pact in Vienna, and yesterday a political coup overthrew the regency of Prince Paul, and his son Peter was proclaimed King. How long now until the Germans move into Yugoslavia?


*Monday, March 31, 1941.*    Another anniversary. Today Frau Goldmann said to me:

"Can you imagine, it was one year yesterday that my Trudi got married!"

It seems incredible.


*Friday, April 4, 1941.*    When I mentioned to Dr. Landau that all the yelling and running around in our house made me dizzy, he gave me a strange look. We were sitting in Horowitz' back room while Horowitz was waiting on a customer outside.

"Dizzy, eh?" Dr. Landau said. "Do you ever get short of breath?"

I remembered all the times I had had to pause climbing a flight of stairs or walking up a steep street.

"Everybody gets short of breath here," I said defiantly. "It's the altitude."

"We'd better make sure it's the altitude. Why don't you call on me, let's say tomorrow, and let me take your blood pressure?"

"There's nothing wrong with my blood pressure! Just because those two brats get me upset . . ."

"How old are you?" Dr. Landau interrupted me.

"How old am I? You know how old I am! I'm sixty-three."

"Have you taken a look at yourself in the mirror lately?"

"I look at myself every day when I shave."

"Well, you should look at yourself from your chin down once in a while. You've gotten very fat."

"It would be politer to say that I've gained a little weight," I said with dignity.

"I'm not a polite person. You've gotten fat. It isn't good for a man your age. Not if you get nauseous and dizzy and out of breath. It's the heavy Jewish food that does it."

"You may say what you will about Frau Kramer, but I won't have you say a bad word about her cooking. It is first rate!"

"That's the trouble. It's too good. Listen, Professor Bernstein, I've just had an idea. You say the children make you nervous, and I say the food isn't good for you. Why don't you move?"

"What?"

I suppose I gaped as though Dr. Landau had suggested that I take a trip to the moon.

"Look, it isn't as if you'd arrived here yesterday. You know your way around Esperanza now. You speak the language. You no longer have to stick close to the people with whom you came here. And you're not married to Frau Kramer, are you?"

The idea of moving out was still too novel for me to digest it quickly. It had simply never occurred to me that I was free to do so. I was, on a

modest scale, financially independent. I could even take a small apartment and live by myself. The trouble was that the prospect had lost
its appeal.

"And where would I move?" I asked Dr. Landau.

"Why not move in where I live?"

"In Frau Steinberg's pensión? Deliver myself into her clutches out
of my own free will?"

"You're not such a catch as you think you are," Dr. Landau said
wryly.

"Besides, I would get the same type of food you claim is not good
for me," I said.

"That's what you think. Frau Steinberg only cooks that way for
catered affairs, when she is paid special prices. Her boarders she feeds
what I wouldn't feed my worst enemy."

"And you tell me to move in with her!"

"So you'll eat less. It will do you good. No, but look, let's be serious.
What sort of life do you lead with the Kramers? What do you talk about
at mealtimes? At least at Frau Steinberg's there's a little variation! You
would have me there" (he smiled in self-mockery) "and Dr. Vogel and
his wife, you know, Lipschitz's business partner, and two Swiss gentlemen who work for Pan American Oil; Dr. Braun recommended them.
Until last week the Fleischers were living with us too. Frau Fleischer
did not feel like going to business and running a household, but when
she heard that the young Kramers were renting a house she had to have
a house too. You know how people are. Frau Steinberg has a vacancy
now. And imagine: no children!"

At this point Horowitz came into the back room to make tea for us.
When I told him about my problems he said with satisfaction that he
had nothing of the sort. He was quite happy living with the Goldmanns, and there was no chance of their moving in with their grandchildren or vice versa.

This remark led us into discussing Trude's pregnancy. Dr. Landau
said angrily that Levy ought to have had more sense than to get his wife
pregnant so soon after the first child.

"At his age, he has to make hay while the going is good," Horowitz
said.

"At least he managed to get himself married," Dr. Landau sneered. "How about you? You could afford to support a wife now!"

"The pot calling the kettle black," Horowitz said.

After some bantering about who of the two was getting to be the richer one, Horowitz brought in a small, velvet-lined sample tray and showed me some new merchandise he was handling: men's and ladies' gold wrist watches.

I asked him where he had got them.

"Where do I get my stuff? Who gives me these ideas? Aronoff!"

What amuses me is that even though Aronoff is the direct cause of his prosperity, Horowitz still speaks his name as if he were the Evil One.

*Monday, April 7, 1941.*   The foreseeable has happened: German troops, which for the past days had been reported massing on the German, Hungarian, Rumanian and Bulgarian borders, have poured into Yugoslavia and Greece. But there is one unexpected note in the news. Russia has officially placed the blame for the spread of the war on her German allies.

Horowitz, who for quite a while now has been dissociating himself from the Russians, had loud words of praise for them in the Centro. And even Goldmann has begun to exhume his long-forgotten idea that there might still be a war between Russia and Germany.

But to keep us from getting too hopeful, there is also some bad news. The Italians, reinforced by Germans and commanded by General Rommel, have opened an attack against the British in Libya and have forced them to abandon their recent conquests. So far the British have been able to maintain their stronghold in Ethiopia and they took Addis Ababa yesterday.

All we can do is hope the best for the future.

*Thursday, April 10, 1941.*   I feel like a man who is contemplating adultery. Ever since Dr. Landau suggested that I move out the idea has been gnawing at my mind.

Really, what is to hold me here now that Eva no longer lives in the house? Frau Kramer's cooking? But this is exactly what Dr. Landau says I should eschew. Besides, the dizziness and shortness of breath persist.

I am not sure any more that this condition is caused by the Lipschitz brats, though today they had themselves another feast of mischief. Again poor Don was their butt. They kept teasing him and throwing stones at him until he jumped over the garden wall (a feat he had never accomplished before) and ran away. He has not come home since and Frau Kramer is already mourning him for dead.

Personally, I don't think Don is dead. I just think he has more sense than I and knows when enough is too much. The scene this afternoon impressed me even more with the necessity for moving out. Still, I shall put off talking about it to Frau Kramer until after the Passover holidays, which start tomorrow evening.

*Sunday, April 13, 1941.*  The strange thing is that every year for the duration of the Seder—and by that I mean during the reading of the Haggadah and the ritual washing of hands, drinking of wine, eating of eggs, boiled potatoes and bitter herbs—I have the feeling our emigration never took place. We might still be sitting around the festively set table in Vienna, or even back in Poland.

But the moment the meal is being served and normal conversation is resumed I am right back in Esperanza.

Yesterday the main topic of conversation was the miscarriage which Trude had suffered the previous night. Eva appeared unusually subdued and repeated several times how sorry she felt for Trude. Dr. Lipschitz maliciously said not to worry, Levy would have Trude pregnant again in no time.

"Well, for a man his age he's doing all right," Frau Ruth said, looking at her husband.

*Monday, April 14, 1941.*  Another interesting political development: the Russians and the Japanese have signed a nonaggression pact.

We all interpret this as a Russian act of hostility directed against the United States. Horowitz' stock is down again.

*Thursday, April 17, 1941.*    This afternoon I dropped in on Dr. Landau. The reason for my visit was twofold. First, I wanted Dr. Landau to take my blood pressure. Unfortunately, his suspicion was right. He said that my pressure was up but that I had nothing to worry about —yet.

While I was there I took the opportunity to inspect Frau Steinberg's pensión. Frau Steinberg was out doing her marketing—an unexpected stroke of luck—and Dr. Landau acted as my guide.

Though I had called for him a few times during Josef's last illness I had never stopped long enough to give the house a second look. Now, upon closer inspection, I realized that it was as huge as it was hideous, something like a gnarled version of Josef's fairy-tale castle.

Apparently the original owner, while still living in the house, had kept adding new wings as his offspring increased in numbers, trying out a new style on each wing.

This monster of a house sat in a lovely garden, large enough to be almost a park and neglected enough to look like a forest. Perhaps three hundred feet to the right, among the trees, I noticed another, smaller building. Dr. Landau explained that this used to be the servants' quarters but that it was empty now. Frau Steinberg kept her sleep-in muchacha in the house, and two other girls came to help out during the day only.

Inside, the house looked spotlessly clean. Dr. Landau showed me through the cavernous rooms on the first floor. Then he took me over an intricate network of stairways to his quarters, located in the turreted medieval fortress.

By the time we reached his room I was puffing. He led me through his bedroom (austerely furnished but warm with afternoon sun) into his office. I was surprised to see that he had really fixed it up to look something like a doctor's office, with the whitewashed walls, the secondhand instrument cabinet with the white enamel flaking off the rusting metal, and the frightening contraption of a chair which doctors use to examine patients.

"I know it's all illegal," Dr. Landau said when he saw me look around in amazement, "but I have quite a practice now. And not only refugees. Ever since I treated Herr Blumenthal, Coronel Jiménez has been calling me in on his family. And you know how large families are in Esperanza. One sends you to another . . . I really don't like it. One day I'll end up in jail. You wouldn't believe it, but last week I was called to the sister of the president. Don't mention it to anyone, I don't want trouble. And sit down and roll up your sleeve."

Dr. Landau took my blood pressure, listened to my heart, made me cough, pinched me, and repeated that I was disgustingly fat.

"Look, you're over sixty. Your pressure is up. You're getting to look like a stuffed pig, and if you don't watch yourself, it will sooner or later affect your heart and then you'll go like that!"

He snapped his fingers, as if to impress me with the speed with which a human life can be snuffed out. But I knew that he was exaggerating in order to scare me, and I was touched that he should be concerned for me not only as a doctor but as a friend.

"All right, I'll try to lose a few pounds, just to please you."

"Don't do me any favors," Dr. Landau said dryly while he put his instruments away.

He invited me to stay a little while, but I was in a hurry to get out before Frau Steinberg came home. If I was going to make up my mind to move here, I wanted to do it without her assistance.

Dr. Landau let me out through a side door of his office and showed me down an open stairway leading directly into the garden. (This approach was mainly used by his female patients, some of whom did not like to be observed coming and going.) We took a path which led us past the abandoned servants' quarters to a small gate in the garden wall. Stepping out into the street, I noticed that the garden house had a second entrance and two windows, boarded up with wooden shutters.

"That would make a nice, private accommodation for somebody," I remarked without much thinking.

"How about you?" Dr. Landau asked bluntly.

"And what would I do with so much privacy? Didn't you just caution me to lead a sedate life? No, if I move here—and I'm not saying yet that I will—I want to live with all the other people. I have already passed the stage when a man wants to be alone. Now I want to enjoy my garrulous old age."

*Sunday, April 20, 1941.*    A perfectly abominable day. Although the rainy season should be drawing to an end now, it has been pouring all day long. None of us has been able to set foot outside, and the Lipschitz brats, confined in their domain of activity, have turned the house into a shrieking inferno.

I have tried to hide in my room and read the newspaper, but I am unable to concentrate. (The Yugoslav government capitulated this week after holding out against the Germans for only twelve days. But the newspapers say that they still keep up guerrilla warfare against the Italians and the Germans.)

Bang! Something in Frau Kramer's household—something precious, I hope—has been smashed by one of her grandchildren. Now I can hear her voice rising in a loud whine as she calls for her daughter to relieve her of the two monsters.

I will eventually have to speak to her about my plan to move out. The period of grace which I allowed myself for putting off the talk— the Passover holidays—ended last night.

*Thursday, April 24, 1941.*    Bad news: the Germans have reoccupied Sollum and Bardia and have encircled Tobruk. The Greeks have signed an armistice with Germany. I have still not spoken to Frau Kramer.

*Monday, April 28, 1941.*    Several times during the past few days I was on the verge of telling Frau Kramer that I wanted to move out, but I always lost my courage when it came to the point of speaking up. Today Walter unexpectedly offered to relieve me of that awkward task.

He had come for a brief visit to his parents after lunch ("Now he rations his visits like a prime minister," Herr Kramer said, aggrieved) and I met him in the downstairs hall just as we were both on our way out. The Lipschitz household seemed unusually quiet, and I even entertained the hope that Frau Ruth had finally strangled her offspring when their cheerful voices began shrilling from the back yard. As if reminded by their yelling, Walter told me that Don had moved in with Eva and him.

"Mama says the children teased him until he ran away. I told her I found Don wandering in the street and took him home. He seemed to prefer to stay behind when we moved out, and now I haven't the heart to tell Mama that he has changed his mind."

Since Walter had broached the subject of the Lipschitz children, I lightly mentioned that I, too, wished to move out of his mother's place. I was already steeling myself for his remonstrances when he surprised me by welcoming my proposal.

"You know, I've thought for some time of asking you to move," he said. "I just didn't know how to put it to you. Oh, nothing personal of course. We're all very fond of you. But you must realize that it isn't like it used to be when we first came here. How does it look, my mother keeping a boarder while Alfred and I are making good money?"

And I, fool, had always imagined that the Kramers thought of me as a friend rather than a boarder!

*Wednesday, April 30, 1941.*    "You're not satisfied with your room perhaps? The food isn't to your liking?"

With these words Frau Kramer assaulted me this morning.

"The room couldn't be better and the food is excellent," I said.

"Then why do you want to move out?"

I did not consider it wise to mention Frau Kramer's grandchildren as the cause for my leaving. Instead I said beguilingly:

"You're too good a cook, Frau Kramer. Dr. Landau thinks I should eat less and have a lighter diet. But I couldn't trouble you with preparing special meals for me. It would be different if I moved into Frau Steinberg's pensión; after all, it's her business to please her boarders. In your house I feel more like a guest. I wouldn't want to make a pest of myself."

I could see Frau Kramer mellowing under my flatteries. She had not wanted so much to retain me as a boarder as to make sure that my leaving was no slight on her housewifely skills.

In the afternoon I called on Frau Steinberg to see what accommodations she had to offer me. She showed me the two rooms in the modern section of the house which had formerly been occupied by the Fleischers. One of the rooms had a small lavatory with running water, and I said this was the one I would consider taking. Frau Steinberg broke into lamentations over what she would do with the other room but finally consented to let me have the room of my choice.

"And may I ask why you're leaving your present accommodations? Perhaps Frau Kramer isn't such a good cook?" Frau Steinberg prodded hopefully.

I could not very well tell her that, on the contrary, I wanted to move in with her mainly because she was the worse cook of the two. Instead I said that I had not been feeling too well lately and that I wanted to live near Dr. Landau.

I thought that with this I was through for the day explaining my wish to move, but I had underestimated the communications system of Esperanza. I had hardly set foot in the back room of Goldmann's Casa Elsa when Frau Goldmann asked me:

"Is it true that you're leaving the Kramers?"

I said it was.

"Did you have a fight?" Goldmann asked eagerly.

"What's the matter with you, Herr Goldmann, can't people just part on a friendly basis?"

"So, why are you moving out if you didn't have a fight?"

I had already endured too many questions, and in sudden anger I told Goldmann the truth.

"First of all, I no longer have the patience to live in the same house with two small boys. Secondly, Walter feels it does not look right any more for his mother to keep a boarder."

I could literally see Frau Goldmann pricking up her ears.

"You hear that, Markus?" she said.

*Monday, May 5, 1941.*     "A fine friend you are! My enemies should have such friends!" Horowitz greeted me today when I came to his store for our weekly tea party.

"What did I do?" I asked, bewildered.

"Why do you have to go around shouting all over town that you're moving from the Kramers'?"

"Now look here, Horowitz! First of all, I didn't go around shouting the news all over town. These rumors just get around. In the second place, I don't see why I should make any secret of it. Not that you can have secrets in Esperanza. And, besides, I don't see how my moving from the Kramers concerns you!"

"You don't see how your moving concerns me!" Horowitz mimicked my voice, dancing with excited, mincing steps through his back room. He looked the way he used to look some time back, during his heated, political tirades. "So Frau Kramer doesn't want to keep a boarder any more? So what do you think happens next? Frau Goldmann doesn't want to keep a boarder either!"

I began to understand.

"I'm terribly sorry, Horowitz," I said.

*"You* are sorry! What about me? Where am I going to live if I move out from the Goldmanns'?"

"Why not move into Frau Steinberg's pensión, just like Professor Bernstein?" Dr. Landau suggested pleasantly.

"Move there after what you told me about her cooking!" Horowitz screeched.

"The food hasn't killed me yet," Dr. Landau said.

"You! You're not human! You would eat anything as long as it doesn't cost much!"

"If you're so liberal with your money you can always eat out if you don't like the food," Dr. Landau said.

"What sort of a life is it if a man can't eat at home!"

"If it's home cooking you want, why don't you get married, Horowitz?" Dr. Landau mocked.

But Horowitz was too furious to reply.

*Friday, May 9, 1941.* It seems that after all the screaming and vituperating Horowitz has decided to move into Frau Steinberg's pensión. Dr. Landau told me that he came to inspect the house today, wrinkling his nose and making faces as if he were about to enter a dungeon. After he had sniffed around in all the rooms, Horowitz announced that the only one he wanted was the one I had already picked. Frau Steinberg tried to induce him to take the room next to mine, but he insisted that he must have running water. The only other room with running water which would be available in the near future—rooms, rather—were the rooms of the two Swiss gentlemen from Pan American Oil, Frau Steinberg explained. The Swiss were being transferred to Venezuela in another three weeks, and then Horowitz could have their quarters, provided he took both rooms. Horowitz said he would take both rooms only on the condition that he did not have to take his meals in the pensión. Frau Steinberg said that such a thing was out of the question, but finally was whittled down to excuse Horowitz from dinner.

"At least once a day I don't want to look at Dr. Landau's face when I eat," Horowitz said.

It looks as if after all this time the three graces (as Eva sometimes calls us)—Horowitz, Dr. Landau, and I—are going to live together.

*Tuesday, May 13, 1941.* I am to move out from the Kramers' by the end of this week. Now that the decision is irrevocable I am beginning to feel qualms and regrets, like a man who has been granted a divorce and now wonders whether the next wife will not turn out worse than the one he is leaving.

Frau Kramer too seems to have regrets and shows her feelings by cooking all my favorite dishes.

"Eat, eat. Such food you won't get at Frau Steinberg's," she keeps urging me.

I must have put on another five pounds in the past few days. Dr. Landau is very angry with me.

Herr Kramer also said that he was sorry to lose me. Somehow Herr Kramer had always struck me as a self-centered silly little tyrant. This show of emotions only proved that one should never hold anybody incapable of feelings.

"I am not a man who makes friends easily," he said. "But you have seen so much of our troubles" ("zores" was the word he used) "that I think of you as more than a friend. I think of you as a member of the family. A closer member than some others," he added bitterly. "It will be lonesome in the house without you."

I don't see, though, how a house that is haunted by young masters Kurt and Paul Lipschitz can be lonesome for long.


*Saturday, May 24, 1941.*   With my few belongings moving ought to be a simple matter. Still, it took me over a week to get settled in my new quarters.

This delay also has to do with the change of my routine. I find that with more people in the house I have less time for myself. There is a tendency to remain sitting around the dining-room table or in the sala after a meal is over. Though the conversation is trivial, mostly gossip (or perhaps because it is gossip), nobody wants to be the first to leave. Thus the big meals, lunch and dinner, take up anywhere from two to three hours.

The food is as bad as Dr. Landau promised it would be. Leftovers, if there are any, are always conscientiously used the next day, disguised with some suspicious-looking brown sauce which tastes as vile as it looks. On the whole, the effect of the food has been salutary. I have already taken off the weight which I put on during my last week with Frau Kramer.

Except for the food, I am quite comfortable here. The room next to mine is still unoccupied and I share the upstairs bathroom only with the Vogels.

I can hear them getting up at about seven o'clock each day, Dr. Vogel urging his wife in his high, rasping voice to hurry up as he stands waiting outside the bathroom door. I had almost forgotten that Eva used to call him the whooping crane. Frau Vogel looks as plain as ever with her mousy hair and her thin, unpainted lips. Compared to her even Walkyrie-sized Frau Steinberg appears almost tempting.

But with Dr. Landau in the house and Horowitz moving in in a few days I shan't be too badly off—though admittedly they are a poor substitute for Eva.

*Monday, May 26, 1941.*    Today Dr. Landau dropped in my room to see how I was getting along. He inspected my collection of books, tested my bed, peeked into my closet and my linen drawers (I could not help the feeling that he was counting my shirts), and then walked over to the window to check on my view. As he glanced out I saw a perplexed look spreading over his face.

"You're facing back," he said, almost reproachfully.

"Anything wrong with that?"

I went to stand beside Dr. Landau and looked out. From where I stood I could see a large part of the garden, and off toward the right the unoccupied garden house shimmering white among the trees. To my left, half a story above me, lay the bay window of Dr. Landau's office in the medieval fortress. The stairway that leads up to his back door, curving around the tower, starts almost directly beneath my window.

"You can see my stairway," Dr. Landau said unhappily.

"Is that such a misfortune?" I asked, puzzled by his crestfallen mien.

"I'll be frank with you," he said. "The view from your window didn't matter so much while the Fleischers lived here. They used to be away during my office hours. So is practically everybody else in the house. You're the only one who might be at home at odd hours. You're liable to see some of the ladies who call on me."

"Well?" I said.

"What I would like to ask you . . ." Dr. Landau seemed more embarrassed than was warranted. "I mean I would appreciate it if you wouldn't talk about any patients you see coming and going. Some of the women just don't like it known that they have been to see me."

"You don't think I'm going to lie in wait all day, spying on your patients! And if I see a woman once in a while, I certainly won't mention her name."

My promise seemed to calm Dr. Landau. But I still don't understand what all the fuss was about.

*Thursday, May 29, 1941.*     Catching up on political news: two days ago President Roosevelt proclaimed a state of unlimited emergency in the United States. Perhaps this means that the Americans are getting ready to enter the war.

*Monday, June 2, 1941.*     More news, this time on the depressing side: the remnants of British troops have been evacuated from Crete. (About two weeks ago German parachute troops had invaded Crete.) What worries us now is that the Nazis—with their mechanized divisions standing at the Egyptian border—have a stronghold so close to Palestine.

*Friday, June 6, 1941.*     Today Dr. Vogel dished up the rumor for lunch that Walter has bought a car. He had it from Dr. Lipschitz, who ought to know. Walter confirmed the news when I met him in the afternoon in the Casa Elsa.

Frau Goldmann has recently added the manufacture of men's shirts to her output, and Walter was one of her first customers.

"A dozen shirts he's ordering," Frau Goldmann said to me. "Who would have thought only a year ago that he would be able to afford three shirts!"

I said that this was not the only sign of Walter's prosperity; I had heard talk of his buying a car.

"You haven't!" Frau Goldmann exclaimed, stepping back and leaving her tape measure draped around Walter's neck while she gazed at him with awe.

Walter said coyly that in Esperanza one did not even have the satisfaction of breaking one's own news. But his face, set in a grimace of modesty, was illuminated with inward pride. Being able to afford a car was no mean achievement, and Walter knew it. Only Señora Blumenthal, Herr Levy, and Aronoff among our people owned cars. ("Big deal, Aronoff, with his father's money," had been Horowitz' comment.)

Prosperity sat well on Walter. He wore a new, double-breasted, pin-striped suit with wide, padded shoulders. His shoes were polished, and he had a good haircut. Only the frayed cuffs of his shirt spoke of worse times, but he was about to remedy that.

When Walter saw me looking him over he said defensively that business had been good—better than expected for the beginning—and that all concerned were satisfied. (I could not held wondering whom he meant by "all concerned" and what they were satisfied with.)

"And Eva, how does she like working?" Frau Goldmann asked with just the right amount of acid in her voice.

"She just loves it. It's amazing how fast she catches on to everything. I never knew she was so clever with her hands," Walter said.

"She must be very busy," Frau Goldmann continued, always with the acid undertone. "When Trude was pregnant with her first baby she used to call on her every day. Now, after this . . . misfortune," Frau Goldmann wiped away an imaginary tear, "she's visited her once. Once!" she repeated.

I considered this a good moment to mention that I had not seen Eva either since she and Walter had moved out and asked if Walter was holding her captive. Walter colored just enough to betray that I had hit a sore spot.

"Why don't you visit her in our factory? I'd have thought you of all people would display a little interest in our new enterprise," he said.

I told him that I had no idea where the factory was located. In fact I didn't know his new home address. Which prompted Frau Goldmann to ask Walter if he hadn't manners enough to invite his old friends to call.

"Or perhaps you are no long interested in your old friends?" she added.

Walter bit his lips.

"Look, as soon as we're entirely furnished we're going to throw a party," he said. "The biggest party Esperanza has ever seen! Everybody will be invited! In the meantime, Professor Bernstein, how about a visit to our factory?"

We decided that Walter would pick me up next Tuesday in his new car and drive me to his place of business.


*Saturday, June 7, 1941.*    This morning, when I visited the Jungle Café after a fairly long interval, I ran into Aronoff. He asked me to sit down with him and have a tinto, and in the course of our conversation he mentioned that he would like to move out to the suburbs. He was getting tired of city living and wanted accommodations where he would have a garden and a chance to sit in the sun.

As he talked, something rang a bell inside of me and I remembered Frau Steinberg's unoccupied garden house. Aronoff seemed quite interested and said that he would call one of these days to inspect it.

If I no longer have use for the seclusion of the quarters, he certainly has.


*Tuesday, June 10, 1941.*    As he had promised, Walter picked me up this morning and drove me over to his factory. He had not told me that it was located in the same house where the Schwarzkopfs live and when he saw my surprised face he said quickly that the house was really too large for two people; that this way they saved on rent for the factory and that, with the apartment upstairs, the women could always retire and lie down for a while when they felt weary.

No wonder I had not seen Eva for such a long time! This house was really self-contained: factory, home, and what not.

We stepped inside, walked through the still empty showroom on the main floor, and entered the workroom for the two women. There the natural daylight was augmented by several naked, brightly lighted bulbs, hanging down from the ceiling on long cords. Along one wall two girls sat bent over buzzing sewing machines. Next to the window two long tables had been placed alongside each other. Facing each other across the tables, Frau Katja and Eva were cutting pieces of material from a huge bolt.

Frau Katja was the first to see me come in.

"Well, well, well, we have a visitor!" she exclaimed in her exuberant fashion.

The two girls at the sewing machine stopped working to gape at me, and Frau Katja yelled sharply at them to go on with their work. Eva too swung around to see who had come in. Now, as she stood facing me, I hardly recognized her.

Her hair, which formerly had fallen soft and golden down on her shoulders, was swept up high on her head and pinned into several stiff-looking curls. Her deep tan had faded, and without the softening frame of hair around her face her cheekbones looked sharper and her eyes larger.

"Eva, your hair!" I exclaimed with dismay even before I greeted her. She patted her curls self-consciously.

"Yes, I changed it."

"It is very becoming," Frau Katja said quickly, giving me no chance to make a remark to the contrary. "It gives her a look of dignity. She cannot run around here looking like a wild kid, not with customers coming in to buy for thousands of pesos."

As so often Frau Katja's logic eluded me, but no doubt she had a good reason for liking Eva's new hairdo: it made her look at least five years older.

Frau Katja proposed a tour through "her" factory. Eva stayed behind to watch the two girls while Walter and Frau Katja stepped down with me through a side door of the workroom into the adjoining garage. There the two doors had been unhinged for the day to make more room for the men who were hammering and sawing on unfinished pieces of furniture. All the men seemed to look alike with their Indian features, their blue-black, slicked-back hair, and their tattered shirts and trousers. The garage was filled with the odor of their unwashed bodies mingling with the smell of glue and sawdust.

While Walter proudly showed me a finished mahogany chest, Frau Katja inspected the pieces in progress, pointing out a faulty joint here, studying the color of a varnish there, showing the upholsterer how to tighten the fabric properly over the seat of a chair. Walter watched her with admiration.

"Katja knows the business inside out, and I still have to see her tired or discouraged," he whispered to me. "Really a woman to help a man get ahead."

This reminded me that I had not seen the man whom Frau Katja supposedly was helping to get ahead, namely, her husband. I did not miss him enough to ask for him but was not spared meeting him upon our return to the workroom. He was sitting behind a large desk which had been unoccupied when we first came in, and his eyes rested on Eva across the room with a doglike devotion for which I could have pitied him if I did not loathe him so.

He jumped up when he saw us and came toward me, hand outstretched and all affability, greeting me as though I were an important customer. Frau Katja proudly told me that "her" Otto was their salesman and that all the ladies were simply mesmerized by his charm and good looks.

Glancing across the room, I saw Eva smile sarcastically as she measured a piece of fabric. I walked over to her and asked her how she liked her work.

"I just love it. It's so rewarding to do something productive." Her smile was sincere now.

I ached at seeing how eager she was to produce something but could not help thinking that instead of this job she should have had a baby.

I took my leave, and Walter and Schwarzkopf showed me out of the house. On the doorstep I nearly fell over a dog stretched out there. Cursing, I looked down and saw that it was Don. Walter said that he followed them to the factory every morning and went home with them again in the evening.

"Sometimes he also spends the night here," Schwarzkopf said like a fool. "He's a good little doggie."

*Saturday, June 14, 1941.*    I am beginning to understand why Dr. Landau was so unhappy about the view from my window. As I casually glanced out yesterday afternoon, I saw Trude puffing her way up the spiral staircase to Dr. Landau's office door.

All it takes now is for Goldmann to start cursing the fertility of his son-in-law to confirm me in my suspicion that Trude is pregnant again.

*Tuesday, June 17, 1941.*    Another omen: yesterday the United States government ordered the closing of German consulates throughout the country. We interpret this as a sign that the United States is moving closer toward war.

*Friday, June 20, 1941.* "That empty house in the garden has been a thorn in my side for the longest time," Frau Steinberg said to me today. "A number of people have looked at it before, but they always found some fault with it. Either they didn't want to walk across the garden for their meals or they didn't want to walk across for their baths. And how many people would take a cold shower in this climate? You can't imagine how much I appreciate your sending me a boarder!"

She gazed at me fondly, her strong, fleshy fingers squeezing my arm as a sign of her gratitude.

"There's only one thing that worries me," she said. "That Aronoff, I understand he has quite a reputation. Perhaps some of my other boarders might object to what goes on in his quarters."

"Look, Frau Steinberg, Herr Aronoff will be living at the other end of the garden. He's got a private entrance from the street. There are shutters on his windows. How can people possibly object to what they can't see and therefore can't know is happening?"

"Ah, but you don't know people," Frau Steinberg sighed, grievously underrating my knowledge of human nature. "Besides, the other gentleman is going to live in the house. I hope you won't mind if I put him in the room next to you."

"Rudi Brueck next door to me!" I exclaimed.

Frau Steinberg seemed somewhat taken aback by my surprise.

"Herr Aronoff said that he needs the entire garden house to himself. It isn't nearly as large as it looks from the outside. Part of it is taken up by the garage, where he wants to keep his car, and by a large storage room where I used to keep my firewood and where he wants to install his soap factory, as he calls it. So you see the other gentleman will have to live in the house! Do you think he'll want to bring women in here?" Frau Steinberg asked worriedly.

I told her that Rudi Brueck seemed to prefer ladies who would rather entertain in their own homes.

"How do you mean?"

"Well, he once mentioned to me that he prefers . . . ah . . . mature women."

I still don't know what self-preservatory instinct made me confide this fact to Frau Steinberg. At any rate, a sharp glitter of interest came into her eyes and she let go of my arm.

"You don't say," she said, her full face under the coiled, blond braids betraying an anticipation quite unseemly in a respectable landlady.

*Monday, June 23, 1941.*    Our excitement over the war in Europe seems to be following a pattern of high and low tide. Since yesterday the tide is again at its highest: the German armies have invaded Russia along a 2,000-mile front, stretching from the White to the Black Sea!

Now, as an afterthought, everybody knows that this was an inevitable development. Especially Goldmann walks around with his chest puffed with pride. Didn't he always say that the war between Russia and Germany would break out in June? What he neglects to add is that he said the Russians would be the attackers and that his prediction was made for June, 1939.

Still, Goldmann is so filled with the glory of the prophet that he made only cursory mention of the other event in his life: Trude's third pregnancy. Fortunately he doesn't know that even this bit of information is no longer news to me.

*Friday, June 27, 1941.*    George Klein said good-by to me this afternoon. I hardly recognized him when he came to my table in the Centro. He did not wear his glasses and he had grown a mustache, which made him look like a criminal trying to hide his identity.

"I've been looking for you for days," he said, aggrieved. "Where have you been?"

He made it sound as though I had broken a contract by failing in my daily visits to the Centro. I told him that my schedule had been upset by my moving and asked him what he wanted to see me about.

"I wanted to say good-by to you. I'm leaving on Saturday."

It is always hard to find something to say to a person whose departure one has already taken for granted.

I extended my hand, hoping that my good wishes could be combined with the farewell, but Klein did not take my hand. He sat down opposite me and told me all about his plans for the future. He was going to volunteer for service as soon as he got to the United States.

"With my knowledge of languages I'll be sent overseas right away and I'll be killed," he said.

He spoke in a studied, flat voice to heighten the dramatic effect of what he was saying, but I felt more inclined to laugh than to commiserate with him.

"Not everybody who goes to war gets killed, Herr Klein. Especially not in a war that has not broken out yet. So why mourn your death prematurely?"

"You'll see, with my tough luck I'm going to get killed. That's why I wanted to say good-by to Eva before leaving. Where can I find her?"

I had been afraid all the time that he would get around to Eva, and I felt that just now she was in enough trouble without having to deal with Klein.

"Look, Eva is busy working in her new factory. Walter brings her there and takes her home again. I doubt that you would find a chance to see her alone."

"Yeah," Klein said dejectedly. "It all turned out the way I thought it would. Money, that's what she wanted. To be rich and to have things. What does she care for love? I don't know why I should want to say good-by to her. Well, if you see her, tell her I left. Tell her she doesn't have to be afraid any longer to show her face in the street. Tell her she did a good job on me. Tell her . . . I'm sorry for her. Yes, tell her that!"

He got up, reached across the table, grabbed my hand and squeezed it furiously. There were tears in his eyes and he did not look at all as if he was sorry for Eva. He looked as if he was sorry for himself.

*Sunday, June 29, 1941.* Aronoff has begun to move his belongings into the garden house. I came upon him this morning when I left through the side gate in the garden wall. He was carrying boxes and suitcases, but he stopped briefly to chat with me, handing over his bundles to Rudi Brueck, who seems to act as his valet.

After we had dutifully commented on the weather I said:

"So your cousin has left us."

Aronoff made a face as if I had said a dirty word.

"The idiot," he said. "Now he has to go to the United States! He's going to join the air force if they'll have him. No woman is worth such lunacy!"

"Did he tell you that he was leaving because of a woman?" I asked, startled.

"He didn't have to tell me. I've known George long enough to guess what's going on in his mind. He was always mixed up in unhappy love affairs, even back in Vienna. It seems this time he got really hurt. If there wasn't a war on he would just be fool enough to join the Foreign Legion."

I was tempted to ask Aronoff if Klein had told him who the woman was, but remembering that he had been one of the first to see through Eva's wiles, I refrained from committing a major indiscretion. Instead I asked him:

"Don't you think that your cousin might feel that he has a stake in this war, even aside from running away from a woman?"

"What stake?"

"In a way it's our war too, isn't it?"

"Is it? Well, you'll have to excuse me, but I have to finish unloading my stuff."

He turned away abruptly and walked into the house, leaving me wondering what had made him so angry. Perhaps I had touched a sore spot. Perhaps he too had asked himself whether he did not have a stake in this war.


*Thursday, July 3, 1941.*    Now that Aronoff, Brueck, and Horowitz have moved in, our meals at Frau Steinberg's are quite lively. What with Dr. Landau and Aronoff alternately heckling Horowitz, and Horowitz blowing up time and again like an active volcano.

Of course all the talk revolves around the war in Russia. The Germans have taken Grodno, Brest-Litovsk, Vilna and Riga, and the Russians continue to retreat with heavy losses. At the outbreak of the hostilities Churchill made the brave but futile gesture of offering the Russians all possible aid, but no such help has as yet been forthcoming.

Horowitz, rediscovering his old sympathy for the Russians, has taken it upon himself to agitate for volunteers for the Russian cause. This has led to several arguments between him and Aronoff.

Today their quarrel started right after lunch, while I went to my room to get my cigarettes. When I came back, Horowitz had already reached the shouting stage.

"So who needs you here in Esperanza!" he was yelling at Aronoff. "Why don't you go to the United States, like your cousin Klein, and join the army?"

"My cousin Klein is an idiot," Aronoff said calmly.

"I don't think he's an idiot," Horowitz said. "I think he's very brave to want to fight for our cause!"

"Jesus, Horowitz, how can you talk such nonsense! Where do the Jews get the idea that this war is being fought for them? It isn't our war. Nobody lifted a finger for us when Hitler marched into Austria and Czechoslovakia! If he hadn't attacked Poland nobody would be lifting a finger for us even now! I don't see why I, or my cousin Klein for that matter, should go and fight their war?"

"You're using the arguments of a coward," Horowitz said with bitter triumph.

I was surprised to see that this remark failed to make Aronoff angry. He smiled, a little sarcastically, and said:

"Look, Horowitz, I don't have to prove to you that I'm a hero. I proved to myself once or twice that I'm not exactly a coward, and that's enough for me. I want to live through this war, and if I have to stay in Esperanza for the duration of it, I'll stay here. I don't say that I wouldn't join up if I were in the United States today, but I'm not in the States. And I don't see any point in going there if I don't have to. As I said before, I don't feel that this war is being fought because of us, and its outcome will hardly be influenced by another hundred, or five hundred Jews joining the Allied forces. A few years ago, before I left Vienna, I might have felt differently. But that's how I feel now."

"And why would you have felt differently a few years ago?" Horowitz asked.

"Because a few years ago it would have been our war. Do you remember the long line outside the American consulate after the Germans had marched into Vienna? One day I went there and stood in line with the rest of the people in order to get an application blank for my visa. It was one of the most dangerous spots for a Jew to show himself in those days. Almost every day the SA and the Gestapo would haul people out of the line and cart them off to concentration camps. And still people went there.

"The day I went there two guys in front of me were talking. One said to the other: 'Why doesn't President Roosevelt give all the Jews in Austria American citizenship? He doesn't even have to let us in! Just give us citizenship, and we would be safe here!' It sounded so simple, but of course it couldn't be done. You see, we were in danger then and they were safe. Now they're in danger and we are safe. I just don't feel that I owe them a debt of gratitude."

"Debt! Gratitude!" Horowitz shouted. "You should want to go out of idealism, because this war is being fought against Hitler!"

"Tell me, Horowitz, if you're such an idealist, why don't you volunteer?"

Horowitz looked momentarily confused.

"But I'm too old," he finally sputtered. "If I were your age I'd certainly go."

"You don't look your age. As a matter of fact, you could easily pass for younger. I think they might still take you if you tried hard enough."

Horowitz looked quite uncomfortable now and did not know what to say.

"You know, Horowitz, you're just another one of those idealists who send other people to do their fighting," Aronoff said.

Horowitz' anger helped him overcome his confusion.

"Tell Herr Aronoff," he screamed at me, "that I will do business with him, if I must. But I don't have to speak to him!"

And Horowitz strutted out of the room with the satisfaction of an actor who had had the last, most dramatic line.

*Tuesday, July 8, 1941.* Of course Horowitz has not stopped speaking to Aronoff. There is one topic which fascinates him beyond any self-imposed restraint in his dealings with Aronoff: women. He has tried to goad Aronoff into naming names and giving details, so far without the slightest success.

"They say you've been to bed with every pretty woman in Esperanza," Horowitz said today. (Meaning, no doubt, every pretty woman in our Jewish colony.)

"Is that what they say?" Aronoff said in an innocent tone. "Why, that's very nice of them!"

He chuckled softly to himself and walked away, leaving Horowitz to turn crimson with frustration.

"All exaggerations!" Horowitz said to me, his voice shaking with rage. "It's just his bragging!"

"I didn't hear him say a word, Horowitz."

"That's just it! He could have denied it!"

Poor Horowitz! He cannot get over the disappointment that Aronoff will not entertain him with lewd, real-life bedroom stories. Considering that he surely has quite a number to tell, Aronoff has shown admirable reticence. But, then, he does not have to brag. The ladies he has favored do it for him.

Even our two ladies, Frau Steinberg and Frau Vogel, have changed since the young bachelors moved into the pensión—though the change, I should guess, is due more to the presence of Rudi Brueck than of Aronoff. Not that Aronoff's attractions have been lost on the ladies. They look at him with the longing with which one might look at the stars, captivated but aware that they are out of reach. With Rudi Brueck it is different: he is available.

A couple of days ago I noticed the unprecedented appearance of lipstick on Frau Vogel's plain face. What's more she, who has always hung on every word of her husband's, has begun to show signs of impatience when he interrupts Rudi in the telling of one of his crude jokes.

But an even greater metamorphosis has come over Frau Steinberg. She now cooks party fare for her boarders! The food she puts before us is so good that I have again put on weight. My blood pressure is up too, and Dr. Landau is very angry with me.

*Saturday, July 12, 1941.*     Life in the Villa Carmen has really become quite pleasant now. Adding to the enjoyment of the excellent food, Rudi Brueck puts on a show for us every evening. He plays his accordion and sings songs which bring a pretty blush of modesty to the faces of our two ladies.

Today I asked Rudi where he had learned to play the accordion.

"I picked it up from a musician friend of mine. I used to associate a lot with artists."

I believe that, like so many others here, Rudi Brueck is also rearranging his past to suit his imagination. Another figment of his fantasy is the title which he has bestowed upon himself: chemical engineer. (This in connection with the soap he is making.) I suspect that the only claim Rudi can lay to an academic education is via his thorough knowledge of ribald student songs.

Yet in spite of his fibs Rudi is a very likable fellow. Whenever I look at him—the little cherub's head with the guileless blue eyes sitting on his tremendous shoulders—he puts me into a cheerful mood.

This morning Frau Steinberg and I visited him in the garden house to watch him brew his soap. He stood stripped to the waist, with only a leather apron covering his chest as he stirred some liquid in a steaming kettle. His skin was red from the heat, and I could see that his muscles were beginning to get buried under a layer of fat. Frau Steinberg's good food is telling on him too.

When he saw his landlady he broke into a roar of laughter, as though her face reminded him of something funny.

"Listen, I just remembered another two stanzas of the song I sang for you last evening," he said.

And he sang them right in front of the steaming kettle.

Frau Steinberg giggled and blushed. Rudi, beside himself with mirth, jabbed her in the ribs. She playfully slapped his hand and he, entirely carried away now, forgot himself and smacked her on her impressive buttocks. Frau Steinberg coquettishly stamped her foot and said: "Now behave yourself, Herr Brueck!"

With their ruddy, laughing faces and the plump bodies they looked like something out of a Frans Hals painting.


*Wednesday, July 16, 1941.*    Not much news to report here. I have settled back into my old routine: mornings in the garden; afternoons in the Centro; an occasional visit to the Jungle Café; and once a week lunch with Señora Consuelo.

These luncheons always have me ill at ease, but they are a ritual Señora Consuelo will not relinquish.

The war in Russia goes badly. The Russians are still retreating. A couple of days ago a mutual aid pact was concluded between Great Britain and Russia, but all this is just so many promises on paper.


*Monday, July 21, 1941.*    Today Frau Steinberg and Rudi sealed *their* pact of friendship in Rudi's room.

When I woke up from my nap in the afternoon the rain was coming down in buckets. The clouds were hanging so low that it looked closer to nightfall than to noon. So instead of getting up I just rolled over on my side and closed my eyes again.

Suddenly I was awakened by what, in my drowsy state, I could only interpret as an earthquake. My whole bed was rocking, and the lamp on my night table was on its shivering course to falling down.

Again I experienced the frightening stab of panic which I had felt the day the earthquake caught us in the Centro. In a move to call on God for help I raised my eyes ceilingward, only to find that the large chandelier, remnant of the better times the Villa Carmen has seen, was hanging motionless. I let my eyes travel over the other objects in the room, realizing that every thing except my bed, my night table, and the lamp was in a perfect state of repose.

Gradually it began to dawn on me—I was wide awake now—that the shaking of my bed was not caused by a terrestrial upheaval but by something that went on in Rudi's room.

Perhaps with any other two people such proximity of lovemaking would have stirred my imagination. But the idea of Rudi Brueck and Frau Steinberg cavorting next door only filled me with such merriment that I lay in my rocking bed and laughed like a madman.

*Friday, July 25, 1941.* With the instinct of the jealous rival Frau Vogel has found out what is going on between Rudi and our landlady. Today she drew me aside, her freshly painted lips set in a thin line of bitter envy.

"I think it's a disgrace!" Frau Vogel said. "This is supposed to be a respectable pensión. She ought to be ashamed of herself, a woman her age!"

Still, the shocking discovery has not stopped Frau Vogel from making eyes at Rudi.

*Tuesday, July 29, 1941.* "You just keep it up and you'll eat yourself into your grave," Dr. Landau said to me this morning after he had taken my blood pressure.

"What do you want from me, Dr. Landau? What pleasures have I left in life except eating?"

"I'll tell you what your trouble is," he said. "Not lack of pleasure but lack of occupation. What's the matter with you anyway? Everybody else has found himself something to do! Just because Goldmann keeps supporting you, you feel that you don't have to find an occupation!"

"Well, what would you have me do?" I asked miserably. "Should I offer to sell ladies' underwear in the Casa Elsa?"

"You ought to be ashamed, striking the pose of the shlemiel. A man with your background, an intellectual, a professor no less! Why don't you go back to teaching?"

"Teaching!"

"Why not? Look, Professor Bernstein, it isn't as if we'd arrived here yesterday. You speak the language now, and I'm quite sure they would offer you a chair at the University of Esperanza if you told them that salary was of no consequence."

Somehow this suggestion struck a chord, but there was a dissonance in it which I could not pinpoint until later.

Perhaps the answer came to me during my afternoon nap. At any rate, the cause of the dissonance was clear to me when I woke up.

If I wanted to be a good teacher I would have to be able to establish a rapport between me and my students. A sort of mutual understanding of purposes. And such a rapport could never exist, for it would have to be based on an understanding of the Parameños, an understanding in which I am completely lacking. The people here are as strange to me today as they were when I first arrived. I know little about their heritage, the way they live in their homes, the way they think, their aspirations. The fault for this does not lie with them but rather with us. They have not purposely kept us out of their society. We did not choose to associate.

Josef was right, after all: wherever the Jews go they carry their own ghetto with them.

No, I could never teach here. I could teach in Vienna—even as a stranger—for there was always at least a smattering of Jewish students in my class. They were not necessarily my best students or my favorite students, but their presence was important to me. They were a part of my people, a part of my heritage, a part of myself; proof that I was not alone amidst strangers. I would be alone here, totally alone. And imparting knowledge without human contact is not enough.

Perhaps if I had gone to the United States—

I must be going mad! Dr. Landau has so stirred up my discontent that I am contemplating another emigration at my age! Of course that is out of the question.

But be that as it may, I will have to do something about my partnership with Goldmann. It doesn't seem fair that he should still share his profit with me fifty-fifty.

*Saturday, August 2, 1941.* Herr Kramer, whom I met in the Centro this afternoon, reminded me that today is Tisha B'ab. He complained that in spite of the day of mourning, attendance at the Sabbath services had been poor, as always.

"Why should we pick one particular day for mourning?" I said. "If the Jews want to mourn they can find a reason any day."

"To me it looks more as if the Jews of Esperanza were thinking of nothing but celebrating," Herr Kramer said dourly.

(There is again talk about an anniversary ball in the Centro.)

Actually, we have little cause for celebrating. The Germans are still advancing in Russia.


*Wednesday, August 6, 1941.*    Before speaking to Goldmann about my plans to quit as his partner, I thought I ought to have some concrete idea of what I want to do with my share which, according to the last accounting, has mounted to the fantastic sum of five thousand dollars.

I could not think of a better person to ask about my problems than Aronoff.

"Well," he said, thoughtfully rubbing his chin, "you could try to get some interest on your money."

"You mean putting it in a bank?"

"No, I don't mean putting it in a bank. A bank would pay you only three per cent a year, not enough for you to live on. But if you would lend it to some businessmen they would pay you anywhere from one to two per cent a month."

"Is that legal?" I exclaimed.

Aronoff shrugged.

"Legal or not legal, it's general practice here. You ask any of them, Levy, Grushka, Dubrovsky, why, even your friend Horowitz, how much interest they're willing to pay you, and they'll tell you."

"Don't tell me that people like Levy need *my* money!"

"Everybody needs money," Aronoff said dryly. "Considering that they make up to one hundred per cent on some of their merchandise, why shouldn't they take up all the money they can get for two per cent a month?"

Still the idea of turning into a moneylender did not appeal to me.

In the afternoon I spoke to Walter Kramer in the Centro. He made a suggestion that was more to my liking. Why not buy some real estate and wait for the value to go up? He had it from a confidential source that the city of Esperanza was going to start urbanization toward the north within the next year. All the plans for the streets and sewers were already drawn up, but most people were as yet ignorant of the plan and land in the north could still be had for a song. Eventually the price would double, triple, perhaps go up to ten times its present value.

All this sounded quite exciting but I still had reservations.

"Suppose something goes wrong and the city drops the plan for urbanization?" I asked.

"They can't drop it. Esperanza is expanding, and there is no place to expand to but toward the north."

The thought of making a lot of money in a speculation fascinates me, but it also frightens me. I was never a gambler. And suppose I did invest my money, how would I make a living until I could reap the profits?

*Thursday, August 7, 1941.*　　I have figured out a way of earning my living if I should decide to freeze my money in real estate. I think Goldmann would be willing to pay me a hundred pesos a month for taking care of his books. Now, if I could find another three or four clients, perhaps Levy, Horowitz, Fleischer and Walter Kramer, who would hire me at an equal salary, I could cover my living expenses. But before talking to any of them I must speak to Goldmann.

*Monday, August 11, 1941.*　　"I hear you are dissolving your partnership with me!" Goldmann greeted me when I set foot in the Casa Elsa.

"Perhaps you could have done me the kindness to inform me first before shouting the news all over town!"

I felt positively stunned.

"All I did was ask two people what they considered a sound investment."

"So what more do you need to do, especially if one of the two is Walter Kramer?"

"Look, Herr Goldmann, since you already know about it, this is exactly what I would like to discuss with you."

"To be quite frank, I have also wanted to talk about it for a long time," Goldmann said craftily. "Only I didn't know how to put it to you without making you think me an ingrate. Nobody can say that about Markus Goldmann!"

"In other words it is also convenient for you to terminate our partnership," I said with relief.

"Who talks about terminating! Just putting it on a different basis!"

"Now look, Herr Goldmann, we both know that you don't need my money any longer," I said (with the idea of tripling it in the back of my mind), "so why not sever our uneven partnership in the best of friendship. You pay me out, and from now on all the profit belongs to you. Of course I shall gladly continue looking after your books, for a small monthly salary," I added cautiously.

"What do you think of me! I'm going to pay you out! I'm going to have people say that Markus Goldmann pushed his benefactor out of his business now that he no longer needs him! What would you do with the money if I paid you out? How would you make a living? I tell you what I'll do: you leave the money with me and I'll pay you one and a half per cent a month, like everybody else in Esperanza!"

This was exactly what Aronoff had suggested and what I had not liked.

"Maybe I want to invest my money," I said to Goldmann.

"Invest it? Where would you invest it?" Suddenly a gleam of suspicion came into his eyes. "I know who's behind all this! Horowitz! He's been wanting to expand his store for a long time!"

"Herr Goldmann, I assure you Horowitz has nothing to do with my decision!"

But Goldmann was struck with temporary deafness.

"This sneaking Communist of a Horowitz!" he raged. "Living in my house for years, eating at my table, and now he's trying to steal my partner! How much did he offer you a month? Two per cent? All right, if Horowitz will pay you two per cent, so will I, but not a penny more!"

What can you do with such a man? I just had to leave my money with him.


*Friday, August 15, 1941.*    Yesterday Roosevelt and Churchill issued a joint declaration of peace aims in a document called the Atlantic Charter.

"They haven't won the war yet and they're already talking about peace aims!" Horowitz ranted. "Instead of talking, the Americans ought to send troops over!"

But he was careful not to make these accusations within earshot of Aronoff.

*Wednesday, August 20, 1941.*    Little news here in Esperanza, and nothing encouraging from the Russian front. The Germans have now conquered all Ukrainian territory with the exception of Odessa.

The Americans are finally beginning to show real war jitters. President Roosevelt has signed a bill which will keep service men in the army eighteen months longer.

"And my idiot cousin had to join just now!" Aronoff exclaimed when he read the news.

*Monday, August 25, 1941.*    Another bit of news that startled us so soon after President Roosevelt had extended the draft: yesterday Churchill pledged British aid to the United States if she should become involved in a war with Japan.

Why Japan? It seems that our entire interest is so focused on the war in Europe that we simply cannot perceive of the threat of war in any other part of the hemisphere.

*Thursday, August 28, 1941.*    A sign of how fed up some people are with life in Esperanza: although the general feeling is that the United States will soon enter the war, Fleischer today confided in me that he plans to emigrate there in the not so distant future. I ran across him this morning only a few blocks from the Villa Carmen. When I asked him what he was doing in my neighborhood, he told me that he had been to the American consulate to apply for a quota number.

"You're not planning to go to the United States now, on the eve of war?" I asked.

He shrugged.

"Even if there should be a war, I'm past draft age. Besides, I may not be leaving here soon. I just want to make sure that I don't have to go through another period of waiting if I should want to leave."

We still talked politics for a while, and then Fleischer asked if Walter's factory wasn't somewhere around. He said he'd like to drop in and see what was going on. I could tell by the expression on his face that he did not mean the work that was going on there.

"You know, I haven't seen Eva in ages," he said. "I just would like her to remember that I'm still alive and willing."

*Monday, September 1, 1941.* Today is the second anniversary of the outbreak of the war in Europe, but people were more concerned with rehashing the incidents at the ball Saturday night. The stories have become so repetitious that I no longer listen to them: which woman wore what, who flirted with whom, and who got stinking drunk.

What I considered more interesting and significant of our state of mind was Dr. Lipschitz' complaint that nobody wants to buy a plot in the cemetery which Josef has bequeathed to the Centro.

"What good does the land do us if we can't convert it into funds for the Centro! But you wouldn't believe it, even the older people refuse to make provisions. Whenever I broach the subject—and, mind you, it isn't an easy subject to broach, telling people that they might, God forbid, drop dead suddenly—I get the same answer: 'I don't intend to die in Esperanza.' Where, I ask you, do they all intend to die?"

He glowered at me accusingly.

"Now don't look at me as though you expected me to become your first cash-and-carry customer, Dr. Lipschitz," I said.

"I didn't mean anything personal. You're in good health, thank God," he said regretfully. "But not everybody is so lucky. I can't help thinking of Herr Blumenthal. By the way, in another couple of months it will be time to set his stone. Perhaps you could speak to Señora Consuelo about it."

I promised to do so the next time I visited her.

*Monday, September 8, 1941.* I notice that a full week has elapsed without my making an entry. And even now all I can think of to record is that the Germans have begun a siege of Leningrad.

It seems that ever since Eva moved out of my field of vision I find it less and less worth while to keep a journal.

*Thursday, September 11, 1941.*    My complaints about having nothing to report were premature. At the moment I even wish they were valid again. My last visit with Señora Consuelo has thrown me into a state of near panic. It seems that everybody—except myself—is agreed that I am to be buried in Esperanza.

Yesterday, at my ritual luncheon with Señora Consuelo, I brought up the matter of the stone for Josef's grave. She told me that she had already ordered it, and after the meal she called for her car and we rode over to the stonemason's to see how the work was progressing.

Since I had forgotten to warn her that there must be no decorations, I felt relieved when I saw that she had ordered a simple stone.

"I sent my lawyer to your padre," she said (meaning Schapiro, our Rosh Hakol) "I know how strict are the rules of your religion and I did not want to make a mistake. I so wanted José to have two angels."

Even without the angels the stone was impressive, hewn out of rare, dark-red marble and shaped like a broad obelisk, resting on a low platform. After inspecting it from all sides, Señora Consuelo suggested that we drive to the cemetery to visualize how the stone will look on Josef's grave.

We rode up the steep street through which I had not passed since Josef's coffin had been transferred to its permanent resting place, pulled up by the wall, and entered through the unlocked gate into the cemetery grounds. As on previous occasions, I was struck by the beauty of the spot. I thought irreverently that the view of the blue mountain ranges and the snow-topped peaks was wasted on the dead.

Señora Consuelo walked ahead of me toward Josef's grave. Where there had been a naked mound of earth there was a patch of well-kept green turf now, bordered by a low fence made of wooden stakes. A small bed of pansies and blue irises gave the grave an almost gay appearance.

It was then I noticed that an identical plot had been staked out next to Josef's. I had only one explanation for it: Señora Consuelo had reserved a resting place for herself next to her husband.

I knew it would be very difficult to tell her what I had to tell her.

"Señora Consuelo, I don't want to hurt your feelings . . . I know how attached you were to Josef . . . but this is a Jewish cemetery and you are a Catholic."

She looked at me and I could see that she did not understand. Pointing at the empty lot, I said:

"This plot . . . you could not be buried here."

"Ah, pero no es para mi. Es para Ud," she said. "Ah, but it is not for me, it is for you. It was José's last wish that you be buried next to him."

I was so taken aback that I did not know what to say. Surely some expression of gratitude for the gift was in order, but I just could not think of anything. All I could think of was that I did not want to be buried in Esperanza.

What am I to do?

Ever since my return from the cemetery I have been unable to shake a superstitious fear. It seems that after charting the course of my life for me Josef also made provision for where it should end.

But I don't want to die here!

*Wednesday, September 17, 1941.* I have made a desperate move: I have taken out an application blank for a visa to the United States and I had my name put on a waiting list for a quota number.

It was not so much the discovery of my burial ground as a chance encounter with Eva which prompted me to do so. I ran across her in the street on my way to the Centro yesterday afternoon. She politely stopped to chat with me but was cool and distant, a stranger with her upswept hair and her tan all but completely faded. I don't know what she wanted to prove by her supercilious manner—perhaps that she was above the gossip she has caused recently—but I still did not see why she should act so cold toward me and I felt hurt and depressed after she had walked on.

I sadly realized that another reason for my staying in Esperanza had vanished. I think it was then that I decided to apply for a visa.

Still, I felt like a traitor when I sneaked up to the United States consulate this morning, hoping all the time that nobody would see me and that my intentions would remain a secret as long as possible. How would I explain to all the people I had brought here that I wanted to leave?

To the best of my knowledge I managed to enter the consulate unobserved. There I sat in the antechamber for half an hour without anybody asking me what I wanted. With my inbred fear of authority I did not want to make a nuisance of myself, but in the end I got up the courage to rap on the window in the wall that separated the antechamber from the offices.

A window opened and a tall, bony girl in a skirt and sweater peeked out. I could hear voices and laughter, and behind her I saw a table with cups and a coffee pot. The girl gave me a friendly smile and asked me in stumbling Spanish if I had been waiting long. I nodded.

"Well, why didn't you bang on the door, honey?" she asked. The suggestion left me speechless. Who ever heard of anybody banging on the door of authority?

I finally collected myself enough to ask her for an application blank for a visa, inquiring at the same time how long a wait there was on the Polish quota.

She went back into the room and presently returned with several printed forms which she handed to me.

"Now, about the quota: you might be lucky there," she said. "You know, what with the war, nobody can get out of Poland, so the Poles who are out of the country can get their quota numbers faster, perhaps in a year or two."

I thanked her for her help, resisting the temptation to tell her that I was an Austrian, though born in Poland. Then I hid the application forms in my breast pocket and sneaked home to study them as if they were secret enemy documents.

Last name; first name; sex; age; year of birth; place of birth; name of father; date of birth of father; name of mother; maiden name of mother; date of birth of mother (God, how am I supposed to remember all that!), and so on and so on and so on.

I read everything. The big print, and the small print in the parentheses, and the upside-down print on the back. Of course one thing is clear which so far I have refused to face: I will need an affidavit. And I have no idea who could furnish me with one.

*Saturday, September 20, 1941.* Sometimes the most unlikely people come up with the answer to one's problems.

Just as I was coming out of Horowitz' Casa León yesterday, I met Frau Lipschitz in the Avenida Bolívar. She waved to me across the street, indicating in an agitated manner that she wanted to talk with me. I had hardly joined her when she took hold of my sleeve, bent her face close to mine, and whispered loud enough to be heard from the Manuel Araujo to the 17 de Marzo:

"So you're going to leave us!"

"What?" I said, dumfounded.

"Come, come, you don't have to play games with *me*, Professor Bernstein! Everybody knows you went to the American consulate Wednesday morning."

(And I had been so sure that not a soul had seen me!)

"I just went there to ask for some information," I lied desperately. "Can't a man have any privacy in this town? And even supposing I wanted to go to the United States, where would I get an affidavit?"

"So? You haven't got a famous friend there? Why don't you write to Professor Einstein and ask him to send you an affidavit?" Frau Ruth asked snappishly.

(It seems she has still not forgiven me for once trumping her husband in name-dropping.)

No doubt her suggestion was meant as a mockery, but my desperate mind readily seized on it. If I had been unable before to think of anybody who would provide me with an affidavit, I cannot think of anybody but Professor Einstein now.

I must write him. The big problem is how to frame my request.

*Thursday, September 25, 1941.* I have given myself a period of respite during the holiday season. I shall not make any decisions until after Yom Kippur.

Monday night I was invited to the Kramers' for a Rosh Hashana dinner. The entire family was there, Eva and Walter included. It seems that as an only concession toward her Jewishness Eva is willing to enter into an uneasy truce with her husband's family whenever a holiday approaches.

Watching her across the table, I felt the familiar tug at my heart. Sometimes I compare myself to a drunkard who has sworn off liquor only to realize that he will never be able to break the habit. Still, mixed with the joy in my heart was pain over the change that had taken place in Eva. Her once ruddy cheeks were pale and bony, and though her sharp cheekbones gave her a strangely exotic air, they also made her face appear harder. She was, in her behavior, politer than before, but also cooler and more guarded; no longer a young girl but a woman of the world.

I noticed that the others were watching her too, as though they did not quite trust this new, polite Eva and expected her to relapse momentarily into her former rudeness. But the dinner party passed without any unpleasantness. And yet I would rather have the bickering that marked our early time in Esperanza.

*Thursday, October 2, 1941.* I think some notes about the war are in order.

The Germans have taken Kiev and Poltava and the siege of Leningrad continues. Yesterday Great Britain and the United States signed a commitment to supply Russia with essential war materials for the next nine months. With winter approaching, perhaps this will give the Russians a chance to recover their strength. Goldmann keeps predicting that by June (his favorite month for prophecies) the Russians will have driven the Germans out of Russia.

Just now it has become so dark in my room that I had to turn on the light, though it is only early afternoon. Outside it is pouring so hard that I cannot even see the trees in the garden. The rainy season commenced about two weeks ago, but we had hoped—in vain, it seems—that the weather would clear up for the holidays. Tonight begins Yom Kippur. Frau Steinberg has set dinner for four-thirty in the afternoon, and I can already smell the cooking.

I asked Aronoff whether he was going to fast.

"What for?" he said.

*Wednesday, October 8, 1941.*    Now that the period of grace which I had given myself is over, the letter to Professor Einstein has become an obsession with me. For days I have been writing and rewriting it in my mind.

I cannot decide how to address him. "Dear friend?" Too familiar. "Sehr geehrter Herr Professor?" Too cold and distant. I feel tempted to use the Spanish phrase "Muy distinguido Profesor," but he might think it an affectation.

And what do I write after I have surmounted the obstacle of the opening? "No doubt you remember me from the pleasant evening which we spent together in Frau Aronoff's house in Vienna. We performed the Kreutzer Sonata together."

He must have met thousands of people since that evening. How could he possibly remember me? Still, I will have to bring up our acquaintance before asking him for an affidavit. But how without seeming obnoxious?

I see I shall have to do some more thinking.

*Monday, October 13, 1941.*    I am so tense because of my yet unwritten letter to Professor Einstein that I am having nightmares. Even my afternoon nap was spoiled by a bad dream.

I did not recover until after dinner, when Rudi's songs transported me into a better mood. He seemed to be flirting with Frau Vogel for a change, and Frau Steinberg looked extremely jealous. Perhaps I am not the only one in the Villa Carmen who has problems.

*Friday, October 17, 1941.*    More bad news from the Russian front. The Germans have taken Bryansk, Vyazma, and Odessa. If they keep thrusting forward at the same speed they will soon reach Moscow.

"Don't worry," says Goldmann, who worries just like the rest of us. "Remember what happened to Napoleon!"

*Wednesday, October 22, 1941.* Another shocking bit of news: we have just learned that the Germans retaliated for the assassination of a German officer at Nantes by executing fifty French hostages!

Even now, in the midst of the war, it takes atrocities like these to make the world realize what barbarians they are dealing with.

*Monday, October 27, 1941.* War, already engulfing the world, has now broken out in the Villa Carmen.

I never thought I would live to see two middle-aged Jewish ladies pulling each other's hair and calling each other names. And over Rudi Brueck of all people!

This afternoon, as I was getting dressed to leave, I heard a soft knocking on Rudi Brueck's door, which I attributed to Frau Steinberg. Presently the knocking grew louder and more urgent, and when there was no answer it suddenly stopped.

I waited a few seconds to give Frau Steinberg a chance to move away from Rudi's door before I stepped out into the corridor. By that time Frau Steinberg had indeed moved on, but only as far as Frau Vogel's door several paces down the corridor. There she stood, first knocking but soon banging.

"Open up!" she shouted. "Open up! I know you are in there!"

(I could have walked discreetly away, but being as curious as the next person I lingered awhile at my door to see what would happen next.)

Frau Steinberg, two clean sheets draped over her arm, stubbornly continued her banging until a small crack opened in Frau Vogel's door and her angered voice could be heard outside:

"What's the matter with you, disturbing people during their afternoon siesta! What do you want?"

"I brought you clean sheets," Frau Steinberg said, holding up the sheets which had obviously been meant for Rudi's bed.

"Now? In the afternoon? Why didn't you come in the morning?"

"Don't tell me when to change sheets in my pensión! The laundress is waiting downstairs to pick up the wash. So kindly open the door and let me change the sheets!"

"You can't come in now," Frau Vogel said, trying to shut the door in the face of her landlady.

"And why not?" Frau Steinberg asked threateningly, leaning her not inconsiderable weight against the door to keep it from closing.

"Because I say so!" Frau Vogel said.

"Ah, because you say so! And who are you to tell me to stay out of one of my rooms? Or are you, perhaps, hiding something in there?"

"Go away!" Frau Vogel screeched.

"Aha! So you are hiding something! Let me see!" And Frau Steinberg pried the door open with her elbow.

I could not see what Frau Steinberg saw over Frau Vogel's shoulder, but I could see Frau Steinberg's face.

"Aaahhh!" she cried outraged. "You whore!"

Frau Vogel dropped all pretense and stepped out into the corridor, wearing, as it appeared, nothing under her robe.

"Whore yourself," she said to Frau Steinberg.

"Your husband shall hear about this when he comes home!" Frau Steinberg screamed. "Why, you common prostitute!"

If being called a whore had not particularly fazed Frau Vogel, being called a common prostitute left her bereft of speech. To release her fury she began pummeling Frau Steinberg with her fists. Frau Steinberg let fly and slapped Frau Vogel full in the face. Frau Vogel got hold of Frau Steinberg's high-piled braids and began pulling them. Both women were hissing and howling like embattled cats.

Presently Rudi came to the door, wearing nothing but shorts. He stood there, bow-legged and befuddled looking, scratching his cherubic head.

"Ladies, ladies," he said beseechingly. "No reason to fight! There's enough for everybody!"

Frau Steinberg stamped her feet in fury and let go of Frau Vogel long enough to snatch up one of the sheets which had dropped to the floor and hurl it at Rudi. He fled into the room and slammed the door behind him.

With the help of Dr. Landau, who had come running down from his tower, I finally managed to separate the embattled women. Dr. Landau escorted Frau Steinberg to her room and patched up her scratches. Then he returned to repeat the same Samaritan service for Frau Vogel.

In the meantime Rudi had escaped to his own room and had locked himself in. He did not come down in the evening to join us for dinner; neither did the Vogels. No doubt Frau Steinberg had lain in wait all afternoon to break the good news to Dr. Vogel.

"I hope he gives her a sound beating," she said tearfully.

But I doubt that Dr. Vogel has it in him.

*Tuesday, October 28, 1941.*   One never stops learning. Today I discovered that cause and effect do not always follow each other logically. Instead of driving a wedge between the Vogels, the affair Rudi Brueck seems to have brought them closer together.

From the noise that emanated last evening from their room, one might have drawn the conclusion that Dr. Vogel had indeed been giving his wife a beating. I cannot be sure, for Frau Vogel does not sport a black eye as proof.

Be that as it may, Dr. Vogel left quite an impression on his wife, for she seems to be looking at him with new affection. He, on the other hand, scrutinizes her with curious glances (this in spite of his aggrieved pose) as though wondering whether he had not overlooked some hidden charms in her.

One thing is sure: regardless of how the marriage of the Vogels has been affected by the recent incident, they will have to move out of the Villa Carmen. The same goes for Rudi.

In fact, the last time I saw Rudi was when he made his brief, scantily clad appearance in Frau Vogel's door. He has not shown his face since, and Frau Steinberg says he had better keep away if he knows what's good for him.

"If he dares set foot in my house, I'll throttle him with my bare hands!"

*Sunday, November 2, 1941.*   It seems that Rudi has no intention of exposing himself to the wrath of a jealous woman. For days he has shunned not only the Villa Carmen but also his soap factory in the cottage. The windows through which the steam used to escape into the garden are closed and shuttered, and I wonder whether Aronoff will have to move the factory to a new location.

So far I have had no chance to question Aronoff about his plans, for he takes most of his meals outside now. There is a good reason for this: ever since Rudi left us, the food in the Villa Carmen has again become abominable. Moreover, the meals are very monotonous, with only Dr. Landau, Horowitz, myself, and a grim-faced Frau Steinberg at the table. The Vogels moved out on Friday. With three of her rooms empty, Frau Steinberg has suffered not only insult but injury. She is taking out her chagrin on her remaining boarders by trying to poison them.

"Well, at least I won't have to put you on a diet," Dr. Landau commented philosophically.

But Horowitz was irate.

"You know whose fault all this is? Aronoff's! If he hadn't brought that boor Brueck to live here, we wouldn't have to eat this grub now!"

What Horowitz seems to forget is that if Aronoff hadn't brought along Rudi, we would never have got decent food in the first place.

But perhaps the bad food has another salutary effect upon me: it has strengthened my resolution to write Professor Einstein for an affidavit.


*Thursday, November 6, 1941.*    This afternoon I was kept at home again by rain. When I heard somebody walking around in the room next door, I hoped briefly that Rudi had returned and that the food situation in the Villa Carmen would better itself. But a peek through the door convinced me of just the opposite: Aronoff was moving Rudi's belongings out of the room.

I used the opportunity to ask what would become of the soap factory now that Rudi was gone. Aronoff shrugged.

"I suppose I'll close it down. Lately it hasn't brought in enough to be worth the bother. And now that Rudi has found himself another occupation, I no longer need it."

I was curious to hear what other occupation Rudi had found.

"He's manager of an establishment," Aronoff said.

"A restaurant?" I asked eagerly.

"Well, not exactly a restaurant," Aronoff said with a wry grin. "More of a casa de paseo."

"What's that?"

"A brothel."

"Aronoff, you must be joking!"

"Not at all. Rudi seems to be very happy there. All he wants now is his clothes and his collection of pornographic books."

Since I had nothing better to do I offered to help him carry Rudi's few belongings into the cottage.

I had been inside the factory but this was my first visit to Aronoff's living quarters. As I followed him into his room, I thought how disappointed Horowitz would be if he could see it. This was nothing like the den of vice he had always pictured behind the closed shutters.

Aronoff's room was more than simple, it was austere. Except for a plain, brown desk, two straight-backed chairs, a closet and a large bed, there was no furniture. The two narrow windows were covered with short, mended lace curtains, no doubt originating in one of Frau Steinberg's trunks. The throw on the bed was a rough Indian blanket, the bright pinks and blues on it faded from the sun. A smaller Indian blanket, equally faded, served as a rug in front of the bed.

But what caught my eye was the sign up on the wall directly above the bed. It had obviously been stolen from a restaurant. On it was printed the word "RESERVADO," and beneath it, penciled in red crayon, the additional words: "para figuras raras y dificiles. Reserved for rare and difficult positions."

Following my astonished glance, Aronoff smiled apologetically.

"A thoughtful gift from Rudi," he explained. "I couldn't hurt his feelings by taking it down while he was still around. But now there's no reason to leave it up there. Pretty silly, isn't it?"

He pulled out the tacks which fastened the sign to the wall. Then he looked at it for a moment, almost affectionately, before he folded it in half and carelessly dropped it into the drawer of his desk.

I could not help thinking that for a man of Aronoff's amorous reputation there was nothing lewd about him.

"Here, let me help you get rid of this," Aronoff said, taking the books from me and dropping them on the floor.

Then, as though he suddenly remembered that he was the host, Aronoff invited me to sit down and asked me if I would care for something to eat.

"I wouldn't mind," I said shamelessly. "Since Rudi left Frau Steinberg has been trying to starve us."

"Well, let's see what we can find," Aronoff said.

He opened the drawer into which he had dropped Rudi's sign and pulled out a greasy package which, upon opening, revealed a chunk of Swiss cheese, half a loaf of dark bread, a long kitchen knife, and a nibbled chocolate bar with the wrapper torn off.

"I'm afraid this is all I can offer you," Aronoff said, sitting down opposite me at the desk. He began to cut slices of the bread and the cheese, handing some to me and making a sandwich for himself out of the rest. He ate his share rapidly and hungrily, with little chomping noises of which his refined mother would never have approved.

Breaking off a few squares from the chocolate bar, he handed them to me across the table.

"Have some dessert."

A smile came and went quickly on his remarkably handsome face. Again I noticed how fast he ate, with the gusto of a man who enjoyed food but did not give it much thought before or after a meal. While he stood wrapping the leftovers in the same greasy paper, he already seemed to have forgotten about our simple feast. Perhaps he enjoyed women in the same intense and yet absent-minded manner, and this was why he never talked about them. Though I had seen him almost daily across the table in the Villa Carmen, I really knew very little about him.

"Tell me, Aronoff, what do you plan to do once this war is over?" I asked him on the spur of the moment.

Something in his face changed, as if he had carefully shut a door behind which he kept his hidden thoughts before he answered me.

"Who knows?" he said.

I realized that this was only a polite way of telling me to mind my own business. But if I know anything about Aronoff I know that he probably has a good idea of what he wants from the future.

*Sunday, November 9, 1941.* Now that Kharkov has fallen and the Germans have begun the siege of Moscow, the United States has extended one billion dollars in land-lease credit to the Soviet Union. Do the Americans still hope to buy themselves out of this war?

*Tuesday, November 11, 1941.* Yesterday was the stone-setting for Josef.

I had asked Dr. Lipschitz to see to it that a few of our people should be present. He had rounded up all the functionaries of our assorted clubs and brought them out to the cemetery. There were only men present, except for Frau Fuchs and Señora Consuelo, who was accompanied by her brother.

During the ceremony I tried to stand in such a way that I would not have to look at the staked-out burial ground next to Josef's grave. But the prepared plot did not escape the attention of the others. As we walked out of the cemetery, Herr Kramer pulled me aside and whispered:

"You know her best. You tell her that she can't be buried here."

I am glad that Herr Kramer elected me his messenger. This way at least I will not have to tell anybody that the site is meant for me.

*Saturday, November 15, 1941.* I have drawn up several letters to Professor Einstein but have destroyed them all. At times I ask myself whether I really want to go to the United States. Perhaps this is just a new form of self-torture which I have devised for myself—something to take the place of my former pining over Eva.

*Wednesday, November 19, 1941.* Horowitz was beside himself when I told him today that Rudi Brueck had become the manager of a brothel.

"This I've got to see," he said. "Of course you'll come along."

He also tried to prod Dr. Landau into accompanying us, but without success.

"I have to look at naked women every day," Dr. Landau said. "That's as much as I care to do at my age."

I was a little hesitant about going myself, but finally my curiosity got the better of me and I asked Aronoff if he would take us to Rudi's establishment. We made a date for tomorrow afternoon. I begged Aronoff to keep the visit a secret. I don't want this talked about.

*Friday, November 21, 1941.* Some people are born to their professions, but it might take them a while to find it out. As for Rudi Brueck, he could not have looked more natural in his new habitat.

"Hello, hello, gentlemen, welcome to our house!" was his jovial greeting when we walked in on him yesterday. He was considerably less embarrassed by receiving us in a brothel than I was by visiting him there.

Aronoff had driven us out in his car. The establishment was on the road to the airport, some ten minutes from the city. The house looked inconspicuous enough, well set back from the street in a large, neglected garden. The pillared front porch did not look unlike the portico in front of Josef's house, only the curtain of beaded strings added a special note to the entrance.

"Come in, come in!" Rudi boomed. "Make yourselves comfortable. The ladies will be down in a minute."

We entered a large, dimly lit, musty-smelling room. The decoration was pseudo-Oriental, with a few, grimy sofas along the walls, a couple of tables and chairs, and ripped Japanese lanterns camouflaging the naked light bulbs.

"We have six ladies here with three teeth among them," Rudi said. "Well, at least you won't get it bitten off!"

He roared with delight at his own joke.

Presently the ladies descended from the upper floor, one more sleazy and unappetizing than the next. How desperate did a man have to be to touch these creatures?

"Well, gentlemen, which of them do you want?" Rudi asked.

I hastened to explain that as far as I was concerned this was a social rather than a business call.

"We might as well while we're here," Horowitz proposed.

"You go ahead. But count me out, Horowitz," I said.

In the meantime Aronoff had sat down on one of the sofas and put his feet on the table. One of the women, the youngest, was cowering beside him on the floor, whispering to him. He smiled indulgently and shook his head.

Finally he took a ten peso bill out of his pocket and handed it to the girl.

"Go away and leave me alone," he said.

She stared at the money incredulously, her face almost hurt by Aronoff's refusal. Then she quickly kissed the bill and tucked it in her blouse.

"You can't give her money for nothing!" Horowitz shouted furiously. "What are you trying to do, drive up the rates? At least tell her to come upstairs with me!"

"Tell her yourself if you want to sponge on me, Horowitz."

Horowitz began to argue with the girl, trying to impress upon her, of all things, that taking pay without offering service was not ethical, but she only shook her head.

"You see what you did!" Horowitz danced around Aronoff like an infuriated gnome. "You spoil her! People ought to work for what they get! I'm opposed to charity!"

"If you're so opposed to charity, why don't you pay the girl if you want her instead of trying to sponge on me, Horowitz?"

In the end Horowitz agreed to pay. I suspect he only did it because he had always wanted one of Aronoff's women and this was the only one he could have.

While Horowitz was upstairs, Rudi served refreshments and entertained us with anecdotes about his patrons.

It took almost half an hour before Horowitz came down. He wore a sheepish expression, mumbling something about its being impossible for one man to work off all the money he and Aronoff had paid the girl.

Rudi ushered us to the door and stood waving on the porch as we drove away. He did not seem a less proud and contented patrician than Josef had been in his lifetime. Which goes to prove that every man has to find his nook.


*Wednesday, November 26, 1941.*    It is almost the end of November now, but the Germans are still advancing in Russia. During the past two weeks they captured Kerch and laid siege to Sevastopol. We had hoped that by now their main offensive would have been broken by the Russian winter.

Yesterday Bulgaria joined the Axis powers, but this did not come as a surprise to us. With so much pressure on them, sooner or later all the Balkan states will have to join.

Tomorrow is little Norma's first birthday. I bought a fuzzy, black toy cat for her. These things are terribly expensive in Esperanza, but then how many children do I have named for me?

*Friday, November 28, 1941.* Now I am doubly glad that I bought a gift for Norma. Trude seemed genuinely touched that I had not forgotten her daughter's birthday, though she chided me for walking over to her house in the pouring rain.

"If you had let me know, I would have sent the car for you," she said.

I said that I had wanted my gift to be a surprise. Of course Norma received so many gifts that there could hardly be any surprises left for her. Trude took me into the nursery to show me the shelves bulging with toys.

"Well, soon there will be two to share them . . . God willing," she added.

Then she picked up little Norma from the floor, where she sat playing, and told her to kiss her Uncle Norman and to say muchas gracias.

Norma, propped up on her mother's bloated belly, shyly thanked me and kissed me with great reluctance. I was saddened to notice that she was, if anything, even uglier than she had been as an infant, and wondered whether it was wise of Trude and Levy to people the world with more children of their own.

"Next year, when she'll be two, we'll give her a real birthday party and invite all our friends," Trude said, "even those who forgot her birthday."

She did not mention any names, but I had a good idea that she was talking about Eva.

*Tuesday, December 2, 1941.* Although, as time passes, our interest in the war becomes more and more relegated to the back of our minds, a flurry of excitement was caused by the news that the Russians had managed to recapture Rostov.

We hopefully interpret this as a sign that the Russians have finally begun their winter offensive.

*Friday, December 5, 1941.* "I tell you, regardless of what people say about him, Herr Aronoff is a very fine person," Frau Steinberg said to me today. "He promised to get me new boarders for my three empty rooms. Some friends of his who will arrive here in a week or so."

After the experience with Rudi Brueck, I was a little worried over what sort of friends Aronoff planned to quarter with us this time. But when I questioned him this afternoon he assured me that the new boarders were perfectly respectable people, a married couple with twins. The wife, Aronoff said, was a distant relative of his mother's.

I expressed some misgivings about having children in the house, but Aronoff told me that to the best of his recollection the twins—two girls who ought to be about nine now—were very pleasant children. Considering that my main reason for moving from the Kramers' was the Lipschitz boys, I hope I have not jumped from the frying pan into the fire.

*Sunday, December 7, 1941.* The Japanese have attacked Pearl Harbor!

Not since the Germans invaded Poland has there been such excitement over the war in our colony.

I had gone to the Centro to spend the evening. As always on Sunday when people come from the Cine Paraíso to have dinner, the place was quite crowded. It was after ten o'clock when the strident voice of a newsboy became audible above the din of voices in the main dining room.

Extra! Extra! Los Japoneses atáquan Pearl Harbor y los Philippínos!

I don't know who was the first to dash down to the street, but suddenly the place seemed to be swamped under a deluge of newspapers with the fat, black print still wet on the front page:

## JAPONESES BOMBARDEAN HAWAII, LAS FILIPINAS, GUAM, MIDWAY ISLAND, HONG-KONG Y MALAYA!

The roar in the dining room became deafening. People were repeating news items of the past week to which, in our preoccupation with the war in Europe and Africa, we had paid little attention: Japanese Prime Minister Tojo's statement that the influence of Britain and the United States must be eliminated from the Orient; and only a few days ago Roosevelt's appeal to Hirohito to help preserve peace.

We should have known! And if we—old, experienced readers of bad omens—had not known, who else could have?

But on the whole the spirit is one of jubilation. Now that the Americans are in it, there is no doubt left in our minds that *we* are going to win the war.


*Friday, December 12, 1941.*   Monday the United States officially declared war on Japan, and yesterday Germany and Italy, in agreement with their pact with Tokyo, declared war on the United States.

Of all our armchair strategists Goldmann is the one most beside himself with glee.

"This will be their undoing!" he keeps predicting. "With the Russians starting their winter offensive from one side and the Americans giving them hell from the other, the Germans will be on their knees by next June!"

(When else but in the magic month of June?)

With all the excitement over the American entry into the war the fact that the British have opened a second drive into Libya is given only small space in the newspapers.


*Wednesday, December 17, 1941.*   Yesterday the Russians retook Kalinin, but contrary to our expectations nothing much has yet happened on the American-Japanese front. It seems that the Americans are still stunned by the surprise attack and it will be some time before they rally their forces.

After the first excitement over the news, our lives here have returned to normal and we are again preoccupied with local events.

Two days ago the tenants Aronoff recommended—people named Richter—moved into the Villa Carmen. To think that they escaped from Shanghai virtually by the skin of their teeth makes one's hair stand on end. After we had been introduced, Herr Richter claimed that his brother used to be a student in my class. It is impossible to remember all the students, but of course I pretended to remember him as a very bright boy.

*Saturday, December 20, 1941.*    Today Herr Fleischer unknowingly put balm on my smarting conscience. (I still have not written the letter to Professor Einstein.) I was sitting in Horowitz' Casa León when Fleischer came visiting from his store across the street.

"Did you read in the papers that the draft age in the United States has been extended from twenty-six to forty-four years?" he asked. "That takes care of me. I wouldn't go there now if somebody paid me."

Now that Fleischer has abandoned his idea of emigration I feel better about letting my own plans drift, although I am already far beyond the draft age.

*Wednesday, December 24, 1941.*    The Richters have turned out to be quite pleasant people. The two little girls are delightful, quiet and polite; they look like refugees from a doll shop with their straight, blond pigtails and their round, blue eyes. Everybody in the house is constantly pinching and petting them, and even Horowitz remarked with a sigh that they made him regret having remained a bachelor.

But I suspect that it is Frau Richter who makes Horowitz regret having remained a bachelor. Her presence has brought us the almost-forgotten pleasure of looking at a pretty woman across the table. Frau Richter is not spectacularly pretty—nothing like Eva—nor is she that young. She is in her early thirties, with auburn hair, deep-set brown eyes, and a full, sensuous mouth in her small face. Somehow she evokes the shy beauty of an antelope, with her thin wrists and ankles and the occasional, nervous tossing of her head. Her life seems wrapped up in her children and she does not talk much, leaving this part almost entirely to her husband.

Herr Richter is not nearly so appealing as his wife. He must have been a handsome man once, but now he is bald, middle-aged, and overweight. He often reminds me of Fleischer with his cynical ideas about women, love, and marital fidelity. Especially of the last he seems to take a dim view.

Horowitz has already developed a deep dislike for Richter.

"That swine," Horowitz said. "With a sweet, pretty wife like Frau Richter, why should he want to run after other women?"

*Friday, December 26, 1941.*    Yesterday Hong Kong was captured by the Japanese. The idea of a war in the Pacific is still so novel that all the reports from there seem somehow unreal.

*Wednesday, December 31, 1941.*    Another year gone.

I don't know why I always feel so nostalgic when New Year's approaches. Perhaps because the years here slip away without seasons to mark their passage. It should be winter now. Snow frosting the streets. Week-old Christmas trees glittering behind the lace curtains in the windows. The grass poking brown through the snow on the slopes in the Prater where children have been riding their sleds. The air crisp. Christine in her white fox collar. Youth.

For the past month we have had rain every day. Tonight there is a dance in the Centro. I shall not attend.

*Sunday, January 4, 1942.*    Today I had to think of the blow-by-blow description of what Horowitz termed Richter's "abominable behavior at the New Year's Eve dance in the Centro."

According to Horowitz, Richter first badgered him about an introduction to Eva (the young Kramers had come with the Schwarzkopfs, but everybody seemed to think that there were strained relations between them) and, failing to get Horowitz' cooperation, Richter had settled for Frau Fleischer and had behaved with her in a manner which must have caused his wife no end of embarrassment. "Poor Frau Richter" had, of course, comported herself impeccably.

But I am afraid that Horowitz is being deceived by appearances. Poor Frau Richter is not quite so innocent as she seems at first sight. I have seen her look at Aronoff in a manner for which there is just one interpretation. At the table she will try to catch his eye, hold his glance as long as she dares, and quickly lower her lids the moment her husband turns to her. I can tell by Aronoff's wry smile that he is a knowing participant in the game.

So far neither Herr Richter nor Horowitz has noticed what is going on.

*Thursday, January 8, 1942.*   I am going through a strange period of life. At times I feel as though I were already half dead. The rainy days drag on monotonously and endlessly, and what little excitement there is I derive from the newspapers.

During the past week the Americans engaged in their first close-range battle with the Japanese and lost Manila and Cavite, but they are still holding Bataan and Corregidor. Now that my mind has become accustomed to dealing with Russian and African place names, it has to get used to still a newer variety.

I wish I had something better with which to fill my time. I try to recall what I did last year at the height of the rainy season. Wasn't I planning my trip to the jungle just then? Well, this too was a debacle.

*Saturday, January 17, 1942.*   I have found a way to alleviate the hardship which the boredom of the rainy season combined with Frau Steinberg's rotten food imposes on me: I have begun to sponge on my acquaintances.

Whenever the occasion permits I drop a remark about not having eaten a decent meal in weeks. Addressed to the right people, this usually leads to a lunch or dinner invitation.

Within the past week I was guest at the Levys' and the Goldmanns', and Wednesday I had lunch with Señora Consuelo, as always. She told me that her brother had gone as a delegate to the Inter-American Conference in Rio de Janeiro and that there was a good chance El Paramo would sever diplomatic relations with the Axis powers. She asked me if I thought this would mean war. I said I doubted it.

Yesterday, at the Levys', we also talked about the war (the Japanese are still advancing in the Pacific and have now occupied the Netherlands East Indies), but Trude appeared more anxious to talk about Eva. She claimed she had not seen her friend for months.

Neither have I.

The last time I saw Eva was during the holidays at the Kramers'. Since then it is as though she had disappeared from the earth. I feel a little hurt because she has not yet invited me to her new home. I met Walter in town several times, but he always seemed ill at ease, telling me with an apologetic smirk that he will invite me as soon as he finishes furnishing his house—which apparently will be never.

I am not the only one affected by Walter's poor hospitality. I have heard similar complaints from many of his former friends.


*Thursday, January 22, 1942.*    Today was brightened by sunshine and good news. The Russians continue advancing in their winter offensive, and El Paramo has indeed severed relations with the Axis powers. Brody, the master of the Jungle Café, told me that the German consulate in Esperanza is to be closed within the next few days and that German citizens residing in El Paramo have been told they are no longer welcome here. Brody says they will probably have to move to Chile or Argentina, countries which still sympathize with the Nazis.

I could not help worrying over what would happen to Jews with German passports, but Brody assures me that by now the Parameños have learned to distinguish between Germans and Jews. I am not quite sure whether this works entirely to our advantage. I remember Josef's opening speech in the Centro in which he said that most people here did not know what a Jew was, and he hoped it would remain that way.

But then, what is a Jew?

*Tuesday, January 27, 1942.*     I recall wondering some time ago about Aronoff's plans for the future. Now I know—or at least I have been given some concrete idea.

Herr Richter says Aronoff is engaged to be married!

Of course I was startled, what with the reputation Aronoff has built up in Esperanza. Somehow it seems impossible to imagine him as a married man. But Richter is quite positive. He says that if it were not for the war Aronoff would already be married.

"You've heard of Becker shirts, haven't you?" Richter asked me. "Becker was in shirts what Aronoff was in ladies' lingerie. Only Becker was smarter than Aronoff. Shortly before Hitler came he got all his money out of Austria and went to open a shirt factory in the United States. I hear he's doing even better there than he was doing in Vienna. And Aronoff is engaged to the Becker girl! Just wait till the war ends and you'll see him grab the next plane and go to the United States. He'd be a fool to bow out on so much money. And take it from me, he's no fool!"

I said that Aronoff was well enough off to marry for love if he wanted to marry.

"The point is, Aronoff doesn't love anybody," Richter said dryly. "Oh, I've heard about his whoring around here, but that doesn't mean he's in love. He's smart enough to marry the Becker girl and do all his whoring around on the side. I have to laugh thinking about all the women here who think they can grab him!"

Frau Richter, who sat with her back to her husband, turned white in the face. Her lips trembled and her eyes were savage. I wondered whether Richter had any idea of how much she hated him just then. But one could never tell with him. Perhaps he had only dragged up the talk about Aronoff to hurt her.

(By now he must have noticed what is going on, and if he does not interfere he probably does so because he finds the situation convenient. Since Walter bartered Eva I can believe anything.)

Even Horowitz' eyes have been opened. He could not be more upset if Frau Richter were his own wife.

"That heel!" Horowitz said about Aronoff. "To seduce a perfectly respectable woman while all the time he's engaged to be married!"

*Monday, February 2, 1942.*　I have started on my second round of lunch and dinner invitations. At every house the main topic of conversation is that Eva and Walter have finally set a date for their house-warming.

The first ones to mention the news to me were the elder Kramers.

"I tell you, I won't go," Herr Kramer said in his old, belligerent manner.

"Jakob, how will it look if you, his own father, refuse to come?" Frau Kramer remonstrated.

"I tell you, I won't go. If he wants us, he can invite the family separately. Of course his wife wouldn't make an extra effort for us. But to go there and shake hands and be friendly with that other woman . . . No, I'd rather stay home! If nobody else in this family has any feeling of propriety, I have!"

"You're absolutely right, Papa," Frau Ruth Lipschitz said. "We'll be the laughingstock of the whole town if we go. All the women keep teasing me about my two sisters-in-law!"

"Now let's be sensible," Dr. Lipschitz said. "We can't just keep avoiding our own family. Let us therefore accept facts, put our best foot forward, and show some tolerance toward a status quo which is outside our powers to change anyway."

"In other words, you want to go to the party," his wife said. "And I've a good idea why, too. All the loose women in Esperanza will be there! I could put up with the rest, but not with that Schwarzkopf woman!"

"I don't know what you all have against her," Frau Kramer said suddenly. "She certainly helped Walter more than his own wife did."

"Mama, she isn't even Jewish!" Frau Ruth exclaimed.

They were still arguing and undecided when I left.

*Saturday, February 7, 1942.*　Dinner with the Brauns yesterday. The Brauns, being more sophisticated than Walter's parents, never considered for a moment the propriety of attending Eva's housewarming party. Their mood was one of regret rather than of censure.

"It's saddening to see a person change so much," Frau Irene said. "I've known Eva since she was a child. Even here she used to come to me and pour her heart out. Now I hardly ever see her, and when I do she seems so reserved she makes me feel ill at ease. As though she had suddenly overtaken me and knew more about life than I do." Frau Irene sighed a little. "I wish something could be done about this unfortunate business. I can't help blaming Walter. I still feel Eva is too young to know what she's doing."

Later, when we had a moment alone together, Hans confessed that he felt he was to blame for the Schwarzkopf affair.

"If I had only refused to let the Schwarzkopfs come along on that unfortunate trip last year!" he said. "I can't shake off the idea that it all started then."

I told Hans not to blame himself. I don't believe that opportunity makes thieves. Thieves will find opportunities.


*Thursday, February 12, 1942.*　　Third installment of opinions re the housewarming party at Eva's. This time from Trude and Levy, with whom I dined yesterday.

"Going there is out of the question!" Levy declared, irate. "I wouldn't let my wife, in her condition, mix with these people! Who knows how it would affect the baby!"

Trude, again an amorphous mass of bloated belly and loosely hanging garments, stamped her foot and nearly cried.

"How can you talk such superstitious nonsense, Isak! I wish my baby would look like Eva!"

"God forbid! It might also have all her qualities!"

"Well, you can't stop *me* from going," Trude said. "Eva is my oldest friend here, and if you won't take me I'll go with Professor Bernstein! You will take me, won't you?"

Which forced me to admit that I had not been asked.

Has Eva really forgotten about me?

*Tuesday, February 17, 1942.* I am beginning to feel like a child left out of a birthday party. Wherever I go people are talking about the approaching housewarming. Even the Goldmanns have been asked, but Eva has still not invited me.

"I really don't know if we should go," Frau Goldmann said. (Of course she will. Everybody will!) "You know, the sort of people who'll be there . . . And who wants to witness such goings on!" she added virtuously, the glittering curiosity in her eyes giving the lie to her sanctimonious words.

*Saturday, February 21, 1942.* Today Fleischer extended me an impromptu invitation to have lunch with him and his wife. Frau Fleischer said she was delighted to have me as her guest when we went to pick her up from the store, but warned me that I would have to take pot luck with them. Nevertheless, the meal turned out to be quite good—the table conversation less pleasant. As everywhere else, the burning issue was the housewarming.

"It's going to be very interesting," Fleischer said. "I wonder if all four of them will do the receiving."

"Shut up, Peter," Frau Fleischer said. "Professor Bernstein is a friend of the Kramers."

"Don't mind my wife. Sometimes she pretends she still believes in the stork. Now, if Eva Kramer would act that way . . . You know, the funny thing about that girl is that in spite of everything . . . I mean, we all know . . . and still, to look at her you'd say she is the most innocent creature on earth. I hope one of these days I'll find out just how innocent she is."

"What would she want with a man your age?" Frau Fleischer said.

"She hasn't been prejudiced against age so far!"

"All the more reason to wish her something better. A younger man."

"What younger man? Perhaps a young stud like Aronoff?"

"Why not? He'd be just right for her."

"Well, Dora, you certainly ought to know," Fleischer said facetiously.

They seemed to have completely forgotten my presence. In my embarrassment I stuffed myself with enormous quantities of food.

"Anyway, what makes you think you would even have a chance with Eva?" Frau Fleischer went on.

"It would be just a matter of clever timing. If you ask me, this whole thing isn't going to last much longer. When I dropped by the factory a couple of days ago I noticed that the two ladies were not speaking to each other."

"Are you making periodic checkups?" Frau Fleischer asked.

While the bantering went on for a while, my mind returned to what Fleischer had said. I wondered why Eva and Frau Katja were not on speaking terms and whether that was a good sign. Perhaps the Schwarzkopfs wouldn't even be at the housewarming party! What a joke that would be on everyone!

During the time I had not listened the conversation had taken a novel turn. The next thing I heard was Fleischer saying to me:

"You know, when I first wanted to go to the United States, my wife was dead set against the idea. But since she heard that our friends, the Richters, are going there, she has suddenly changed her mind. Now what do you think makes a woman so fickle?"

"Why don't you shut up, Peter? Professor Bernstein has other things to worry about than your silly questions."

When I left shortly afterward I felt a little sick at my stomach—a sensation not caused by the food I had been served. I asked myself if Eva had any idea of how men talked about her behind her back. I was also annoyed because Fleischer, with his filthy mouth, had been asked to the housewarming, while I was still waiting for my invitation.

In my rage I drafted another letter to Professor Einstein. I have already torn it to pieces and deposited it in the wastebasket.


*Tuesday, February 24, 1942.*    Ah, the childish relief at not having been excluded!

Today Eva called in person to invite Horowitz, Dr. Landau, and me. I could tell by the pleased faces of the other two that they also had been worried.

We sat chatting for a while in Frau Steinberg's sala when Herr Richter wandered in and stared at Eva the way men usually stare at her. He just kept walking round and round as if he were looking for some lost article until, in the end, I saw no way out of introducing him.

"Ah, so you're the famous Eva Kramer," he said (as though he had not known all the time who she was), leaving Eva to interpret the remark as she pleased. "I hear you're throwing a big party next Saturday. You might have invited me too!"

Eva took the hint with a nonchalance she had never displayed as a young girl.

"Then why don't you come?" she said. "One more won't make the slightest difference."

"Two more," Horowitz said angrily. "Herr Richter has a wife!"

"And who said I was bringing my wife along?"

"By all means do," Eva said. "As it is, there aren't enough women to go around."

"I like the way you put that, Frau Kramer," Richter said.

"Just don't interpret too freely," Eva said with a cool smile.

I was glad to see that she had not entirely lost the gift of icy repartee. In spite of it, she left Richter in an alarming state of animation.

"A very beautiful woman," he said after Eva had left. "Is it true what they say about her?"

I kept quiet, waiting for Horowitz or Dr. Landau to answer the question, but neither one deigned to reply. Without so much as a word of agreement we—the old guard—had closed ranks against Richter. If there was any gossip about Eva, it was none of his business.


*Saturday, February 28, 1942.*    The afternoon before Eva's housewarming.

I am curiously excited, as if the party were really a big event. It is rumored that we are to be served some unheard-of delicacies. Also that Walter has hired two professional waiters to do the serving and that he has stocked huge amounts of liquor.

It was the liquor which Dr. Landau cautioned me about when he took my blood pressure today.

"I'm warning you," he said. "Under the pretext of visiting people you've been stuffing yourself for the past two weeks. On top of it, you keep chocolate hidden in your room which you eat between meals. Don't give me that indignant stare, I can smell it on your breath!"

"You are, as always, exaggerating, Dr. Landau."

"Of course. I take profound pleasure in ruining the lives of my patients with unreasonable orders. Everybody does me personal favors by listening to me. Just do me one more favor: don't make a fool of yourself by getting drunk tonight!"

"I was never drunk in my life," I said, with a feigned air of injured dignity. But perhaps Dr. Landau knew more about my inclinations than I knew myself. I was counting on having a good time tonight and getting drunk might be part of it—especially since I really never have been drunk.

"Tell me, what's the matter with you anyway?" Dr. Landau asked.

"What should be the matter with me?"

"I don't know. Sometimes you just sit there and stare off into space. At other times you walk around twisting your fingers and scratching your head and your chin as if you had heaven knows what worries. I never went in much for Freud, but I have a good idea that even your overeating is compulsive. Look, we've been, well . . . you might call it friends for quite a while now. You have no family left in Europe, and with Goldmann providing for you, you should have no worries. But obviously you have. Perhaps if you could tell me what they are, I might be able to help."

"As you said yourself, Dr. Landau, what worries should I have? I assure you, my only worry is to have a good time tonight!"

"In that case remember what I told you: don't overeat; go easy on the liquor; don't smoke too much; look at the young women but don't think about them. And above all, lie down this afternoon and rest!"

When I left him he was still calling advice after me.

But I am too keyed up to rest. Perhaps I should have confided in Dr. Landau. Wouldn't he be surprised if I suddenly told him about the site waiting for me at the cemetery. About the unwritten letter to Professor Einstein. About the visa application hidden in the drawer of my desk. And, above all, about Eva.

Every time I think that my dreams have become completely disentangled from her she moves back into them. Perhaps my need to escape from here is caused not so much by the fear of dying in Esperanza or by the desire to teach again, but by the secret hope that in the United States—in Utopia—there might still be an Eva to give meaning to my remaining years.

I think Dr. Landau is right. I had better lie down and rest now. Why am I so excited? God willing, I shall not make a fool of myself tonight.

# Part Six  ❧  The Bow in the Cloud

*And it shall come to pass,*
*when I bring a cloud over*
*the earth, that the bow shall*
*be seen in the cloud.*

GENESIS 9:14

*Tuesday, June 2, 1942.*    I have come back to life.

Today, for the first time since I am out of bed, I feel the urge to write down what happened. But there are still some blank spots in my memory as though I had intentionally blocked out some recollection—something that happened at the housewarming just before the pain came that made me crumple on the floor.

The effort to remember is something new. Before there was nothing but my prostrate body, helpless under Frau Steinberg's ministrations, my mind tortured by the wish for a wife of many years—the only person before whom a man may lose all his modesty—instead of having to listen to Frau Steinberg religiously discussing my bowel movements.

There are certain things I do remember. The moment when I opened my eyes and recognized Dr. Landau's face bent over me and I knew that I was not dead. The faces of people swimming in and out of my room, looking at me with solemn eyes as if I were already lying in state. Somebody telling me that Trude had had her baby. But all that mattered was that my heart should go on beating.

I remember Eva's face, frightened and almost resentful, as she stood looking at what she thought was death. And Frau Fuchs smiling in sour disappointment because she had been, temporarily, cheated out of the pleasure of washing my carcass. The injections, the medicines, Dr. Landau's soapy smell as he hovered above me . . .

I think I am still incoherent. If I could just remember what happened before. Nobody has mentioned anything to me, and for some reason I am afraid to ask.


*Wednesday, June 10, 1942.*    It is strange how hard I find it to make an entry in my diary after having interrupted the habit for such a long time. As if writing—like shaving or brushing one's teeth—were just another loathsome routine to which one has to get used again.

The spring holidays came and went without my participation. There was a Purim ball in the Centro (why does it hurt so much to think that people go on enjoying themselves while one lies near death?) and I missed my chance of spending another four evenings with Eva at the Passover meals at the Kramers'.

The Russians have recaptured many cities which they lost to the Germans last summer, and the Americans and the Japanese seem to have reached some sort of stalemate in the Pacific, with the battle ranging back and forth. Once United States planes bombed Tokyo, but this did not put the expected fast end to the war. Some two weeks ago the Germans began their second drive into Egypt, and a few days back the Japanese attacked Midway Islands. I think this brings me up to date as far as the war is concerned.

Here in Esperanza the season has changed from rainy to dry. Every day I can see from my window the glory of the blue sky behind the green mountain ranges. I am longing to go for a stroll in the garden, but Dr. Landau will not hear of my climbing stairs.

*Thursday, June 18, 1942.* One thing about receiving visitors in bed, where I am still spending much of my time: you get to see them from a new angle. I notice details which I never noticed when sitting face to face with a person. (Perhaps this has nothing to do with my prostrate position. Perhaps I only search people's faces in self-defense, for they too search my face. Is he more withered, his skin gray, his eyes pale? Has death left its mark upon him?)

Before my sickness I could hardly have thought of the color of anybody's eyes except Eva's. And perhaps Aronoff's, because they are so dark. Now I know them all. And I know their voices, particularly the voices of the women.

This morning, when I heard Eva's voice, I felt elated even before she stepped into my room.

"Is it all right to come in?" she called as she knocked on the door.

I called back that she was always welcome. She came in, bringing the radiance of her youth with her. As on all her previous visits she tried to sound cheerful when she told me how well I looked, but insincerity is not her forte. Her eyes always remain shocked when she looks at me.

She, on the other hand, looked exceedingly well, better than she had in a long time. Soon I realized why: her cheeks had filled out again and her skin had regained its golden tan. I remarked upon the change, asking her when she found time to take sun baths.

"Don't you know that I'm no longer working?" she asked.

I was surprised, but not as much as I should have been. Somehow the news seemed to touch on something I ought to remember and did not. The thing that had happened at Eva's party. I felt I could not ask her outright what had happened; instead I asked her why she had quit working.

"I've learned what I wanted to know," she said, looking down on her fingers as though contemplating their newly acquired skill. But perhaps she was referring to more than her manual dexterity.

"Don't they need you in the factory, Eva?"

"Need me? They never did need me," Eva said candidly. "I just worked there because there were a few things I wanted to learn. Perhaps I learned too much too fast."

Again I had the uneasy feeling of having forgotten something. I also wondered if, by quitting work, Eva had not upset the delicate balance in the relationship with the Schwarzkopfs.

"How about Walter?" I asked with sudden suspicion. "Is he still a partner in the factory?"

"Of course," Eva said. "Why shouldn't he be? He didn't want me to work in the first place."

When she brought up Walter's objections, which she had shrugged off initially, I became even more suspicious. I pretended to drop the topic while actually I only changed my approach.

"Eva, I've never had a chance to tell you how sorry I am for having spoiled your party."

"Don't talk about it!"

"But I would like to talk about it. You see, Dr. Landau had warned me . . . Tell me honestly, Eva, did I overdo it? Sometimes I seem to remember that there was something I wanted to do, something I was going to do, just before passing out. Something that had happened or was about to happen . . . What was it, Eva?"

She stared at me incredulously, as if she could not believe that I really did not know whatever it was that had happened. Then her face quickly shifted into the blank expression which precedes a lie and she said:

"Nothing happened. You're just imagining things."

She turned her head toward the window, and the reflection of the sunlight made her golden skin glow. Perhaps she had also flushed. From my lying position I saw the firm line of her chin, pulled up and thrust out in what I thought was a grim pose of defiance. Whatever had happened at the party, she would not discuss it with me.

I shall have to ask Walter.

*Tuesday, June 23, 1942.*    Today Walter came to see me, together with Herr Kramer. The presence of his father made it impossible for me to ask Walter what had happened at the party. We talked mostly about the war. Churchill has gone to Washington for a conference with President Roosevelt. The Germans have captured Tobruk for a second time and seem to be sweeping straight on in their advance. We can already see Palestine in peril, and we are worried.

*Sunday, June 28, 1942.*    I won't have to ask Walter after all. Sometimes information comes my way in the most unexpected manner.

I have known for quite a while now that the Richters are about to leave for the United States. This afternoon they dropped in to say good-by to me, bringing their children with them. The two little girls with their grave doll faces stood staring at me with the morbid curiosity which sickness seems to arouse in children.

For some reason the farewell affected me more than I should have expected. Perhaps it stirred up the guilty knowledge that I am still toying with the idea of writing to Professor Einstein.

Herr Richter said he was glad to leave, making me wonder whether his affair with Frau Fleischer had meant so little to him that he felt no regrets. Frau Richter was pale and irritable, snapping at the children, who tried to climb up on my bed. When she shook my hand for the last time she seemed close to tears, an emotion that must have been triggered by another farewell still ahead of her. But I did not realize how upset she really was until later at night, when I heard her desperate sobs through the thin wall behind my bed.

I had fallen asleep around ten o'clock, exhausted after Horowitz' faithful evening visit. (Horowitz means well, but his repetitive daily accounts of his dealings with contrary customers are beginning to wear me down.)

Suddenly I woke with a start, my heart pounding before I was able to identify the sound that had wakened me. I felt transported years back when, after a quarrel, Alma's pitiful sobs had pried me out of my sleep, and for a heartless second I was glad that the weeping next door did not concern me.

Then I began to wonder who might be crying. Nobody slept in the room formerly occupied by Rudi Brueck, and my first thought was that perhaps one of the children had hidden there to cry over some injury, real or imaginary. I was about to get up and peek in when I heard the shuffling of slippered feet along the corridor and the soft knocking on the door, preceding the low voice:

"Stop that nonsense and come to bed, Edith!"

The sobbing in the adjoining room only grew louder. Presently the door opened and closed with a faint creaking, and then I heard Herr Richter's voice through the thin partition:

"Get up off that bed and come to sleep, Edith! We have to leave early tomorrow morning."

"But I don't want to leave!"

"Oh, so now you don't want to leave. Very well, stay here if you want to. But the children come with me."

The sobbing continued and so did Richter's hard voice, like the monotonous, maddening dripping of a faucet.

"All right, so you'll stay. What then? Is he going to marry you?"

Only sobs for an answer.

"Of course he won't marry you! And I'll tell you why he won't marry you: not because he's engaged to another girl but because you are too old for him!"

The sobs were rent by a small, desperate scream.

"I thought you had sense enough to know how to handle such an affair," said Richter's bitter voice. "I should have known better! Love affairs with older women always end the same way: the man gets tired and the woman doesn't want to let go. Do you want to wait until he gets tired of you and throws you over for a younger woman?"

Again a little scream of protest that was more than an answer.

"It always happens," Richter said pitilessly. "And it's ugly when it happens. Remember Katja Schwarzkopf? Making a fool of herself, throwing a bottle at her lover's wife in front of all the people . . ."

Of course, I thought. Of course! That was what had happened before I passed out at Eva's party!

Again I saw the savage expression on Frau Katja's face. The way she raised the bottle—not as though she were going to pour a drink from it—and I rushing forward, shouting: "Don't, don't!"

Or perhaps I only wanted to rush forward and shout, and everything was already lost in the pain that overtook me like a runner racing toward the same goal.

With the recollection of that moment other incidents from the party began to reel drunkenly through my mind.

Eva in red—the red of defiance—standing in the doorway to greet her guests. And a few steps behind her, in ill-chosen green that made her skin look sallow, Frau Katja. Everybody avoiding the Schwarzkopfs. Frau Goldmann, wavering between curiosity and disapproval. Trude pregnant to the bursting point. Herr Kramer, managing to make a sharp turn before he had to shake hands with Frau Katja. Frau Kramer, smiling weakly to make up for her husband's rudeness.

The food, the drinks, the cigarette smoke, the babble of voices, the piercing shrieks of laughter, the blaring of the record player.

And everywhere Walter and Eva, gay, laughing, chattering, as if they had broken out of their confinement and the taste of so many people was intoxicating to them.

Fleischer, drunk almost the moment he stepped across the threshold, sprouting six additional arms to throw around Eva. And Schwarzkopf, big and clumsy, with his anxious eyes and his permanently injured air, following her around like a dejected bloodhound.

Most of the older people leaving by midnight, except for me and Dr. Landau (cursing me under his breath and saying that he would stick it out with me).

Walter hopping from woman to woman, slightly tipsy, his homely face red, his eyes avoiding Frau Katja's threatening glances. Men swarming around Eva, trying to pat her, pinch her, brush against her.

Fleischer, senselessly drunk now, throwing himself on the floor before her, hugging her legs and kissing her calves. Schwarzkopf emerging from the bathroom, with eyes red as if he had been crying.

Eva passing from man to man, suddenly finding herself opposite Walter. Both looking at each other, astonished, like two old acquaintances unexpectedly meeting in a strange place. And Walter, flushed and tipsy, saying loudly: "Why, she is beautiful!" Bending forward and lightly kissing Eva's cheek.

A shocked pause in the drunken babble of the room—as if, by kissing his own wife, Walter had committed an act of adultery. Frau Katja, alone at the bar, turning pale, her nostrils quivering, her savage cat's eyes mere slits. Humiliated by her lover kissing his wife in front of all the people. All the people who knew. Raising the bottle . . .

And I, jumping up trying to rush forward, with the food heavy in my stomach, the alcohol roaring in my veins, the thick, smoke-filled air of the room closing in on me . . . Don't, don't, don't!

The memory of the scene made me gasp as I lay in bed. When I recovered my breath I heard that the sobbing next door had ceased. Either Frau Richter had followed her husband back to their room or she had fallen asleep on Rudi's stripped bed.

Early next morning I heard the blaring of the taxi which came to take the Richters to the airport. Later in the day Aronoff dropped by my room. He looked subdued but not heartbroken. I was reminded of what Richter had said the night before. It always ends the same way. The man gets tired first.

*Wednesday, July 8, 1942.* Wednesday is Señora Consuelo's day for visiting me. This to make up for our lost luncheons together. Today she came with her brother, Coronel Jiménez. The coronel immediately launched into a vicious attack on President Castillo of Argentina, who two days ago declared that Argentina would remain neutral.

"Fascistas desgraciados," the coronel said.

Señora Consuelo asked if this war was going to last forever. It is in its third year now with no end in sight. Every summer the Germans seem to be getting stronger. They have begun a new offensive in Russia, retaking all the cities they lost to the Russians during the winter. By now all those places must be devastated.

Perhaps the war will really last forever.

*Tuesday, July 14, 1942.*     Today I had an unexpected visitor: Rudi Brueck.

He had remembered that this was the afternoon of Frau Steinberg's monthly Hadassah meeting and had thought it safe to come to see me. Still, he sent Aronoff in ahead of him to make sure that the coast was really clear, and afterward posted him in the garden from where he could keep an eye on both the front and the side gate.

I was really touched by Rudi's visit. He brought me a bunch of flowers from his garden, wrapped in a piece of wrinkled, green tissue paper. Holding out the gift to me in his two enormous hands, he said bashfully:

"The ladies asked me to bring them to you. They still remember you. El gringo viejo con el pelo blanco. The old gringo with the white hair."

I asked him to thank the ladies for me and invited him to pull up a chair and sit down.

As he sat there, cracking his knuckles and gazing at me with his guileless, blue eyes, I wondered what in the world we would talk about. I felt queasy about asking him the old standby question—how business was—but in the end I did to break the silence. Rudi said that business was good, thank God, he had no complaints. He only hoped he would soon be able to see me among his customers.

I understood that this was his way of wishing me a speedy recovery.

In lieu of anything else to say I repeated how pleased I was by his visit. He said he would have come sooner if he had not been afraid of you know who.

"We're all very fond of you," he said to me in his heavy Viennese dialect, looking a little embarrassed and rubbing the palms of his hands over the leather hearts on the elbows of his old, checkered sports coat.

"Even Aronoff, he's fond of you. It's just you can't tell with him. He don't show how he feels. You'd never think he's sad because his, ah, his lady friend left. He really . . . liked her a lot."

I was astonished at the delicacy with which Rudi picked his words.

"For a while I even thought he'd marry this one," Rudi said. "But Aronoff is a strange one. He's got it all figured out who he's going to marry. You see, he thinks. With his head," Rudi added, tapping his index finger against his forehead.

Then he got up, walked over to the window and looked out worriedly.

"I better don't press my luck," he said. "I like to get home with my scalp intact."

He patted his golden ringlets with a gesture of disarming vanity. Watching him, I thought of a big, friendly Saint Bernard that had never harmed anyone. I could see why Aronoff was so fond of this simple man with whom he had nothing in common.

Rudi backed out the door, rear first as if leaving the presence of royalty, talking to me all the time.

"Now you be good now. And take care of yourself. And don't forget, first time out of the house you come to see me—on business. Just so you can be sure you're really well!"

In a way I envy Rudi his big body and his tiny brain. I wish life were as simple for me as it is for him.

*Thursday, July 23, 1942.* Horowitz of all people reminded me that today, once again, was Tisha B'ab. I asked him if he had been to the synagogue, and from the vehement way he denied it I suspect that he had. Perhaps prosperity has brought back religiousness for Horowitz.

It appears that by predestination Tisha B'ab always falls into a time of disaster. The German summer offensive in Russia is still in full swing and any day now Rostov will fall to them again.

*Wednesday, July 29, 1942.* I had several visitors today. First Señora Consuelo, who comes every Wednesday. We sat together by the window, she with her head slightly bowed and her fingers clasped as if in perpetual prayer. As the sun played over her hair, I noticed a glimmer of white in it. But her graying hair and her black clothes of mourning are the only outward signs of her loss. Her face has remained the ageless face of a Madonna, with the skin clear, translucent, and unlined.

She stayed only about ten minutes so as not to exhaust our meager topics of conversation.

Shortly after she had left I heard something outside my door which sounded like angry whispering. Then Herr Kramer came into the room, followed by Dr. Landau, who remained through his entire visit, leaning against the door like a morose guard.

Kramer talked about a multitude of things, holding his black Homburg in one hand and resting the other on the knob of his cane. But I could tell by the way he absent-mindedly kept tapping his cane on the floor that his thoughts were elsewhere.

It dawned on me only after he had left—throwing a poisonous glance at Dr. Landau—that he had probably come to discuss with me the drawing up of my will. When I questioned Dr. Landau, he reluctantly admitted that this was what all the whispering outside my door had been about.

"Kramer is a fool and a busybody," Dr. Landau said. "I didn't want him to upset you."

"But he is absolutely right! I should draw up a will. A few years ago it wouldn't have made any difference what I did. I had nothing to leave then. Now I have at least a modest sum of money. I shall ask Señora Consuelo at her next visit to send me her lawyer."

"Just don't get upset thinking about it," Dr. Landau said.

Strangely enough, I am upset. To whom shall I will my money? Another problem created by prosperity. If I only had a family!

*Saturday, August 1, 1942.* About my will: I have decided to leave my money to the Centro.

My first thought was to bequeath at least part of it to Goldmann, for having helped me make it. But Goldmann no longer needs my contributions. Next I considered splitting it between my friends Horowitz and Dr. Landau. Aside from the gossip and jealousy such an arrangement might arouse among other people who also consider themselves my friends, both men can do very well without my support. (Horowitz told me last night that he has enlarged his store and has hired two sales-girls. He certainly is moving up in the world.)

For one mad moment I even thought of leaving everything to Eva, but such a move—if it ever became known—would surely cause a scandal.

The Centro still seems the most reasonable solution. Thus my money will someday benefit the entire Jewish colony. My friends will have to be satisfied with my personal belongings.

I can die in peace now. Of course I have no intention of dying after having pulled through this attack.

One more problem has just occurred to me: what to do with the diaries?

*Friday, August 7, 1942.*    I have spent the past few days rereading my diaries. Two things struck me: First, how much our situation here has changed since our arrival. Second, that the diaries are almost as thorough a record of Eva's life as they are of mine.

If I had any sense I would destroy them. Suppose they should fall into the hands of a person like Fleischer! He could cause a tremendous amount of embarrassment to a number of people. But pride in authorship—or is it vanity?—will not let me dispose of the record of so many years.

I believe I have hit upon a sure method of ruling out any indiscretion. I shall leave the diaries to Eva. There is nothing in them which she does not know—except, perhaps, how I feel about her. But this will make little difference after my death. She might value the remembrance, and I am sure she will not betray my trust.

*Thursday, August 13, 1942.*    I don't know why the news that Churchill has gone to Moscow to discuss the opening of a second front should arouse personal guilt feelings in me. I cannot help telling myself that there is a man as old as I, traveling one day to Washington, the next to Moscow, while I am confined to a useless existence in my room. He makes me realize that age, which we all hold ready as a simple explanation for our decay, is no excuse.

*Sunday, August 16, 1942.*    A bit of cheerful news: for the first time today Dr. Landau allowed me to go down to the garden. He and Horowitz guided me down the stairs, and Aronoff, who is stronger than the two of them put together, helped me back to my room.

My elbows still ache from the strong grip of his hands as he slowly, cautiously pushed me up the stairs, more exhausted from bridling his youthful impatience than from the physical exertion of helping me. Before depositing me in my easy chair, he fluffed a pillow and tucked it in behind me. Such little gestures of attention from Aronoff always surprise me. Afterward he stayed for a while to keep me company. He seems to have completely recovered from the loss of what Rudi Brueck called his "lady friend." Such is youth.

*Thursday, August 20, 1942.*    Another afternoon in the garden. I usually sit in a spot from where, through an opening in the trees, I can see the ridge of the Andes. Strange that after thinking of them as prison walls more than once I should have missed them so during my confinement.

While I was sitting in the garden Irene Braun called. She pulled up a chair beside me and in her soothing manner told me all the latest gossip, with the sting and acid removed. Among other things she asked me if I had seen Trude's new baby. I shook my head, and Frau Irene smiled and also shook her head, almost in wonder.

"If I didn't know the baby's grandmother," she said, "I might believe that Trude had misbehaved. It seems impossible that Levy should have fathered such a beautiful child. But then the baby is the image of Frau Goldmann. You must ask Trude to bring the child along next time she comes."

I was happy for Trude. If she had been denied beauty, at least one of her daughters had been better endowed.

After a while our talk veered to Eva—as it always does eventually. Frau Irene remarked that Eva looked very well lately, and that she was glad she had given up working.

"Well, how could Eva go on working after what happened at the party?" I said.

Frau Irene looked at me, surprised.

"So you know. I thought you passed out just before . . . I mean, it happened almost simultaneously. I hope you won't think me heartless if I say that it was, in a way, a lucky coincidence. Most people were pretty drunk by then and everybody was so preoccupied with you that they did not quite realize what had happened. Many thought Katja hadn't thrown the bottle, she had just dropped it with fright."

"Why would a woman do such a thing?" I said.

Frau Irene shrugged.

"You know, we used to be quite friendly with the Schwarzkopfs for a while. We have a common interest in music, and they used to come to our house and we went to theirs. Oh, nothing of the sort" (she blushed without elaborating), "but finally I broke off the friendship. Katja has absolutely no sense of humor and she cannot share people. She likes to consume them. I just couldn't stand for that. I was shocked when I saw what Eva and Walter were letting themselves in for."

"Eva may look palatable," I said, "but I am sure that if somebody tried to consume her he might find her lying heavy in his stomach."

Frau Irene laughed.

"Yes, fortunately Eva is much tougher than she looks. Counting on that, I hope that she and Walter will still make a go of it. They're both young, and we all have to make our mistakes."

*Monday, August 24, 1942.*    Most of the time I feel as though my sickness had not really made me lose touch with the outside world. But then suddenly something happens which makes me realize that all my news is superficial and secondhand.

From what I could gather from my conversation with Walter Kramer this afternoon—and it was a rather confused conversation—he is considering marrying Katja Schwarzkopf. Why, I am at a loss to understand. Perhaps at the beginning of their affair—perhaps even six months ago—but why now?

From what I have heard from my other gossip-bearing visitors, I should have expected just the opposite. All the rumors had it that whatever had been going on between the Kramers and the Schwarzkopfs was drawing to an end.

By now it is common knowledge that Eva has quit work. Frau Goldmann told me, a little piqued perhaps, that Eva is again fast friends with Trude. ("One thing about my Trudi: she doesn't bear a grudge!") Horowitz brought the startling information that he had seen Walter playing cards in the Centro with, of all people, his former boss and adversary, Grushka. Eva and Walter were getting back into circulation. Their former friends, and even their former detractors, seemed relieved.

And then, out of the blue, Walter comes with this—I do not know what to call it! Calamity? Threat? Of marrying Katja Schwarzkopf.

Not that he ever said so outright. But I knew what he was getting at when he tried to sound me out on what I thought about marrying a Gentile.

"Why ask me?" I said.

Finally he hinted that he and Arthur had known all the time about my affair with Christine. Such things get around among students, he said. I was upset even after he assured me that Arthur had understood. (If Arthur approved of his father having an affair with a much younger woman, perhaps I had not brought him up properly.)

But, instead of letting Walter probe my prejudices (and what business did he have prying into my past private affairs?), I asked him to probe his own. How about substituting the word "shickseh" for the word "Gentile"? He winced, revealing his prejudices as being deeper than he had suspected. He would have to love a woman very much to overcome them. And I doubt that he still loves Katja Schwarzkopf. If he did, he would not have kept repeating over and over again something about a man having certain obligations.

God only knows what he meant by that. Obligations toward his mistress, his family, or his wife? In my confusion I forgot to ask him what would become of Eva if he married Katja Schwarzkopf.

*Wednesday, August 26, 1942.*     Acting like a stirred-up anthill, Walter's family descended upon me today.

The first one to come in the morning was Herr Kramer. After only a cursory knocking at my door he burst into the room, grim-faced and angry. I thought he had battled his way past Dr. Landau in a final attempt to discuss my will with me. To spare us both the diplomatic preliminaries preceding such a discussion, I said:

"Calm yourself, Herr Kramer. I have already sent for a lawyer to draw up my testament."

"Who cares about your testament?" Herr Kramer replied with his native diplomatic finesse. "I have come to talk about my son Walter. I know he has been to see you. Instead of talking to his father first, he goes running to you. I hope you didn't encourage him!"

"Encourage him to do what?"

"To marry that woman!"

"Look, Herr Kramer, it is true that Walter visited me a few days ago. He does that from time to time. But we did not discuss anything as personal as his marriage plans."

I enjoyed the look of consternation on Kramer's face. He seemed to think that he had unwittingly let me in on a family secret. But he quickly recovered his poise, or whatever it was.

"All right, so he did not discuss it with you. But you know what I mean. If I don't tell you, somebody else will. I say he wants to marry that Schwarzkopf woman!"

"And what does Walter say?"

"Isn't it enough if he comes around to sound us out on how we feel about mixed marriages? How stupid does he think we are? But I tell you, this time I'm going to put my foot down! Nobody can say that I ever tried to interfere in the affairs of my son" (I could easily think of a few people who would vouch to the opposite) "but if he marries this woman, I am no longer his father!"

For greater emphasis Herr Kramer delivered this entire speech standing up, his black Homburg on his head, his cane menacingly pointed at me.

"And what would you want me to do?" I asked.

"If Walter asks your opinion—and believe me he will—you tell him that you're dead set against a Jew marrying a shickseh!"

"And suppose that does not happen to be my opinion?"

Herr Kramer just stared at me, the tip of his cane quivering in mid-air.

"Look, Herr Kramer, is Frau Schwarzkopf's religion all you have against her? If she were Jewish, would you like the idea of Walter marrying her?" I asked, reversing the argument I had used on Walter.

"Of course I wouldn't want him to marry her! Bad enough he's married to Eva! Does he need a wife twenty years older than he is?"

I did not know whether to be annoyed or to laugh about Kramer's exaggeration. There is no bigger fool than an angry fool.

In the afternoon Frau Kramer came.

"My husband has been to see you this morning. So you know why I am here. I can't talk with Jakob. He is very stubborn. Tell me honestly, do you think it would be so bad if Walter married this . . . lady?"

I made noncommittal sounds.

"She has been very good for him," Frau Kramer went on. "She helped him a lot. And regardless of what Jakob says about her, she respects us. The few times I talked with her, she even mentioned that she has thought of becoming Jewish."

It was my turn now to be surprised. I seemed to remember that Frau Katja was a devout Catholic. But what wouldn't a woman do for love?

"Tell me, Frau Kramer, is this really your only objection? What about the age difference?" I asked, using an argument that her husband had left me.

"What age difference? Three, four years matter nowadays? I tell you, from looking at her you would say she is not older than Eva!"

In the evening the Lipschitzes dropped in. Frau Ruth slumped down on a chair and immediately began dabbing at her eyes.

"My brother will make us the laughingstock of the whole town!"

"Be quiet, Ruth, that is not what's important!"

"Then what is important? How am I going to face the other women if he does such a thing to us? Not enough that she is a shickseh, she's old enough to be his mother! You take my word, under that red dye her hair is completely gray!"

"All this is irrelevant, Ruth! We have not come to discuss Frau Schwarzkopf's hair color! The situation is much more serious than that! Walter is going to jeopardize the reputation of the entire family. What I mean is not only that he proposes to marry a Gentile several years his senior, but he will also have to divorce his wife!"

"A man usually has to divorce his wife before he can marry another woman," I said.

Dr. Lipschitz took my attempt at humor with a blank face.

"Ah yes," he said, "that is usually the case. But what I want to bring out is that in name Eva will still be a member of the family, albeit a divorced woman. Now, you and I being men, Professor Bernstein, know what that means!"

"I have no idea what you're leading up to."

"Come, come, Professor Bernstein, let us not fool ourselves. Eva is a very attractive woman, and with all the men around here, how is it going to look—what I mean is, what will become of her?"

"Who cares?" Frau Ruth said, sniffing. "If I know Eva, she'll find herself somebody. She can always marry Otto Schwarzkopf. He at least is Jewish!"

"Ruth!" Dr. Lipschitz exclaimed, shocked. "The man is old enough to be her father! Besides, this would only confirm what people have been saying all along, that Walter . . . What I mean is, Eva is only a young girl, we have some responsibility toward her as a member of our family."

"And why are you so concerned about Eva?" Frau Ruth asked, with sudden, sharp suspicion. "We came here to talk about Walter and that Schwarzkopf woman, and all the time you keep talking about your precious Eva!"

"Why, God damn it, Ruth," Dr. Lipschitz shouted, and for once in his anger he managed to bring out a straight sentence, "why can't Walter just stay married to her! She's young, she's pretty, she's Jewish! I saw the way she runs her house, she even is a good housewife. So Walter had himself a fling, all men do that at one time or another."

"Alfred!"

One whole day of family arguments was beginning to wear me down. I found myself getting tired and fed up.

"Tell me, Dr. Lipschitz, why do you all come to me with these problems?" I asked.

Dr. Lipschitz stared at me, hurt and taken aback.

"Where else should we go?" he said.

*Wednesday, September 2, 1942.*    The last good report from the war came almost a month ago, when United States Marines landed on the Solomon Islands. Ever since then all the reports have been disastrous. Last week the Germans began their offensive against Stalingrad. Yesterday they crossed the Kerch Straits; and in between they found time to annex Luxembourg, like an afterthought. So far there is no sign of the opening of a second front in Europe.

All this fits in with my general mood. Today we had the first rainfall of the season. Sitting alone in my room, I felt more shut off from the world than ever. I felt so desolate that I would even have settled for the visit of any member of the Kramer family, but none of them came.

Later in the afternoon Señora Consuelo arrived in the pouring rain. Her faithfulness is really touching.

*Tuesday, September 8, 1942.*    I must have mortally offended the entire Kramer family. For almost two weeks none of them has called on me. Even Walter and Eva have not been to see me. I keep worrying about what is going on, but dare not ask any of my other visitors for fear of giving away the secret.

This afternoon Trude dropped in. When I asked her about Eva, she told me that she was seeing Eva practically every day now. I was on the verge of asking her point-blank if she knew anything about an impending divorce—after all, Trude is and always was Eva's only friend here—but refrained at the last minute. (It occurs to me only now that Trude possibly might have been bursting to share her information but, like myself, felt obliged to guard the secret.)

Instead of discussing Eva's marital affairs we talked about Trude's children. I repeated all the wonderful tales I had heard about the beauty of her baby and asked Trude if she was really as pretty as people said she was.

"Don't ask me! To a mother there is no difference between her children!" Trude said with a vehemence that made me doubt the veracity of her protestations.

Before she left Trude gave me a bit of depressing news. Frau Paula Gruen is dying of cancer of the stomach.

"It's very hard on my father, watching her agony without being able to help her. Why do people have to die in such a manner?"

Later I talked to Dr. Landau about Frau Gruen's illness.

"At times I doubt the wisdom of the law which forbids a mercy killing," he said. "I know this is not the proper thing for a doctor to say, but if I knew that I had a hopeless case of cancer, I would kill myself. I have seen too many people rot to death. I wouldn't want to die like that, especially not in Esperanza."

I don't know why we all think that dying in Esperanza would be worse than dying in any other place in the world. I am also surprised by Dr. Landau's confession. He is the last person from whom I would have expected such a defeatist attitude.

Perhaps I ought to be grateful for my heart condition.


*Monday, September 14, 1942.* The Kramers have not forgotten me, after all. If I offended them, they have nevertheless put aside their injured feelings for the duration of the holidays. They all came to wish me a happy New Year. Frau Lipschitz brought me a bunch of flowers and Frau Kramer a generous piece of cake. When Dr. Landau frowned at the cake, she said pleadingly:

"So, a little bit of cake won't kill him. At least for the holidays you might be lenient."


*Saturday, September 19, 1942.* I think I am beginning to understand what Walter meant when he spoke of his obligations. Or at least I am trying to put two and two together.

This afternoon Dr. Landau dropped in to examine me. His face looked uncommonly grave and vexed as he listened to my heart, and I asked with some alarm whether there had been any unfavorable change in my condition.

"No, nothing wrong with you. I'm worried about something else."

He went on muttering about a crazy woman who had just tried to blackmail him into giving her a certificate that she was pregnant.

"But why should she want to blackmail you?" I asked. "Can't you tell when a woman is pregnant?"

"Of course I can tell, provided she will let me examine her. But this one just wouldn't. She told me all she wanted was a certificate stating that she was three months pregnant. When I said I could not give her such a certificate—first of all, because I am not licensed to practice medicine here, secondly because I did not know whether she was pregnant—she threatened to report to the authorities that I had performed an abortion on her. I told her that if she did, we would both be going to jail. Finally I got her to leave, but I'm not at all sure that I have seen the last of her," Dr. Landau said worriedly.

He stayed for a while longer, and I tried to cheer him up by talking about matters as far removed from pregnant women as possible.

Frau Steinberg, who lately drowns her sorrow by dusting and rearranging her unoccupied rooms every other day, must have heard our voices, for presently she knocked on my door and asked if she might join us. She had not been in the room two minutes when she turned to Dr. Landau and asked:

"Tell me, Dr. Landau, is Frau Schwarzkopf very ill?"

Dr. Landau looked taken aback.

"What do you mean?" he said.

"Well, I saw her walking out of the house a while ago, and she was crying," Frau Steinberg said.

Dr. Landau got very angry.

"Frau Steinberg, how often have I asked you kindly not to spy on my patients, and if you must spy, not to mention names! You will get us all in trouble!"

"Don't get so excited," Frau Steinberg said. "I was only wondering."

So am I.

*Tuesday, September 22, 1942.*    I had hoped for a chance to speak to Eva or Walter before Yom Kippur, but neither came to visit me. The longer I think about what Dr. Landau told me the more convinced I become that Frau Katja is trying to blackmail Walter with a fake pregnancy into marrying her.

I just wish I knew what is going on!

*Friday, September 25, 1942.* Today I got an unexpected chance to look for Eva in the Centro—but without any success.

I doubt that Dr. Landau would ever have given me permission to go into town if Trude had not offered to take me and bring me back in her car.

Trude had come in the afternoon to show me her children. Everything people have told me is true: the baby, with her black hair and her black eyes, is the miniature of her beautiful grandmother. Next to her little Norma looked even more like an ugly duckling, in spite of her ruffled, starched dress and the large bow in her straight hair. She waddled around the room on her fat legs, examining everything with great interest and incessantly chattering in Spanish. Trude told me that she also understands every word of German.

"Any day now she'll start speaking it too. She's very bright," Trude said with a sigh.

Remembering how Frau Goldmann used to sigh over her bright and ugly Trude, I had to smile.

Later Dr. Landau came down to cluck over "his children." The way he acts one would think that he not only had delivered but actually fathered them. I took advantage of his benign mood to ask him when he would let me take my first trip into town. He immediately began to lecture me on strain, exertion, altitude, and was I out of my mind, but finally said that if Frau Levy would take charge of me and bring me back within a reasonable time, he did not see why I should not go.

Trude sent the children home with their niñera, and then she and Dr. Landau helped me down the stairs and into the car.

"Where would you like to go?" Trude asked.

"Where does a horse like to go? To the stable! Take me to the Centro!"

I doubt that a trip to the moon could have been more exciting for me. I looked at the hilly, meandering streets, which at one time or another I had thoroughly loathed—especially during the rainy season when the gutters had been running with water and the passing buses had splashed the pedestrians on the narrow sidewalks—and was glad that I had been granted another chance to see them. The Indians, the mules, the women relieving themselves in the middle of the road, all were welcome to my eyes.

Realizing my delight at the outing, Trude told her chauffeur to take us through the Avenida Bolívar. I was childishly pleased at seeing all the familiar stores. The biggest surprise was Horowitz' new Casa León. He had broken through the wall of his old store and had installed a huge plate-glass window in the front.

As is his habit, Horowitz was standing in the door of his shop when we passed. He saw the car, recognized my face in the window, for a moment looked as if he had seen a ghost, and then ran after the car, shouting and gesticulating wildly. People in the street stopped and stared. Trude laughed and said that Horowitz was very fond of me. I am always touched and surprised when I hear that. Why should anybody be fond of me? I am really not a very ingratiating person.

And yet people must be fond of me, or else why should my appearance in the Centro have caused such excitement? Everybody acted as if I were Lazarus risen from the grave. Fleischer almost knocked over Trude's chauffeur to help me up the stairs. The moment I set foot inside the Centro, several people jumped up to offer me their chairs, though there were plenty of empty chairs around. Herr Bloch wanted to serve me free coffee ("An honor to have you as guest of the house!") and was disappointed when I told him that I was allowed only very weak tea. Trude hovered over me like a mother hen, saying time and again: "Please, I promised Dr. Landau."

Horowitz, having learned of my destination through some sixth sense, dashed in a few minutes after us.

"A fine friend you are! First time out, and you don't even tell me about it!"

While people fussed over me I kept craning my neck, hoping that Eva would come out of one of the rooms. If she had been in the Centro she would surely have been attracted by the commotion. I was disappointed when she failed to appear and did not protest when Trude took me home shortly afterward.

On the ride back I mentioned casually that Eva had been neglecting me.

"She's been neglecting me too," Trude said. "I have not seen her for four or five days. Who knows if she hasn't resumed her 'old' friendship."

Trude's remark caused me a jolt of anxiety. I am still worried about what Frau Katja has been up to.

*Wednesday, September 30, 1942.* At times I wonder whether I was meant to be an unintentional eavesdropper. But probably it is my own fault if people have their private conversations within my earshot. For some reason—embarrassment mostly—I always fail to make my presence known after a conversation has gone beyond what is meant for the ears of a third party. To wit: what happened today.

I had given Eva another three days to visit me. When she did not come, I waylaid Aronoff this afternoon and asked him to drive me over to her house. It was around five-thirty, and I was sure that she would be at home. I told Aronoff not to wait for me, and he drove away while I stood pushing the doorbell.

A few minutes later the muchacha leisurely approached the gate and inquired in formal Spanish what I desired. I said I desired to see the señora. The señora was not at home. Neither was el Señor Balter. El Señor Balter had gone to look after one of his projects in the province and would not be back until late at night. La señora never came back from work until after six o'clock.

My heart sank. Trude's suspicion had been correct. But why had Eva gone back to work?

I told the muchacha that I would wait for the señora, and she opened the gate, ushered me into the house, and left me in the sala.

On the previous occasion when I had been in this room (and what a painful memory that was!) it had been crowded with people. Now that I was alone I noticed for the first time how well Eva had arranged everything, but what seemed to be lacking was warmth. Eva's only concession to softness had been the filmy, shirred curtains through which the landscape outside the window took on a dreamlike quality.

I sat down in one of the deep easy chairs facing the window, and for a few minutes gave myself over to the voluptuous feeling of luxury. It was good to be able to look out at an Andean sunset from the shelter and security of such a pretty room. We had come a long way in a few years.

After a while the muchacha stuck her head in and asked if I would mind being left alone while she ran to the tienda for some bread. I told her to go ahead, and after she left I apparently dozed off, as I do so often now, for the next thing I heard was Eva's voice, calling:

"Maruja, Maruja, where the devil is that girl again?" I was about to reply in Maruja's stead when I heard Eva saying outside the door: "No, Otto, you can't come in. We've been over all that before. Can't you get it through your head that it's over? And I'm not coming back to work either. I only came to help out for a few days because Katja had got herself into that mess . . ."

"I won't have you talk that way about Katja! It was your husband who got her into the mess! You don't know what it meant for her to give up that baby. Katja is a very devout woman. For her an abortion is a deadly sin!"

"She didn't have to have an abortion. If anybody had told me what was going on, I would have given Walter a divorce and he could have married Katja!"

"And you would have married me?"

There was a short pause, and then Eva said softly:

"Damn you. Why don't you go to hell? Why do you always have to drive me to a point where I have to hurt you? What pleasure do you get out of it? No, I wouldn't have married you. I never loved you, I never told you that I loved you, and I don't see why you have to keep pretending to yourself that I did. I'm sick of it all! It's over, done with, finished! Just leave me alone! Can't you understand that? Leave me alone!"

There was quiet for a second, and then Schwarzkopf said: "Oh, Eva," in a voice which no man should ever hear another man use.

Presently I heard his heavy tread on the garden path as he walked away, and the next moment Eva stepped into the room. Her face was still contorted with anger and she seemed startled when she came upon me so unexpectedly.

"What are *you* doing here?" she asked without first greeting me. Her voice was harsh, and I felt as if some of her disgust with Schwarzkopf had spilled over on me.

I knew that I must not let her suspect that I had overheard her conversation, so I said quite innocently that I had dozed off while I sat waiting for her in the dark. Her features softened and gradually took on a more composed expression. She bent over to place her handbag on a table, and when she straightened up all emotion was erased from her face.

She sat down opposite me and began to make conversation. How had I got here? She had not known that I was already allowed to go out. I told her that Aronoff had driven me over, and she seemed surprised that he should have shown himself so obliging. Like most people, she thinks that Aronoff lives strictly for his own pleasures.

Her next question was one I had anticipated: why had I come?

Since my original reason had been voided by what I had overheard, I said the next best thing that came into my mind:

"You did not come to see me, so I came to see you. Can a man have a better reason for coming to your house than wanting to see you?"

She shook her head and smiled.

"Professor Bernstein, you're the only man who does not make me suspicious by flattering me."

(Ah, but she is so wrong!)

Eva asked me to wait for Walter and have dinner with them, but I said that if I did not report back to the Villa Carmen Dr. Landau would send out a search party to see if I was lying dead in a ditch. Even so, he was already waiting for me by the garden gate when I returned a half hour later by taxi.

"So you had to go and see Eva Kramer," he said (no doubt Aronoff was his informant). "Was that visit really necessary?"

What should I have told him?

*Thursday, October 1, 1942.* It appears that my outing yesterday had some adverse after effects. I did not feel too well today and Dr. Landau ordered me to stay in bed. He was exceedingly angry and spent some time sitting in my room, mutely glowering at me.

I was tempted to tell him about Frau Katja's capers, but refrained because Dr. Landau had actually never mentioned her name to me. Still, I am sure he would have been interested. How often does one come across a woman who stages the abortion of a baby she has never conceived, right down to the perfectionistic detail of staying in bed afterward?

But perhaps there had been a deeper purpose to her act. Perhaps she had only tried to put a different pressure—the pressure of guilt—on Walter.

*Monday, October 5, 1942.*    Horowitz had told Eva that I had to stay in bed the day after my visit to her, and today she came to make sure that I was all right again.

"If this is the only way I can get you to visit me, I don't mind having a bad day once in a while," I said.

Eva laughed and wagged her finger at me.

"You old rogue," she said.

This was the first time she had ever used any sort of endearing term with me. I was delighted.

She was sitting on the window sill, with the sun drawing a golden halo around her head. I recalled what Fleischer had once said about her: that she looked pure in spite of everything. She was, I thought, the eternal virgin whom so many men crave beneath all their sophistication. It was inconceivable that her life should not be as pure and serene as her appearance.

"Eva, there's something I have wanted to ask you for some time now," I said. "You know how rumors get around in Esperanza . . . Please, don't look so angry before your hear what I want to ask you. Are you and Walter planning to get a divorce?"

Her expression changed from anger to astonishment.

"Of course not! Whatever gave you that idea?"

"As I told you, there are always rumors."

Eva shook her head. "There's no basis for such rumors just now. Quite the contrary."

"The contrary?" I asked hopefully.

She laughed. "I wouldn't tell this to anybody but you. After all, you have lived with us, you know the troubles Walter and I used to have. A few days ago, after all this time, Walter suddenly asked me to run away with him."

"What?"

"Well, he didn't put it exactly that way. He just asked me how I would like to leave everything and go to the United States. Start all over again and that sort of thing."

I could see that Eva was trying to be flippant over something that had touched her.

"Why don't you?" I asked.

"It wouldn't work. Not with me. I'm a funny person. I can't live backward, only forward. I can't erase the past and just turn back to the first page."

"Eva, you looked angry before. You can start looking angry again, for now I'm going to ask you what you thought I would ask you then. Eva, the other thing, is it over?"

She looked me straight in the eye.

"It's over."

"And you say you don't want to give it another try with Walter. Then what will you do?"

Eva turned up the palms of her hands as if expecting manna from heaven.

"Hope for the best," she said.

She left a little later. I stood by the window, watching her walk to the side gate. She walked swiftly and a little awkwardly, like a long-legged colt, and halfway down the path she almost bumped into Aronoff, who was headed toward the house. They tried to make room for each other on the narrow path, but, weaving from side to side, still kept blocking each other's way. Finally Aronoff took her by the shoulders and swung her around him. There was something decisive in his action which made me think of young Alexander cutting the Gordian knot.

Eva gave a short laugh, turned around and walked through the gate without glancing back. Aronoff looked after her briefly and then continued on his way toward the house.

*Tuesday, October 13, 1942.*    Dr. Landau says that I am his bane. I keep bothering him to allow me a greater range of activities. He does not object so much to my going into town as to my climbing stairs. I am still dependent on the strong arms of Frau Steinberg or Aronoff to help me upstairs when I return from one of my outings.

This afternoon Aronoff gave me a ride into town. I am reluctant to make a nuisance of myself, but he offered to take me along. Before dropping me outside Goldmann's Casa Elsa, he told me that he would take me home again if I would look for him in the Jungle Café in about two hours.

Goldmann was so overjoyed to see me that he transferred his denture from his breast pocket to his mouth.

"For me he wouldn't do that!" Frau Goldmann complained.

The Goldmanns immediately made me sit down, and next my state of health was discussed at great length. (I am beginning to understand all chronic hypochondriacs. There is hardly a more interesting topic of conversation than one's ailments. For the duration of such a discourse one is the center of the universe and nothing else matters. "Every patient loves his sickness," Dr. Landau says.)

But all good things must come to an end, and eventually Goldmann asked me if I felt up to inspecting the books, a task to which I had not attended for months. Goldmann said that he had done his best but that looking at numbers made him dizzy.

"He needs glasses, that's why he gets dizzy!" Frau Goldmann said. "But would he wear them? No! He would carry them in his breast pocket to keep his teeth company!"

Goldmann had made a complete mess of the books. Figures were crossed out or corrected in an illegible manner, and frequently the totals at the bottom of a column were closer to fiction than to fact. Still and all, it seems that I have made an additional fifteen hundred dollars since I was taken ill.

"So who else is getting richer while he is flat on his back?" Goldmann asked boastfully. But the moment I said that I was beholden he began to belittle his achievements.

Goldmann agreed that I ought to take the books home to put them in order, but he looked worried when, a little later, I started out for Horowitz' store with his account books under my arm. I had to promise that I would hide them from Horowitz' prying eyes.

"Now that he's making money himself, he begrudges everybody else his income! You mark my word, that Communist won't be satisfied until he is richer than all the rest of us put together!"

Horowitz certainly seems on his way—if not to outstrip, at least to equal some of our business tycoons. Unlike his old cubbyhole, his new store extends almost the entire length of the building, the large show window admitting some light from the street. Inside, Horowitz has added a few glass showcases similar to those in the Casa Elsa, where he displays his merchandise with his typical neatness, but with an utter lack of artistic taste. All his articles are lined up in symmetrical order like soldiers on parade. Only his two salesgirls appear to have escaped his mania for neatness. Although he has forced them into aprons, they still manage to wear their hair in an unruly manner which accentuates their swarthy, Latin good looks. (I suspect that Horowitz hired them for their looks in the first place. He has repeatedly hinted that they have shown themselves very accommodating.)

I stayed for about an hour with Horowitz and then went looking for Aronoff in the Jungle Café. He sat at a table in a booth, the latest edition of the *Día* spread out before him. While he waited for his check, we talked about the war. (The Germans have annexed Slovenia, but the Russians, starting their winter offensive early, have attacked the German armies northeast and southeast of Stalingrad. We hope that this time they will finally drive them all the way back into Germany. By June, Goldmann had said when I visited him in his store.)

After Aronoff had paid, we left.

On our way home we passed Eva waiting at a bus stop. Aronoff stepped on the brake, backed up and told her to get in.

Eva looked surprised and all the way home hardly said a word. I could see that this was the first time Aronoff had ever offered her a ride. I was sitting between them, and what little conversation they carried on they directed at me without looking at each other.

When we stopped in front of Eva's house, Aronoff got out and opened the door for her, holding her elbow as she climbed out of the car. She looked up briefly at him and he immediately dropped her arm.

"Well, thanks for bringing me home. It was very nice of you to go out of your way," Eva said. There was a little edge of irony in her voice.

"My pleasure," Aronoff replied. His voice too sounded mocking.

He climbed back into the car without waiting for her to unlock the gate.

I cannot understand this strange hostility between them. Unless, of course, they are beginning to be interested in each other.

*Sunday, October 18, 1942.*    I must say Eva's new concern for me is touching! To sacrifice a Sunday morning in order to visit me!

She spent most of the time standing at my window, looking in the direction of Aronoff's garden house. But he did not make his appearance until a half hour after she had left.

Perhaps I am just imagining things.

*Thursday, October 22, 1942.*    Another visit from Eva. This time I could not resist teasing her about her sudden show of concern.

"If you don't want me to come, you just have to say so," she said testily. "I remember only a little while ago you complained that I did not come to see you often enough!"

I quickly assured her that she was always welcome, adding in my mind: whatever her motives.

Actually, her motives are anything but clear to me. Although I was under the distinct impression that she was waiting for Aronoff (she had dropped in shortly before lunch, at about the time when, as I had mentioned to her, he would come to help me down the stairs), she rose the moment he came into the room and announced that she was in a hurry to get home.

"If you're in such a hurry I can drive you home," Aronoff said politely. "I'll just run downstairs and tell Frau Steinberg not to start serving before I get back."

He turned and disappeared into the corridor before Eva could stop him. She remained with her hand outstretched and the word "don't" dying on her lips.

"That's all I need! To have him tell Frau Steinberg that he is driving me home! A woman only has to cross the street with Aronoff and people will say that she has slept with him."

I have never seen Eva so squeamish about her reputation. But I can vouch for it that Aronoff returned directly after bringing her home. The trip took him exactly eleven minutes. I know. I looked at my watch.

*Tuesday, October 27, 1942.* In our tight little pool the smallest motion can cause a ripple. Today Walter came to ask me with some alarm if Eva had been seeing Aronoff. Again I countered with my old defense. "Why ask me?"

"Because I understand that she comes here to meet him!" Walter said.

"To the best of my knowledge Eva comes to see me."

"And Aronoff incidentally, perhaps?"

"Whatever gave you that idea, Walter?"

"Do I have to tell *you* how rumors get around here? He's been seen driving her home twice!"

"Exactly. Once I was with them. He was driving me home and we picked Eva up at a bus stop. The second time he took her home when she was visiting me. I can assure you that he was right back for lunch."

Walter was only half listening to me. There was a frown on his face as he stood furiously twisting horns out of his hair.

"I won't have it!" he said. "Not this time! I know Aronoff's reputation. Besides, he's engaged. If Eva ever gets involved with another man he's going to marry her!"

This statement struck me as so funny coming from a husband that I had to laugh. Walter looked startled.

"You don't seem to understand what I mean. People are holding me responsible for what is happening to Eva, for what she is . . . turning into. I suppose it's as much my fault as hers if our marriage is wrecked beyond repair, but I won't have her ruining her life! I won't have that on my conscience!"

In spite of my reassurances, Walter was still angry when he left. I suspect that by trying to stop Eva from getting involved with Aronoff, he wants to make her atone for his own sins.

*Monday, November 2, 1942.* Something to take my mind off Eva and Aronoff: Frau Katja came to visit me today.

It was shortly after lunch and I was sitting in the garden with Horowitz and Dr. Landau when she walked in. She hesitated briefly when she saw that I was not alone, but then strutted forward, her head with the metallic red hair held up defiantly. Planting herself before our little group, she crossed her arms and said in the tone of one delivering an ultimatum:

"I have come to see Professor Bernstein."

Horowitz and Dr. Landau, who for reasons of their own are both afraid of her, rose simultaneously to attend to some urgent matter inside the house.

Frau Katja pulled up a chair and sat down opposite me, her knees almost touching mine, her gaze so intent on my face that I had the weird sensation that she was trying to mesmerize me.

"I know I should have come to see you sooner," she said, "but I thought you might not want to see me."

It would have been easy to agree with her, but with such a woman the truth will never do.

"You need not apologize, Frau Katja," I said. "I know how busy you are in the factory, especially now that Eva has quit working."

I noticed my blunder too late. At the mention of Eva's name Frau Katja's green eyes began to glitter.

"Ah, yes, our precious Eva! But she is not the person from whom one can expect gratitude. She always used to make fun of me because she had a better education than I, but what good did all her education do her? It was me who taught her a trade so that she would never again have to be afraid of starving to death! And her thanks was to ruin our lives! Mine and Otto's and Walter's . . . yes, Walter's too!"

I did not know what to say. I had expected her to get around to abusing Eva—indeed, the reason for her visit must have been the urge to pour her heart out rather than concern for my health—but not so soon.

"She broke Otto's heart, that's what she did. Why shouldn't I tell you? It is no secret that he loved her. First she destroyed our marriage and then she broke his heart. How do you think it makes me feel to see my husband sitting by his desk, staring at Eva's empty worktable while tears run down his cheeks?"

I was so embarrassed that I literally wished to sink into the ground. But then it is Frau Katja's special talent to cause embarrassment.

"Please, Frau Katja, I am not at all well yet and what you tell me does not really concern me," I pleaded with her.

"Oh, yes, it does! Everybody comes running to you, telling you stories! But I want you to know the truth when people tell you lies about me. I know what they say! They say that Walter Kramer finally ditched the shickseh!"

"Frau Katja!" I protested.

"Of course it isn't true. What really happened was that Walter asked me to marry him and I told him I couldn't do that. I couldn't abandon Otto to Eva! She would ruin him. Besides, she would never give Walter a divorce. It was she who told him not to marry 'the shickseh'!"

Frau Katja had bent forward and gripped my wrists. Her hands were surprisingly strong and I thought she could easily strangle a person. But I was not frightened so much by her strength as by the fact that she had abandoned all logic and was talking like a madwoman, contradicting her own statements in the same breath. I looked toward the house in the hope that either Dr. Landau or Horowitz would come to my rescue, but they had fled permanently.

"Of course you don't believe me," Frau Katja said bitterly, to my great relief releasing my wrists. "She has bewitched you too. And why should you believe me? I am only a shickseh! I should have listened to my father when he begged me not to marry a Jew. 'Katja,' he said to me, 'you are my favorite child. I love you more than all my other children. Katja my darling, don't marry the Jew! You don't know the Jews! With all the crooks among them they are proud of being Jewish! They'll spit on you.' I should have listened to him. If I had not married a Jew I would not be here today. I would not be suffering this humiliation."

I was shocked beyond words. It seemed that no matter how deep a prejudice has been buried, in the end it will out.

And yet—and yet I had to remind myself of Christine, of her culture, her polish, her beautiful manners and brilliant mind to keep myself from judging Frau Katja ill for being a Gentile.

"Frau Katja, there is something I want you to know," I said with difficulty. "For many years I had a . . . very dear friend who was not Jewish. And it was she who broke off our relationship in the end. I never thought she did it because I was a Jew."

Frau Katja looked at me unblinkingly. With her short nose and her slanted eyes she looked like a cat frozen in a pose.

"But you don't understand," she said. "Walter did not leave me. He wanted to marry me. It was Eva who would not let him. She has some hold on him. She has a hold on Otto too. I don't know what it is. I only know that her heart is as cold as her body. She has nothing to give and still they love her."

I was quite desperate now, and still nobody came from the house to rescue me.

"Tell me, Frau Katja, why did you come here? What do you think I can do?"

"You can tell everybody the truth! People will believe you. They say you are the only person in town who never starts a rumor. I want to be able to walk through the streets holding up my head!"

I felt very sorry for her. Her pride, which had been so deeply hurt, would not let her realize that her private life had ceased to be of interest to anybody but herself.

I finally got her to leave by promising that I would defend her reputation if anybody should dare attack it in my presence. But I doubt that I shall have to fulfill my promise. For most people the affair Schwarz-kopf-Kramer is closed.


*Friday, November 13, 1942.*    Politically a very exciting week. It seems that a second front in Europe may not remain a wild daydream after all. British troops under General Montgomery have finally driven Rommel's divisions from Egypt, and five days ago Anglo-American troops under the command of General Eisenhower—a new name to us—have landed in Algeria and Morocco. By Wednesday the French garrisons in Casablanca, Oran, and Algiers had surrendered and an armistice was arranged by French General Darlan. (He is not to be trusted, Goldmann, our military brain, maintains.)

In the meantime the Germans have taken over control of unoccupied France. But now we permit ourselves the hope that with the Americans just across the Mediterranean, the German rule in France will soon come to an end.

Yesterday we were further cheered by the news that the United States has won a three-day naval battle in the Solomon Islands.

As is the case with those who live in absolute safety, I hear that some of our people in Esperanza are already planning a dance in the Centro to celebrate "our recent victories."

*Tuesday, November 17, 1942.*    I am to go on another trip!

This time Dr. Landau made all the plans for me. For several weeks now we have had a running argument over how much activity he would permit me. I kept complaining that I would lose the use of my legs if he would not let me take the long walks to which I had been accustomed before my heart attack, and he said he would have no objection if it were not for the great altitude at which we live. If I could go to a spot some three to four thousand feet below Esperanza I could do all the walking I wanted. The only such place where one can go is Aguas Calientes, but Dr. Landau said he would never allow me to travel by the rickety overland bus which is the only connection there.

Today he came to tell me that my trip was all arranged.

"Aronoff is going to take you along in his car. He'll be leaving some time early in December," Dr. Landau announced.

I said that I had already imposed enough upon Aronoff—he still helps me up the stairs whenever he is around—and I would not go unless I was sure that I would not interfere with his plans.

"You mean you don't want to disturb him if he's taking a woman along," Dr. Landau said. "Well, he isn't."

"How do you know?"

"I asked him."

"I must say, Dr. Landau, you have some nerve!"

"Instead of criticizing me you ought to be grateful. After all, I only acted as your physician. Besides, you were driving me crazy with your constant whining and complaints. This way at least I won't have to look at you for a week or two."

*Wednesday, November 25, 1942.*     Eva appeared unduly upset when I told her that I was going to Aguas Calientes with Aronoff.

"But you can't go!" she said. "There's a dance next week Saturday in the Centro."

"I am afraid my dancing days are over, my dear," I said.

She looked quite unhappy. Of course I am not fool enough to imagine that I am the cause of all this unhappiness. Eva must have counted on Aronoff's attendance. I wonder whether deep inside she still carries the hope of meeting her Prince Charming at a ball.

*Saturday, November 28, 1942.*     Yesterday was little Norma's second birthday.

To make up for her neglect last year, Eva brought her an enormous Panda. There were quite a lot of small children at Norma's party, most of whom I did not know. All the children had come with their niñeras, and the constant loud chatter in Spanish made me feel as if I had wandered into a strange place. The children too spoke Spanish, rapidly, faultlessly, and without an accent. It made me realize again how often, among Jews, every third generation speaks a different language.

Trude and Eva spent much of the time huddling in one corner, whispering and giggling like young girls. I was glad to see Eva so cheerful again.

*Monday, November 30, 1942.*     Never underestimate the cunning of a woman!

Since I did not want to keep Goldmann's account books at home while I was away, I went to return them today. Levy was in the store when I mentioned that I was going to Aguas Calientes.

"So we'll be meeting there," he said.

"You're going too?" I asked.

"Going? I'm being dragged! Would I go at this time of year? But my wife wants to go, so I have to go too! For months, ever since the baby was born, I've been begging her to take a vacation. But no, she would not leave the children alone, although Mother Goldmann" (this is the title upon which Levy has finally settled for his mother-in-law) "offered to take care of them. Of course now that Eva wants to go, my wife suddenly can leave the children!"

"Eva is coming too?" I asked incredulously.

"Is she coming? It's all her idea in the first place! If not for the ball in the Centro we would be leaving this weekend already. But the women have to wear their new ball gowns, so we won't be able to leave before Monday. I tell you, Professor Bernstein, these women can drive a man crazy! Half the time they don't know what they want!"

I have a pretty good idea though that Eva does.

*Wednesday, December 2, 1942.* From what Walter told me this afternoon when he sat down at my table in the Centro I can see that Eva has become a regular Machiavelli.

(Aronoff had driven me into town. I had fought off the temptation to tell him that Eva was coming to Aguas Calientes. I want to see his face when she walks in. For some reason I have the idea that he is avoiding her. When I remarked that he would be missing the ball in the Centro, he said that this was strictly intentional on his part. He was sick and tired of balls in the Centro.)

Walter, obviously unaware that I also am going to Aguas Calientes, mentioned Eva's pending trip.

"I'm glad Trude talked her into going," he said. "It will do her good to get away from Esperanza for a while. She hasn't been away since . . ."

He broke off, but I knew what he was thinking about.

"I've always wanted her to go to Aguas Calientes. It's such a lovely place, and I can get special rates in the hotel. But I suppose Eva did not want to go without company."

It becomes increasingly hard for me to keep my mouth shut. But why should I tell Water that Aronoff is going to Aguas Calientes if I did not tell Aronoff that Eva was going?

*Thursday, December 3, 1942.* Horowitz has got wind of my plan to go away, or, as he bitterly calls it, my "dastardly attempt to sneak off with Aronoff behind his back."

"You could have invited me too!" he said to me.

"How could I invite you if Aronoff invited me?"

"From him I would not accept an invitation," Horowitz said haughtily.

Nevertheless, I suspect that we shall see Horowitz in Aguas Calientes some time after the ball, which he would not miss for anything in the world.

*Saturday, December 5, 1942.* A very relaxing trip with Aronoff; quite unlike my two previous trips in chauffeur-driven cars. Aronoff drives carefully and talks little. From time to time he asked me if I was comfortable and if he was driving too fast. I am always newly amazed by his show of consideration.

In the morning Dr. Landau had escorted me to the car and given Aronoff a number of instructions concerning me, as if I were too feeble-minded to take care of myself.

"Don't let him exert himself. See to it that he rests between walks. Don't let him climb mountains, ride horseback, or overeat."

"If you're so worried about Professor Bernstein," Aronoff said, "why don't you throw a few things into a suitcase and come along with us, Dr. Landau?"

"What, and pay rent in two places?" Dr. Landau said indignantly, putting us in a gay mood for the trip.

The trip to Aguas Calientes did not seem nearly so long as the first time I had made it. When we crossed the last mountain range and the fertile valley came in sight—the bright green fields of sugar cane; the shabby, wooden shacks raised on stilts above the ground; the smell of moist, heavy air steaming up from the black earth—I had a strange feeling that I was coming home.

It took me a while before I was able to sort out my feelings. For the first time since our emigration I was returning to a place I had visited once before. I had almost lost the use of the phrase "going back."

But now I have gone back. Perhaps going back is, after all, not so impossible as Eva thinks it is.

*Sunday, December 6, 1942.* I have secured one of the few rooms located on the main floor of the hotel in Aguas Calientes. This way I have to climb only three or four steps from the dining room.

There is a narrow balcony outside my room from which I can overlook the paved patio below (the ground slopes away from the house, rendering the location of my room higher than it appears from the inside) and at a distance of about fifty feet the elevated structure of the swimming pool.

Aronoff spends most of the day lying by the pool and baking himself to a deep brown. I think he is heavier than he was a few years ago, his figure that of a man rather than a boy. His youth and strength make me feel doubly old and decrepit.

Until now there are not too many people in Aguas Calientes to appreciate Aronoff's good looks. The only other guests in the hotel are the Vogels. Dr. Vogel looked apprehensive and Frau Vogel blushed when she saw Aronoff walk in with me yesterday afternoon, but when the Vogels realized that Rudi Brueck was not with us they relaxed again.

After dinner I took a short walk with Aronoff. We walked in the dark —the roads around Aguas Calientes are not lighted—and I had to be careful not to stumble. Aronoff picked his way with the surefootedness of a cat. He was humming off-key, as if he were trying to join in the song of the cicadas.

Mindful of Dr. Landau's instructions, Aronoff soon took me home. I thought he would go out again after depositing me in the dining room, but he went upstairs to sleep. When I asked him if he would be able to fall asleep so early in the evening, he said he could fall asleep any hour of the day or night.

Ah, youth, youth!

This morning Aronoff was up bright and early, swimming back and forth the length of the swimming pool in a slow crawl, while I sat watching him from my balcony. Then he climbed up on the diving board, shook himself like a wet dog and lay down to sun himself.

From downstairs I heard the voice of Herr Mayer addressing his wife, whom I could not see but who must have been standing in the open dining-room door:

"Why don't you go in the kitchen and see to it that the girls get breakfast ready, stupid goose. Aren't you ashamed to stand here gaping at a man his age!"

Later Herr Mayer told me that he was glad there were more guests coming on Monday.

"It's not only the business," he said. "But an empty place makes for idleness. And idleness always leads to mischief."

Frau Mayer, who is a dumpy fifty, ought to feel flattered that her husband still considers her capable of mischief.


*Monday, December 7, 1942.*     As I had expected, Horowitz arrived today with the Levys and Eva.

It was late in the afternoon when Levy's car pulled up in front of the hotel. Aronoff and I were sitting at a table near the dining-room window, having coffee. When we heard the sound of voices we both bent forward and looked out.

The first two out of the car were Levy and Horowitz. Together with the chauffeur they immediately began pulling out bundles, packages and suitcases and piling them on the ground. In a minute it looked as if a band of gypsies had descended on the hotel. Herr Mayer rushed outside to greet his new guests and to add to the general confusion.

Next Trude emerged and stood behind the pile of luggage, pulling at a piece of cloth which turned out to be her coat on which the men had heaped the suitcases. Eva was nowhere to be seen. I was beginning to think she had experienced a last-minute change of heart when I saw her rounding the rear of the car.

Aronoff, who up until now had seemed amused by the commotion outside, leaned back and shot me a quick, suspicious glance.

"Did you know they were coming?" he asked.

"Well, yes. Levy mentioned that he might come down with his wife. And Horowitz . . . you know Horowitz! The moment he heard that we were coming he had to come too!"

I did not say anything about Eva and he did not ask. He sat stubbornly with his back to the door and would not even turn around when he heard the party walking in.

Upon discovering me, Horowitz broke into loud jubilation as if he had not seen me for several years. Levy waved briefly, too busy instructing his chauffeur what to do with the luggage to come and shake hands. Trude took one look at me and Aronoff and quickly turned around to glance at Eva, who had come in last.

Eva was wearing slacks and looked fresh even after the long trip in the crowded car. She put down her little overnight bag and came to the table to greet me. When she moved into his field of vision Aronoff gave her what can only be described as a small, hostile smile.

"Oh, you're here too," Eva said to Aronoff as if she had had no idea. "Well, I'd better go and see if Herr Mayer gave me a nice room."

I wonder whether I will ever understand women.

Eating dinner at a table for four with the Levys and Horowitz, Eva turned only once to look in our direction. But Aronoff had sat down with his back to her. He was sullen all evening and hardly said a word on our after-dinner stroll.

The Levys and Eva had already retired to their rooms when we returned, and only Horowitz was sitting in the deserted dining room.

"So, it would have been beneath your dignity to ask me to come along for a walk?" he said.

*Tuesday, December 8, 1942.*　　Now there is a lot of activity around the swimming pool.

Levy and Trude, both equally white-skinned, have already acquired severe sunburns. In the evening they tried to outdo each other, showing off their blisters.

This was my first chance to see Levy minus his clothes. He has spindly legs and a chicken breast but, surprisingly, something of a paunch which never showed beneath his coat.

Trude has not changed much since she was a young girl. A bathing suit is still not the most flattering attire for her.

Horowitz, short, wiry, and with a much better figure than I had expected, has turned out to be a frustrated athlete. He always dives head first into the pool, with more determination than grace, and he has taken to walking on his hands, looking like a trained poodle with his bushy hair standing about his head. If he is out to impress Eva he will soon discover that he has a formidable, though to all appearances unwilling, rival.

After a long time I can again feast my eyes on Eva in a bathing suit. She is more beautiful than ever.

For some reason Aronoff does not seem to enjoy looking at Eva. Perhaps he finds it annoying that his is no longer the only beautiful body around the swimming pool. Only he and Eva stayed in the sun long after all the others had prudently retired, as though engaged in a secret competition.

In the evening they ignored each other again. I am utterly baffled by their behavior.


*Thursday, December 10, 1942.*     I keep remembering the longing glances Eva used to give Aronoff years ago, when he seemed unattainable. Now that he has moved within her orbit, she acts as if she were afraid to reach out for what she really wants. I simply cannot believe that she is as indifferent as she pretends to be.

Yesterday morning she refused to go with the men for a swim in the warm-water pool, pretending that she preferred to stay behind with Trude. In the evening we all went for a walk. It was a dark, moonless night, lit only by the glimmering of countless glowworms. Eva was laughing and flirting with Horowitz, misleading the poor fellow into thinking she was interested in him. Aronoff had walked ahead with

Levy, talking business. Even Trude was puzzled and wondered aloud what Eva was suddenly seeing in Horowitz after all these years.

This morning Herr Mayer told us that there was an even hotter spring to be found a half hour's walk from Aguas Calientes. In a whispered aside he added that it was supposed to have miraculous effects upon a waning virility. Horowitz and Levy immediately set out on a pilgrimage there, accompanied by Trude, who said she wanted to keep her husband from overdoing it.

"Poor Trude, she's afraid she will have to get her maternity clothes out the moment she comes home," Eva said.

With the others gone and the Vogels preferring the sensible shade of the patio to the broiling sun, Eva and Aronoff had the pool to themselves. Eva lay down on the towel she had spread on the tile platform by the pool. Aronoff mounted the diving board at the opposite end of the pool and stretched out flat on his belly, his arms crossed beneath his chin. After about half an hour he got up, raised his arms overhead, and dived into the pool. When he hit the water a column of drops rose into the air and splashed on Eva's back. She squealed in surprise and shook like a cat that had got wet. Then she sat up on her towel and began to rub sun-tan lotion over her exposed skin.

Aronoff had come out at the far end and started on a slow, deliberate stroll around the pool. Just as he passed Eva, she was trying to squirm into a position in which she would be able to oil her back. He watched her struggle for a minute, then without a word he took the lotion bottle from her, shook some of the liquid into the palm of his hand, and began to rub it over her back.

Eva—the same Eva whom I still remembered as flinching from the touch of strangers—sat motionless, with her eyes closed and a little smile about her lips while Aronoff knelt behind her, rubbing her back. He stopped as suddenly as he had started, screwed the top back on the bottle and abruptly handed it to Eva. The little smile around her lips became tinged with irony, and I could imagine the defensive edge of sarcasm in her voice as she thanked him for his assistance.

Dr. Vogel, who also sat watching them, said glumly:

"Don't let him fool you, he's going to make a pass at her."

Not until Dr. Vogel put into words what had been in the back of my mind all the time did it occur to me that I had been acting the part of the matchmaker. My amused detachment gave way to a nagging sense of responsibility. I began to watch Eva and Aronoff for any further physical contact, but they did not go near each other again until evening, when Aronoff sat down to play poker with Levy and Horowitz. It was alarming to see Eva, who had never displayed any interest in cards, watching a game of poker for such a long time.

Later, when we went for our evening walk, I also noticed a slight change in our distribution. This time Trude walked with Horowitz, Eva beside Aronoff, and Levy with me. Once Eva stumbled and Aronoff gripped her arm to steady her. The contact lasted only a second, but it seemed to transmit itself to me like an electrical shock wave.

When we got back to the hotel I did something very foolish. I took Aronoff aside and asked him to let Eva alone.

"What makes you think I am interested in her?" he asked.

"I don't know. You are both young, you are on a vacation, it seems like the natural thing . . ." I stammered in confusion.

"Don't worry. I'm particular about my predecessors," Aronoff said, with unexpected viciousness.

But his remark only added to my worry. Such anger can hardly be caused by indifference.


*Saturday, December 12, 1942.*    Levy has turned into a compulsive handwasher.

It all began last evening when Eva went for a walk in the rain with Aronoff and Levy came to tell me that he was washing his hands. He has not stopped washing his hands since.

When I woke up yesterday morning, the sky was a foamy gray and the mountains were dark blobs behind swirling clouds. Fine, sharp raindrops were piercing tiny holes into the smooth surface of the swimming pool. The frogs were croaking in broad daylight (whatever there was of it) and the mists in the valley had a yellow tinge, as if they had been tainted by the vapors of the warm springs. There was no breeze and the air reeked of sulphur.

At breakfast everybody was glum and irritable. Because of the dampness the women had put up their hair in curlers and wore scarves. Dr. Vogel was trying to hold Herr Mayer responsible for the bad weather.

"What do you want, you were lucky until now!" Herr Mayer said. "This isn't the good season yet. In May I could have guaranteed you sunny skies every day!"

"So you think I wanted to come now?" Levy said. "My wife and her crazy girl friend, *they* had to come! The way they acted you'd think God knows what they would be missing if they didn't come to Aguas Calientes just now!"

Aronoff gave Eva a furtive glance and she flushed slightly.

With nothing else to do, the men sat down to a poker game shortly after breakfast. They played until lunchtime, and when I came down from my afternoon nap the game had already been resumed.

For a while I amused myself watching the players: Dr. Vogel, his small eyes darting quick looks left and right, as if trying to peek at the cards of the other players, agonizing over every bid, calling God as witness to his bad luck, even intimating that his wife, who had objected to his playing, had cast an evil eye upon him; Horowitz, his porcupine hair quivering on his nervously twitching scalp, his complexion turning from red to purple as he continued to lose to Aronoff.

"Look who's winning! Our money he needs! Without our money he wouldn't be able to pay for another meal!"

"Shut up and play, Horowitz."

Aronoff was playing seriously, inscrutably, not even smiling when he won. Every time he raked in a big pot he wore an odd expression, as if he had just proved that man can forge his own luck.

Levy played quietly, only occasionally chewing his nails with quick, nervous bites like a squirrel. The only time he showed real irritation was when Trude looked into his hand.

Except for the bids of the poker players it was very quiet in the dining room. From outside came the croaking of the frogs and the faraway lament of a mule in the rain. Frau Vogel was knitting, trying to make the needles give off an ominously threatening sound, which was lost on her husband. After Levy had snapped at her (they were really and truly married now) Trude retired into a corner to read. Eva sat quietly beside Aronoff and watched the game.

Thus passed a dreary afternoon.

After dinner Horowitz was all for going back to the card game—he must be a masochist—but both Frau Vogel and Trude raised their voices in protest, and Aronoff said he had had enough, he was going for a walk.

"What, in the rain?" Horowitz exclaimed.

"Why not? It's only water, though perhaps not of the invigorating kind which you prefer. Anybody else want to come along?"

"If you'll wait a minute, I'll get a wrap and come with you," Eva said.

We were all so startled by her sudden decision that no one made a remark until after she had left with Aronoff. Horowitz was the first to voice his qualms.

"I should have gone with them. Really, what is a little rain? We should not have let her go out alone with Aronoff. What are people going to say?"

"What people?" Trude said. "We're the only people here."

"I don't think he's going to bite her," Levy said without conviction.

"If you ask me, he's going to make a pass at her. He was just waiting for a chance like this," Dr. Vogel said.

"Look, let's not make something of nothing," I said. "Eva is old enough to defend herself. Besides, it is raining," I added foolishly.

The speculations were dropped for the time being. But after half an hour had gone by and Eva and Aronoff had not returned, Trude began to look thoughtful, Horowitz exasperated, Dr. Vogel slyly triumphant, his wife indignant (as if she had never strayed from the path of virtue), and Levy plainly upset.

"Where are they? What are they doing out in the rain?" he kept repeating as he looked at his watch.

"Levy, for heaven's sake, will you relax?"

"I brought her down here! I'm responsible to her husband! You are my witness, Professor Bernstein: she did not ask my consent! I am washing my hands of this whole business!"

Five minutes later Eva and Aronoff walked in.

My companions in the dining room immediately began to scrutinize them as if they had returned from the execution of a major crime. Was Eva's blouse properly buttoned? Her hair disarranged beneath the scarf?

And Aronoff? Were his pants zippered? Was there lipstick on his face, his shirt collar, his earlobes? Did he look lewd, animated, tired, relaxed, secretive, as if he covered some hidden knowledge of infamy?

Both Eva and Aronoff looked as they always looked, except that they were wet. Eva coolly returned the stares of the reception committee in the dining room and asked:

"Say, what's the matter with you? Did a ghost come in with us?"

Everybody looked away and resumed a strained conversation. But the moment Eva went upstairs to change, Dr. Vogel whispered to me that you could never trust a woman and Levy came to repeat that he was washing his hands, definitely and absolutely.

Aronoff had picked up the magazine which Trude had read in the afternoon and sat down by the open window. But I doubt that he was reading. I strongly suspect that he was just grinning behind the raised magazine.


*Monday, December 14, 1942.*     Yesterday the weather was good again and the hotel guests spent most of their time around the swimming pool, watching Eva and Aronoff. The two seemed to be talking more than before, and Aronoff taught Eva how to swim the width of the pool underwater. But aside from that they showed no signs of familiarity under the vigilant stares of the others.

Today Aronoff confounded the watchdogs by appearing with two horses which he had rented after breakfast to take Eva for a ride. Levy instantly came rushing to me to tell me that he was washing his hands.

"I am responsible for her. Aside from everything else, she might break her neck," he said hopefully.

He made me think of the time before Eva's marriage to Walter, when Herr Kramer had considered himself her guardian. But whereas Herr Kramer had restricted himself to watching Eva as long as she kept within the range of his naked eye, Levy outdid him by borrowing binoculars from Herr Mayer through which he could follow Eva and Aronoff's progress on horseback.

Aronoff had hinted that they wanted to ride up to the crest of one of the lower mountains—a flat-topped, dead volcano covered with low brush which would leave a rider clearly visible—from where they would have a view of the valley below.

In spite of Trude's remonstrances ("Don't act like a fool, Isak, it's none of your business"), Levy, his lips grimly compressed, kept the binoculars trained on the mountains.

"They're nowhere to be seen. I knew the horses were only an excuse so that they could get away together. Ah, here they are. They're heading up the slope. Aronoff is riding ahead. Eva is following him. She's holding on to the reins with both hands. I'm sure she is going to fall and break her neck. Aronoff is way ahead now. He's stopping to wait for her. She is catching up with him."

Thus Levy gave us a blow-by-blow description of their ascent, until Trude angrily snatched the binoculars from him.

"All right, you know now that they're riding up the mountain. What more do you want?"

But the moment Levy turned his back, Trude raised the binoculars to her eyes and began to scan the slope herself. There was an expression of wonder on her face, not unlike that of a child pondering the mysterious origin of a snowstorm within a crystal ball. After all these years she was still impressed by the fact that Eva was everything she was not and did everything she would never dare to do.

Against my will I also found myself looking up at the mountain, but all I could see were two small black dots making their way between the greenery of the shrubs.

I was distracted from the view by Horowitz' acrimonious voice. He had sat down at the foot of my deck chair, facing me. His face was nicely tanned and he did not look bad at all—for Horowitz.

"That's Aronoff for you," he said bitterly. "All the time he wasn't interested in Eva. Even here he did not give her a second glance until he noticed that I was making headway with her. Then he had to have her! He's like a pasha, he can't stand seeing another man get a woman. He has to have them all!"

Horowitz made a sweeping gesture which included Trude, Frau Vogel and, no doubt, even Frau Mayer inside the house. Now at least he was able to blame his failure to impress Eva on Aronoff instead of having to blame it on himself.

*Thursday, December 17, 1942.*    This morning Eva brought Levy to the edge of apoplexy when she announced that she was not going home with him on Saturday.

"But I have to bring you back!" Levy protested. "Remember, Madame Eva, I brought you down here!"

"And I'll never forget it as long as I live, Isak," Eva said. (This was the first time I had heard her call Levy by his first name.) In spite of her effort to sound mocking, her voice was astonishingly sincere, almost tender. She had to be very happy to feel tenderness even for Levy, I thought.

"But how are you going to get back to Esperanza?" Levy asked, as if it were not perfectly clear how Eva was going to get back.

"I'll come home with Professor Bernstein and Aronoff." Eva diplomatically mentioned my name first. "There is no reason why I should rush back if I have a chance to stay another few days."

"And what will I tell your husband?" Levy asked tartly.

"The truth of course," Eva said, with a grin, leaving it to Levy to interpret the truth any way he saw it.

She had barely stepped out of earshot when Levy informed me that he was washing his hands.

"You are my witness, Professor Bernstein! I asked her to go home with us. But if she doesn't want to go, I can't force her. I should never have taken her along in the first place! How am I going to explain to Walter?"

"But you don't have to explain a thing to Walter," I said. "Just tell him the facts. You know what facts are? Things of which you have positive proof."

Levy gave me an indignant look and stalked away.

A little later Trude came to pour out her heart to me.

"Eva shouldn't have done that," she said. "Personally, I don't care what she does, but Isak is furious. He almost made a scene! He says I let myself be used by Eva; that she dragged us down here only because she wanted to run after Aronoff. But I don't believe that Eva would run after anybody, not even Aronoff.

"I wouldn't dare say such a thing in front of Isak," Trude went on, "but in a way I admire Eva's courage. She isn't even trying to conceal what she is doing. What if Walter should kick her out?"

I said that I hardly thought Walter would "kick" Eva out. And even if he should threaten her with a divorce, Eva was no longer dependent on him.

As I talked to Trude, something that had baffled me for the past two years became clear in a sudden flash. I was beginning to understand why Eva had consented to the Schwarzkopf affair.

Some women sold their bodies and souls for clothes, furs and jewelry. Eva had been willing to sell hers—temporarily—in order to gain independence. For she was independent now, not only financially but also morally. There was no need any longer for her to conceal her affairs. If Walter had agreed once on the basis of an exchange, he could not very well object to Eva's venturing out alone without admitting that he had used her. And even if he should object, she could simply leave him. She no longer needed him. If Eva had reached her aim by design —and I was almost sure that she had—it had been a very bold design indeed. Perhaps ruthless would be a better word. If I was appalled by this newly discovered facet of her personality, I was also impressed.

"To tell the truth, Trude," I said, "I am myself admiring Eva for what you call her courage. If her morals are somewhat unconventional, at least she is willing to stand and fall by them."

"That's exactly how I feel," Trude said.

But I am afraid we were thinking of entirely different aspects of Eva's morals.

*Saturday, December 19, 1942.*    This morning Levy left, taking with him all the guests except Eva, Aronoff and me. As soon as the Vogels had learned that Eva was staying behind, they had insinuated—at first slyly and then not so slyly—that Levy give them a ride home. After some hedging Levy had grudgingly consented.

Eva and I sat in front of the hotel, watching the departure. Aronoff had disappeared somewhere on a mysterious errand.

The stowing of all the passengers and their luggage in the car was a complicated affair. This accomplished, Levy came back once more to say good-by and to tell me that he was washing his hands. For Eva he had only a curt nod.

"Remember, Madame Eva, I asked you to come home with us."

"Sure, Isak, you did your duty."

To escape her mockery Levy sprinted toward the car and squeezed into the front seat next to Trude and the chauffeur. The sputtering of the motor drowned out the farewell shouts, and then the car started jolting wildly down the road until it disappeared in a cloud of dust.

"Well, that's that," Eva said. She leaned back in the deck chair and closed her eyes with a smile of contentment.

Ten minutes after the car with the other guests had departed Aronoff returned, asking cautiously whether they had gone.

"Good," he said. "Now we'll have the place to ourselves."

I suppose he included me in this statement, for neither he nor Eva seemed the least bit inhibited by my presence. They spent the rest of the morning at the swimming pool, lying side by side. If they did not talk much it was obviously because there was little need for words between them. Their coming together was as natural as the meeting of two rivers which had meandered over different fields before their waters finally flowed into each other.

After lunch Eva rose first (she now eats at our table), said that she was going to rest for a while, and went upstairs. Soon Aronoff retired too, presumably to join her, though he did not indicate this intention with either a word or a smirk. Still, the young know no hours for love.

In the evening they invited me to join them on their walk. We walked in the dark as we had done on the previous nights, picking our way over the ruts in the road. Eva walked between me and Aronoff. It was too dark for me to tell if they were holding hands, but I think they were, for they moved as one person.

Back in the hotel, Eva was again the first to go upstairs. Aronoff waited a decorous ten minutes and then followed her. He seemed neither lewd nor excited nor animated, and his calm irritated me. I felt tempted to throw his remark about his predecessors up to him, but I checked myself in time.

Now, after practically bringing him together with Eva, I cannot help being jealous of him.

*Tuesday, December 22, 1942.*     No doubt Eva is happy. She shows her happiness in small ways.

Yesterday Herr Mayer mentioned in passing that today was his wife's birthday. Eva went into the village in the afternoon, ostensibly to get a few items from the pharmacy. She soon came back with a rather large parcel wrapped in newspaper.

This morning it turned out that the package had not contained toothpaste and soap but a round earthen bowl, such as the Indians sell in the market place, and a bunch of flowers. Eva had cut the flowers and arranged them artfully so that they looked as if they had just come from an exclusive flower shop. She put this arrangement on Frau Mayer's breakfast table as a birthday present.

Frau Mayer was so touched that she wept. She struggled vainly for some words of gratitude and finally settled on embracing Eva.

"Such a sweet girl," she said to me afterward. "Wasn't it thoughtful of her to get me a surprise? What a pity that she gives people cause for gossip."

Even in her joy Frau Mayer could not forgo a note of censure.

This was the first time I had ever known Eva to make a spontaneous effort to please anyone, especially a virtual stranger. Her action gave meaning to David's phrase: my cup runneth over.

I began to look at Aronoff with new respect. How had he been able to succeed in such a short time where the others had failed? How had he made her cup run over so that some of her happiness even spilled on Frau Mayer?


*Thursday, December 24, 1942.*     I have almost forgotten about my heart trouble. No doubt the difference in altitude between Esperanza and Aguas Calientes is having its effect. Although I accompanied Eva and Aronoff on a long walk today, I felt hardly tired when I returned to the hotel.

We have only another two days left, and the young people wanted to make the most of them by visiting the hot sulphur spring to which

Levy and Horowitz had made their devout pilgrimage. (Horowitz would have said with bitter glee that even Aronoff was beginning to feel the need for its invigorating powers, but as it turned out he went only to look, not to bathe.)

Herr Mayer had warned me that the path to the spring was narrow, running uphill all the way, and suggested that I hire a mule to take me there. But my last experience with mules is still so vivid in my mind that I preferred to trust to the power of my own two legs.

Eva and Aronoff walked very slowly on my account. Though the air was clear, it was heavy with the dampness peculiar to Aguas Calientes and its surroundings. The blue of the sky and the lush green of the cone-shaped mountains seemed to lie behind the haze of a fine gauze curtain. There had been no rain since the day Eva and Aronoff took their first walk together, and the ocher-colored earth of the narrow path was hard and crusty. As we made our slow ascent we gradually left the eucalyptus trees and weeping willows behind. Presently the only vegetation was bushes with tiny yellow blossoms. They gave off a heady perfume which was blotted out by the sharp fumes of sulphur as we got nearer our destination.

After the next bend in the road we came to the place from which the unpleasant smell originated. The path we had followed suddenly declined sharply, leading with a few, crudely hewn steps down to what looked like a depression among the surrounding hills—a hole as if the earth had been sucked in by a mysterious force. At the lowest point of the depression we saw a small pool, perhaps twelve by fifteen feet, filled with a yellow liquid not unlike that in the warm pool in Aguas Calientes. Only here the liquid seemed denser and more violently agitated, burping up thick bubbles which exploded on the surface of the pool. Here and there the water churned like a miniature whirlpool, shooting up thin columns of vapor. The air smelled like rotten eggs.

"This," Eva said, "is definitely the bottom of hell! And to think that men come here to stimulate their virility!"

Aronoff curled his lips, as if the whole idea were ludicrous. He was, no doubt, still at the height of his brutal young strength, and I almost felt sorry for him when I thought that someday his moment of disappointment would come as it came for all of us.

Except for an Indian couple there were no people in the pool. The Indians had piled their clothes on the ground beside the pool, and they watched us with expressionless, dark eyes, obviously afraid we might snatch away their belongings while they were bathing. The woman had opened her long hair and it was floating on the water. I wondered when she had last taken a bath or washed her hair before immersing herself in a public pool, and I could tell from Eva's grimace that she had similar thoughts. She remained standing beside me while Aronoff climbed down the steps, surefooted as a goat, to stick one finger into the yellow water.

"Come on down and try it!" he called up to us. "It's boiling hot!"

"No, thank you!" Eva called back. "I'll wait until after I'm dead!"

Aronoff climbed up to us and we started back for the hotel. The descent went faster than the trek uphill. We walked in single file most of the time and there was little conversation. Still, I noticed that Eva and Aronoff did not address each other by their first names in my presence and that they phrased whatever they had to say in such a manner as to avoid the familiar "thou." They seemed to be clinging to some private rules of discretion, but occasionally Eva dropped her guard as she looked at him, and I could see that she was very much in love. I could not tell about Aronoff. But for some reason it did not seem to matter.

# Part Seven ❧ Leave-Taking

*And God spake unto Noah, saying,*
*Go forth of the ark, thou,*
*and thy wife, and thy*
*sons' wives with thee.*

GENESIS 8:15, 16

*Sunday, January 3, 1943.*    A new year has begun and with it our colony in Esperanza has gained a new topic of conversation.

It seems that in spite of all his hand-washing Levy has been unable to keep from spreading his version of the truth (which, incidentally, happens to be the truth).

Dr. Landau's second question upon seeing me (his first had been a reluctant inquiry about my health and a grudging admission that apparently the money for my vacation had been well spent) was whether what he had heard was indeed true. Had Aronoff finally worked his way around to Eva Kramer?

I suggested that Dr. Landau go ask Aronoff, who was certainly as handy for information and, no doubt, better informed than I was.

My next questioner was not to be put off so easily. I had hardly finished eating my breakfast the day after our return from Aguas Calientes when Walter Kramer walked in on me.

"You knew it all the time!" he said accusingly. "All the time we were talking about Eva's trip to Aguas Calientes, you knew that Aronoff was also going there! You might at least have warned me!"

"There was nothing to warn you about then," I said, adding quickly, "and I doubt that there is anything now."

"Good God, Professor Bernstein, you are almost a freak with your old-fashioned discretion. I don't see why you should deny something which Eva does not try to hide!"

"You might be misinterpreting Eva's behavior . . ."

"Unfortunately, she didn't give me a chance to misinterpret her behavior. When I told her that I wouldn't tolerate this . . . escapade, she didn't even deny my accusations. She just said I could not stop her. And what's more, she is right too. I can't stop her. If I divorced her now, people would say that Walter Kramer will close an eye only when he can get something in exchange. You know what they'll call me? A pimp!"

Oh, how clever she was, I thought. Had she herself suggested the word? But then I remembered the mellow mood in which Eva had been lately. She felt safe now. There was no need for her to hurt other people. Somebody else must have thrust this lance into Walter.

"If at least I could know that he will marry her in the end," Walter said.

"What makes you so sure that he won't?"

"Not Aronoff! Everybody knows that he has a rich bride waiting for him in the States. The moment the war is over he is going to leave Esperanza and forget Eva. There's no doubt in anybody's mind about that!"

I asked Walter whether it had ever occurred to him that all those people who pretended to be so well-informed about Aronoff's plans were people who hardly knew him.

"How can people be so sure that Aronoff will do thus and thus if probably he himself has no idea what he is going to do?" I said to Walter.

"Just you wait and see," Walter said gloomily.

In a way it endeared him to me that he should be worrying about Eva's future happiness, though she herself seemed perfectly satisfied with the present.


*Sunday, January 10, 1943.* Not much news from the home front, but events have been moving in Europe since we left for Aguas Calientes.

Goldmann derives great personal satisfaction from the assassination of Admiral Darlan, whom he never trusted ("The old collaborator, the cur!"), at the end of December. To the rest of us it is a much greater source of satisfaction that the Russians are inflicting one defeat after the other on the Germans. By now the Russians have again retaken Kharkov and have finally broken the siege of Leningrad after seventeen months. Goldmann says for sure this year by June . . . God willing. It is really high time.


*Friday, January 15, 1943.* Walter's skeptical attitude toward Eva and Aronoff—just you wait and see—is one which generally prevails.

Today Frau Goldmann said wasn't it a shame about Eva, and why now when Walter was doing so well? (Which confirms my old suspicion that women consider it only half a sin if a wife is unfaithful to a husband who is unable to support her in style.) Later in the day Dr. Lipschitz remarked that it was really unfortunate that his brother-in-law should be married to a nymphomaniac. And the worst part of it was that Aronoff would not marry Eva. (As if, by marrying her, he could wipe the blot off the family honor.)

In the evening when I came out of the assembly hall in the Centro I almost bumped into Frau Katja.

She must have read surprise in my face at meeting her in the Centro, for she informed me defiantly that she and her husband were having dinner with the Fleischers.

Taking my arm so I could not escape her, she steered me toward their table. Her husband's eyes were fixed on some distant spot in the room, and his gaze was so intent that I turned to see what he was staring at. I discovered Eva sharing a table with Trude. Once her eyes met Schwarzkopf's and she gave him a pleasant and impersonal smile, which must have hurt him more than complete indifference. But suddenly her expression changed, and I saw that Aronoff had come in.

He looked around and his eyes also lit up briefly when he saw Eva, but immediately clouded over as if he had given away a secret. He stopped at her table, said a few words, and then proceeded toward the card room without sitting down. I could see that they were still obeying their own rules of discretion.

But Frau Katja seemed to interpret Aronoff's display of coolness otherwise.

"I know all about him! He'll make her pay for the suffering she caused other people!"

If Frau Katja seemed pleased with the image of Aronoff as executioner, her husband appeared more concerned with the suffering he was causing him now than with the suffering he supposedly was going to cause Eva. When we got closer to the table, I noticed that Schwarzkopf squirmed as he listened to Fleischer discoursing freely on Eva's love life. Finally he could no longer take the suggestive talk and rose with tears in his eyes and retired to his last place of refuge, the bathroom.

"Don't get upset, Otto!" his wife called after him. "He'll teach her a lesson!"

"Oh, shut up," Schwarzkopf mumbled gruffly, and Fleischer looked pleased with all the unpleasantness he had instigated.

I excused myself and fled to Eva's table. She greeted me with her new warmth and pushed a chair over for me to sit down. I was conscious of all the people in the room looking in our direction and whispering, but Eva seemed oblivious of the new ripples of indignation she was causing. This time she simply is just too happy to care.

*Wednesday, January 27, 1943.*    Now that Eva and Aronoff have finally come together, there is hardly anything worth reporting left in Esperanza. All the news—and, thank God, it is good news for a change—comes from the war theaters.

President Roosevelt and Winston Churchill have announced that during their conference in Casablanca they worked out plans for an Allied offensive this year which should secure the unconditional surrender of the Axis powers. So far this is only a promise, and yet we feel as if the walls confining us in Esperanza were slowly being pushed back. We don't dare talk too much about it, but most of us still want out.

*Monday, February 8, 1943.*    More good news from the war: the Russians have forced twenty-two German divisions to capitulate, the first major German debacle in this war. It warms our hearts. And yesterday General Eisenhower, in whom we have developed great confidence, was appointed commander of the theater of operations in North Africa. We hope that any day now the invasion of Europe will begin.

*Saturday, February 20, 1943.*    I have gone back to the routine I kept before my heart attack, among other things resuming my position as treasurer for the Centro and the Zionists. With the accounting I do for Goldmann, this provides me with a semblance of activity.

Dr. Landau no longer objects to my taking walks and even permits me to navigate stairs at a snail's pace. Frau Steinberg cooks for me what she calls a "special diet," which tastes even viler than what she puts before her other boarders. I try to find respite from her kindness by having myself invited to other people's houses, but now I eat with moderation even if the food is most tempting.

Wednesdays I still lunch with Señora Consuelo. Nothing has changed in Josef's house. Like the castle of the Sleeping Beauty, it has fallen asleep with his death. Señora Consuelo still wears deep mourning, with only the silver crucifix around her neck to break the monotony of her black clothes. Even Ruth Lipschitz has stopped asking when she will get married again. (Though a little while ago Frau Kramer suggested that I might marry her. "After all, she was married to a Jew for such a long time, she's practically Jewish herself!" As if this were the most valid inducement for marriage.)

At our last lunch together I asked Señora Consuelo if she would never come out of mourning. I felt that our long acquaintance gave me the right to ask such a question.

"If you mean will I remarry," Señora Consuelo said, with startling comprehension, "I never will. Not unless I could find another husband like José, which is impossible. And to marry one of my own countrymen—no. Todos nuestros hombres no valen. All our men are no good. The husbands of my sisters . . . my own brother . . . all philanderers. They have a wife to bear them children and a mistress for their pleasure. I could not live like that. Los Judios son marídos buenos. Jews are good husbands. A woman needs to be respected by her man to be able to respect herself. Para respetárse a si misma," she said.

*Tuesday, March 2, 1943.*     Yesterday I had lunch with Eva and Walter. They seemed on the friendliest of terms, as if, after all this time, they finally knew where they stood. There is no longer any emotional tie between them, not even the complicity which bound them together during the Schwarzkopf affair. Their relations have become casual and comradely. But Walter still takes pride in the possession—if in name only—of a beautiful wife.

Don had wandered into the sala after lunch, and Eva rose to chase him out. When she returned she stood for a moment on the sunny terrace outside the door. Once again it struck me that daylight, which is not kind to most women, was really the most felicitous illumination for her. Her hair gleamed, her skin had a golden glow, and her eyes were incredibly blue.

"Love has made her very beautiful," Walter said wistfully, as if he regretted that he had never been able to bring out that glow. "Maybe I'm a fool for not giving her up, but I am one of those people who love having beautiful things around them. It gives me pleasure just to look at her."

I thought this was perhaps the best kind of pleasure a man could derive from a beautiful woman: a pleasure wholly devoid of pain, like the pleasure one gets from looking at a lovely painting.

*Saturday, March 13, 1943.*    The war is going well for us. The Germans have lost some of their holdings in Tunisia, and yesterday we learned from the newspapers that the winter offensive in Russia cost them more than 500,000 men.

"Half a million criminals less, may the Russians tear them limb from limb," Goldmann says.

*Sunday, March 21, 1943.*    Yesterday there was a Purim ball in the Centro.

Eva and Aronoff set a precedent by appearing together. Eva wore her white gown and looked happy. People kept staring at them as they danced together all night. Those who were benevolent said they made a beautiful couple. Those who were malevolent said it would not last. So far it has lasted four months.

The Schwarzkopfs came with the Fleischers. Rumors have it that Walter is about to sell out his share in the factory to Fleischer. Some people already whisper that the Fleischers have taken over the former roles of Eva and Walter. But this substitute does not seem to have lessened Frau Katja's hatred for Eva. As the evening wore on, she looked ready to throw another bottle at her. Fortunately, Eva and Aronoff left early.

Watching them, Trude said fervently:

"I hope to God he marries her! They would have such beautiful children."

*Wednesday, April 7, 1943.*    Eva and Aronoff continue to conduct their affair without any regard to the rumors around them. They are seen riding together in Aronoff's car, going to the movies, and frequenting cafés other than the Jungle Café.

But they do not always resort to public meeting places.

When I came home from lunch with Señora Consuelo today, I saw a dog lying on Aronoff's doorstep. His muzzle was covered with his paws and I thought he was fast asleep, but when I approached, his tail began to beat out the rapid tattoo of recognition.

It was Don.

*Friday, April 16, 1943.* Had lunch today in Trude's house. Levy is still sputtering with indignation at the mere mention of Eva's name.

"She used us. She uses everybody. If you ask me, a very dangerous woman!"

"Oh, stop talking nonsense, Isak! You make her out a regular Lucrecia Borgia!"

Levy did not argue the point, whether because he was not sure who Lucrecia Borgia was or not to upset Trude in her condition, I don't know. It seems that the miracle-working sulphur spring in Aguas Calientes has had a belated effect. Trude is pregnant again.

I hope, for Levy's sake, that this time it will be a boy.

*Thursday, April 22, 1943.* It seems incredible that it should be Passover again, our fourth in Esperanza. I celebrated both Seders with the Kramers, as always. The entire family was assembled, even Eva and Walter.

Eva was composed, polite, and a little supercilious, as if she were granting a royal favor by her presence. Walter's family has now reached a point at which they look at Eva not so much with hatred as with a dull awe.

*Friday, May 7, 1943.* I seem to have lost all impetus for writing. There is really very little to report. The war in Russia has reached a stalemate, and in Africa "we" have already won. Last month there was a flurry of excitement when President Roosevelt visited Avila Camacho in Mexico, and some people began to speculate whether he would also come to El Paramo. But what reason on earth would Roosevelt have for visiting El Paramo?

My life is all routine now, with my morning strolls (fortunately we are again in the glory of the dry season), my afternoon visits to the Centro, my bookkeeping, my weekly lunches with Señora Consuelo, and my habitual tea chats in Horowitz' back room. I have traced the beginning of this apathy back to the first months of Eva's affair with Aronoff. Since then I feel as if a certain tension had gone out of my life. There is nothing left to wait for, though the others are still waiting for the end of the affair.

*Sunday, May 16, 1943.* Today I felt ambitious and cleaned out my desk. I came across the application blank for the American visa. The empty spaces among the small print glared at me accusingly. I never did fill out the application, though somewhere in Washington my name is on a waiting list for a quota number.

I also found a letter I had begun to write. "Most esteemed Professor Einstein, you probably don't remem . . ." I tore it up, but I kept the visa application blank. One never knows.

We all seem to be waiting for the invasion of Europe. For a miracle. For some new beginning. We have been waiting all these years, but now the feeling has become intensified.

I also listen for grumblings in my heart. But all is quiet.

*Monday, May 24, 1943.* My notebook is almost filled and there is space left for only a brief entry.

Yesterday the Third International was dissolved. Horowitz, who has long ceased talking about Communism, unexpectedly came in for quite a bit of ribbing in the Centro.

"Well, Comrade Horowitz, you're entirely on your own now. No more directions from Moscow on how to get rich in Esperanza!"

Horowitz only glowered at his tormentors and then turned his back on them, as if he considered it beneath his dignity to answer.

*Monday, August 9, 1943.*    I have let more than three months pass without making a single entry. Running out of writing space in my last notebook was only a poor excuse for my sloth. I put off buying a new book until I finally managed to forget all about it.

Perhaps my inertia was also caused by the fact that there has been only good news for the past few months. Strange that good news makes so much duller reporting than bad news.

Although the Germans attempted a new summer offensive in Russia, they were weakened by their great losses and soon their advance was stayed. Early in July Allied forces invaded Sicily, half of which they occupy by now. Later in July Mussolini was forced to resign and Marshal Badoglio declared the Fascist party dissolved. The jubilation in Esperanza was beyond description, with everybody shouting "Hitler next!"

Here at home the weather was splendid, and I was able to spend a lot of time out of doors. My heart gives me no trouble and I have resumed all my old activities. I go for my daily strolls, and often when I return I find Don lying on Aronoff's doorstep. Now that the novelty of the affair has worn off and people do not pay so much attention to her, Eva seems happier than ever. And yet she must know that this cannot go on forever. But perhaps she does not care. Perhaps she has the good sense to be satisfied with her moment of happiness.

It is hard to say what made me sit down today and break the lazy spell of the past three months. Perhaps it is apprehension. This morning Herr Kramer mentioned to me that tomorrow is Tisha B'ab, the great day of mourning. I remember that in recent years it has fallen in a period of disasters.

But everything seems to be serene just now, and perhaps I am just superstitious.


*Saturday, August 14, 1943.*    My foreboding was not without justification. This morning Horowitz burst into my room, bristling with excitement and glee.

"I knew it, I knew it, I knew it!" he cried. "It just had to happen and it did!"

"What?" I asked.

"He's leaving! Aronoff is leaving!"

"Don't go spreading foolish rumors, Horowitz! You know Aronoff will not leave before the war is over."

"This time it's no rumor. I have it from the most reliable source: Aronoff himself. I wanted to place an order for some merchandise, and he told me he could not accept any more orders, he was leaving in a few weeks."

Although I pretended not to believe Horowitz, I did not doubt for a moment that he had spoken the truth. I had myself been expecting this event from day to day, but somehow I had always connected it with the end of the war. (The end of the war would necessarily mean the beginning of a new era for all of us. All excuses for staying on in Esperanza would be removed, and we would have to decide whether we wanted to remain of our own volition or go elsewhere.) But Aronoff has made his decision ahead of us. Why is he in such a hurry?

All through lunch my eyes kept wandering to him. I had come to take him for granted as one of my table companions. I would miss him.

He must have noticed my staring, for once or twice he raised his eyebrows, and after lunch he moved over to my side and asked if anything was troubling me.

"Is it true?"

He understood my question, and I could feel the curtain coming down over the secret compartment of his mind. I knew I would get nothing but impersonal answers.

"Yes, I'm leaving," he said.

"Why now? I always thought you were willing to sit out the war in Esperanza."

"The war will soon be over."

"But it might still last long enough for you to be drafted."

"That is a chance I will have to take."

"What difference would another few months make now?"

"There are things which cannot be put off forever," Aronoff said crossly.

"Like the girl who is waiting for you to marry her? You are going to get married, aren't you?"

He glared at me as if I had asked him an insolent question, but instead of the sharp reply I had expected he said:

"I never broke off my engagement."

He did not sound happy. I wondered whether he chose to leave because he was afraid that if he did not leave now he would never leave.

I wanted to ask him if he was running away from Eva; if he had finally fallen in love with her. But I doubt that in all Esperanza there was one person who would ask Aronoff such a question—perhaps not even Eva herself.

"Only a few more weeks, isn't it?" I asked.

"Yes. And I still have a lot of business to wind up."

Nothing about how sorry he was to leave. I suppose he talks like that to everybody. People will gloat and say they knew it all the time, just like Horowitz. Eva does not mean a thing to Aronoff. He is leaving her.

But I am convinced that they are all wrong. Aronoff is not leaving Eva. He is leaving because of her.


*Friday, August 20, 1943.* Now that Aronoff's impending departure has become common knowledge, everybody's curiosity is again focused on Eva. How will she take it?

Most people can judge the reactions of others only by the reactions of which they themselves are capable. Especially the women. Frau Katja seems to expect Eva's complete disintegration. Possibly she hopes that Eva may kill herself. Frau Fleischer, who has had her share of amorous adventures in life, shrugs and says Eva will get over it; one always does. Trude has confided the secret hope that at the last minute Eva will run off with Aronoff. Obviously she has retained a romantic heart inside her enormous, pregnant body. Frau Braun says that there is always a price to be paid for happiness, but if it is real happiness it does not matter. Frau Goldmann just casts her eyes heavenward and asks what the younger generation is coming to and whether men have lost all sense of honor. The entire Kramer family, male and female Lipschitzes included, are of the opinion that it serves Eva right.

The men, on the other hand, seem to speculate mainly on who is going to be the next one. Horowitz has gone and ordered himself two suits of hard-to-get British wool. This might be strictly accidental, but I don't think that it is.

Only the person who has caused all the guesswork—Eva—is as serene as if nothing were about to happen. She acts as if she had never heard that Aronoff was leaving. But perhaps she simply puts off facing reality.

*Wednesday, August 25, 1943.*    Strangely enough, Walter seems more troubled than Eva by the fact that his wife's lover is leaving. Today, once again, he voiced his misgivings about Eva's future.

"What is going to become of her? She can't just keep on drifting from man to man. If you ask me, Aronoff is an idiot for not marrying her. She loves him. But perhaps he can't appreciate what that means," Walter said, with regret.

Walter might also be worried over how Aronoff's departure will affect his own home life. By now he must have become used to a marriage of convenience, with a wife who is just a beautiful fixture and a good housekeeper, but who leaves him to lead his own life as he pleases. There was nothing wrong with his acting the libertine while Eva was having an open affair, but once she returns to the fold of domesticity, Walter might feel cramped in his new freedom.

*Sunday, September 5, 1943.*    Only four days left until Aronoff's departure.

Eva has gone into complete seclusion. I used to meet her occasionally in the Centro or shopping along the Avenida Bolívar, but now the only sign of her existence is Don, lying cross-pawed on the doorstep of Aronoff's garden house. I have yet to see Eva arriving or leaving, but I know that she is in there.

*Wednesday, September 8, 1943.*    Aronoff has said good-by to me. He is to leave early tomorrow morning by plane.

After dinner he came to my room and sat on the window sill. He appeared ill at ease and kept getting up and sitting down again, picking up an ashtray here, a book there on his short, erratic strolls. I felt that he had been brought only by some vague sense of duty and that he wished he could find words which would speed his departure. I tried to help him.

"All packed?" I asked.

"Yes, all packed. There wasn't too much to pack, anyway. I sold most of my stuff. My suits were getting too small for me, and I'm going to buy new ones when I get to the States. All I really need I'm carrying right here."

He tapped his fingers against his left breast pocket, which bulged with what must have been his papers and his checkbook, but for a moment I was misled into thinking that he was pointing at his heart.

"Well, I guess I'd better say good-by now," he said.

He came toward me with his hand outstretched and I took it. Since we had been living in the same house and our comings and goings had always been casual, this was the first—and probably the last—time that I had occasion to shake hands with him. His grip was firm, and my regret at seeing him leave was joined by the faint, physical pain of the pressure on my hand. I was surprised at the strength of his long, white fingers.

"Well, good-by," he repeated, for there was little else to say.

I could feel his fingers relaxing their grip on my hand, but I would not let go yet. For a moment, as we looked at each other, his eyes seemed to grow misty, as if some of his feelings had welled up from the secret compartment. I felt myself growing emotional, and quite without intending to I asked him:

"Will I see you again?"

"Of course! I'll be coming back from time to time."

"For a man my age and in my condition that is small guarantee that I will see you again."

"Don't talk nonsense," he said, almost gruffly, "you'll live to be a hundred and twenty."

I wondered where he had picked up this typically Jewish prediction. Perhaps from Grushka around the poker table.

"I hope you'll visit us soon," I said.

"I hope so too."

"I'll miss you. Others will miss you too."

There was no need for either of us to mention Eva.

"Well, good-by once more," Aronoff said and I let go of his hand.

He turned and walked out of the room without looking back. There was something quite definite about his leaving. I am almost sure he will never come back here.


*Friday, September 17, 1943.* Neither death nor parting can make time stand still. The hours turn into days and the days roll by. It is over a week now since Aronoff left.

We still talk about him around the table. Frau Steinberg enumerates the dishes he liked to eat, lacing her account with lamentations that now she would never again get rid of the garden house. Dr. Landau says he enjoyed seeing Aronoff across the table; his good looks gave him hope for the future of the Jewish race. Even Horowitz grudgingly admits that he misses him.

"Aronoff was the one person who could get you any kind of merchandise you wanted. He had a good Jewish head on his shoulders. More sehel than a rich man's son usually has."

On the other hand, Horowitz said, he was glad that Aronoff was gone.

We all know what he means by "on the other hand." But Eva seems to have vanished from the face of the earth. It must be close to three weeks now since I saw her last. Sometimes I feel the urge to visit her, but I would not know how to explain such an impromptu visit and I keep putting it off.


*Thursday, September 23, 1943.* Now that Aronoff has gone and Eva has retired into seclusion, we talk again mainly about politics. With every Allied victory we feel as if the walls surrounding us in Esperanza were being pushed back a bit farther.

Early this month the Badoglio regime surrendered unconditionally, but Mussolini, who had been held a prisoner near Rome, escaped and established a separate Fascist government, backed by the German army of occupation. Though the Allied forces have almost reached Naples, the Germans still hold Rome and cities north of it. It seems that now, with winter approaching, the war in Italy is far from over. We—by this I mean the Austrian Jews—cannot wait to see the Allied armies crossing the border into Austria.

Goldmann, who is as powerful an armchair strategist as ever, has developed this new theory:

"You'll remember what I said: the way the Russians have been advancing, they'll be in Vienna before the Americans ever get there!"

Most of us do not care who gets there first, as long as they drive the Nazis out. With all the interest we take in the war, the climax of our revenge still remains the liberation of Vienna—even for those who do not have the slightest thought of returning there.

*Saturday, October 2, 1943.*    I was sorely disappointed not to see Eva for Rosh Hashana. I had expected to meet her at the Kramers', but this year the Kramers suddenly decided to celebrate the holidays in the house of their daughter, and Dr. Lipschitz, who has the memory of an elephant and does not easily forget a grudge (dating back to the time when he came to me for advice in the Schwarzkopf affair), did not ask me. In the end I was only too glad to accept an invitation to the Brauns', instead of spending a dull holiday with Frau Steinberg and Dr. Landau.

I saw Walter in the synagogue, but I had no chance to go near him and ask about Eva. It is now so long since I have seen her that I am beginning to be seriously worried.

*Sunday, October 10, 1943.*    Another Yom Kippur gone by.

The rain poured down all day and I did not even go to temple. I spent the time in my room, fasting, headachy, wallowing in reminiscences which the rainy weather always seems to bring out in me. I thought a lot about Josef. He has been dead for three years now. I also thought about my burial plot staked out next to his.

In the afternoon Dr. Landau dropped in on me. Though he does not keep any other holiday, he always fasts on Yom Kippur. None of us can completely break with tradition. We talked about our experiences in Esperanza as if we had been living here for the past hundred years. He asked in passing whatever had become of Eva Kramer. I said I had no idea. She is still invisible.

*Friday, October 22, 1943.*    Today I met Walter in the Centro. He has recently sold his part in the factory to the Fleischers, but he is still busy and hardly finds time to speak to his former friends. More and more often I notice the sign Walter Kramer, Arquitecto, on the new structures that I pass on my morning stroll. Walter is slowly getting to be *the* architect in Esperanza.

I waved him over to my table, but even before he sat down he told me that he had only a few minutes and that he must be off presently. I told him all I wanted to know was how Eva was.

Walter shook his head with a puzzled air.

"I'll be damned if I understand her," he said. "After living with her for so long, I still don't know a thing about her. I thought that she was just keeping up a brave front and that she would go to pieces after Aronoff left. But no . . . Her mood seems pleasant enough, her appetite good, and she keeps herself busy around the house. The only thing is that she refuses to go anyplace."

"Perhaps she wants to give herself time to forget," I said.

"I wish I was sure she *wants* to forget," Walter said. "I only hope she isn't just sitting at home because that is the best place to nurture her memories. My God, she's only twenty-one! I wish something would happen to jolt her out of her unnatural complacency. Anything would do, even a minor earthquake!"

Sometimes I think Walter's many shortcomings are completely canceled out by his astounding loyalty.

*Sunday, November 7, 1943.*    Walter's wish has come true, though fortunately not in the form of an earthquake. Last night Trude gave birth to a boy!

If nothing else, this should be enough to lure Eva out of her seclusion. I cannot imagine that she would not visit her old friend to congratulate her on the happy event. Besides, there is the circumcision coming up next week. Levy intends to throw a party to end all parties. He says he is going to dispense with invitations and just hold open house.

"Anybody at all who wants to attend is welcome! There will be plenty of food and drink. No one should say that Isak Levy is a tightwad when it comes to celebrating the birth of his son!"

Whatever people have called Levy, I doubt that anybody ever called him a tightwad. Stinginess is certainly not one of his faults. I am sure that there will be enough food to satisfy a hungry battalion, and enough spirits to enebriate a horde of sailors who have not seen land for months.

Perhaps Eva will use the occasion to make her first public appearance.

*Sunday, November 14, 1943.*    What a party!

I would have enjoyed it even more if Dr. Landau had not followed me around like a bloodhound, lecturing me on every clandestine bite of food I tried to sneak into my mouth.

But more than the food I enjoyed mingling with all the people. The crowd was in high spirits, with no trace of the somber mood that had been the undercurrent at the circumcision of the Braun boy three years ago. Then the war and our emigration had been in their early, bitter stages.

The entire Jewish colony of Esperanza seemed to be present, everybody who could have been expected, and even some unexpected guests. Grushka, the smuggler, and Brody, the master of the Jungle Café, looked a little out of place, but the one who really created a stir when he walked in was Rudi Brueck. He had accidentally passed the house, had seen all the people entering, and upon his inquiry had been told that Levy was holding open house with free food and drink for everybody. This was all the inducement Rudi needed to join the party.

Still wearing his old sports jacket, patched at the elbows with leather hearts, he looked somewhat odd among the dressed-up guests, but he could not have been more at ease if he had been wearing a morning suit. He got drunk in due course and began to belt out some of his ribald student songs. Levy wanted to throw him out, but Trude argued that he was contributing to the entertainment, and with such a mentor Rudi was allowed to stay.

It was strictly Trude's day, and the circumcision of her son seemed incidental rather than the cause of the party. People kept congratulating her on the birth of a male heir as if Levy and the miracle-working sulphur spring in Aguas Calientes had had nothing to do with the event. This time Trude had recovered swiftly from her accouchement, and though still rotund she moved freely among her guests. On her simple, navy-blue dress she wore a large, new diamond pin, which seemed to cause disquiet among the ladies.

In the meantime Rudi, his spirits rising by the minute, cornered me and whispered at the top of his voice how disappointed he was that I had never visited him at his place of employment. Fortunately the attention of the other guests was distracted just then by the arrival of Eva.

There was a faint ripple near the entrance, and the heads of the people at the far end of the room turned like leaves swung in the same direction by a breeze. With the perception of the alert hostess Trude began heading toward the door, and as a path opened for her, I could see Eva walk in. Walter was beside her, lightly holding her arm, and seeing them walk so close together seemed almost indecent. The smiles on the faces of some of the people were barely above a snicker, but nobody really did snicker—whether out of respect for their hostess, whose friend Eva was, out of respect for Walter, who had now attained a certain position of prominence, or simply because Eva looked so beautiful, I cannot say. I remembered how self-conscious she had been as a young girl, at a time when there had been no doubt about the impeccability of her reputation, and I marveled at her composure now that she faced all those people who questioned her conduct. If she had been cocky before, she was sure of herself now.

Trude fairly beamed as she walked arm in arm with Eva about the room. What I found most remarkable was that even those ladies who had severely criticized Eva did not try to cut her. Perhaps they secretly envied her the courage to do what they only dreamed of doing. I noticed that she did not stay too long with any one group, as if she wanted to inoculate herself in small doses after her long abstinence from people.

Several times I saw Horowitz, in one of his new suits, beating a path through the crowd to Eva's side. She seemed amiable enough as she talked with him, but apparently would not be induced to join him at the bar.

Later, when the crowd had thinned out and only the intimate friends of the family remained, I found a moment alone with her. We stood at the window, our backs toward the room, looking out at the mountains.

"Have you heard from Aronoff?" I asked.

She shook her head.

"No. We decided not to write each other."

She spoke calmly, and yet she sounded as if she had said she had decided to cut off one arm. I was so shocked that by sheer reflex I asked her if she was all right.

"Oh, I'm fine," she said. "I just keep telling myself that I won't be seeing him today, but I'll see him tomorrow. This way the passing days seem less hopeless."

I could not imagine that she should be satisfied for long in such a make-believe world.

"Do you think this is wise, Eva?" I asked.

"No," she said, "but it works. I'll worry about the wisdom of it later on."

Walter is right. She is an enigma.


*Saturday, November 27, 1943.*     Today was Norma's third birthday. Trude decided to give her a big birthday party, the second party in her house this month.

"After Robertito's circumcision, and with everybody gushing over how pretty Yvonne is, I just couldn't let Norma's birthday pass quietly. Poor thing, she feels so neglected."

Trude, well established, loved and contented now, has still not forgotten how it feels to be an ugly duckling. Looking at Eva sitting cross-legged on the floor between her two daughters, she shook her head and sighed.

"It seems like such a waste."

I could not tell whether she meant Eva's beauty or the fact that Eva had no children of her own.

*Wednesday, December 8, 1943.*     We are going through another period of dull waiting.

The war, which promised to be over soon after the invasion of Italy, drags on. Perhaps now, after the Teheran Conference, we will soon see the opening of a second front in Europe. (Goldmann keeps insisting on June.)

Sometimes the boredom becomes suffocating. The daily rains severely restrict my activities.

*Friday, December 17, 1943.*     I am perplexed at myself for having consented to go to Aguas Calientes in the middle of the rainy season. This time I do not even have the excuse of taking the trip for the sake of my health. I suppose what lured me into the project was simply my vanity.

Yesterday afternoon I met Eva in the Centro. She has gone back to what might be called a normal life. She no longer keeps to herself, and I understand that she has even volunteered to help with the bazaar which the Women's Federation has planned for this month.

As always, I felt a little jolt of joy at coming upon her unexpectedly. I was pleased that she should disengage herself from a group of ladies and come to join me at my table. For a while we talked about insignificant matters. The weather (we have a particularly abominable rainy season this year) and dutifully about my health. But all the time Eva appeared distracted as she stared out the window beyond which hung the rain in gray, depressing monotony. Though the Centro was quite crowded, the air in the room felt damp and raw.

Suddenly Eva said:

"How would you like to come with me to Aguas Calientes?"

The invitation came as such a surprise that I did not question her motives for wanting to go there.

"Now, in the middle of the rainy season?"

"It can't be worse there than it is here! At least it will be warm there, and if we're lucky we might even get a few hours of sun every day."

"And how do you propose that we get there?" I asked, interested in spite of myself.

"We can rent a taxi. I talked to some people who did, and it isn't nearly as expensive as I thought it would be."

I could see that she had already planned all the details and I uneasily remembered Levy's constant chant that Eva was using people. But what could she possibly want with—and from—me?

"After all the good the last trip did you, why not come again?" Eva tempted me.

When she saw that I was still hesitant, a mischievous sparkle which I had not seen there in a long time came into her eyes and she said:

"Well, Professor Bernstein, how would you like the good Jews of Esperanza to say that you went to Aguas Calientes with Eva Kramer?"

It was a bait I could not refuse.


*Thursday, December 23, 1943.* We have postponed our trip to Aguas Calientes until after the first of next year. The ladies, who for so long were perfectly able to do without Eva's help, have found that her assistance with the bazaar is indispensable.

The great event is to take place next week, beginning Tuesday morning and ending Thursday evening, when the large assembly hall of the Centro has to be cleared for the New Year's Eve ball. Eva says she will not attend the ball and we will be free to leave Saturday morning, but it would be foolhardy to entrust our lives to an Esperanza chauffeur the morning after New Year's Eve. Since there is no particular hurry, we have agreed to leave on Monday.

In the meantime I have another week left for daydreaming.


*Aguas Calientes, January 6, 1944.* Strange how certain situations which keep recurring in one's daydreams are so completely different when they turn into reality. How often had I wishfully thought of taking a trip with Eva to some romantic, conveniently desolate place? But now that we are here in Aguas Calientes—the only guests in the deserted hotel for the past three days—it is not at all the way it used to be in my dreams. Yet how could it be?

We have not come here as lovers but rather as friends. Or not even that. Old acquaintances would be a better word. I suppose love might sooner be possible over the gap of years between us than friendship. Although Eva will readily use me as a father confessor, she would be deeply shocked if I should suddenly begin to reciprocate her confidences.

Since there is a drizzle most of the day and we cannot go out, we spend much time just sitting and talking. Occasionally Frau Mayer steals into the dining room to look at us thoughtfully, perhaps in an attempt to puzzle out our relationship. It was simple enough for her to accept the combination of Eva and Aronoff. But Eva and Professor Bernstein, aged sixty-five?

Even if Frau Mayer dared eavesdrop on our conversations, she would be disappointed. Like certain blossoms, Eva will not open up until after dark, when we go for our evening stroll. These walks in the dark trigger her memory more than anything else, and at times I can almost feel Aronoff walking with us like a third presence. We talk about him in the most natural manner, not at all as if he had been a partner in an illicit love affair.

"Most people say that I was only attracted to him by his looks," Eva said. "I won't deny that physical attraction played a big part, but if his character had proved disappointing, the attraction would soon have worn off. Some even say I was dazzled by his money." She chuckled softly. "He came here with less money than many other people. You know that, don't you?"

Remembering what Aronoff had told me long ago when we had talked about his cousin Klein, I nodded in the dark.

"Do you know what impressed me most about him? That he was not afraid! I don't mean not afraid like a fool who doesn't know fear, but not afraid like a man who knows his own potentialities. And he never used what happened to us as a crutch or an excuse."

"I'm not sure I know what you mean," I said when she stopped talking.

"Of course you know what I mean! I mean all those people who had been only mild successes before Hitler, but who now claim that they would have been much bigger successes if not for Hitler. 'If we hadn't been thrown out, if we hadn't come here, we would have achieved this or that!' Aronoff never claimed that his education had not prepared him for the life he had to lead, and he probably had more reason to complain than most other people. But he was sure that he could make his way in Esperanza—or in any other place, for that matter. He never blamed success or failure on circumstances. I often had the feeling that if the heavens should fall, he could hold them up above me."

"You loved him very much, Eva, didn't you?"

She was silent, but then the question did not beg an answer.

"And did he love you?"

"I don't know. At times I thought he did, but I really don't know."

"Didn't he ever tell you that he loved you?"

"You know something, Professor Bernstein, I have found that only weak men talk easily of their love. Strong men are very shy when it comes to showing their feelings."


*Friday, January 7, 1944.* Since I know that Eva is not the person to bestow her confidence easily, I am doubly touched that she should go on revealing herself to me. Tonight we returned to the theme we had opened yesterday like a forbidden door: love.

As soon as we walked away from the hotel in the evening, it was almost as if Eva were taking up a conversation that had been only briefly interrupted.

"No, I never was really sure that Aronoff loved me. He cared though. The only mistake in my life which he seemed unable to understand or to forgive was the Schwarzkopf affair. Klein he could understand, he said. Klein at least had been my own age. But why Schwarzkopf?"

"Why indeed?" I asked.

"It's hard to explain. At that time I had completely lost hope of myself. I was willing to settle for being loved instead of loving; for any man who just loved me and wanted me badly enough to make up in feeling what I lacked. It seemed like the nearest thing to love. Of course it isn't.

Regardless of how passionately anybody loves you, if you can't return his love, it is as bad as lying dead on a marble slab and having people come to worship you."

She stopped as if she had said more than she intended, but after a minute she went on:

"Then there was the business end. I wanted to learn a trade, even if there were conditions to being taught. I wanted to be independent.

"But the worst part was that Katja hated me. I knew it long before she began admitting it to herself. If you spend so much time with one person whom you cannot love and another who hates you, you end up despising yourself. There was little I could say to Aronoff to justify myself: just that I had to pay for my independence."

"Perhaps the price was too high?" I said.

"Perhaps. But then it is usually inexperience that makes you overpay."


*Saturday, January 8, 1944.*    We seem to be keeping up a running conversation from night to night.

"There was something else about the Schwarzkopf affair," Eva said. "Walter needed Katja badly. He really needed her badly in the beginning, needed her exuberance. But that very exuberance which attracted him at first repelled him in the end. There has to be a measure even for love and lovemaking, and Katja was insatiable, emotionally and physically. In a way she had consumed Otto, and when Walter escaped her, she blamed it on my sinister, magic powers and on the fact that I was Jewish and she was not."

"Tell me honestly, Eva, don't you think that Walter might have been influenced by the circumstance that Frau Katja was Gentile?"

"If you're asking me if Jews are bigoted, you know as well as I that they are among the most bigoted people in the world. But in Walter's case it didn't make any difference. You see, he was quite willing to marry Katja in the beginning, when the opposition to such a marriage was the strongest. What held him back was not her religion but the age difference. In the end, when she became nearly crazed with possessiveness, he would have left her regardless of her age, race or religion."

"Frau Katja did not seem to think so," I said. "One day she came and poured her heart out to me."

"I don't want to sound cruel," Eva said, "but at that time Katja was pouring out her heart to anybody who would listen."

"Perhaps you are too young to appreciate what a pathetic creature Frau Katja really is, Eva," I said. "Isn't it heartbreaking to have so much love to give and nobody to give it to?"

"Don't think that I am not pitying Katja! Much more now than I used to. I can even understand and pity my mother-in-law now for hating me, because I took away the only young man she ever loved. Sometimes I ask myself whether I regret any of the things I did. I don't think I really do, but if I had a second chance I would perhaps try to hurt fewer people."

"Eva," I said, "Eva, Eva. You *have* come a long way."


*Tuesday, January 11, 1944.* "Tell me, Eva, didn't you ever attempt to make Aronoff change his plans?" I asked tonight. I thought we had reached such a point in our confidences that I might risk the question.

"No, never."

Her quick, unhesitating answer took me by surprise. I could not quite believe that she had not tried to persuade him to stay.

"Didn't you think it might have been worth trying?" I asked.

"It was not at all a question of whether it was worthwhile or not. I knew that Aronoff could not be persuaded, and I would not put my conviction to the test. Let's say I was too much of a coward to try."

"I don't know a lot about Aronoff," I said, "but I doubt that his leaving had anything to do with how he felt about you."

"It's a funny thing, Professor Bernstein. Sometimes I play a game with myself: I ask myself whether it would have made me happy if he had broken off his long engagement without going to see his fiancée. And the answer is no. It would have been out of character for him. I would have completely lost confidence. For, after all, if he once backed out of his obligations without even trying to fulfill them, how could I be sure that he would not act the same way with me? I probably would have ended up begging him to leave, just to make sure that there were no doubts and reservations in his mind if he came back."

This was the first time Eva had mentioned the fact that Aronoff might come back.

"Did he say anything about coming back to you?"

"No. Nothing beyond all the vague things one says while saying good-by."

"You know what amazes me about you, Eva? That you don't seem the least bit resentful!"

"Resentful! Why on earth should I be resentful when I have so much to be grateful for! I don't know what I gave Aronoff—or if I gave him anything—but he certainly gave me a lot: he gave me back hope. He showed me that I could love by making it possible for me to love him. He gave me back my self-respect. What more can one ask?"

Again I was dumfounded by the way her mind had developed during the past year.

"But, Eva, you won't be able to go on living the rest of your life with just a memory!"

"Don't you see that I don't have to! Don't you see that now that I know I can love I have at least the hope that I might love again. Oh, not today or tomorrow, but perhaps after a while . . . who knows?"

For a while we walked in silence. It had stopped raining earlier in the evening, but we could still hear the dripping of the water as it fell from the leaves of the trees by the roadside. A full moon above the thick layer of clouds turned the air a misty blue, through which the glow-worms weaved their way like lost souls. The croaking of the frogs was like the pounding of surf.

I thought about what Eva had said. What prospect did she have of finding another rewarding love affair in Esperanza? As if she were tuned in on my mind, Eva suddenly said:

"I have been thinking. There is no future for me in Esperanza. If I stay here I will just keep on drifting from day to day, like everybody else. Mañana and mañana and mañana. But I don't have to stay. Not any longer. I am free to leave. I am no longer afraid! I know that I can make a living, if not one way then another. Aronoff has given me that much confidence in myself. I must make the break while Walter and I are still young, while we still have a chance to carve out a new life for ourselves—separately."

"Eva, what are you saying!"

"I am saying that I have decided to get a divorce," she said calmly.

"But why now? There seems no reason in the world why you should want to get a divorce right now!"

"That is exactly the reason: because nobody will be able to say that there is a reason. Nobody will be implicated or hurt. It will all be perfectly clean and simple."

"And what will you do afterward?" I asked, dismayed by the turn our talk had taken.

"Afterward I will do what so many people here dream of doing but don't have the courage to do. I will get out of Esperanza. I will go to a country where, I hope, time has not come to a complete standstill and people are not satisfied to drown in their own inertia· the United States."

*Sunday, January 16, 1944.* We arrived back in Esperanza late this afternoon.

Almost from the moment I stepped out of the taxi, Horowitz has been dogging my steps in an attempt to find out what Eva and I did in Aguas Calientes. If I were a younger man, he would not hesitate to make up his own explanation.

"You say the weather wasn't good. So what did you do all day long?" Horowitz insisted.

"We talked."

"All the time?"

I can understand that Horowitz should be incredulous. But that is exactly what we did all the time: talk. I realize now that Eva needed me as a sounding board for her thoughts. She had to say them aloud to find out whether they were really valid. I suspect that the idea of getting a divorce did not occur to her until that night in Aguas Calientes. But by the time we left, everything seemed quite clear in her mind—so clear indeed that she dropped the pose of grown-up sophistication which she had maintained since the beginning of the Schwarzkopf affair.

When I came down for breakfast in the morning—our last breakfast together in Aguas Calientes—I was startled by her changed appearance. I had become so accustomed to seeing her with an upswept hairdo that at first I hardly recognized her. She had taken all the pins out of her high-piled curls and had brushed her hair down, wearing it loose to her shoulders the way she had as a young girl. Her face looked soft and round again, and I thought that now that she was grown up she could afford to look youthful; she no longer had to wave her superiority like a banner.

Where the roots of her hair had been covered by the high-piled curls, they had turned darker and had lost some of their golden gloss. Seeing the direction of my glance, Eva touched her hair and asked:

"Well, how do you like it?"

"I like it very much. To tell the truth, Eva, I always liked you better with your hair down. And don't worry about the top. The hair will fade back to blond in the sun."

She shook her head.

"No, it will never again be the color it was when I was seventeen. You see, I'm getting older too."

Before I could make some profound remark about age, the muchachas came to carry our suitcases out to the taxi. Just as we got in, the sun broke through the foaming clouds, instantly lifting the lush colors of the subtropical vegetation out of the monotonous gray which had choked them. Once again the wreath of cone-shaped mountains stood green around us, sprinkled with the yellow tufts of blooming bushes. We looked back through the rear-view window until the sight was blocked out by the bend in the road. I wonder whether Eva too felt as though we had just finished a chapter of our lives.

*Sunday, January 23, 1944.*     Eva's request for a divorce seems to have hit Walter out of the blue. Today he came rushing into my room just as I sat buried beneath a pile of newspapers, trying to catch up on the information I had missed during our stay in Aguas Calientes. (The Russians are still advancing, and two days ago Allied forces landed at Anzio.)

It turned out that Walter had come not so much to seek my counsel as to accuse me of having instigated this new trouble.

"Not a word about a divorce before Eva left for Aguas Calientes! And now, only a week later, she is so set on her idea that she won't even discuss an alternative. Tell me, what on earth did you talk about in Aguas

Calientes to make her decide that she 'can't go on like that'?"

Walter glared at me suspiciously.

"My dear Walter, if you're accusing me of trying to steal your wife, why don't you come right out and say so, and I'll feel extremely flattered!"

"Oh, don't talk nonsense," Walter snarled, making my blown-up vanity collapse in an instant. "I'm not accusing you of anything, except perhaps of filling her mind with all sorts of crazy, philosophical ideas."

"Such as what?"

"Such as that we can't go on using a marriage of convenience to fall back on whenever we want to avoid making a decision. Such as that I might meet a woman whom I would want to marry if I were free, but would not for fear of having to give up a marriage which was very comfortable, though utterly immoral. Such as putting off life—real life—for a sham existence!"

"Are these the reasons Eva gave you for wanting a divorce?"

"Well, that's about the gist of it, aside from what she said about the necessity for mutual love, respect and self-respect. But I just can't see her as a divorced woman. If Aronoff were here, if he were willing to marry her, it would be different. But the idea that she should go to the United States and live there as his mistress . . ."

"Walter, I think I can assure you that Eva has no intentions of going to the States in order to live there as Aronoff's mistress! She doesn't even know where he is!"

"Then why does she want to go there?"

"Because she feels she could make a new beginning there. Walter, are you going to refuse her a divorce?"

"Of course not! On what grounds could I refuse her? I have nothing to offer her but a measure of security, a sheltered life, and comradely relations. But Eva won't settle for such a life, and nothing I say can dissuade her from her plans, not even when I point out to her the risk she is taking by going alone to a strange country. You know what her answer is? One can't go through life not taking chances!"

"Walter," I said, "you simply have to accept the fact that Eva is no longer a child. And while you give her credit for a mind of her own, you might also ask yourself if her judgment is not better than yours—or mine, for that matter. I think Eva is right. We have to take chances. We can't keep time at a standstill. It will move on and we have to move with it, whether we like it or not."

*Saturday, January 29, 1944.* A little local excitement, if one can refer to all South America as "local."

This week an espionage plot of Axis agents was discovered in Argentina, which made the Argentine government finally sever relations with Germany and Japan. The news caused Frau Goldmann to unearth her long-buried suspicion that Rudi Brueck was a Nazi spy. When we all laughed at her, she said somewhat piqued:

"I don't see what you find so funny! Seriously, do you really think that a Jew would consent to become manager of such a . . . house?"

*Monday, February 14, 1944.* When Eva first said to me that now was a good time to get her divorce because nobody would suspect her of ulterior motives, she had overestimated the generosity of our friends. Now that her plans have become known, it is amazing how many people seem to share Walter's opinion that Eva only wants to go to the United States in order to be with Aronoff.

"To give up a beautiful home, a good existence, and for what? To become the mistress of a married man!" said Frau Goldmann, wringing her hands and casting dramatic glances heavenward.

Levy said glumly that he felt guilty of having been the instrument steering a woman onto a road which could only lead to a life of depravity. But he does all this breast-beating behind the back of his wife. With a romantic optimism which is certainly not based on any experience in her life, Trude keeps insisting that Aronoff will eventually marry Eva. You'll see!

Strangely enough, the people who have always felt that Walter's marriage was a mistake—his closest family—are not at all pleased now that his divorce appears imminent. Herr Kramer feels aggrieved because Walter did not start the action but waited until his wife "ran off after another man." Frau Kramer, whom I had expected to be deliriously happy over the news, is actually morose. Now that Eva has finally ceased to be a rival for her son's affection, she will have to begin worrying over her next daughter-in-law.

To my surprise both Dr. Lipschitz and his wife say that lately they have become quite fond of Eva.

"She turned into such a nice person this past year. And now that she's finally become a mensch they have to get divorced!"

One person who is wavering between wild joy and deep apprehension is Frau Katja. On the one hand, she is convinced that Eva will starve to death and end in the gutter after her divorce; on the other hand, she seems to worry—like Frau Kramer—about the woman who will be Walter's next wife. What might also disconcert her is the renewed look of hope in the eyes of her husband.

Eva herself is the calm center of the new turmoil. She is even a little amused by all the speculations, not bitterly but mildly amused.

"Whatever people will say about me after I have left, one thing they'll have to admit: I always gave them their money's worth of entertainment."


*Wednesday, February 23, 1944.*    Today I turned the tables on Eva: I went to seek her advice.

This is what happened: when I came home from my morning stroll I found a letter from the United States consulate in my room. (Frau Steinberg told me later that it had been delivered by messenger.) Immediately my legs began to shake and my hands trembled so that I could hardly open the envelope. The letter said in brief, concise official language that my quota number had arrived from Washington and that I had better make use of it lest I lose my privilege.

But I was not at all sure that I wanted to go to the United States! In fact I had long ago put the idea out of my mind, even though I had never destroyed the application form for the visa. With the inertia we have acquired in Esperanza, I felt that as long as I did not urge my business at the consulate, nothing would be done for me. In other words, I had felt safe from having to make a decision. Now that the matter was unexpectedly thrown back in my lap, I did not know how to handle it.

I would have loved to talk to somebody—Dr. Landau, Horowitz—but for some reason I felt reluctant to discuss my plans with them. How, after all these years, could I admit that I wanted to turn into a traitor, a deserter?

I thrust the letter into the drawer of my desk and shut it quickly, hoping that I could shut the problem from my mind.

All through lunch I was very irritable, and when Frau Steinberg announced challengingly that I had received a note from the United States consulate I came up with a bland lie. I said that I had inquired after a former colleague, but that the authorities had been unable to locate him for me. Back in my room I took the letter out again and read it over and over until the print swam before my eyes.

I tried to decide whether I really wanted to leave Esperanza. Who could possibly advise me? Who else was planning to emigrate to the United States?

I was dumfounded that I had not thought of Eva sooner. Without first taking my afternoon nap, I set out for her house.

Eva was startled when I descended on her unannounced, more startled yet when I blurted out the news to her.

"What? But I had no idea that you considered going to the United States! But this is wonderful!"

Her enthusiasm was so genuine that I momentarily forgot the doubts and reservations with which I had come. Perhaps it was really not such a bad idea for me to get out of Esperanza. I too could start a new life in the United States. And I would be able to see Eva now and then. If we planned it cleverly, Eva said, we might manage to leave together.

"Imagine, Professor Bernstein, people will say that I ran away with you when all the time they thought I was running after Aronoff!"

Her glee had a sobering effect upon me.

"Eva, to me this is not a prank," I said. "You can take the idea lightly, but I am forty years older than you. For me to move again is a serious decision."

Her mood changed instantly.

"I know you have a nice income here," she said, "but is this really enough to satisfy you? Sometimes I wonder about all the lawyers and doctors who came here—yes, and about you too—all the professionally trained people who simply put everything they learned aside and decided to forget about it. Not just temporarily, but for good, forever. Tell me, don't you ever think of teaching again?"

I had to admit that I had not thought of it in a long time. I had become Professor Bernstein, the South American, who rested on his former reputation and lived off the capital another man had made for him. And although common sense told me that I was safe and well off in Esperanza, some of Eva's discontent and fighting spirit transmitted itself to me. I wished I had the courage to take her advice, but at the same time I continued to look for obstacles.

"It isn't so simple to get a visa, Eva, even if you have a quota number. I would need an affidavit, and how would I get one?"

"The same way I am going to get one! You must have a dozen friends in the United States! Why not write to one of them and ask for an affidavit?"

"But, Eva, how can I ask for an affidavit if I haven't written to any of these people in years?"

"You see, that's another thing: we have cut ourselves off here. Do you remember when we first came here those religious, daily trips to the post office? But by and by we stopped all our correspondence. Oh, we said the war, and the times, and you can't get a letter through to Europe —but there were plenty of people in the States to whom we could have written! Don't go on taking inertia for an excuse, Professor Bernstein! If I thought of somebody who might send me an affidavit, so will you. Promise me!"

I had, of course, thought of Professor Einstein long before our conversation.

Why not write him? Why indeed not? Suppose I should go to the United States and not like it there, I still have what Eva calls the alternative of the coward: I can always come back to Esperanza.

*Thursday, March 2, 1944.* For the past week I have been playing the childish game of omens. I promised myself that if the Allies had one major setback during the week, I would not write to Professor Einstein for an affidavit. But things have kept on going well.

The entire month of February was a month of advance for the Allies —slow advance, but advance. The Russians have penetrated Estonia and are now on the border of prewar Poland, trapping on the way ten German divisions whose members were either killed or taken prisoner. About the middle of February part of Italy was returned to the jurisdiction of the Italian government, the first government to be re-established. And the Americans, who early in February landed on the Marshall Islands, have now begun the invasion of the Admiralty Islands in the Pacific.

Even the excuse that only a fool would leave Esperanza while the war was going badly is no longer valid. I will have to draft my letter to Professor Einstein.

*Monday, March 6, 1944.*   I have embarked upon a new course of self-torture. Yesterday I mailed my letter to Professor Einstein. Now begins the period of waiting for an answer.

After I had made up my mind to write him, it was really not so difficult to ask for an affidavit. There is something to being able to say: I am not a poor man; I will not become a burden to anyone. My mood was quite different from before, when I had tried to write Professor Einstein in a fit of rebellion and self-pity.

The truth is, I take great stimulation from the thought that Eva too is going to the United States.

*Monday, March 13, 1944.*   Saturday there was another Purim ball in the Centro.

I went with the idea in the back of my mind that this was perhaps the last Purim ball I would attend in Esperanza. People were surprised to see me, and I was asked so often what had brought me out of my seclusion that I almost ran out of lies.

Of course I did not tell anyone that I was planning to leave. The longer I am able to keep the news from getting around, the longer I will preserve my peace of mind. I have not yet steeled myself to the accusations which my move is bound to bring down on my head.

*Friday, March 17, 1944.* Still no answer from Professor Einstein.

I am beginning to get worried. Perhaps my letter was not properly addressed. Perhaps it was lost or mislaid. Professor Einstein must be getting hundreds of letters a week.

I am tempted to run to the post office every day, but since air mail gets to Esperanza only three times a week—now, during the rainy season, when the flying weather is bad, sometimes only twice—there is no point to it. Besides I don't want to arouse suspicion by showing my face too often at the post office. People, their minds sharpened by boredom to notice any minor variation, would soon deduce that I am waiting for some important letter.

*Tuesday, March 21, 1944.* All Esperanza knows that I am planning to desert!

Although I had taken the greatest precautions not to let anyone see that I was mailing a letter to Professor Einstein, there were no possible precautions I could take to keep any of the five people with whom I am sharing our apartado from finding his answer.

As was bound to happen, I arrived this morning at the post office to discover Dr. Lipschitz standing in front of the unlocked apartado, turning a letter over in his hand.

"It's for you," he said, without relinquishing the letter. "From the United States. It says here it's from Albert Einstein, Princeton, N.J."

"I can read," I said, trying to wrest the letter from him.

"From Professor Einstein?" Dr. Lipschitz asked, overawed.

"Yes, from Professor Einstein. Do you mind?"

I snatched the letter from him and slipped it into my pocket.

"Aren't you going to read what he writes you?" Dr. Lipschitz asked indignantly.

"I prefer to read my correspondence in private," I replied testily.

But where was I to find privacy in the city? Certainly not in the lobby of the post office!

Dr. Lipschitz had already walked away from me, insulted, and was talking to Fleischer, who was on his way down from mailing a letter. Both men were looking at me. No doubt Dr. Lipschitz was telling Fleischer that I had received a letter from Professor Einstein. Before returning to his store, Fleischer was sure to drop in on Horowitz to tell him the news. Horowitz in turn would pass the tale on to Goldmann; Goldmann to Levy; Levy to whomever he would meet in the Jungle Café while having his morning tinto; and some of these people would further spread the news during lunch in the Centro. By early afternoon the story would be all over town.

I decided that the only place where I could read the letter in peace was at home, and I took the next bus back. I managed to sneak up to my room unobserved, and there I opened the letter.

Professor Einstein wrote that he often recalled with pleasure our musical adventure. In fact he had only recently mentioned it to one of my former colleagues, Professor Ungar, who had taught physics at the University of Vienna. Ungar had told him that I had gone to some remote country in South America, he did not know which. Imagine his surprise when he suddenly received a letter from me!

He would certainly do his best to provide me with an affidavit. If he himself was unable to send me one—he had sponsored so many of his friends and he was not a wealthy man—he was sure he would be able to persuade Professor Ungar or some other colleague to come to my help. We would talk about finding me a teaching position as soon as I got to the United States. In the meantime I had better brush up on my English.

It was such a positive letter that the last doubts were instantly removed from my mind, and I already saw myself packing my suitcases. What gave me a little pause was the reminder to brush up on my English. My English is indeed poor, and I will have to find somebody to give me lessons.

In the meantime my more immediate worry was how to break the news to my friends, for there would be no putting it off beyond lunchtime.

As soon as I ventured out of my room I was cornered by Frau Steinberg, who demanded to know what was in the letter from Professor Einstein. (She had the information from Frau Fleischer, whom she had met in the market place.)

"I will tell you at lunch," I said.

"You're leaving us!" Frau Steinberg exclaimed, divining my plans with the mysterious sixth sense of a woman. To my great consternation she began to cry.

"Please, Frau Steinberg, I shan't be leaving for several months. In the meantime I would ask you to let me break the news to Horowitz and Dr. Landau."

Dr. Landau had been out on sick calls and came in with Horowitz. They both bore down on me immediately, and Horowitz asked without any preliminaries:

"So what did he write you?"

"Gentlemen," I said solemnly, "I have big news for you."

"I know it!" Horowitz cried. "You have been secretly working on some new mathematical theory and you have sent it to Professor Einstein . . ."

"No, no," I interrupted him, "I'm sorry to say that I have done nothing of the sort. Gentlemen, I am going to emigrate to the United States!"

Dr. Landau looked stunned for a moment and then he cried:

"Bravo! Good for you!"

Horowitz just stared at me with a blank face.

"You are joking," he said finally.

"No, no, I am serious."

"What about your quota number? You were born in Poland!"

"I already have my quota number. I applied for it some time back."

Horowitz looked at me and then at Dr. Landau.

"Behind our backs," he said. "Behind our backs!" And then he added what I had feared: "You traitor!"


*Wednesday, March 29, 1944.* A new period of waiting has begun, the waiting for my affidavit.

I am glad now that I wrote to Professor Einstein at the beginning of the month, without waiting for any further omens. In the meantime the Allied advance in Italy has come to a halt at Cassino, and German troops have occupied Hungary. But at least the Russians keep advancing and have already reached the Rumanian border.

Even with a setback here and there, we are all convinced by now that the war will soon be carried right to the Germans.

*Sunday, April 9, 1944.*  Once more it is Passover. Another holiday I am crossing off as probably my last in Esperanza. At the Seder the Kramers looked at me with premature nostalgia. Walter was there, but Eva had refused to come.

"She never liked these family gatherings," Walter said, "and now that we're getting divorced, she no longer has to attend."

I said that I could understand her point, but it would be a lie to pretend that I was not disappointed.

*Tuesday, April 18, 1944.*  For once I have stolen the limelight from Eva.

The interest in her divorce has been pushed into the background, while people keep stopping me in the street to ask whether it is really true that I am leaving. Perhaps this is all for the best. It gives Eva peace in which to settle her private affairs and forces me to take a more positive stand every time I repeat that the rumor is indeed true. Without knowing it, people are helping me to cut off my retreat.

On the whole, the attitude is congratulatory, and I even seem to have stirred some of the others out of their inertia. At least that is what Horowitz keeps accusing me of.

"I knew it would happen," he said. "They could disregard such madmen as Aronoff and his cousin Klein before him, but once Professor Bernstein says he is going to leave, everyone else will want to leave too!"

I tell Horowitz that he exaggerates, as always, but he insists that during the past days there has been a literal run on the United States consulate.

"What's wrong with El Paramo? The country has been good to us through the war years! Why run away now?"

Thus reasons Horowitz—but he is reasoning for his own cause. He does not want to give up what he has achieved here, and the threat of a mass exodus makes him feel guilty. Perhaps he feels he is not right in wanting to stay.

But I believe the time has finally come for each of us to make his own decision as an individual, not as the member of a group. The time of imminent danger is over. We will have to learn to think for ourselves again.

*Thursday, April 27, 1944.*    I was without word from the United States for so long that I was beginning to get frantic. What if after I had told everybody that I was leaving, I should not get an affidavit after all?

Today finally the long-expected, thick envelope arrived by registered mail. It contained not one but two affidavits: one from Professor Ungar, the other from a Professor Weil, whom I do not know. Perhaps I am now being rewarded for helping strangers like Dr. Landau and Horowitz. Still I am touched and surprised that people who barely know me should go to such trouble for me.

All that is left now is to apply for my visa and wait for confirmation from Washington. I have made an appointment at the consulate for next week Thursday. After that the world.

*Thursday, May 4, 1944.*    Today I spent two hours at the American consulate.

The secretary had gone out on some business of her own, and the vice-consul himself filled out the forms for me and took my fingerprints. It was a messy business, and the consul, a nice young man from New Mexico, was very apologetic about it.

"It's really a disgrace, fingerprinting immigrants like criminals," he said. "A barbaric law. But with so many people coming into the country each year, how are we to keep track? Still, once you get your visa you are free to go anywhere you please and do anything you want."

I was about to tell him that Jews had gone through considerably worse humiliations than being fingerprinted to obtain a visa. But in the end I did not say anything. I believe our problems are not nearly so interesting to others as they are to us.

*Monday, May 15, 1944.* Hans Braun has found me an English teacher, an American writer whom he met on several occasions in the home of his boss, Dr. Zwingli. The young man readily agreed to give me lessons. He said he could use the money. I am to meet him at the Brauns' this coming Saturday.

*Sunday, May 21, 1944.* Wherever did I get the idea that all Americans were tall and lanky and had such names as Cooper or Grant or Stewart? (From the movies, I suppose.) My new English teacher is short and dark, with a mobile, Latin face, and his name is DiMarco.

I was so surprised when Hans first introduced him to me that I thought I had misunderstood and kept looking around for a tall, blond American to come in.

The misunderstanding was aggravated by the ensuing conversation, which was in English. I believe Mr. DiMarco said that he was Italian, but perhaps I did not understand him properly, for he talked very fast. We are to have our first lesson on Thursday. I will have to ask him to talk a little more slowly.

*Tuesday, May 30, 1944.* I never thought I would enjoy my English lessons so much. We study informally, without any books or attention to grammar. Mr. DiMarco brings along old newspapers from which we read together. When I run across a word I don't understand I look it up in the dictionary or he tries to explain the meaning to me. My main purpose is to get my ear attuned to the language, a purpose Mr. DiMarco fulfills perfectly. He much prefers talking with me to teaching me, and today he asked me to call him by his first name, Tom.

"Everybody calls me Tommy," he said. "It makes me feel queer to hear you call me Mr. DiMarco."

I asked for an explanation of the word "queer" and for no reason at all he laughed. I think he is a little crazy. It still takes some effort to call him by his first name. I would never think of calling Dr. Landau and Horowitz by their first names, even though I have known them for years and consider them my friends. But I suppose I will have to get used to American informality.

*Saturday, June 10, 1944.* It is as if an epidemic had seized our little community; as if we were all running a high fever. Tuesday, the sixth of June, British and American forces began the invasion of Normandy!

Everything else is forgotten: Eva's pending divorce, my planned emigration. All we can think of doing at the moment is reading the newspapers and endlessly discussing the reports. We are advancing, we are winning, we can smell victory in the air!

Even Tommy, my English teacher, does not talk about anything but the war. He keeps throwing words like "Omaha Beach" and "Utah Beach" at me (I knew he was crazy, there are no such beaches on the coast of Normandy!) and constantly wails that he ought to be there now with the troops. That this was the stuff great books would be made of someday.

"Well, then, why aren't you there?" I finally asked him.

"You don't expect me to volunteer, do you?" he said indignantly. "I'm not that crazy! Ah, I can see you wondering why I wasn't drafted. I'll let you in on a little secret: I'm past the draft age. I don't look it, but I'm forty-four. But don't let my looks fool you. It's only a boyish face hiding an ancient soul," he said with a sarcastic grin.

He made me think of all the talks about idealism which I used to have with Horowitz. It seems that when it comes to protecting your hide there is little difference between nationalities.

*Monday, June 19, 1944.* After the jubilation of the past few weeks, after the invasion of Normandy, after the Americans entered Rome, after the Russian advances and the American gains in the Pacific, we have suffered a shocking setback. The Germans, whom we had already thought of as finished, have begun to bomb British cities with what seem to be pilotless planes. From the first reports the new weapon sounds quite frightening, and in spite of our recent optimism we have to think of the Blitz of 1940.

The worst part of it is that in spite of our deep hatred for them, we cannot deny the Germans an amount of grudging admiration. We just pray that all the plants in which they produce these new, infernal weapons will soon be destroyed.


*Wednesday, June 28, 1944.*   To our great relief, the British are standing up admirably under the recent German attack.

"You have to hand it to the British," Goldmann said. "For the way they're behaving now, I could almost forgive them Munich."

Yesterday Cherbourg, the first major city in France, fell into Allied hands. But victories seem to have a reverse effect on our minds. Instead of satisfying us, they fill us with an even greater impatience to see the war finished.


*Friday, July 7, 1944.*   My English lessons continue to be fun, for me as well as for Tommy. From the questions I ask him he must think me a complete fool.

Today, after we had plowed through a page of newspaper, he came back to one of his favorite topics—himself. He told me that he had always wanted to go to Europe to write, but that he had never had the money for it.

"Then an old aunt of mine died and left me some money, and what happens? The war breaks out in Europe! Here I was all ready to go to Paris or Rome, settle down and write the great American novel, and the war had to break out! So I finally ended up in South America."

I asked if he could not just have stayed at home to write the great American novel.

He looked at me, slapped his thigh, and laughed so hard that I thought that he was hysterical.

"Professor, you slay me," he said.

I begged him to explain.

"You slaughter me, you kill me, I'm dying in a fit of laughter."

"I can see that much," I said.

I waited for him to calm himself and to explain why he found my remark so funny. But he never did explain. And I still think that the logical place to write the great American novel is America.

*Tuesday, July 18, 1944.* A few days ago Tommy complained that he had not had a decent cup of coffee since he came to South America. (He seems to attach tremendous importance to what he calls "a decent cup of coffee.") I offered to take him to the Centro, a rash move that did not fail to bring on repercussions.

"So we are no longer good enough for you," Horowitz said after seeing me with Tommy. "You're going to America, right away you have to have American friends! Goyim to boot!"

*Saturday, July 29, 1944.* Again Tisha B'ab.

We Jews have a predilection for days of mourning. There is always somebody to remind me of it. This time at least the reminder came in a positive form.

"Nothing to mourn about this month, thank God," Dr. Lipschitz said to me when I met him coming home from the synagogue.

The Allies keep advancing in Normandy, and the Russians have finally driven the Germans from the last important Russian city, Pskov. Before long now they will reach the Prussian border.

*Friday, August 11, 1944.* Tommy has become a regular at the Centro. He no longer needs my patronage to go there. What's more, he seems to have tried to pick up Eva on one of his recent visits. I must have looked quite put out when she told me about it, for she clapped her hand over mine and said soothingly:

"Don't worry, Professor Bernstein. I am not going to get involved. I've learned how to handle men. Now the look in their eyes is enough to bolster my vanity. I don't need any further proof that I appeal to them."

*Friday, August 25, 1944.* Another two weeks of good news: the Allies have captured Florence, landed on the French Mediterranean coast, and yesterday their troops began entering Paris. The extent of our joy is comparable only to the extent of our sorrow when Paris fell, four years ago.

Goldmann, who ever since the sixth of June feels that every single victory is due to his military genius, has invited all his friends to celebrate the event in his house tomorrow evening.

*Monday, September 4, 1944.* More good news!

Last week the remnant of German forces in Paris capitulated. Saturday Brussels fell to the Allies. And today the American consul dropped by in person to inform me that my papers have come back from Washington, all approved.

"Now you can go to the United States any time you please," he said. "But you have to make use of your visa within a year. God, how I envy you!" he added spontaneously.

For the first time it occurred to me that he too was living in exile.

*Sunday, September 17, 1944.* Tomorrow night begins Rosh Hashana.

Now that I have my visa I can tell myself in good faith that this is to be my last Rosh Hashana in Esperanza. There is just the slightest twitch of nostalgia attached to the thought. I think I shall pray more fervently this year than all the previous years. Not only because I shall need God's help for the future but also because I—like the rest of us here—have much to be thankful for. Early this week the event for which we have been waiting so long has finally taken place: the Americans have crossed the German border near Eupen.

The war has come to Germany.


*Thursday, September 28, 1944.*   Today I tried to question Tommy about life in the United States. He was not too encouraging.

"I'll hand that much to you people, you've got guts!" he said. "Packing yourselves up and emigrating to the United States without even knowing what you're letting yourself in for. The rush, the pressure, the competition, the whole rat race . . . Perhaps I should go home too. To tell the truth, I haven't done much writing since I came to Esperanza. I don't know, but the environment doesn't seem propitious." (Two difficult words; I had to look them up in the dictionary.) "Perhaps you're right, Professor. Perhaps the best place to write the great American novel is in America."


*Wednesday, October 4, 1944.*   I have finally set a date for my departure. That is, Eva has. This afternoon, when I met her in the Centro, I asked her whether she had heard from Aronoff.

"Not a word. But I got my affidavits yesterday, and I am applying for my visa next week. Professor Bernstein, when are we going to leave?"

She was pushing me into a decision I was still trying to put off. After all, my visa was good for one year. But if I really wanted to leave Esperanza, procrastination would not do forever.

"You set a date, Eva," I said.

"Well, I still have to wait for my divorce to come through, and it might take a couple of months before my papers come back from Washington. Besides, I want to sell most of my things. You know, my china, my pots and pans, my bedding—I won't need all that. I think if I allow myself six months, everything will be straightened out. How about May? Will you be ready by then?"

"All right, Eva. May."

I should be glad about having made up my mind, but the date, though still some time off, looms ahead like doomsday. I am only beginning to be frightened.


*Wednesday, October 18, 1944.*   Tom told me that I will have to find myself another English teacher. He is going home.

When I asked him what had brought about the sudden decision, he shrugged and said:

"You know, Professor, years ago I had a college instructor in creative writing who told me never to use the phrase 'Suddenly he came to realize.' But that's exactly what happened to me: suddenly I've come to realize. Life doesn't always stick to the strict rules of fiction."

Saying good-by to Tom is just one more good-by to me. Every day now is a day of mental and verbal leave-taking. I am like a man who, on the verge of breaking with a woman, notices details about her to which he has been blind for years: the color of her eyes, the way her hair sparkles in the sun, certain movements of surprise, joy, sorrow.

Thus it is with me. I cannot remember when I was last consciously impressed by the beauty of the craggy line of the Andes against the blue sky. Now, every time I look at the Grampico in the morning, I think nostalgically that soon I will trade this sight for a row of prosaic houses opposite my window. I have become insensitive to the banks of clouds piling up on the mountains until their weight makes them sink into the valley to dissolve into rain. The word "winter" has, in my mind, through the process of metamorphosis turned into rainy season without sounding alien any more.

Perhaps the lack of changing seasons has blunted my perception. I realize that for years I have been looking at some of my closest associates (perhaps with the exception of Eva) without seeing them. Only the knowledge that I will soon leave them has brought their faces back into focus, and I have been shocked by some of the changes I find.

Yesterday I had lunch with the Kramers. I noticed that Frau Kramer's hair, an iron gray when we arrived, is almost white now. Herr Kramer has shriveled with his useless existence, and his former belligerence has turned into garrulousness. He finds fault with everybody, nags, and quarrels constantly with his wife, even in front of strangers. But both he and Frau Kramer profess to be heartbroken over the prospect of losing me.

"One of the few friends we have here," they said.

Though I felt flattered by their regret, I could not help marveling at the flexibility of the word "friendship." Had the Kramers and I really been friends?

Frau Goldmann gives way to unabashed tears every time she sees me. "That you should walk out on us!"

There again is the open accusation which brands me a deserter.

Frau Goldmann too has aged. Her hair is not so black as it once was. The white streak in the middle has spread, tinging the temples and the sides. But her face has changed little; it is smooth and unlined, possibly because she has gained weight and plumped out all over.

Her husband, on the other hand, has become thinner, looking more than ever like a scarecrow. Now as before he prefers to carry his denture in his breast pocket, and his cheeks are puckered and crinkled. But he still brags about his virility.

Beneath his lewd and obscene talk he hides a heart of gold. Today, when I spoke to him about withdrawing my capital from his business, he offered to keep on paying me interest and to deposit my earnings for me in the United States.

"Look, Professor Bernstein, why not leave at least part of your money with me?" he said. "You don't know how soon you will find a teaching position. In the meantime you won't have to live off your capital."

Some people might say that Goldmann wants to hold on to my money, but I doubt that he really needs it any longer.

As I say my mental good-bys, I find that I have a multitude of acquaintances, but only a few friends. Perhaps I might claim the Brauns as friends. And Walter Kramer. Certainly Horowitz and Dr. Landau.

Dr. Landau keeps repeating that he is glad for me in spite of himself.

"It's good for you to get down from this altitude. If I weren't so selfish, I should have advised you to move to Rioverde long ago."

I told him that I would not have been happy in Rioverde. What I did not mention was the secret fear that perhaps I would not be happy in the United States either.

Frau Steinberg alternately grieves and sulks.

"First Aronoff, now you! How am I supposed to fill my pensión if all the bachelors are leaving?"

I said that, God willing, the war would soon be over and there would be a new wave of immigration to South America afterward. I was surprised at Frau Steinberg's hostile face.

"Who knows what sort of people those newcomers will be?" she said.

I was reminded of Grushka's resentment when we first arrived in El Paramo. Now we too have turned into old-timers, closing ranks against anybody who might come after us. Like fossils, I thought. We form a layer, turn into stone, and nothing but brute force will penetrate us.

Perhaps it is all for the good that I will leave before turning into a fossil.

*Sunday, October 29, 1944.*    I feel as if I were carried toward the date of my departure on a wave of victories.

Athens has been occupied by the Allies. Belgrade has fallen before the Russians, and in the Pacific the Americans have made good General MacArthur's promise from the beginning of the war and have landed on Leyte.

I go to the movies more often now than in all the previous years, just to see the newsreels. Beneath all the horror of witnessing those terrible scenes of destruction, my heart glows. These victories are our victories.

In comparison, life in Esperanza seems doubly dull and humdrum. I am passing through a period of great restlessness, and sometimes I wish that Eva had set our departure earlier. Even the idea of sitting down for a few minutes to make an entry in my journal annoys me. Most of what I have to record does not seem worth the effort.

*Wednesday, November 15, 1944.*    This morning I met Eva and Walter in town. They were walking together, engrossed in conversation, and they almost passed without seeing me. But when they did notice me, they bore down on me with what struck me as a mischievous air, and Walter said gaily:

"Come on, Professor Bernstein, we're going to the Hotel Excelsior to celebrate."

"Celebrate what?" I asked suspiciously.

"Our divorce has just become legal this morning," Eva said. "We never had a chance to celebrate our wedding. At least let's celebrate our divorce!"

All this sounded quite frivolous, but I realized that both Eva and Walter were trying to hide a certain sadness beneath their gaiety.

We had a very good lunch in the Hotel Excelsior (none of our people was there to frown at the unorthodox twosome) and Walter ordered wine for the occasion. I did not drink, but he and Eva got slightly tipsy. Raising his glass to her, he said:

"To my beautiful ex-wife! May she make my lucky successor very happy!" Then he turned serious. "Isn't it a pity? She gets more beautiful the older she gets. What would you say if I asked you to remarry me?"

Eva smiled and shook her head.

"After the way we've been living, this would almost be incest."

"You see, not only beautiful but bright too."

"Yes, a very unfortunate combination," Eva said. "It makes life too complicated."

Later she told me that Trude and Irene Braun had both suggested that she move in with them after her divorce. Again she laughed and shook her head.

"Even people who ought to know better don't seem to realize that a divorce can't make the slightest difference in our relationship. Of course we'll go on living in the same house until I leave. I can't think of any place where I would be safer."


*Monday, November 27, 1944.* Today was little Norma's fourth birthday.

Trude, who has turned into a regular party-giver, made a big occasion of it. The house was swarming with small children and their niñeras, shouting back and forth in Spanish. The mothers, who had also been invited, sat in the sala and spoke German among themselves.

Watching them, I realized that all these women, though still young, would forever remain foreigners in Esperanza, and I was doubly glad at having decided to leave. But then perhaps even moving will not help me shake the old Jewish curse. We were strangers in Egypt. It seems that we will remain strangers forever everywhere.

*Saturday, January 20, 1945.* I cannot remember ever having experienced such a feeling of impatience.

Time and the world move on, but here in Esperanza everything seems at a standstill. Eva's sale of her household articles proceeds slowly, and she still has not received her papers from Washington. At times I wonder whether it was wise for me to tie up my departure time with hers, but I have neither the will nor the courage to leave before her.

About the war: after the setback of the Battle of the Bulge last month, Allied armies in Europe are again sweeping forward. The Russians have taken practically all Poland, and the Germans were forced to abandon their defenses along the Vistula. It is beginning to show only now how much the raids on their factories during the past year have weakened German resources. Daily the noose around Germany is becoming tighter.

"They'll squeeze the life out of them like this!" Goldmann predicts, clenching his fist tightly around his thumb.

But even his absurdities fail to amuse me. On top of everything else, the rainy season increases my morbid feeling. The high excitement of the first weeks after receiving my visa has now given way to the nagging fear that I will never get out of Esperanza. If I could only work up the will to get out on my own! I often think of what Josef said to me when he lay dying: "It is not lack of opportunity but sloth which keeps most people from realizing their dreams."

*Friday, January 26, 1945.* My depression increases from day to day, especially since the atrocious reports about extermination camps and gas chambers have begun trickling into Esperanza. Though none of us can quite visualize the horror (or rather none of us wants to, for aren't we guilty for being alive?), we are gradually giving up hope of ever again seeing those friends and relatives who stayed in Europe.

*Wednesday, February 14, 1945.* At long last! Eva has received her visa!

This morning she came rushing over to the Villa Carmen to tell me the good news.

"There's no reason now why we should not be leaving in two, three weeks," she said.

After we had talked for a while, she calmed down a bit.

"Lately I feel more and more guilty about having frittered away six years of my life. When I imagine what happened to the Jews in Europe, it seems like such a crime to have drifted along on waves of mañana. Now I realize doubly that life is not to be wasted but to be lived. Oh, God, I just can't wait to get out of Esperanza!"

*Saturday, February 24, 1945.* Eva has talked me into going with her to the Purim ball in the Centro tonight.

"This time it will really be our last Purim ball in Esperanza," she said. "My first ball as a free woman! I'll wear my prettiest dress, flirt with all the men, and leave a maze of the most confusing rumors behind me."

She was brimming over with carefree mischievousness. I am beginning to think that she has really got over Aronoff.

*Monday, March 5, 1945.* Of course I was mistaken. I am always mistaken. Eva has anything but got over Aronoff. Now that she has learned that Aronoff is coming back, she has even ceased all talk about leaving Esperanza at the earliest possible date.

It seemed only fitting that the first one to know about his return should be the same person who had first told me about his intention to leave, namely, Horowitz.

Two days ago, Horowitz came into the Centro with a visible air of triumph about him. I could tell by the swift way in which his head with the porcupine hair kept swiveling from side to side that he was looking for somebody. No sooner had he spied Eva sitting at a table with me than he descended on us.

"So you thought you could keep it a secret!" he said to Eva. "Not from Horowitz you can't! I know he's coming back!"

"Who?" Eva asked weakly, as if it were not clear who was meant.

"Who, who?" Horowitz mimicked her in the way he has when excited. "You see the act she's putting on? Aronoff of course!"

I had seen Eva blush before, but never so violently and deeply. No doubt Horowitz attributed her change of color to the fact that he had found her out. But I knew better. Eva had had no idea that Aronoff was coming back; this was the first she had heard of it. What I could not understand was why Aronoff should have informed his friendly enemy Horowitz instead of writing to Eva.

"How did you find out, Horowitz?" I asked.

"I got a letter from him today. He writes me he wants to bring in some typewriters, if I would be interested in buying them from him. Of course I'm interested! Nobody has been able to get his hands on a typewriter since the first years of the war. But leave it to Aronoff! I always said he has a good Jewish head on his shoulders."

"And how soon do you expect these . . . typewriters?" I asked cautiously.

"In a month or two, Aronoff writes me. And *you* thought you could fool us!" Horowitz said to Eva.

Eva did not say a word. The blood had receded from her cheeks and she had turned pale beneath her tan. She seemed to struggle to keep back her tears. Fortunately Horowitz was still under the misapprehension that she was upset because he had found her out.

Eva managed to keep herself under control until after Horowitz had gone back to his store. Then she burst out:

"But this is terrible!"

"Eva, aren't you glad he is coming back?"

"It's not a question of whether I am glad or not! Just imagine the situation! I don't even know if he is married. He does not know that I am divorced. You saw how Horowitz interpreted the news! Everybody will say that Aronoff is coming back to marry me. He will just walk into these rumors, and it will look as if I had set a trap for him, as if I were trying to coerce him into something."

But when I suggested that we could always leave before Aronoff's arrival, Eva looked at me as if I were mad. Beneath her shock and anxiety, her happiness was almost palpable.

"He should have let me know. It's a bad sign that he did not write to me," Eva muttered, as if trying to discourage herself from expecting too much.

I did not know what to say to ease her mind. I don't know what to think myself. But then Aronoff has always been something of a puzzle to me.

*Friday, March 16, 1945.* I remember reading somewhere that a way to increase the effectiveness of torture is to give the victim a short, physical respite in which he can build up in his mind an even greater horror of the pains to follow. Thus I am affected by the manner in which Eva keeps pushing the date of our departure back and forth.

I had thought that by this time I would be in the United States, yet I am still in Esperanza. Eva has abandoned her original plan to leave in May and has taken refuge in vagueness and excuses. Of course, I realize that all this procrastination has to do with the fact that she does not know exactly when Aronoff will return.

Again I have the feeling of dallying at the sidelines while the world moves forward. Since my last entry in my journal the Americans have crossed the Saar River and recently the Rhine at Remagen. The Russians are standing at the gates of Berlin. Whenever I read the newspaper, the victorious reports sound like a mighty overture to my getting out of Esperanza. I keep telling myself that these last few weeks are just a final trial of my patience. More than ever before I am struck by the symbolism in the name of the place of my captivity: Esperanza. Esperar —to wait, to hope.

*Tuesday, March 27, 1945.* Eva was right when she thought that people would say Aronoff was coming back to marry her. There is not a person who thinks differently. The opinions range anywhere from approval to severe misgivings. Even Walter is in a mood of anticipation.

"It would be a burden off his conscience to hand me over to a new keeper," Eva complains.

To avoid curious questions and stares, Eva has gone back into seclusion. I asked her why she had become so sensitive all of a sudden. People had linked her with Aronoff before.

"Don't you see that it's different now?" she said miserably. "If he is not married and I am divorced, there won't be anything to fall back on. No more excuses for keeping up the game of star-crossed lovers. We will just have to reach some sort of definite decision!"

"Don't you want to make a decision, Eva?"

She looked unhappy.

"It will mean giving up the dream for reality," she said.

*Monday, April 9, 1945.*　My restlessness seems to have spread to our entire colony. This is due partly to anticipation of the end of the war, partly to what people expect of Aronoff's return. For a while it had looked as if Eva, after all the fireworks she had caused over the years, would quietly slip from them. Now people feel that they will not be cheated of a grand finale after all.

Horowitz had another letter from Aronoff in which he writes that his arrival will be delayed until early in May. He is trying to lay the foundation for some sort of business in New York. So it appears that his trip to Esperanza is really nothing but a business trip. Or perhaps he just wants to make it look that way.

We will simply have to persevere another month to find out.

*Friday, April 13, 1945.*　A great shock to all of us: yesterday President Roosevelt died at Warm Springs.

I keep remembering the news photo from the Yalta Conference. How tired and drawn he looked in his black cape, sitting between Churchill and Stalin. Now he is gone, and though none of us has ever laid eyes on him, we feel as if we had lost a personal friend. Such is the intimacy one can feel only with greatness. The most tragic part is that he did not live to see the end of the war.

*Wednesday, May 2, 1945.* The events of the last few days have flooded our Jewish colony in Esperanza with a joyful hysteria.

The excitement started last week Thursday, when the American and Russian armies met at Torgau, and reached a feverish pitch Monday, when we learned that Mussolini had been captured by his own Italians and shot without a trial. The same day the remaining German divisions in Italy were forced to capitulate, and in Austria, which had already been occupied by Allied armies, a provisional government was set up. The rule of the Nazis was over.

But all stops were pulled out today when the news reached us that the Russians had fought their way into Berlin and that Hitler was reported dead.

Hitler dead!

In the evening everybody who could walk or crawl congregated in the Centro. People who had hardly exchanged a word before kept shaking hands and shouting at each other:

"We outlived him! We outlived him!"

Even Herr Kramer forgot himself so far in the excitement that he embraced his old archenemy, who had succeeded him as Rosh Hakol, Schapiro. For a short while everybody loved everybody, and people acted as if they had never spoken ill of one another.

And yet the war is not over. The Allies will not accept anything but the unconditional surrender of Germany, and here and there German divisions are still fighting. But it can only be a matter of days now until they too surrender.

*Tuesday, May 8, 1945.* I do not know to which news to give preference: the end of the war in Europe or the return of Aronoff. If I were a mystic I would certainly attribute some symbolic meaning to the fact that both events took place on the same day.

I had gone into town early this morning to order a large crate for my belongings which I want to forward by steamer. (Ironically, all the crates we brought from Europe have been converted into furniture, tokens of permanence.) I want to ship everything but the merest essentials ahead, so that I will have my belongings waiting for me upon my arrival in the United States.

It was about ten o'clock in the morning when I turned from the Calle Flores, where the carpenter has his shop, into the Avenida Bolívar. There was an unusual crowd of people in the street for this early hour, most of them headed in the same direction, toward the Plaza de la Libertad. When I saw Horowitz darting out of the Casa León and starting in the same direction, I called out after him. He looked back and stopped to wait for me, impatiently skipping from one foot to the other, like a person in a hurry to reach the bathroom.

I stepped up my pace and was so out of breath when I caught up with Horowitz that I literally gasped:

"What's going on? Where is everybody running?"

"Don't you know?" Horowitz said. "The news is up on the black-board outside the *Día!* The war is over! I just have to go and see it with my own eyes!"

He took my arm and began to drag me along with him, past the Plaza de la Libertad and up the steep road to the post office, which is located across the street from the El Día Building. I felt my heart pounding, not only from the fast pace at which we proceeded but also with emotion, and I remember thinking vaguely that all this excitement was really not good for me. Dr. Landau would certainly disapprove of our sprint.

We had not quite reached the corner of the post office when we heard Goldmann shouting behind us:

"Wait for me, wait for me!"

He too was out of breath. We were all panting when we finally rounded the corner. And there, opposite us, mounted on the crumbling wall of the old building was the blackboard, with the lettering on it in bold, white chalk:

ARMISTICIO! SE ACABA LA GUERRA EN EUROPA!

"Well," Goldmann said, "so we won."

There were tears in his eyes and he unabashedly rubbed them away with his hands.

The street was filled with a mob now, largely made up of our own people. The crowd kept spilling over into the gutter, and the cars, rounding the steep corner in low gear, furiously honked their horns to disperse the human barricade. People were mounting and descending the steps to the post office like the angels in Jacob's dream, and stranger talked excitedly to stranger.

I saw Eva coming out of the post office, and I left my companions to battle my way to her. She wore her blue dress, and with her blond hair blowing about her head, she looked to me like the goddess of victory.

"Well, Eva, the day has come at last," I said when I reached her. "We never could quite believe that it would come, could we?"

"It seems that all days come sooner or later: those one dreads and those one looks forward to."

She gazed thoughtfully across at the blackboard, then down on the crowd washing over the stairs, then toward the left where the street dipped sharply downhill.

"What brought you into town so early?" I asked her.

"I heard the plane coming in in the morning and I went to see if I had any mail from . . ."

She stopped and the expression on her face changed abruptly.

Even before I turned to look, I knew that Aronoff was coming up the street. He wore a light suit and his wavy, black hair gleamed in the sun. His progress was slowed down by people stopping him to shake his hand and ask him questions. Eva stood spellbound, waiting for him to see her. When he finally discovered her, he broke away from the last person who had stopped him and quickly came up the stairs to where we stood.

I thought I should step aside to give them privacy to greet each other, but awkwardness kept me from moving. Aronoff briefly touched my arm in greeting, as if he had seen me only yesterday, and then he turned to face Eva. For a few seconds they just stood looking at each other. Then he said:

"You changed your hairdo."

"Yes," she said, "I did."

There seemed to be no need for them to acknowledge the end of their separation in a more elaborate manner. I could see that I was not wanted, and I left them in their walled-off cubicle of happiness in the middle of the crowd.

*Saturday, May 12, 1945.*    Aronoff has moved back into the Villa Carmen, but this time he has not rented the garden house. He said it would not pay for the short stay he had planned.

The first chance I had to speak with him alone I pulled him aside and asked him whether he had got married.

"No. I am still a free man," he said, with a wry grin.

"But when you go back . . .?"

He shook his head. "It's over," he said.

I thought it was too early to press him for details and let it go at that. Horowitz was not so tactful. Bristling with curiosity, he opened his attack on Aronoff at our first meal together.

"Why did you come back to Esperanza, Aronoff?"

"Don't you know that I only came back to bring in some typewriters for you so you could become the richest Communist alive?" Aronoff said.

This remark got Horowitz' hackles up (he has not mentioned Communism in a long time) and he said belligerently:

"People say you have come back to marry Eva Kramer. If you ask me, it would be the decent thing to do!"

"I'm not asking you, Horowitz, but someday I might surprise you by doing just that," Aronoff said.

But his flippant voice made the statement sound like a mere joke, and we know as much about his plans and the motives for his return as before.

*Wednesday, May 16, 1945.*    We have set June 4 as the tentative date for our departure. By now Eva has sold most of her household articles, and the carpenter has promised to deliver my crate by the end of the week, con seguridad. All that remains now is to make our flight reservations. This is to be our first flight! Eva is not nearly so excited as I. At the moment there are other things that excite her more.

She has resumed her affair with Aronoff as if he had never been away.

Or perhaps she has gone on to a new beginning, as she said she would. They are seen everywhere together, and I understand that he has had dinner at her house several times. Although Eva is divorced now and perfectly free to do as she pleases, people still cannot get over the shock of seeing her with Aronoff. What makes this reaction more ridiculous still is that both behave as decorously in public as if they were an old married couple.

*Monday, May 21, 1945.* Today, while he helped me with my packing, I had a long talk with Aronoff.

The carpenter had delivered my crate in the morning—three days after the promised date—and two Indians had carried it up to my room, chipping the walls in the corridor, much to Frau Steinberg's chagrin. Aronoff had directed the complicated maneuver of getting the bulky crate through the narrow door, and once it was deposited in my room, had offered to help me with the packing.

"It will save you a lot of running around and bending over," he said in one of his surprising flashes of consideration.

I began to empty my closets and drawers, getting more depressed with every item I added to the pile on my bed. As I looked at my books and the few objects of art which I had brought along from my former home, I thought that I had little to show in material possessions for my long life —and not too much in spiritual possessions either. I said something to that effect to Aronoff, but he chided me for my regrets.

"It doesn't pay to have regrets," he said. "You just have to decide what you want most out of life, and then go after it. That's all there is to it."

I asked him what he wanted out of life.

"Before you left you seemed to have some idea of what you wanted," I said. "But obviously you have changed your mind."

He shrugged and grinned an embarrassed smile.

"Well, sometimes you think you know what you want, until you're about to realize your plan. And then you find that it isn't what you wanted at all."

"Aronoff, it's none of my business, but why did you break off your engagement after so many years?"

"Just as I told you: I found out that it wasn't what I wanted after all. I always thought that I wanted certain qualities in the girl I was going to marry, aside from the obvious ones, like being pretty. What I mean is a background similar to mine, good breeding, a quality of . . . well . . . innocence, or rather not too much sophistication; perhaps also a kind of submissiveness. I thought I had found all that in the girl to whom I was engaged. Oh, don't misunderstand me! I didn't just go out and pick her for these qualities. I went with her for quite a while before I left Vienna, and I was, well, yes, you might say I was in love with her. I thought that everything that happened here didn't really count, and that one day I would go back and marry her. But then, when I saw her . . ."

"Had she changed so much?" I asked.

"No, she hadn't changed. That was the trouble. She had not changed at all. She was still the sweet, pretty, submissive girl she had been years ago. She still dressed the same way; she still talked the same way; she still told her mother what time she would be home when she went out . . . Why, she had not even had a date with another fellow in all that time! No, she had not changed. I had.

"You know, when I came to the town where she lived—her father has a factory in a small town in South Carolina—everything was just as I had imagined it. They had a beautiful home, servants, two cars in the garage, a sweater factory with three hundred employees. They had already picked out a lot to build a home for us. They had had an architect draw up the blueprints, and had selected the furniture and the rugs. My future father-in-law showed me my office in the plant, complete with desk and secretary. All I had to do was get married and step into a ready-made position.

"And then I realized that this was exactly what I did not want. That it would be Esperanza all over again: no challenge but, to make it worse, no freedom either. Every time I stepped out of the house my fiancée asked me where I was going and when I would be back. I could just imagine our marriage: whenever I wouldn't be able to account for my whereabouts, she would tell me that during all the years of our engagement she had not once been out with a fellow. She would run home to mother, and her parents would come and remonstrate with me and hint that I was indebted to them.

"That's when I said I wanted out. All this . . . security which they had to offer did not mean a thing to me. I wanted to make it on my own. As for money, I have money. There's got to be more to a marriage than money."

"And didn't you try to explain all this to your fiancée, Aronoff? After waiting for you for so long, wouldn't she have been willing to move wherever you wanted to move and live with you the way you wanted to live?"

He looked down on his hands, thoughtfully flexing his long, beautiful fingers.

"No, I didn't talk it over with her. You see, there was something else I found out about myself: I cannot marry a woman I don't love."

I knew that at this point I could ask him what Horowitz had asked without seeming impertinent.

"Are you going to marry Eva?"

He was still flexing his fingers.

"I suppose I will," he said reluctantly.

And this answered a question I did not have to ask.

*Friday, May 25, 1945.*    As if having made me his confidant had placed an obligation upon him, Aronoff has taken over entirely the arrangements for my departure.

Suddenly the preparations which seemed like insurmountable obstacles have lost their terror for me. Aronoff has filled out the papers which must accompany my crate, has seen it through the customs inspection, and shipped it off to the railroad station. He has offered to convert my pesos into dollars, purchase my travelers' checks, and make my flight reservations. (I have postponed my departure once more, until the second week of June, when Aronoff will be ready to leave with Eva and me.)

I can see now why a marriage to his fiancée in the United States would never have worked out. Aronoff is the born provider. You cannot defraud a man like that of achieving his own success. I also understand why he was the natural choice for Eva after all the weak men she had known. No woman is so emancipated that she would not like to shift responsibility to somebody else's shoulders, provided those shoulders are stable enough.

*Wednesday, May 30, 1945.*   Although I have not repeated to anybody what Aronoff told me, people seem to have learned through osmosis that he is planning to marry Eva. They no longer ask "Are they going to get married?" but "When are they going to get married?"

Today Aronoff asked me indignantly whether I had spread the rumor. I swore by everything that is holy to me and a few things that are not that I had not said a word.

"Then what makes people so sure that I am going to marry her?"

"Look, Aronoff, if people keep guessing long enough, it is only natural that once in a while they should guess correctly. Deep inside they won't be convinced of your honorable intentions until they get a look at the signed and sealed marriage certificate. By the way, when are you going to get married?"

He laughed.

"Not before we get to the United States. If we want to make a new beginning, we might as well make it in a new country. It's too bad that our friends here will be cheated out of the circus they expect!"

*Tuesday, June 5, 1945.*   The last days are slipping away fast.

Again I am living in a state of apprehension. I keep making up lists of people to whom I must not forget to say good-by. My blood pressure is up, and Dr. **Landau** repeats again and again that I ought to keep calm.

Trude has told me that she is planning to give a farewell luncheon for Eva and me the day before we leave.

"Only our closest friends will be invited," she said. "The people who came over on the boat with us, and those you helped bring here. This will be a really intimate party. Who knows when we'll be seeing you again?"

Though all this upsets me, it relieves me at the same time from having to call on a number of people. I have tried to figure out who will be at

Trude's party. The Goldmanns, of course. The Kramers. The Lipschitzes. Walter, Eva, Dr. Landau and Horowitz. (Aronoff told me that he declined the invitation. "I have nothing in common with these people.") With the Levys and me that makes thirteen.

I wonder whether Trude forgot to count her guests or whether she is not superstitious. Perhaps I ought to try to persuade Aronoff . . . But no. Eva said he cannot be persuaded.

*Monday, June 11, 1945.* I have said good-by to the Fleischers and the Schwarzkopfs. After some consideration I felt that I ought to call on the latter too.

Herr Fleischer seemed wistful when he shook my hand.

"You have more courage than I have, Professor Bernstein. Do you remember when I met you on my way from the American consulate? At that time I was all decided to leave Esperanza at the soonest possible date. But now that we can leave, I am scared."

Frau Fleischer dabbed at her eyes and said that all the nicest people were leaving. What nice people? Did she ever have an affair with Aronoff?

In the afternoon I visited the Schwarzkopfs in their factory. They have expanded their working quarters and seem to be very busy. When I told them that I was leaving Esperanza on Friday, Frau Katja wrinkled her cat's nose and compressed her lips in a thin line of disapproval.

"I hope you won't regret it," she said gloomily. "Some people don't know what's good for them." (This, no doubt, in reference to Eva's still-unforgiven desertion.) "I hope you will find that this is what you really want."

I thought of what Aronoff had said about wanting the wrong thing all the time. I remembered Trude wanting romance and settling for security. Eva wanting to be loved, only to discover that what she really wanted was to love. Aronoff wanting stability and a submissive bride, until he found that what he needed was self-forged success and the challenge of a woman as exasperating as Eva.

Of course we never know what we want until we see it. Most of what we think we fancy is nothing but a puerile dream.

*Wednesday, July 11, 1945.*   This will be my last entry in Esperanza. I still have to unwrap the package in which I keep all my previously filled journals and add this one. Then the package will go into my large briefcase with the rest of my valuables.

(An incident occurred during the packing of my crate: as I kept sorting what was to be packed, I took the wrapped and sealed parcel out of my desk and placed it on my bed, with the inscription down. I briefly went to get something from my closet, and when I turned around I saw Aronoff standing by the bed, weighing the parcel in his hand.

"Do you want this packed too?" he asked, ready to stow it in the crate.

"No, no, I want to keep it with me!"

I startled him by literally pouncing on him and snatching the parcel from his hand.

"Anything valuable in it?"

Valuable? Who was to judge the value of the memories of six years? What price would I put on it if it were lost?

"I don't think you would call it valuable," I said. "Just some old letters, photographs, diplomas; that sort of thing."

The lie came easily and he did not question it. Fortunately he had not turned the package over and discovered my instructions that in the case of my death it was to be delivered, sealed, to Eva Kramer.

I wonder how he would have reacted. The few times he has mentioned my trip to Aguas Calientes with Eva, his voice sounded a bit testy. Could he really be jealous of me? The fabulous Aronoff jealous of ancient Professor Bernstein? He must truly be in love with Eva.)

I do not know why my mind insists on dwelling on that incident now. Perhaps to distract me from more upsetting thoughts.

Today I said farewell to Señora Consuelo. Our relationship has always remained stylized, like the movements of characters in a Japanese play. But beneath this formality flows real affection.

"Entonces se va de veras. Que pena!" Señora Consuelo said. "So you are really leaving. What a pity."

I remembered how, at one time, Frau Kramer suggested that I might marry Señora Consuelo, and I wondered whether not having done so would someday prove another cause for regret. But Señora Consuelo soon brought me back to reality, saying that surely I would want to say good-by to Josef before I left.

Though a trip to the cemetery was the last thing I craved today I would not hurt her feelings by refusing to accompany her. It was the first time since Frau Gruen's death that I had driven out there. The sloping meadow behind the high adobe wall was still covered with yellow buttercups, and aside from Josef and Frau Gruen's graves, there were only two other graves of older people whom I had hardly known to mar the ground like an acne.

For a while I stood quiet behind Señora Consuelo as she knelt praying at Josef's grave, in her black widow's clothes. With her bent head, her long, white neck, and her fine profile, she looked more than ever like a Madonna. A Madonna in a Jewish cemetery, I thought.

All the time I kept my eyes averted from the staked-out site next to Josef's grave. It had always lurked in the back of my mind like a menace. But day after tomorrow I would escape it forever. I was not going to be buried in Esperanza.

And yet, as I looked at the blooming flowers on Josef's grave, I felt a little wistful. Who would ever tend so lovingly to my grave?

But these are morbid thoughts, and Dr. Landau has cautioned me that I must keep serene. He would not tell me what my blood pressure was when he took it an hour ago. He only said he wished Frau Levy had not planned that party for tomorrow.

"You will eat very moderately. You will not drink. And after lunch you will retire to a quiet room and take a rest," he said to me.

He treats me like a moron. I shall miss him terribly.

One good thing about the party: when I stopped by the Brauns' in the afternoon to say good-by, Frau Irene told me they would be seeing me again tomorrow in Trude's house.

We will not be thirteen at the table after all.

# Epilogue

*And all the days of*
*Noah were nine hundred*
*and fifty years: and*
*he died.*

GENESIS 9:29

Professor Bernstein never left Esperanza. Shortly after dinner in Trude Levy's house he began to complain of nausea, and two hours later he was dead of a second heart attack. The heavy meal, the excitement of his impending departure, and the years of living at that high altitude had been too much for him. He was sixty-seven years old when he died.

He is buried in the Jewish cemetery of Esperanza, next to Josef Blumenthal. His headstone bears the simple inscription, proposed by his friends Dr. Landau and Horowitz:

NORMAN BERNSTEIN

HIJO DE MOSES Y DEBORAH BERNSTEIN

1878–1945

HE WAS A GOOD MAN

## ABOUT THE AUTHOR

Stella Wilcheck was born in Vienna, Austria in 1922 and attended the Real Gymnasium in that city until the outbreak of World War II. The next eight years she spent as a refugee from Hitler in South America, before coming to the United States. With her husband she lives at present in Greenwich Village, New York City. *Ararat* is her first novel.

*Set in Granjon*
*Format by Betty Anderson*
*Manufactured by American Book–Stratford Press*
*Published by Harper & Brothers, New York*